For the Roses

G·K
Hall
&Cº

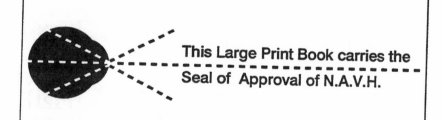

For the Roses

JULIE GARWOOD

G.K. Hall & Co.
Thorndike, Maine

Published in 1996 by arrangement with Pocket Books,
a division of Simon & Schuster Consumer Group, Inc.

This book is a work of fiction. Names, characters, places and incidents are products of the author's imagination or are used fictitiously. Any resemblance to actual events or locales or persons, living or dead, is entirely coincidental.

G.K. Hall Large Print Romance Collection.

The text of this Large Print edition is unabridged.
Other aspects of the book may vary from the original edition.

Set in 16 pt. News Plantin by Minnie B. Raven.

Printed in the United States on permanent paper.

Library of Congress Cataloging in Publication Data

Garwood, Julie.
    For the roses / Julie Garwood.
      p.   cm.
    ISBN 0-7838-1639-1 (lg. print : hc)
    1. Adoptees — Identification — Fiction. 2. Family — Montana
— Fiction. 3. Montana — Fiction. 4. Large type books.
I. Title.
[PS3557.A8427F67   1996]
813'.54—dc20
                                                            95-47887

No man is an island, entire of it self; every man is a piece of the continent, a part of the main; if a clod be washed away by the sea, Europe is the less, as well as if a promontory were, as well as if a manor of thy friends or of thine own were; any man's death diminishes me, because I am involved in mankind; and therefore never send to know for whom the bell tolls; it tolls for thee.

— John Donne
Devotions upon Emergent Occasions
Meditation XVII

Prologue

New York City, 1860

They found her in the trash. Luck was on the boys' side; the rats hadn't gotten to her yet. Two of the vermin had already climbed onto the top of the covered picnic basket and were frantically clawing at the wicker, while three others were tearing at the sides with their razor-sharp teeth. The rats were in a frenzy, for they smelled milk and tender, sweet-scented flesh.

The alley was the gang's home. Three of the four boys were sound asleep in their make-do beds of converted wooden crates lined with old straw. They'd put in a full night's work of thieving and conning and fighting. They were simply too exhausted to hear the cries of the infant.

Douglas was to be her savior. The fourth member of the gang was taking his turn doing sentry duty at the narrow mouth of the alley. He'd been watching a dark-cloaked woman for quite some time now. When she came hurrying toward the opening with the basket in her arms, he warned the other gang members of possible trouble with a soft, low-pitched whistle, then retreated into his hiding place behind a stack of old warped whiskey barrels. The woman paused in the archway, gave a furtive glance back over her shoulder toward the street, then ran into the very center

7

of the alley. She stopped so suddenly her skirts flew out around her ankles. Grabbing the basket by the handle, she swung her arm back as far as it would go to gain momentum and threw the basket into a pyramid of garbage piled high against the opposite wall. It landed on its side, near the top. The woman was muttering under her breath all the while. Douglas couldn't make out any of the words because the sound she made was muffled by another noise coming from inside the basket. It sounded like the mewing of a cat to him. He spared the basket only a glance, his attention firmly on the intruder.

The woman was obviously afraid. He noticed her hands shook when she pulled the hood of her cloak further down on her forehead. He thought she might be feeling guilty because she was getting rid of a family pet. The animal was probably old and ailing, and no one wanted it around any longer. People were like that, Douglas figured. They never wanted to be bothered by the old or the young. Too much trouble, he guessed. He found himself shaking his head and almost scoffed out loud over the sorry state of affairs in general, and this woman's cowardice in particular. If she didn't want the pet, why didn't she just give it away? He wasn't given time to mull over a possible answer, for the woman suddenly turned around and went running back to the street. She never looked back. When she was almost to the corner, Douglas gave another whistle. This one was loud, shrill. The oldest of the gang members, a runaway slave named Adam, leapt to his feet with the agility and speed of a predator. Douglas pointed to the basket, then took off in pursuit of the woman. He'd noticed the thick envelope sticking out of her coat pocket and thought it was time he took care of a little business. He was, after all, the best eleven-year-old pickpocket on Market Street.

Adam watched Douglas leave, then turned to get the basket. It wasn't an easy task.

The rats didn't want to give up their bounty. Adam hit one squarely on the head with a jagged-edged stone. The vile creature let out a squeal before scurrying back to the street. Adam lit his torch next and waved it back and forth above the basket to frighten the other vermin away. When he was certain they were all gone, he lifted the basket out of the garbage and carried it back to the bed of crates where the other gang members still slept.

He almost dropped the thing when he heard the faint sounds coming from inside.

"Travis, Cole, wake up. Douglas found something."

Adam continued on past the beds and went to the dead end of the alley. He sat down, folded his long, skinny legs in front of him, and put the basket on the ground. He leaned back against the brick wall and waited for the other two boys to join him.

Cole sat down on Adam's right side, and Travis, yawning loudly, hunkered down on his other side.

"What'd you find, boss?" Travis asked, his voice thick with sleep.

He'd asked Adam the question. The other three gang members had elevated the runaway slave

9

to the position of leader one month ago. They'd used both reason and emotion to come to their decision. Adam was the oldest of the boys, almost fourteen now, and logic suggested he, therefore, lead the others. Also, he was the most intelligent of the four. While those were two sound reasons, there was yet another more compelling one. Adam had risked his own life to save each one of them from certain death. In the back alleys of New York City, where survival of the fittest was the only commandment anyone ever paid any attention to, there simply wasn't room for prejudice. Hunger and violence were masters of the night, and they were both color-blind.

"Boss?" Travis whispered, prodding him to answer.

"I don't know what it is," Adam answered.

He was about to add that he hadn't looked inside yet, but Cole interrupted him. "It's a basket, that's what it is," he muttered. "The latch holding the top closed looks like it could be real gold. Think it is?"

Adam shrugged. Travis, the youngest of the boys, imitated the action. He accepted the torch Adam handed him and held it high enough for all of them to see.

"Shouldn't we wait for Douglas before we open the thing?" Travis asked. He glanced over his shoulder toward the entrance of the alley. "Where'd he go?"

Adam reached for the latch. "He'll be along."

"Wait, boss," Cole cautioned. "There's a noise coming from inside." He reached for his knife. "You hear it, Travis?"

"I hear it," Travis answered. "Could be something inside's gonna bite us. Think it could be a snake?"

"Of course it couldn't be a snake," Cole answered, his exasperation evident in his tone of voice. "You got piss for brains, boy. Snakes don't whimper like . . . like maybe kittens."

Stung by the retort, Travis lowered his gaze. "We ain't never gonna find out lessun we open the thing," he muttered.

Adam nodded agreement. He flipped the latch to the side and lifted the lid an inch. Nothing jumped out at them. He let out the breath he'd been holding, then pushed the lid all the way up. The hinge squeaked, and the lid swung down to rest against the back side of the basket.

All three boys had pressed their shoulders tight against the wall. They leaned forward now to look inside.

And then they let out a collective gasp. They couldn't believe what they were seeing. A baby, as perfect and as beautiful as an angel from above, was sleeping soundly. Eyes closed, one tiny fist in mouth, the infant occasionally suckled and whimpered, and that was the noise the boys had heard.

Adam was the first to recover from the surprise. "Dear Lord in heaven," he whispered. "How could anyone deliberately throw away anything this precious?"

Cole had dropped his knife when he spotted the baby. He reached for it now, noticed his hand was trembling in reaction to his worry over what might be hiding inside the basket, and shook his

11

head over what he considered cowardly behavior. He made his voice sound mean to cover his embarrassment. "Course they could throw the baby away. People do it all the time. Rich ones and poor ones. Makes no difference. They get tired of something and just toss it out like dirty water. Ain't that right, Travis?"

"That's right," Travis agreed.

"Boss, didn't you listen to any of the stories about the orphanages Douglas and Travis were telling?"

"I seen lots of babies there," Travis announced before Adam could answer Cole's question. "Well, maybe not lots, but some," he qualified in an attempt to be completely accurate. "They kept them up on the third floor. None of the little buggers ever made it that I recollect. They put them in that ward, and sometimes they just plumb forgot they were there. Least, I think that's what happened." His voice shivered over the memories of the time he spent in one of the city's refuge centers for displaced children. "This little mite wouldn't never make it living there," he added. "He's too small."

"I seen smaller down on Main Street. The whore, Nellie, had one. How come you think it's a boy baby?"

"He's bald, ain't he? Only boys come bald."

Travis's argument made perfectly good sense to Cole. He nodded agreement. Then he turned to their leader. "What are we gonna do with him?"

"We ain't throwing him away."

Douglas made the announcement. The other

three boys jerked back in reaction to the harshness in his tone of voice. Douglas nodded to let them know he meant what he'd just said, and added, "I seen the whole thing. A fancy-dressed man in coat and tails climbs out of this expensive-looking carriage. He's got this here basket looped over his arm. He's standing under the streetlamp, so of course I see his face real clear. I seen the woman's face too. She'd been waiting on the corner for him, I figured out, when he gets out of the carriage and goes right to her. She keeps trying to hide her face by pulling the hood down over the top of her head, and the way she's acting makes me think she's good and scared. The man starts getting angry, and it don't take me long to figure out why."

"So? Why was he getting angry?" Cole demanded to know when Douglas didn't immediately continue.

"She didn't want to take the basket, that's why," Douglas explained. He squatted down next to Travis before going on. "She keeps shaking her head, see, over and over. The man's talking up a storm and pointing his finger in her face. Then he pulls out a fat envelope and holds it up in front of her. She comes around then. She snatches it out of his hand as quick as lightning, which makes me think that whatever is inside the envelope is important, and then she finally takes the basket. He climbs back inside the carriage while she's tucking the goods in her pocket."

"Then what happened?" Travis asked.

"She waits until the carriage rounds the corner," Douglas told him. "Then she sneaks into our alley and throws the basket away. I didn't pay the basket much attention at all. I thought there was maybe an old cat inside. Never guessed it could be a baby. Don't think I would have left if I'd known . . ."

"Where'd you go?" Cole interrupted to ask.

"I'd gotten mighty curious about the envelope in her pocket, so I followed her."

"Did you get it?" Travis wanted to know.

Douglas snickered. "Of course I got it. I don't have the reputation of being the best pickpocket on Market Street for nothing, do I? The woman was in a hurry, but I got into her pocket in the thick of the crowd pushing their way onto the midnight train. She never knew I touched her. Stupid woman. Bet she's just about now figuring out what happened."

"What's inside the envelope?" Cole asked.

"You ain't gonna believe it."

Cole rolled his eyes heavenward. Douglas liked to draw things out. It drove the others crazy. "Honest to God, Douglas, if you don't . . ."

Travis interrupted his threat. "I got me something important to say," he blurted out. He wasn't the least bit interested in the contents of the envelope. His thoughts were on the baby. "We're all agreed we ain't throwing the little fella away. So now I'm wondering who we're gonna give him to."

"I don't know anyone who'd want a baby," Cole admitted. He rubbed his smooth-skinned jaw the way he'd seen the older, more sophisticated thugs do. He thought the action made him look older and wiser. "What's he good for?"

14

"Probably nothing," Travis replied. "Least ways, not yet. Maybe though, when he gets bigger . . ."

"Yeah?" Douglas asked, curious over the sudden excitement that came into Travis's voice.

"I'm thinking we could all teach him a thing or two."

"Like what?" Douglas asked. He reached out and gently touched the baby's forehead with his index finger. "His skin feels like satin."

Travis was warming to the possibility of educating the baby. It made him feel important . . . and needed. "Douglas, you could teach him all about picking pockets. You're real good at it. And you, Cole, you could teach him how to be mean. I seen the look that comes into your eyes when you think someone's wronged you. You could teach the little fella to look like that too. It's real scary."

Cole smiled. He appreciated hearing the compliment. "I stole me a gun," he whispered.

"When?" Douglas asked.

"Yesterday," Cole answered.

"I seen it already," Travis boasted.

"I'm going to get good shooting it as soon as I steal me some bullets. I'm gonna be the fastest gun on Market Street. I might be persuaded to make the little fella second best."

"I could teach him how to get things," Travis announced. "I'm good at finding what we need, ain't I' boss?"

"Yes," Adam agreed. "You're very good."

"We could be the best gang in New York City. We could make everyone afraid of us," Travis

15

whispered. He was so enthralled over the possibility, his eyes shone bright. His voice took on a dreamy quality. "Even Lowell and his bastard friends," he added, referring to the rival gang members they all secretly feared.

The boys all took a moment to look at the pretty picture Travis had just painted for them. Cole rubbed his jaw again. He liked what he was imagining. He had to force the eagerness out of his voice when he spoke again. "Boss, you could teach him all about them books your mama taught you about. You could maybe make him as smart as you are."

"You could teach him how to read, and he wouldn't get whiplashes across his back for learning the way you did," Travis interjected.

"If we keep him, the first thing we got to do is take that sissy dress off him," Douglas announced. He glared at the long white gown and shook his head. "No one's ever gonna laugh at him. We'll see to it."

"I'll kill anyone who even snickers," Cole promised.

"All babies wear those things," Travis said. "I seen them before. It's what they sleep in."

"How come?" Douglas asked.

"They don't need walking clothes because they don't know how to walk yet."

"How we gonna feed him?" Cole asked.

"You can see the bottle of milk someone put in the basket. When it's empty, I'll get him more," Travis promised. "He probably don't have teeth yet, so he can't eat real food. Milk will do for now. And there are also some dry nappies —

16

I'll get him some more."

"How come you know so much about babies?" Cole asked.

"Just do," Travis answered with a shrug.

"Who changes him when he piddles?" Douglas asked.

"I say we all gotta take turns," Cole suggested.

"I seen them nappies hanging on the lines behind McQueeny's house. There were little clothes hanging out to dry too. I could get the little fella some. Say, what are we going to call him?" Travis asked. "Anyone got any ideas?"

"What about Little Cole?" Cole suggested. "It's got a nice ring to it."

"What about Little Douglas?" Douglas asked. "It's got a nicer ring to it."

"We can't name him after one of us," Travis said. "We'd fight about it if we did."

Douglas and Cole finally agreed with Travis. "All right," Cole said. "The name's got to be something real important sounding."

"My pa's name was Andrew," Douglas interjected.

"So?" Cole asked. "He dumped you at the orphanage after your ma died, didn't he?"

"Yeah," Douglas admitted, his head downcast.

"We ain't gonna name the little fella after anyone who would throw a kid away. It ain't right. We got standards, don't we? This one already got himself tossed in the trash. No use reminding him with your pa's name hanging over his head. I say we call him Sidney, after that fancy fella who used to run the numbers over on Summit Street. He was a real mean one, Sidney was. You

17

remember him, don't you, Douglas?" Cole asked.

"I remember him all right," Douglas replied. "He was mighty respected."

"You got that right," Cole said. "And he died of regular causes. That's important, isn't it? No one snuck up on him and did him in."

"I like the sound of the name," Travis interjected. "Let's take a vote on it."

Douglas raised his right hand. It was coated with dirt and grime. "In favor?"

Cole and Travis both raised their hands. Adam didn't move. Cole seemed to be the only one to realize their boss hadn't offered much to the conversation in the past several minutes. He turned to look at their leader. "What's wrong, boss?"

"You know what's wrong," Adam answered. He sounded old, weary. "I have to leave. I don't stand a chance of surviving in the city. I've stayed far too long as it is. If I'm ever going to be free and not have to worry about my owner's sons finding me and taking me back, I have to go West. I can't live any kind of life hiding in alleys until the dark of night. A man can disappear out in the wilderness. You can understand, can't you? I shouldn't have a vote about the baby. I won't be here to help raise him."

"We can't make it without you, Adam," Travis cried out. "You can't leave us." He sounded like a frightened little boy. His voice cracked, then broke on a loud sob. His fear of being abandoned by his protector terrified him. "Please stay," he begged in a near shout.

The noise jarred the baby. The infant flinched

18

in reaction and let out a whimper.

Adam reached into the basket and awkwardly patted the baby's stomach. One touch and he immediately pulled back. "This baby's soaked through."

"Soaked through with what?" Cole asked. He started to reach for the bottle to see if there was a crack in the glass.

"Piddle," Travis answered. "Best get the nappy off him, boss. Otherwise his backside's gonna get sore."

The infant was struggling to wake up. The boys all stared in fascination. None could remember ever being this close to anything this tiny.

"He looks like he's full of wrinkles when he squiggles up his face like that," Douglas whispered with a snort. "He's a cute little bugger, ain't he?"

Cole nodded, then turned back to Adam. "You're the boss for now, Adam. You got to take that nappy off."

The oldest didn't shrug off the responsibility. He took a deep breath, grimaced, and then slid his hands under the baby's arms and slowly lifted him up out of the basket.

The baby's eyes opened. In the light from the torch Travis held up, they could all see how blue the color was. "He could be your little brother, Cole. You both got the exact color of eyes."

Adam's arms were rigidly extended in front of him. He had a pained expression on his face. Sweat beaded his forehead. He was obviously terrified holding the infant. He didn't know how hard to squeeze, and heaven help him if the little lad started to cry. He didn't know what in God's name he would do then.

In a hoarse whisper he asked Cole to please lift the gown and undo the nappy.

"Why me?" Cole complained.

"Travis is holding the torch and Douglas is too far away to get around my arms," Adam answered. "Hurry now. He might start squirming again. I'm afraid I'm going to drop him. He's so light, it's like holding air."

"The little fella's a curious one, ain't he?" Travis remarked to Douglas. "Look how he's studying each one of us. So serious for such a tiny bit of a thing."

"Douglas, reach around me and wipe my brow," Adam requested. "I can't see for all the sweat pouring down into my eyes."

Douglas snatched up a rag and did as he was requested. Adam was acting as though he were holding a piece of delicate dynamite. His concentration was intense and almost painful to watch.

Travis was the only one to see the humor in the boss's reaction. He let out a hoot of laughter. "He ain't gonna explode, boss. He's just like you, only smaller."

Cole wasn't paying any attention to the chatter going on around him. He held his breath while he worked on the nappy. Touching the soggy cotton made him want to gag. When the thing was finally released, it fell in a heap on the ground next to the basket. The boys all paused to look down and frown at the offending garment. Cole wiped his hands on his pant legs, then reached up to pull the gown back down over the baby's chubby thighs. He completed the task before the truth dawned on him.

And then he looked again, just to make certain.

Sidney was a baby girl. A bald baby girl, he qualified. He immediately got good and angry. Just what in thunder were they going to do with a useless, no account, never-amount-to-anything girl? He started to shake his head. His mind was made up all right. He wasn't going to have anything to do with her. No, sir, not him, not ever. Why, they ought to toss her right back into the trash.

She changed his mind in less than a minute's time. He was in the process of working up a real scowl when he happened to glance up at her face. She was staring right at him. He leaned to his left, out of her immediate line of vision. She followed him with her wide-eyed, trusting gaze. Cole tried to look away. He couldn't. He didn't want to keep staring at her, but he couldn't seem to make himself stop.

Then she went in for the kill. She smiled at him.

He was lost. The bond was formed in that instant.

The others fell like dominoes.

"We got to do it right." Cole's voice was a bare whisper. The other boys turned to look at him.

"Do what right?" Travis asked the question the others were thinking.

"There can't be any more talk of us being the best gang in New York City. We can't keep the baby here. It wouldn't be right. She needs a family, not a bunch of street thugs bossing her around."

"She?" Adam almost dropped the baby then and there. "Are you telling me you think Sidney's a baby girl?"

"I don't just think it, I know it," Cole announced with a nod. "She don't have the necessary parts to be a boy baby."

"God help us," Adam whispered.

Cole didn't know what he found more amusing, the look of horror on Adam's face when he implored his Maker's assistance, or the strange sound he made in the back of his throat when he croaked out his plea. He sounded as if he were choking on something big, like a chicken leg.

"I don't want no girls around," Travis muttered. "They ain't good for nothing. I hate every last one of them. They're just a bunch of complainers and crybabies."

The other boys ignored Travis. Douglas and Cole were both watching Adam. Their boss was looking ill.

"What's the matter, boss?" Cole asked.

"A black shouldn't be holding a lily white baby girl," Adam said.

Cole snorted. "I watched you save her from getting eaten up by the rats. If she was older and understood, she'd be mighty appreciative."

"Mighty appreciative," Douglas agreed with a nod.

"Besides," Cole said. "She don't know if you're black or white."

"You saying she's blind?" Travis asked, stunned

by the very possibility.

"She ain't blind," Cole muttered. He let the youngest member of the gang see his exasperation. "She's just too little to understand about hating yet. Babies aren't borned hating anything. They have to be taught. When she looks at Adam, all she's seeing is a . . . a brother. Yeah, that's what she's seeing, all right. And big brothers protect their little sisters, don't they? Ain't that a sacred rule or something? Maybe this little one already knows that."

"I made a promise to my mama," Adam told the other boys once again. "I gave her my word I would run as far west as I could until I found a place where I'd be safe. Mama told me there was a war coming, and when it was all over and everything was decided, there's a good chance she'll be free. She promised to come after me then. I just have to keep myself alive until that day comes. I promised her I'd survive, and a son doesn't break a promise to his mama. I have to run for her."

"Take the baby with you," Cole told him.

"They'd hang me for sure," Adam scoffed.

"Hell, they're gonna hang you anyway for killing the bastard who owned you, remember?" Cole said.

"If they catch you, Adam," Douglas interjected. "And you're too smart to let that happen."

"I'm feeling a might brotherly toward the baby too," Cole announced.

The other boys immediately turned to look at him. He became embarrassed over the way they were staring at him. "There ain't no cowardice in admitting it," he quickly added. "I'm strong, and she's just a puny little thing who needs brothers like Adam and me to see she grows up proper."

"Proper? What do you know about proper?" Douglas asked. There was a snicker of disbelief in his voice.

"Nothing," Cole admitted. "I don't know nothing about being proper," he added. "But Adam knows all about it, don't you, Adam? You talk good, and you read and write like a gentleman. Your mama taught you, and now you can teach me. I don't want to be ignorant in front of my little sister. It ain't right."

"He could teach all of us," Douglas said. He wasn't about to be left out.

"I don't guess I'd hate her if I was her big brother," Travis grumbled. "I'm gonna get real strong when I'm all growed up. Isn't that true, Douglas?"

"Yeah, it's true all right," Douglas confirmed. "You know what I think?"

"What's that?" Adam asked. He smiled in spite of his worries, for the little one had just given him the silliest grin. She was sure pleased with herself. She seemed to like being the center of attention. For such a tiny thing, she held considerable power over all of them. Her smile alone made him feel all warm and comforted inside. Her easy acceptance of him was melting away the painful knot he'd been carrying around in his belly ever since the day he'd had to leave his mama. The baby was a gift magically given into his care, and it was his duty to see that she was nurtured and protected and cherished.

"I sometimes wonder if God always knows what He's doing," Adam whispered.

"Of course He does," Douglas replied. "And I think He would want us to come up with another name for our baby. Sidney don't seem right now. I sure hope she grows some hair. I don't cotton to the notion of having a bald little sister."

"Mary," Cole blurted out.

"Rose," Adam said at the very same time.

"Mary was my mama's name," Cole explained. "She died having me. I heard tell from neighbors she was a right good woman."

"My mama's name is Rose," Adam said. "She is a right good woman too."

"The baby's falling asleep," Travis whispered. "Put her back down in the basket, and I'll try to slip another nappy on her. Then you two can argue about her name."

Adam did as he was instructed. They all watched as Travis awkwardly put a dry nappy on. The baby was sound asleep before he finished messing with her.

"I don't think there's anything to argue about," Douglas said. He reached over to cover the baby while Adam and Cole both muttered their reasons again for wanting the baby named after their mothers. Douglas knew a full-blown argument was developing, and he wanted to stop it before it went any further. "I say it's all settled. Her name is Mary Rose. Mary is for your mama, Cole, and Rose is for your Mama Rose, Adam."

Cole was the first to see the rightness in the name and the first to smile. Adam quickly agreed.

Travis started to laugh, and Douglas hushed him by shoving his elbow in his side, so he wouldn't wake the baby.

"We have to make plans," Douglas whispered. "I think we should leave as soon as possible, maybe even tomorrow night, on the midnight train. Travis, you got until then to get the things we'll need for Mary Rose. I'll buy the tickets for us. Adam, you'll have to hide in the baggage car with the baby. Is that all right with you?"

Adam nodded. "You figure it all out, and I'll do it," he promised.

"How are you going to buy the tickets?" Cole asked.

"The envelope I took from the woman who threw Mary Rose away was stuffed with money. There were some old-looking papers with fancy writing and seals on the paper, but I can't make out any of it because I can't read. I know money when I see it though. We got us enough to get as far as Adam needs to go and stake us some land."

"Let me see those papers," Adam asked.

Douglas pulled the envelope out of his pocket and handed it to their boss. Adam let out a whistle when he saw all the money tucked inside. He found two papers and pulled them out. One was filled with numbers and scratches he couldn't make out, and the other sheet looked like a blank page torn from a book. There was only a little bit of handwriting on the top, giving the baby's date of birth and her weight. He read the words out loud so the others would know what he'd found.

"It weren't enough they threw her away. They even thrown out her papers," Douglas whispered.

"I didn't have papers when I was dumped at the orphanage," Travis said. "It's a good thing I already knew my name, isn't it, Cole?"

"I suppose so," Cole answered.

Travis shrugged off the matter as unimportant. "I got a suggestion to make now, so don't interrupt me until you hear me out. All right?"

He waited until everyone nodded before he continued. "I'm the only one of us who knows for certain I'm not wanted by the law, and nobody's looking to find me, so I say Mary Rose should carry my last name. Fact is, if we're gonna do it right, like Cole says we should, then everyone should take my last name. Brothers and sisters are all part of the same family, after all, and they all got to have the same last name. So I'm saying, from this minute on, we're all Claybornes. Agreed?"

"No one's going to believe I'm a Clayborne," Adam argued.

"Who cares what anyone else believes?" Cole asked. "We ain't asking for approval, just to be left alone. If you say you're a Clayborne, and we say you're a Clayborne, whose to say you ain't? Anyone who challenges you has to get through the rest of us first if he wants to make trouble. And remember," he added, "I got me a gun now. Soon enough I'll be able to handle any trouble that comes our way."

Douglas and Travis nodded. Adam let out a sigh. Douglas put his hand out over the basket,

27

his palm down. He looked at each of the other gang members.

"I say we run for Mama Rose and we become a family for our little Mary Rose. We're brothers," he whispered.

Travis put his hand on top of Douglas's. "Brothers," he vowed.

Cole was next. "We run for Mary Rose and Mama Rose," he pledged. "We're brothers until we die."

Adam hesitated for what seemed an eternity to the other boys. And then his mind was finally made up. His hand covered Cole's. "Brothers," he vowed in a voice shaking with emotion. "For the Roses."

July 3, 1860

Dear Mama Rose,

I'm writing to you in care of Mistress Livonia, and I pray this letter finds the two of you in good health. I'm going to share with you all the wonderful adventures I've had heading West, but first I have something very important to tell you. It's about your new family. You have a namesake now, Mama. Her name is Mary Rose . . .

Love,
John Quincy Adam Clayborne

1

Montana Valley, 1879

The baby was finally coming home.

Cole waited next to his wagon for the stagecoach to round the last bend in the road. He was so excited, he could barely stand still. The cloud of dust coming from above the hill indicated she was close. He couldn't wait to see her. He wondered if she'd changed much in the past months, then laughed out loud over the foolish notion. Mary Rose had been all grown up when she'd left for her last year of school. Other than acquiring a few more freckles on the bridge of her nose, or letting her hair grow a little longer, he couldn't imagine any significant changes.

Lord, he'd missed her. They all had. Life on the ranch kept them running from sunup until sundown, and it was only at dinner that they all ached to have her around trying to boss them into eating something new and different she had prepared for them. She was a fine cook when she didn't stray from the familiar, but none of them could abide the fancy French sauces she liked to pour over everything.

The stagecoach was over an hour late, which meant that crusty old Clive Harrington was doing the driving. He would have had to catch up on all the gossip with Mary Rose before they started

30

out. Clive would demand her full attention, and knowing what a soft heart his sister had, Cole knew she wouldn't rush him.

They were fast friends, but no one in Blue Belle could understand why. Clive Harrington was a cantankerous old buzzard who constantly scowled, snapped, and complained and was, in Cole's estimation, a thoroughly disagreeable son-of-a-bitch. He was also as ugly as sin. The walkways in town would clear at the first sight of him, unless Mary Rose was around. A magical transformation took place then. Clive went from ferocious to meek. Not only did he act as though he were everyone's best friend, he also wore a ridiculous, ain't-life-grand grin from morning until night. Harrington made a complete fool of himself doting on Mary Rose, and all because she doted on him. She really cared about the old coot. She took care of him when he needed caring, made certain he was included in their holiday dinners, and personally mended all of his clothes for him. Harrington always took ill once a year, usually around roundup time, but sometimes a full month before. He'd appear on their doorstep with his hat in one hand and a dirty handkerchief in the other, asking for a bit of advice about how to cure his latest mysterious ailment. It was all a ruse, of course. Mary Rose would immediately park old Clive in the guest room and pamper him for the full week it always took before he felt fit again.

Everyone in town called Harrington's week of infirmity his annual getaway, and from the way the old man was dabbing at the corners of his eyes and rubbing his nose with his handkerchief while he slowed the horses, Cole surmised he was already planning his next holiday.

The stagecoach had barely rocked to a stop when the door flew open and Mary Rose jumped to the ground.

"I'm finally home," she called out. She picked up her skirts and ran to her brother. Her bonnet flew off her head and landed in the dust behind her. She was laughing with sheer joy. Cole tried to maintain his somber expression because he didn't want Harrington spreading the rumor he'd gone soft. Cole liked having everyone in town fear him. His sister's laughter proved contagious, however, and Cole couldn't control his reaction. He smiled first, then burst into laughter. Appearances be damned.

Mary Rose hadn't changed at all. She was still just as dramatic and uninhibited as always, and, heaven help him, she'd be the death of all the brothers, who constantly worried about the way she always wore her heart on her sleeve.

She threw herself into his arms. For such a little thing, she had the grip of a bear. Cole hugged her back, kissed her on the top of her head, and then suggested to her that she quit laughing like a crazy woman.

She wasn't offended. She pulled away, put her hands on her hips, and gave her brother a thorough inspection.

"You're still as handsome as ever, Cole. Have you killed anyone while I was at school?"

"Of course not," he snapped. He folded his arms across his chest, leaned back against the wagon, and tried to frown at her.

"You look like you grew another inch or two. Your hair seems more blond too. When did you get that scar on your forehead? Did you get into a fight?"

Before he could answer her questions, she turned to Harrington. "Clive, did my brother shoot anyone while I was away?"

"Not that I recollect, Miss Mary," he called back.

"Any knife fights?" she asked.

"I don't think so," Clive answered.

Mary Rose seemed convinced. She smiled again. "I'm so happy to be home. I've made up my mind. I'm never leaving again. Adam isn't going to make me go anywhere, no matter how good it might be for my mind or my soul. I'm all refined now, and I've got the papers to prove it. Lord, it's warm for spring, isn't it? I love the heat and the dirt and the wind and the dust. Has Travis gotten into any fights in town? Never mind," she added in a rush. "You wouldn't tell me if he did anything wrong. Adam will though. He tells me everything. He wrote more than you did, by the way. Is the new barn finished? I got a letter from Mama Rose just the day before school ended. The mail arrived right on time too. Isn't that something? We live in such modern times. What about . . ."

Cole was having trouble keeping up with his sister. She was talking as fast as a politician. "Slow down," he interrupted. "I can only answer one question at a time. Catch your breath while I help Harrington unload your baggage."

A few minutes later, her trunk, boxes, and three valises were packed in the back of the wagon. Mary Rose climbed up on the flatbed and started sorting through her things.

Cole told her to wait until they got home to find what she was looking for. She ignored his suggestion. She closed one box and turned to the second one.

Harrington stood next to the wagon, smiling at her. "I sure missed you, Miss Mary," he whispered. He blushed like a schoolboy and gave Cole a quick look to make sure he wasn't going to laugh at him.

Cole pretended he hadn't heard the confession. He turned away before he rolled his eyes heavenward. His sister was obviously pleased by Harrington's admission. "I missed you too, Clive. Did you get my letters?"

"I surely did," he replied. "I read them more than once too."

Mary Rose smiled at her friend. "I'm happy to hear it. I didn't forget your birthday. Don't leave just yet. I have something for you."

She was diligently sorting through her trunk and finally found the box she had been searching for.

She handed it to Clive. "This is for you. Promise me you won't open it until you get home."

"You got me a present?" He looked flabbergasted.

She smiled. "Two presents," she corrected. "There's another surprise tucked inside the first."

"What is it?" Clive asked. He sounded like a little boy on Christmas morning.

Mary Rose took hold of his hand and climbed down out of the wagon. "It's a surprise," she answered. "That's why I wrapped it in a box with such pretty paper. Thank you for the ride," she added with a curtsy. "It was very lovely."

"You ain't mad because I wouldn't let you ride up on the perch with me?"

"No, I'm not angry," she assured him.

Harrington turned to Cole to explain. "She begged me to let her sit up there with me, but I didn't think it would be fitting for such a dignified young lady to be riding shotgun."

Cole nodded. "We need to get going, Mary Rose."

He didn't wait for her agreement but turned and got up on the seat of the wagon. He took the reins in his hands and asked his sister to quit dawdling.

She had to chase after her forgotten bonnet first. Clive was clutching his present with both hands while he slowly walked back to his coach. He acted as if he were carrying a priceless treasure.

They were finally on their way home. Cole answered her questions while she removed most of the evidence proving she was a refined lady. She took off her white gloves first, then pulled out the pins holding her prim bun together at the back of her neck. She wasn't satisfied until the thick, blond mass floated down her back.

She let out a sigh of pleasure while she threaded her fingers through her curls.

"I'm so sick of being a lady," she said. "Honest to heaven, it's such a strain."

Cole laughed. Mary Rose knew she wouldn't get any sympathy from him.

"You wouldn't laugh if you had to wear a corset. It binds a body up as tight as a coil. It isn't natural."

"Did they make you wear one of those things at school?" Cole was horrified by the idea.

"Yes," she answered. "I didn't though. No one could tell, after all. I never got dressed in public."

"I hope to God not."

He had to slow the horses when they started the steep climb up the first ridge. Mary Rose turned around so she could watch to make sure her trunk didn't fall off the back of the wagon.

Once they'd reached the crest, she turned around again. She took off her navy blue jacket, draped it over the back of the bench, and started unbuttoning the cuffs of her starched white blouse. The collar was chafing her neck. She unbuttoned the top three buttons.

"Something odd happened at school. I didn't know what to make of it."

"Make of what?" he asked.

"A new classmate arrived in January. She was from Chicago. Her parents came with her to help her get settled."

"And?"

Mary Rose shrugged. "It's probably nothing."

"Tell me anyway. I can hear the worry in your voice."

"I am not worrying," she said. "It was just so peculiar. The girl's mother was born and raised in England. She thought she knew me."

"She can't know you," he said. "You've never

been to England. Could you have met her some-place else?"

Mary Rose shook her head. "I'm sure I would have remembered."

"Tell me what happened."

"I was walking across the commons. I smiled at the new arrivals, just to be polite and make them feel welcome, and all of a sudden, the girl's mother lets out a scream loud enough to frighten the stone gargoyles on top of Emmet Building. She scared me too."

"Why's that?" he asked.

"She was pointing at me all the while she was screaming," Mary Rose explained. "I became quite embarrassed."

"Then what happened?"

"She clutched her chest with both hands and looked like she was going to keel over."

"All right, Mary Rose. What'd you do?" He was immediately suspicious his sister wasn't telling him everything. She had a habit of getting into mischief, and she was always astonished by the trouble that would inevitably follow.

"I didn't do anything wrong," she cried out. "I was acting like a perfect lady. Why would you jump to the conclusion I was responsible for the poor woman's condition?" she asked, sounding wounded.

"Because you usually are responsible," he reminded her. "Were you carrying your gun at the time?"

"Of course not," she replied. "I wasn't running or doing anything the least improper. I do know how to behave like a lady when I have to, Cole."

37

"Then what was the matter with the woman?"

"When she finally calmed down, she told me she thought I was a woman she used to know. She called her Lady Agatha Something-or-other. She said I was the spitting image of the woman."

"That isn't peculiar," he decided. "Lots of women have blond hair and blue eyes. It's not unusual."

"Are you saying I'm plain?"

He couldn't resist. "Yeah, I guess I am."

It was a lie, of course. Mary Rose was the complete opposite of plain. She was really very beautiful, or so he'd been told over and over again by every eligible man in town. He didn't see his sister that way. She was sweet and good-hearted most of the time, and a little wildcat the rest of the time. She used to be a brat, but now that she was all grown up, he guessed she wasn't such a pain after all.

"Adam assures me I'm pretty," she argued. She shoved her brother with her shoulder. "He always tells the truth. Besides, you know very well it's what's inside a woman's heart that really matters. Mama Rose thinks I'm a beautiful daughter, and she's never even seen me."

"You about finished being vain, Mary Rose?"

She laughed. "Yes."

"I wouldn't worry about the coincidence of looking like someone else."

"But that wasn't the end of it," she explained. "About a month later, I was called into the superior's office. There was an elderly man waiting for me. The headmistress was there too. She had my file on her desk."

"How'd you know it was your file?"

"Because it's the thickest one at the school," she answered. "And the cover's torn."

She looked at her brother and immediately knew what he was thinking. "You can quit smiling that know-it-all smile of yours, Cole. I will admit that my first year at school didn't go well. I had a little trouble adjusting. I realize now I was simply homesick and was trying to get thrown out so you'd have to come and get me. However," she hastily added, "I have had a perfect record ever since, and that should count for something."

"Tell me about the man waiting in the office," he said.

"He was a lawyer," she said. "He asked me all sorts of questions about our family. He wanted to know how long we'd lived in Montana and why our mother didn't live with us. He wanted me to describe to him what my brothers looked like too. I wouldn't answer any of his questions. I didn't think it was any of his business. He was a complete stranger, after all. I didn't like him at all."

Cole didn't like him either. "Did he explain why he was asking all these questions?"

"He told me there was a large inheritance at issue. I think he went away convinced I wasn't a long-lost relative. I've made you worry, haven't I?"

"A little," he admitted. "I don't like the idea of anyone asking about us."

She tried to lighten his mood. "It wasn't all bad," she said. "I hadn't studied for my English

39

exam because Eleanor kept me up half the night complaining about some latest slight. Since I was in the office, I got to wait until the following day to take the test."

"I thought you weren't going to put up with Eleanor again."

"I swear to you I wasn't," Mary Rose replied. "No one else would take her for a roommate though, and the mistress practically got down on her hands and knees begging me to take Eleanor in. Poor Eleanor. She has a good heart, honest she does, but she keeps it hidden most of the time. She's still a trial of endurance."

Cole smiled. Eleanor had been the one wrinkle in his sister's otherwise perfect life. Mary Rose was the only student at school who would suffer the young woman's presence. The brothers loved hearing Eleanor stories. They found the woman's antics hysterically funny, and when any of them needed a good laugh, an Eleanor story had to be dredged up.

"Was she as ornery as ever?" he asked, hoping his sister had a new story to tell.

"She was," Mary Rose admitted. "I used to feel guilty telling all of you about her, but then Travis convinced me that since no harm was done and she'd never find out, it was all right. She really can be outrageous. Do you know she left school a full week before everyone else? She didn't even say good-bye. Something was wrong with her father, but she wouldn't tell me what it was. She cried herself to sleep five nights in a row, then she left. I wish she'd confided in me. I would have helped if I could. Her father wasn't ill. I asked the headmistress after Eleanor took off. She wouldn't tell me anything, but she puckered her lips, and she only does that when she is really disgusted about something. Eleanor's father was going to donate a large sum of money so the mistress could build another dormitory. She told me it was all off now. Do you know what she said?"

"No, what?"

"She said she'd been duped. What do you suppose she meant by that?"

"Could be anything."

"Just the night before Eleanor left, I told her that if she ever needed me, all she had to do was come to Rosehill."

"Why'd you go and tell her that?" Cole asked.

"She was being pitiful, crying like a baby," Mary Rose explained. "I wouldn't worry about her showing up at the ranch though. It's too uncivilized out here for her. She's very sophisticated. But she hurt my feelings when she didn't say good-bye. I was her only friend, after all. I wasn't a very good friend though, was I?"

"Why do you think you weren't?"

"You know why," she replied. "I tell stories about her and that isn't at all nice. Friends shouldn't talk about each other."

"You only told us about incidents that really happened, and you defended her to everyone at school. You never talked about her there, did you?"

"No."

"Then I don't see the harm. You've never criticized her, not even to us."

"Yes, but . . ."

"You also made sure she was invited to all the parties. Because of you, she was never left out."

"How did you know I did that?"

"I know you. You're always looking out for the misfits."

"Eleanor is not a misfit."

"See? You're already defending her again."

She smiled. "After I've talked matters over with you I always feel better. Do you really believe the lawyer will quit asking about us?"

"Yes, I do," he answered.

She let out a sigh. "I missed you, Cole."

"I missed you too, brat."

She nudged him with her shoulder again. The talk turned to the ranch. While she'd been away at school, the brothers had purchased another section of land. Travis was in Hammond getting the supplies they needed to fence in a portion of the vast expanse so the horses would have enough grazing space to see them through the winter.

Cole and Mary Rose reached Rosehill a few minutes later. When she was just eight years old, she had named their home. She'd found what she believed were wild roses growing out on the hillside, declared it was a message sent to them from God telling them they were never supposed to leave, and all because her name was Mary Rose and so was her mama's. Adam didn't want to dampen her enthusiasm. For that reason, he didn't tell her the flowers were pink fireweed, not roses. He also felt that naming their ranch might give his sister an added bit of security. The name stuck, and within a year, even the residents of Blue Belle were referring to Clayborne homestead by the fanciful name.

Rosehill sat in the very middle of a valley deep in the Montana Territory. The land was flat around the ranch for nearly a quarter of a mile in every direction. Cole had insisted on building their home in the very center of the flat expanse so he would be able to see anyone trespassing on their land. He didn't like surprises; none of the brothers did, and as soon as the two-story house was finished, he built a lookout above the attic so they would always be able to see anyone trying to sneak up on them.

Majestic, snowcapped mountains provided the backdrop on the north and west sides of the meadow. The east side of the homestead was made up of smaller mountains and hills, which were useless land for ranchers because of their need for rich grazing pasture. Trappers worked the eastern slopes, however, as beaver and bear and timber wolf were still quite plentiful. Occasionally a worn, weary trapper would stop by the house for food and friendly conversation. Adam never turned a hungry man away, and if their guest was in need of a bed for the night, he'd put him in the bunkhouse.

There was only one easy way into the ranch, and that was from the main road that led over the hill from the town of Blue Belle. Outsiders were pretty worn out by the time they reached even the riverboat stop though. If they used wagons to haul their possessions, it usually took

43

them a good day and a half more to reach Blue Belle. Most didn't bother to go farther than Perry or Hammond; only rugged, determined souls, or men on the run, ever continued on. While there were occasional whispers of gold hidden in the mountains to the north, none had actually been found, and that was the only reason the land had stayed uncluttered. Decent, law-abiding families, hoping to homestead free land, crossed the plains in prairie schooners or took their chances on any one of the multitude of river-boats navigating the Missouri River. By the time most of these families got to a large town, they were happy to stay there. It was somewhat civilized in the larger towns, which of course was a powerful lure to the eastern, church-going families. Honest folks cried out for law and order. Vigilante groups heard the call and soon cleaned out all the riffraff hanging around the larger towns, including Hammond.

In the beginning, the vigilantes were a solution, but later they became an even more threatening problem, for some of the men got into the nasty habit of hanging just about anyone they didn't like. Justice was swift and often unserved, hearsay was all the evidence needed to have a man dragged out of his house and hanged from the nearest tree limb. Even wearing a badge gave one no protection from a vigilante group.

The real misfits and gunfighters looking for easy money, who were quick and cunning enough to escape lynching, left the larger towns like Hammond and settled in and around Blue Belle.

For that reason, the town had a well-earned

seedy reputation. Still, there were a few good families living in Blue Belle. Adam said it was only because they had got settled in before they realized their mistake.

Mary Rose was never allowed to go into Blue Belle alone. Since Adam never, ever left the ranch, it was up to Travis or Douglas or Cole to escort her on her errands. The brothers all took turns, and if it wasn't convenient for any of them to leave their chores, Mary Rose stayed home.

Cole slowed the horses when they reached the crest of the hill that separated the main road into town from the Clayborne estate. Mary Rose would ask him to stop the minute they reached the last curve that led down into their valley below.

She was as predictable as ever. "Please stop for a minute. I've been away such a long time."

He dutifully stopped the horses and then patiently waited for her next question. It would take her a minute or two. She had to get all emotional first, then her eyes would fill up with tears.

"Do you feel it? Right now, do you feel it the way I do?"

He smiled. "You ask me that same question every time I bring you home. Yes, I feel it."

He reached for his handkerchief and handed it to her. He'd learned a long time ago to carry one just for her. Once, when she was still a little girl, she'd used the sleeve of his shirt to wipe her nose. He wasn't about to ever let that happen again.

They had a panoramic view of their ranch and the mountains beyond. No matter how she re-

45

membered it, every time she came home, the first sight of such beauty would fairly overwhelm her. Adam told her it was because she gloried in God's creation and was humbled by it. She wasn't so certain about that, but the vibration of life coming from the land did stir her as nothing else could. She wanted her brothers to feel it too, this link between God and nature, and Cole would admit, but only to her, that yes, he did feel the pulse of life beating all around them. The land was never quite the same from glance to glance, yet always enduring.

"She's as alive and beautiful as ever, Mary Rose."

"Why is it you and Adam both call Montana a woman?"

"Because she acts like one," Cole answered. He didn't blush or feel embarrassed talking such foolishness, because he knew his sister understood. "She's fickle and vain and won't ever be tamed by any man. She's a woman all right, and the only one I'll ever love."

"You love me."

"You're not a woman, Mary Rose. You're my sister."

She laughed. The sound echoed through the pine trees. Cole picked up the reins and started the horses down the gentle slope. They had lingered long enough.

"If she's a woman, she's taken us into her embrace. I wonder if my roses are beginning to wake up yet."

"You ought to know by now the flowers you found aren't roses. They're pink fireweed."

46

"I know what they are," she replied. "But they're like roses."

"No, they aren't."

They were already bickering. Mary Rose sighed with contentment. She kept her attention focused on her home. Lord, she was happy to see her ranch again. The clapboard house was rather unimposing, she supposed, but it was still beautiful to her. The porch, or veranda, as Adam liked to call it, ran the length of the house on three sides. In the summer they would sit outside every evening and listen to the music of the night.

She didn't see her eldest brother working outside. "I'll bet Adam is working on his books."

"What makes you think so?"

"It's too nice a day to be cooped up inside unless there was book work to do," she reasoned. "I can't wait to see him. Do hurry, Cole."

She was anxious for the reunion with all of her brothers. She had gifts for everyone, including a box full of books Adam would treasure, drawing paper and new pens for Cole to use when he was designing a new building to add to the ranch, medicine and brushes for Douglas to use on his horses, a new journal for Travis to keep the family history in, several catalogues, seed for the garden she, under Adam's supervision, would plant behind the house, chocolates, and store-bought flannel shirts for all of them.

The reunion was every bit as wonderful as she knew it would be. The family stayed up well into the night talking. Cole didn't tell his brothers about the attorney who had visited Mary Rose's school until after she had gone up to bed. He didn't want her to worry. He was worried, however. None of them believed in coincidences, and so they discussed every possible reason the lawyer could have to want information about the Clayborne family. Douglas and Cole had both done unsavory things when they were youngsters, but time and distance from the gangsters they'd preyed upon had convinced them their crimes had been forgotten. The real concern was for Adam. If the attorney had been hired by the sons of Adam's slave master to track him down, then trouble was coming their way.

Murder, they all knew, would never be forgotten. Adam had taken one life to save two others. It had been accidental, but the circumstances wouldn't be important to the sons. A slave had struck their father.

No, the father's death would never be forgotten or forgiven. It would be avenged.

An hour passed in whispered discussion, and then Adam, as head of the household, declared it was foolish to worry or speculate. If there was indeed a threat, they would have to wait to find out what it was.

"And then?" Cole asked.

"We do whatever it takes to protect each other," Adam said.

"We aren't going to let anyone hang you, Adam. You only did what you had to do," Travis said.

"We're borrowing trouble," Adam said. "We'll keep our guard up and wait."

The discussion ended. A full month passed in peaceful solitude. It was business as usual, and Travis and Douglas were both beginning to think that perhaps nothing would ever come from the lawyer's inquiry.

The threat finally presented itself. His name was Harrison Stanford MacDonald, and he was the man who would tear all of their lives apart.

He was the enemy.

November 12, 1860

Dear Mama Rose,

Yore sun wanted me to show off my writing skil and so I am writing this her letter to you. We all work on gramer and speling afther Mary Rose goes to sleepe. Yore sun is a fine teecher. He dont lauf when we make misteaks and he always has good to say when we dun fore the nite. Since we are brothurs now I gues you belong to me to.

Yore sun,
Cole

2

Harrison Stanford MacDonald was learning all about the Clayborne family without asking a single question. He was a stranger in town and therefore should have been met with suspicion and mistrust. He had heard all about the wild and rugged, lawless towns dotting the West and read everything he could get his hands on as well. From all of his research, he'd learned that strangers inevitably fell into one of two groups. There were those men who were ignored and left alone because they kept to themselves but looked intimidating, and those men who got themselves killed because they asked too many questions.

The code of honor that existed in the West perplexed Harrison. He thought it was the most backward set of rules he'd ever heard. The inhabitants usually protected their own against outsiders, yet took it all in stride when one neighbor went after another. Killing each other seemed to be acceptable, providing, of course, that there was a hint of a good reason.

On his journey to Blue Belle, Harrison considered the problem he would have finding out what he needed to know and finally came up with what he believed was a suitable course of action. He decided to use the town's prejudice against strangers to his own advantage by simply turning the tables on them.

He arrived in Blue Belle around ten o'clock in the morning and became the meanest son-of-a-bitch who ever hit town. He acted outrageously suspicious of everyone who dared to even look his way. He wore his new black hat down low on his brow, turned up the collar of his long, brown trail duster, kept a hard scowl on his face, and sauntered down the middle of the main road the residents called a street, but which was really just a wide dirt path, acting as if he owned the place. He gave the word "sullen" new definition. He wanted to look like a man who would kill anyone who got in his way, and he guessed he'd accomplished his goal when a woman walking with her little boy caught sight of him striding toward her and immediately grabbed hold of her son's hand and went running in the opposite direction.

He wanted to smile. He didn't dare. He'd never find out anything about the Claybornes if he turned friendly. And so he maintained his angry hate-everyone-and-everything attitude.

They loved him.

His first stop was the always popular town saloon. Every town had one, and Blue Belle wasn't any different. He found the drinking establishment at the end of the road, went inside, and ordered a bottle of whiskey and one glass. If the proprietor found the request odd for such an early hour, he didn't mention it. Harrison took the bottle and the glass to the darkest corner in the saloon, sat down at a round table with his back to the wall, and simply waited for the curious to come and talk to him.

He didn't have to wait long. The saloon had

been completely empty of customers when he had entered the establishment. Word of the stranger's arrival spread as fast as a prairie fire, however, and within ten minutes, Harrison counted nine men inside. They sat in clusters around the other tables spread about the saloon, and every single one of them was staring at him.

He kept his shoulders hunched forward and his gaze on his shot glass. The thought of actually taking a drink this early in the morning made his stomach want to lurch, and he didn't have any intention of swallowing a single sip, so he swirled the murky amber liquid around and around in his glass and tried to look as if he were brooding about something.

He heard whispering, then the shuffle of footsteps coming across the wooden floor. Harrison's hand instinctively went for his gun. He pushed his coat out of the way and rested his hand on the butt of his weapon. He stopped himself from pulling the gun free, then realized that what he'd done instinctively was actually what he should have done if he were going to continue his hostile charade.

"Mister, you new in town?"

Harrison slowly lifted his gaze. The man who'd asked the ridiculous question had obviously been sent over by the others. He was unarmed. He was also old, probably around fifty, with leathery, pockmarked skin, and he was about the homeliest individual Harrison had ever come across. Squinty brown eyes the size of marbles were all but lost in his round face, for the only feature anyone was ever going to notice was his gigantic potato-

53

shaped nose. It was, in Harrison's estimation, a real attention getter.

"Who wants to know?" he asked, making his voice as surly as possible.

Potato-nose smiled. "My name's Dooley," he announced. "Mind if I sit a spell?"

Harrison didn't respond to the question. He simply stared at the man and waited to see what he would do.

Dooley took his silence as a yes, dragged out a chair, and sat down facing Harrison. "You in town looking for someone?"

Harrison shook his head. Dooley turned to their audience. "He ain't looking for anyone," he shouted. "Billie, fetch me a glass. I could use me a drink, if this stranger is willing to share."

He turned back to Harrison. "You a gun-fighter?"

"I don't like questions," Harrison replied.

"Nope, I didn't think you were a gunfighter," Dooley said. "If you were, you would have heard Webster left town just yesterday. He was looking for a draw, but no one would oblige him, not even Cole Clayborne, and he's the only reason Webster really came to town. Cole's the fastest gun we got around here. He don't get into gun-fights anymore though, especially now that his sister came home from school. She don't abide with gunfights, and she don't want Cole getting himself a bad reputation. Adam keeps him on the square," he added with a knowing nod. "He's the oldest of the brothers and a real peacemaker, if you ask me. He's book smart too, and once you get over what he looks like, well, then, you realize he's the man you should go to if you got a problem. He usually knows what's to be done. You thinking of maybe settling around here or are you just passing through?"

Billie, the proprietor of the saloon, strutted over with two glasses in his hands. He put both of them down on the table and then motioned to a man sitting near the door.

"Henry, get on over here and shut your friend up. He's making a nuisance of himself asking so many questions. Don't want to see him killed before lunch. It's bad for business."

Harrison gave only half answers to the questions that followed. Henry joined them, and once he'd taken his seat, the proprietor pulled out a chair, hiked one booted leg up on the seat, and leaned forward with his arm draped across his knee. The three men were obviously fast friends. They liked to gossip and were soon interrupting each other with stories about everyone in town. The threesome reminded Harrison of old-maid aunts who liked to meddle but didn't mean anyone harm. Harrison filed away every bit of information they gave him, never once asking a question of his own.

The talk eventually turned to the availability of women in the area.

"They're as scarce as diamonds in these here parts, but we got us seven or eight eligible ones. A couple of them are right pretty. There's Catherine Morrison. Her pa owns the general store. She's got nice brown hair and all her teeth."

"She don't hold a candle to Mary Rose Clayborne," Billie interjected.

Loud grunts of agreement came from across the room. Everyone inside the saloon, it seemed, was listening in on the conversation.

"She ain't just pretty," a gray-haired man called out.

"She's a knock-your-breath-out-of-you looker," Henry agreed. "And as sweet-natured as they come."

"Ain't that the truth," Dooley said. "If you're in need of help, she'll be there to see you get it."

More grunts of agreement followed his statement.

"Injuns come from miles around just to get a swatch of her hair. She gets real exasperated, but she always gives them a lock. It's as pretty as spun gold. The Injuns think it brings them good luck. Ain't that right?" Henry asked Billie.

The proprietor nodded. "Once a couple of half-breeds tried to steal her off her ranch. They said they got themselves tranced by her blue eyes. Said they were magical, they did. You remember what happened then, boys?" he asked his friends.

Dooley let out a hoot of laughter. "I recollect it as sure as if it happened yesterday. Adam weren't no peacemaker that day, was he, Ghost?"

A man with stark white hair and a long, scraggly, white beard nodded.

"No, sir, he weren't," he shouted. "As I recall, Adam almost tore one of the half-breeds clear in half. No one's tried to steal her since."

"Miss Mary don't get herself courted much," Billie said. "It's a shame too. She should have two or three babies pulling at her skirts by now."

Harrison didn't have to ask why she wasn't courted. Dooley was happy to explain. "She's got herself four brothers none of us is willing to take on. No sir*reee*. You can't get to her without going through them. That's why she ain't married up yet. You'd best stay clear away from her."

"Oh, she won't have nothing to do with him," Ghost shouted.

Dooley nodded. "She only takes to the bumbling ones and the weaklings. Seems to think it's her duty to look out for them. It's because she's so sweet-natured."

"I already told him that," Henry said.

"She drives her brothers crazy the way she drags home the pitiful ones. Still, they got to put up with it," Billie said.

"She likes us, and we ain't weaklings." Dooley obviously wanted to set the record straight.

"No, of course we ain't," Henry agreed. "We wouldn't want you to get the wrong idea, mister. Miss Mary likes us because we've been around so long. She's used to us. You can get yourself a gander at her in a couple of hours. We like to line up in front of the store around noon so we can get a good, close look at her. She's always got something real nice to say to each one of us. I'm hoping her brother Douglas rides shotgun with her today."

"Why's that?" Billie asked.

"My mare's acting fussy again. I need the doc to take a look at her."

"If you're in need of a good horse, Douglas has a stable full," Dooley told Harrison. "He tames the wild ones and sells them every now

57

and then. He's got to like you though. He's peculiar about who gets hold of his horses. He ain't a real doctor, but we like to call him such."

"He don't like it none, Dooley. Says he ain't a doctor and we shouldn't be calling him one," Ghost called out.

"I know that," Dooley shouted back. His exasperation was apparent in his tone of voice. "That's why we never call him Doc to his face. He's got a special way with animals though, and he's good with his remedies."

"What kind of business are you in?" Billie asked Harrison. "I'm just being neighborly, mister," he added.

"Legal work," Harrison answered.

"That won't make you enough money to put food in your belly, at least not on a regular basis. You do anything else?"

"I hunt."

"Then you're a trapper," Henry decreed.

Harrison shook his head. "Not exactly," he hedged. He was on a hunt now, but he wasn't about to tell these men he was searching for a stolen child. She would be a fully grown woman by now.

"You're either a trapper or you ain't," Henry said. "You got any equipment to trap with?"

"No."

"Then you ain't a trapper," Henry told him. "What about ranching? You ever try your hand at ranching? You've got the build for it. I don't recall ever seeing anyone as big as you are, or as wide across the shoulders. A couple of the Clayborne brothers come to mind, and Johnny

Simpson, of course, but I think you might be a half a head taller than any of them."

"You willing to tell us your name?" Henry asked.

"Harrison," he answered. "My name's Harrison MacDonald."

"You got a last name for a first name, don't you?" Dooley remarked. "Will you take offense if I call you Harrison, or do you want to be called MacDonald?"

"Call me Harrison."

"Guess I should if you're gonna be settling here. You got yourself a real different-sounding twang in there with your words," he added. He hastily put his hands up. "I don't mean you no insult. I'm just wondering now where you come from."

"California?" Henry guessed.

"I'm thinking Kentucky," Ghost called out.

Harrison shook his head. "I was born in Scotland and raised in England," he answered. "Across the ocean," he added in case they didn't know where those countries were located.

"The town could use a lawyer," Billie interjected. "We don't have any around these parts. If Adam Clayborne doesn't know the answer, then we got to go all the way to Hammond to get the help we need. Hanging Judge Burns will be happy to have you around. He gets upset when he has to work with . . . what does he call us?" he asked Dooley.

"Ignorant."

"That's the word. If you ask me, the law's gotten mighty tricky. There are too many papers to file with the government."

"Ain't that the truth," Ghost called out. "Getting a piece of land used to be easy. You just squatted there and it was yours. Now you got to pay money and fill out papers."

"So you going to settle here then? I'll bet Morrison will rent out the storefront across the street from his store. You could put your shingle out and maybe earn a couple of dollars every month."

Harrison shrugged. "I'm not sure what I'm going to do yet. I might settle down here, and then again, I might not. It's too soon to tell."

"You got enough money to hold you over until you decide?" Henry asked.

Harrison knew better than to admit he was carrying money. "No," he answered. "I don't suppose I have enough to last more than a couple of days."

"You'll get along," Dooley advised. "You're big and you got muscle. You can always hire out and work to keep food on your table."

"That's what I figured," Harrison lied.

"What exactly are you doing in Blue Belle?" Billie asked. "I know it isn't any of my business, but I'm curious to know. You mind telling us, mister?"

"Call me Harrison," he said again. "I don't mind telling why I'm here. I'm on what I'm pretty certain is a wild-goose chase. At least the man I work for believes my trip will end up running after a dream."

"You already got yourself a job?" Dooley asked.

"I've taken a temporary leave."

"So you could end up staying here. Is that the way of it?" Henry asked.

"I suppose I could."

"I say you should stay," Billie announced. "Don't work for anyone but yourself. That's our way. You don't have to answer to anyone."

"You mind answering a question about the law?" Ghost asked.

"What is it you want to know?"

"I'm thinking hard about stealing a horse," Ghost announced. He stood up and walked over to the table. "The fella I'm thinking about robbing stole my woman years back, so, the way I see it, I ain't really doing nothing wrong. The law's on my side, right?"

Harrison leaned back in his chair. He stopped himself before he smiled. The question was amusing, but he didn't want Ghost to think he was laughing at him.

"Sorry to disappoint you," he said. "Pride might be on your side, but the law isn't."

Dooley slapped his hand down on the tabletop and let out another hoot of laughter. "That's what I told him," he announced in a near shout. "Pride will get him hung by the vigilantes if he steals Lloyd's horse."

Ghost didn't like Harrison's answer. He walked away from the table muttering to himself. His question opened the door for others, however, and for the next hour, Harrison dispensed free legal advice. Although he'd been educated at Oxford and had done his apprenticeship in England, he also worked for a man who owned two manufacturing plants. Because the company regularly shipped to the American east coast, Harrison had had to familiarize himself with the laws regulating

61

export and import.

The difference between the way the law was interpreted by the courts in England and in America fascinated him. He tirelessly pored over any material about unusual decisions and cases that he could get his hands on.

His associates thought it was dry reading indeed, especially the older cases he'd wanted to discuss with them. He was told it was boring material at best, and it reminded them of all the mandatory reading they'd had to suffer through while at university. Harrison didn't agree. He loved reading the philosophers, especially Plato, and he enjoyed reading the opinions of the scholars who founded his country's government as well. But most of all, he loved the law. The discipline of the court system appealed to him. He thought it was imperative to keep up with all the latest decisions so that he could eventually become one of the best in his field. Good wasn't enough for him. Harrison strove for excellence in everything he undertook. Unfinished puzzles drove him crazy. Whatever he started, he finished.

His passion for the law and his compassion for his fellow man had made him unpopular in many circles. Because he worked for the powerful Lord Elliott, he had never actually been blackballed, although he'd certainly come close on several occasions, and all because he took on unpopular cases. He was rapidly getting a reputation for being a champion of the less fortunate in London's slums. He hadn't set out to become anyone's champion, of course, and if anyone had told him at school that he would eventually become a criminal lawyer, even on a part-time basis, Harrison would have thought he was out of his mind.

The unsought distinction had cost him his engagement to Lady Edwina Horner, who informed him in a letter that she couldn't abide being married to a scandal-setter, whatever in God's name that meant. Men who still called themselves his friend tried to warn him that he had to get over his ridiculous notion that the poor in England should be entitled to the same rights as the rich. Harrison, however, refused to accept such an elitist, self-serving view.

"Maybe them laws in England are different from our laws," Ghost suggested. He strolled back across the room and gave Harrison a hopeful look. "I'm thinking that maybe I wouldn't get hanged, if I stole the horse, because Lloyd started the dirt first."

Harrison shook his head. Ghost, it appeared, wasn't ready to give up his plan.

"I've studied enough American law to know you'll still be found guilty."

"Even though he wasn't on the square and he started the dirt first?"

While Harrison wasn't familiar with either of those odd expressions, he still felt he was giving sound advice. "Even so."

Another round of questions followed. All the curious who'd started out watching him from across the saloon had filed over to Harrison's table and now formed a half circle. None of them seemed to be in any particular hurry to get on with their day.

The doors to the saloon suddenly flew open.

"Miss Mary's coming. Cole's riding behind her."

The man who shouted the announcement bounded off at a trot down the walkway.

The reaction to the news was astonishing to witness. Every single one of the men jumped to his feet and ran outside. Dooley was almost knocked to his knees in the stampede. He eventually regained his balance and turned back to Harrison.

"Ain't you coming along? You ought to at least take a peek at our Miss Mary. She's worth your time."

Because Dooley might have thought it peculiar if Harrison hadn't shown an interest, he got up from the table and followed the old man out the doorway. Harrison wasn't in any hurry to meet the young woman, however, and Dooley was already down the block and halfway across the street before Harrison reached the hitching post in front of the corner building.

His hunt could very well end in just a few minutes. Harrison was suddenly filled with all sorts of conflicting emotions. He had made a promise to Lord Elliot that this adventure would be his last attempt to solve this puzzle, and if Elliot turned out to be correct, then traveling all this distance had been just another wild-goose chase.

He let out a weary sigh. The facts, Elliot had argued, were indisputable. Mary Rose Clayborne couldn't possibly be his daughter. Victoria was an only child. Mary Rose had four older brothers. Yet while that information had been verified by the attorney in St. Louis, the man had also included several other comments Harrison found intriguing. Mary Rose had been on her guard throughout the interview and refused to give even the names of her brothers. The attorney reported that although she'd been extremely polite, it was apparent to him that she was afraid. The superior hadn't been able to persuade the young lady to cooperate.

The headmistress had proven most helpful however. She told the attorney that two of Mary Rose's brothers had traveled with their sister to the school at the beginning of each term. She hadn't met either one, hadn't even seen them at a distance, and, therefore, couldn't describe the gentlemen. She had heard a disturbing rumor about one of the brothers, but she refused to give the attorney any details.

She declared she wasn't a gossip and that Mary Rose was a model student, once she'd made the adjustment to life in a boarding school, and the vile rumor one of the girls had started was quickly stopped. No one would ever have believed it anyway, of course. Gossip was for peasants and not for proper young ladies.

She couldn't be pressed for more.

Harrison shook his head. Gossip couldn't be relied on, of course. It was probably just as Elliot had predicted it would be. Another case of two women looking somewhat alike. Elliot had urged Harrison to let it go, as the older man himself finally had, and accept the soul-destroying evidence that little Victoria Elliott had died shortly after she'd been taken. In his heart, Harrison knew Elliott was right, but every time he looked at the man who had protected Harrison's father for so many years, he would become compelled to go on just one more hunt.

Harrison believed he was a realist, yet even so, his gut instinct had told him to go to Montana and find out the truth for himself. He wasn't completely grasping at rainbows. He had already been in America when he had received the wire regarding the latest sighting, and Chicago was just a day's ride away from where he'd been staying. It didn't take him any time at all to go to the outskirts of the city to talk to the woman who believed she'd met Elliott's daughter. After talking to Mrs. Anna Middleshaw and hearing the report of the attorney he'd then had interview Mary Rose, he decided it would be worth his while to go into the wilderness. Mrs. Middleshaw didn't appear to be a woman given to theatrics or emotion. She was actually quite level-headed. She believed with all her heart that she had seen Lady Victoria. Her argument was valid. No one, she said, could look that much like another without being related. Harrison wanted to believe she was right.

He braced himself for disappointment and stepped off the wooden walkway. The gleam of metal caught his attention. He half turned to look back down the walkway and saw what looked like a shotgun barrel protruding from an alley about fifteen feet away. Whoever held the weapon had it trained on the group of people standing in front of the general store.

Harrison recognized Henry and Ghost and Dooley, but there were three other men he'd never seen before standing in a circle on the opposite walkway. A man with light yellow hair stood next to Henry, but when he took a step back, the barrel of the rifle came up. Yellow Hair moved again almost immediately, however, and Dooley inadvertently blocked him from ambush. The barrel of the rifle, Harrison noticed, lowered once again.

He decided he would interfere. The group of men filed inside the general store. Harrison removed his coat on his way across the road, tossed it over the hitching post in front of the walkway, and then went inside.

The scent of leather and spices filled the air around him. The store was large, about the size of one of Elliott's stables back home. There was a wide aisle that ran the length of the store, and two other smaller aisles on either side. Weighted-down, bowed shelves were lined with jars of food, piles of clothing, leather goods, picks and shovels, and so much more the eye could barely take it all in. The entire store was built out of several different kinds of wood, though mostly pine, just like the rest of the buildings in town.

Harrison had never seen such a disorganized, stuffed-to-the-rafters establishment in all his life. His obsession with discipline and order made him mentally blanch at the chaos before him. Bolts of colorful fabric were haphazardly stacked into a lopsided pyramid on top of a round table in one corner of the store, next to three giant-size pickle barrels. He watched an unkempt man reach down and take out a large pickle from the brine, then wipe his wet hand on the edge of a lace fabric that drooped down from a bolt over the side of the table. The material fell to the floor, barring the man's path, and so he simply stepped over the bolt on his way back to the front of the establishment.

Working amid such chaos would have driven Harrison out of his mind. How in God's name did the proprietor ever find anything?

Harrison let out a sigh, put the matter out of his mind, then moved to the side of the entrance where he planned to stay until he spotted Yellow Hair in the crowd.

Where in thunder was the man? Harrison was at least a head taller than everyone else inside the store, yet still couldn't find Yellow Hair. He couldn't have disappeared into thin air, though in this mess Harrison guessed anything was possible.

Dooley waved to him from the left side of the store. The old man stood in front of a counter, talking in a whisper to a pretty brown-haired young lady. She had to be the owner's daughter, the one named Catherine Morrison. Dooley motioned for him to come over to the counter, but Harrison shook his head and stayed right where he was. He didn't want to take the chance of missing Yellow Hair. If Dooley thought his behavior was rude, Harrison neither minded nor cared.

A few minutes later he heard Dooley say something about "being shy." Since Dooley was looking at him when he made the comment, Harrison assumed he was referring to him. The notion was ridiculous.

The Morrison woman caught his attention when she waved at him. She leaned halfway over the countertop and gave him a provocative, come-and-meet-me smile. He didn't smile back. He wasn't in the mood to be social right now, for he felt that warning the stranger was more important.

He didn't normally interfere in another man's affairs, but he fervently believed in equal treatment and fair play. Ambushing an unsuspecting man was a damned cowardly thing to do, and Harrison could never abide a coward.

He ran out of patience. He decided he was going to have to go find the man, but just as he started to move, Yellow Hair appeared at the end of the main aisle, carrying a sack of wheat or flour he'd hoisted up on one shoulder. While Harrison waited for him to get to the entrance, a young woman skirted her way around Yellow Hair and came hurrying toward Harrison.

Dear God, she was Lady Victoria. The beautiful young woman walking toward him had to be Elliott's long-lost daughter. She was the spitting image of the man's late wife. At the first sight of her high cheekbones and her brilliant blue eyes, Harrison took a deep breath and forgot to let it out. Astonishment paralyzed him. His heart started thundering inside his chest until it became painful, and he was finally forced to breathe again.

He couldn't believe what he was seeing. The lovely woman looked as if she had just stepped out of the oil portrait of Lady Agatha that hung above the fireplace in Elliott's library. The clothes were different, yes; yes, of course they were, but by all that was holy, even the spray of freckles across the bridge of her nose seemed to be identical. Harrison suddenly didn't care how many brothers she had. It was just as Mrs. Middleshaw had said. No one could look this much like another without being related.

Mary Rose Clayborne. The closer she got to him, the more subtle differences became discernible. Her eyes were a little paler in color than her mother's in the portrait of her as a young woman. Harrison let out a sigh of frustration. The exotic, almost almond shape of her eyes and her facial bone structure seemed to be the same as her mother's; yet, now that she was coming closer to him, he couldn't be absolutely certain. Hell, she even looked a little bit like Yellow Hair. She had the same color of hair. No, the color wasn't quite the same. Hers was a lighter yellow streaked with honey-colored strands throughout. God, she was beautiful, but she could still be Yellow Hair's younger sister, and hell and damnation, how could that be possible when she looked so much like Elliott's wife?

He'd been too young when he'd last seen Lady Agatha to remember significant details now about her physical appearance. He had been only ten when she and her husband left for America to attend the grand opening of their plant near New York City. He remembered foolish little-boy things about her, such as the wonderful way she smelled, like flowers after the rain, and the way she smiled at him, with such love and kindness in her eyes. He remembered the warmth and tenderness of her hug, but all of those memories, treasured though they were by a boy who had lost his own mother, weren't going to help him.

He had never seen Lady Agatha again. After her return to London, she'd stayed in her bedchamber day and night, clothed in black, he'd been told, and closeted away in darkness while she mourned the disappearance of her four-month-old daughter.

Was the woman walking toward him Lady Victoria? God help him, he didn't know.

His mind frantically sought for a way to find the truth. Then he remembered what Dooley and the other men had told him about Mary Rose Clayborne. She was the champion of the weak. Hadn't Dooley also told him that she drove her brothers crazy because she was constantly dragging misfits home with her?

Harrison suddenly had a new plan.

He was no longer going to be the meanest son-of-a-bitch who ever hit town. That charade had gotten him the information he needed and acceptance by the men in the saloon. The pretense wouldn't work now, at least not with Mary Rose Clayborne. She liked odd ducks, and so he decided to become just that. He was going to be a bumbling, naive city boy who didn't have enough common sense to stay alive. He only hoped he could pull the deception off.

Mary Rose Clayborne noticed the stranger almost immediately. He had his arms crossed in front of his chest and was leaning against the ledge of Morrison's window. He was a giant of a man, impossible, really, not to notice, with dark brown hair and wonderfully expressive gray eyes.

He was handsome, she supposed, in a rugged, outdoors way, but appearances weren't important to her. He certainly looked unhappy to her. Honest to heaven, he looked pale enough to make her think he'd seen something very distressing.

Like a ghost, she thought to herself. She smiled then, because it was such a silly notion. Only Ghost ever saw spirits from the other world, and only after he'd dipped into his homemade brew that guaranteed visions. A ghost, indeed.

Still, she wished he didn't look so unhappy. She decided to introduce herself to him. Perhaps he would tell her what was worrying him. She might be able to help.

Just as quickly as the idea to meet him came to her, she decided against it, because she'd finally noticed he was wearing one of those fancy gunbelts around his hips. A six-shooter was neatly tucked into the holster. Mary Rose realized the stranger could very well be just another gunfighter in town for the sole purpose of antagonizing her brother into a gunfight, and, by God, if that was the case, she wasn't about to be gracious or helpful. Why, she might even shoot him herself.

She knew she was jumping to conclusions. She decided her best course of action was to ignore him. She reached the entrance and tried to open the door for her brother. Cole was right behind her, but his hands were occupied holding the sack on his shoulder.

Harrison quickly moved to block her exit. He leaned against the door and waited for her to look up at him.

She took her sweet time.

"I wouldn't go outside just yet, ma'am."

"You wouldn't?"

He shook his head. "No, I wouldn't."

She stared stupidly up at his face. He finally smiled. She almost smiled back. She stopped herself in time. She stood only a foot away from him and, therefore, had to tilt her head all the way back so she could get a close-up look at his eyes. There was a definite sparkle there, she noticed. She couldn't imagine what he found so amusing. His color was back as well, and he smelled quite nice to her. Like the outdoors and leather, she decided, and because his skin was so bronzed, she knew he spent a good deal of time in the sun.

Mary Rose shook herself out of her stupor. "Why don't I want to go outside?" she asked.

Harrison knew he was going to have to quit staring at her so he could answer her question. God, she was pretty. He noticed her scent, so light and faint, very like the scent her mother used to wear, and, hell, he knew he was behaving like a schoolboy, but he couldn't make himself stop. He couldn't stop smiling down at her either, because she was so damned lovely, of course, but also because it was both possible and impossible for her to be Elliott's daughter.

Reality was quick to bring him back to the present.

"Open the door, Mary Rose," Yellow Hair ordered. He was staring at Harrison when he muttered the impatient command.

"This gentleman doesn't want us to leave just yet," she answered. She turned to her brother and lifted her shoulders in a shrug. "I don't know why."

Cole glared at Harrison. His tone was scathing when he said, "Look, mister, there are easier ways of getting an introduction. If you want to meet my sister, wait until I unload this. Then maybe I'll let you talk to her."

Mary Rose couldn't let the stranger be misled. "He won't let you talk to me though," she explained. "My brother never lets me talk to strangers. My name's Mary Rose Clayborne. And who are you, pray tell?"

"Harrison Stanford MacDonald."

She nodded. "I'm pleased to meet you, Mr. MacDonald. May I go outside now?"

"I'd like to talk to your brother first," he said.

She backed up a space and stepped on her brother's foot. "Are you a gunfighter?"

She made the question sound like an accusation. She didn't give him time to answer, having obviously concluded that he was. She frowned up at him and shook her head.

"You can just forget about getting my brother into a draw. He isn't at all interested. I suggest you leave Blue Belle, sir. You aren't welcome here."

"For God's sake, Mary Rose. I can talk for myself. You a gun-fighter, mister?"

Harrison shook his head. He was thoroughly bewildered by the turn in the conversation. "No," he answered. "I'm not a gunfighter." He turned back to Mary Rose. "Exactly what is it you think I'm here to draw?"

Her eyes widened. "Cole, he doesn't know what

74

a draw is. Where are you from, Mr. MacDonald?"

"Scotland."

She frowned over his answer. "Why are you in Blue Belle?"

"I'm looking for a place to settle down."

"Then you aren't here to fight my brother?"

She stopped frowning at him, but her voice was still filled with suspicion. It was apparent she wasn't completely convinced.

He decided to answer her question with one of his own. "Why would I want to do that, ma'am. I don't even know your brother."

She let out a happy sigh. "Well, then," she whispered. She brushed her hair back over her shoulder, in an action he found utterly feminine, and smiled sweetly up at him.

"I didn't think you were a gunfighter, but I couldn't be absolutely certain. When I think . . ."

Cole wouldn't let her finish the complaint she was about to make. "For God's sake, Mary Rose. Open the door."

"But I haven't introduced you to Mr. Mac-Donald yet," she protested.

"I don't need to meet him," Cole muttered. "Douglas is waiting out front with the wagon. Just open the door."

Mary Rose didn't seem to be at all affected by her brother's surly tone of voice. She continued to smile up at Harrison and acted as if she had all the time in the world to talk to him. "My brother's name is Cole Clayborne. He has a middle name, but he's sensitive about it, and he'd kill me if told you what it was. Cole, I'd like you to meet Mr. Harrison . . ."

"Mary Rose, I swear to God I'm gonna drop this heavy sack of flour right on top of your head."

She let out a sigh. "My brother's really very nice, sir, once you get to know him."

Harrison wasn't convinced. Cole didn't look like the sort who could ever be nice. The scowl on his face seemed to be a permanent fixture. Only one thing was certain. Mary Rose's brother wasn't going to wait much longer. Harrison decided he'd better hurry up and tell him about the ambush before the impatient man went storming through the closed door. He looked strong enough and irritated enough to do just that.

"There's a rifle trained on you," he began. He kept his voice low so the other customers wouldn't overhear him. "Whoever wants to shoot you is hiding in the pass-through across the street. I thought you might want to know."

Cole immediately lost his irritation. "You get a look at the fella?"

Harrison shook his head. "I considered trying to shoot the rifle out of his hands, but the truth is, I only just purchased this gun and I haven't tried it out yet. I probably would have ended up hurting someone."

"That's the general idea," Cole told him, his exasperation obvious in his tone of voice.

"Sorry I couldn't help you out," Harrison said then. "But until I learn how accurate . . ."

He let the sentence trail off uncompleted. He would let Mary Rose and her brother draw their own conclusions.

He didn't have to wait long. Mary Rose let

out a little gasp. "You're wearing a gun and you've never used it before?"

"Yes, ma'am."

He hadn't had to lie to her again, but he hadn't told her the truth either. He deliberately withheld pertinent information, knowing full well she would be led down the path he wanted her to take. The way he was manipulating her didn't sit well with him. Still, he would do what was necessary in order to gain her confidence so he could find out what he needed to know, and since she took in the misfits, he concluded he would have to become one.

"Are you out of your mind?" she asked him then.

"I don't believe so," he answered.

"Dear God, don't you know any better than to walk around town armed? As big as you are, you're bound to get into a fight. You'll get yourself killed in no time at all. Is that what you want, Mr. MacDonald?"

Her hands moved to her hips, and she was looking at him as though she thought he didn't have a lick of sense. She reminded him of a teacher reprimanding one of her students. He never had any teachers who were this young or pretty though. Most were old and dusty and as dry as dead leaves.

She was obviously concerned about him. Odd, but he liked the attention she was giving him. Being a misfit wasn't going to be so terrible after all.

Harrison tried to look worried. "No, ma'am. I don't want to get killed. I want to learn how to use my new gun. I can't do that, can I, if I keep it packed away."

Cole let out a loud sigh. Harrison immediately turned back to him. "Would you like me to carry that sack outside for you? I could put it in your wagon and go find the sheriff."

"We don't have a sheriff in Blue Belle," Mary Rose explained.

Harrison didn't have to pretend surprise. "Then who keeps the order here?"

"No one," she answered. "That's why this town is such a dangerous place for someone like you. You were raised in the city, weren't you, sir?"

He tried not to chafe over the pity he heard in her voice. "Yes, as a matter of fact I was raised in the city. Please call me Harrison. *Sir* and *mister* are too formal for out here."

"Fine," she agreed. "I'll call you Harrison. Please take your gun-belt off. You really shouldn't be wearing one. I'll bet someone told you it was fashionable attire in our territory, didn't he? Or did you read that it was?"

"I read that it was necessary equipment."

She let out a sigh. "Oh, dear."

Cole had waited long enough. He leaned over, propped the sack of flour against the wall, stood back up, and then rolled his shoulders like a bear to get rid of the crick in the side of his neck.

Harrison and Mary Rose moved out of his way when he reached for the door. Cole didn't seem to be overly concerned about the ambush. He nudged his sister further away from the opening, took his gun out of his belt, and then opened the door just enough to let a crack of sunshine in.

Douglas was waiting out front. Cole's brother stood on the street, next to their wagon, leaning against a hitching post. He appeared to be sound asleep. Cole whistled to get his attention.

Harrison watched Mary Rose. Her behavior puzzled him. The second her brother reached for his gun, she covered her ears with her hands and stared up at the ceiling with a resigned expression on her face.

"Douglas, hit the ground."

Cole barked the command a scant second before he leaned out the doorway, took aim, and fired three rapid shots. The sound of exploding gunfire ricocheted around and around the store. The glass window shivered from the noise.

As quick as lightning he put the gun back in his holster. "That ought to do it."

And then he picked up the sack of flour and strolled outside. His casual attitude was a little surprising, of course, but what most amazed Harrison was the fact that the majority of patrons inside the establishment weren't showing the least bit of curiosity. If they thought it was peculiar for Cole Clayborne to fire his weapon out the doorway, they certainly weren't letting it show. Did this sort of thing happen every day? Harrison was beginning to think that maybe it did.

"Cole, you forgot to thank Harrison," Mary Rose called out.

"Thanks for the warning," Cole dutifully called over his shoulder.

His gratitude sounded shallow to her, but she

didn't take issue with her brother. She knew it was difficult for him to ever say thank you to anyone, and he must have found it grating indeed to know a stranger had saved his life.

"Who was trying to ambush you, Cole?" she asked.

"You're welcome," Harrison called out at the very same time.

Cole tossed the sack of flour into the back of the wagon with the other supplies they'd already purchased, then turned to answer his sister's question.

"It was probably Webster. The son-of-a . . ." He stopped himself before he completed the rest of his dark opinion of the vermin waiting to ambush him. "He was sore because I wouldn't fight him last week. Guess I should have killed him then. He'll only try again. I winged him though, so he'll have to mend first. You about ready to leave, Mary Rose?"

"In just a minute."

She turned back to Harrison. "It was very kind of you to warn my brother. He's really very appreciative. It's just difficult for him to show it. He doesn't like owing anyone anything, even gratitude."

"Your brother doesn't owe me gratitude. Anyone would have done what I did."

"I wish that were true," she replied. "Perhaps in Scotland one neighbor helps another, but around Blue Belle, things are different."

He nodded, accepting what she told him as fact, and continued to stare at her while he tried to think of something else to talk about. It didn't take him long to start feeling like a simpleton. She was slipping right through his fingers, but he couldn't think of a single thing to say to keep her near him for just a few more minutes.

The irony of the situation wasn't lost on him. He was a lawyer, for God's sake, a man who spent his days debating, cajoling, and arguing in order to make a living, yet now he was speechless. If that wasn't a contradiction, he didn't know what was.

Lord, she had lovely eyes.

The second the thought popped into his head he realized he was in trouble. The young lady smiling so sweetly up at him was turning his mind into mush. He was thoroughly disgusted with himself. He knew better than to let a physical attraction get in the way of his plans.

Mary Rose supposed she had lingered long enough. She didn't want to go home just yet, however, and she told herself it was only because she was concerned about the kindhearted stranger.

"I was wondering . . ."

"Yes?" He blurted out the word like a little boy about to receive a gift.

"Why do you want to learn how to shoot?"

Hell, he was going to have to lie to her again. It was becoming difficult for him. Perhaps if she hadn't been looking at him with such trust and innocence in her gaze, it would have been easier.

The truth wasn't going to help him now, because he knew that if he admitted he was actually quite skilled with a gun, she'd go sailing out the doorway and never look back.

It was galling to his pride to pretend to be

inept. He'd won awards at university for his accuracy on the range and in the field, and while he'd served in the military, he'd learned how to be fast. Six-shooters were the common man's choice of weapons, however, and as much as he disliked the gun, he had still made it a point to learn how to use it. He had to admit the gun had come in handy, and his speed had saved his hide more than a few times.

"Please tell me, why do you want to learn how to use a gun?" she asked him again.

"I'm thinking about becoming a rancher," he told her. "I believe the weapon will be useful."

"We have a ranch a few miles outside of town. It's called Rosehill. Have you by chance heard of it?"

It was a ridiculous question, and she was sorry she'd asked it as soon as the words were out of her mouth. Of course he hadn't heard of Rosehill. The man had only just arrived in town. Still, the inquiry was all she could come up with to keep him talking, and, Lord, how she loved hearing him speak. His unusual accent was almost musical to her, with its deep, vibrant burr.

"No, I haven't heard of your ranch," he answered.

They continued to stare at each other for another minute before Mary Rose once again turned to leave. She had made it all the way out the front door when she stopped.

Cole and Douglas were both watching her. Her brothers were leaning against the back of the wagon. Both men had their arms folded in front of their chests, and each, she noticed, had one booted ankle crossed over the other. They had resigned expressions on their faces.

They were used to Mary Rose lingering.

She smiled at the two of them before turning back to Harrison. She was happy to see he'd followed her outside. He was looking at Douglas and probably wondering who he was, she supposed. She would have to remember to introduce him after she finished telling him her plans for his immediate future.

She simply had to do something to help the man. He looked so alone and lost.

"I simply cannot leave you here on your own."

She gained his full attention with her announcement. "You can't?" he asked.

She glanced over her shoulder to see if her brothers were still watching her and saw that both weren't only watching, they were also frowning with obvious disapproval. She smiled at them, just to let them know she was quite happy to be talking to the stranger, and then she took hold of Harrison's arm and motioned for him to walk with her away from the entrance. She wanted to put some space between the two of them and her brothers. She also needed privacy for their discussion, because she knew her brothers would try to interfere if they had any idea of what she was planning to do.

"No, I certainly can't leave you here. You're going to get into trouble if I don't do something."

"Why do you think I'll get into trouble?"

"Why?" she repeated.

She couldn't believe he needed to ask. Still, she could see how puzzled he looked. Heaven help him, the poor man didn't even realize his own jeopardy. It was her duty to explain his circumstances to him, she decided.

"You've all but openly admitted you don't know how to defend yourself. I'm certain several customers inside the store heard you. Everyone in town seems to make it their business to know what everyone else is doing and saying. Word will get around, Harrison, and as much as it pains me to admit it, our lovely town does have a fair number of mean-headed bullies. As soon as they hear you're vulnerable, they'll come after you. You won't be safe here."

"Are you suggesting I'm inept?" He looked astonished.

She decided she was going to have to be blunt with him. Even though she was probably going to hurt his feelings, the truth was for his own good.

"You are inept."

He had to remind himself he was pleased by the way things were progressing. She was making him her responsibility. Dooley and Henry had been right about her. She really did take to the weak and the vulnerable.

Still, his pride was taking one hell of a beating. It was damned grating for any woman to think of him as a weakling.

He decided to make a fainthearted protest just to appease his own ego. "Ma'am, I don't remember telling you I couldn't take care of myself."

She pretended she hadn't heard him. "I'm afraid you're really going to have to come home with me."

He tried not to smile. "I don't believe that's a good idea. I'm bound to get the hang of using this new gun of mine. I paid a lot of money for it. I'm sure it's accurate."

She looked exasperated. "Guns aren't accurate. Men are. Coming home with me is a sound solution. Please try to understand. You're such a big man, and you're therefore a fair target. People here have certain expectations."

He didn't know what she was talking about. "What does size . . ."

She didn't let him finish. "It's expected that you'll fight to protect yourself and your possessions, and if you don't learn how to use your fists and your gun, you'll be killed before the end of the week."

She deliberately softened the truth so he wouldn't become overly alarmed. Actually, she didn't believe he'd last a full day on his own.

"I'm certain my brothers will be happy to teach you everything you need to know. You did save Cole's life, after all. He'll be pleased to offer you instruction on shooting so you can take care of yourself."

Harrison had to take a deep breath before he spoke. He knew his own arrogance was getting in the way of his plans now, but God help him, he couldn't stop himself from arguing with her. He was certain he could act a little vulnerable. He wasn't about to pretend to be completely inadequate. Damn it all, there had to be an easier way.

"I really can take care of myself. I'm not certain how you got the idea I couldn't. I've used my fists before and I'm . . ."

She didn't want to hear it. She shook her head at him, added a pitying expression, and then said, "Thinking and doing are two different kettles of fish, Harrison. It's dangerous to believe you're skilled when in fact you aren't. Have you ever been in a gunfight before?"

He had to admit he hadn't.

"There, do you see?"

She acted as though he should have figured everything out by now. He wondered if being in a gunfight was some sort of ritual required before she would believe he was adequately prepared to live in Blue Belle.

"Have all the men who live here been in gunfights?" He sounded incredulous. He couldn't help it. A lawyer should never be led around in circles, and Harrison had never had it happen to him before, but this delightful woman was doing just that, and he was in a quandary trying to figure out exactly how it had happened.

"No, of course not," she answered.

"Then why did you ask me if I'd ever been in one?"

She gave him an exasperated look.

"Surely you noticed that the men inside the store weren't wearing gunbelts," she said. "Most don't. A message goes right along with the weapon, Harrison. If you wear a gun, you have to be prepared to prove you can use it. I'm pleased to know you haven't been in any gunfights, and I sincerely hope you never have to kill anyone. Guns shouldn't be used for sport or vengeance. We kill snakes and other vermin, not men. Un-

86

fortunately, some of the people living here, and others drifting through, well, they don't seem to know the difference."

"I noticed your brother was wearing a gun."

'That's different," she insisted. "Cole has to and you don't. Gunfighters looking for a reputation pester my brother all the time, because they believe they're faster than he is. Their arrogance eventually gets them killed, though not by Cole's hand. He hasn't killed anyone in years. He's not a gunfighter," she added in an emphatic tone of voice.

She seemed to want him to agree with her. "I see."

"He has to wear the gun to protect himself."

"I understand."

"He only became proficient so he could keep all of us safe. It wasn't his fault he was fast. You're going to have to learn how to defend yourself too, if you want to settle down out here. Besides, if you're serious about wanting to learn how to ranch, Rosehill is the ideal place for you. You'll have wonderful teachers. Adam might even pay you to work for us, and you can learn as you do."

"Adam?"

"My oldest brother," she explained. "I have four. I'm the youngest in the family, then Travis, Cole, Douglas, and Adam."

Since she was being so open with him, he decided to ask her as many questions as he could.

"Are you parents still living?"

"My mother is," she answered. "She lives in the South right now, but she'll be joining us soon.

You should go and get your things. If you like, I'll walk with you."

"Don't you think you should ask your brothers before you offer their services?"

From past experience, she knew that asking their permission wasn't a good idea. "No, I'll ease them into agreeing. Do call me Mary Rose, or just plain Mary, like everyone else in town does. Do you have a horse and wagon, or did you ride into Blue Belle on the stagecoach?"

"I have a horse."

"Shall we go then?"

She was obviously through discussing the matter. She stepped off the walkway, smiled at her brothers as she passed them, and headed for the stables. Harrison must have taken a minute or two to make up his mind, because he didn't catch up with her until she was halfway down the road.

"The gentleman next to Cole is my brother Douglas," she told him. "I believe I'll wait a little while before I introduce you to him. His mood is bound to improve."

"He does look irritated about something," Harrison remarked.

He'd given the man a close inspection when he strolled past him. Harrison walked by Mary Rose's side, with his hands clasped behind his back, while he considered a delicate way to ask her about Douglas.

"Is Douglas a stepbrother?" he asked in what he hoped was a casual tone of voice.

"No. Why do you ask?"

"He doesn't look like you or Cole. I never would have guessed he was related. He reminds me of a friend of mine named Nicholas. He was born and raised in Italy."

"I don't believe Douglas is Italian. He might be Irish. Yes, I believe he is."

"You believe he is?"

She nodded but didn't offer any additional information. Harrison was thoroughly confused. "Did your father marry a second time?"

"No. Cole and I are the only ones in the family who resemble one another."

He waited for her to tell him more. She didn't say another word about her brothers, however, and, in fact, turned the questioning around on him.

"Do you have any brothers?"

"No."

"Any sisters?"

"Afraid not."

"What a pity," she concluded. "Being an only child must have been terribly boring for you. Who did you fight with while you were growing up?"

He laughed. "No one."

No wonder the poor man didn't know how to defend himself. It was all making perfectly good sense to her now. He didn't have any older brothers to teach him all the necessary things he needed to know.

Harrison glanced back over his shoulder to get yet another look at Douglas.

His conclusion didn't change. He still didn't believe Douglas was related to Mary Rose. Everything about his physical appearance was different from Cole's. Douglas had curly black-brown hair and dark brown eyes, a square chin, and wide, yet pronounced, cheekbones. Cole's facial features were more patrician in structure, and his nose was almost hawklike. Harrison couldn't tell which one was older. Odd, but they appeared to be about the same age. Perhaps only a year separated their births, he reasoned, and perhaps too, Douglas was simply a throwback to one of their ancestors.

Anything was possible, he knew, and damn but he was anxious to find out if he was wasting his time or not.

"You don't look Irish."

"I don't?" She smiled up at him and continued walking. She was obviously unwilling to discuss the matter further.

"Mary Rose, where in thunder are you going?"

Her brother, Douglas, shouted the question. She turned around. "I'm going to the stables," she answered in a near shout of her own. She hurriedly turned around again, quickened her pace, and only then called out the rest of her explanation.

"Mr. MacDonald will be joining us for supper."

The two brothers watched their sister all but run away from them. Cole waited another minute and then put his hand out, palm up, in front of his brother.

Douglas let out a low expletive, reached into his pocket, and pulled out a silver dollar.

"Never bet against a sure thing," Cole advised.

Douglas slapped the piece of silver into his hand. His gaze stayed on the stranger. "I don't get it," he muttered. "He looks fit enough to me. He towers over Mary Rose. Hell, he's over six feet tall, and he's got muscle, Cole. You can see he does."

"I see," Cole replied, laughing.

"He moves like you do, I noticed right away, and his gaze doesn't miss a thing. Honest to God, I can't understand what she sees in him. He looks kind of normal."

Cole was gloating because he had won the wager. Douglas found his behavior irritating.

"Damn it, he's wearing a gun. I'd be wary of him if I met him in a dark alley."

"It's a new gun."

"So?"

"He's never used it."

"Then why is he wearing one of those fancy new gunbelts?"

Cole shrugged. "I guess he figured he should. There isn't a single nick on the leather. It's got to be brand-new too."

"Is he stupid then?"

"Seems so."

Douglas shook his head. "He's gonna get himself killed."

Cole's smile widened. "And that's why our sister is bringing him home."

Douglas wanted his money back. "You knew all this before you made the bet?"

"You could have asked. You didn't."

Douglas accepted defeat. His gaze went back to the stranger. He watched until he disappeared around the corner of the stable.

"Dooley told Morrison he's from Scotland. Said he was book smart too."

"Then he's a city boy?"

Cole nodded. "Seems so," he agreed. "He can't shoot his new gun, and I don't think he can fight. You didn't see any scars on his face, did you?"

"No, I didn't see any scars. I guess he'd have some if he'd been in any knife fights."

"My point exactly," Cole said. "I talked to him for a couple of minutes. He sounds educated, but he doesn't seem to have any common sense. He told me he was afraid to shoot at Webster. Said he was worried he might hurt someone."

Douglas laughed. Cole waited until he'd calmed down, then said, "If he had any sense at all, he wouldn't be wearing a gun. He's giving everyone the notion he's qualified."

"It's a shame," Douglas remarked. "Someone that big ought to be able to fight. He could be a real mean one if he only knew how."

Cole agreed. "It's a crying shame all right."

"What did Mary Rose say his name was?"

"MacDonald," Cole replied. His grin was wide when he added, "A-Crying-Shame MacDonald."

February 11, 1861

Dear Mama Rose,
   We got into a little trouble in St. Louis.
I was carrying Mary Rose on my hip and
a troublemaking man came along and tried
to bother us. The baby's got curls now, all
over her head, and she's right friendly to
anyone who looks at her. Well, she smiled
at the man, showing off her four front teeth
and drooling down her chin, and he starts
in wondering in a loud voice how come she
don't look nothing like me. He kept trying
to take her from me too, but Cole came
along and of course he looks just like
little Mary Rose's brother what with the
same yellow hair and blue eyes. Anyways,
he snatched our baby up in his arms and
tells the mister to mind his own business.
   The troublemaker got us all thinking we
should keep on going until we find us a place
where people mind their own business.
Adam's thinking the prairie might be far
enough away from folks, so we're packing
up our lean-to and heading out tomorrow.
It's a shame you can't write back to us yet,
but just as soon as we get ourselves situated,
we'll send you our whereabouts.
   Adam's looking over my spelling now and
he says to tell you we got to get us a proper
cabin. Mary Rose is crawling everywhere and
the dirt we call a floor inside the lean-to

is sticking to her hands and knees. She tries to eat the dirt when we aren't looking. None of us know why she does that. She sure is a happy little thing though. We all got to take turns putting her down for her nap. She sleeps with one of us every night and I got to tell you, I'm getting sick of waking up with her piddle on me. She wets through everything we put on her. Guess that's usual though, isn't it?

We sure wish we could see you so we'd know what our mama looks like.

Love,
Your favorite sun, Douglas

3

Douglas was vastly amused by his brother's nickname for Mary Rose's latest charity project, but his mood drastically changed when he got a good look at Crying-Shame's stallion. He suddenly wanted to kill the man. It didn't matter to him that MacDonald might not be able to defend himself. If the son-of-a-bitch was responsible for the mount's pitiful condition, then, by God, he deserved to die.

Cole had ridden down to the stables in the wagon with his brother. The owner, a red-haired, potbellied giant of a man named Simpson, told them Mary Rose and the stranger were out back by the corral. Cole was going to collect his and Mary Rose's horses, but Simpson kindly offered to saddle the gelding and the mare and bring them out, and so Cole rode with Douglas around the corner to where MacDonald's horse was being housed. They'd only just rolled to a stop when Douglas tossed Cole the reins and reached for his shotgun. The weapon was propped on the seat between the two men. Cole was quicker than his brother. He snatched the shotgun out of Douglas's hand and threw it into the back of the wagon.

He knew what his brother was thinking. "Find out first," he suggested in a low voice. "Then you can kill him."

Douglas agreed with a curt nod, then jumped to the ground. He stormed over to the corral, where Mary Rose and MacDonald stood watching the animal.

She had been stunned speechless at her first sight of the horse but was quick to recover. She kept her attention on the stallion while she tried to understand why anyone would treat him so maliciously. White, puckered scars covered almost every inch of his coat. She couldn't imagine how the poor thing had managed to survive.

She decided she'd better get the particulars. "How long have you owned the horse?" she asked in a voice strained with worry.

"Almost three weeks now."

"Thank God," she whispered. She was going to ask him another question, but then she spotted Douglas coming toward them and she immediately hurried to put herself between the two men. She could see rage on her brother's face.

"He's only owned the horse three weeks, Douglas. Just three weeks."

Harrison found her behavior puzzling. "Why are you shouting?"

"It was important for Douglas to hear me. I didn't want him to kill you."

If he was startled by her bluntness, he didn't let it show. His attention turned to her brother. He noticed how red and mottled Douglas's face was and immediately understood. Douglas was staring at the stallion, enraged on the animal's behalf.

"Douglas has become an expert in the care of most animals," Mary Rose said. "Ranchers come from miles around just to get his advice. My brother has a particular fondness for his horses. He's also extremely protective, and when he saw the scars on your animal . . ."

"He only saw the scars."

"Yes," she agreed. "Someone used a whip on him, didn't he? Do you know, I thought his coat was white until I got closer, then I could see a hint of gold. Who did this to him?"

Douglas had reached the two of them and now stood with his hands fisted at his sides while he studied the animal and listened to the conversation. He was trying to get rid of his anger and finding it an almost impossible task.

"I don't know who was responsible," Harrison replied. "I asked, but no one knew. I forget about the scars. I just see MacHugh."

"MacHugh? What a peculiar name," she said before she realized she might be insulting him. "I mean to say, what a fine name," she hastily corrected. "Peculiar and fine," she ended, with a nod so he'd believe she was sincere.

She was going to great lengths not to injure his feelings. He smiled in reaction. She really was a sweetheart and appeared to be completely unspoiled. If that was the case, then she was going to be a refreshing change from all the other women he'd known in the past.

He wondered if she realized how incredibly lovely she was.

He pulled himself back to the topic at hand. "I named him after a crusty ancestor of mine. I saw certain similarities."

"You did?"

"That's one damned ugly horse."

Cole made the judgment from behind. Harrison didn't turn around when he answered him. "Get past the scars and you'll see he's one damned fine horse."

"You think he's fine?" Mary Rose whispered the question.

"Yes."

She let out a barely noticeable sigh. She could feel her heart melting. Harrison was a good and decent man. It was such a rarity for any man to ever look beyond the surface, at least that was the conclusion she'd come to after having to fend off several arrogant, opinionated suitors, and she could really name only four other men who had conquered the ability to look deeper, into a person's heart. Her brothers were all good and decent, even when they didn't want to be, and perhaps Harrison was too. Lord, she hoped she was right. Good men were so difficult to find these days, especially in Montana Territory.

They also tended to die young. Their high standards and their values got them killed. But not this one, she vowed. Come heaven or purgatory, she was determined to help him learn how to get along in the wilderness. Besides, it really wasn't all that difficult once you got the hang of it.

MacHugh was busy putting on a show for his audience. He was rearing up and snorting and acting as if he had just been fed a bucket full of crazy weed. Harrison was used to his theatrics. He knew MacHugh was trying to intimidate them, and from the worried look on Mary Rose's face

98

when the stallion came charging toward the fence, he concluded she was duly impressed. She moved toward her brother Douglas, seeking his protection without even realizing it.

Harrison found himself wishing she'd moved toward him.

"Does he let you ride him?" she asked.

Douglas had calmed down enough to join in the discussion. "Why would he buy him if he couldn't ride him, Mary Rose? Use your head, for God's sake," Douglas instructed her.

"I would have purchased him anyway, even if I couldn't ride him," Harrison said.

"Well, now, that's plain stupid," Cole remarked.

Harrison didn't take offense. "Perhaps."

"Because of the similarities you saw?" she asked.

He nodded. "Tell me what they were," she said then.

"The horse is every bit as stubborn as my ancestor was reported to be," Harrison said. "There was fire in his eyes, but something else too. Patience, I guess, for the men who didn't understand him."

She sighed again. "Patience," she whispered.

Harrison nodded. He couldn't imagine what had just come over her. Her eyes had taken on a dreamy, faraway look. He wondered what she was thinking about.

She thought she might be falling in love. It was a fanciful, schoolgirl notion. She didn't care. As long as she didn't tell anyone what she was daydreaming about, it was all right, wasn't it?

"I figured I could learn a few things from him," Harrison told Douglas. "I'm short on patience."

He really would make a wonderful husband, Mary Rose decided. He wanted to be patient.

"He's got strong legs," Douglas said. He moved closer to the fence. "Actually he's quite sound. Did you look him over? In his mouth?"

"Yes."

"No diseases you know about?"

"None."

"Where did you get him?"

"Right outside of Hammond, at Finley's place. Have you heard of it?"

Mary Rose's eyes widened. "You went to Finley's? Dear God, he only buys horses he's going to kill for the meat he sells. How much did you pay for him?"

"Twelve dollars," Harrison answered.

"Then you were robbed, MacDonald." Cole happily volunteered his opinion.

Douglas disagreed with his brother. "I'm not so sure he was, Cole. He might have gotten a bargain."

"I did get a bargain," Harrison insisted. "And I was extremely fortunate. If I'd been an hour later, MacHugh would be dead."

"And that is why you would have purchased him even if you couldn't ride him."

Mary Rose was smiling over her conclusion. She turned to Cole. "Isn't he sweet?" she whispered.

"He's stupid," Cole whispered back.

Harrison heard the exchange. He shrugged and

then walked around to the gate. MacHugh followed him. The horse acted as if he wanted to tear Harrison from limb to limb, yet when he walked inside the corral, MacHugh gave him only a hard nudge before settling down.

He stayed meek and willing until Douglas tried to get near him. Harrison grabbed hold of the bridle and soothed the panic away.

Mary Rose's brother shut the gate behind him and walked forward. The horse immediately started fussing again.

"Stand where you are," Harrison called out. "Let him come to you. If you don't move, he won't hurt you."

Douglas agreed with a nod. He stood with his legs braced apart and waited to see what the stallion was going to do.

He didn't have to wait long. As soon as Harrison let go of the bridle, the stallion came charging across the corral. Mary Rose was certain MacHugh was going to kill her brother. She wanted to scream a warning, and it took all her discipline to keep quiet. Cole was sure he could see fire in the stallion's eyes and immediately reached for his gun. By God, he'd shoot the damned thing before he'd let it trample his brother to death.

"Don't you have any sense, Douglas?" Cole whispered.

MacHugh stopped a few inches away from Douglas. He wasn't through with his terror tactics, however, and had to rear up twice before he finally decided to behave.

Mary Rose's knees had gone weak. She moved

closer to Cole and leaned against him.

"You can touch him now, if you want to," Harrison told Douglas. He walked over to stand next to the stallion. "I told you he wouldn't hurt you. He just likes to put on a show. Are you all right?"

He added the question when he noticed how pale Douglas's complexion was. Mary Rose's brother had to swallow before he could answer. "You forgot to mention he was going to scare the hell out of me."

He reached out to pat the stallion. MacHugh promptly shoved him back a good foot. Douglas let out a hoot of laughter. Then he tried again. "Up close, I can see how fine he really is. You just have to get past the scars first. He's one of the soundest animals I've come across in a good long while." There was grudging admiration in his voice when he added, "You chose well."

Harrison couldn't take the credit. "I didn't choose. He did."

He didn't elaborate, and Douglas didn't ask. He seemed to understand.

"He's almost seventeen hands, isn't he? — and surprisingly gentle for a stallion," Douglas remarked.

"We've got bigger in Scotland," Harrison replied.

"Is that where you're from?"

Harrison nodded. "I understand you're Irish," he said, hoping to get Mary Rose's brother to talk about his background.

Douglas looked surprised. "Who told you that?"

"Your sister."

The brother smiled. "Then I guess I am . . . sometimes."

What the hell was that supposed to mean? Harrison wanted to ask, but he wisely chose to turn the topic back to the stallion, for he could see the brother was already closing up on him. The flash of a smile vanished as quickly as it had appeared. He looked wary now.

"Don't let MacHugh fool you. He's only gentle when he wants to be. He can be deadly, especially when he's feeling cornered."

Douglas filed the information away. "A lot of men feel the same way."

He introduced himself then and told Harrison he didn't mind having him come home for supper. A tenuous bond formed between the two men. Douglas's love for all animals and Harrison's obvious affection for MacHugh had given them something in common.

Cole had stood idle for as long as he was going to. He wasn't about to let his brother one-up him. If Douglas could get near the hellish animal, then he could too.

A few minutes later he had suffered through the same godawful ordeal that Douglas had gone through. It took Cole a little longer to get his color back.

Mary Rose wanted to be next. Both brothers ordered her to stay outside the corral.

"MacHugh is partial to women."

Harrison's casually mentioned remark didn't sway Cole or Douglas. They were both diligently shaking their heads when their sister came marching inside.

"She never listens to us," Cole muttered.

Douglas thought he should defend her. "She's got a mind of her own," he told Harrison.

"I can see she does."

Mary Rose stopped right inside the gate and tried not to look afraid. She wanted to close her eyes, but she didn't dare. Her brothers would laugh then, and she'd be mortified because Harrison was watching.

The stallion ignored her. She waited several minutes before she finally moved closer.

MacHugh finally trotted over to her. She patted him and cooed to him and treated him very like a baby, and he responded in kind. It was obvious he liked her scent, and he seemed greedy for her affection.

"You're going to like Rosehill," she whispered. "You might even want to stay with your friend, Harrison, for a long, long time."

She knew she was daydreaming about impossible things. She'd only known the man for twenty or thirty minutes, and one of the first things he'd told her was that he was only *thinking* about settling down in the area. He could decide the life was too harsh here and pack up and leave before winter set in.

She peeked around the stallion to look at Harrison. Then she became a little breathless again. She couldn't imagine what was the matter with her.

She didn't believe her bizarre reaction to the man was due to the fact that he was handsome. Granted, she did find him attractive, but that wasn't what made her breath catch in her throat.

It was because he was such a nice man. It hadn't taken her any time at all to come to that conclusion. He was extremely kindhearted as well. MacHugh was living proof of that fact.

She couldn't stop staring at him. Could an infatuation strike this quickly? All the girls at boarding school insisted that it did, but she hadn't believed their foolishness.

Now she wasn't so certain. Her brothers had insisted that eventually she would get married, and in her heart, she knew they were probably right. Yet until today, the mere possibility of being saddled with the same man day in and day out for the rest of her life had always made her feel nauseated. She wasn't feeling at all sick to her stomach now, however. Everything was suddenly different. No man had ever made her feel breathless. She thought the condition might very well be a requirement one had to suffer through when one was caught up in an infatuation.

The way she would feel if and when he ever kissed her was another requirement, she supposed. She had been kissed only a couple of times. The experiences had been as pleasant as being kissed by jellyfish. She had been completely repulsed.

Mary Rose decided she would have to find out how Harrison kissed. She let out another little sigh just thinking about it. She knew she was being shameless. She didn't care.

She gave MacHugh one last pat and then turned around and walked out of the corral. The stallion meekly followed.

Both brothers had noticed their sister gawking

at Harrison. He had noticed too and was now trying to understand what had come over her.

Then they all heard her singing.

"What the hell's the matter with her?" Cole asked his brother.

"She's daydreaming," Douglas speculated.

Harrison didn't say anything. He continued to stand in the middle of the corral and watch Mary Rose. She was acting peculiar all right. When she was staring at him, she had a bemused expression on her face. What had she been thinking about? It bothered the hell out of him that he didn't know.

She was beginning to show signs of being unpredictable. Harrison didn't like seeing that trait in anyone.

Knowing what others were thinking was essential in his line of work. Granted, he wasn't a mind reader, but he was a good judge of character and could usually predict reactions.

"Give it up, MacDonald," Cole said before heading for the stables. He had waited long enough for old man Simpson to get off his rump and saddle his horse. He would take care of the chore himself.

"Give what up?" Harrison asked Cole.

Douglas was walking toward his wagon. "Trying to understand her," he called over his shoulder. "You're never going to figure Mary Rose out."

Cole turned around when he reached the back door of the stable. "Harrison, don't you think you'd better catch up with your horse? He's trying to follow my sister home."

Harrison let out an expletive and started running. What in thunder was the matter with him? He hadn't even noticed MacHugh had left.

From the surprised look on Harrison's face, Cole knew he hadn't noticed. He had a good laugh at Crying-Shame MacDonald's expense, and he didn't particularly mind at all that he was being downright rude.

Cole certainly hadn't been surprised by MacHugh's turnabout in loyalty. The stallion wasn't acting any different from most of the other creatures who roamed the area. They knew a good thing when they spotted it.

Man or beast, it didn't seem to matter. They all followed Mary Rose home.

She lived in the center of paradise. Harrison stopped when he reached the rise above the Clayborne property. He stared down in fascination and wonder at the valley below. Lush spring grass covered the floor of the valley and swept upward into the mountains beyond. The green was so brilliant and intense, it was almost more than the eye could take in, and he found himself instinctively squinting against it. It looked as if the sun had fallen to the earth and turned itself into emeralds. Everywhere he looked, the grass sparkled with leftover dew. Splattered against the glorious carpet were pink and yellow, red and orange, and purple and blue wildflowers, so plentiful in number it wasn't possible for anyone to count them. All the flowers were ablaze with their own rich hues. Their sweet perfume mingled with the clean fresh air of the valley.

Mountains as old as time stood regal and proud on the north and west sides of the valley, and a wide, clear blue stream meandered down the eastern slope.

The land was breathtakingly beautiful and so much like his glen back in the Highlands, he was suddenly melancholy for Scotland and the home he'd been forced to leave.

How could one piece of heaven remind him so much of another? He wouldn't have believed it was possible, yet there it was, spread out before him like one of God's exquisite robes.

The melancholy vanished as quickly as it had come, and he was suddenly feeling tremendous peace and contentment.

Tranquility wrapped around him like a warm, heated blanket. He was comforted and soothed and replenished. His hunger for home abated with each breath he drew.

He could stay here forever.

The realization jarred him. He immediately forced himself to block the traitorous thought. His heart belonged to Scotland, and one day soon, when he was wealthy enough and powerful enough, he would go back and take what belonged to him.

He finally turned his attention to the Clayborne ranch. He had imagined they would live in a log cabin, similar in style to all the others he'd seen on his travels, but the Claybornes lived in a two-story, white clapboard house. It was quite modest in both proportion and design, yet he still found it quite regal.

A veranda, supported by white posts, circled

the house on three sides. Everything appeared to have been freshly painted.

There were two large barns behind the house, though still some distance away. The buildings stood about fifty or sixty yards apart and were surrounded by corrals. He counted five in all.

"How many horses do you have?"

"It seems like hundreds at times," she answered. "Our income depends on our horses. We raise them and sell them. We really never have more than sixty or seventy, I suppose, and sometimes as few as thirty. Cole brings in wild mustangs every now and then. We also have cattle, of course, but not nearly the number Travis thinks we should have."

"And Travis is the youngest brother?"

She thought it was terribly sweet of him to try to keep everyone straight in his mind.

"Yes, he's the youngest brother."

"How old was he when you were born?"

She gave him a curious look. "He was nine, going on ten. Why do you ask?"

He shrugged. "I just wondered," he replied. "Does Travis look like Douglas, or does he resemble you and Cole?"

"He looks like . . . Travis. You ask a lot of questions, Harrison."

"I do?" he replied for lack of anything better to say.

She nodded. "What do you think of my home?"

He turned to look at the landscape once again before answering her. Simply telling her that her valley was beautiful wouldn't adequately describe the feeling the wondrous area gave him. He didn't understand why it was so important for him to find the right words, but it *was* important somehow, and he was determined to be as exact as possible. Paradise deserved more than a moment's reflection. It demanded recognition.

And so he ended up speaking from his heart. "Your land reminds me of Scotland, and that, Mary Rose, is the highest praise a Highlander can give."

She smiled with pleasure. The look in Harrison's eyes indicated his sincerity. She suddenly felt like sighing again. Dear heavens, how she liked this gentle man.

She leaned to the side of her saddle so she could get a little closer to him. "Do you know what I think?" she whispered.

He leaned toward her. "No," he whispered back. "What do you think?"

"You and I are very much alike."

He was instantly appalled. She was out of her mind if she believed they were anything alike. Why, they were complete opposites in his estimation. He'd already figured out she was all emotion. He sure as hell wasn't. He rarely let anyone know what he was thinking or feeling. He was also extremely methodical in everything he undertook. He hated surprises; in his line of work they could be deadly, and so he carefully thought out every plan of action before he made any decisions. He demanded order in his life, and from what he'd heard about Mary Rose, he could only conclude that she thrived on chaos. She was also sweet-tempered, terribly naive, and openly hospitable to strangers. And trust — good God Almighty, the woman seemed to trust everyone she met. It hadn't taken her more than five minutes to make the decision to take him home with her. For all she knew, he could have been a cold-blooded killer.

Oh, no, they weren't anything alike. He didn't trust anyone. He was a cynic by nature and by profession.

She couldn't possibly understand how she'd misjudged him, however, because she didn't know anything about him. She had innocently accepted what he had told her, and as long as he continued to pretend to be an unsophisticated city boy who wore a gun only because he thought he was supposed to, then she was going to continue to believe they really were soul mates.

"Don't you wonder why I think we're alike?" she asked.

He braced himself. "Why?"

"You look at things the same way I do," she answered. "Do quit frowning, Harrison. I haven't insulted you."

The hell she hadn't. "No, of course not," he agreed. "Exactly how do we look at things?"

"You see with your heart."

"I learned a long time ago to put logic and reason above emotion," he began. "My philosophy of life is really very simple."

"And what might your philosophy be?"

"First with the mind, then with the heart."

She wasn't impressed. "So you never allow yourself to just . . . feel? You have to think about it first?"

"Of course," he agreed. He was pleased she

understood. She would do well to follow his rule, he thought.

"How exact you are, Harrison."

He smiled. "Thank you."

"And rigid."

"Yes."

She rolled her eyes heavenward. "Adam's going to like you," she predicted.

"Why is that?"

"My brother shares your philosophy. I believe I drive him crazy sometimes. I'm sorry he worries so, but I can't help the way I am. When I look at my valley . . ."

She suddenly stopped. And then she started to blush.

"Yes?" he asked.

"You'll think I'm crazy."

"I won't."

She took a breath. "You may laugh if you want, but sometimes I feel a bond with the land, and if I'm real quiet and just let myself listen and feel, I can almost hear her heart beating with life all around me."

She watched him closely. He didn't smile, but she thought he looked as if he wanted to. She felt the need to defend herself.

"I thought you felt it too, Harrison. I'm still not so certain you . . ."

"Mary Rose, will you get moving? Honest to God, I've wasted the entire day waiting on you."

Cole bellowed the order from behind. Mary Rose immediately nudged her mount forward.

"My brother doesn't have much patience for

112

dillydallying. He's really very easygoing. He just likes to hide it."

That had to be the contradiction of the year. Harrison didn't think Cole had any patience at all. He found himself wondering why someone hadn't killed the man by now. Her brother wasn't just hot-tempered; he was also the most abrasive individual Harrison had ever come across.

And that seemed to be his better quality.

The youngest brother met them outside of the main barn but had to wait for an introduction. Harrison had already dismounted and was busy trying to talk MacHugh into going inside the stable. The stallion wasn't in the mood to co-operate. He reared up several times and then started snorting and stomping and slamming his head into Harrison's shoulder.

Harrison ordered MacHugh to behave. The animal must not have liked his tone of voice. MacHugh pushed him again, but put more muscle into it. Harrison landed on his backside in a cloud of dust.

His lack of control over the animal was damned humiliating. Mary Rose was sympathetic. She kept pleading with her brothers to do something to help. They were smart enough to stay away from the beast. Douglas was smiling. He was polite enough not to laugh, even when Harrison landed on his backside a second time.

Cole wasn't as reserved. He laughed until tears came into his eyes. Harrison really wanted to kill him. He couldn't, of course, at least not if he wanted to stay for supper and find out who the hell these people really were. He had already figured out the redheaded brother standing behind Mary Rose was either Adam or Travis.

Cole's laughter caught his attention again. Perhaps Harrison could just put his fist through the obnoxious brother's face and, hopefully, break a few bones. What was the harm in that? It took all Harrison had not to give in to the urge. Reason prevailed. Mary Rose would probably get upset if he beat the hell out of her brother. She'd also realize he could take care of himself.

God, he hated that deception, and right this minute, he hated Cole Clayborne just as passionately.

Harrison had had enough of MacHugh's temper tantrum. He let the stallion win. He let go of the reins and walked over to the corral. MacHugh let out another loud snort, stomped around a bit, and then followed him.

The horse trotted into the center of the ring and stood as still as a stone while Harrison stripped him of his gear.

"If you jump the fence, MacHugh, you're on your own. You got that?"

"Harrison, come and meet Travis," Mary Rose called out.

"What kind of name is Harrison?" Travis asked in a voice loud enough for Harrison to hear.

"A family name," Harrison called back. He draped the saddle and the blanket over the fence, shut the gate behind him, and walked over to meet the youngest of Mary Rose's brothers.

"What kind of name is Travis? Irish?"

Travis smiled. "Could be," he replied in a gratingly cheerful tone of voice.

What the hell kind of answer was that? He couldn't ask because Mary Rose had already jumped into an explanation of how she had met Harrison and how kind and thoughtful he was because he'd warned Cole of an ambush.

Harrison watched Travis during her lengthy explanation and one thought kept running through his mind. No way in hell. This man couldn't possibly be a relative. He didn't look anything like any of the others, though the more Harrison thought about it, not looking like the others seemed to be the one trait they all shared. Hell, Travis looked more like MacHugh.

The comparison made Harrison smile. Travis had reddish brown hair and green eyes. His face was square shaped. Mary Rose had a perfectly oval face. Travis was about the same height as Douglas, but he didn't have his bulk. The youngest brother was reed thin, and he lacked Cole's muscle.

Harrison decided nothing more could surprise him. If she tried to tell him Travis happened to have a twin brother who was a full-blooded Crow, he wouldn't bat an eye. He might even be able to keep a straight face when he asked the twin if he happened to be Irish too.

He started paying attention to the conversation when Mary Rose told Travis that he would be staying for supper. Her brother didn't look irritated by the announcement. In fact, he looked resigned.

Harrison had only just decided this brother wasn't nearly as abrasive as Cole, but the man quickly changed his mind.

"You've got guts to ride such an ugly horse."

"Travis, don't be rude," Mary Rose ordered.

"I wasn't being rude," he replied. "I was giving Harrison a compliment. It does take guts." He turned to his guest. "Sorry if you took offense."

"Harrison, are you gonna saddle up MacHugh tomorrow?"

Cole shouted the question from the back of the wagon.

Harrison was immediately suspicious. "Why?" he shouted back.

The brother lifted the sack of flour onto his shoulder before answering. "I want to watch."

Harrison knew he would regret it if he said anything at all, and so he forced himself to keep silent. It almost killed him.

He watched Cole cross the veranda and go inside the house and only then noticed the tall, black-skinned man leaning against the pillar. The stranger was quite impressive looking, with wide shoulders, silver-tipped hair, and round gold-framed spectacles that made him appear scholarly. He wore a muted red plaid shirt open at the collar and dark brown pants. He looked very relaxed and thoroughly at home.

Harrison wondered if he was another lost soul Mary Rose had taken under her wing and invited home for dinner. If that was the case, the man had obviously decided to stay on.

"Don't pay any attention to Cole, Harrison. He likes to tease. That's all. He doesn't mean to hurt your feelings. He's actually a very gentle, understanding man."

She smiled up at him to let him know she

116

really expected him to believe that nonsense. It took a good deal of willpower not to laugh right in her face.

"For heaven's sake, Mary Rose, Harrison's a man, not a little boy." Travis gave the brotherly criticism and fell into step beside their guest. "You'll get used to my sister, but it's gonna take a while. She's always worried about everyone's feelings. She can't seem to help it. Just ignore her. We do."

After giving him that sage advice, he ran on ahead.

"Just one more brother to meet, and then you'll know everyone. Hurry up, Harrison. Adam's waiting for us."

Mary Rose ran up the steps, but stopped next to the stranger. Harrison assumed she wanted to introduce the other guest to him before they went inside to meet Adam.

He was mistaken in his assumption.

"Adam, I'd like you to meet my friend, Harrison MacDonald. He's from Scotland."

Adam moved away from the pillar to face Harrison. "Is that right?" he replied. "Welcome to Rosehill, Mr. MacDonald."

Harrison was too stunned to speak. He glanced down at Mary Rose, then looked back at Adam. He didn't know what he was supposed to do or say now, and neither one of them was giving him any clues. They simply stared back at him and waited to see how he was going to react to the announcement.

He would have loved to have had a detailed explanation as to why the black-skinned man was

117

calling himself her brother and why she was accepting him as such.

He finally gathered his wits about him. It wasn't his place to ask any questions, and they certainly didn't need to explain. He just wished to God someone would.

"It's a pleasure to meet you, sir. Your sister very kindly invited me to stay for supper. I hope it won't be an inconvenience." Harrison extended his hand in greeting. Adam seemed surprised by the gesture. He hesitated for a second or two, and finally shook his hand.

"It won't be any bother at all. We're quite used to Mary Rose inviting strangers home for supper." He paused to smile at his sister. "Scotland's a long way from here."

Harrison agreed with a nod. "Supper's waiting," Adam announced. "You can wash up inside."

He led the way. Mary Rose followed. Harrison stood where he was and tried to sort out all the wild possibilities rushing through his mind.

He couldn't get anything to make any sense. How in God's name had she ended up with four such diverse, couldn't-possibly-be-related brothers?

Mary Rose held the screen door open and patiently waited for him.

He finally shook himself out of his trance.

"About Adam . . ." she began.

"Yes?" He braced himself for another one of her surprises, fully expecting to be flabbergasted again.

"You haven't asked yet, but I thought I would

118

tell you anyway."

He felt like cheering. Finally. He was going to get some real, honest-to-God explanations.

"Yes?"

She smiled up at him. "He isn't Irish."

July 1, 1862

Dear Mama Rose,

We're having an awful time trying to get the baby to quit wetting her drawers. Being boys like we are, we do things different. The baby caught Travis one afternoon, and she's been standing up ever since. We tried to explain to her that girls don't do it that way, but she won't listen to reason, and now we're starting to think maybe she doesn't understand she's a girl. Adam swears she's as smart as a whip, but she's also as stubborn as Cole, and you know how mule-headed he can be. We all figured we needed a woman to help us out with the problem. Adam thought he should take the baby over to Belle's shack, since she's the only woman in the entire area. Cole pitched a fit over the idea. He didn't want little Mary Rose hanging around a whore, but I thought it ought to count for something that Belle was so good-hearted. Besides, everyone knows she hates what she has to do to put food on her table. Why, she hates whoring so much, she tells every man who calls on her how sad and blue she is. It's gotten so folks don't even call her a whore anymore. No, they call her Blue Belle . . .

Your loving son,
Douglas Clayborne

120

4

Supper became an interrogation. The tables were neatly turned on Harrison, and while he was pretty certain he could have taken control of the questioning at any point, or at the very least put a stop to it altogether, he chose to go along with the game and be as accommodating as possible. He had an ulterior motive. The questions asked by the Clayborne brothers and their reactions to his answers gave him a good deal of information and insight into the family.

Each man used a different approach. Cole tried to be as blunt and intimidating as possible, Douglas was direct and often offered personal bits of information about the family, and Travis was both methodical and diplomatic. Adam was the most elusive. He maintained a rather stoic expression throughout dinner. Harrison was never given even an inkling of what he might be thinking.

Adam was the antithesis of his sister. Mary Rose was as easy to read as an elementary primer. Her every reaction showed on her face and in her eyes. Harrison had never met anyone quite like her. She was open and honest and wonderfully tenderhearted, and those qualities made him want to get closer to her.

He was honest enough to admit that he was also physically attracted to her. She was a beautiful woman, and he would have had to be dead not to notice. Her eyes mesmerized him, and that sweet mouth of hers made him want to think about things he had no right to even consider. Not even in his dreams.

But, while her beauty made him notice her, it was her heart that kept him interested.

Luckily, his discipline saved him from making a complete fool of himself. He stopped himself from blatantly staring at her during supper.

Her brothers weren't as controlled in their behavior. They stared at him from the minute the food was placed on the table until the plates had been taken away. They were rude, knew it, and didn't seem to give a damn.

They waited until their coffee cups had been refilled to begin their grilling. Harrison leaned back in his chair and let them have at him.

The pecking order in the family had been established as soon as the family took their seats. Adam sat at the head of the table, a position of importance Harrison found both significant and intriguing. Mary Rose sat on his left side and Cole was on his right. Douglas sat down next to his sister, and Travis, the youngest brother, sat down next to Cole. Harrison was seated at the opposite end of the table and faced the man he silently called the patriarch of the Clayborne family.

"Did you get enough to eat, Mr. MacDonald?" Adam inquired.

"Yes, thank you. The stew was excellent. Please call me Harrison."

Adam nodded. "And you must call me Adam," he suggested. "In England, some men hold titles.

Is this true in Scotland?"

"Yes, it is," he answered.

"What about you, Harrison. Do you have a title?" Douglas asked.

He didn't answer. He felt uncomfortable discussing the topic and had to admit to himself he was even a little embarrassed. A titled gentleman suddenly seemed pompous to him and certainly out of his element in these mountains.

"Well, do you?" Cole demanded to know.

"As a matter of fact, I do," he admitted. "The title has been passed down from generation to generation, a tradition really."

"What is your title?" Adam asked.

Harrison sighed. There didn't seem to be any way out of the admission. "I am the Earl of Stanford, Hawk Isle."

"That's an awful lot to be saddled with growing up," Douglas remarked. "Were you born with the title?"

"No, I inherited it when my father died."

"What do people there call you? Sir?" Cole asked.

"Staff would."

"And others?" Cole persisted.

"Lord."

Cole grinned. "Sounds mighty fancy to me," he remarked. "Do you have lots of money and land?"

"No."

Mary Rose could tell their guest was uncomfortable. She decided to put him at ease by stopping the discussion about titles.

"Adam made the stew for our supper. It was

123

his turn to help Samuel."

"Who is Samuel?" Harrison asked.

"He's our cook," she explained. "You haven't met him yet. He sometimes sits at the table with us, but he was busy tonight."

"No, he wasn't," Cole told his sister. He turned to Harrison. "He pretended to be busy. He hates strangers. You won't see him until he's good and ready to let you see him. What made you decide to leave Scotland?"

The switch in topics didn't take Harrison by surprise. He almost smiled over the ploy. He'd used the same technique many times in court. The goal was to get the witness to drop his guard and answer without even thinking.

"I wanted to see the States."

Cole didn't look as if he believed him. Harrison didn't bother to try to convince him. He didn't say another word, but simply stared back and waited for him to ask another question.

"I understand from Mary Rose that you want to learn how to ranch," Douglas interjected.

"Yes."

"Why?" Travis asked.

"The life appeals to me."

Travis obviously wanted him to go into a more detailed explanation. Harrison refused to accommodate him. He was going to make him work to find out what he wanted to know.

"It's backbreaking work," Douglas told him.

"I imagine it is," Harrison agreed.

"What exactly do you find appealing about ranching?" Travis persisted.

"Being outdoors," Harrison answered. "And

working with my hands."

"There are lots of things you could do to get outdoors," Cole interjected.

"You sound like you've been cooped up in an office," Travis said.

"Yes," Harrison replied. "I do sound like that, don't I?"

"Well, were you?" Travis asked. His frustration in not getting a more satisfactory answer was apparent in his tone of voice.

"Most of the time I was in an office," Harrison admitted. "But lately I've been able to do some traveling on business matters."

"Who do you work for?" Douglas asked.

"Lord William Elliott," he answered. "I've taken a leave from my duties, however."

"So he's got a fancy title too," Douglas remarked.

Harrison agreed with a nod but didn't go into more detail.

And so it continued, on and on and on. Harrison would occasionally give an obviously evasive answer or deliberately go off on a tangent just to find out which brother would bring him back to the question they wanted answered. It was curious and surprising to him that Travis, the youngest brother, proved to be the most doggedly determined. He was also quite analytical.

He would have made one hell of an attorney.

"Why didn't you stay in the states?" Travis asked.

"The 'states'?" Harrison repeated, not certain he understood the question.

"Montana isn't a state," Douglas explained.

"Yes," Harrison said. "I'd forgotten that fact. Do you believe the area will become a state soon?"

"It's only a matter of time," Douglas told him. He was going to expound further on the topic of statehood, but Travis cut him off. "So why did you come all this way?"

They had come full circle once again. Harrison could barely hide his smile.

"I wanted to see the land. I believe I already mentioned that fact, Travis."

"Please quit pestering him," Mary Rose pleaded. She leaned forward then, with her elbow on the table and her chin resting in the palm of her hand, and smiled at Harrison.

"What do you think of our home?" she asked.

Harrison watched Adam while he answered her question. The oldest brother hadn't said a word for quite some time. He looked half asleep, and Harrison was beginning to think he wasn't even paying attention to the conversation, yet the second his sister put her elbow on the table, he slowly reached over and touched her arm with one hand. It was a very subtle reminder. Mary Rose instinctively turned to her brother to find out what he wanted. Adam didn't explain. Harrison knew he didn't want to draw any attention to her breach in manners. He must have applied a little pressure on her arm, however, because she suddenly straightened up in her chair and put her hands in her lap.

Then she smiled at Adam. He winked back at her.

Harrison pretended he hadn't noticed what had just happened. He moved his cup from one spot on the table to another and shifted his position in the hard-backed chair.

"Your home is beautiful," he remarked.

"You haven't seen all that much of it," Douglas protested.

"He saw the first floor," Cole interjected. "And that's all he's ever going to see. The upstairs is off limits, Harrison."

"There are just bedrooms up there," Mary Rose hastily added. She frowned at Cole for sounding so rude, then looked at their guest once again.

Harrison smiled at her. "The house took me by surprise. I didn't expect . . ."

Cole cut him off. "Did you expect us to live like barbarians?"

Harrison had taken about all he was going to take from the abrasive man. He decided to goad him just enough to make him lose his temper.

"Do you believe I would think you live like barbarians because you occasionally act like one?"

Cole started to stand up, but Mary Rose changed his mind.

"He didn't mean to insult you," she told her brother. "You can be intimidating. Some might even call you a bully."

"They do call him a bully," Travis said. "At least in town they probably do."

Cole shook his head. "I can't take the credit for something that isn't true," he said. "People think I'm antisocial, Harrison. Unfortunately I still haven't earned the nickname of bully. I'm working on it."

Cole turned to his sister. "Thanks anyway, Mary Rose."

127

She let him see her exasperation. Then she explained to Harrison. "Out here, being a bully does have certain advantages. People tend to leave you alone, and Cole likes that. Therefore, your remark that Cole acted barbaric was actually a note of praise. Do you see?"

"Are you telling me I just gave him a compliment?" He tried not to sound incredulous, but knew he'd failed when the brothers smiled at him.

Mary Rose wasn't smiling. "Yes, actually you did," she said.

He wanted to vehemently disagree. Yet she had sounded so earnest and was now looking so worried he wouldn't go along with her outrageous fabrication to placate her brother, he decided to play along.

"Then I guess I did."

He didn't choke on the words. He thought that was a laudable effort on his part. She looked relieved, and Harrison decided that swallowing his pride had been well worth the effort.

"What surprised you?" Travis asked.

He couldn't remember what they'd originally been talking about. It was Mary Rose's fault, of course. She was so happy he was trying to get along with Cole, she smiled at him. Harrison didn't believe she was flirting with him or trying to act coy, but she was still twisting his mind into knots all the same. She was so damned sweet and pretty. Provocative too. He couldn't stop himself from imagining what she would feel like in his arms.

"Harrison?" Douglas called his name.

"Yes?" he said. "What did you just ask me?"

"I didn't ask you anything," Douglas replied. "Travis asked."

"If you'd quit staring at our sister, you might be able to concentrate," Cole said.

Travis told his brother to quit baiting their guest and then repeated his question. "I wondered what surprised you about the house."

"It looks very modest from the outside," Harrison explained. "Yet inside . . ."

"It's just as modest," Cole told him.

"If you aren't really looking, I suppose," he agreed. "But I always notice the details."

"And?" Cole asked.

"The attention given to the details surprised me," Harrison admitted. He was careful to keep his gaze away from Mary Rose. He refused to even glance in her direction. "The moldings in the entry are spectacular, and the detail on the staircase is just as impressive."

"Moldings?" Travis repeated.

"The border, or edging, between your ceilings and your walls," Harrison explained.

"I know what they are," Travis returned. "I was just surprised you noticed such a detail."

"I didn't expect to find so many rooms. You have a large parlor, this dining room, of course, and a library filled to the rafters with books you certainly didn't purchase around here."

"Cole designed the house," Mary Rose boasted. "All the brothers helped build it. It took them years."

"He wouldn't let us help with the banister or the walls in the entry though. That's all his work," Travis said.

"You've just given Cole another compliment, Harrison," Mary Rose said.

Harrison was sorry to hear it. He didn't want to find anything impressive about Cole Clayborne. The man had the manners of a boar. Still, his craftsmanship was superior, and Harrison knew it must have taken him months of painstaking work. He had to admire the man's talent and his discipline.

"What else surprised you?" Douglas asked.

Harrison wanted to smile again. From the expressions on the brother's faces, he knew they weren't simply curious about his opinion of their home. They seemed eager to hear praise.

"You have a piano in the parlor. I noticed it right away."

"Of course you noticed it," Cole said. "It's the only thing in there."

"It's a Steinway," Douglas announced. "We got it when Mary Rose was old enough to learn how to play."

"Who taught her?" Harrison asked.

"The piano came with a teacher," Douglas explained. He grinned at Travis before adding, "Sort of anyway."

Harrison didn't know what he was supposed to conclude from that odd remark. He decided not to ask. He would save his questions for more important issues.

"How old were you when you began your lessons?" he asked Mary Rose.

She wasn't certain. She turned to Adam to find out. "She was six," he answered.

"I was seven," Harrison said.

"You play the piano?" Mary Rose looked thrilled over the notion.

"Yes."

"Of course he plays the piano," Cole scoffed. "He can't fight or shoot, but, by God, he can play the piano. Well, piano playing isn't going to keep you alive out here."

"He could play in Billie's saloon," Douglas said.

"And get himself shot in the back like the last one?" Travis argued.

"Why'd he get shot?" Harrison asked the question in spite of his decision not to make inquiries unless the answers gave him information about the family.

"Someone didn't like what he was playing," Cole told him.

Harrison nodded. "I see," he said, though in truth he really didn't understand.

"Why did you learn how to play the piano? That seems peculiar to me," Cole said.

"It was all part of my education," Harrison explained. He wasn't offended by Cole's attitude. He was actually a little amused. The brother seemed to think that playing the piano was something men didn't do.

"Then you were sorely educated," Cole said. "Girls play the piano. Not boys. Didn't your father ever take you out back and teach you how to use your fists?"

"No," Harrison answered. "Did yours?"

Cole started to answer the question, then changed his mind. He leaned back in his chair and shrugged.

"Have you ever heard of Chopin or Mozart,

131

Cole? They were composers," Harrison said. "They wrote music and they played it . . . on the piano."

Cole shrugged again. He obviously wasn't swayed by Harrison's argument.

Harrison decided to change the topic. "Where did you get this china?"

"There are only six cups, and two don't match. We don't even have plates. I got the cups in St. Louis so Mary Rose could have tea parties."

"I was much younger then," she said. "Serving tea was part of my education."

"And who taught you?" Harrison asked, smiling over the picture of Mary Rose as a little girl learning how to be a proper lady.

"Douglas did," she answered.

"We all had to take turns," Douglas hastily added.

From the look Douglas gave his sister, Harrison surmised he wasn't at all pleased she had told him about their tea parties. Mary Rose pretended she hadn't noticed Douglas's glare.

"Our fascination with your reaction to our home must seem odd to you," she said. "We don't usually ask our guests to tell us what they think, but you're very worldly and sophisticated."

He raised an eyebrow over her opinion of him. She interpreted his look to mean he didn't agree.

"You are sophisticated," she insisted. "The way you speak and the way you look at things tells me so. You have obviously been raised in a refined atmosphere."

"You seem the type who would appreciate quality," Douglas said. He was damned thankful they had gotten away from the subject of tea parties. "Most of the people around here don't care about the finer things in life. I don't fault them. They're busy carving out a living."

"Hammond is becoming refined," Travis said. "We get the rejects here in Blue Belle."

"Because it's lawless out here," Cole interjected.

Everyone nodded. "I guess we wondered if you thought we measured up," Travis said. "Douglas is right. The folks around here haven't even looked inside our library, and they sure haven't asked to borrow any books. Adam would let them, but they don't seem to have the time or the interest."

"Have you read all the books in your library?" Harrison asked.

"Of course we have," Cole said.

"Travis failed to mention that the majority of our neighbors don't know how to read, and that's why they haven't asked to borrow any books," Mary Rose said.

Harrison nodded before turning to Travis again. "You asked me if I thought you measured up," he reminded the brother. "To what standard? Yours or mine? If you filled your house with treasures for the sole purpose of impressing others, then no, in my opinion, you haven't measured up to any standard. But you didn't begin with that goal in mind, did you?"

"How do you know we didn't?" Cole asked.

"Simple deduction," Harrison replied. "The piano isn't in the parlor collecting dust and admiration. You purchased it with the intent of training your sister. You could have used the

133

money to buy other things, but you chose a piano instead. You all wanted your sister to have an appreciation for music, and that tells me you understand and value education in all forms. Admitting you've read the books in your library is another indication. As for being sophisticated or cultured, well I think perhaps you're far more sophisticated than you want anyone to believe. Without a doubt, you're all well educated. The titles you've chosen to read told me that."

"None of us went to a university the way you did," Douglas pointed out.

"Going to university is only one avenue to gain knowledge. There are others. A degree isn't insurance against ignorance. Some of my colleagues have proven that."

"You're complimenting us, aren't you?" Travis asked.

"Yes, I suppose I am."

Mary Rose sighed loudly enough for everyone to hear. Harrison turned to smile at her. She immediately smiled back.

"The piano is my favorite possession," she said. "Did you have one special thing back home you hated to leave?"

"My books," Harrison answered.

Adam nodded. "I'm partial to my books as well," he admitted. "It seems we have a common interest."

Harrison was pleased the eldest brother had once again joined the conversation. Adam was proving to be an extremely reserved man, and therefore he was the most difficult to understand. Harrison wanted to draw him out so that he could

134

find out more about him, but he knew he would have to proceed with caution.

"I noticed the meditation you have framed in your library," he remarked.

"The what?" Travis asked.

Before Harrison could answer, Douglas asked, "Do you mean the poem Adam put up on the wall?"

"Yes, it is one of my favorites," Harrison said.

Cole decided to challenge him. "You've really read it? I don't know what book Adam found it in, but it took him hours to copy it down just right and put it in a frame. He made sure he wrote at the bottom where it came from so folks wouldn't think he was trying to take credit for writing it."

"Of course I've read it, many times in fact. I probably have it memorized by now."

Cole didn't look like he believed him. "Let's see if you know it by heart," he challenged. "Recite the poem from start to finish."

Harrison decided to accommodate him, even though he thought it was a bit childish.

"No man is an island . . ."

He missed only one line. Adam supplied it for him. The eldest brother was still impressed, if his smile was any indication, and Harrison began to think that of all the brothers, he and the eldest were probably the most alike.

Mary Rose was smiling like a proud teacher, pleased with her student's performance.

Harrison felt like an idiot.

"Well done," she praised. "Adam plays the

piano," she blurted out. "You share that interest as well."

"Now, why'd you go and tell him that?" Cole demanded. He looked as if he wanted to throttle his sister.

She didn't care for his glare or his surly tone of voice. "You've been terribly rude tonight," she said. "You know better, Cole. Harrison is our guest. Kindly keep that in your mind."

"I don't need you to tell me how to act or what to say, Sidney. Why don't you keep that in mind?"

She let out a gasp. "You're insufferable," she whispered.

Harrison wasn't certain what had just happened. Mary Rose was furious with her brother, and if glares could kill, Cole would have been slumped over in his chair by now. The reason for her anger didn't make sense, however. Calling her by a man's name seemed to be the cause, yet he couldn't imagine why.

Curiosity made him ask. "Did you just call your sister Sidney?"

"I did," Cole snapped.

"Why?"

"Because she was starting to act a little too uppity."

"She was?"

"Listen, Harrison. Out here, it's dangerous to ask questions. You should remember that."

Harrison began to laugh. It wasn't the reaction Cole expected. "What's so amusing?"

"You're amusing," Harrison said. "You've spent the last hour questioning me."

Cole smiled. "It's our house. We make the rules. You don't."

"Will you stop being so inhospitable?" Mary Rose demanded.

She was going to continue to berate her brother, but Adam changed her mind. He leaned forward in his chair and looked at her. Mary Rose immediately sat back and closed her mouth. Then Adam turned to look at Cole. The abrasive brother immediately sat back too.

Adam had obviously demanded a truce, and what impressed Harrison was the fact that he hadn't said a word.

"If you aren't too tired, Harrison, I'd certainly like to hear about Scotland," Adam said. "I've never had the opportunity to go abroad, but I've done a fair amount of traveling with my books."

"Do you think you'd like to visit Scotland one day?" Mary Rose asked.

"Yes, of course I would, but I'd see my home first."

"And where is home?" Harrison asked.

"Home is Africa," Adam replied. "Surely you noticed the color of my skin."

His smile was sincere. He wasn't mocking Harrison; he was simply being blunt.

"Were you born in Africa?" Harrison asked.

"No, I was born into slavery down south, but as soon as I was old enough to sit still and listen, my mother and father told me wonderful stories about their ancestors and the villages they came from. I would like to see the land before I die."

"If it's still there," Cole interjected. "Villages get burned down."

"Yes, 'if,' " Adam agreed.

"You won't go to Africa," Douglas said. "You never go anywhere."

"I think you'd like Scotland," Harrison predicted, bringing the topic back to what Adam wanted him to talk about. "There are similarities between this valley and sections of the Highlands."

"Tell us about your home," Travis said.

Harrison did as he was requested. He spent another five or ten minutes talking about the land and the estates, and ended by saying, "My father's bed was always in front of his windows so he could look out at his land. He was content."

He stopped himself from saying more. "I apologize for rambling. You've figured out by now that it's dangerous to ask a Highlander to talk about his home. He's sure to bore you for hours."

"You weren't boring," Cole said.

"You were eloquent," Adam assured him.

"You mentioned your father's bed was in front of the window," Cole said. "Was he bedridden?"

"Yes."

"For how long?"

"For as long as I can remember. Why do you ask?"

Cole was feeling as low as a worm. He remembered asking Harrison why his father had never taken him into the backyard to teach him how to use his fists. The reason was apparent, of course. The father couldn't. God, he was disgusted with himself.

"I was just curious," Cole answered. "What happened to your father?"

138

"A bullet pierced his spine."

Cole visibly winced. "Then he was paralyzed?"

"Yes."

"Was it an accident?"

"No." Harrison's answer was curt.

"But you stayed with him, even when you were old enough and could have taken off," Cole said.

The remark bordered on obscene in Harrison's estimation. "Yes, I stayed with him. I was his son, for God's sake."

"He might not have stayed with you if you were the one in the bed day and night. Most fathers wouldn't."

"You're wrong," Harrison said. "Most fathers would stay. Mine certainly would have."

"You did your duty by staying," Cole said with satisfaction. He seemed to have worked everything out in his mind.

Harrison was insulted. "It wasn't a duty."

"Are you getting hot under your collar?" Cole had the gall to smile when he asked the question.

Harrison suddenly wanted to smash his face in. His voice was biting when he said, "You insult my father's honor and mine, voicing such a twisted opinion."

Cole shrugged. He wasn't impressed with his guest's anger. He turned to Adam. "We have to toughen him up. Are you willing to take him on?"

"Perhaps," Adam allowed.

"He's got enough bulk, but he also needs gumption," Douglas interjected.

Cole snorted. "He stayed with his father, didn't he? That's proof enough he's got gumption.

Travis, what do you think?"

"It's all right with me. He seems a little too interested in our sister though. That could be a problem."

"Everyone takes an interest in Mary Rose. I'd wonder if Harrison didn't. I say we give it a try."

The brothers nodded consent. Mary Rose couldn't have been happier. She clasped her hands together and smiled at Harrison.

He couldn't believe they had all discussed him as though he'd already left the room. Their rudeness was so outrageous, it was almost laughable.

Mary Rose stood up. Harrison immediately did the same. None of the others moved.

"You've been invited to stay with us," she told him. "This time everyone is agreeing. It's amazing, really," she added with a nod. "Cole usually doesn't agree with anyone. He likes you. Isn't that nice?"

He couldn't resist giving a dose of honesty. "Not particularly," he said.

Everyone laughed, including Mary Rose. "You have a wonderful sense of humor, Harrison."

He hadn't been jesting, but he decided to leave well enough alone. Mary Rose walked around the table so she could face him. "I'll show you where you'll be sleeping. Adam, may we be excused?"

"Yes, of course. Good night, Harrison."

She turned to leave. Harrison thanked the brothers for supper, added his good night, and then followed their sister. None of the brothers followed him. He was somewhat surprised, especially after Travis had voiced his concern about his interest in their sister.

Neither he nor Mary Rose said a word until they were on their way to the bunkhouse. There were at least a thousand stars in the sky to light their way.

"You like my brothers, don't you?"

"Some of the time," he replied. "They're a strange group."

"Not strange, just different."

He clasped his hands behind his back and slowed his step so he could walk by her side. He considered several ways to gently broach the topic he wanted to discuss and finally settled on being blunt.

"May I ask you something?"

"Yes?"

"Why didn't you warn me?"

"About Adam?"

"Yes, about Adam."

"Why would I warn you? You would either accept him or you wouldn't. The choice was yours."

"None of you are related by blood, are you?"

"No, none of us are. We're still a family, Harrison. Blood doesn't always determine bonds."

"No, of course not," he agreed. "You became a family a long time ago, didn't you?"

"Yes," she replied. "How did you guess?"

"You act like siblings. You're protective and loyal to each other, yet argue over minor, inconsequential things. The way you treated each other during supper told me you've all been together a long, long time."

"We have," she agreed. "Isn't it beautiful out here?"

He didn't want to talk about how pretty it was. She was deliberately changing the subject, however. He decided to let her have her way. There had been enough questions for one evening. He'd find out more tomorrow.

"Yes, it is beautiful. The air clears the mind."

"If that is all you noticed, you've been living in the city too long."

He was in full agreement. "You can't always see the stars in London. The air is filled with dirt and fumes. It clouds the view."

"It's very like that in New York City," she remarked.

He missed a step. His heart felt as though it had just stopped beating. "What did you say?"

She repeated her comment. "You seem surprised," she said.

He guessed he hadn't done a very good job of masking his reaction. He forced a smile. "I was surprised," he remarked in what he hoped was a casual tone of voice. "I didn't realize you'd ever been in New York City."

"I was just a baby, so of course I don't remember what the city looked like, but my brothers remember. They told me it was very crowded with factories and smoke and hordes of people milling about."

Harrison took a deep breath. The puzzle was coming together. He still needed to find out who had taken her from her parents and who had helped the boys get all the way to Montana Territory.

"Only parts of New York City are crowded," he said. "It's actually a very interesting place."

"You have to be careful there, don't you?"

"You should be careful everywhere."

"You're sounding like Adam again. He's always telling me to be careful. I sometimes don't pay attention to my surroundings," she admitted. "Travis was amazed I didn't get robbed in St. Louis while I was at school. It's safe here though, on the ranch. I never want to leave again. I become terribly homesick."

He didn't want to hear that. "You might like England and Scotland," he suggested.

"Oh, I'm sure I would. I know there are beautiful places I've yet to see. I would miss my valley though. There's so much to do and see here and never enough hours in one day. I'm constantly finding out new and interesting things. Do you know I just heard about a woman living all alone up on Boar Ridge. Her family had just gotten settled in when they were attacked by Indians. Her husband and son were killed. She was scalped, and left for dead. But she survived. Travis told me he heard Billie and Dooley whispering about her. Everyone thinks she's crazy. The poor woman has been all alone for years and years, and I only just heard about her. I'm going to go and see her, as soon as I can get Adam to agree."

"If she's crazy, she might be dangerous, Mary Rose. You shouldn't . . ."

"You're sounding just like Adam again," she interrupted. "Now that I know about the woman, I have to try to help her. Surely you understand."

Harrison turned the topic just a little. "I could

143

be content living in your valley. I think perhaps you could be content living in Scotland or England, once you made the adjustment."

"Why? Because it would remind me of home? Isn't that very like loving one man because he reminds me of another? I would appreciate Scotland, Harrison, but I don't believe I would ever become content. Home really is best."

He let out a sigh. "You're too young to be so resistant to change."

"May I ask you a personal question? You don't have to answer if you don't wish to."

"Certainly," he agreed. "What is it you want to know?"

"Have you kissed very many women?"

The question caught him off guard. "What did you just ask?"

She asked again. He didn't laugh because she looked so damned sincere.

"What made you think about kissing?"

She wasn't about to tell him the truth. Every single time she looked at him, she thought about kissing. From the moment she'd witnessed how kind and gentle he'd been with his temperamental stallion, she'd thought about little else. She wanted him to kiss her, and even though she knew that what she wanted was quite brazen, she didn't care.

"I was just curious. Have you?"

"I guess I have."

"Do you think about kissing someone first, then you kiss her, or is it all more spontaneous?"

"You think about the strangest things."

"Yes, I do."

They reached the entrance to the bunkhouse. He put his hand on the doorknob and turned to look at her.

"Do you remember what I told you earlier in the day when we were looking down at your valley? React first with the mind, then with the heart. There's your answer. I always think before I act."

She looked disappointed. "You're a very disciplined man, aren't you?"

"I like to think I am."

She shook her head. He didn't know what to make of her obvious disapproval. Being disciplined was an asset, not a liability. Didn't she understand that basic principle?

"I'm not so disciplined."

He nodded. He had already come to the same conclusion. He opened the door and backed up a space so she could go inside first if she was so inclined.

She didn't move from the doorstep. "There are twelve beds inside, but you'll be all alone tonight. If you need anything, please let one of us know."

"Where does Douglas want MacHugh bedded down?"

"Put him in the first stall on the left," she answered. "There's more room. I imagine his feed is waiting for him. Do you think he'll be more agreeable to going inside now that he's had time to get used to us?"

"Yes."

"What about you, Harrison? Are you getting used to us?"

Her question made him smile. "Yes, I am."
She smiled up at him. God, she was pretty.
"May I ask a favor of you?"

She was standing just a foot away from him,
with her face turned up toward his, and, Lord,
her eyes had turned into the color of sapphires
in the moonlight. He didn't dare look at her
mouth. He knew he'd forget his control if he
did, for even now he was thinking about what
she was going to feel like pressed up tight against
him. The urge to taste her was making him rigid.
Her softness and her warmth beckoned him to
lean down and take what she wasn't even offering.

He was out of his mind. "What favor do you
ask?"

His voice sounded brittle to him. She didn't
seem to notice. She obviously didn't realize the
effect she was having on him either, or she
wouldn't have leaned up on her tiptoes so
she could get closer. She smelled wonderful. Like
wildflowers after the rain. She rested the palms
of her hands against his chest. His heart began
to hammer a wild beat inside.

"Will you think about kissing me?"

He hadn't thought about anything else.

"Hell, no, I won't think about kissing you."

His rejection stung. She thought he acted as
though she'd just asked him to think about kissing
a goat. She was immediately embarrassed by her
boldness. Her hands fell to her sides. She had
made a complete fool of herself, but she was going
to have to wait until later to die of mortification.
Now the only important issue was trying to maintain a little dignity.

It took work on her part. And, Lord, it was a terrible strain. She wanted to pick up her skirts and run like lightning back to the house, but she wasn't about to act like a child. She stood her ground and forced herself to look up at him again, just the way a fully grown-up woman would.

"I couldn't help but notice how appalled you sounded. Was the idea atrocious to you?"

"I wasn't appalled. Men don't become appalled."

He sounded angry now. She didn't ask him if he was, though, because she supposed he would only tell her men didn't ever get angry either.

"Good night, Harrison. Sleep well."

She wasn't jesting with him. The crazy woman didn't have a clue what she had just done to him. Sleep was out of the question.

He leaned against the doorframe and watched her walk back to the house. She acted as if she didn't have a care in the world. She had just turned his mind into mush and his stomach into knots, and, damn it all, he wouldn't have been surprised if she'd started in humming.

He wondered how blasé she would be if he told her what he really wanted to do to her, and what he wanted her to do to him with her sweet, provocative mouth.

He could stop himself from wanting to take her to his bed. He reminded himself he was a man, not an animal, and he could certainly control his primitive urges. He had almost convinced himself too, but then he happened to notice the gentle sway of her hips when she walked, and his imagination immediately filled his mind with all sorts of carnal images.

Sleep well? Not bloody likely.

August 4, 1862

Dear Mama Rose,

We had a terrible scare last week. Mary Rose got real sick. We should have known she wasn't feeling good earlier in the day, but none of us even considered that sickness could be the culprit for her unusual foul mood. She always acts real cheerful, but Tuesday last, she started out behaving like a hellion. She got worse by afternoon. Douglas had washed her favorite blanket, the one she likes to hold up against her nose while she sucks on her thumb, and when she spotted it drying on the bushes, she threw a tantrum none of us will ever forget. Our ears are still ringing from her piercing screams. She missed her nap altogether and wore herself out crying. She wouldn't even let Adam comfort her, and she wouldn't eat a bite of her supper. Since she usually has a good appetite, we finally realized something was wrong. By midnight, she was burning up with fever.

We all took turns sitting with her and sponging her off, and when we weren't holding her hand or rocking her in the chair, we were running into each other while we paced.

The fever lasted three days and nights. She looked so little and helpless in her bed. She needed a doctor, but there weren't any to be had, not even in Hammond.

I don't believe I've ever been so afraid in all my life. Cole was frightened too, but he hid it behind his anger. He went on and on about how wrong we had been to bring a baby into the wilderness. He was wrung out with his guilt, and so were we. We knew he was right, but what were we supposed to do back then? Leave the baby in the garbage so the rats could get to her?

Loving someone this little and fragile scares all of us. She depends on us for every little thing. We always have to remember to cut her meat into tiny squares so she won't choke, and making sure she doesn't step on a snake takes everyone's constant attention. Some days I get so scared inside worrying about her, I can barely get to sleep.

I prayed all the while she was sick. I even tried to bargain my life for hers. I guess God wanted us all to stay around a little longer though, because on Saturday morning, the fever broke and Mary Rose came back to us.

Douglas and Adam and I were so relieved, tears came into our eyes. I'm not ashamed to admit it because no one saw us. Cole hid his tears too. He ran outside and didn't come back home for almost an hour. We all knew what he'd been doing. His eyes were as red as ours were and just as swollen.

Keep praying for us, Mama Rose. We can use all the help we can get. We're sure praying for you. Now that the fighting is getting so close to you, we're more afraid for you than ever. The papers we get are full of old news, but Adam's trying to keep us up with all the battles being fought. The way it looks now, the South might win this war no one will officially call a war yet. Stay safe, please. We need you.

Your son,
Travis

P.S. I almost forgot the good news. Just two weeks ago, the Morrisons arrived. They plan on building a general store down the road from Blue Belle's shack. Everyone is mighty pleased about that, of course. It's going to be a luxury to be able to order our supplies so close by. The mail will eventually be delivered to the store as well, though still only just once a week.

The Morrisons have a daughter named Catherine. She's about a year and a half older than our Mary Rose. Our sister needs a friend to play with, at least Adam says she does, and since the Morrisons seem to be decent folks, Cole doesn't have any objections about getting the little girls together.

5

$\mathcal{H}$arrison was up at the crack of dawn. He hadn't slept well at all. He had awakened during the night when Cole crept into the bunkhouse and searched through his things, and after he had left, Harrison couldn't go back to sleep. He'd thought about asking Cole what it was he was looking for, but after mulling the idea over, he decided to continue to pretend to be asleep.

He hadn't been worried Cole would find anything significant. Harrison wasn't carrying any important papers or files with him. All the information he had gathered, along with the report he'd received from the attorney in St. Louis, had already been posted back to London. He was still damned irritated, and depending upon his mood later in the day, he might or might not decide to make an issue out of the intrusion.

His mood didn't improve. After he washed and dressed, he went to the barn to take care of MacHugh. He then spent at least twenty wasted minutes trying to coax the stubborn animal into leaving his stall.

He wanted to take the horse back to the corral. MacHugh wanted to stay where he was. He knocked the bridle out of Harrison's hands, and when Harrison had picked it up and started toward the stallion again, MacHugh tried to trample him. The ungrateful beast was making enough noise to wake the household. Harrison finally ran out of patience. He cursed the animal for several minutes, and in several languages, and although it didn't make MacHugh settle down and behave, Harrison still felt a hell of a lot better for having vented his frustration.

He finally threw his hands up in defeat. If MacHugh wanted to rot in the stall, that was fine with him. He left the gate open, turned to leave, and came to a quick stop. Cole and Douglas were standing just inside the entrance to the barn, and from the ugly grins on their faces, Harrison knew they had witnessed MacHugh's tantrum.

"There's food up at the house," Douglas informed him. "When you've finished eating, Cole's going to put you to work."

"Doing what?" Harrison asked.

"I was going to let you help me break in a couple of mustangs, but from the way I just saw you handle your horse, I've changed my mind. Why don't you stay in the house and play the piano?"

Harrison's temper ignited. He remembered Cole's reaction when Mary Rose blurted out that Adam had also learned how to play the piano, and Harrison decided to give the arrogant brother a little well-deserved prodding.

"Do I play before or after Adam has a turn?"

Cole came rushing toward him. He stopped just inches away. The brother didn't look angry, however. He looked worried. Harrison was confused by the reaction.

"Listen, MacDonald, the only reason Adam learned how to play was so that Mary Rose would.

He had to act like he was enjoying learning. You got that straight? He didn't want to; he had to."

Douglas also felt it necessary to defend the eldest brother's motives. "We don't want you getting the idea Adam isn't manly. He can hold his own in any fight. Can't he, Cole?"

"Damned right he can. What do you think about that, MacDonald?"

Harrison didn't even try to be diplomatic with his answer. "I think the two of you are crazy." He figured they had to realize they were out of their minds because they held such stupid prejudices. Any kind of prejudice was just plain ignorant, and in Harrison's estimation, it was also completely unreasonable and illogical. Therefore, it was crazy.

Douglas turned bright red in response to Harrison's opinion. Cole kept his reaction hidden. Harrison gave up on the two. He tried to walk past them and go outside to get some fresh air. He was thoroughly disgusted.

Cole blocked his path. Douglas nudged him out of the way. "Don't hit him yet," he told his brother. "I want to ask him something."

"Why do you think we're crazy?" He sounded bewildered.

"You both believe that only women should be allowed to play the piano, isn't that right?"

Neither brother answered. Harrison shook his head. "Your attitude is both ludicrous and completely illogical. Adam is an accomplished man," he continued. "It's to his credit that he is so well-educated."

He turned his full attention to Cole. "You, on

the other hand . . ."

Douglas interrupted him before he could finish. "I don't want any roughhousing in my barns," he announced. "The horses get riled up. Cole, I don't see why Harrison can't help with the mustangs."

"I'm certain I'm capable enough," Harrison interjected. "It can't be all that difficult, and it sure as hell can't require much intelligence."

"Why do you say that?" Douglas asked.

Harrison smiled. "Cole does it, doesn't he?"

It took a second or two for the insult to register. Harrison patiently waited. He expected Cole to either go for his gun or use his fist. He was prepared for either reaction.

Cole's eyes widened. He took a step back, shook his head, and then burst into laughter.

Harrison was severely disappointed. He wanted to fight.

"You're an easy man to like, Harrison," Cole told him. "Honest to God, you are."

"Next time you go through my things, I'll shoot you."

Cole looked surprised. "You heard me last night?"

"Damned right I did."

"You're getting sloppy, Cole."

"I guess I am. I didn't think I made a sound."

"Exactly what were you looking for?" Harrison asked.

"Nothing really," Cole replied. "I was just curious."

Douglas rushed to explain. "You should understand his curiosity," he said. "It was difficult for us to believe you couldn't fend for yourself, as big as you are. Of course, once you mentioned you played the piano, I understood how it was."

"Exactly how was it?"

"You know . . . with your father sick and all . . . Cole, you shouldn't have gone through his things. It wasn't hospitable."

"You told me to," Cole reminded his brother.

Douglas couldn't remember making such a suggestion. The two brothers got into a rather heated argument. One thing led to another, and before long they were arguing about something that had happened years ago. If Harrison had been standing close to a wall, he was certain he would have started slamming his head into it by now. The Clayborne men were making him crazy.

He decided to take control of the conversation. "I can fend for myself," he snapped, forcing the two of them to leave their childhood grudges behind. "I do want to learn about ranching, but you two don't have to waste your time teaching me how to fight or shoot. If you'll step outside, I'll be happy to prove it."

Cole laughed. "How are you going to prove it? Shoot us?"

Harrison shook his head. "The idea does have merit," he admitted. "However, I've decided I'll just beat the hell out of the two of you."

Douglas gave him a pitying look. "Not knowing how to defend yourself isn't anything to be ashamed of, Harrison. We'll teach you what you need to know. I'm happy to see you've got a temper though. You'll have to be a little hotheaded if you want to get along with people."

"That's ridiculous."

"Maybe," Cole agreed. "But it's also the way it is around here. You want some respect or don't you?"

Harrison gave up trying to reason with the mule-headed men. He knew he was responsible for planting the misconception in their heads that he was inept. It had seemed like a good idea at the time. Mary Rose took weaklings in, and so he pretended to be just that.

It suddenly dawned on him that he was being as illogical as the brothers. He was getting exactly what he wanted. He should have been pleased.

He wasn't though. And all because he didn't want Mary Rose to think he was weak.

What in thunder was the matter with him? Harrison left the brothers and went to the house. He forced himself to concentrate on the real reason he had traveled all the way to Montana. Lady Victoria. He didn't have any doubts left. Mary Rose had to be Lord Elliott's long-lost daughter.

He wished he could just pick her up, toss her over MacHugh's able back, and drag her back to England where she belonged. There were, however, several giant obstacles barring his path. First, he had to find the mastermind behind the kidnapping. Until the culprit or culprits were found, the Elliott family wasn't safe.

The other obstacles standing in the way of re-uniting the grieving father with his daughter were the Clayborne brothers.

Damn it all, he wished he didn't like them. Even Cole was beginning to make him smile with his ridiculous notions about life. All the brothers' obvious love for their little sister was something he had to admire. And respect. And so was their loyalty to one another.

None of them was going to let her go without putting up a fight. And just what the hell was he going to do about that?

Harrison didn't believe Mary Rose would prove to be too much of a problem. She wouldn't fight the inevitable; at least, he didn't think she would. Granted, she wanted to stay in her valley for the rest of her life, but he knew her feelings would change when she found out she had a father waiting for her back in England. She was simply too kindhearted not to go and at least meet the man. Getting her to stay in London would be her father's problem. Harrison's work would be done.

He quit mulling the matter over in his mind, picked up his step, and was just about to turn the corner so he could go directly into the kitchen from the back door, when he spotted Mary Rose hurrying in the opposite direction. She was headed toward the smaller barn, and from the indirect path she was taking, it didn't take him long to realize she didn't want to be noticed by anyone. She carried a brown wicker basket with a rounded handle looped over her arm.

"Good morning, Harrison," Travis said from behind.

Harrison turned around. "Morning," he replied. "Where's your sister going? She seems to be in quite a hurry."

Travis smiled. "She's sneaking off. I know where she's headed though. I'm going to give her a couple of minutes, then follow her. Adam's going to be angry when he finds out."

"Finds out what?"

"Mary Rose is paying a call on Crazy Cornelia."

"Is she the woman who survived the Indian attack?"

"You already heard about her?"

"Your sister mentioned her last night."

"Corrie's the one, all right. Word has it she's crazy as a loon. Guess if you got scalped, you would be too. Even the Indians stay away from her now. They're afraid of her. So are most of the people in Blue Belle. They're talking about burning her out."

"Burning her out of what?"

"Her cabin," Travis explained. "A trapper thought the place was deserted. She almost blew his head off with her shotgun when he tried to get near the door. Corrie's been holed up there since the attack, and that was over fifteen years ago. Anyway, now that Mary Rose knows about her, she's determined to pay a visit. She thinks the woman could use a friend. Adam told her she couldn't go. He said it was too dangerous. No telling what the woman will do. I knew Mary Rose wouldn't listen though. She never does. There she goes now. Honest to God, Adam's going to kill her."

Travis took off at a trot. "Tell my brothers where I'm going, all right?" he called over his shoulder.

The brother was armed for trouble. Harrison was pleased to know that all the Clayborne men watched out for their little sister.

159

He heard Travis mutter something about being damned tired of being inconvenienced, and found himself smiling in reaction.

It was the last moment of joy he experienced for a long, long while.

Breaking in mustangs wasn't difficult. It was impossible. Harrison didn't get the knack of it for a full week, and during the days in between, he suffered one indignity after another. He was black and blue everywhere His humiliation was just as painful for him. He spent more time on his backside and shoulders in the dirt than on his feet and, in general, provided a vast amount of entertainment for the Clayborne family.

Cole's timing was superb. No matter what task he was involved in, he always happened to be near the corral whenever Harrison went flying off the saddle. The brother always reacted the same way. First he would give an exaggerated wince for Harrison's benefit, then shake his head and say, "That's going to hurt." Laughter inevitably followed.

Harrison wanted to kill Cole, of course. Going after him would have required strength, however, and he simply didn't have any to spare.

He couldn't make up his mind which time of day was worse. In the evenings, his entire body throbbed in agony, and in the mornings he felt as if rigor mortis had set in. He walked around like an old, bowlegged man. Honest to God, he even groaned like one.

Mary Rose came to the bunkhouse late one evening, but fortunately he still had his pants on. He'd gotten his torn shirt off, then collapsed onto the bed, facedown. He didn't even lift his head up when she walked inside.

"Oh, Harrison, your back is a mess," she whispered. She sat down on the side of the bed and gently patted him. "Adam sent some liniment to soothe your muscles. Would you like me to put some on your shoulders?"

He needed it on his backside, but he knew it wouldn't be proper for him to ask.

"Thank you."

"You're all tuckered out, aren't you?" she asked.

He didn't answer her. Mary Rose opened the bottle and poured some of the cold liquid on his back. Then she started to massage the aches away. She wrinkled her nose in reaction to the scent and hoped Harrison wouldn't notice.

"What in God's name is that stench?"

He looked toward the open doorway, thinking the odor must have been coming from outside.

"It's the liniment," she explained.

"God, it's foul."

"The horses seem to like it."

He lifted his head. "You use this stuff on your horses?"

She pushed his head back down on the pillow. "It's all right to use on people too. The smell will fade in a minute. Try to relax. Let me work the liniment into your muscles. You're going to feel better in no time at all."

He didn't believe her. His backside was still going to ache. "Leave the bottle," he suggested. "If the liniment works, I'll put some on my . . . leg."

161

"All right," she promised. "Close your eyes and try to rest."

Five minutes later, he thought he'd died. Her hands were magical against his skin. His muscles were soothed, but he wasn't the least bit aroused by her closeness or her touch, and in his mind, that could only mean he was already dead.

He groaned with pleasure so she wouldn't stop soothing him.

She thought he had fallen asleep. His face was turned toward the doorway. He looked peaceful to her, and ruggedly handsome. His hair had fallen down to cover his forehead. There was a day's growth of a beard, a shadow really, and she was suddenly filled with curiosity to know what it felt like. She felt safe enough because he was sound asleep and wouldn't know how brazen she was being. She touched his forehead first, then grew a little bolder. She noticed a bruise on the side of his temple and slowly circled it with the tips of her fingers. His skin was smooth and warm to her touch.

She grew bolder and traced the profile of his perfectly formed nose and cheekbone. She trailed her fingers down the side of his face to his neck. The bristles from his growth tickled her. She wanted to touch his mouth, gave into her urge almost immediately, and slowly explored it just as fleetingly with her fingertips.

There wasn't anything about the man she didn't like, she realized. He really was as beautiful to her on the outside as he was on the inside, where it mattered most. In his heart.

She leaned closer and kissed his forehead. She

couldn't believe how audacious she was being. She was usually very reserved, sometimes even shy around men, but tonight . . . with Harrison.

She let out a little sigh and kissed the side of his cheek. Then she straightened up and began to massage his shoulders once again. She didn't want to stop touching him. What was the matter with her? She could feel herself physically reacting to Harrison, but because of her inexperience, she didn't have the faintest idea what she should do about it.

Stop, she supposed. She didn't stop though, because she liked the way his skin felt under her fingertips. He was warm and muscular. Her stomach tingled and quivered like she was filled with butterflies.

And when she thought about kissing him again . . .

"What are you doing in here with a half-naked man? Don't you have any sense at all, Mary Rose?"

Cole made the criticism from the doorway and walked over to the side of the bed.

"Keep your voice down," she whispered. "He's asleep. I left the door open so it would be proper for me to be in here. Besides, he may be half naked, but he's also harmless. I won't take advantage of him. I promise."

She didn't think it was a good idea to mention she'd already taken advantage. Cole wouldn't understand her curiosity. How could he when she couldn't?

"Don't talk like that. It isn't ladylike. I never thought you'd take advantage of him. You

163

wouldn't know how."

"I should though, shouldn't I? Don't you think it's about time you explained a few facts to me?"

"Later, Mary Rose. We'll talk about all that later."

"You always say that," she whispered. "Never mind. I've figured it all out on my own."

Cole wanted to change the topic to a less delicate one. He squatted down next to Harrison so he could get a closer look at his face, then stood up again.

"I can't tell if he's breathing. Is he?"

"Of course he is."

"He looks dead."

"He isn't," she assured her brother. "At least not yet. When are you and Douglas going to let up on him?"

"We're teaching him what he needs to know if he's going to take up ranching."

"You're killing him."

He smiled over how incensed she'd sounded. "No, we aren't. Harrison's tougher than he looks."

She let out an inelegant snort. "No, he's softer than he looks," she corrected. "Has he gotten any better at breaking in the horses yet?"

Cole sighed. "Douglas keeps telling me he has. I can't see any improvement though. Harrison's a touch loco, Mary Rose."

"Why do you think that?"

"He talks to the mustangs. Douglas says he lays it all out for them, then gets up in the saddle and expects them to understand and cooperate.

He never raises his voice either, and the only time he curses is after he's finished for the day. You better come on back to the house. It's late."

Cole started to leave, then changed his mind. "By the way, Catherine Morrison's father told Douglas that Catherine wants him to ask Harrison if he would like to court her."

Mary Rose was astonished. And furious. She hid her reaction from her brother and applied herself to the task of soothing Harrison's muscles.

"That's ridiculous," she said. "The Morrisons don't even know Harrison."

"They're going to invite him for Sunday supper," Cole told her.

"He can't go."

"Why can't he?"

"He's going to be busy."

"Travis sure isn't going to like hearing about Harrison getting an invitation. Your brother's kind of partial to Catherine."

"I can't imagine why. I don't like her at all."

"Why not?"

"She's uppity and a flirt," Mary Rose said. "She's brazen too."

"I never noticed."

"You're a man. Of course you never noticed. Men never notice such things. Besides, she never flirts with you. She's afraid of you."

Cole grinned. "It makes you kind of mad, doesn't it?"

"What makes me mad?"

"Some other woman taking an interest in Harrison."

"I am not angry."

If Harrison hadn't been pretending to be asleep, he would have disagreed. The gentle massage she'd been giving him had turned into a pounding. He didn't know how much longer he was going to be able to put up with the beating.

"Someone has to look out for Harrison. He's very naive, you know."

"You don't say."

"He's overly trusting too."

"Is that right?"

"I'm serious, Cole, so you can quit smiling like that. Harrison is a kind, gentle man. Surely you've noticed."

"I can't say I have," Cole replied.

"All of us should be watching out for him. He's our responsibility."

"Exactly what is it you think Catherine's going to do? Bite him?"

"I wouldn't put it past her," Mary Rose said. She knew she was being unreasonable. She didn't care. "I realize I'm being uncharitable, but I do believe Catherine can turn into a viper. I think you should tell the Morrisons Harrison isn't interested."

Cole rolled his eyes heavenward. "Harrison and I are going to town tomorrow to pick up a couple of harnesses. He can tell Morrisons yes or no about Sunday supper when he's invited. The decision is his to make, Mary Rose."

"I'm going to town with you."

Harrison had taken all the pounding he was going to. He opened his eyes just as Cole turned around and walked out the door.

"You can stop beating on me now," he said.

166

She jumped a foot when he spoke to her. "You're awake."

He didn't think it was necessary to agree. "Do your shoulders feel better?"

The sting in his muscles was actually worse because of her overly enthusiastic pounding. "Yes, thank you."

She recapped the bottle, put it on the floor next to her, and stood up.

"When did you wake up?" she asked, trying to sound only mildly curious. She was in a panic, wondering how much of the conversation he'd overheard. Dear Lord, what if he hadn't been asleep at all? What if he'd only been resting? Did he know she'd kissed him?

"Just now," he lied. "Why?"

She was blushing. Harrison wanted to laugh but he didn't because he knew she'd become even more embarrassed. He rolled off the bed and stood up. His bare feet were cold against the wooden floor. He was standing entirely too close to her, knew he should move, but couldn't seem to make himself.

"I wondered if you heard Cole," she stammered out. "He came inside to check on you."

"Thank you for worrying about me."

She looked startled again. "Why do you think I'm worrying about you?"

"The liniment," he replied.

She relaxed. She turned toward him. "Harrison?"

"Yes?"

"I was telling Cole I'm going to make a very special supper Sunday. I'm cooking everything

167

myself. You'll be sure and be here, won't you? I'm going to an awful lot of trouble. I might even invite Dooley, Henry, Billie, and Ghost."

He was trying hard not to laugh. "That sounds nice."

She smiled. "Would you like to meet my friend one day? I think she'll like you."

"Crazy Corrie?" He was immediately intrigued.

"Please don't call her crazy," Mary Rose asked. "She isn't, you know. She's shy, and cautious. Wouldn't you be if you'd been attacked by Indians?"

"Yes," he agreed. "Did she talk to you?"

"No, but she's getting ready to," she answered. "I could tell."

"If she didn't talk to you, how could you tell she was going to? Did she smile at you or . . ."

"Oh, I didn't see her. She wouldn't let me."

"Then how could you possibly know she's not crazy?"

"She didn't shoot me."

He closed his eyes and counted to ten before he started questioning her again.

"Tell me exactly what happened. Did you knock on the door? Did you go inside?"

"I never got near the door. I didn't even get as far as the porch. She really is very shy, Harrison."

"How close to the cabin did you get?"

"I made it as far as the clearing in front," she answered. "She shot the ground in front of my feet. She deliberately missed me. She was letting me know she didn't want me to come any closer."

"Then what did you do?"

168

"I told her who I was and that I had only just found out about her. I also mentioned how difficult it had been finding the cabin. It's hidden, you know. Anyway, then I visited with her. I told her about my family. I had to shout every word, of course, so she could hear me, and when I knew my voice was going to give out, I told her about the basket I had for her. There were jars of jellies and baked bread, and cookies too. I asked her if I could please leave it for her. I made certain she didn't misunderstand my motives. I wasn't offering charity, just friendship. Every woman has a little bit of pride. I didn't want to offend her. I believe she understood. She let me walk a few feet closer. I didn't try for more. I left the basket and told her I'd come back tomorrow with another basket full of welcoming gifts. I also asked her to please leave the empty basket in the clearing so I could take it back home."

"Do you plan to go there every day?"

"No, I couldn't do that. There wouldn't be enough time for anything else, and I have so much to do around here. Once Corrie starts talking to me, and we've gotten to know one another, then I'll probably go just once a week for a nice long visit. I believe we'll become good friends. You haven't told me yes or no yet."

"About having dinner on Sunday?"

She nodded. "If you're going to go to the trouble to cook a special meal of course I'll be here." He paused. "Adam was angry you left without telling anyone where you were going, wasn't he?"

"He wasn't angry. He was disappointed." She

169

let out a sigh. "That's far worse. If he yelled at me, I wouldn't have felt as guilty."

"Are you going to tell him about your plans for tomorrow?"

"We already discussed it. I have his approval. Understand, Harrison. He doesn't want me to ask his permission to do anything. He realizes I'm capable of making my own decisions. He just wants me to be cautious. I promised never to go there alone. You're going to catch a cold," she added. "You should put a shirt on. Good night."

She turned to leave. He wanted her to stay a little longer. He grabbed hold of her arm and said, "Wait."

She turned back to him. "Yes?"

"I've never met anyone like you."

God, he couldn't believe he'd said that. He felt like a simpleton. "You're very kind," he said.

Mary Rose remembered all the terrible things she'd said to Cole about Catherine Morrison just a few minutes before and couldn't in good conscience go along with Harrison's misconception.

"No, I'm not kind," she admitted. "I try to be, but sometimes I turn into a shrew. I can even be cruel."

Harrison didn't let go of her arm. He started to pull her closer to him. He knew he had lost his mind, because for the first time in his life he couldn't and wouldn't let good sense prevail. He had already decided not to get personally involved with Mary Rose.

He was still going to kiss her.

"What are you doing?"

"Bringing you close to me."

"Why?"

"I want to kiss you."

She was astonished. "Are you serious?"

"Yes."

He'd drawled out the word, made it sound incredibly seductive. She almost sighed out loud, but stopped herself in time.

"Do you want me to kiss you?"

"That isn't the issue." She paused. "I don't understand," she admitted then. "You have barely spoken to me all week, or even looked my way . . . and now you want to kiss me? Harrison, I don't believe you're being very logical."

She sounded stunned by her own conclusion. He laughed. "I'm not being logical."

"Why do you think you want to kiss me?"

She'd turned the tables on him. Now she was being the analytical one.

"I believe in fair play."

She still didn't understand. He pulled her up tight against his chest, lowered his head, and kissed her forehead. Then he took hold of her hands and put them around his neck.

She didn't resist. She still looked thoroughly puzzled, but not at all uneasy. He hadn't put his arms around her yet, and wouldn't if she gave him any indication of fear or refusal.

"You kissed me," he explained. "Several times I recall. Now it's my turn, and that, Mary Rose, is what I call fair play."

"Oh, God, you weren't sleeping, were you?"

She sounded mortified. She turned her gaze to his chest. Harrison nudged her chin back up with

171

his hand. He kissed the side of her cheek, just the way she'd kissed him, then kissed her on the bridge of her nose.

She got over her embarrassment almost immediately. "You must have enjoyed it," she whispered.

"No, I didn't," he told her.

"You didn't? Why not?"

"You were driving me crazy. You kiss like a girl."

Her fingers began to toy with his hair. She was surprised by how silky it felt. She let out a little sigh and moved closer to him. She loved the feel of his skin against her. The heat, and strength, radiating from his body warmed her.

"Show me how you would like to be kissed, Harrison."

He finally put his arms around her. Then he told her to open her mouth.

She tried to ask him why, but then his mouth settled on top of hers and she forgot all about asking him anything. A shiver passed down her spine and she instinctively tightened her hold on him.

It was the most amazingly wondrous kiss she'd ever experienced. His mouth was almost hot against hers, demanding and yet gentle, and then his tongue moved inside her mouth to rub against hers. The passionate way he kissed her made her weak with pleasure. She clung to him, squeezing herself tight against his chest. She felt embraced everywhere. Her softness was surrounded by his arms and his thighs. She felt him shudder, knew then he was just as affected by the kiss as she

172

was, and suddenly realized she was every bit as powerful as he and just as much in control of what would or wouldn't happen.

His mouth slanted over hers hungrily, with blatant ownership, but all of her inhibitions were gone now, and she kissed him just as eagerly.

He ended the kiss much before she wanted him to, but she refused to move away from him even when his hands dropped down to his sides. She rested the side of her face against his chest. She heard the thundering of his heartbeat. Or was it hers hammering inside her head?

He was breathing as raggedly as she was. "I didn't want to stop."

Her whispered confession sounded bewildered. Harrison took a deep breath, trying to regain some semblance of control. He was still reeling with his own bewilderment and astonishment, for in truth, he'd never felt such instantaneous hot passion with any other woman.

"Did you want to stop?" she asked.

She sounded breathless. He was pleased to know she'd been just as affected as he was.

"No, I didn't," he admitted. "And that's exactly why I did. Let go of me, Mary Rose. It's time for you to go home."

She didn't want to leave, but she guessed she would have to. It wouldn't have been polite or ladylike to try to nag him into kissing her senseless again. She slowly turned around and walked to the doorway.

She looked back at him when she reached the step. She wanted to tell him good night. The words got trapped in her throat, however, and she simply stood there staring at him. He looked so amazingly perfect. He stood in the glow of the oil lamp, and in the light, his skin took on a golden tone. He leaned against the bedpost, and when he shifted his position, she could see the muscles ripple under his skin. Douglas had told her Harrison had the strength of three men, yet she knew he would never use his physical power against her.

"I feel safe when I'm with you."

She was surprised she'd said the words out loud. Harrison smiled. "You should feel safe with me. I would never hurt you, Mary Rose."

"Did I kiss like a girl again?"

He shook his head. "No, you kissed like a woman. What happened tonight can't happen again. I never should have started something I can't finish."

He threaded his fingers through his hair, his frustration apparent with the action. "We can't become involved."

"We're already involved."

"No, we aren't," he said, his tone hard, unbending.

She didn't understand what had come over him. She nodded, then turned and walked away. She tried to reason it through while she got ready for bed. After an hour of trying to sort it all out, she finally gave up. She knew Harrison was attracted to her, for the way he'd kissed her told her so. She wasn't the patient sort, but she decided she would have to try to be patient until she figured out what his problem was. There had to be a good reason why he didn't want to pursue a relationship with her. The man had a reason for everything he did. She guessed she would have to wait until he told her what it was.

And then she would find a way around whatever obstacle was holding him back.

She put on her slippers and her robe and went downstairs to the library. Adam was inside, re-reading one of his favorite books.

Her brother was sitting in a worn, brown leather easy chair. A fire crackled in the hearth, warming the room.

"Adam, may I interrupt you?"

Her brother looked up and smiled. "Of course," he agreed. He closed the book he'd been reading and put it on the table next to his chair.

There was another identical brown leather chair flanking the other side of the fireplace, but she walked past it and sat down on the footrest next to Adam's feet.

"I wanted to talk to you about Harrison."

"Is something wrong?"

"No," she assured him. "Nothing is wrong. I like him . . . very much. I think he likes me too. He seems to, anyway."

"Then what's the problem?"

She looked down at her lap. "I asked him to kiss me last week. He finally got around to agreeing tonight."

She looked up at her brother to see how he was taking her confession. Adam didn't show any reaction. He took his spectacles off, carefully folded them, and put them on top of the book.

"He kissed you."

"Yes," she replied.

"And then what happened?"

"He told me he wasn't ever going to kiss me again."

"I see." A slow smile eased his expression. "Did he tell you why?"

"Yes, he did," she answered. "But his explanation didn't make any sense at all. I know he enjoyed kissing me. He looked like he did, and he felt like he did, but he only kissed me once, and now that I've had time to think about it, maybe he didn't like it as much as I did."

"You said you liked kissing him. I think we need to talk about that."

"I did like kissing him, very much. I like him, Adam. He told me we couldn't become involved, but he wouldn't give me any reason why we couldn't. Maybe he's trying to protect me from heartache," she continued. "Perhaps he knows he's going back to Scotland, and he doesn't want to begin a relationship only to leave. He might also be like Cole."

"How exactly is your brother?"

"Cole doesn't want to be trapped by any woman. He's always telling me he'll never get married. Do you think Harrison feels the same way?"

"I don't know him well enough to answer your question, but I do know Cole. He's all talk, sister. He just needs time to meet the right woman. Then his attitude will change."

"Why do men think of marriage as a trap? Women aren't taking away their freedom, for heaven's sake."

"In some ways they are," Adam replied. "Once

married, always married. If a man has made the wrong choice, he's trapped, isn't he?"

"I suppose, but the woman is also trapped."

Adam's mind began to wander. He was thinking about Harrison now. He realized he needed to find out more about their guest. If Mary Rose was becoming involved, it was Adam's duty to make certain Harrison didn't hurt her.

"Adam?"

"Yes?"

"What were you thinking about just now?"

"Harrison," he answered. "I realized we don't know all that much about him. I believe you should give yourself some time to get to know him better before you ask him to kiss you again."

She agreed with a nod. "I'll try."

"Cole told me I needed to have a talk with you about men and women and . . . ."

"Intimacy." She supplied the last word before he could.

"Yes, intimacy."

"We already had our talk years ago."

"I remember, and I thought you remembered too, but your brother said you asked him to tell you all about the facts of life again. He doesn't think you understood. Didn't you?"

"Yes, you made it all perfectly clear."

"I thought I had. You certainly asked a lot of questions."

"And you patiently answered every one of them. You're the only brother who made any sense. Travis started out giving me all sorts of parallels about trees and bees, and then he jumped into a couple of parables from the Bible. When he recited the one about the loaves of bread multiplying, I was completely lost. He told me I was like a loaf of bread and that one day I would also multiply. I asked him how. He threw up his hands and sent me to Douglas."

"And what did Douglas tell you?" Adam had heard all of this before, but he enjoyed the retelling just as much.

"He told me to use my head. He was extremely gruff. The topic made him terribly uncomfortable. He wouldn't even look at me. He reminded me that I lived on a ranch, kept adding, 'for God's sake,' and suggested I look around me. Then I'd be able to figure it all out. I told him I had been looking around for all of my eleven years and I still hadn't figured anything out. In desperation, he pointed to the horses and told me that when I was all grown up, I'd be just like a filly and a man would come to me just like a stallion."

Adam laughed until tears came into his eyes. "Now tell me again how you reacted to his comparison."

"I was highly insulted, of course, and disgusted. That's when he sent me to you."

He dabbed at the corners of his eyes with the backs of his hands and finally calmed down. "If you remembered our talk, why did you ask Cole to explain?"

"I couldn't stop myself," she admitted. "His reaction is so amusing. He blushes, Adam, really blushes. He gets all flustered too, and that's very unusual for him. I'll probably ask him again and again, until he finally catches on."

178

Adam laughed again. "Go right ahead. I'm dying to know what comparison he'll eventually come up with. It's bound to be a dandy."

He let out a sigh, then turned to a more serious issue. "And now I think we had better talk about how you felt when you were kissing Harrison."

And so they did. Mary Rose didn't feel the least bit uncomfortable or embarrassed because she was with Adam. He always put her at ease. There wasn't any subject she couldn't discuss with him. She could say whatever was on her mind and not worry he would be appalled or disappointed. The bond between brother and sister was as strong as iron, and her trust in his judgment was absolute.

He was concerned she might have been frightened by her physical reaction to Harrison. Passion was sometimes misinterpreted, and often, what one didn't understand, one feared. He didn't want his little sister to be afraid of anything or anyone. She should embrace life, not hide from it, the way he'd had to all these many years.

"A man can want to bed a woman without loving her. Do you understand?"

"Yes, I understand. A woman can behave in the same manner, can't she?"

"Yes, she can."

"You want me to realize that wanting and loving don't always go hand in hand."

"Yes."

"Don't worry about me. You're worried because I'm innocent, but remember, being innocent doesn't mean I'll be foolish."

"Exactly right."

They talked for a few more minutes, until she became too sleepy to stay up any longer. She kissed her brother good night.

"I wish Mama were here. I miss her."

"Someday soon she'll be joining us," Adam promised. "Her nightmare can't continue much longer. Mistress Livonia may have a change of heart and let her leave. I doubt Mama would want to go anywhere until after Livonia dies. She's totally dependent on Mama now."

"I cannot imagine what it would be like to be blind. I don't believe I would turn mean, though, the way Livonia did."

"She needs your mama more than you do, Mary Rose . . . for now, anyway."

"Are her sons so very cruel that they would really turn their backs on their mother?"

"You know the answer to that," he said. "They'll do anything to get her money. Rose and Livonia have their own cottage behind the property the sons already sold off. They're getting along all right now. As long as Livonia's sons leave them alone, no harm will come to either one of them."

"You send them money regularly, don't you?"

"We do what we can. Go on up to bed now. I want to finish this chapter on the Constitution. I plan to nag Harrison into a debate tomorrow night, and I want to be prepared."

"I'm going to write Mama another letter tonight before I go to sleep. I need to tell her about Harrison. She'll want to know every detail."

"I thought you already told her about him."

"Yes, but that was before he kissed me. I need

180

to tell Mama about that. Good night. Love you."

"Love you too, sister."

Mary Rose went to bed a half hour later. She fell asleep thinking how perfect her life was. She lived in a beautiful valley with wonderful brothers, and now she had a dashing suitor who would eventually pursue her. She would lead him a merry chase first, of course. Then she'd let him catch her.

Her plans were grand, and, oh, how perfect her life was. She was falling in love.

May 17, 1863

Dear Mama Rose,

We've heard so many conflicting reports about the war, we don't know what to think. Both the North and the South are taking credit for every victory. By the time we get any news, it's all so convoluted, it doesn't make sense. All we know for certain is that thousands of young men are dying. We're all trying hard to do as you say and not worry about you, but it's difficult. You're in our thoughts, in our prayers, and in our hearts.

Your letter was a blessed relief. We were so thankful to hear from you after nearly a month of waiting, we celebrated with a special dinner. Cole made squirrel stew, Douglas made biscuits, and I cut up fresh vegetables from our garden. For dessert we had baked apples and a piece of peppermint candy. After we'd eaten our fill, we took turns singing. I thought Cole and I weren't too bad, but Douglas and Travis were plumb awful. No one was as horrible as little Mary Rose. Your namesake doesn't actually sing; she screams. I've been toying with the notion of getting her a piano when she's older. We would have to find a teacher, of course, to give her the necessary training. Now I'm not so certain it's such a good idea. If she can't carry a tune, maybe we would be just wasting our time. Still, it's important for her to have a well-rounded education, and an appreciation of music is important. Her brothers and I talk about the advantages we want her to have. Travis insists that she learn how to speak French. He says all well-educated men and women know at least one other language. Right now we're concentrating on English. The baby's grammar is still pretty raw. She's forever getting her verbs mixed. We took your advice and don't overdo correcting her though, and we always try to praise her for every little task she completes. She likes to please us, and when she's happy and smiles at us, well, it seems as though sunshine has just come inside our cabin. She lights up a room, Mama, like a thousand candles burning bright.

Cole showed us a design he'd made of the house he wants to build. We were stunned by the detail. None of us knew he had so much talent. I think he's taking on more than he can chew though, but I didn't squelch his enthusiasm. The design is for a two-story house with five bedrooms, and it's as grand as any of those fancy plantations down South. I did suggest he make the outside as plain as he could so we wouldn't draw attention to the family. People see an expensive home and they start to wonder what's inside. Then they become resentful, at least from my experiences watching people that's the conclusion I've hit upon. If someone has something better, they think they should have it, even though they aren't willing to work hard. Folks in Blue Belle aren't like city folks, however. We all tend to appreciate anything anyone else has. I've got seven books in my collection now, and Travis wants to go to Hammond next week and see what goods he can barter for there. Douglas has started breaking in a couple of wild mustangs he and Cole captured. Douglas has a knack for communicating with animals. He says they don't actually talk to him, but they let him know when something's wrong.

We're all slowly figuring out what we can do to contribute to the family. It's interesting to me how God gave each one of us a special talent. I've got a head for numbers, so I keep the records straight. There's quite a lot of paper work involved in filing for land, and I also started a ledger and write down every bit we spend. Morrison has started offering credit to us. He says we only need to pay him once every other month for the supplies we take, but he charges interest on his kindness, and in my mind, that's a loan pure and simple. If we don't have enough money in the cigar box, then we go without. I don't ever go into town. I've taken your advice and try not to draw too much attention to myself. Everyone has come out here to meet me, and I believe they've gotten used to me. New arrivals are a little surprised when they hear there's a black man living amongst them, and when they meet the rest of the family, I'm sure they're befuddled. Cole says that because everyone else in Blue Belle accepts me as ordinary, the new ones figure it must be all right. Winning the Morrisons' friendship helped, of course. They got into real trouble when their roof caved in. I went into town then to help build a new one. Mrs. Morrison kept Mary Rose for us, and even though our sister insists little Catherine hit her and pulled her hair, we all are sure she had a good time playing with a new friend.

I've strayed from my topic, haven't I? I was telling you how God gave all of us a special talent. Then I started bragging about myself. Now I'll tell you about the contributions my brothers are making. Cole's still practicing with his gun so he can protect us and kill game for supper, and while I think he's got a talent for being quick and accurate, none of us want him to become a gunfighter. I'm happy to report he also has a talent for building. He helps everyone else too. Douglas works with the horses they caught, and Side Camp has already said he'll buy one as soon as my brother gets him saddle trained. Douglas wants to build a barn before starting on the house. He and Cole are still arguing about what is going to come first. Cole will let Douglas win, but he's going to make him suffer before he gives in.

Travis has become the procurer for the household. The boy can talk anyone out of anything. Whenever we need something, we tell him and he finds a way to get it for us.

We don't know what special talent the baby has yet. It sure isn't in the area of art though. I've enclosed a drawing she made for you. It's supposed to be a picture of our little cabin, but I don't think you're going to be able to tell. It looks like a bunch of scribbles to me. She was proud of her work, and so of course we all praised her and told her how fine it was. She doesn't like us to call her baby anymore. She won't answer to the name Mary either. We have to say her full name if we want her to answer us. It seems foolish to call her Mary Rose Clayborne all the time, but it means a lot to her and so we go along.

She asks about a hundred questions a day. I still think she's smarter than the rest of us put together, and from the way she gets us to do things for her, my brothers believe I'm right.

We don't let her misbehave too much. If she won't obey, we make her sit by herself until she's ready to be part of the family again. She doesn't like to be left out, and she looks plumb pitiful. Cole always wants to give in because he has such a soft heart, but he too understands the importance of helping her understand certain behavior won't be tolerated.

I'm not so certain about how miserable she feels sitting all alone though. Just yesterday, she and I were working in the garden together. She wanted me to stop work and take her inside and get her a piece of peppermint candy. When I told her no, she went in the cabin and got it anyway. She knew she was going to get into trouble because she didn't just eat one of the pieces. She ate every last one of them. A few minutes later, she came outside again wearing the evidence of her misdeed (her face was covered with pink coloring), and she was carrying her blanket and the rag doll Travis had made for her. She marched right past me and went all the way across the yard and sat down on a log. Then she started in wailing and acting pitiful. She's got all of us figured out, Mama. I had to turn my face away from her because I couldn't quit smiling.

I'll stop for now. Travis and Douglas have already given me their letters to you, and Cole's just finishing his. We sure appreciate the way you include a sheet for each one of us with our names written on the fold. We all like having a private minute with you, and when Mary Rose is older and can read her own, I'm sure she'll appreciate your thoughtfulness too.

My brothers have been talking about joining up and doing what they can to help the North win the war. I get angry every time one of them mentions it, and I think I finally convinced them that although their hearts are in the right place, they can't leave. We all made a promise to our sister, and we all have to put her first. Travis didn't think the baby needed all four of us, but after I pointed out how each one of us makes an important contribution, he felt better. It's true, Mama. It takes four almost grown-up men to look after Mary Rose. It's a hard life out here. It takes everything a man has inside just to survive.

We pray for those good Northern soldiers every single night.

I don't want to end this letter on a sad note. We were surprised the pretty locket you sent

187

actually got here. The package wasn't even torn. Mary Rose caught us looking at it. We told her you had sent it to her, but that she wasn't supposed to have it until she turned sixteen years old. Well, Mama, she threw quite a tantrum. None of us gave in though. We did come up with a compromise. We promised she could look at it every night before she goes to bed. Now we have another ritual to add at night. We're up to three. She has to have a sip of water, a bedtime story, and now she has to look at the locket.

She sure is a piece of work, and my, how she makes us smile.

I love you,
Adam

6

*G*entle, sweet-natured Harrison turned into a raging maniac right before Mary Rose's eyes. She couldn't believe how terrible the day turned out to be. At supper that night, she told Adam her entire day had been a nightmare.

And it was all Harrison's fault. She was so furious with the man, she still couldn't speak to him.

The morning had started out pleasantly enough. She spent a good hour getting ready to go into town. She wanted to look as pretty as possible for Harrison. She didn't believe she was being vain, and usually what she wore only had to be functional for her to be happy. Today was different, however, because the man of her dreams had kissed her the night before, and she wanted to look beautiful for him. She knew she was probably being silly, but she couldn't seem to care. After trying on three different outfits, she ended up wearing a pale blue riding skirt with a white blouse. She tied her hair back with a blue and white ribbon. She wasn't overly thrilled about her appearance, but it was the best she could do with the looks God had given her.

She soon realized she needn't have gone to all the trouble. Except for a terse good morning, Harrison didn't pay her any attention at all.

Everyone but Adam went into town with her.

Travis wanted to pick up a package, Cole and Harrison were going to collect the new bridles, and Douglas rode along so he could talk to the blacksmith about shoeing a couple of horses. Mary Rose had a shopping list of supplies she thought her new friend, Corrie, could use.

Being ignored by the stubborn guest was fine with her. She was furious with him because he refused to listen to reason. He insisted on wearing his gunbelt and gun and gave Cole the ridiculous argument that he'd loaded up his old, reliable gun and would be just fine if trouble came their way. She couldn't believe how muleheaded he was being. Granted, her own brothers were armed, but they were all skilled and wore the weapons for protection. The ignorant gunfighter named Webster, and some of his misfit associates, were still on the prowl, and until the Claybornes were certain they had all left the territory, the brothers needed to stay on their guard.

Because it was Thursday, no one in town was expecting to see any of them. Mary Rose had diligently prayed that Catherine Morrison had stayed home today and wasn't in the store helping her father. Mary Rose didn't want to have to watch the woman flirt with Harrison because such blatant tactics were bound to make her nauseated. Harrison was so naive. Most men were when it came to the ploys used by certain women. Harrison wouldn't know what Catherine was up to, but Mary Rose would. Women understood each other. Catherine wanted to snare Harrison. Finding a man wasn't difficult in the valley. They outnumbered women by well over a hundred to one. Finding a good man was another matter altogether. They were as scarce as diamonds.

Mary Rose didn't believe she was jealous. She was just looking out for Harrison. He was her guest, after all. Catherine Morrison was just going to have to find someone else to chase.

On the way into town Mary Rose must have asked Cole and Douglas at least five times to look after Harrison. The two brothers soon got tired of promising her they would. They told her to quit nagging them. She would have asked Travis, but he and Harrison were riding their mounts side by side, and she didn't want the man she wanted protected to know she didn't think he could take care of himself. He couldn't, of course, but she didn't want him to know she realized it.

Luck was on her side. Catherine wasn't in the store. Mary Rose saw Harrison talking to Catherine's father, but the conversation lasted only a minute or two, and then Harrison was being introduced to Floyd Penneyville, another new resident, and the topic turned to the annual cattle roundup that had ended just three weeks before. Both Floyd and Harrison were sorry they'd missed all the excitement.

Dooley caught up with her just as she was leaving the store. She was on her way to the stables to collect Douglas. Cole and Travis and Harrison were all talking to Floyd.

"Morning, Miss Mary. My, you look right pretty today."

"Thank you, Dooley."

"Henry chased me down," he said. He remem-

191

bered his manners then and immediately took his hat off. "We'd already sent word to Cole that Webster had some cronies with him. I guess, from seeing the brothers, he's expecting trouble."

"One must always be prepared for any eventuality," Mary Rose told her friend. She was quoting Adam, of course. He was always telling her to be prepared.

Dooley followed her outside and walked by her side down the wooden walkway.

"Anyways, Henry told me you were taking supplies to Crazy Corrie. Was he fibbing me or telling the truth?"

"He was telling the truth," she said. "Corrie isn't crazy. I would appreciate it if you'd tell your friends so. She's my friend, Dooley."

"That's exactly what Henry said you'd say. I got some bad news for you, Miss Mary. Bickley and some of his vigilante friends is going up to the ridge to burn Corrie out. They think she's a danger to folks."

Mary Rose was appalled. "How dare they," she cried out. She grabbed hold of Dooley's arm. "Have they left yet?"

"No, but they're getting ready to," Dooley explained. "Henry and Ghost are keeping them busy bragging. You know how Bickley is. He likes to boast about hisself. He's the devil's own brother, Miss Mary. I wish he'd go on back to Hammond where he belongs. He's got no business trying to be a big man here. Some of his friends got to be bad to the core. One's so ugly, he makes me want to puke just looking at him. Calling themselves vigilantes, like they're something special."

The old man paused to snort. He would have spit, but he didn't think Miss Mary would appreciate it.

"Where are they now?"

"Inside the saloon. They're itching to leave though. Henry's running out of questions to ask, and you know how Ghost is. Ever since he started making his own brew he's been acting real funny. It takes him a long time to figure out what folks are talking about. He can't concentrate is what it is, cause he's got all them spirits talking to him all the time. Course, getting hit by lightning didn't help him none, but I'm still saying he'd be right in the head if he'd stay away from liquor. Miss Mary, where are you dragging me?"

"To the saloon."

"You aren't thinking about going inside, are you?"

"If I have to, I will," she said. "I've got to put a stop to this."

They were running down the walkway. Dooley was soon out of breath. "Let me fetch your brothers, Miss Mary," he begged between gasps. "You wait right here."

Mary Rose saw the wisdom in getting some assistance. She agreed to wait and had only just sat down on a bench outside of the warehouse when Bickley and his cohorts strutted outside. Their horses were waiting, their reins tied to the hitching posts in front of the saloon.

She didn't dare wait any longer. She prayed to God the men weren't liquored up. She didn't know Bickley but she'd heard stories about him, and none of them were worth repeating. His appearance was every bit as nasty as his character. He had long, stringy, brown hair and beady eyes. He looked like a sneak, she thought to herself, and from all accountings, that's exactly what he was. Bickley was only a couple of inches over five feet. Adam said he was a little man trying to be big.

"Bickley? Might I have a word with you?"

Mary Rose stood on the corner of the walkway and waited for the leader to acknowledge her. She hoped he would come over to her alone and that his friends would wait by the doors of the saloon.

He turned at the sound of her voice. He gave her a grin, squinted his eyes against the sunlight, and sauntered over to her. She was sorry to see his friends followed him.

"What might I do for you, Miss Mary?"

Bickley was sour from the stench of liquor and old sweat. She wasn't surprised he knew her name. There were so few women living in Blue Belle that all the men who lived in the town and in the surrounding area knew who the women were. She was even known as far away as Hammond.

"Are you and your companions going up to Boar Ridge?"

"That's where we're headed, all right. We're going to burn out that crazy woman before she kills someone. We respect the law, and since Blue Belle don't have a sheriff, I figure it's our duty to take care of things around here."

"I can't imagine why you would think anyone around here is your responsibility," she said. "You live in Hammond, not Blue Belle. We take care of our own here."

She wanted to tell him to go back where he belonged and start minding his own business, but she didn't offer the suggestion for fear she'd antagonize him into doing something rash.

"There's a sheriff in Hammond," he said. "He don't want my help. Folks around here will be more . . . appreciative."

One of his cohorts chuckled. Mary Rose diligently tried to control her temper. She took a deep breath and then tried to reason with the vile creature.

"Just yesterday I went up to the ridge and had a nice long visit with the dear woman. Corrie isn't crazy. She's shy. She doesn't like outsiders trying to pry into her life. No one does. Corrie only likes people who live around Blue Belle."

"You're trying to keep us from doing our duty, aren't you?"

"Corrie is my friend. I want you to leave her alone." Her tone had taken on a hard edge.

"I don't have to listen to you. I got my mind set. Don't I, boys?"

Mary Rose couldn't keep her temper contained another second. "If you bother that sweet woman, I shall personally go to Judge Burns and sign a petition. I'll charge every single one of you with attempted murder, and my friends in Blue Belle will appreciate watching you hang."

Bickley didn't cotton to being threatened. Especially by a woman. Liquor made him forget

195

all about the Clayborne brothers. It was time someone took the uppity bitch in hand. He was just the man to see the duty done. He would shake some sense into her and have her quaking with fear in no time at all.

"Who do you think you are to talk to me like that?" he asked in a shout that caused spittle to drip down his chin.

"I'm a woman who knows an ignorant fool when she sees one," she replied.

Bickley wasn't overly intelligent, but he was certainly quick. Before she realized his intent, he grabbed hold of her upper arm, squeezed hard, and tried to pull her toward him. She kicked him soundly in his leg, right below his kneecap. Pain shot up into his thigh. He used the back of his hand and struck her across the face, and when she didn't cry out, he used his fist to hit her again.

"Are you plumb loco, Bickley?" one of his friends asked in a nervous whisper. "Let go of her before her brothers start shooting."

"I ain't letting go of her until she begs me real nice. I'm hurting her all right. I know I am. I'm gonna keep squeezing her arm until I snap her bone clear in half if she don't start telling me how sorry she is for sassing me. If her brothers try to stop me, I'll shoot every one of them. Just see if I don't."

Mary Rose had been temporarily stunned by the attack, but she quickly recovered. She could taste blood in her mouth and knew the corner of her lip had been torn. Her chin felt wet too, and she thought blood was pouring down from the injury. She didn't waste time worrying about it. Her mind had cleared sufficiently for her to remember what her purpose was. She was going to keep Bickley from going up on the ridge, no matter what the cost. She kicked the horrible man once again, much, much harder this time, and when he doubled over, she used her fist to knock him clear off his feet. Adam had always told her she had a mean left hook. She meant to prove she was worthy of the compliment.

She expected Bickley to let go of her, but he held tight until he had almost hit the ground. Then he sent her flying into one of the hitching posts. She struck the side of her head and collapsed to the ground.

She was knocked unconscious. She awakened a minute or two later, with pain exploding inside her head. She closed her eyes and tried to concentrate on making the throbbing inside her skull stop. There was a horrid roaring sound ringing in her ears.

She couldn't make it go away. The sound intensified, even after she'd opened her eyes and her vision began to clear. She thought she was feeling better because she wasn't seeing sparkling lights everywhere. Men were suddenly tripping over her to get to their horses. One man kicked her in the stomach. She cried out and doubled over and tried to roll onto her side. Another man used her hip as a stepping stool in his haste to get up on his horse. He tore her skirt with his spurs.

She was still in too much of a daze to protect herself. It was a miracle she wasn't trampled to death by the horses or the cowards trying to run away. She couldn't seem to make her eyes stay open. She felt someone lift her, and then her mind went black again. She floated between darkness and light for several minutes, and when she next awakened, everyone was running away. She sat up just in time to see Bickley kick his horse into a full gallop. She tried to stand up, thinking she had to go after him before he hurt Corrie, and she almost made it to her knees, but what happened next so surprised her, she fell back on her bottom again.

Sweet and gentle Harrison had been transformed into a barbarian. He appeared like an avenging angel out of thin air and literally leapt up into the air to attack Bickley. The bellow of rage she was hearing came from Harrison.

He was in a fury. He plucked Bickley from his saddle and threw him halfway down the road. Then he went after him. Everyone was shouting at the same time. Mary Rose wished to God the racket would stop. The noise made her head hurt all the more. Harrison wasn't making any noise now. He was fully occupied killing Bickley with his bare hands. From the look of deadly calm on his face, she didn't have any doubt about his intentions. If someone didn't stop him, he would kill the man who had attacked her.

She was stunned speechless. Harrison's expression sent chills down her spine. He looked so . . . methodical. He certainly didn't fight like a gentleman. For that matter, neither did Bickley. He tried to pull his gun out and shoot his tormentor, but Harrison kicked the weapon out of his hand. Bickley reached for his knife then. Harrison seemed pleased by his tactic. He actually smiled. He waited until Bickley lunged toward him, then moved as quick as lightning and snatched the knife out of his hand.

A rifle shout sounded in the distance. Mary Rose spotted Douglas walking toward her. He had the shotgun propped against one hip and his six-shooter cocked and ready in his other hand. The men who'd tried to get away weren't riding their horses now. They walked back to the saloon in front of her brother. Douglas must have caught them in front of the stables, Mary Rose concluded.

Cole stood behind Harrison. He had his arms folded across his chest and smiled with satisfaction as he watched Bickley try every dirty trick possible.

Travis was suddenly kneeling by Mary Rose's side. He gently lifted her into his arms and stood up.

"Dear God, sister. Are you all right?"

He sounded frightened. She didn't nod for fear the movement would make her head hurt more. "I'm fine, really. You've got blood on your shirt. Are you all right?"

"It's your blood, not mine. It's all over the side of your face. He really belted you, didn't he?"

"Travis, what took you so long to get here? I've been waiting and waiting."

"Mary Rose, it all just happened. You must have gotten knocked senseless. Are you sure you're all right?"

"Why is Harrison pounding Bickley? He isn't

supposed to know how to fight. Go and stop him before he gets hurt. Bickley's mean enough to kill him, Travis."

"Now, why would I want to do that? We all saw what the bastard did to you. Harrison's fast, isn't he? He was on top of Bickley before Cole or I could even get to the corner."

"Please put me down. I can stand on my own."

"You'll only go after Harrison if I let go of you. He won't kill Bickley," he promised. "Cole probably will though. Just wait until he gets a gander at your face. You're a real mess, little sister. You've got blood spewing out of your forehead and more pouring out of the side of your mouth."

Henry and Ghost hovered like old-maid aunts behind the pair. Travis turned to the men. "Watch my sister while I go help Harrison, will you?"

"Give her to us," Henry said. "We'll protect her. Won't we Dooley?"

"Of course we will," his friend promised. He was still panting for breath. He had only just reached the general store to get the brothers when Bickley came outside and started hurting his Miss Mary. "Everything happened mighty fast."

"That's the truth," Henry agreed. "Lickety-split was how quick it happened."

Henry lifted Mary Rose into his arms and held her tight against his chest. In his attempt to comfort and shield her, he was inadvertently making it impossible for her to breathe.

"She don't weigh more than a feather," he remarked.

"Please put me down. Let me lean against you and Dooley."

"All right," he agreed. "But if you get dizzy, I'm picking you up again."

"Make her promise to stay here," Dooley suggested.

Henry thought that was a grand idea and made his hostage give him her word.

Ghost had come outside the saloon and was standing near the doorway. Henry turned to him. "Go and fetch a chair for Miss Mary, will you, Ghost? We'll sit her down against the wall. Then get us a bowl of water and some clean towels. They're behind the bar. We got to clean up Miss Mary before Cole sees her."

"I'm thinking you should be more concerned about that Harrison fella. He's a bigger worry than Cole."

"He's already seen her," Henry said. "Why do you think he's so mad?"

"Looks like he's about finished with Bickley. Think he killed him?"

"No. Bickley's still wiggling in the dirt."

"Could be the death wiggle," Dooley suggested. He rubbed his jaw and squinted at the man writhing on the ground.

"Knowing Harrison and how he feels about the law, I don't think Bickley's a goner."

Dooley didn't agree. "Make you a nickel wager."

"You got it."

"If Bickley's dead, I win."

Henry nodded. Mary Rose sincerely hoped both men would stop talking. She kept her attention focused on Bickley's cohorts. Douglas was forcing the five men to walk toward Harrison. They were still armed, and she was worried one or two of them might decide to try to shoot Harrison or Cole.

"I saw one of them fellas kick our Miss Mary right in her gut," Henry whispered. "Another one stepped on her, hard. Yes, sir, he did. Ain't it a pity for men to treat a lady like that?"

Dooley agreed it was a pity. He thought about it a few seconds more and then felt compelled to tell her brothers and her avenger what the men had done. He hurried over to the edge of the walkway.

"Harrison? Cole? One of them fellas kicked your Miss Mary right in her gut. The ugly one stepped on her. Hard too. Almost killed her, he did. Someone else tore her pretty dress. Yes, sir, that's what they did all right."

Mary Rose wanted to strangle Dooley. He was deliberately inciting Harrison and her brothers. Before she could hush Dooley, it was too late. Harrison had heard every word. He didn't say anything. He didn't have to. His expression said it all.

"Why'd you go and tell Harrison? Cole's better with a gun," Henry remarked almost absentmindedly. He half dragged Mary Rose closer to the road so he'd have a better spot from which to watch the fight brewing.

"I told Harrison and Cole," Dooley said. "But I'm thinking Harrison's much meaner. You see how he took after Bickley. Besides, Cole heard what I had to say. Those men do anything else to you, Miss Mary?"

She gave Dooley a scathing look. If Bickley's friends had done anything else to her, she wasn't about to tell the town crier. She pulled away from Henry and made it past Dooley before they realized she'd gotten away.

"Catch her," Henry called out. "If there's shooting, she'll get herself done in trying to interfere. She's still in a daze, Dooley. You can see she is."

Dooley caught her around her middle and pulled her back to stand next to Henry again.

"What was I supposed to fetch?" Ghost asked the question from the doorway. Henry patiently reminded him what his errand was while Mary Rose once again edged her way to the corner.

She never took her attention away from Harrison. He stood ten or fifteen feet in front of Cole and Travis. Her brothers protected his back and had their attention on the men coming toward them.

The ugliest one of the bunch reached for his gun. Cole shot the weapon out of his hand before it had completely cleared his waistband.

The other men immediately raised their hands. They apparently didn't want to get into a gunfight.

Harrison turned to Cole. "Stay out of this," he ordered. "They're all mine."

Cole grinned. Travis shook his head. "You'll get killed and Mary Rose will get real pissed," he whispered so only Harrison and Cole could hear him.

Harrison had already turned back to Bickley's

friends. "Take your guns off," he ordered.

He waited until they had complied with his order, then removed his own belt and gun and tossed both to Travis. Cole kept his six-shooter trained on the group. He had five bullets left, and that was all he needed to kill every one of them if they tried anything underhanded. He wouldn't put anything past the vile creatures. One could very well have another gun tucked away. He hoped to God someone did. He really wanted to shoot at least one of them.

He was denied the opportunity. Harrison beckoned to the men to come to him.

"Is he going to take all of them on at once?" Travis asked his brother.

Harrison answered. "Damned right."

Cole smiled again. Both he and Travis stepped back to give Harrison more room.

"This ought to be good," Cole drawled out.

Mary Rose suddenly wished she had her gun with her. If it had been handy, she was certain she would have shot everyone in the street, including her brothers and Harrison. Cole actually looked as if he was enjoying himself. She'd shoot him first.

She refused to watch any longer. Harrison disappeared into the middle of the group of men. Then bodies started flying.

She had seen enough to give her nightmares for a week. She turned around and walked inside the saloon. She sat down in one of the chairs near the window but refused to even glance outside. Ghost was standing in front of the bar, having a drink. When he spotted her, he put the bottle down, scratched his head, and tried to look bewildered instead of guilty.

"What was I supposed to fetch, Miss Mary?"

"Never mind, Ghost. Enjoy your beverage."

"It's a might better than my brew."

"Don't you want to watch the brawl like everyone else in town?"

"I'm getting ready to watch," Ghost said.

Mary Rose closed her eyes. She ached everywhere. She felt like crying. Lord, she'd actually looked forward to today's outing. Oh, well, at least things couldn't get any worse. She found some comfort in that belief.

She was wrong though. She wasn't through being tormented.

"You can come on outside now, Miss Mary. You really ought not to be in the saloon. What would Adam think?"

Dooley asked the question from the doorway. "Ghost, ain't you fetched . . ."

"What was I supposed to get?"

"Water, bowl, towels," Mary Rose wearily supplied.

Ghost smiled. "Now I remember." He poured himself another drink while he nodded. "Yes, sir, I do remember."

"Here comes Harrison and your brothers," Dooley said.

If there had been a back door, she would have used it. She didn't want any of them to see her like this. At least that was the excuse she gave herself. She didn't want to think about the real reason. Harrison had completely changed his behavior. She didn't know how she felt about that.

He'd looked so ruthless. Honest to God, she hadn't thought he had it in him.

"I don't want Harrison to see me, Dooley. Make him wait outside."

Dooley hurried over to her. "He already seen you good, Miss Mary. Who do you think it was who moved you? He made sure you was breathing and all, and then he went after Bickley."

Cole and Travis both came inside just as Dooley finished his explanation. Harrison followed.

"I don't remember," she admitted. She kept her gaze on her lap, still not certain how she was going to react when she looked at Harrison again.

"You were knocked out, Mary Rose. Of course you don't remember. You should have killed him, Harrison, or at least let me at him," Cole muttered.

"Harrison broke Bickley's hand," Mary Rose said.

"No, he didn't. He just twisted it peculiar," Henry told her. "Douglas is dragging them all into the warehouse while Morrison gets some rope."

"How come?" Dooley asked. "Are we going to have us some hangings?"

"No," Henry returned. "Some of the folks are going to drag them back to Hammond. The sheriff there will probably lock them up."

"Isn't there a doctor around here we can take Mary Rose to?" Harrison asked.

Cole shook his head. "Closest one lives in Hammond."

"That's too far," Travis interjected. "Let's take

206

her to Morrison's house. Mrs. Morrison will take care of her."

"I would like to go home."

"In a little while," Cole promised. He squatted down next to his sister. In a whisper he asked, "Why won't you look at us?"

"I don't want to," she answered. "I want to go home. Now."

"Are you mad at us?"

She nodded, then promptly winced over the pain the movement caused. She never should have sat down, she realized. She'd gone all stiff. She wasn't even sure her legs would work.

"Then why don't you yell or something?"

"It would hurt too much," she admitted. She tried to stand up and promptly let out a loud groan.

Cole was suddenly shoved out of the way. Harrison scooped Mary Rose up into his arms. He was incredibly gentle with her. When that fact registered in her mind, she could almost look at him.

"What's the matter with her?" Travis asked. "Is she scared?"

"No, she's mad," Cole told him. "I don't want to be around when her temper explodes."

"I'll wager you've never seen anything like it, Harrison," Travis said.

He and Cole both burst into laughter. Mary Rose was offended by their callous attitudes. "I cannot imagine what you two find so amusing," she snapped.

"We're laughing because we're happy you weren't killed," Travis said.

She didn't look as if she believed him. Cole tried to calm her down. "Look at it this way. The day has to get better, doesn't it?"

She grasped the hope. Yes, things did have to get better.

Unless Harrison started showing off again.

September 1, 1863

Dear Mama Rose,
Your daughter has quite a mouth on her. Yesterday morning she told Cole to hush up, and just a few minutes ago, she told Travis to mind his own business. We're always so astonished to hear her talk like that, we have to work real hard at not letting her know how funny we think it is. She loves to try to boss us around, and lately she's been repeating cuss words she's heard Cole say. We all learned an important lesson, of course, and we're trying hard not to say anything improper. She's spending quite a lot of time sitting by herself, and, Lord, can she cry. She can be a little stinker all right.

We have started taking turns teaching her the alphabet. She's still too young to get the hang of it, but she enjoys having the attention. Travis got her a chalkboard and two boxes of chalk. She ate one of the pieces of chalk, and that made her sick. I don't think she'll eat any more of them.

Everyone's worried about you, Mama Rose. What with the war going on, and none of your letters getting through to us, we get anxious. We pray you and Miss Livonia are safe. It sure would help us get through the days if we'd get a letter from you. We know you write, but the post service is in such a confusion now, we aren't even sure you're getting any of our letters. I believe God will look out for you, and that when this is over, you'll be a free woman, and you can come join your family. The baby needs you so . . .

God protect you,
Douglas

7

She never should have tempted fate. Things progressed from worse to horrible. Ten minutes after she'd suffered her humiliating attack, she found herself in the most ludicrous position. She was seated in a chair with her feet propped up on a stool in the Morrisons' parlor. She was all by herself. Everyone else had disappeared into the kitchen. Catherine's mother had gone to fetch cloths and water so she could clean up Mary Rose's face, while her daughter entertained their other guests at the kitchen table.

Mary Rose told herself she deserved the misery she was suffering. She had made unkind remarks about Catherine, and even though most of the uncharitable opinions were true, she couldn't complain when Catherine lived up to her every expectation. At first — when Mary Rose walked inside the house, anyway — Catherine had pretended sympathy. She'd had an audience then. She gave quite a grand performance. Why, she even became tearful over what she kept calling her dear friend's hideous condition. Mary Rose wasn't fooled. She'd figured Catherine out years ago. Even as a little girl, Catherine pretended to be the perfect child in front of her parents and Mary Rose's brothers, but the second their backs were turned, she'd grab hold of Mary Rose and take a bite out of her. Time, unfortunately, hadn't improved her disposition or her behavior. Her sympathy for Mary Rose ended the minute Mrs. Morrison ushered the men into the kitchen. Catherine haphazardly slapped a towel her mother had given her against Mary Rose's face and went chasing after Harrison.

Travis, Cole, and Harrison were all seated around the kitchen table eating portions of the blackberry cobbler Mrs. Morrison had only just taken out of the oven. Dooley joined them. From where Mary Rose sat, she could see Harrison clearly. And Catherine, of course. She was hanging all over him. When she served him some dessert, she put her hand on his arm and draped herself over his shoulder to place the bowl in front of him. It took her an eternity to straighten back up. Harrison didn't seem to mind.

Having to watch Catherine flirt and not being able to do anything about it was purgatory. Travis wasn't about to be left out. He was competing for Catherine's attention, throwing out one perfectly stupid compliment after another. Catherine preened like a cat.

"It sure was something the way you got so mad, Harrison," Dooley praised. "I thought you were out of your mind taking on all them fellas, and I'll bet you didn't even feel the punches you were getting."

Harrison shook his head. "No, I wasn't out of my mind. I knew exactly what I was doing."

Dooley wasn't finished talking about the excitement in town. "Who would have thought it possible," he remarked. "A fancy lawyer like you being able to fight so mean."

Cole went completely still. "He's a lawyer?"

"Sure is," Dooley said.

Cole slowly put his spoon down and turned to Harrison. Then he punched him in the side of his jaw.

Harrison flinched in reaction. The punch stung. He rubbed his jaw and glared at Cole. "What'd you do that for?"

"Cause you're a lawyer," Cole answered.

He picked up his spoon again, turned to his bowl of cobbler, and then said, "Why in thunder didn't you tell us you were a lawyer?"

"It weren't no secret," Dooley blurted out. He walked over to the stove and leaned against the edge of it. There weren't any seats available unless he went into the parlor, and he wasn't about to leave the kitchen for fear he would miss some important piece of gossip.

The old man shoveled in another heaping spoonful of dessert and then said, "Everyone in town knows what Harrison does for a living, Cole. We even talked over the notion of him opening an office across the street from the general store. Yes, sir, we did."

"You hit me again, and I'll flatten you," Harrison said.

"I hate lawyers."

"Apparently so," Harrison said dryly. "Mind telling me why?"

"I would have punched you myself, but Cole was quicker," Travis muttered.

"Cole pretty much hates everyone, Harrison. Ain't you figured that out yet?" Dooley asked.

Travis finally answered Harrison's question. "We hate lawyers because they're always poking their noses in where they don't belong. Someone ought to round them all up and hang them. We could have a picnic after."

"We almost had us a bunch of hangings this morning, Miss Catherine," Dooley said.

Harrison looked into the parlor to see how Mary Rose was doing. He'd been looking every other minute just to make certain she was all right. Mrs. Morrison was taking forever getting her supplies ready so she could take care of Mary Rose, and Harrison had about used up all his patience waiting for someone to help her.

"What are you staring at?" Cole asked him.

"Your sister," he admitted. He started to stand up. "I think I'll go see if I can help . . ."

"Let the Morrison women see to her," Travis advised. "Women like other women nursing them."

Harrison sat back down again. In a low whisper, he said, "It's taking the women a hell of a long time to get to it, isn't it?"

"All in good time, Harrison," Travis said. He glanced over his shoulder to look at his sister, then turned back to the table. "She's fine. Don't worry about her."

"Someone has to worry," Harrison stubbornly insisted. "You and Cole act as though she skinned her knee. She was knocked out, for God's sake. She could be . . ."

"Don't let her know you're concerned."

Cole gave the warning. Travis grinned. "Sound advice, Harrison. You'd do well to remember it."

214

Harrison couldn't believe how unfeeling the brothers were. Cole guessed what he was thinking when he saw how incredulous he looked.

"She's little, but she's tough."

"She's probably feeling like hell," Harrison said.

"For God's sake, don't ask her how she feels," Travis warned.

"Why not?"

"You're a lawyer, you figure it out," Cole answered. "You really thinking about giving up on the law and learning to ranch?"

"Yes," Harrison replied. "That's exactly what I'm thinking about."

"Mr. MacDonald, I just love the way you talk," Catherine Morrison said. She leaned forward to brush against her guest while she put a linen napkin down in front of him. "It's so unusual. Isn't it, Travis?"

"I think he sounds like he's got something caught in his throat," Travis muttered. He wasn't at all happy to hear Catherine say anything nice about another man since he was thinking about becoming interested in her in the future.

"Oh, Travis, you're just adorable when you tease like that."

Cole and Harrison shared a look of exasperation. Harrison thought the young woman had taken coyness to a new height. She was extremely transparent. Cole wasn't as kind in his opinion. He thought Catherine was acting like a desperate, husband-hunting old maid.

Travis thought she was about the sweetest little thing in Blue Belle.

Catherine wasn't finished flirting, but Mary

215

Rose was finished listening. She couldn't stomach sitting in the parlor any longer. She wanted to go home and get some comfort and some care. If the cuts on her forehead and her mouth hadn't stopped bleeding on their own, she figured she'd be dead by now for all the attention she was getting. Probably no one would even notice she'd died, at least not until they ran out of cobbler. She knew she was feeling sorry for herself. That was all right. She might even decide to wallow in self-pity for the rest of the day.

Sitting in the chair had made her stiff. She stood up and almost lost her balance. She staggered forward, straightened up, and then turned to look in the kitchen to see if anyone noticed. They hadn't. She wasn't surprised, of course, for everyone was still fully occupied gobbling down cobbler.

She went outside and saw the horses were tied to the fence. Douglas came riding up just as she stepped off of the porch.

"You look a sight, Mary Rose."

"Is it any wonder? I was attacked, Douglas. When I think of all . . ."

He stopped her before she could really get into her list of ills. "Now, now, no use complaining."

Her brother dismounted and started toward the porch. "Where is everyone?"

"Inside, having some of Mrs. Morrison's mighty fine cobbler. I wouldn't know, of course. No one offered me any."

"There you go again. Complaining won't make you feel better."

He reached her side and awkwardly patted her on her shoulder.

"Yes, it will," she assured him. "I like to complain."

"I know." He sounded resigned.

Then he smiled at her. His amusement set her off again. What in heaven's name did she have to do to get a little sympathy around here?

"When I think about all I've been through today, I . . ."

"Where were you going all by yourself?"

"Home," she answered. "And don't you dare try to stop me."

It finally dawned on him that she really was feeling miserable. She looked close to tears. "All right," he soothed. "We'll go home. You wait right here. I'll go get the others. We'll all ride together. I'll hurry, I promise."

She pretended to agree so he would leave her alone. She knew what was going to happen. Douglas's promise was sincere, but once he got into Mrs. Morrison's kitchen, he was going to forget all about taking her anywhere.

Men. They were all so incredibly easy to sway. Pat them on their heads, give them something to eat, and they'll follow you anywhere. Add a smile and a few stupid compliments, and they'll immediately forget all about their other responsibilities.

Like a sister dying on the front porch, she thought to herself.

By God, someone was going to comfort her, even if she had to go all the way to Hammond and hire a complete stranger to be sympathetic.

217

It took her a long while to get comfortable in the saddle. Then she started for home. She forced herself to brush off her bad mood. She didn't feel all *that* bad. Mary Rose was a big believer in measuring each awful incident with something else awful that had happened in her life. Each painful and or humiliating trauma was immediately categorized in her mind as being as bad as, or not as bad as, or worse than something else. And as bad as being attacked by Bickley was, it still wasn't as bad as the bee attack. To date, nothing had even come close.

She'd almost died from the bee stings, at least Adam told her she'd been standing at heaven's door. She didn't have any recollection of being that ill. She just remembered the pain. She hadn't complained, even when her brothers begged her to.

"Mary Rose, slow down and wait for us."

Douglas shouted the order. She did as he demanded, but when he reached her side and she noticed he was wearing several crumbs of cobbler at the corner of his mouth, she gave him a hard frown and then ignored him.

"Can she ride on her own?" Harrison asked her brother from behind.

"She's trying," Mary Rose answered.

"Would you feel better if you rode with me?" Cole shouted the question.

"I doubt it. My backside is killing me. You've obviously forgotten what happened."

"And you're gonna remind me, right?"

She almost smiled. She stopped herself in time. She didn't want any of her brothers to catch on to her game. It would ruin all the fun for her if they realized that one of the reasons she complained was because they hated it so.

"I was brutally kicked and . . ."

"No use going over it, Mary Rose."

Cole reached her side and took her into his lap. "There. Now you'll feel better."

She might have agreed if he hadn't sounded so damned cheerful. He was acting as though nothing out of the ordinary had happened. All the men were, even the showoff, Harrison. She decided to make Cole miserable and immediately started complaining again. Her brother really was trapped with her. She could whine all she wanted, and he couldn't do anything about it. Usually, the minute she started listing her grievances, everyone would leave. She'd figured that out years ago. And that was exactly why she'd begun her game. Whenever she wanted privacy, she would start complaining, then sit back and watch her brothers trip all over themselves in their haste to get away from her. Her ploy was effective, and when something worked, one didn't mess with it.

Her goal now was to get back on her horse and be left alone. She needed privacy so she could think about Harrison's bizarre behavior. In the blink of an eye, his entire personality had changed. It was as though he'd been caught up in some sort of a spell. What in heaven's name had happened to the gentle man she'd liked so much? She was going to have to sort it all out in her mind before she could look at him again without getting angry.

Cole didn't want to let her ride on her own, but he soon got tired of listening to her. He gave her to Douglas. He didn't even last five minutes. Then Travis got stuck with her.

Three down and one to go, she thought a bit smugly.

"Listen, Mary Rose, you're making my teeth hurt listening to you," Travis muttered. "Why don't you wait until we get home and then sit down and write a long letter to your mama. You can tell her all about how poorly you're feeling."

"No, I can't," she replied. "Mama doesn't want to hear it. She told me it wasn't proper for a young lady to complain, even when she enjoys it so."

Travis laughed. "You used to write and tell on us, didn't you?"

"I was very young then," she defended. "Mama made me stop. She said I wasn't being loyal to my brothers and that I shouldn't ever tattletale. Mama would be sympathetic if she could see me now. Why, I was punched and . . ."

"Harrison, you want to take a turn?" Travis shouted.

"Never mind," Mary Rose whispered. "I'm finished complaining."

Travis didn't believe her. He all but tossed her into Harrison's lap. She let out a loud groan when she landed on his hard thighs.

He told her to lean against him. Once she had adjusted to his steel-like frame, she finally relaxed just a little. She kept her gaze directed on the trail ahead and thought about the tender way he was holding her in his arms.

Her mind began to wander. She suddenly realized she must look a fright. What an odd thing to think about now, she decided. Her foolish worry about her appearance was yet another contradiction floating around in her head. She knew she wasn't being logical about Harrison. She couldn't make herself look at him just yet. Granted, he had all but scared the curl out of her hair when he'd gone after Bickley and his friends, but then, ten minutes later, she hadn't been able to stomach watching Catherine flirt with him.

She must still be befuddled from hitting the side of her head against the post.

Harrison couldn't stand the silent treatment any longer. He moved her hair out of his way and leaned down close to her.

"Are you in pain, Mary Rose?"

"No."

"You need a physician," he announced. "I could ride to Hammond and get one."

"I don't need a doctor," she assured him. "I feel fine, really."

He gave her a little squeeze. "Try to relax."

A few minutes later he whispered her name again with that intoxicating brogue of his, and she suddenly wanted to sigh and shiver at the same time. She diligently resisted both urges.

The hit on her head must have knocked her senseless. She was angry with Harrison, wasn't she?

"Why won't you look at me? Did I scare you?"

He sounded amused. He was being kind and

221

considerate now and very, very sweet. She wanted to kick him.

She wouldn't answer him. Harrison let out a sigh. "Forget I asked," he said. "I must have been mistaken."

Several more minutes passed in silence. Guilt finally forced her to tell him the truth.

"You weren't completely mistaken. I wasn't afraid of you. I was afraid of what had happened to you. You told me you could take care of yourself, but I didn't believe you. I don't like men who fight."

"You must hate your brothers then."

"I love my brothers. I don't love you."

He knew she didn't love him. Of course she didn't. Still, it bothered him more than he cared to admit to hear her tell him so.

"I'm still not certain what came over me," he said.

"Are you given to spells, Harrison?"

She sounded genuinely concerned. He tried not to laugh. "I don't think so. When I picked you up in my arms, something snapped inside me. I can't explain it. You were limp and bloody, and I couldn't tell if you were breathing. I didn't know . . ."

She was astonished by what he was saying. She couldn't stop herself from interrupting. "You picked me up? Dooley said you did, but I didn't believe him."

"You were out cold," he explained. "So you can't possibly remember. You were in danger of being trampled by the horses. I had to do something to protect you. I know, I was a little late

222

getting to you, wasn't I? You were sprawled out on the ground and you weren't even trying to protect your head, for God's sake."

The memory of seeing her in such a helpless state made him shudder.

He instinctively tightened his hold on her, and she realized Harrison had been afraid.

"After you picked me up, what did you do?"

"I noticed you were still breathing before I lifted you off the ground. I should have calmed down then, but I didn't. Something snapped inside of me. I put you down where I knew you'd be safe, and then I went after the bastard."

She was barely paying attention to what he was saying now. She was too busy gloating. Hadn't she told him they were very alike? And my, how he'd argued with her. She remembered every word he'd said. She also remembered quite clearly how appalled he'd looked.

She wondered if it would be rude to say she'd told him so. It was about time he admitted she'd been right.

"So you, in fact, didn't take time to think about the situation? You just reacted, didn't you?"

He knew exactly where she was headed with her question. He gave a shrug and tried not to smile. Lord, she was clever.

"I didn't say I was . . ."

"Yes, you did say. You got your philosophy a little turned around, didn't you? You remember. First with your heart, then with your head."

"It's the other way around."

"I know," she answered, a smile in her voice. "I think you must have forgotten. Do you realize

223

what a lovely compliment you've just given me?"

"Really? You just insulted me."

She laughed. She obviously wasn't the least contrite. The sound of her joy reached her brother, Cole. He nudged his horse forward so he could ride alongside them. He immediately noticed how close Harrison was holding his sister. He appeared to be hugging her.

"Aren't you holding Mary Rose a little too tight for respectability?"

"Mind your own business, Cole," Harrison said.

Mary Rose smiled. Cole looked startled. He wasn't used to being sassed by another man. All her other guests had been too timid to talk back to any of her brothers. Harrison wasn't like anyone she'd ever known before.

Cole decided not to press the issue. He turned to his sister. He gave her a wide smile. She thought he was trying to be sweet, a rarity for him. When he continued to smile, she realized something else might be the cause.

"Why are you grinning at me like that?" she asked suspiciously.

He wasn't about to tell her the truth. His poor sister looked downright pitiful. Her hair was practically standing on end. The blue and white ribbon was dangling down the front of her neck. Dried blood caked her forehead and her chin. There was more on her neck. She was going to have heart palpitations when she looked at herself in a mirror.

"I'm happy you're feeling better," he told her.

He continued to ride by their side. Mary Rose wanted him to leave her and Harrison alone. She wasn't finished making Harrison tell her how he'd felt. He wouldn't say another word as long as Cole was hanging around. She needed privacy all right, and there was only one sure way to get it.

"I'm not feeling better."

"You just laughed. I heard you."

"I was delirious. I'm in terrible pain. Have you forgotten what happened to me? My head throbs and my hip is . . ."

She didn't need to go on and on. Cole took off. She watched him take over the lead and let Travis trail behind him. Douglas stayed well behind the group so he could protect their backs from any surprises.

"Now then, what were you telling me?"

"Mary Rose, I'm really concerned about you. Are you in terrible pain? You need a doctor," he once again insisted.

She patted his hand. "I'm fine, really. Now I remember," she continued. "You just can't help it, can you, Harrison?"

"You're sure you're all right? You sounded so weak and ill when you were telling Cole how poorly you felt. I'm really going to have to insist you see a physician," he said again.

She patted his hand. "It's sweet of you to worry. I'm fine, really. You can't help it, can you?"

"Help what? Being sweet?"

She smiled. "No, you can't help caring about me."

Now he would tell her what he was feeling in his heart.

"Of course I care about you. I care about your

brothers too. You all took me into your home and fed me. You gave me a bed and . . ."

"Pat them and feed them, and they'll be forever beholding."

"What did you just say?"

"Never mind."

"Are you going to look at me?"

"I'm getting ready to," she said. "Promise me something first."

"What is it?"

"Don't have any more spells. Be who I think you are. All right?"

"I don't have spells, Mary Rose, and I'm going to have to figure out what you think I am before I can accommodate you."

She believed that was fair enough. She finally turned to look at him. She quickly wished she hadn't bothered. Harrison looked startled, but only for a second or two. Then he gave her the same silly grin Cole had given her just minutes before.

He explained his behavior before she could ask. "You kind of remind me of Ghost."

"That bad?" she whispered.

He tried to organize her curls. They seemed to be everywhere. She reached up to help him. "Didn't I look like this in town? You weren't smiling then?"

"I was upset in town. I'm not upset now. Besides, your hair . . ."

"What about my hair?"

She pushed his hand out of her way so she could smooth her curls properly. "Is it standing on end? Oh, Lord, do I really look like Ghost?"

"No, his hair has a part on the side. Yours doesn't."

"Mary Rose? You'll never guess who's waiting for us," Cole shouted. "Clive Harrington's standing in our front yard."

Cole shouted the news from the lookout above the ranch. She immediately forgot about her appearance. She told Harrison to hurry and catch up with her brother.

"Clive must be sick," she called out.

Cole shook his head. "I don't think he is."

Travis was the next one to reach the rise. "Now, what is his stagecoach doing in our front yard?"

Something must have happened. Mary Rose was sure of it. Clive had a strict policy. He never drove his vehicle onto anyone's property. He said it went against his principles. He left his passengers at the various crossroads along his route. It was up to them to figure out how to get home. Guests received the same treatment. Clive didn't concern himself about strangers getting lost. He didn't worry about their baggage either. He told Mary Rose he had more important matters to think about.

He had hinted he'd change his rule just for her, of course, but she insisted he treat her like everyone else. She didn't want special consideration. Clive thought she was an angel, sent down from heaven to help him keep to his standards.

She and Harrison finally reached the vantage point above the valley. She spotted Clive right away, pacing back and forth in front of his horses.

"Something terrible has happened," she announced. "Look how agitated poor Clive is."

227

"Where's Adam?" Travis wondered.

"He must be inside the house," Douglas guessed from behind.

"It's terrible all right."

"Don't borrow trouble, Mary Rose," Harrison advised. "It could be just the opposite. Something wonderful could have happened and the stage-coach driver is anxious to tell you all about it."

She half turned in his lap so he could see how exasperated she was by his ludicrous suggestion.

"Maybe he got robbed," Travis speculated.

"I doubt it," Cole replied. "Everyone around here knows he never carries anything of value."

"Please hurry," Mary Rose pleaded. "I have to help Clive. He's in trouble."

"It might not be bad news," Cole argued. "Harrison could be right."

"After the morning I've had. Of course it's bad. I deserve it."

"Are you going to start in again?"

"I said some mean things about Catherine," she told her brother. "Everything I said was true, but I still shouldn't have said them. In my defense, I will tell you that if you had any idea what I had to suffer growing up with her for my only companion, you would get down on your knees and beg my forgiveness. Yes, you would. Why didn't you just give me a rattlesnake to play with? I would have been safer."

Travis smiled at Harrison. "Mary Rose is still mad Catherine cut her hair. She likes to hold a grudge."

"The haircut was the least of it. Either start down the hill, or please get out of my way."

The brothers finally moved. They reached the ranch a few minutes later. Clive hurried over to help her down to the ground.

"Lordy, Lordy, what happened to you, Miss Mary?"

"Bickley punched me."

Clive became outraged on her behalf. "I'm gonna kill him for you. Just see if I don't."

"Now, Clive, don't get all riled up. It isn't good for your digestion. Bickley and his friends are being taken back to Hammond. The sheriff will take care of them. It's very sweet of you to be concerned about me. You're such a dear friend."

"Are you in pain, Miss Mary?" Clive asked. He wasn't convinced he should let the matter drop.

"No, no, not at all," she assured him. "Once I wash my face and change my dress, you won't be able to tell anything happened to me."

"And comb your hair," he suggested.

She immediately tried to smooth her curls down again. "Now, tell me why you're here. Is something wrong?"

"Something's wrong all right," he answered. "I'm so thankful you're finally home. You got no business going into Blue Belle today, Miss Mary. It ain't Saturday. Did you forget?"

"No, I needed supplies to take to another friend. It was a special circumstance."

"All right then, if it was special," he muttered. His mind returned to his dilemma. "Even though you look like you got yourself run over, you're still a sight for these sore eyes. I need your help something desperate. You just got to help me. You just got to."

She shot her brothers an I-told-you-it-was-trouble look before giving Clive her full attention again. "Of course I'll help. Just tell me what's wrong."

"You got to get her out of my stagecoach. She won't budge. She wouldn't even let Adam get near the door. She started in shouting at him. She said she wasn't going to let no hired hand greet her. It weren't proper. That's precisely what she said, all right. I tried to tell her how things were around here, but she wouldn't listen. She won't believe Adam's your brother. I could understand her doubt. She ain't from around here, so she ain't used to things. Adam finally gave up and went on back inside. He didn't want to get shot. She was threatening to do him in if he got near the coach again. Your brother offered me a comfortable chair and a cool drink. I didn't dare take him up on his offer though. I couldn't leave her out here alone. No telling what she'd do to my coach if I turned my back on her. I tried to soft talk her out, Miss Mary. Nothing worked. She demands a proper greeting, and she says she ain't getting out until she gets what she wants. She's been roosting in there a good two hours. She's something else, Miss Mary."

"Who do you have inside?" Douglas asked. He had already tried to look in the window, but a dark drape blocked his view.

"Miss Border." He shuddered when he whispered the name.

"Eleanor?" Mary Rose was thunderstruck. She

couldn't believe what Clive was telling her. What in heaven's name was Eleanor Border doing in her front yard?

Douglas whirled around and stared at his sister. "*The* Eleanor?"

Clive tugged on her arm before she could answer her brother.

"You just got to take her off my hands. I swear I'll do anything you ask. I'll even beg if you want me to."

Cole was the only brother who was amused by the news. His eyes sparkled with delight. "You're already begging," he said. Then he started laughing. The notorious roommate they'd heard all those outrageous stories about, the woman who had made Mary Rose miserable for years now, had come to pay her respects.

"What is she doing here?" Travis demanded. He was good and angry.

"Did you invite her?" Douglas asked.

"Sort of," she hedged.

"What does 'sort of' mean?" Douglas asked. He stomped over to stand in front of his sister. "Well?"

"I did invite her, but only because I was certain she wouldn't ever take me up on my offer. She doesn't like the frontier. She thinks it's barbaric and uncivilized. Douglas, do quit glaring at me. What's done is done."

"Has that woman ever been west of St. Louis before?" Travis asked.

"No, but she still doesn't like it," Mary Rose explained.

"I want you to tell me she isn't the same Eleanor

231

you've been talking about all these past years," Douglas demanded.

He latched on to her other arm and wasn't going to let go until she gave him what he wanted.

"You know perfectly well she's the same Eleanor," his sister whispered. She tried to pry off his hand so she could go and get her houseguest.

"I could wring your neck for inviting her, Mary Rose," Travis muttered.

"You're acting like a child," she said. "And lower your voice. I don't want her to hear us talking about her. She has tender feelings."

Cole burst out laughing again.

"Clive, take her back to Blue Belle," Douglas suggested. "She can stay in one of the rooms above the saloon."

"Be reasonable, for heaven's sake. Only drunks stay above the saloon. Eleanor's a delicate and refined lady."

"I don't think any of you understand my problem here," Clive cried out. "I got to get rid of her if I'm ever going to make Morton Junction before nightfall. People are waiting on me."

"Yes, of course," Mary Rose soothed. "We'll help you."

Clive wasn't listening. He was on a roll and wasn't about to stop. He'd been storing up his frustration for two long hours. It was time to get it all out.

"If folks around here find out I broke my own principles and brung her right to your front door, I'll never be able to hold my head up again."

He turned to the brothers. "I'm telling you,

men, she's something else. I ain't going against her. She already put a hole in my best hat. Thank the Lord it weren't perched on my head at the time. She told me she'd shoot me down like a dog if I misbehaved on her. I don't know about her being delicate, Miss Mary. I only know you got to do something quick. I want to get out of here."

"I'll get her out right this minute," she promised. "Douglas, please let go of me. We have to be hospitable. We've already been rude by making her wait."

Harrison stood by MacHugh's side and watched. He was astonished by everyone's reaction to the unwanted guest. Needless to say, Eleanor Border had captured his curiosity.

"Do you think I'm going to let you welcome her after she was rude to my brother?" Douglas asked.

"She didn't understand."

"Exactly what didn't she understand?" Travis asked. "You heard Clive. He said he told her Adam was your brother."

"She obviously didn't believe him," Mary Rose countered.

"She threatened to shoot him too," Clive interjected.

Cole quit smiling. "She what?" he said in a near shout.

"I never told anyone about my family. Cole, calm down. You insisted I keep quiet about everyone. Remember? All of you told me over and over again not to mention any details about our family." She lowered her voice when she added,

233

"Eleanor probably thought Clive was trying to dump her."

"I was trying to dump her," Clive shouted.

Mary Rose closed her eyes. Douglas was still tugging on her arm, and Clive was on her other side pulling on her hand. Honest to heaven, she wasn't up to this today. She hurt all over, and she really didn't want to waste time trying to fix something that couldn't be fixed. They were stuck with Eleanor Border whether they liked it or not.

"She'll apologize to Adam," she promised.

"Or what?" Travis asked.

"Or she'll leave," Mary Rose promised.

"What about me, Miss Mary? She called me an ignorant mule. She said I didn't know what a bath was. She said a lot of other nasty things about me too, but I ain't gonna repeat them. She's got the sting of a hornet, I'm telling you. And for what? All I did was try to pitch her out at the junction. Was that a crime, I ask you? You know I've got my standards."

"Yes, I know. No one's ever going to find out you broke your policy to bring her here. None of us will tell anyone. Eleanor's going to apologize to you too, Clive. She'll pay for a brand-new hat. Will that make you feel better?"

Clive looked like he wanted to weep with gratitude. Mary Rose patted him.

"You're a good man to put up with her. I know how she can be. She was my roommate at school. I'm so sorry you were inconvenienced."

Clive leaned forward. "And terrorized, Miss Mary. I ain't afraid to admit it."

Cole rolled his eyes toward heaven. "I say we set the coach on fire. She'll get out fast then. I'll buy you a new one, Clive."

Mary Rose closed her eyes again. She decided not to waste any more time soothing anyone. She pulled away from her brother and ran over to the side of the stagecoach.

Clive backed up all the way to the steps leading up to the porch. Mary Rose knocked on the door and then tried to open it. It wouldn't budge.

"Eleanor, I'm home now. Please open the door," she called out. "It's Mary Rose."

She heard the click of the bolt as it was unlocked. She opened the door then and climbed inside. Before anyone could see inside, she shut the door behind her.

There was enough of a crack between the curtains for light to filter inside the coach. Mary Rose took one look at Eleanor and was immediately flooded with guilt over all the stories she'd ever told about her. Her old roommate looked terrified. She was huddled in the corner of the coach and was visibly shaking with fear. Tears streamed down her face.

Mary Rose sat down on the bench across from Eleanor and started to lean forward to take hold of her hand. She noticed the gun then. Eleanor was holding it in her lap. The barrel was pointed at Mary Rose.

She wasn't alarmed. Just nervous. Eleanor was looking at her, but Mary Rose didn't think she was really seeing her.

"When did you get a gun?" she asked.

"Last week."

"Do you know how to use it?"

"Not yet. I'll learn."

"Guns are dangerous, Eleanor. You shouldn't be carrying one."

"I cut my hair. Do you like it?"

Mary Rose wasn't at all surprised by the question. Eleanor had always tended to be a little self-involved. Her appearance came before everything else — apparently even terror.

The poor woman was so frightened, her hands were shaking. She had a wild look in her eyes, and Mary Rose was suddenly reminded of a deer trapped in a tangled mass of brier.

Eleanor was a strikingly pretty woman with dark black-brown hair and vivid green eyes. Her hair used to be shoulder length but now only just covered her ears. It was curly everywhere and very pretty.

"Yes, I do like your hair. It's lovely."

She kept her voice whisper soft. She didn't want to startle Eleanor, and her movements were slow and measured as she reached over and turned the weapon until the barrel pointed toward the floor. She then gently pried the gun out of Eleanor's hand. Her friend watched what she was doing, but didn't try to stop her.

"You don't have to be afraid any longer. You're safe now. Everything's going to be all right."

"No, it isn't going to be all right. Nothing can ever be the same. I didn't want to come here. You know how I dislike primitive conditions."

"If you didn't want to come here, why did you?"

"I didn't have any other place to go."

She finally really looked at Mary Rose. Her eyes filled with fresh tears.

Eleanor looked miserable and still very afraid. Mary Rose decided to find out what had caused her to become so frightened. Her friend had always been quite unemotional at school and somewhat coldhearted. Except late at night, Mary Rose remembered. She would hear Eleanor weeping then.

"You're a contradiction, Eleanor," she remarked. "Tell me about your father. Weren't you going to Europe with him after you finished school?"

"It was all a lie," Eleanor answered. "Father ran away. He didn't even tell me he was leaving. He just . . . ran."

"Why?"

"The authorities came to the school to question me. I found out what Father had done then. I had to leave the school of course. The headmistress was furious. It seems that Father had promised her funds to construct a new building."

"She couldn't just toss you out," Mary Rose protested.

"She did," Eleanor insisted. "The last of the fees hadn't been paid. The investigators told me Father had taken money from other people. All these past years he's been stealing from his clients with one scheme after another. He lived high and mighty. He was always impeccable in his dress, always insisted on wearing the latest fashions. He must have had over fifty suits in his wardrobe. Father always had a young woman latched on to his arm."

"And?" Mary Rose prodded when she didn't continue.

"He didn't want me dampening his social position. I was a constant reminder to others how old he was getting. He stuck me in boarding school so he wouldn't have to have me around."

"You can't know if he wanted you or not."

"Yes, I can know. He told me so many times, I got sick of hearing it. He never wanted me. My mother tricked him into marriage by getting pregnant. She died having me, but she had a ring on her finger, so she was probably content."

Mary Rose was appalled by what she was hearing. Her heart went out to Eleanor. She was careful not to show her compassion openly, for Eleanor would undoubtedly think she was feeling sorry for her.

Mary Rose was feeling sorry for the poor woman, but she didn't want her to know it.

Pride. It certainly got in the way of practical solutions.

"I thought you and your father lived an exciting life. Did you go to all those exotic places on your vacations . . . ?"

"No, I never went anywhere. I stayed with the housekeeper at home."

"But the stories you told me about . . ."

"I read about all those places. That was all. I wanted to impress you."

"Why?"

Eleanor shrugged. "I don't know."

"Why didn't you just tell me the truth?"

"I had my appearances to keep up," she muttered. "Like father, like daughter, I suppose. Besides, you would have pitied me."

"What happened to your father? Where is he now?"

"I don't have any idea. No one does. The authorities are still looking for him. I should be thankful he paid some of my tuition, but I'm not. He used other people's money. He didn't leave me a note telling me where he went. The police didn't believe me. I was taken to a jail and had to stay there for two nights. It was horrible. They finally had to release me. It is all a big scandal, of course. people as far away as Chicago hate me because I'm related to him. Everyone seems to think I know where he's hiding. The authorities were watching the house night and day. It was unbearable. I hid behind the drapes and tried to pretend nothing had happened."

"I'm so sorry," Mary Rose whispered.

Eleanor didn't seem to hear her. "I thought we owned the house, but we didn't. Our landlady threw me out. I didn't know where else to go. You told me I could come to you if I ever needed you. Did you mean it?"

"Yes, of course I meant it."

"You won't send me away?"

"No, I won't send you away," she promised. "Were you worried I wouldn't let you stay because you and I haven't always gotten along?"

"You're the only person at school who put up with me at all. I know I can be difficult. I was hateful to you because I knew you were feeling sorry for me."

"I didn't feel sorry for you. Are you about

239

ready to get out of the coach?"

"Yes."

Eleanor reached for the door handle. Mary Rose stayed her hand. "Wait just one minute," she asked. "I'd like to talk to you about my brothers before you meet them. Adam . . ."

"The man with the black skin?"

"Yes," she answered.

"You aren't going to believe what that horrid driver told me. He said the dark man was your brother. Can you believe such outrageous . . ."

"Adam is my brother. Because he is the oldest in our family, he is also the head of the family."

Eleanor's mouth dropped open. "You can't be serious."

"I'm perfectly serious. You're going to have to apologize to him before you can come into our house."

Eleanor was flabbergasted. She leaned back against the cushions and stared at Mary Rose. "How in heaven's name . . ."

"How isn't important," Mary Rose insisted. "Adam is my brother, and I love him with all my heart."

"He can't be your brother."

Mary Rose was weary of trying to convince her. "He is," she insisted abruptly, for what she decided was the last time. "Adam and my other brothers raised me from the time I was an infant. We're a family, Eleanor, and family comes before everything else."

"Do people around here accept all of you?"

"Of course."

"Why?"

Mary Rose let out a sigh. "We've been here a long time. I suppose everyone's used to us. Well? Are you going to apologize?"

Eleanor nodded. "I didn't mean to offend him. I didn't say anything mean, Mary Rose. I thought the driver was lying to me. He had already tried to toss me out in the middle of a dirt road. Can you imagine?"

"The driver's name is Clive Harrington. He's a good man. You're going to have to apologize to him too. You really shouldn't have shot at him."

Eleanor shrugged. She obviously wasn't overly contrite. "I didn't mean to shoot at him, but I don't believe I want you to tell him that. He might get angry if he knew the gun just sort of went off."

"He's already angry."

"It was an accident," Eleanor insisted. "Why do I have to apologize to him for something I didn't mean to do?"

"You could have killed the man."

"I didn't."

"You also inconvenienced him," Mary Rose told her. "And you hurt his feelings. I promised him you'd say you were sorry. I also gave my word that you would purchase a new hat for him. You put a hole in the only one he owns."

"I can't buy him a hat. I don't have enough money."

"Then I'll give you enough," Mary Rose said. "Just don't let Clive know. Pretend you're going to buy the thing with your money."

"Why do you care about his feelings?"

241

"Clive is my friend."

"Oh, all right," Eleanor muttered. "I can tell you're going to be stubborn about this. I'll apologize and I'll buy him a new hat. Why didn't you tell me about Adam? Were you afraid I would tell the other girls?"

Mary Rose shook her head. "Why would I care if you told anyone or not?"

"Because you would have been shunned."

Mary Rose's patience was worn thin. All she wanted was a hot bath and a little comfort. She knew she wasn't going to get either of those things until she got her houseguest situated.

"We know all about prejudice, Eleanor. Being shunned by a group of ignorant girls means little to me. Frankly, my brothers and I have learned not to waste our time on people who hate. All my brothers are wonderful, proud men. I'm not ashamed of my family."

"Then why didn't you say anything?"

"Family is private," Mary Rose explained, repeating what she'd been told over and over again by her brothers. "Who we are and what we do isn't anyone else's business."

"Now that I think about it, you never told me about your other brothers either," Eleanor said. "I knew you had four, but that's all I ever knew. Are they . . . like Adam?"

"Yes," Mary Rose replied. "They're just as kind and good-hearted. Douglas and Cole are a little more stubborn though."

Eleanor couldn't seem to get her wits about her. She was still reeling inside from the shock Mary Rose had given her.

"We can get out now."

"In a minute," Eleanor whispered. "Things are different out here, aren't they?"

"Conditions are different here than in the city," Mary Rose replied. "But family is family, no matter where home is."

"What in heaven's name is that supposed to mean?"

"Now that I know about your father and what your family life was like, I can well understand why you wouldn't understand. Once you get used to all of us, I think you'll like living here. It's stifling inside, Eleanor. Can't we get out?"

"Adam is head of your household and for that reason, I shall respect him. I give you my promise."

Mary Rose shook her head. "No, you will respect him because you should. His position in the family isn't important. Meet him, Eleanor. I promise you that once you get to know him, you'll respect him because of who he is, not what he is."

"Honestly, Mary Rose, you're always trying to mix me up. Adam's the only one who can make me leave, isn't he?"

Mary Rose gave up trying to reason with the woman. "Oh, for heaven's sake," she muttered. "I want a bath. Will you please stop arguing with me and get out?"

Eleanor finally noticed how horrid Mary Rose looked. "What happened to you?"

"A difference of opinion," she replied.

"Your brothers didn't . . ."

"Of course not. Honestly, Eleanor, we aren't

barbarians. I'm getting out before I faint."

"It is hot in here, isn't it?"

Mary Rose reached for the door latch. "You will be gracious to everyone, won't you?"

She wouldn't have demanded the promise if she hadn't known just what Eleanor was capable of. "Don't you dare try any of your nonsense on my brothers. They won't put up with it."

"What nonsense?"

"You know what I'm talking about."

"Give me an example."

"The look of disdain you give everyone," Mary Rose said. "And the . . ."

"Oh, all right. I'll be nice. Lord, I only hope I know how."

Mary Rose wondered the very same thing. She finally opened the door and tried to get outside. The heat had made her weak, and the burst of fresh air was as refreshing as a drink of cool water after a day in the garden.

The door knocked Harrison. He'd been standing close by, waiting to see if Mary Rose needed his help. He offered her his hand and helped her step down to the ground.

He looked worried. She smiled to let him know everything was all right. She still had Eleanor's gun in her hand, but kept the weapon pointed to the ground until Harrison spotted it and took it away from her. He tossed it to Cole who immediately tucked it into his gunbelt.

Eleanor climbed out of the stagecoach a minute later and stood next to Mary Rose's side. She squinted against the sunlight and kept her gaze directed on her friend.

244

Because Harrison was the closest, Mary Rose introduced him to Eleanor first. Then she made her brothers come forward to meet their new houseguest.

Clive was standing by the steps. He still looked as though he wanted to string Eleanor up from the nearest tree.

Eleanor and Mary Rose walked over to face the driver. Eleanor finally whispered an apology.

Clive wasn't satisfied. "You got to say it loud and clear so every one will hear, and you got to call me Mr. Harrington, real respectful-like."

Mary Rose had to nudge Eleanor into complying. Clive never smiled, but Mary Rose could tell he was pleased by Eleanor's apology because his scowl wasn't as dark.

"Miss Mary, will she keep her word about buying me a hat?"

"Yes," Mary Rose promised.

Clive nodded. He strutted back to his stagecoach, muttering under his breath all the while. Mary Rose knew his bluster was all for the men's benefit. Clive couldn't act relieved, not if he wanted to keep his mean reputation intact.

The driver climbed up on the perch, took the reins in his hands, and then called out to Mary Rose. "I was feeling a bit poorly early in the week, but now . . ."

He paused in his explanation to glare at Eleanor. "Now I ain't too sure how I feel. How long is she gonna stay?"

"For a spell," Mary Rose answered. "There's always room for you, Clive. You know that."

"I'm feeling better," he said. "I might be able

to fight off this illness . . . for a spell. Bye now, Miss Mary."

"What was that all about?" Eleanor asked.

Mary Rose waved to her friend before answering. "He's telling me he won't get sick until you leave. Why don't you go and sit in one of the chairs on the porch while I go inside and talk to Adam. It's going to take a while," she predicted. "He's going to have to welcome you before you can set foot in our house."

"What if he won't welcome me?"

Mary Rose didn't want to think about that possibility. "Adam is compassionate. I'll have to tell him what happened to you. Will you mind?"

"Will he tell everyone?"

"No," she assured her.

Eleanor agreed. "Do I have to sit there alone?"

Mary Rose looked around her for someone to keep Eleanor company. Harrison became her only candidate for the task, but only because he was the slowest one getting away. Cole had already reached the main barn, and both Travis and Douglas were hot on his heels.

Harrison didn't particularly want the duty, but he was gallant enough to do as Mary Rose asked.

He made her beg first, however, which she thought was extremely rude of him.

She had to chase after him too. "Will you slow down?" she demanded when she finally reached his side. "Why are you frowning like that?"

"I was concerned about you," he admitted. "You shouldn't have gotten inside. She had a gun, Mary Rose. You could have been hurt. She already shot at Clive," he reminded her.

"Eleanor wouldn't hurt me, or anyone else for that matter. She's afraid, Harrison. She's had a bad time lately. Be kind to her."

Harrison knew he was going to have to be a gentleman about this. He shouted to Douglas to come and get MacHugh, and when the brother arrived, he followed Mary Rose over to the porch.

She was finally able to go inside the house. Adam was in the library, sitting behind his desk. He was diligently working on one of his ledgers and didn't notice her standing in the doorway for a minute or two.

She patiently waited, and all the while she fought the tears gathering in her eyes.

She finally gave up trying to remain composed. She was fighting the inevitable, after all. For as long as she could remember, she'd been disgustingly predictable. Regardless of the severity of the insult or injury done to her, she could always control herself and maintain her dignity until she got home and spotted her oldest brother.

Then she would fall apart.

Today she proved to be as predictable as a downpour during a picnic. All it took was for Adam to notice her.

"Oh, sister, what happened to you?"

Mary Rose promptly burst into tears and threw herself into her big brother's arms.

February 13, 1864

Dear Mama Rose,
We just finished poring over a month-old newspaper Travis traded some skins for up near Perry, and a gentleman by the name of Benson reprinted Lincoln's speech he made in Gettysburg. We had already read about the battle there back in July, where so many brave men gave their lives. Benson said our President made the speech on the site of the cemetery he dedicated on the site of the battlefield. Adam wept when he read the words, and he copied it all down just right so we could send it to you.

Cole thinks you've probably already read it, Mama, but we all think it's too important not to read at least twice.

You and Lincoln are in our prayers.

Douglas

8

Mary Rose threw herself into Adam's arms and wept like a little girl. He put his arms around her and patted her until she calmed down. It took her several minutes to regain control. Then she sat on the edge of the desk and poured her heart out. She told him all the horrid details of everything that had happened to her in town. She lingered over the Catherine Morrison episode. Adam examined her injuries while he listened, calmed her with his gentle voice as he said, "Is that so?" over and over again. In no time at all she was feeling fine again.

Her brother took her to the kitchen and washed her face so he could get a better look at the wounds to determine if stitches were going to be necessary. She held her breath until she heard the verdict, then smiled with relief over his decision. Stitches weren't needed after all.

She was finally ready to get on with the business of the day. She started to give Adam his handkerchief back, noticed it was soaked with tears and old blood, and tossed it into the laundry basket instead.

Her brother suggested she go upstairs and get cleaned up. He returned to the library to finish his work. "Relax this afternoon, Mary Rose. You've had enough excitement."

She chased after him. She couldn't pamper herself with a bath as long as Eleanor was sitting on the front porch fretting. She needed to get her settled in, and then she was going to take the supplies she'd purchased to Corrie. She had made the woman a promise to return today, and Mary Rose didn't want to break her word.

"I've indulged myself in childish self-pity long enough," she told her brother. She stood in the doorway and watched Adam take his seat behind his desk once again. She noticed the ledgers were open, knew then she was interrupting his work, but decided he was just going to have to be patient a little longer. The books could wait. Eleanor couldn't.

"Don't forget to put some medicine on those cuts."

"I won't forget," she said. "We need to talk about Eleanor now. She's waiting on the porch. I told her she couldn't come inside until you gave permission. Will you talk to her . . . in private? She wants to tell you what happened to her before you make up your mind to let her stay or not."

Adam was surprised by the request. "In all of your life, have you ever known me to send anyone away?"

"No, but Eleanor's a different situation. She's going to throw the family into chaos for a little while. Are you in the mood to put up with her?"

"What about your brothers? Shouldn't they have a say?"

"They'll do whatever you think is right," she countered. "Cole will be difficult, of course, but he'll figure out a way to avoid her until she settles down."

Adam leaned back in his chair and gave his sister a speculative look. "Exactly how long is Eleanor going to be staying with us?"

She couldn't look at him when she gave her answer. "For a spell."

"Is that right? And exactly how long is 'a spell,' Mary Rose?"

She shrugged. "I wish I knew," she whispered. "Talk to her, please? She's scared. She needs a safe place."

Adam let out a sigh. He stood up and came around the desk. "All right," he agreed. "Go on upstairs now. I'll take care of Eleanor. Her last name is . . . ?"

"Border," Mary Rose answered. "Shouldn't I stay down here while you talk to her?"

Adam shook his head. "That isn't necessary."

She started up the stairs to the second floor. Adam was almost to the front door when she turned and called out to him.

"I want to make certain she . . ."

He turned around and looked up at her. "She what?"

"Apologizes to you. She insulted you, Adam, and I don't want her to come inside my house until she tells you she's sorry."

"Oh, for heaven's sake, go on upstairs. You're giving me a headache. I'll deal with Eleanor."

Adam opened the screen door. Eleanor was sitting in one of the wicker chairs talking to Harrison. Their other houseguest wasn't sitting. He was leaning against the post with his arms folded across his chest, looking both irritated and bored.

Adam waited until Eleanor had finished complaining to Harrison about the heat.

"Miss Border, will you come inside to the library with me? I'd like to talk to you."

He raised an eyebrow over her reaction to his request. He hadn't raised his voice, but she acted as though he'd just shouted at her. She jumped to her feet so quickly, she toppled over her chair in the process.

Harrison reached down and straightened the chair back up again.

Eleanor started toward Adam, then suddenly stopped. She clasped her hands together. "I can't come inside, Mr. Clayborne."

"You can't? Why not?" Adam asked.

"Mary Rose told me I couldn't until I apologize to you. I'm sorry, truly sorry, if you were offended. I didn't believe that horrible driver. I thought he was lying to me so he could get rid of me. I certainly didn't wish to give you the impression that because you're . . . you know, well, that I couldn't . . . because that wasn't it at all. I didn't even believe that man had driven me to Mary Rose's house."

She eventually had to pause for breath. Adam hadn't blinked an eye during her explanation. Harrison was impressed. He couldn't stop smiling. He wanted to ask her to explain exactly what Adam was, just to watch her squirm, but because he was a gentleman, he didn't give in to the urge.

Cole didn't have any such reservations. Being a gentleman obviously didn't rank high on his list. He had just reached the steps leading up

252

to the porch when Eleanor started her convoluted apology.

"Adam's a 'you know'? What's that?" he asked her.

She turned to frown at the brother. "I was apologizing because I didn't believe Adam was Mary Rose's brother. She only told me she had four older brothers and a mama who lived in the South somewhere, but she never gave me any details. I will admit, I never asked."

She paused to look Cole up and down. "Your sister was obviously jesting with me in the stagecoach when she said you and the other two were just like Adam. You aren't, of course."

She dismissed the brother from her thoughts then and there and turned back to Adam. "May I still come inside, sir?"

"Please," Adam said. "You're welcome to stay with us."

"Wait a minute. I still want to know . . ."

"Let it go, Cole," Adam suggested. His tone didn't leave room for argument.

Eleanor walked over to the doorway. She waved her hand in Harrison's direction, in an action that reminded him of England's queen.

"Fetch my bags out of the dirt and put them in my room," she commanded.

Cole grinned at Harrison. He smiled back at the brother. Then Harrison turned to Eleanor. "Sorry, Miss, but I can't fetch for you," he announced. "I'm not allowed on the second floor."

Harrison went down the steps. "Guess that leaves you to do the fetching," he drawled out on his way past the brother.

"Be sure to dust them off before you bring them inside, Kyle," she commanded.

Harrison heard a blasphemy and decided then and there that the day was beginning to look better. He spotted Douglas running out of the barn. MacHugh was chasing him. The stallion was obviously in one of his moods and was taking his bad temper out on the brother. Yes, sir, the day was looking better and better.

"Adam, I want to talk to you about something important," Cole called out. He had to shout at his brother so he'd hear him above Harrison's laughter.

Adam let Eleanor walk past him before answering Cole. "I won't be long," he promised.

"What do you need to do?"

"Talk to Miss Border," he answered. "It shouldn't take any time at all."

Adam was partially correct in his estimation. The talk with Eleanor didn't take any time at all. It took three long hours.

The private discussion started out strained. An hour later Adam found himself in the most ludicrous position of getting the front of his shirt all wet again. Eleanor turned out to be a little like Mary Rose. After vehemently insisting she never, ever cried, she wept all over him.

Cole got tired of waiting for Adam to finish up. He was determined to talk to him about Harrison. Finding out their houseguest was an attorney had rattled him. He wanted to get Adam's take on the situation before he made a real issue out of the discovery.

He heard all the commotion inside the library, opened the door to find out what was going on, and then stood there watching in stunned disbelief. Eleanor had her arms wrapped around Adam's waist and was sobbing and trying to talk at the same time. Cole couldn't make out any of the words. It all sounded like gibberish to him. Adam's reaction was amusing to watch. He stood there in the center of the library with his hands up in the air, looking as though he'd just been told to reach for the sky. Cole's brother appeared to be horribly uncomfortable, and definitely helpless.

Adam finally reached down with one hand and awkwardly patted Eleanor on her shoulder. He noticed Cole watching from the doorway, glared at him because he was smiling, and then motioned him to leave.

Cole immediately closed the door.

Neither brother mentioned the incident during supper. Eleanor had chosen to stay in her room. Mary Rose had taken a tray of food up to her and a fresh pot of tea she hoped would calm the overwrought woman.

She was the last to join everyone at the dining room table.

"Sorry I'm late," she said. "Eleanor isn't going to come down and eat with us tonight. She's all tuckered out."

She took her seat adjacent to Adam. "She certainly likes you," she whispered to her oldest brother. "Of course, she doesn't realize yet how stubborn you can be."

"I don't believe she likes Adam at all," Douglas

interjected. "Fact is, I think she might be prejudiced."

Cole shook his head. He had thought the same thing until he saw her with her arms wrapped around Adam. She wouldn't be holding on to someone she hated.

"No, she's just rude," he told the family.

"You sure?" Douglas asked. "I don't want her around here if you aren't sure."

"I'm sure."

"What do you have a bee in your bonnet about, Mary Rose? You're frowning like you're stewing over something or other," Travis asked.

"I refused to give her permission to ride up to the ridge this afternoon," Adam said.

"I am not a child. I don't understand why you think . . ."

"We have a houseguest," Adam said. "Kindly remember that."

She immediately closed her mouth and turned to Harrison.

"Can't we start? I'm starving," Douglas asked. He reached for the bowl of potatoes but stopped when Adam asked him to wait another minute.

"Harrison? Do you happen to speak French?"

"Yes. Why do you ask?"

"I'd like you to indulge us for this evening."

"Certainly," Harrison agreed without having the faintest idea what the brother had just asked of him.

Adam turned to the family. "We've been remiss, these past weeks and have gotten out of the habit of saying our blessing. Mary Rose, would you like to lead us in grace?"

She nodded agreement, then bowed her head and folded her hands together in prayer.

"Au nom du Père . . ."

Harrison was once again astonished by the Clayborne family. Each and every one of them spoke French throughout the meal. Mary Rose, he noticed, had the strongest vocabulary, and he assumed she had studied the language while attending boarding school. Understanding French and Latin would have been requirements. She wasn't simply skilled, however. Both her accent and her ease in speaking the language indicated to him that she'd been studying for a long, long time.

Travis was amusing to listen to, for while he was fluent, he had a noticeable twang in his voice. He slaughtered some pronunciations. A Frenchman would have cringed hearing them.

The prayer Mary Rose had recited before supper was familiar to Harrison, but he couldn't quite put his finger on where or when he'd heard it before.

"May I ask a question?"

"Again? What now, Harrison?" Cole asked.

Harrison ignored the brother's sarcasm. "The prayer you all said is familiar, but I can't remember where I've heard it before."

"It's a Catholic prayer, called grace," Mary Rose answered. "We recite it before meals."

"Good God Almighty, you're Catholics."

He hadn't realized he'd spoken the thought out loud until he noticed everyone was staring at him. They were looking quite astonished and mystified.

"What have you got against Catholics?"

"Nothing," Harrison answered. "I was just surprised. I don't know why, but I assumed you'd be . . . something different."

"We are," Mary Rose told him.

"You're what?" Harrison asked.

"Different. We aren't always Catholics."

He leaned back in his chair. His mind was still reeling over the news. Lord Elliott was bound to be horrified. Their family didn't just belong to the Church of England. They owned the front pew.

And why in heaven's name did Harrison think the Claybornes would have joined the Church of England?

He smiled over his initial reaction to hearing the news. Lord Elliott was going to love Mary Rose just as much. He would, however, diligently try to convert her.

It finally registered with him what Mary Rose had just said about being Catholics some of the time. She wasn't making a lick of sense.

"Wait just a minute," he said. "You can't be Catholics some of the time. It's all or nothing. I know. My best friend is Catholic."

"Yet you still dislike . . ." Cole began.

Harrison wouldn't let him finish his comment. "I do not dislike Catholics. I was surprised to find out you were Catholic. There isn't any more to it than that."

"Why can't we be Catholics some of the time?" Travis asked.

"We are," Mary Rose insisted.

Harrison decided to play along. He would slowly force them with logic and patience to re-

258

alize they couldn't jest with him.

"All right, let's assume you're Catholics some of the time. Mind telling me when you are?"

"April, May, and June," she replied.

He didn't bat an eye. "What about July, August, and September?"

"Lutheran," Travis told him.

Harrison was impressed. The brother hadn't cracked a smile.

"And the next three months?"

"We're different again. We're Baptists, or at least try to follow their rules."

Harrison had had enough. "Mary Rose, are you about finished . . ."

He was going to ask her if she was finished jesting with him. She wouldn't let him complete his question, however.

"No, I'm not finished," she interrupted. "Now where was I?"

"January," Cole reminded her.

"Jewish in January, February, and March, and in April . . ."

"Jewish in January?" He practically shouted the words.

"Now, what in thunder do you have against the Jewish religion?" Cole asked. "You seem to have a lot of grudges against an awful lot of people."

Harrison closed his eyes and counted to ten. Then he once again tried to wade through the mire of confusion the Claybornes had just tossed him into and find some sort of reasonable explanation.

"I do not have any grudges," he snapped. "I'm

just trying to make some sense out of you people. None of you can be all of those religions. It's a mockery to each and every faith if you only believe their sacred doctrines three months of the year."

Adam finally took mercy on him. "We're learning all we can about the different religions, Harrison. We believe it's important to understand and respect another man's beliefs. Do you believe in the existence of God?"

"Yes, I do."

"So do we," Adam replied. "We don't belong to an organized church, however."

"Probably because there aren't any in Blue Belle," Douglas interjected. "Folks talk about building a church, but then they start arguing over the kind it will be, and so nothing gets done."

"You were probably raised to be a member of your father's church, weren't you?" Travis asked.

"Yes, I was," Harrison agreed.

"As a child, it wouldn't have occurred to you to think about joining any other church. None of us had fathers around to guide us. We do what we can, Harrison."

He couldn't fault their reasoning. "Self-education," he said.

"And understanding," Adam supplied.

Harrison nodded. "There are many different religions. Will you try to learn about all of them?"

"Even after we have committed our minds and our hearts and our souls to a specific religion, we will continue to keep an open mind about the beliefs of others. Knowledge is freedom, and

260

with freedom comes understanding."

"There are several Jewish families living in Hammond. We visit with them as often as possible. Some of the residents there dislike them. As ridiculous as it seems, they tend to dislike what they don't understand. Some even mock. Their ignorance is shameful. None of us were born Jewish, and we are therefore unable to become practicing Jews; at least from the information the families have shared with us that is the conclusion we have reached. Their traditions are rich and meaningful to them, and we find that the more we know about their faith, the richer we become. Any man who lives by his beliefs is to be admired, not mocked. Now do you understand?"

"Yes," Harrison returned. "Now tell me why you speak French," he continued. "Do you wish to understand how the people in France live?"

Even though he was seated at the opposite end of the long table from his host, Harrison could still see the sparkle that came into Adam's eyes.

He prepared for frustration once again.

"We speak French because it's Thursday."

"And?" Harrison prodded with a grin.

Mary Rose smiled at him. "And we always speak French on Tuesdays, Thursdays, and Saturdays."

Here we go again, he thought to himself. He knew exactly where this conversation was headed. "Is this discussion going to be like the one we had about the Irish?"

"Perhaps," she allowed.

261

"What did he mean about the Irish?" Travis asked.

Mary Rose turned to her brother to explain. "Harrison wanted all of us to be Irish. I can't imagine why it was important to him, but it was. I simply tried to be accommodating. He is our guest, after all. I wanted him to feel welcome."

"So that's why you told him I was Irish," Travis said with a nod.

"You are Irish, Travis."

"I know that, Cole. I only wondered why it was important to him. He's a strange duck, isn't he?"

Cole nodded. Then he turned to Harrison. "Maybe he wanted us to be Irish, and then again, maybe he didn't. You'd think, being from Scotland and all, he'd want us to be Scots, and not Irish at all. Exactly what have you got against the Irish, Harrison? What have they ever done to you?"

Harrison suddenly had the urge to pound his head against something hard. He couldn't imagine how the conversation had gotten twisted into a defense of the Irish.

He took a deep breath and tried to be reasonable once again. "I don't care if you're Irish or not," he said.

"Why not?" Cole demanded.

Harrison glared at the offensive brother. He decided that trying to have a normal conversation with any of the Claybornes was simply too difficult for him. He was ready to concede defeat.

"I pray to God I never have to cross-examine any of you in a courtroom," he remarked dryly.

"Now what's wrong with us?" Douglas asked. "We've been real hospitable, haven't we?"

"You people are completely illogical, that's what's wrong with you," Harrison announced. He didn't care if he insulted them or not. Frustration, after all, had its limits.

"Maybe we're just a little too logical for you," Cole reasoned. "Ever think of that possibility?"

"I simply wondered why you speak French three nights of the week," he replied.

"Tuesdays, Thursdays, and Saturdays," Cole had the gall to remind him with a grin.

The brothers were all enjoying his frustration. Harrison was slow to catch on this evening, but he wasn't completely dimwitted. He decided they had all had enough sport.

He deliberately changed the subject. "Mary Rose, are you feeling all right?"

"Yes, thank you," she answered.

"She took quite a pounding this morning," Harrison told Adam.

"Apparently so," Adam agreed. His voice was mild, pleasant.

"She looks better," Douglas remarked.

"Better" didn't adequately describe how she looked to Harrison. He thought she was just as beautiful as ever, bruises and all. Her forehead had a bump near her temple the size of a small rock. He couldn't see the cut, however, because her curls covered it. The corner of her mouth was also swollen. It probably stung, he thought. It didn't matter to him. He still wanted to kiss her.

"He's doing it again, Cole."

"Who's doing what, Douglas?"

"Harrison's gawking at Mary Rose."

"I was simply taking inventory of her injuries," Harrison defended. "You're very resilient, Mary Rose. You're to be complimented for your stamina."

"I'm not at all delicate," she replied. She gave Adam a quick frown before she added, "My brothers can't seem to understand that fact."

"Don't start with us, Mary Rose," Cole warned.

"Don't start what?" she asked, looking as sweet and innocent as a babe.

"You look delicate," Harrison admitted out loud.

"Well, I'm not, so don't get the notion you can tell me what to do. I get enough of that nonsense around here."

Harrison raised an eyebrow over the vehemence in her tone of voice. Mary Rose obviously was in a rotten mood. He wasn't certain what had set her off, but he was intelligent enough not to ask her to tell him what the problem was. She looked as if she wanted to tear someone's head off. His, he decided, was fine right where it was.

"Don't ask her any questions," Cole said in a loud whisper.

"I wouldn't dare," Harrison replied.

"What was it you wanted to talk to me about?" Adam asked Cole.

"Harrison," Cole answered. "I wanted to talk to you about our houseguest. I got tired of waiting for you to finish talking with Eleanor, so I went back to work. Anyway, I know now why Harrison asks so many questions. He just can't help it. You heard what he said about cross-examining us in a courtroom, so you've figured out by now . . ."

"He's a lawyer," Travis interjected before his brother could finish.

Cole frowned at his brother because he'd stolen his thunder. Then he put the rudeness aside and continued on.

"He thought he had told us, but I think maybe he forgot on purpose. He must have guessed we wouldn't have allowed him to stay with us if we'd known what he did for a living. We got our standards, after all."

Douglas looked stunned by the news. Cole was puzzled by his reaction.

"Weren't you listening to him a couple of minutes ago? Only lawyers cross-examine people," Cole said.

"I wasn't paying attention," Douglas admitted. "Why didn't he admit it to us? He had plenty of opportunities."

"It's extremely rude to talk about a guest when he's in the room," Harrison interjected.

"Isn't it better than waiting for him to leave and then talking about him behind his back?" Cole asked.

"You shouldn't talk about him at all," Harrison instructed.

"Why didn't you tell us?" Douglas asked.

"He thought he had mentioned it," Cole said. "Everyone in town knows, even Dooley."

"Well, we didn't know, now did we?" Douglas

said. "Honest to heaven, I'm mad enough to hit him."

"I already did," Cole boasted.

"Yes, he did," Mary Rose said. Her frown was scorching. "Right in Morrison's kitchen. Your brother has excellent table manners, Adam. Wouldn't you agree, Harrison?"

Everyone at the table turned to see whose side he was going to take. Harrison decided to be completely honest with his answer. "Perhaps," he allowed. "However, I will admit I was going to hit him back, but then I noticed you were watching."

"You knew I was watching?" she asked.

He nodded. Her frown intensified. "Yet you still let Catherine Morrison drape herself all over you?"

"She wasn't draped all over me, was she, Cole?"

Since their guest had defended him a minute ago, Cole felt he had to do the same.

"No, she wasn't. She was just being polite, wasn't she, Travis?"

"Maybe a little too polite for my liking," Travis said. "But she was real polite with me too, so I guess it was all right."

"In other words, she was also draped all over you," Mary Rose snapped.

Harrison happened to look at Adam then. He was surprised to notice he was smiling. Mary Rose's reaction to Catherine obviously amused him.

"Why do you care what she does to Harrison?" Cole asked.

"I happen to believe a hostess should be a little

less hospitable," she muttered.

"She was hospitable all right," Cole replied.

"Mary Rose, if you'd quit being stubborn and let go of your grudge against Catherine because of the things she did to you when you were little girls, you'd see what a nice woman she's become. Why, she's sweet and innocent and kind-hearted."

Adam suddenly changed the subject.

"I have a question I'd like to ask all of you," he announced. He waited until he had everyone's undivided attention, and then said, "I'm curious to know where all of you were while Mary Rose was getting beaten. Anyone mind telling me?"

Everyone started explaining at the same time. Cole was so rattled by what he felt was implied criticism, he forgot to speak French while he gave his list of reasons why he wasn't looking out for their sister.

Mary Rose was right in the middle of the shouting match. She kept insisting she was perfectly capable of looking out for herself. No one paid any attention to a word she said.

Harrison was fascinated by the change that had come over Adam. He was, as an Englishman would say, bloody furious. It was the first time the oldest brother had ever shown real emotion. The look in his eyes was every bit as chilling as his voice. Travis was coming up with some dandies for why he wasn't watching out for his sister. Cole wasn't making much sense at all, and Douglas was still trying to get his excuses in.

Just as surprising to Harrison was his own behavior. He hadn't simply joined in the argument. He was in the thick of it. He was every bit as loud and obnoxious as Cole was each time he tried to be heard over the others.

He was having the time of his life. Suppers back home were always dignified. And boring. No one ever spoke above a whisper, and no one ever interrupted anyone else to make a point. Only unimportant issues were ever discussed, and Harrison hadn't realized until now how terribly dull his life had been, and how very, very controlled.

"Adam, will you please listen to me," Mary demanded in a near shout. She pounded her hand on the table to get his attention. "I want you to acknowledge that I am a fully grown woman and can take care of myself. Don't you realize how insulting this discussion is to me?'

She didn't like his answer. "You may be excused now, sister. Why don't you go into the parlor and practice your music? I haven't heard you playing in a long while."

She wanted to protest. The look on her brother's face changed her mind.

Everyone stood up when she left the dining room. They were following Harrison's lead. As soon as their sister was out of sight, they sat back down and started yelling again.

Harrison didn't continue to fight for Adam's attention. He leaned back in his chair and watched the brothers battle it out.

Cole had calmed down sufficiently enough to speak French again. He was now cursing in the language. He seemed to know every colorful blasphemy in the French vocabulary.

"Honest to God, she was there one minute,

then she was gone. All I did was turn around and she disappeared on me."

His explanation was the only one that made any sense. Travis was still hedging with his excuses, and nothing he said was at all plausible. Douglas was fully occupied accusing Cole of not paying attention. He reminded his brothers that he was inside the stable and therefore couldn't possibly have been expected to watch Mary Rose. No man could be in two places at the same time.

"Then why did you expect me to be inside the general store and outside at the same time?" Cole asked.

"All right, all right," Travis shouted. "I was on my way over to see Catherine. I should have stayed in town, but I thought you were watching her, Douglas."

Adam turned his gaze on Harrison. "And what were you doing?"

He didn't give any excuses. "I take full responsibility. I got involved in a discussion about the cattle roundup and simply didn't notice her leaving the store."

Adam nodded. He scanned each face before he spoke again. "This cannot happen again. Mary Rose can take care of herself. I realize we aren't her keepers. She also shares the blame because she went searching for trouble. She knows better. She didn't even have a gun with her," he added with a shake of his head. "Our sister let her anger get the better of her. However, now that she's inside the parlor and unable to protest, I'll remind you that she is indeed delicate. She may not like her physical limitations, but that isn't important to us. She could have been killed."

"Yes, she could have," Cole agreed. "Bickley's short, but he's more than twice her weight and muscle."

"His friends were big," Douglas said.

"His friends? There were other men hurting her?"

The brothers flinched over the roar of Adam's displeasure. Cole and Travis turned to Harrison for help. Douglas stared hard at his coffee cup.

"No one else struck her," Harrison explained. "I was able to convince Bickley not to run away. Your brothers would have done the same thing. I just happened to be the first to get to her."

"How did you convince Bickley?" Adam asked. He'd calmed down enough to speak in a normal tone of voice.

"With my fists," Harrison admitted. "I lost my temper. I'm not sorry about that. I could have killed all of them, but I didn't. The men are being taken back to Hammond. The authorities will deal with them."

"What makes you think the sheriff will do anything?" Adam asked.

"Are you saying he won't?" Harrison asked.

"It's doubtful. We live in Blue Belle. The folks in Hammond take care of their own. God only knows, the sheriff has enough to contend with. He'll probably slap their hands and let them go."

"Do you think they'll come back to Blue Belle?" Harrison asked.

"Eventually," Adam said. "Trash always drifts through our town. I don't think Bickley will come

270

after Rose though. You'd be his target, Harrison. I believe all of us should stay on our guards."

The brothers couldn't agree fast enough. Adam smiled. "I'm glad we cleared the air. Harrison, about a month ago, we purchased three hundred head of cattle from a rancher who lives near the falls. Will you be staying around long enough to help us bring them to Rosehill?"

He wasn't given sufficient time to come up with an answer. Douglas gave his opinion first. "He doesn't know how to rope a steer, Adam. Do you, Harrison?"

"No. But I . . ."

"Let me guess," Cole drawled out. " 'It can't be all that difficult,' right? Isn't that what you said about breaking in the horses?"

"I was perhaps a bit inept," Harrison conceded. "However, I'm certain that if you give me a rope and show me how to use it, I'll get the hang of it in no time at all."

"He's a glutton for pain, isn't he?" Douglas remarked.

"When are you going to realize you're completely out of your element?" Cole asked.

"Just after I smash your face in, Cole."

Everyone laughed. They didn't think he was serious. "Yes, sir, you sure are easy to like," Cole said.

"Why is that?" Harrison asked.

"You're the only one who stands up to him," Douglas explained. "That's why he likes you. You might not be too smart, but you sure have courage. Cole isn't used to anyone talking back to him."

Harrison shrugged. "How far away is this rancher with the cattle you purchased?"

"About two days' ride," Cole answered. "You can start working with a rope the day after tomorrow. You have to finish up with the mustangs first. You've still got that stubborn one to break in. Remember?"

Harrison let out a sigh. "I remember. The speckled one. He hasn't been ready to listen to reason yet. He's getting there though. I can feel him warming to the idea. He's a lot like you, Cole. Real stubborn. I'll probably have better luck with him tomorrow."

"You'd already be finished if you didn't waste so much time talking everything over with the horses first. They don't understand a word you say to them. You must realize that."

"I'm getting them used to my voice," Harrison explained. "They're stubborn, yes, but also frightened. I'm not the only one who talks to the horses. I've heard Douglas."

"He's right," Douglas admitted. "I do talk to them."

"Douglas, will you please go and remind Mary Rose it's her turn to clear the table? Harrison, you can have the duty tomorrow night."

"Certainly. What does the task involve?"

"Haven't you ever had to clean up the dishes before?" Cole asked.

"No, I haven't."

"You sure were pampered, weren't you?" Travis remarked.

"I suppose I was."

Douglas had gotten up from his chair and

272

walked over to the door. He paused at the threshold, then turned around and hurried back to the table.

"I'm not going in there. You go get her, Travis."

Douglas sat down just as Travis stood up. "She's playing Beethoven," Douglas warned.

"Which one?" Travis asked.

"The Fifth."

He sat down again. "Let's send Harrison."

All the brothers laughed. Cole explained what was amusing. "You don't want to mess with Mary Rose when she's playing Beethoven."

"Meaning?"

"She's in a real sour mood," Cole explained. "Whenever we hear 'The Fifth,' we run the other way. You're safe if it's Mozart or Chopin," he added. "She's really pounding it out tonight, isn't she, Adam?"

His brother smiled. "Yes, she is," he agreed. "Harrison, are you ready to go into the library?"

Harrison agreed with a nod and stood up. He followed Adam out of the room.

The two men had fallen into the habit of capping each evening with a spirited debate. Harrison looked forward to the mental sparring. The first few times he allowed Adam to win, or at least he believed he'd allowed him the victories, but eventually his own competitive nature demanded he take a few wins as well.

Debating Adam was challenging. Harrison thoroughly enjoyed it, almost as much as Adam did.

He took his seat in one of the two soft leather chairs in front of the hearth and picked up the notebook from the side table. He moved the ink bottle and pen closer to his reach.

Adam poured each of them a shot glass filled to the brim with brandy. He handed Harrison his drink and then sat down across from his guest.

Harrison propped his feet up on the footstool. "What's our topic tonight?"

"I've given the matter a good deal of thought, and decided on the final invasion of Carthage." He seemed to savor each word he said.

"We can't talk about the end until we have examined the beginning," Harrison replied.

Adam slapped his knee. "Precisely so," he said. "The Greeks, you must realize, were a proud and highly intelligent people."

His opening statement established his position. Harrison countered with his thesis. "As were the Spartans. They were also invincible fighting men, with superior skills in every area, including battle plans. Their superiority cannot be disputed."

Thus the debate began. The two men argued for well over an hour. When Adam finally suggested a halt, Harrison counted up the points each had had to concede to the other. He and Adam were disappointed to find out the evening had ended in a draw.

Adam stayed in the library to read before going up to bed. Harrison said good night and started back to the bunkhouse.

Mary Rose was waiting for him on the front porch. Her golden hair was a beacon in the moonlight.

"Why aren't you in bed? It's late."

"I needed some air," she answered. "I'll walk with you."

Harrison waited for her at the bottom of the stairs. They walked side by side across the yard.

"I'm restless tonight."

"Didn't Beethoven help you get rid of your anger?"

She could hear the amusement in his voice. She smiled in reaction. "I wasn't angry, just frustrated. My brothers can be overbearing. They're forever trying to interfere."

"I don't think they interfere enough," he told her. "It's dangerous out here."

"And I'm a weak, little woman, right?"

He shook his head. "I'm not about to get into that discussion. I don't have a piano in the bunkhouse, and that would leave me to take the pounding."

"Then you believe I'm incapable . . ."

"I didn't give an opinion one way or another," he said. "You do have one habit that irritates me to no end, Mary Rose. You always jump to conclusions before you have all the facts."

Her hand brushed against his. "I do?" she asked.

"Yes, you do."

She deliberately brushed against him again. He didn't take the hint. The man was either shy or dense, she decided. Subtlety was wasted on him. She guessed she would have to be bold if she was going to get him to cooperate, and that conclusion irritated her to no end.

She grabbed hold of his hand and moved closer to his side. Harrison would either have to fling

275

her aside or shove her, and he was simply too much of a gentleman to behave in such an ungentlemanly fashion. He was stuck with her, whether he liked it or not.

Her show of affection took him by surprise. He didn't pull his hand away. He squeezed hers instead and held on tight.

"You spend an awful lot of time talking to Adam," she remarked in what she hoped was a casual tone of voice. She was nervous about bringing up the subject, and she didn't want him to notice.

"You think so?"

"Yes, I do."

He didn't say another word. She kept hoping he would explain why, and when he continued to keep silent, she decided to prod him.

"I wonder why you talk to him every night," she began again.

Her voice was strained. He looked down at her to find out if she was just worried about something or actually afraid.

All he could see was the top of her head. She was staring down at the ground and wouldn't look at him. Her hand was trembling though, indicating she was very concerned about something or other.

He knew better than to take the direct approach to find out what was wrong. The only way to get Mary Rose to make sense was to go in through the back door.

"I enjoy talking to him."

"I thought you did."

"Yes."

"What do you talk about?"

"This and that."

"Be more specific."

"Why? What is it you want to know?"

"I was curious."

"We talk about all sorts of things."

"Like what?"

"Like the war between your states, and why no one ever called it a war while it was going on. What did you think we were talking about?"

"I thought you might be asking him questions. You do tend to be overly curious by nature."

"What would I ask him questions about?"

"His background."

"No, I didn't ask him about his background."

It wasn't until he'd given the admission that he realized how telling it was. He hadn't asked her brother one single question about his past. He had deliberately wasted perfect opportunities to try to find out more about the family.

He was astonished by his own behavior. He hadn't kept his priorities straight, and the realization appalled him. He had come to Montana Territory in search of the truth, yet now, when there was just one vital piece of information needed to fit the entire sequence of events together and find the culprit responsible for the kidnapping, he had ceased and desisted.

He understood the reason for his reluctance. The truth was going to tear the Clayborne family apart. Honest to God, it was tearing him apart just thinking about the pain he would cause all of them.

Mary Rose was holding on to his hand now,

letting him feel her affection for him, but he knew that when she found out why he had stayed with her family, she would despise him.

He didn't want her hatred; he wanted and needed her love.

Harrison quickened his step. He was suddenly furious with himself. He needed time alone to think things through and come to some sort of resolution. He'd become emotionally involved with the Clayborne family without even noticing what was happening to him. He liked all of them, cared about them, worried about them. Hell, he even enjoyed disliking Cole.

Oh, yes, he had a lot to think about tonight.

"Harrison, I didn't mean to insult you by suggesting you would pry," Mary Rose whispered.

"I didn't think that," he replied.

"You aren't angry?"

"No, of course not." He slowed his step and tried to calm down.

"Then do quit squeezing my hand."

He immediately let go of her. "It's cold tonight. You should go back to the house," he said abruptly.

"I'm not cold," she said. It finally occurred to her that he might be trying to get away from her.

She fervently hoped she was wrong. "Are you worried about something?"

"Like what?" he asked.

"That I might kiss you again."

Her remark was absurd. He couldn't help but laugh. "I kissed you," he reminded her.

"I assisted."

"All right, we were both culpable."

"Culpable," she repeated. "You're a lawyer all right. I wish you weren't."

"Explain."

"Lawyers bother us."

"Why?"

She shrugged. She wasn't going to explain any further. Harrison didn't let go of his question. He decided it was high time he got a suitable answer.

"Were you worried I would ask Adam questions about the family or about his background?"

They had stopped walking and now faced each other. The moonlight cast a golden canopy all around them.

"I just didn't want you to bother him. Adam doesn't like to talk about parts of his growing-up years. He was in bondage, Harrison. That is all you need to know."

"What does he like to talk about?" he asked. "Is the time he spent in New York City off limits for conversation as well?"

"No."

"How about the time he spent getting here? Will he talk about the journey, or should I avoid the subject altogether?"

"I don't believe he would mind talking about the journey. My brothers are quite proud of what they accomplished."

Harrison couldn't stop himself from taking hold of her and pulling her closer to him. It wasn't a physical response to her this time. He just wanted to keep her close for as long as he could.

She seemed to understand what he needed, for she put her arms around his waist and hugged him tight.

"You were very lonely growing up, weren't you?"

"If I was, I didn't know it," he answered. His chin dropped to rest on the top of her head. He closed his eyes and let himself feel the pleasure she was offering him.

"Until now?" she whispered into the collar of his shirt.

"Yes, until now."

She was trying to comfort him. Harrison was almost overwhelmed by her gentleness and her understanding. She had so much love inside her. She made him feel . . . complete somehow. Life had been empty, hollow, terribly cold. Mary Rose, sweet, loving Mary Rose. What in God's name was he going to do about her?

He finally forced himself to let go of her. Getting her to let go of him took a little longer. He had to pull her hands away from him.

"I'm not going to ask you to kiss me. You needn't worry about that."

"You need to go home, Mary Rose. Come on, I'll walk with you."

"But I just walked you to your home."

"Good night then."

"Good night."

She turned to leave. Harrison clasped his hands behind his back and watched her. He was completely caught off guard when she suddenly turned again and threw herself into his arms. She wrapped her arms around his neck, leaned up on her tiptoes, and gave him a long, thoroughly inadequate kiss.

He couldn't stop himself from taking over. His arms wrapped her in his embrace, and then he showed her how he wanted to be kissed. His mouth was hot, open, devouring. His tongue moved inside to mate with hers, and, heaven help him, he couldn't seem to get enough of her.

The kiss turned carnal. He never wanted it to stop. The husky little sound she made in the back of her throat intoxicated him. Everything about her was magical to him, and when he realized he wanted much, much more from her, he immediately pulled back.

She stared up at him, her lips rosy and swollen from his kisses, her eyes misty with passion, and all he wanted to think about was pulling her back into his arms again.

"Good night." Her voice was a throaty whisper.

She didn't move. Harrison was inordinately pleased with her bemused state of mind. He understood that passion was new to her, and because she didn't have any experience to guide her, she was vulnerable because she trusted him. Mary Rose was a strong woman. She wouldn't allow any man to take advantage of her. She had high values and morals, but she was nonetheless vulnerable with him. It was, therefore, his duty to keep her from being hurt.

Harrison watched her until she reached the house and went inside. And still he didn't move. What in God's name was he going to do? Mary Rose was falling in love with him. He could have stopped the infatuation before it became more serious. Yet he had done nothing at all to discourage her.

Why hadn't he? Harrison blanched over the truth. It had been staring him in the face for over a week now. He knew exactly why he hadn't discouraged her.

He was in love with her.

August 2, 1864

Dear Mama Rose,

We read in the Hammond paper about another battle that was fought right around where you and Mistress Livonia live. Of course we all started worrying. We've heard so many terrible stories about the riots for food and medical supplies. A week after we read the paper, your letter arrived telling us you were doing just fine. You're probably shaking your head over our foolishness. You keep telling us to have faith in God and let Him do the worrying, but sometimes it's hard to hand things over to Him. We try, Mama. I guess that ought to count for something.

We're sure sorry to hear the new treatment didn't improve Mistress Livonia's eyes. Don't you think all those beatings her husband inflicted on her might have something to do with her blurred eyesight now? I remember seeing her all bruised and bloodied. Please tell her we're thinking about her and praying for a recovery from the cross she's been given.

I hope her sons are leaving the two of you alone. Some of the things they've done to their own mama makes us sick inside. How can her sons be so cruel? Cole's worried the boys will try to bother you the way their father did, but I told him to have more faith in you. As long as you keep on your guard and stay close to their mother, they won't dare come after you. I pray I'm right.

There was another of Lincoln's fine speeches reprinted in the paper. He gave the talk several years ago, Mama. Did you know he called us Black Men instead of slaves? Black seems more dignified to me than some of the other names I've heard. Cole wonders why everyone can't be just called men and women. He doesn't see any reason in having to be more specific. I wish it were all that simple, but people have strange notions about anyone who isn't just like him. Why does being a different color make people hate?

One night all of us brothers got into a discussion about the differences in the races. I asked Travis if he thought the men who wrote the Declaration of Independence for us worried about the color of a man's skin. It says in our laws that all men are created equal. I told my brothers I didn't believe Jefferson was thinking about including black men when he wrote down his rules for government, but Douglas said it shouldn't matter. Equal is equal, no matter what color your skin is or what religion you practice, and so on. We all ended up agreeing on one thing. A lot of southern folks never took the time to read the Constitution.

Mary Rose likes to help with the dishes now. She's careful with the two china cups Travis got for her. He promised her that as soon as he could barter for a couple more, he'd show her how to have a proper tea party. He's trying to find a teapot now, and knowing

Travis, he won't fail. He doesn't know anything about what's proper, of course, but he is sure Mrs. Morrison will be happy to show him how it's done, and then we can teach our sister. Cole swears he isn't having any part in tea parties, but he'll change his mind. He always does.

Cole finally started work on our house. One thing after another prevented him from beginning the project last year. First there was the barn for Douglas, then winter set in before he could put in the cellar, and the following spring, he had to spend all his time hunting for food and horses to barter. We sold every one of the mustangs he captured. The mountains are filled with opportunities. Cole can't work on the house while his brothers work gathering up horses. He knows our income depends on catching the wild ones and training them before anyone else does. Douglas is getting a reputation around Blue Belle. Folks come from miles around to get his opinion on what should be done about an ailing cow or a persnickety hen. My brother does have a gift of knowing what should be done.

We've all started working hard to clean up our language because Mary Rose is swearing all the time now. Cole came up with the idea of writing a new word on the chalkboard every morning. We all have to use the word sometime during the day. He thought it would be good for all of us to increase our vocabulary, and of course sister will also benefit. She doesn't like to be left out of anything.

I'm enclosing everyone's personal notes to you. I'll write again real soon, Mama.

God keep you safe,
Adam

9

Friday turned out to be another lesson in humility. Harrison was up bright and early. He was determined to get the last of the horses he'd been assigned calmed down and decent before noon.

He missed his deadline by several hours, but by late afternoon, and at least ten bruises later, the speckled mustang was finally obeying.

Douglas was impressed with Harrison's patience and endurance. He shouted to Cole to come over and see for himself what a fine job their houseguest had done.

"Look how sweet and docile Speckle is now," he remarked to his brother. "Harrison calmed him down all right."

Douglas had his arms draped over the top of the fence. He motioned for Harrison to ride Speckle over so he could give him a word of praise.

"You've done a remarkable job," he praised.

"I used patience and understanding," Harrison replied. He stared at Cole during his boast. "You would do well to learn a little of both."

Cole scoffed. "Patience and understanding? Hell, Harrison, you talked and talked until that poor animal would have done anything to get you to shut up."

Harrison refused to be goaded into an argument. He had better things to think about than Mary

287

Rose's stubborn, never-give-an-inch brother.

He dismounted and removed both the saddle and blanket. Speckle followed him over to the fence. Harrison draped the equipment over the top, then took hold of the bridle and led the animal over to the largest of the corrals, where the other mustangs were being kept.

Going inside the fenced area with Speckle turned out to be a mistake. It took him a long, long time to get the bridle off the horse, for the other mustangs were crowding around Harrison and nipping each other in their attempt to get his undivided attention. Each horse apparently craved a little notice, and Harrison couldn't leave until he had patted and praised every one of them.

He took the long way around the corral so he wouldn't have to get into another discussion with Cole, picked up the blanket and saddle on his way, and continued on across the yard and into the barn.

Douglas and Cole both stared at the horses.

"Did you notice?" Douglas whispered to his brother.

Cole smiled. "I noticed all right." Then he shook his head. The mustangs were so besotted with Harrison they had circled the inside of the fence in a cluster and kept pace with their master as he walked around the outside.

"I've never seen animals act like that before," Douglas said. "Are you willing to admit Harrison's talking might have worked a little magic?"

Cole shrugged. "I'll admit it, but not in front of Harrison. I wonder if he'll try to sweet-talk the steers into following him home."

"Probably will," Douglas replied. "Have you seen Travis?" he asked then.

"He's hiding in the barn."

Douglas didn't have to ask why their youngest brother had taken shelter inside the barn. The reason was sitting on the front porch.

Eleanor Border was rocking back and forth in Adam's favorite chair, while she fanned herself with Mary Rose's treasured, only-used-on-special-occasions fan.

Douglas and Cole both turned to frown at their unwanted guest just as their sister came hurrying outside with a fresh glass of juice for Eleanor.

"That woman sure is running Mary Rose ragged," Cole commented.

Douglas agreed with a nod. "Do you think she'll ever let our sister leave for the ridge?"

"I doubt it," Cole replied. "At least not today. Mary Rose has been trying to leave since early morning and it's going on three now."

"It's her own fault, letting the time get away from her," Douglas remarked. "She's going along with Eleanor's bossing. Mary Rose carried up two trays to her this morning. Eleanor didn't like the first breakfast cook prepared, so our sister fixed her another one."

Cole shook his head. "She never lets us boss her around," he said. "Besides, she shouldn't have fixed her anything. Eleanor wouldn't be acting like a persnickety princess if she wasn't being treated like one."

"I think we should talk to Adam tonight," Douglas suggested. "He's being unreasonable about Eleanor staying here. You and Travis and

I could gang up on him. We'll vote to give Eleanor the boot. Mary Rose and Adam will vote to let her stay, of course, but it won't matter. Majority rules."

Cole's conscience got in the way of his agreement. He couldn't block the memory of seeing Eleanor in such an anguished state. The poor woman had sounded plumb pitiful as she wept against Adam's chest. Even though Cole hated to admit it, the memory gave him a heartache.

"Let's not jump the gun, Douglas. I say we wait a couple of days before we put it to a vote. Adam must have had some sound reasons for letting the woman stay with us."

"Why hasn't he told us his reasons?"

"I guess he isn't ready to," Cole replied. "Maybe Eleanor will quit complaining in a day or so. She's about covered every topic around."

"She'll just start over," Douglas predicted. "She sure likes to hear herself whine, doesn't she?"

Cole smiled. He stared at the woman under discussion and couldn't help but notice how pretty she might be if she ever tried to smile. "It's the red in her hair," he told his brother. "Makes her temperamental."

"Travis has red in his hair, and he isn't temperamental."

"He's hiding in the barn, isn't he? That sounds a might temperamental to me."

Harrison walked over to join the two men. Douglas turned to him. "Can you believe it? Cole's defending Eleanor."

"I only said we should give her a couple of days before we take a vote to toss her out," Cole countered. "I think she's scared and that's why she acts bossy."

Harrison nodded agreement. "I believe she's frightened too. Being difficult must give her some sense of control over her current situation."

Douglas shook his head. "I think you both have turned into milk toast. I'm going with Travis over to Hammond to barter and sell a couple of my horses. Are either of you interested in tagging along?"

"Will you be stopping by Pauline's place?" Cole asked.

"Who is Pauline?" Harrison asked.

"She runs a house outside of the town," Douglas said. "Just past Sneeze Junction."

"She's . . ." Harrison began.

"Friendly," Cole supplied.

Harrison declined the invitation. Cole, Travis, and Douglas left for the junction a short while later. The brothers had made the assumption that because of the lateness in the day, their sister wouldn't still want to go up to the ridge to take Crazy Corrie supplies.

They were mistaken in their assumption. The duty of escorting Mary Rose would fall on Adam's or Harrison's shoulders.

Adam let Harrison decide. He called him into the kitchen and explained the situation. "One of us has to stay here and keep Eleanor company. The other one has to go up to the ridge with Mary Rose."

"I thought you never left the ranch," Harrison remarked.

"Where did you hear that?"

291

"In town. Dooley or Ghost mentioned it."

"I only avoid going into town, Harrison. The mountains are my home. I often hunt with Cole, and fishing is my favorite pastime," he added with a nod.

"I would rather go with Mary Rose," Harrison said.

"Can you use a gun or did you exaggerate? I don't mean to insult you, but I need to know you can protect my sister if the need arises."

"Yes, I can use a gun," Harrison assured him. "If it will make you feel better, I'll carry two."

"Strap a rifle behind the saddle as well," Adam suggested. "We've had only one bad run-in with a bear in all the time we've lived here, but this time of year they're roaming for food. You might take one by surprise."

"I'll be prepared for any eventuality."

"Mary Rose can hold her own, of course. I wouldn't want you to get the notion she wasn't educated. Cole taught her how to shoot to kill. Thank God, she hasn't had to use her expertise."

"We should get going," Harrison said then.

"Just a minute more, please," Adam requested. "I'm going to be blunt instead of dancing around the issue," he said. "Mary Rose is attracted to you, and from the way you look at her during suppers, I have to assume the attraction is mutual. I expect you to behave as a gentleman. I realize I'm insulting you, but Mary Rose is more important than your feelings right now. Do I have your word?"

Harrison wasn't offended. Adam was acting like

292

a loving brother. Harrison wouldn't have expected less.

"You have my word. I'll keep Mary Rose safe, or die trying, Adam, and I will assuredly protect her honor."

Adam shook his hand and then walked with him to the front door. "I wish she'd wait until tomorrow, but she's stubborn, Harrison."

"I noticed."

Adam smiled. "Yes, of course you noticed. I'll be curious to get your take on this Corrie woman. Mary Rose tends to see only the good. Watch out for her when she's talking to her new friend. I don't like the idea of a rifle being pointed at my sister all the while she's talking."

Eleanor stood up when the two men walked out onto the porch. She nodded to Harrison and turned her attention to Adam.

"Are you letting her go, Adam? It looks like rain. She'll ruin her clothes if she rides off into a thunderstorm. I do wish you'd tell her she has to stay home."

"Where is Mary Rose?"

"She's in the barn," Eleanor answered.

"Why don't you come inside with me. You can keep me company while I prepare supper."

Eleanor looked thankful for company. She eagerly nodded and followed Adam inside.

It took Harrison and Mary Rose two hours to reach the secluded cabin tucked up high on the ridge. The climb was slow, for the trail was broken in spots and nonexistent in other sections they needed to cross.

The time passed all too quickly for Harrison.

The landscape held him in constant awe. It kept changing with every turn he made, as did the colors and the aromas, and it required his full concentration to keep his eye on Mary Rose too. His gaze wanted to linger on the cascading waterfall to the right of the zigzag path and the rolling hills on the left, thick with heavily scented pines, with clusters of small meadows tucked in between. Wildlife was plentiful in the area. The animals had come down from the higher peaks to shed their winter coats and feed on berries and sweet spring grass. There were deer and elk, mule bucks and red squirrels as thick as cottontails. A whitetail fawn, more curious than afraid, didn't move at all when they passed within inches of the animal. If Harrison had reached out, he was certain, he could have touched her brown, velvety nose.

Mary Rose became his eager guide in the wonderland. She gave names to all the wildflowers he'd never seen before and pointed out several plants the locals used to cure their aches and pains. When the trail was wide enough to accommodate both horses, they rode side by side. She stopped several times to point out animals and views she thought would interest him.

Her love for the land became more evident the higher they climbed. She pointed to a cow moose and calf feeding near a spring and whispered her opinion that they were simply adorable.

She stopped once again near the top of the ridge and motioned to the hill below.

"Brown bears," she whispered. "On the left of the stream. Do you see them, Harrison? One's just going in the water. If there were enough time, I would insist we watch them fish. They're much better at it than we are."

"How do you know they aren't grizzly bears?"

If she thought his question was foolish, she didn't let him know it. "A grizzly has a distinctive hump behind his head," she explained. "We don't see too many around here. Don't be disappointed. They can be troublesome."

"I read that some men who live in the mountains like to hunt the grizzly."

She rolled her eyes heavenward. "I'll bet you read that in a dime novel, didn't you? Those stories are all made up. Men hunting grizzly bears? Only very foolish men perhaps," she allowed.

The tiny frown that creased her brow as she gave the earnest explanation and the enthusiastic tone of voice as she instructed him made him smile.

He suddenly realized he was as much in awe of her as he was of the land.

"Why are you smiling? Don't you believe me?" she asked.

"I believe you. I'm smiling because you make me happy."

She was inordinately pleased with his compliment. "Thank you," she said.

"Mary Rose?"

"Yes?"

"Why are we whispering?"

The look of surprise on her face told him she hadn't realized they had been whispering. She laughed with delight.

"Adam and I used to whisper whenever we were up here. I was much younger then, and he tended to let me have my way."

"But why did you want to whisper?" he asked.

"You'll laugh," she predicted.

He assured her he wouldn't. Then he had to promise. She made him.

"I whispered because I thought I was in God's backyard."

"You what?"

"You haven't been around many children, have you, Harrison?"

"No, I suppose I haven't. You really thought you were in . . ."

"Yes, I did," she interrupted. "It seemed appropriate to whisper to show my respect."

"And now that you're all grown up? What do you think now?"

She decided to be completely honest with him. "That I'm still in God's backyard."

He burst into laughter. She had to wait for him to quiet down before she spoke again. "I like it when you laugh, even though you promised you wouldn't. Whenever you smile, which is a rare occurrence indeed, the worry lines at the corners of your eyes crinkle up. It's very appealing. You do worry too much."

"I do?" He was actually surprised by her opinion. He couldn't imagine anyone worrying too much. The notion seemed foreign to him. When a man worried, he stayed on edge, always ready, always prepared for any eventuality.

"Oh, yes, you worry too much."

She softened her criticism by smiling at him. He immediately smiled back. And still they lingered. Neither one of them wanted to move. The moment suddenly became filled with promise. A new intimacy flowed between them, in this peaceful interlude when the outside world couldn't invade. Just now she belonged only to him. He didn't have to share her with anyone.

A clap of thunder sounded in the distance, but Harrison ignored the warning. So did Mary Rose. She was fully occupied staring at him. He was just as content to stare at her.

A twig snapped behind them. Harrison reacted with lightning speed. He turned in the saddle, his gun drawn and cocked, and waited for the next sound. A rabbit raced across the trail then, and Harrison put his gun away.

Mary Rose watched him in astonishment. She hadn't ever seen anyone move that fast, except Cole, of course, but brothers didn't count, and she couldn't help but worry about where and why he had developed the skill. Or was it instinct?

He was making her nervous again. There was definitely more than one layer to the man, and she didn't know how she felt about that.

"Now you're frowning. What's wrong?" he asked.

"The way you moved just now. That's what's wrong. You're used to being on your guard, aren't you?"

He didn't answer her. She shook her head. "You're a complicated man. You behave one way and then do something that changes what I'm supposed to think you are. I wish you'd stop it."

"Surprises can be good, can't they?"

"How?"

"Intrigue," he replied. "Occasionally surprising someone could be . . ."

She didn't let him finish his argument. "I'm already intrigued. I like you just the way you are."

"You like me the way you think I am."

"You're driving me crazy, Harrison."

He laughed. "You make me crazy too, Mary Rose."

She turned away from him. "I won't get into a discussion of the flaws in your personality now. There isn't enough time. It's getting late, and if we don't hurry, I won't have any time at all to visit with my friend. Please quit dawdling."

Harrison wasn't about to let her have the last word. "I have never dawdled in my life."

Her unladylike snort was her rebuttal.

He wasn't irritated. In fact, he couldn't stop smiling. He hadn't felt this good in a long, long time. Peace and contentment seemed to radiate from the mountain. And when he looked into Mary Rose's eyes and saw the joy there, he felt as though he could do anything he ever wanted to do, no matter how impossible the obstacle. He felt . . . complete when he was with her, and all because of the trust in her gaze, and the acceptance.

Acceptance. Hadn't he spent his life trying to gain that? Wasn't that the true reason he had become so obsessed with his hunt to find Lord Elliott's daughter, so that he would accept him as an equal? Or was it all a payback for his kindness?

Harrison didn't have any answers. He knew

298

he was grateful to Elliott for taking care of his father; yes, of course he was. He was the one man who didn't turn his back on his friend when everyone else in London did. He gave them money and took over the payment of the taxes, and when constant nursing became mandatory, he saw that they had the best staff available. Thanks to his generosity, neither his father nor he ever went without. Elliott had even financed Harrison's education.

He owed a tremendous debt to Elliott, and because of honor, he would spend his life repaying. Harrison didn't shirk his responsibilities. And he certainly could never ask for anything more . . . even happiness.

Mary Rose. Lord, how she'd made him think about things that could never be. He was in love with her, and he had absolutely no one to blame but himself. He knew better than to get involved, and yet he'd done exactly that.

Elliott had made plans for his daughter within a month after her birth. Harrison hadn't been part of her future then, and he knew that when they returned to England, nothing would change.

Honor kept him from asking for her hand in marriage. He was neither worthy enough nor financially secure enough to give her his name.

He didn't want to think about his future. He decided he would appreciate the time he had with Mary Rose so that he could savor the memories on all the cold nights ahead.

He was thankful when they reached Corrie's cabin because there wasn't time to wallow in his misery.

Mary Rose wouldn't let him get close to the clearing. In fact, she made him stay a good half mile away. She explained she didn't want Corrie to become upset, and the first sight of him might very well upset just about anyone. He took immediate insult, of course.

"Exactly what do you think is wrong about my appearance?"

"You've got a day's growth on your face and your hair has been in dire need of a trimming for two weeks now."

"So?" he demanded.

"I shall have to be blunt," she said. "You look menacing and . . . scruffy. I find you appealing. She won't."

He snorted with disbelief, then laughed over the sound he just made. Heaven help him, he was starting to act like her.

"I'm sorry if I've stomped on your tender feelings," she said.

"I do not have tender feelings."

"Yes, well, as soon as you open your mouth and speak, everyone knows how cultured and refined you are."

"Cultured and refined people can also be killers, Mary Rose. You make it sound as though an education ensures decency."

She shrugged. She didn't want to waste any more time arguing with him. The heaviness in the air indicated a storm was closing in on them, and she didn't want to get soaked until after she had a nice visit with her new friend.

She wouldn't even let Harrison carry the supplies into the clearing. She made three trips and finally finished stacking all of her gifts in a pile in the very center of the clearing.

Mary Rose was thrilled that Corrie let her get much closer to the porch this time. She saw that as real progress in their relationship.

She didn't mind at all that the shotgun was pointed at her the entire time she stood there. She was just thankful Harrison wasn't close enough to notice. He was bound to make a scene if he thought she was in danger.

He hadn't stayed where she'd put him, however. Without making a sound, he moved to a spot where he was both concealed by the foliage and yet had a clear view of the front of the cabin.

When he spotted the barrel of the shotgun protruding from the window, his heart damned near stopped beating. It was aimed at Mary Rose's middle. His initial reaction was to pull his gun free and shoot the barrel. It took extreme willpower not to interfere. He broke out in a sweat, of course, but after ten, then fifteen minutes passed, he realized the shotgun was all for show. He still wasn't going to take his gaze off the threat, of course, but he was finally able to breathe normally again.

Mary Rose's behavior and her one-sided conversation for the next hour were both bizarre and endearing.

She would never have gone on and on if she'd known he was listening, of course, and he didn't plan to ever let her find out.

After she had placed the last of the jars in her stack, she stood up and mopped her brow with the edge of her sleeve.

She apologized because she hadn't been able to keep her word and visit the day before.

"I always keep my word, Corrie, unless something terrible prevents me from doing so, and after I've told you about all the sorry things that happened to me, you'll understand my tardiness," she assured the woman. She then gave a full accounting of her time. Harrison noticed she didn't mention the reason why she had gone after Bickley. He assumed she didn't want Corrie to worry that the vigilantes might still come up to the ridge to burn her out. Mary Rose said only that she had a difference of opinion and tried to use reason when she conversed with the man. One thing led to another and another, and before she knew what was happening, she was being attacked.

Her recollection of the events made him smile. She didn't linger on the injuries or the pain she endured, or on the fact that she damn near got killed. No, she spent the time telling all about the lovely skirt that got ripped and how frightful her hair looked.

She wasn't finished telling about her woes. She went into a long explanation about her experience waiting in Catherine Morrison's parlor. That was when Harrison found out Mary Rose considered him her exclusive property. He didn't have to guess. Mary Rose told Corrie all about her right to "have" him. She even outlined all the reasons why he belonged to her.

"I took him home with me before he got himself killed. When I think of what could have happened to the poor thing, well, my heart just aches. Can he help it if he's inept or awkward? No, of course he can't. He's terribly naive too, Corrie. The man wore a gun into town and didn't even know how to use it. Can you imagine such idiocy. I swear he needs a keeper. God love him, he doesn't know how incompetent he really is. No one has the heart to tell him, except Cole. Harrison did fight those men after they tore my dress and messed my hair, but they were scrawny little men, so Harrison was able to get in a couple of solid punches. I worried about it for a while, seeing him fight and all, and then I thought about it and realized anger had made him stronger and luck had been on his side. He took me by surprise on the way up here, and then I had to think it through and realized I shouldn't have been surprised at all. You see, he thought he heard a noise, and he drew his gun lickety-split. He was fast all right, but the fact is he probably couldn't shoot his way out of a barn. Being quick isn't worth a sneeze out here if you can't hit anything, now is it?"

She paused to let out a long, exaggerated sigh. Harrison could feel his face heating up. He wanted to stomp into the clearing and set the little woman straight. By God, he wasn't that inept.

Mary Rose wasn't through tearing his pride to shreds, however. "You should have seen him trying to learn how to break in some horses for Douglas. It was a pitiful sight, all right. I hid up in my room and watched from the window so he wouldn't be more humiliated than he already was. It's a blessing he didn't break his neck, Corrie, bless his heart."

Harrison gritted his teeth together and started counting to ten. His temper had reached the simmering point.

"I don't want you fretting about Harrison," Mary Rose continued. "I only told you about him because he came with me up to the ridge. He's supposed to protect me. That's why I wore my gun, Corrie. I can keep him safe enough. Anyway, he won't bother you. He'd kind and sweet-natured, and you should know me well enough by now after our last visitation to understand I wouldn't put up with him if he were mean. Did I tell you about Catherine Morrison throwing herself at him?"

She guessed she hadn't told the woman and went into a long, blown-out-of-all-proportion explanation about all the wrongs the woman had done to her over the years. Mary Rose had stored up a lot of complaints about Catherine and she proceeded to tell Corrie about each one, going all the way back to their early childhood. Since Corrie couldn't or wouldn't tell her to stop, she became Mary Rose's dream come true. A trapped listener who couldn't run away.

Harrison had started out worried that Corrie would shoot Mary Rose because the woman was as crazy as everyone said she was, but by the time the one-sided conversation was finished, his concern had changed. Now he couldn't figure out why Corrie didn't shoot her just to shut her up.

Mary Rose kept interlacing comments about Harrison. His ego took one hell of a beating, and if she "blessed his heart" just one more time, he swore he was going to have to throttle her.

Her voice finally gave out. She promised her friend that she would return as soon as she could for another long visit and turned to leave. She suddenly remembered she hadn't mentioned her newest houseguest yet and promptly stopped in her tracks.

Both Corrie and Harrison then listened to another long discussion, about Eleanor.

"She's going to settle down real soon," Mary Rose predicted. "She may even turn out to be a good friend once she gets over feeling sorry for herself. My, how the time has flown. Do get your supplies inside before the rain comes. Bye now, Corrie. God keep you safe."

Harrison stayed where he was until Mary Rose left the clearing. The rifle barrel was moved from the window a minute later. He backtracked, making a wide circle around Mary Rose, and was back to the spot where she'd told him to wait before she got there.

"Did you have a nice visit?" he asked.

"Oh, yes," she answered. Her voice sounded hoarse. "She's a dear woman."

He couldn't imagine how she knew that. "Did she talk to you?" he asked.

"No, but she's getting ready to," Mary Rose assured him. "We should get going, Harrison. It's late."

"How do you know she's getting ready to talk to you?" he asked, ignoring her suggestion to leave.

"She let me get much closer to the center of the clearing," she explained. "We're obviously friends now."

"Because she didn't shoot you."

"Yes," she said, pleased he understood.

He thought she was making as much sense as a two-year-old having a tantrum.

"You're being completely illogical," he told her. "You do know that, don't you, Mary Rose?"

She shook her head at him. "Is it illogical to look for the good in people? Everyone has feelings, Harrison. 'No man is an island.' Remember the passage both you and Adam are so partial to?"

"Yes, of course, but . . ."

"We cannot exist without each other. Do the words, 'any man's death diminishes me, because I am involved in mankind' mean the same thing to you that they mean to me? We're all part of the same family, Harrison. Corrie has needs just like the rest of us. Now do you see?"

"Point taken, Miss Clayborne."

Her smile was radiant. "I do believe this is the first argument with you I have ever won."

"We weren't having an argument," he replied.

"It seems like one. We need to leave now." She started toward her horse and glanced up at the sky above. "We're really in for a soaking. You do love to dawdle, don't you?"

He lifted her up into the saddle and gave her the reins. She folded her hands on top of the saddle horn. Harrison started to turn away, then changed his mind. He reached up and covered her hands with his.

She looked into his eyes to find out why he suddenly wanted to linger. His smile captured her full attention. Lord, how she loved it when he was happy. His eyes turned as warm and welcoming as sunshine. She felt the heat all the way down in her belly.

"You have a very good heart, Mary Rose."

She felt as if he had just caressed her. She was just about to thank him when he went and ruined it.

"I try to remember that whenever you make me crazy."

He let go of her and turned to go to MacHugh. In one fluid motion he swung up into the saddle. The gracefulness in the action impressed her. She guessed all the time he'd spent climbing back up onto the horses after he'd been pitched to his backside had taught him something useful after all.

"What is that comment supposed to mean?" she asked.

"It means I know what your game is. You're the one who spent entirely too long talking to Corrie, and so you've decided to blame me if we get soaked. I dawdle? I think not."

"You're too clever for me, Harrison." She lifted the reins and turned to lead the way home. "I never said I was perfect, did I?"

"No, you never did," he agreed with a laugh.

"You aren't perfect either. You're extremely argumentative, but of course you must realize that. You're also given to spells, but I doubt you can help that."

"You constantly jump to conclusions based on insufficient information. You do know that, don't you? And I don't have spells, woman."

"Most of the time you're a perfect gentleman, but in the blink of an eye, you can turn into a

307

raging lunatic." What else could she call his affliction? The man had spells, and that was that. She wasn't going to argue about it now. She wanted to discuss something else just as important.

"You refuse to understand that sometimes one must act before one has gathered hundreds of documents to support a possible thesis. If I had waited until I had every bit of information about you before I invited you to come home with me, you'd probably be dead. So would I," she added. "From old age."

"In other words, you leap before you look. Isn't that right?"

"At least I dare to leap."

"That attitude is exactly why so many people die young out here."

"Action is often more effective than words."

"In an uncivilized world, perhaps. Remember, Mary Rose, we are all accountable for our actions."

"We don't live inside a courtroom."

"We should behave as though we did."

"It would kill you to agree with me, wouldn't it, Harrison?"

She laughed after she asked her question. He smiled in response. "Perhaps," he allowed. "I like to win."

"Life isn't about winning. It's about surviving."

"In my line of work, surviving and winning are the same thing."

She had to think about what he had just said for a long while before she gave him her rebuttal. She was obviously enjoying sparring with him.

He was having just as much fun. He found her comments invigorating and refreshingly honest, even when she wasn't making a lick of sense.

The hell he had spells.

"I believe you should find another line of work."

He ignored the suggestion. "One really shouldn't get personal when one is debating."

"Is that what we're doing?"

"Debating?"

"Yes. Are we debating?"

"I thought we were. What did you think we were doing?"

"Getting personal."

He laughed.

"Exactly what were we debating?"

He didn't have the faintest idea. He wasn't about to tell her so, however, and so he decided to make up something that sounded reasonable just so he could continue to argue with her.

"We are debating the differences in our philosophies of life."

"We and our? My, but those words do imply getting personal to me."

"Point given, Miss Clayborne."

She gave him a regal nod.

"I can sum up the differences between us in just two words."

"So can I," he assured her.

"Ladies first?"

"Of course."

"Experience and observation. I experience life. You observe it. I'll wager you were going to say the very same thing."

"You'd lose your wager then," he countered. "I would say logical versus illogical, order versus chaos, sanity versus insanity . . ."

"Lawyers do love to go on and on, don't they?"

"Some do."

"You do realize you just called me illogical, insane, and chaotic?"

"You do realize you just said I only observe life? It isn't true."

"It's raining. I think we should stop."

Lightning lit up the sky. "It's going to get worse," he predicted.

"Probably. There are caves about a quarter of a mile from here. We have to backtrack just a little, and we should hurry now. The trail's going to become too dangerous for MacHugh and Millie."

He didn't want to stop, but darkness was already closing in on them, and it would have been foolish to try to go on. He had hoped to reach the peak above her home before night caught up with them. The trail was much wider there, safer for the horses. They could find their way back to the barn with or without light. Instinct and hunger would guide them.

Spending the night with Mary Rose was just as dangerous for him as treading over slick stones would be for the horses.

He would, of course, behave like the gentleman he had been trained to be. He had given Adam his word, and he meant to keep it. He would have acted honorably regardless of his promise, however. Behaving wasn't the issue. Frustration was going to be the problem, but there didn't seem to be any way to avoid it. He was going to have to suffer through the unnecessary test of endurance, no matter what. He gritted his teeth in anticipation of the miserable night ahead of him.

"Hurry up, Harrison," she called after him. "It's only a fine mist now, but in a few more minutes it's going to become a downpour. I don't want to get soaked if I don't have to."

Harrison thought she was exaggerating. A short time later, when he was soaked through to the bone and freezing, he had to admit she'd been right.

The cave they found was little more than a long, narrow overhang of rocks. There were two reasons they went inside. One, it wasn't occupied, which was a problem to be considered given the nightly habits of some of the animals in the area, and two, the floor was dry. The air was as damp and welcoming as sleet, but not too drafty, and so it would have to do.

MacHugh refused to go to the back with Millie. Harrison stripped the stallion of his gear and let him stand near the mouth of the cave. The horse changed his mind and moved to the back as soon as Mary Rose got a fire going with the twigs and branches Harrison had collected. He'd tried for ten minutes to get the damp wood to ignite. She was more experienced than he was, however, and knew how to stack the wood just right with dried leaves she'd gathered from the floor of the cave.

Harrison dried off the horses as best he could, then caught water in a makeshift bucket he fash-

311

ioned out of the canvas he'd been intelligent enough to bring along, and gave the water to Millie. When she'd had her fill, he let MacHugh quench his thirst.

Mary Rose worked on drying the damp bedrolls and then made up beds for the night. She placed the blankets side by side.

He wanted his on the opposite side of the fire, but he didn't complain because he knew she was only using good sense. They would need to stay close together to share their warmth during the night.

She took off her boots, moved them away from the fire, then pulled out the gun he hadn't noticed until now tucked into the waistband of her skirt, and put it under the fold in her bedding.

Harrison went to the other side of the fire and stood there, trying to warm himself.

"Have you camped outside much?" he asked.

"No."

"You act like you have."

She knelt down and added a few more twigs to the fire. "I prefer my own bed, but one does what one has to do to stay warm out here. Isn't that right?"

"You aren't at all squeamish."

"Heavens, I hope I'm not squeamish. Did you think I would be?"

He shook his head. She didn't understand the world he had come from, where gently bred women fainted over the slightest suggestion of impropriety. So fragile was society, reputations could be ruined by inconsequential whispers. Queen Victoria set the standards for the day, of course, and she rigidly emphasized prudence in every undertaking, sobriety, and caution. Yet while she also showed the world what an independent thinker she was, the women in England Harrison associated with still didn't educate themselves to emulate her.

He and his best friend, Nicholas, were running with the wrong crowd. The women they associated with depended on others for their every need, including amusement. If any of them became bored, it was someone else's fault.

God, what a miserable, restrictive life he had known. It was too damned bleak to think about.

Mary Rose Clayborne. What a breath of fresh air she was. He hadn't believed she could take care of herself. Now that he had time to think about it, he realized he had made several erroneous conclusions about her, based on his own narrow-minded knowledge of the women from his past.

She certainly proved him wrong. He was impressed with her no-nonsense approach to their situation. He was beginning to think she had more common sense than he had believed.

Then she took her clothes off. His knees almost buckled under him when he realized what she was doing. His opinion changed in the blink of an eye. The naive woman didn't have any sense at all.

"What in God's name do you think you're doing?" His roar of outrage echoed around the stone walls.

"Undressing. Why?"

"Put your blouse back on."

313

She ignored his command. She finished removing the garment and then bent down to take off her socks. She stood on her blankets so she wouldn't get her feet dirty.

She straightened up again, her wet socks in her hands, and smiled at him.

He was staring at her. She thought he might be looking at her locket.

"It's a pretty locket, isn't it?"

"What?"

"My locket. I thought you were looking at it."

"I was," he lied. "Where'd you get it?"

"My mother sent it to me. It was a gift for my sixteenth birthday. The locket doesn't open, but I don't mind. Can you see the engraved rose on the front?"

She started to walk to him so he could get a closer look. He put his hand up.

"I can see it."

"She said she chose the heart-shaped locket because our hearts are entwined. Isn't that sweet? One day I shall pass it down to my daughter."

"It's very nice," he remarked.

She nodded. "When I wear it, I feel closer to her, so of course I wear it all the time," she explained.

She patted the locket, let out a little sigh, and returned to the business of getting warm.

She handed her socks to Harrison across the fire. "Hold these for me please. They're just a little bit damp. Don't let them hang too close to the flames."

He was happy to help her because he thought

she wanted her hands free so she could put her blouse back on.

"Don't stand too close, Harrison. Travis will be furious if I ruin them."

"You wear your brother's socks?"

He didn't know whether to laugh or shake his head. She smiled at him while she worked on undoing the ribbon at the back of her neck. He tried to stare at the ledge behind her right ear and not think about the white lacy underthing that was plastered against her skin. Every single time she moved, the swell of her breasts caught his attention. He could feel himself breaking into a cold sweat.

"Only when I can sneak them off the line before he notices."

What in thunder was she talking about? "Sneak what off the line?"

"His socks."

"Why don't you wear your own? Don't you have any?"

"Of course I have socks. I prefer wearing my brothers' though. They're thicker. I don't care what they look like. I only wear them with my boots, so no one ever sees them. Besides, they keep my feet warm. Isn't that all that should matter?"

She was only being practical, but he still didn't want her wearing any man's socks, not even her brothers'. That thought immediately led to another one. He wouldn't mind if she wanted to wear his socks. Fact was, he'd like it.

God help him, his mind had snapped. Happy now? he wanted to ask her. It was all her doing,

315

driving him to distraction with every little movement she made.

"Put your blouse back on," he snapped.

She ignored him again. She spread her hair out behind her shoulders so the curls wouldn't clump together and take forever to dry, dropped the pink ribbon on the blanket, and only then gave him her full attention.

"Why would I want to put my blouse back on? I only just took it off. It's wet," she reminded him. "Oh, for heaven's sake. Quit looking like you want to strangle me. I'm only being practical. Do you want me to catch my death? You'd better get over your embarrassment and take your clothes off too. You'll get consumption, and then I'll have to take care of you. Do you think I want that duty? No, I don't, thank you. You would do nothing but complain the entire time."

Her hands had settled on the tilt of her hips while she argued her case, but once she'd made her position clear, she started fiddling with the back of her waistband.

His mind was simply too befuddled to realize what she was doing. He was occupied trying not to look at the front of her and turned his gaze to the fire a scant second after her skirt dropped to the ground. He should have kept staring at the wall, because the path his gaze took gave him an ample view of her legs. They were incredible. Long, shapely, perfect.

Exactly how much was he supposed to endure before this godawful night was over? Harrison didn't know, but he was certain his situation couldn't get any worse. This hope was all he had, he decided, and so he grasped it with the desperate determination of a drowning man clinging to a rope.

He stomped over to his saddlebag to see if he could find something for her to put on. He muttered obscenities about his lack of discipline all the while he searched.

He tried to get angry so he wouldn't think about anything else. Like her legs . . . her tiny waist . . . her creamy skin . . .

"Embarrassment has nothing to do with the problem of your undressing," he gritted out, just to set the record straight.

He tossed her a dark flannel shirt and barked out the order for her to put it on.

"Won't you need this to keep warm?"

"Put it on."

His tone of voice didn't suggest she argue with him. She put the shirt on. She had to roll the cuffs back twice, and after she'd secured all the buttons, she felt warm again. The shirt was gigantic on her, of course, and covered most of her thighs.

"Thank you."

He ignored her gratitude. He sat down across from her with the fire between them and stared into her eyes. She sat down, folded her legs just the way he had, covered them with her blanket, and then picked up her blouse to hold it close to the fire so it would dry.

"I cannot help but notice you're glaring at me. Your voice was downright surly too. Have I done something to offend you?"

The look he gave her made her toes curl.

Scorching didn't adequately describe it.

"I am not one of your brothers."

"I didn't think you were." She thought she sounded reasonable.

He thought she was as dense as a rock. "I'm not going to be able to take much more."

"Much more what? For heaven's sake, haven't you ever had to sleep outside? Haven't you ever been caught in a storm before? I can't help it if you're feeling uncomfortable."

He unbuttoned his shirt, took it off, and then held it up by the fire.

"I'm extremely comfortable."

"Are you going to take your pants off?"

"Hell, no."

"You don't have to get angry. Aren't they wet?"

"Not wet enough."

"I don't believe it's necessary for me to put up with your bad mood."

"You really don't understand, do you? No, I don't believe that, not for one second. You know damned well I want you, and you're deliberately tempting me. Stop it immediately, and I'll get over my bad mood."

The light was slow to dawn, but once it had, she found she wasn't embarrassed about her stupidity.

He wanted her. And she'd been wearing her brother's socks. Her face turned pink with mortification. Oh, God, she was dressed like a lumber lug. She just bet Catherine Morrison never wore her father's socks. No respectable, eligible woman with marriage on her mind would.

"Are we agreed?" he demanded.

"Yes, we are agreed."

Silence followed the truce. Mary Rose waited several minutes so he would have time to get over his anger.

"I usually wear silk stockings with lace around the tops," she blurted out.

He couldn't imagine why she wanted him to know that. She wasn't quite finished discussing her clothes, however.

"I rarely wear my brother's socks. I certainly wouldn't want you to get the idea I like wearing men's clothing. I don't."

"The thought never crossed my mind."

"Good, because I don't."

"This shirt is never going to dry."

Harrison turned the shirt over and only then looked at her face. Her complexion was as red as the flames.

"Are you feeling, all right?"

"Yes, of course.

"Move away from the fire. Your face looks like it's getting burned."

The man was an idiot. And thank God for that, she thought to herself. She scooted back from the fire, hoped her blush would eventually fade, and tried to think about something inane to talk about. She wanted him to forget all about socks.

"I'm going to have to do dishes for a week."

"Why?" he asked.

"I didn't use the word of the day."

"What word?"

"The word printed on the chalkboard. I don't even know what it is."

Harrison closed his eyes and pictured the

kitchen. Then he smiled.

"Infelicity."

"You're sure?"

"I'm sure."

"How did you . . ."

"Adam took me into the kitchen. I noticed the word then. I still haven't seen the cook, by the way. I don't think he exists."

"I don't know what it means."

"It means I think you made him up."

"The word, Harrison. What does infelicity mean?"

"Unhappiness."

She smiled with pleasure. "I used it."

"But not in front of any of your brothers," he pointed out.

"Of course we have a cook. When he's ready to meet you, he'll show himself. Until then I suggest you give him a wide path. He's somewhat prickly. It's because he's led a life of infelicity."

Harrison laughed. "He's infelicitous, is he?"

"Most assuredly. You will be my witness. Testify on my behalf tomorrow night during supper."

"Your brothers will have tried to kill me by then."

"Why?"

"We're spending the night together."

He couldn't believe he had to remind her of their circumstances. "If I were your brother, I'd become angry enough to kill someone."

"My brothers trust us," she argued. "Adam would never have let you come with me if he believed you were a lecher."

"Wasn't lecher the word last week?"

"Tuesday," she said. "You aren't at all lecherous."

He shook his head. "You have been properly educated." He caught himself before he added the thought that her father was going to be very pleased with the effort her brothers had shown.

He put his shirt flat on his saddle with the hope the air would dry it during the night and sat down on his bedroll. He leaned back against the stone wall and closed his eyes. The stone wasn't comfortable against his shoulders, but he didn't mind enough to move.

"Are you hungry?"

"No, are you?"

"No."

She turned to look at him. "Don't worry about my brothers getting the wrong idea. Cole's the only one who will try to make an issue out of our situation, but he'll have to work at it. He'll probably hit you. That's all."

"No, he won't hit me."

"He won't?"

"I won't let him. Once was enough."

"He might not see it that way."

"It won't matter. I won't let him hit me."

She let out a sigh. "I'm pleased to see you haven't lost any of your confidence," she remarked. "Spending the last week on your backside didn't affect your spirits at all."

"I did not spend the last week on my backside."

"If you say so."

"Let's talk about something else, shall we?" he asked.

"Yes," she agreed. "I just want you to know that Cole is actually the easiest of my brothers to roll over for me. He's really a very nice person."

"I didn't say he wasn't nice," he countered. "You've got him wrapped around your little finger, don't you?"

"No. He just doesn't like to see me unhappy. If he can take my side, he will."

He thought his interpretation was more accurate. "Was it difficult for you growing up without a father and mother?"

"I have a mother," she replied. "Mama Rose."

"Why doesn't she live with you and your brothers?"

"She can't . . . not yet. She'll join us as soon as possible."

"Do all of your brothers call her Mama?"

"Yes, they do. Why do you ask?"

"I just wondered. What about your father?"

"I don't have one of those."

"Don't you miss having one?"

"How could I miss what I've never had?"

Mary Rose decided her blouse was dry enough. She folded it and put it behind her, then went to work on her skirt.

Harrison watched her every movement. He thought she was an extremely graceful woman, wonderfully feminine and yet very practical. It was a fascinating combination.

"You're as unspoiled as your paradise."

"I am?"

"Mama Rose is Adam's mother, isn't she?"

"And mine as well."

"But she gave birth to Adam."

"Yes. How did you know?"

"Simple deduction. She lives in the South. You've never seen her, have you?"

"Not deduction, you guessed," she countered. "You don't know where my other brothers came from. They could have lived down south too. No, I haven't ever seen Mama, but I know her very well. She writes to me at least once a week, sometimes more. She never misses, not once since I started writing to her. During the war, when I was too young to read or write, she did miss sending letters a couple of times. I don't remember the time, but my brothers were very worried. She survived, of course, just like we did. When the time is right, she'll join us."

"But the time isn't right yet."

"No."

The quickness in her reply told him not to press the issue. He let it go.

Several minutes passed in companionable silence. He kept thinking about how pretty she looked wearing his shirt.

She kept thinking about how awful she'd looked wearing her brother's socks.

"What are you thinking about, Harrison?"

"How pretty you look."

She laughed. "You've been away from the city too long if you think I look pretty tonight. My hair's a mess and I'm wearing a man's shirt, for heaven's sake."

You're wearing my shirt, he silently corrected. And that made all the difference in the world

323

to him. Seeing her in his favorite, worn-out shirt made him feel extremely possessive toward her. Everything about her aroused him. He wanted to protect her from harm, comfort her, hold her, love her. And in his heart, he wanted the same from her.

Harrison tried to think about his life back in England. Nothing about his daily routine appealed to him now, however. How cold and empty his life had been. Until he had come to Montana, he hadn't known what it was like to feel alive. He had always felt as though he were standing on the outside of life, looking in. He observed. Hadn't Mary Rose used just that word to describe him? He wondered if she had any idea how accurate her evaluation was.

"Now what are you thinking about? You look worried. Are you?"

"No."

"I was bemoaning the fact that I wore such a heavy skirt. It's taking forever to dry. Now it's your turn to tell me what you were thinking about. I shall only hope your thoughts weren't nearly as boring."

"You were thinking about practical matters. I wasn't. I was thinking about my life back in England."

"Don't you mean to say Scotland?"

"All my work is in England. I have a town house in London. I rarely have enough time to go back to the Highlands."

"Because of all of your work?"

"Yes."

"You miss the Highlands though, don't you?"

"I miss what it represents."

"What is that?"

"Freedom."

He hadn't realized he was going to use that specific word until he said it.

"You've let duty become your chains, haven't you?"

"A man has to repay his debts before all other considerations."

"Do you owe your employer this debt? Is that why you've never had enough time to pursue your own dreams?"

"Yes and no," he answered. "Yes, I owe him a debt. But it's more complicated than that. My dreams have changed. I used to love what I was doing. I don't any longer. I think maybe you're right, Mary Rose. Winning isn't everything."

"I'm pleased to hear you admit it," she said. "You like our paradise, don't you?"

"Yes."

"And you're happy here."

"Yes."

"Then quit making everything so complicated. Stay and be happy. See how simple it is?"

"No, it isn't simple at all."

"I'll only ask you one more question," she promised. "If it were simple, would you stay here?"

"In a heartbeat."

She knew she'd just promised not to ask any more questions, but she couldn't stop herself from asking one more. "Have you made up your mind to leave then?"

She was gripping the edge of her skirt, praying

he would tell her what she desperately wanted to hear.

"I haven't made up my mind about anything. I'm not being evasive, just honest. I don't have enough information yet to know what road I should take."

"I don't understand."

Her arms were aching from holding up the skirt to dry. She finally gave up and put it away. Then she moved back, covered her legs, and leaned against the rock wall next to Harrison. She sat so close to him her upper arm pressed against his.

She stared into the fire and let it mesmerize her. She didn't want to think about the possibility of Harrison leaving, not when she was just about to decide to fall in love with him, and so she tried to think about something else.

"I know you must be hungry. I'll be happy to find something to eat."

"Where?" he asked.

"Out there," she answered with a wave of her hand toward the mountain.

"I'm not that hungry. If you are, I could go outside and find something for you to eat."

She smiled but didn't look at him. Harrison had sounded arrogant when he spoke.

"You haven't had to stay out overnight much, have you?"

"Actually, when I was in service, I did," he replied.

"Do you mean the military?"

"Yes."

"Tell me about London. What's it like living there?"

"It's beautiful. The architecture is remarkable. Cole would appreciate the quality and the workmanship. I think you would like living in London," he added. "Once you got accustomed to the differences."

She couldn't imagine living in a city. Paradise was all she needed, or wanted. Why couldn't Harrison understand?

"Have you ever had to stay outside with a woman in the Highlands or in England?"

The question made him want to laugh. "I'd be married now if I had."

"Why?"

"The woman's reputation would have been ruined. Marriage would be the only honorable solution."

"But what if nothing happened? What if the circumstances were as innocent as ours are tonight?"

"It wouldn't make any difference," he answered. "She would still be condemned."

"What about the man? What would happen to him?"

"Not much," he admitted after a moment's reflection. "It isn't all absolute, of course. If she comes from a powerful family, or if an influential friend decides to help, there is a chance she wouldn't be shunned. A remote chance," he added. "But still a chance. Before you judge too harshly, I'll remind you that your society in New York is similar."

"It isn't my society," she argued. "Out here, we don't have time for such nonsense."

A sudden thought made her smile. "If what

327

you say is accurate, then you would have to marry me tomorrow if we were in the wilderness in England. They do have their own paradise, don't they?"

"Yes," he assured her. "They do. There are untouched areas just as breathtakingly beautiful."

"Honestly?"

"Honestly."

"What about my other question? Would you have to marry me?"

She turned to look at him. He slowly turned to look at her. She saw the sparkle in his eyes and something else she couldn't quite put her finger on.

"Probably not," he told her. "My employer is a very powerful man in England. He would come to your aid."

She looked disgruntled by his answer. Harrison laughed.

She was getting a crick in her neck. She moved again, got up on her knees to face him, then leaned back against her ankles. The side of her thigh touched his.

He tried once again not to think about her closeness or her lack of attire. It helped if he stared at her forehead — not much, of course, but he was a desperate man. He would take what he could.

"Now why are you frowning? Tell me what you're thinking about?"

"Approaching sainthood."

She didn't understand. He wasn't going to enlighten her. "You're a puzzling man, Harrison. One minute you're laughing, and the next you're frowning like a bear."

"Bears don't frown."

"I was being metaphorical."

"Another word on the chalkboard?"

She nodded. "I like the word. It sounds . . . intelligent."

"You're going to make me go stand outside, aren't you, Mary Rose?"

"Why?"

"You're being provocative."

"I am?" She was pleased with his remark.

"I haven't just given you a compliment. You're deliberately tempting me. Stop it."

She couldn't hide her smile. "Now you're gloating," he muttered.

She had to agree. She was gloating. "A woman likes to know she's appealing," she explained. "But I shall stop flirting with you just as soon as I figure out what it is I'm doing."

"You could start by taking your hand off my thigh."

She hadn't realized where her hand was draped. She immediately pulled away.

"What else?"

"Quit looking at me that way."

"What way?"

"Like you want me to kiss you."

"But I do want you to kiss me."

"It isn't going to happen, so stop it," he ordered again.

She tucked the covers around her legs, then folded her hands together in her lap.

"What would happen if we weren't discovered?"

"Where?"

"In England, after spending a night together," she said.

He thought they had finished discussing the subject. She was obviously still curious about the workings of his society, however, and so he answered her.

"We would be discovered. Gossip travels like the plague. Everyone always knows everyone else's business."

"Then do you know what I might do?"

"No, what?"

"I'd give them all something to talk about. The people must be terribly bored, after all, to be concerned about everyone else all the time. I would become indiscreet. If I loved the man I was spending the night with, and if I knew he wanted to marry me and I wanted to marry him, well then I would . . ."

His hand covered her mouth. "No, you would not. You would have your own honor to protect. You would be true to yourself, to who you are."

It took her a long minute to finally admit he was right. "Yes, I would," she said. "Still, being a fallen woman does hold a certain fascination. I'd probably wear red all the time."

He shook his head. "Look at the cost," he suggested.

She rolled her eyes heavenward. "Ever the attorney," she whispered. "All right. We'll look at the cost. You're going to tell me all about it, aren't you?"

He nodded. "If you give up parts of who you are, eventually you give up everything."

"Yes, Harrison."

He didn't realize she was agreeing with him. "If you lose yourself, you've lost everything."

"In other words, you aren't going to kiss me."

"You've got that right."

"You have bruises all over your chest. And your neck. I'll bet your backside's black and blue."

"You aren't going to find out."

She reached over and touched a bruise near his left shoulder. Her fingertips were warm against his skin.

He didn't think she had any idea of what she was doing to him. She was frowning with obvious concern over the beating his body had taken.

When she touched the bruise next to his navel, he grabbed hold of her hand.

"You'd better start taking care of yourself," she said. "I don't think you should go with my brothers to get the cattle we purchased."

"Why not?"

"Because you'll probably break your neck."

"You've got a lot of confidence in me, don't you?"

"I believe in you."

Her words came out in a soft whisper, and, oh, how they touched his heart. Her belief in him was humbling.

They stared into each other's eyes for a breathless moment, then each looked away. Neither was willing, nor ready, to take the next step. Harrison knew he loved her but couldn't profess his love for her because they would be empty words indeed without a future together. He would have to declare his intentions to Lord Elliott first and only after he had proven himself financially stable enough to provide for his daughter in the style Elliott would demand.

Mary Rose was afraid to fall in love with Harrison. She was trying to protect her heart from being crushed. He had been very open and honest with her about the possibility of leaving, and who was she to keep him from pursuing his destiny and his dreams?

I am very practical, she decided with a good deal of self-disgust. She wouldn't allow herself to grasp any possibility until she was assured of the outcome. She desperately wanted to protect herself, yet even now she was close to weeping over a future without Harrison.

"What are you thinking?"

She pulled her hand away from his before she answered. "Here today, gone tomorrow. What were you thinking?"

"That it would take me years to become financially equal to my employer."

They both sounded disheartened.

"If we were living in the city of London, I would probably have complete confidence in your ability to take care of yourself."

He raised an eyebrow. " 'Probably'?"

She smiled. She loved it when he sounded outraged. She knew it was forced, of course, and assumed he was also trying to move back into a safer, more casual conversation.

"No, not 'probably,' " she qualified. "I'm certain you could look after yourself."

"I would hope so."

"I don't think less of you. No, of course I

332

don't. I believe in you, Harrison. It's your experience we're talking about now."

"What's wrong with my experience?"

"You don't have any."

She patted his knee in mock sympathy. "You've never worked with cattle before. I doubt you even know how to use a rope. Therefore, it would be dangerous for you. Have I injured your feelings again?"

"Go to sleep."

She decided not to take offense over the gruff order. "I am tired," she admitted. "Running up and down those stairs got old fast."

"Why were you running up and down the stairs."

"I had errands to complete."

"Eleanor, right?"

She didn't answer him. Harrison shook his head. He understood how difficult the demanding woman was. He'd seen Eleanor in action when she'd taken on Travis. She wanted him to fetch something for her, and by God, after ten minutes of hounding, the brother had given in. He told Harrison he would have done anything to shut her up.

Mary Rose straightened her blankets and then stretched out on her side. She kept her back close to Harrison's thigh, tucked her hands under the side of her face, and closed her eyes.

"How long are you going to let Eleanor run you around in circles?"

"For heaven's sake, she only just arrived. She hasn't been running me in circles. I'm merely trying to help her get comfortable."

"When the two of you are together and no one else is around, is she pleasant to you then?"

Mary Rose thought about the question a long while before she finally answered.

"No."

"Then why do you put up with her?"

She rolled onto her back and looked up at Harrison. He was scowling down at her. The man became upset over the oddest things.

"Why do you put up with MacHugh?"

"Why? Because he's a sound, reliable horse."

"So is Eleanor. She's sound and reliable."

"You can't know that for certain."

"You couldn't have known for certain your horse was sound and reliable either. You went with your instincts, didn't you?"

"No, I didn't. One look at MacHugh and I fully understood why he was being difficult. His scars speak for him."

"So do her scars," she reasoned. "Eleanor carries them inside, and perhaps, because people can't see them, the injuries done to her are even more damaging. She's often misunderstood."

Harrison moved down, stretched out on his back, stacked his hands behind his head, and stared up at the stone ceiling of the cave while he thought about Eleanor.

"Travis is getting ready to toss her out."

"No, he isn't."

"He can't hide in the barn until she leaves, Mary Rose. Douglas, I couldn't help but notice, is doing the same thing. You're asking too much from your brothers. They should have the same rights you have."

"They do have the same rights." She turned toward him, propped her elbow on the blanket, and then rested her chin on the palm of her hand so she would be comfortable while she argued with him.

"My brothers aren't very patient men," she began. "Still, they know they can't toss her out. It wouldn't be a decent thing to do. They're all honorable men, every one of them."

"There is an easy way to get Eleanor to behave," Harrison said. He turned his attention from the ceiling to her eyes and allowed himself to be mesmerized by their intense, bewitching color.

She scooted closer to him and leaned up. "How?" she asked.

"If something no longer works, you try something else, right?"

"Right," she agreed.

"Does Eleanor expect breakfast to be served to her in bed every morning?"

"She said she did."

"What would happen if no one carried a tray up?"

"She'd be furious."

"And hungry," he predicted. "She would have to come downstairs."

"I wouldn't want to be around when she did. Her anger is often quite worrisome."

"Bluster."

"Bluster?"

"In other words, it's all for show. Ignore her anger. Simply state your position, give her the rules of the household, and . . ."

"What rules?"

"When you eat, when you don't," he said. "That sort of thing."

"I see. And then what should I do?"

His grin was devilish. "Run like hell. You might try hiding in the barn with your brothers."

She laughed. "Everyone's going to love Eleanor once they understand her."

"She should have responsibilities to take care of for as long as she is here, assuming, of course, Eleanor plans to stay for a long while."

Mary Rose sat up and leaned over him. "If I tell you something, will you promise not to tell Travis or Douglas or Cole?"

"What about Adam?"

"He already knows."

She put her hand flat against his chest. His heart felt as if it had just flipped over. He couldn't stop himself from touching her and put his hand on top of hers.

"What don't you want your other brothers to find out?"

"Eleanor won't be leaving."

"Do you mean to say she won't be leaving soon?"

"I mean to say, not ever."

"Oh, Lord."

"Exactly," she whispered. "She doesn't have any other place to go. Now do you understand? She doesn't have any family. Her father ran away from her and from the authorities. He's done terrible things to other people, and the law finally caught up with him."

"What terrible things?"

"He took their money. He pretended to be an

336

investor. He wasn't."

"He took their savings."

"Yes."

"What about Eleanor's mother?"

"She died a long time ago. Eleanor's an only child, the poor thing."

"Aren't there any aunts or uncles she could turn to?"

"No," she answered. "Most of the people in her town turned against her. She didn't have any friends to speak of."

"I'm not surprised."

"Show some compassion."

"Why? You have enough for both of us, sweetheart."

Her eyes widened. "You called me sweetheart."

"Sorry."

"Don't be. I liked it. Say it again."

"No. We were talking about Eleanor," he reminded her.

"We shouldn't talk about anyone. It isn't polite."

"I just wanted you to be aware of Travis's current frame of mind. He really is getting ready to call for a vote and toss your houseguest out. You'd better talk to him."

She pulled her hand away from his and then reached up to stroke the side of his face. She felt the day's growth of whiskers under her fingertips and smiled over the pleasure the tickling sensation gave her.

He didn't stop her caress. He liked it too much. His hand cupped the back of her neck. His fingers threaded through her silky hair.

And then he pulled her down on top of him. He kissed her long and hard. He forced her mouth open by applying pressure on her chin. He was deliberate in his seduction, for the lure of tasting her once again overrode all thoughts of caution. There wasn't any harm in kissing her good night, or so he reasoned, and he was certainly experienced enough to know when to stop.

She opened her mouth for him as soon as she realized what he wanted. His tongue moved inside hers to take complete possession. She seemed to melt against him then. His mouth trapped her whispered sigh. And only then did he deepen the kiss. His mouth slanted over hers again. He was hard and hot against her, his tongue hungry to give her the taste of him inside her.

They mated with their mouths, their tongues, until she was overwhelmed by passion. Desire such as she had never known before swept through her body. Each time his tongue slid in and out of her mouth, she silently begged for more. Her nails dug into his shoulder blades, and her body rubbed against his, telling him without words how much she wanted him.

The sound she made in the back of her throat made him hungry to give her more.

A single kiss and yet, when he finally called a stop, they were both shaking with raw desire.

He buried his face in the crook of her neck and tried to regain his senses. He took a deep, shuddering breath, inhaled her wonderful light fragrance, and became more intoxicated by her. God, she was perfect. She felt so good, so right in his arms.

"Harrison, I can't breathe very well. You'll have to move a little."

He was on top of her. How in God's name had that happened? His arms were wrapped around her waist. He hadn't remembered putting them there. He had to take her with him when he rolled to his side so he could pull his hands free.

His lack of control appalled him. And yet he still held on to her. His knee was wedged between her thighs. He couldn't feel her skin through the fabric of his pants, but he knew she was silky everywhere. It made him even harder thinking about it.

Her arms were wrapped around his neck. Her fingers were driving him to distraction because she was still stroking him.

She leaned up and kissed his chin. She tried to let go of him. It was the decent thing to do, given their circumstances. She couldn't make herself behave, though. He felt too wonderful against her.

She tucked her head under his chin and closed her eyes. "Could we please sleep like this? We'll stay warm," she promised. "Just for a little while?"

He kissed the top of her forehead. "Just for a little while," he agreed.

She leaned back so she could look at him when she whispered her goodnight. She stared into his eyes, saw the tenderness there, and felt her heartbeat quicken in reaction. "Your eyes have turned as dark as night. You're a very handsome man."

His hands moved to cup the sides of her face.

"And you're a very beautiful woman."

His thumb rubbed across her lips. They were rosy and swollen from his kisses. Her eyes were still misty with passion, and, God help him, he couldn't stop himself from kissing her again.

"You are so amazingly soft," he whispered a scant second before his mouth settled on top of hers. It was hard, demanding, incredibly arousing. Passion ignited within each of them. She was every bit as wild as he was in her bid to explore the taste and texture of him.

His hands caressed her neck, her shoulders, then moved lower until he was cupping her sweet backside. She moved restlessly against him. Her pelvis pressed against his knee. A surge of pleasure poured over her. He angled his head to the side and kissed her again, then shifted his position. He moved his knee away and gently forced her to straddle him. He pressed his groin against the junction of her thighs, caught her gasp with his mouth, and growled with his pleasure. He was mindless now to everything but pleasing her.

Passion flowed between them with an intensity of white-hot lightning. He couldn't seem to get enough of her. His hand slipped beneath the flannel shirt to caress her more intimately. He pushed the light fabric of her chemise out of his way and boldly took one full breast into his hand. His thumb rubbed across her nipple again and again, until it had become a hard nub ready for his mouth to devour.

She loved the way he caressed her. She moaned and arched up against his hand, silently pleading for more.

She never wanted to let go of him. She craved his closeness, the tenderness in the way he held her. She could feel his strength in the corded muscles under her fingertips and glorified in the knowledge that with each of her own gentle caresses, she gave him as much pleasure as he gave her. His nonsensical, sweet, loving words against her ear told her so.

She was overwhelmed by him. She knew he had enough strength to crush her, yet also knew he would give up his life to keep her safe. She tasted the saltiness in his skin as she placed wet kisses along the column of his neck, inhaled his male scent, entwined now with her own, and heard his heart beating wildly and in perfect harmony with her own racing heartbeat.

His caresses became more demanding, for her soft whispers of pleasure drove him now. He became desperate to get closer to her heat, to touch and stroke what he most wanted to possess. His hand moved down between her thighs, and he shuddered with yet another burst of uncontrollable passion. Her skin was as silky and sweet as he knew it would be. His fingers slipped underneath her clothing and found her at last. When he touched her and felt the warm dampness in her soft curls, he forgot all about holding on to his discipline. He stroked the fire inside her and burned with his own. His fingers brushed across the very spot he knew would drive her wild. He nearly came undone when she arched up against him and let out a soft cry of ecstasy.

He wasn't going to stop. He started to undo the buttons of his pants. His hands were shaking so much he could barely get the top one unhooked.

She felt his hard arousal pressed against her, and yet she didn't become afraid or worried. In her heart she knew he would stop touching her the minute she asked him to.

Her trust in Harrison was absolute. He was an honorable man. He would do whatever she asked of him, as long as it was honorable.

Dear God, what was she asking of him now? Wasn't he going to sacrifice his honor to please her?

She was sickened with shame. She didn't know if she had the power to destroy him, but she cared about him too much to risk the possibility.

She went completely still and squeezed her eyes shut so she wouldn't be able to cry.

"We have to stop now."

Her voice was a ragged whisper against the side of his neck. The words registered in his mind almost immediately. It took him a little longer to react.

And then he let out a loud, shaky breath, clenched his jaw tight, and forced himself to move away from her. It almost killed him.

The physical agony of his own frustration, and his stupidity, made him furious. What in God's name had he been thinking? Lust had driven him beyond any semblance of control. He hadn't been thinking at all. No woman had ever been able to get to him the way Mary Rose did. She was different all right, and dangerous.

She was having trouble catching her breath. The second Harrison had rolled away from her, she felt abandoned, alone. She shook with cold and with regret. Her shameful conduct humiliated her. No man had ever touched her so intimately. He had stroked her breasts, her belly, her backside, her . . . Oh, God, she was out of her mind. She couldn't stop the tears from forming in her eyes.

What if she hadn't asked him to stop? She knew the answer. He would marry her.

The thought didn't please her. No, it horrified her. Because of his integrity he would do the right thing. God only knew, he was used to the weight of responsibility. His shoulders should be stooped by now, for she knew he'd been carrying obligations from the time he'd been just a little boy. Responsibility had robbed him of his childhood.

She wasn't about to take anything more from him. She felt sick to her stomach and almost doubled over with her guilt. Trapping a man into marriage with lust was beyond shameful. It was unforgivable.

She sat up with her back toward Harrison and stared at the wall while she straightened her blankets. Her hair was hanging down over her face. She impatiently brushed it back and only then realized her hands were still shaking.

She knew she had to say something to him, offer him some sort of apology or explanation for her behavior, but she couldn't seem to find the right words to convey to him her feelings. Nothing she came up with seemed to be even barely adequate.

Harrison couldn't get comfortable. He sat up,

moved back, and then leaned against the stone wall. He let the frigid rock cool his shoulders.

He still burned for her. He could taste her in his mouth and tried not to think about how good she'd been, how sweet and hot, and wet and . . .

"Hell." The word came out in a low groan.

She turned to look at him. He was staring at her. The coldness in his eyes shamed her even more than her own guilt.

He continued to stare at her for a long minute, until he realized she was making him hard again. Her eyes were still misty with passion, and her lips were swollen from his kisses. He'd scratched her face with his whiskers. He found the marks aroused him too. He knew that if he pulled her back into his arms, he would inhale his own scent.

Hell, he'd been all over her. He turned his gaze to the ceiling and tried to burn a hole through the rock.

"Do you understand what almost happened?"

She flinched over the anger in his voice. "Yes," she answered. "I understand. I suggest we don't ever let ourselves become . . . involved again. It's too dangerous."

"Damned right it's dangerous."

"I'm sorry," she whispered.

He didn't have anything to say about that. She turned to look at him again. Another clump of her hair fell over her left eye. She impatiently brushed it away.

His hair was as tousled as hers was. He looked as though he'd just awakened. She thought he was the most handsome man on earth.

She turned away from him. The silence was making her nervous. She looked at the fire, realized it was nearly out, and immediately added more twigs to the flames.

"Are you going to stay angry for long?"

"Go to sleep, Mary Rose, before I forget all about protecting your honor."

She whirled around to look at him. "Is that why you stopped?"

"No," he answered. "I stopped because you asked me to."

He looked at her again and immediately lost some of his anger. There were tears in her eyes. It finally hit him that he hadn't been thinking about her tender feelings at all. He was too busy being self-centered. God, he was a cad. She had never experienced raw passion before, the way she'd responded to him was proof of that truth, and the burning need inside her must have scared the hell out of her.

"Then what does my honor have to do with anything? You said you stopped because I asked you to stop."

He let out a sigh. He couldn't believe he had to tell her. "Sweetheart, I damned near took your virginity and your honor. A couple of minutes more and I would have."

It wasn't what he said but how he said the words that soothed her. His tone was softer, more civilized. And almost loving. She instinctively relaxed her shoulders and stopped gripping her hands together.

"So that is why you became angry?"

"Yes."

She took a deep breath. "I beg to differ with you."

"You do?" The sudden outrage in her voice made him smile.

It wasn't the reaction she was looking for.

"You're being very smug and male about this, aren't you?"

"I don't believe I am."

"Then I shall enlighten you. You didn't almost take anything. I could have given you my virginity and my honor. I chose not to. I'm the one who asked you to stop. You were busy unbuttoning your pants. Remember?"

He was astonished by the vehemence in her voice. He could feel himself getting angry again, and all because she reminded him of his own lack of discipline.

"Tell me why you stopped."

She shook her head. "You're a lawyer. You figure it out."

"You were afraid."

"No."

"Look, I know you wanted me. You were as hot as I was. I can still feel the marks your nails made on my shoulders. You do remember where your hands were, don't you?"

She could feel herself blushing over his reminder of how she'd behaved. She watched him draw one leg up and drape his arm over his knee. Every movement he made seemed to arouse her.

God, she was despicable. She wasn't any better than a rabbit in heat.

"Of course I remember. I'm not sorry."

"Neither am I."

The emotion in his admission made her shiver and feel warm at the same time. Her reaction to him didn't make any sense to her. She decided it was his fault. The man was deliberately making her crazy.

"Stop looking at me like that."

"Like what?"

"You know."

He did know. He turned to look at the fire. "You still haven't told me why you asked me to stop."

"And you aren't going to let up until I do. Isn't that right?"

"Yes," he agreed. "If you weren't afraid, what was it? You liked the way I touched you. Don't pretend you didn't. I remember how your body reacted. You were hot and wet for me."

Her gaze flew to his. He was staring at her again, and the look in his eyes made her want to melt. "Stop talking like that," she ordered in a voice that sounded horribly weak to her.

"Tell me why you stopped," he ordered once again. "Then I'll stop reminding you."

She closed her eyes. It was the only thing she could think to do to get away from him.

"For a lawyer, you're really dense. It wouldn't ever occur to you that maybe, just maybe I stopped because of your honor, not mine."

"My honor?"

She knew he didn't believe her. She told herself she didn't care. Were all men as arrogant as Harrison and her brothers were? Heavens, she sincerely hoped not.

"Yes, Harrison, your integrity," she said again.

"You are serious, aren't you. . . . My honor." The words came out in a whisper.

Well, hell, he still didn't know if he believed her or not. Yet when she opened her eyes and looked at him again, he could see the sincerity. He was thunderstruck and humbled.

"Your honor," she whispered back. Then she rolled her eyes heavenward and turned away from him.

She was obviously disgusted with him now. He didn't have time to think about that. He was fully occupied trying to figure out how he felt about her protecting him.

"You've got more discipline than I do."

It almost killed him to admit it. She thought he sounded offended by the possibility.

"How like a man to think he's the only one to ever consider such noble things as honor and integrity. Believe it or not, women can be protective too. It isn't a novel concept. It's plain reality. Haven't you ever heard of Joan of Arc? She gave her life for France's honor, and for her own."

"Joan of Arc?" He would have laughed over the comparison, but he didn't want to get killed. "I don't believe she ever did what we just did, Mary Rose."

"Of course she didn't. The woman was a saint, for heaven's sake. I'm not. I wasn't comparing myself to her. I was simply saying that I knew you couldn't have lived with yourself if you had been intimate with me."

"I *was* intimate with you. Remember where my fingers were?"

"Oh, go to sleep."

She moved over to the edge of her blankets so she could get as far away from him as possible. She pulled the covers up, closed her eyes, and tried to get some rest.

He knew he should have stopped tormenting her, but her reaction was so incredibly pleasing to him he couldn't resist. The prettiest blush came over her cheeks when she got flustered.

He was also thankful she was irritated with him. He'd tried to make her angry on purpose, and knew that if they had continued to argue with each other, he would have succeeded. He wasn't being a cad. No, he was being noble, or at least he believed he was. If she was angry, she'd stay away from him. No woman wanted to kiss a man she was thinking about killing. It all made perfectly good sense to him.

Hell, who was he kidding? He was really trying to protect himself. She had already proven she had more discipline than he had. It wouldn't take much to make him forget all about his good intentions. All she had to do was crook her finger in his direction, and he'd be all over her again. He had gotten a taste of heaven, and he had to try to pretend he hadn't loved it.

He didn't sleep much during the night. He kept his gun in his hand near his side and listened for every little sound. He drifted off twice. The first time, the soft flutter of wind awakened him. Someone or something was inside the cave with them. Harrison stayed perfectly still. He opened his eyes only a sliver and saw the woman then. His reaction was immediate. His hand tightened on the gun tucked under the cover. It took all he had not to shoot her, and he thanked God she wasn't looking at him now. She had a quilt in her arms and was standing over Mary Rose, looking down at her.

Crazy Corrie. One look at her and Harrison couldn't imagine why she hadn't gone insane. She was so grossly disfigured, he wanted to turn away from her. He didn't, of course. He didn't move at all. He simply waited to see what she would do.

The woman had finally taken her fill of watching. Without making a sound, she covered Mary Rose with the quilt. She left as silently as she had entered.

He wanted to call after her, to say thank you at the very least, but he didn't make a sound. If the woman had wanted to be seen, she would have done something to make certain they'd awakened. She obviously wasn't ready, and he would respect her wishes.

He felt tremendous guilt over his initial repulsion at the sight of her. And then he closed his eyes and drifted off to sleep once again. Mary Rose had moved closer to his side, but he was still feeling safe in the knowledge he wouldn't have to worry about temptation and his own appalling lack of control.

He woke up with her face in his groin. He thought he'd died and gone to heaven, but as soon as the mist of sleep wore off, he knew he'd gone straight to purgatory instead. Mary Rose wasn't seducing him. She was sound asleep. Her feet were tucked under his chin. She was simply trying in her sleep to get warm.

It took him forever to move her away from him without waking her up. Then he got up as quietly as he could. He walked barefoot outside and stood in the rain.

It didn't help one damned bit.

July 11, 1865

Dear Mama Rose,

Today is my birthday. I wish you were here to celebrate the day with me. Now that the war is over, you'll be able to come to your family, and that will be the best present a son could have.

We pray for Lincoln's soul every night. I try not to get angry anymore about his senseless death, and I'm consoled by the words from his last inaugural address. Here's the part I like the most:

"With malice toward none, with charity for all, with firmness in the right as God gives us to see the right, let us strive on to finish the work we are in, to bind up the nation's wounds, to care for him who shall have borne the battle and for his widow and his orphan, to do all which may achieve and cherish a just and lasting peace among ourselves and with all nations."

Love you,
Travis

10

Some son-of-a-bitch took a shot at them on their way home. Harrison was paying attention. He rode by Mary Rose's side, and the second he spotted the glint of metal through the pines directly ahead of them just where the crook in the trail began to turn, he shoved Mary Rose off her horse, drew his six-shooter, and fired a scant second too late.

The enemy's bullet passed through his right side. Harrison barely reacted to the sting of pain. He was leaning close to Mary Rose's saddle now, his gaze fully directed on the forest ahead. Had she been riding her mount, the bullet he caught most certainly would have killed her.

And that realization sent him right over the edge.

"Stay down," he ordered.

He didn't take time to find out where she'd landed. He goaded MacHugh into a full gallop. Harrison's only determination was to find the bastard and destroy him with his bare hands.

He got a good look at the coward's face, but when he reached the next bend in the trail, the culprit was gone. Harrison followed the tracks and was disappointed to see they ended near the cliff above the river. The coward had obviously jumped. Harrison only hoped he drowned.

He backtracked and found Mary Rose sitting

on a rock with her gun in her hand. She didn't seem to be the least upset by what had just happened.

"Are you all right?" His voice was gruff, angry.

"Yes, thank you." Her voice was as bland as a drink of water. "Would you please fetch Millie for me?"

Harrison nodded, then went after the mare. When he returned, Mary Rose was standing in the center of the trail. She'd put her gun away and was trying to smooth down her hair.

He gave her the reins, then started to dismount so that he could help her, but she was quicker than he was. She got settled in the saddle, smiled at Harrison, and then nudged Millie into moving.

Honest to God, she looked as if the ambush had been an everyday occurrence.

"Are you really all right?" he asked again.

"Yes. My backside's going to be as black and blue as yours though. I landed hard. You did throw me into the bushes, Harrison. Next time I would suggest you merely tell me to duck."

Harrison let her ride ahead of him. He didn't want her to notice he was looking over his injury. He could feel the wetness under his shirt, and when he glanced down, the stain of blood was oozing downward.

It didn't feel like much of an injury to him though. Blood wasn't gushing out, and he took that as a good sign. He was thankful the bullet had gone through.

He took the time to get his leather vest out of his saddlebag. He put it on as quickly as he could. He grimaced over the pain that shot up his side when he moved his arm, then forced a smile because Mary Rose turned in her saddle to look at him. He nudged MacHugh so he could catch up with her now and ride by her side.

"Are you cold? You could use Corrie's quilt if you are," she suggested.

"I'm all right," he answered. "Aren't you cold?"

"No, my clothes dried out. They're wrinkled but warm. Did you catch whoever was trying to kill us?"

"No." He gave her a hard look. He couldn't help but remark on her composure. "You act as though this sort of thing happens all the time. Does it?"

"No, of course not."

"Then why are you acting so calm?"

She waited for him to catch up with her before she answered. "Because you aren't."

"I'm not what?"

"Calm."

He thought he looked and sounded perfectly calm. He guessed he didn't.

"The expression in your eyes makes a mockery of your tone of voice."

"What's wrong with the look in my eyes?"

"Cold . . . angry . . . you're furious you didn't catch the man, aren't you?"

"He jumped over the cliff. I hope he drowned."

"He probably did."

"Weren't you afraid at all?"

"Yes, I was."

"I applaud you then. You hide your feelings better than I do. I thought I was the master of that game. I guess I'm not."

"Is it important to be a master?"

"In a courtroom it is."

She smiled and reached over to pat his knee. "I'm certain you do very well in a courtroom."

"You're something else, Mary Rose. Honest to God, you are."

She didn't know if he'd just given her praise or not. He was smiling though, and so she decided to take his remark as praise.

"Living with Cole has taught all of us to be prepared for surprises. It's all part of our lives out here."

"Your brothers will be home by now."

"Probably. We'll reach the ranch in another half hour or so."

"What do you think he wanted?"

"Who?"

"The coward who tried to kill us."

"Our horses or our money. He might be hoping for both."

"Hell."

"Quit fretting about him. He's gone now. Let's talk about something else. I still can't get over Corrie's thoughtfulness. She had to walk a fair distance to bring us the quilt. It took courage, don't you think?"

"She wanted you to have the quilt. Not me," he corrected.

"You can't know that for certain," she argued.

Harrison smiled. He did know Corrie had covered Mary Rose up, but he hadn't admitted he'd seen the woman. His reason was probably foolish. Corrie belonged to Mary Rose. He wanted her to be the first to see her friend . . . if and when Corrie was ever ready to present herself.

"You still look angry, Harrison."

He couldn't help that. "Damn it, Mary Rose, you could have been killed. I've got a right to be angry. If anything ever happened to you . . ."

She turned to look at him. "Yes?"

He let out a sigh. "Your brothers would kill me."

"Would it kill you to admit you'd miss me?"

"No, it wouldn't kill me. Of course I'd miss you."

She was extremely pleased. She changed the subject once again. "I've considered what you said about Travis, and I've decided I will have a talk with him. I don't want him to become overly upset about Eleanor. I'll have a firm talk with her too. She can't boss my brothers around. Travis will listen to me. Eleanor probably won't. Still, I'll try. Travis's birthday is coming up soon. He'll be on his best behavior so I'll give him a nice present."

"When is his birthday?"

"July eleventh," she answered. "I've almost finished knitting a sweater for him. I think he'll love it. The color complements his eyes. He won't care about that, of course. He'll love it because it will keep him warm. When is your birthday?"

"February seventeenth," he answered.

He didn't ask her to tell him her birthday. He assumed she didn't know the actual date and that her brothers had made one up so she would have her own celebration.

Besides, he already knew the date of Lady

357

Victoria's birth, January second.

"January second."

She said the words a scant second after he'd thought them. He couldn't believe he'd heard right. Then he thought he had inadvertently said the date out loud.

"Did you just . . . What did you say?"

"January second," she repeated. "My birthday. Is there something wrong with January second? You look a little stunned. Honestly you do."

He couldn't answer her. His throat had already closed up on him. Stunned? That had to be an understatement. His mind was reeling with all his impossible possibilities. How in God's name could she know her actual birthday?

"Adam's birthday is November twentieth, Cole's is April fifteenth, although to be perfectly honest with you, he really isn't sure of the date because he doesn't have any proof, but a neighbor remembered him and thought he was born then, so he decided to use it for his celebration date, and Douglas's birthday is the very last day of March. I didn't leave anyone out, did I?"

He shook his head again. "Did you make up your date for your birthday or do you have proof you were born on January second?"

"I have proof," she answered. "I came with papers."

Harrison leaned back in his saddle. The words were echoing in his mind over and over again.

She came with papers.

Everyone was waiting for them. Eleanor was pacing back and forth on the porch, Adam was standing in the doorway, and Douglas and Travis were both sitting on the porch railing, leaning against the posts.

Cole had just walked out of the main barn when Douglas shouted to him and pointed in their direction.

The hotheaded brother's hand, Harrison was quick to note, immediately went to his gun. The expression on his face indicated he was thinking hard about using it.

Harrison let out a weary sigh. Honest to God, he didn't have time for this nonsense. He felt like hell. His side was on fire now. His day wasn't going to get any better though, because he had finally made up his mind not to wait any longer. One way or another, Mary Rose's future was going to be decided before he went to bed. He was going to tell the brothers about their sister. He would get the information he needed first, of course, and if he had to resort to shooting a couple of them in order to find out what he wanted to know, then by God, that's exactly what he was going to do.

He wouldn't procrastinate any longer. He'd be married with six children if he didn't do something soon.

"Harrison, don't frown."

"Sorry. I was thinking about shooting your brothers."

"Please don't," she whispered. "Smile, for heaven's sake."

"They look like a lynch mob."

She turned to look at her brothers again. Harrison was right. Three of the four did look like they wanted to string Harrison up from the nearest tree. Eleanor appeared to be ready to fetch the rope. Her hands were on her hips, and she was glaring at them.

"Adam looks happy to see us. I'm sure he'll be reasonable. Just give your explanation quickly before Cole . . ."

"Sweetheart, we didn't do anything wrong."

"Then why do I feel like we did?"

He smiled when he realized he felt the same way. "I'll take on Cole. You start on the others."

"You take on Cole, and I take on four? Sounds fair to me," she teased.

She turned to watch him head for the barn. Millie wanted to follow, but Mary Rose forced the mare to move toward the house.

"Take off your gun," she suggested to Harrison in a loud whisper. "Cole doesn't usually like to shoot an unarmed man."

Harrison shook his head at her and continued on. He slipped off MacHugh when he was about a yard or so away from Cole. The stallion continued on into the barn. Harrison would see to his needs after he'd dealt with the brother.

Cole came storming over to face him. "You low-down son-of-a-bitch. If you . . ."

He'd reached Harrison before he finished his threat and decided to punch him instead.

Harrison was ready for him this time. He caught Cole's fist in the palm of his left hand and held on tight. Then he started applying pressure.

"If I what?" he challenged in a voice as cold as January.

Cole's expression went from rage to astonishment in the blink of an eye.

360

"If you . . . Damn, you're quick. Let go of me. You're squeezing my trigger finger."

"Are you going to try to hit me again?"

"No. I'm thinking about shooting you now. Then I'm gonna shoot Mary Rose."

"I'll kill you first."

"Hell."

"Nothing happened, Cole. We got caught in the rain, that's all. Walk with me into the barn. I got shot. I want to find out how much damage there is without letting Mary Rose know."

Harrison let go of Cole's fist and walked inside. His legs felt weak to him, but he was certain food would take care of that.

"What happened to you? Did you try something with Mary Rose? Did she shoot you?"

"Of course not," he snapped. He paused near the kerosene lamp and waited until Cole got the flame going.

"Where'd you get hit?"

"In my side. The bullet just nicked me. It passed through."

"Let me have a look."

Cole was all business now. He moved Harrison's arm out of his way and slowly pulled his shirt up. Then he bent down to get a closer look at the injury.

He inwardly blanched when he saw how serious the wound was.

"It's just a scratch, isn't it?"

Cole straightened up. He wondered if Harrison knew how puny his voice sounded. He was fading fast and in need of immediate care.

"Just a scratch," he agreed.

361

Harrison started to retuck his shirt in his pants. "Some coward tried to ambush us near the ridge. I went after him, but he'd already jumped into the river."

"Did you get a look at his face?"

Harrison nodded. Then he started to walk outside. "I should talk to Adam before I clean up."

Cole moved to his left side and put Harrison's arm around his shoulder. He forced him to lean into him.

His voice was mild. "He'll give you something to put on your puny cut. You were a gentleman, weren't you? I sure as certain wouldn't have been if I'd been with a pretty girl. Of course my sister's different. I would have had to kill you if you'd touched her."

"I'll be sure to let you know if I do," Harrison replied.

Cole thought it was strange Harrison didn't seem to notice he was holding him up. His worry intensified. It wasn't like Harrison to be so agreeable.

"I'm taking you to the bunkhouse. Adam will come to fix you up. The little scratch is actually deeper than I let on. It's still puny, of course, but you being a city boy and all, well, it should be looked after. I'll go save Mary Rose this time. You've already had a turn with the bushwhacker."

"What are you going to save her from?"

"My brothers. Why do you think everyone was upset? You took Mary Rose off and left us with the witch. I don't know if I can ever forgive you for that. She took a shot at Douglas. She said it was an accident, but he doesn't believe

362

her, not after she 'accidentally' shot at the stage-coach driver. None of us believe her. We're giving her the boot before she kills one of us."

Harrison managed a weak smile. "Then you weren't worried about your sister's virtue?"

Of course he'd been worried, but he wasn't about to admit it. He'd seen the way Harrison stared at his sister. Mary Rose had been just as busy staring at Harrison.

"No, I wasn't worried about you two. I was going to say that if you go off with Mary Rose and leave us with Eleanor again, we'll all take turns killing you. That's what I was going to say. I decided to punch you instead. I figured a good punch would get my point across much quicker."

Harrison staggered, regained his balance, and continued on. He thought he'd stepped on a rock and that made him stumble.

"Ah, hell, you're going to make me carry you, aren't you?"

Harrison didn't answer Cole. He couldn't. He'd already passed out in his arms.

Mary Rose let out a shout, picked up her skirts and came running toward them. Everyone followed her.

"What did you do to him. Dear God, what did you do?"

"I didn't do anything," Cole shouted back.

She didn't believe him. "What happened to him?"

She bent down and looked at Harrison's face. She saw how pale he was and promptly burst into tears.

Douglas was the next one to reach them. "Did you kill him, Cole?" he demanded.

"No."

The injury was serious, but it wasn't life-threatening, and in Cole's mind that meant Harrison was still fair game.

"What happened?" Adam asked.

Cole's grin was devilish. "He fainted."

January 15, 1866

Dear Mama Rose,
Yur suns are mean to me. Adam make me sit by myself at the table just kause I kicked Travis. Adam is a bad boy. Tell him I don't have to sit there by myself. I made a picture for you.

Mary Rose

11

𝒯hey were never going to let him live it down. No sir, not ever. Fainting was apparently something mountain men never did, and all of the brothers, including Adam, took fiendish delight in telling him so over and over and over again.

Harrison suffered through it, but only because he didn't have any choice. He was too weak to strike back, and once he'd finally regained his strength, three of the four brothers had taken off. Adam stayed home, of course, but Harrison left him alone. The oldest brother had to keep Eleanor calm, and Harrison believed that was enough punishment for any man to suffer.

Now that he'd made up his mind to tell the brothers about Elliott's daughter, he was impatient to get it said. He was forced to wait for all the brothers to come back to the ranch, because he felt it was the only decent thing to do. It wouldn't be right for any of them to get the information secondhand. No, Harrison was determined to tell all of them at the same time.

Waiting made him surly. Adam went up to the ridge with Mary Rose on two separate occasions so she could visit with the woman she now referred to as her dearest friend, and both times they were away, Harrison got stuck entertaining Eleanor. It wasn't a difficult chore, just mind muddling. All he had to do was sit on the front porch and pretend to listen to her complaints.

It took him a good two weeks to get his strength back, and just when he was beginning to feel fit, he got stuck taking Eleanor into Blue Belle.

Cole had finally returned from his hunting trip. On his way home, he had taken time to pick up a couple of items Harrison had requested he look for if he was near Hammond, and so Cole thought he was due a favor in return. He wanted Harrison to accompany him into town. Travis and Douglas had also gone hunting with their brother, and they were now waiting in town for the two of them. Several strangers had arrived in Blue Belle, and Cole wanted Harrison to look them over. If one of them was the bastard who had shot him, well then, Cole would take care of him.

Harrison was more than ready to go anywhere as long as he could get away from Eleanor. He was sitting on the porch with his booted feet propped up on the railing when Cole suggested the outing. Eleanor was seated next to Harrison. She was fanning herself with a week-old newspaper while she complained about the heat.

Cole ignored the woman. He had gone into the kitchen to get something to eat and came back out a few minutes later. He leaned against the post while he told Harrison what he wanted him to do. Eleanor stopped complaining long enough to listen.

She decided she wanted to tag along. "I believe I shall go with you. I have to buy that rude man a new hat."

"No, you can't come with us." Cole gave the denial in a downright mean tone of voice. It was the first time in over two weeks that he'd spoken directly to Eleanor.

She didn't pay any attention to his refusal. She stood up, tossed the newspaper on the floor, and marched inside. "We'll just see about that," she muttered.

"See how easy it was?" Cole remarked. "Am I the only one who can handle Eleanor around here? I said no and she left."

Harrison smiled. "She went inside to get Adam. He'll make us take her."

Cole laughed. He obviously didn't believe him. A minute later, Mary Rose came rushing outside. She spotted the newspaper on the floor and hurried to pick it up.

"May I please go with you and Eleanor into town? I have some errands to do."

Harrison and Cole told her no at the very same time.

She became flustered over the abrupt refusal. She reminded Harrison of an absentminded angel. She wore a dark blue dress with a pale yellow apron. Her hair was pinned up on top of her head. The curls didn't want to stay put, however, and several strands had already fallen down to float around her face.

Cole thought she looked all worn out and told her so.

She ignored his criticism. "Please let me go with you. I won't make you wait on me. I swear I won't."

"Two women are too much for Cole and Harrison to look after, Mary Rose. You should stay home today," Adam suggested from the doorway.

"Two women?" Cole asked his brother. He was already frowning, for he knew where this was headed.

Harrison smiled. "I told you so," he taunted.

Mary Rose didn't want to give up. She obviously thought she still had a good chance of being included because she was taking her apron off and trying to tuck the hair back in her pins at the same time.

She sure looked pretty today. Harrison tried not to stare too long at her. Cole was bound to notice. Harrison had kept as far away from Mary Rose as possible while he was recovering. It hadn't been easy. She wanted to hover over him to make certain he was healing properly. His only defense was to pretend to be asleep whenever she came into the bunkhouse. He wondered why she didn't think it was strange for him to sleep day and night. She didn't though, and he counted that as a blessing.

"Adam, I can't let Eleanor go into Morrison's store alone. None of us will ever be allowed inside again if she acts up. Please reconsider. I won't get into any trouble."

Adam looked at Cole. He shrugged. "There are strangers in town. Two women might be too much to handle. What if he has another fainting spell? He still looks sickly."

"You get to ride with Eleanor in the wagon," Harrison promised in retaliation.

Cole shook his head. Harrison turned to Adam. "Mary Rose is perfectly capable of looking after herself as long as she thinks before she acts."

"She wasn't thinking when she charged after Bickley, was she?" Adam asked. He shook his head while he thought about the result of her actions. "We're lucky she didn't get killed."

"Yes, we are," Harrison agreed. "She's a very beautiful woman. Men are prone to do stupid things when they see a pretty face. We can't predict how these strangers will react. Therefore," he concluded, "Mary Rose and Eleanor should stay home."

He thought he had presented a sound case. He still didn't win. Adam let the women go.

Mary Rose hurried to get ready. Eleanor was already upstairs changing her dress. Harrison couldn't imagine why she needed to put on a fresh one. She hadn't done a damned thing to get the gown she'd been wearing dirty.

Adam waited until both women were out of sight and then came out onto the porch and sat down next to Harrison.

"I don't know if I'm using good sense or just giving in to desperation. A few hours of peace and quiet is a powerful lure."

"Eleanor's driving you crazy too, isn't she?" Cole asked.

Adam reluctantly nodded. "She's pleasant to me. I shouldn't complain, but . . ."

"She has the household in an uproar," Harrison concluded.

"Yes," Adam agreed.

"She isn't stupid, just mean," Cole said. He paused to smile. "I kind of appreciate that quality in a woman," he admitted.

"Which one? Stupid or mean?" Harrison asked just to goad him.

"Mean, of course. Eleanor isn't going to bite the hand that lets her stay."

"I wish she'd stop causing so much trouble." Adam sounded weary and bewildered.

"You're going to have to do something about her," Cole told his brother.

"Like what?"

Harrison stood up. "Let me take a swing at her. Cole, you're going to have to help."

"I don't like to hit a woman. Fact is, I never have. It doesn't seem right."

"I didn't mean literally." Harrison caught Cole's grin and realized he was jesting.

"Mary Rose says Eleanor's afraid," Adam remarked. "I've spent quite a lot of time with the woman and I guess I agree."

"And that's why the two of you have been so patient with her. It isn't working," Harrison said.

"Tell us something we don't know, City Boy."

"Cole, quit baiting him. He's trying to help. Did you have a particular plan in mind, Harrison?"

"Yes. A little terror tactic."

Eleanor's shout of anger floated down to the porch. Cole closed his eyes in reaction. Adam clenched his jaw.

"God, she's got a shrill voice," Cole muttered. "Does she have to scream all the time?"

Harrison didn't believe Cole's question needed an answer. He told the brothers the plan and waited to hear their arguments.

There weren't any. "So I get to be the savior," Cole remarked. "What about Mary Rose? She won't go along with this."

"We wait until we're on our way back from town. Travis and Douglas will ride with Mary Rose ahead . . . way ahead," Harrison said.

"Why can't I be the one to dump her out on the ridge?" Cole asked. "I'm better at being mean."

"Because I don't want her to hate you. She can hate me," Harrison explained.

"Then you have to ride with her in the wagon. I'll go get it hitched up," Cole said.

Mary Rose came downstairs a few minutes later, but Eleanor didn't come down for another half hour.

Harrison waited in the front hall with Mary Rose. Adam had gone into the kitchen to help prepare their supper.

Eleanor finally presented herself. She was wearing one of Mary Rose's dresses. Harrison remembered it because Mary Rose had looked so pretty in its particular shade of blue.

Mary Rose looked startled when she saw what her houseguest was wearing. She didn't say anything about it, however, and Harrison decided to let it go, for now.

Eleanor didn't look half bad wearing the dress. If he didn't dislike her behavior so thoroughly, he would have taken the time to appreciate the fact that she was a fine-looking woman. She had pretty hair. It was short and very curly. He didn't know if she had a nice smile though, because he'd never seen her smile. Her lips were always puckered with disgust, as though she had just swallowed a dose of castor oil.

"Are you ready to leave, Eleanor? Cole's waiting out front."

"Is there a restaurant in town? I'll probably want to refresh myself with a spot of tea and some biscuits before we head back. I'll need additional funds, Mary Rose. Be a dear and give me more money."

"The only eating establishment is the saloon, and we can't go in there."

"How uncivilized. Why can't we go inside?"

"Because it isn't proper. Shall we go?"

Harrison held the screen door open for the women. Eleanor went outside first but came to an abrupt stop. Mary Rose bumped into her.

Eleanor had spotted the wagon at the end of the path and was now shaking her head. Cole was on his way back to the barn to get the other horses.

Eleanor shouted to him. "You, there. Fetch the buggy. The wagon won't do."

Cole stopped in his tracks. And then he slowly turned around to look at Eleanor. His expression showed how furious he was.

"Didn't you hear me, boy? Fetch the buggy."

Harrison could have sworn he saw smoke coming from Cole's eyes. The brother was smoldering with his anger.

"Won't the wagon do, Eleanor?" Mary Rose asked. She was trying to head off a confrontation. "You're making my brother angry. Do try to get along."

Harrison stood behind the two women with his

hands clasped behind his back and a wild, isn't-life-grand grin on his face. He was thoroughly enjoying Cole's anger, because the brother couldn't do a damn thing about it.

"You cannot be serious, Mary Rose," Eleanor replied. "My skin will get burned if I ride in the wagon. Do you want me to become afflicted with freckles?"

"I have freckles," Mary Rose said.

"Yes, dear, I know."

Mary Rose let out a sigh. Then she turned to Cole. "Please cooperate," she called out. "I'll help you hitch up the carriage."

Cole said something, but they were too far away to hear. Harrison guessed it was a nasty expletive.

"I'll help him," Harrison volunteered. "You ladies wait here. Mary Rose?" he said her name on his way down the stairs.

"Yes, Harrison."

"I like your freckles."

Harrison did ride with Eleanor, of course, and by the time they reached Blue Belle, getting drunk was beginning to have a certain appeal.

His ears were ringing from her criticisms. The woman never let up. He was going too fast. He wasn't going fast enough. He was sitting too close to her. He was surly with his remarks. He was rude because he wouldn't talk to her.

Travis and Douglas were inside the saloon. They hurried outside as soon as they spotted Cole and Mary Rose riding past. Douglas was given the responsibility of watching out for their sister. He agreed before he spotted the buggy and realized he had just gotten stuck with Eleanor too, and then he started complaining.

No one paid any attention to him. Travis hurried back inside the saloon. He wanted to keep his eye on the three ugly-looking strangers to see if one of them reacted when Harrison came inside.

Mary Rose and Eleanor walked side by side down the street. Douglas stayed well behind them.

"When we go inside the store, you might notice a young woman working behind the counter. Her name's Catherine Morrison. Her father owns the place," Mary Rose said.

"Is she important?"

"What do you mean?"

"Never mind," Eleanor replied. "Why are you telling me about her if she's just a clerk?"

"She's interested in Harrison," Mary Rose said.

"I'm certain the woman could do better."

"What's wrong with Harrison?"

"So many things I don't know where to begin," Eleanor said. "Let's see. He can't engage in a decent conversation. He mumbles one-word replies, and he frowns all the time. He's quite intimidating too. Surely you've noticed."

"I noticed he's wonderful and kind and thoughtful and loving," Mary Rose replied. "I don't want Catherine flirting with him."

"And?" Eleanor prodded.

"I just thought that if you happen to see Catherine hanging around Harrison, you would . . . you know."

"Interrupt them?"

"Yes."

"Why would I want to do that?"

"To help me," Mary Rose cried out, her exasperation obvious. "It won't kill you, Eleanor, to lend a hand every now and then. Oh, never mind. Forget I even mentioned Catherine. You should have asked me if you could wear my dress before you put it on, by the way."

"It's too tight for me."

Eleanor didn't apologize, but Mary Rose hadn't really expected her to. They reached the general store. Mary Rose held the door open and let Eleanor go inside first.

Douglas made certain there weren't any unsavory characters inside, then went back out and stood by the door. He was going to make his sister control Eleanor's behavior.

Harrison spotted the man who had tried to ambush him as soon as he walked into the saloon. The son-of-a-bitch quickly looked away. Harrison pretended he hadn't recognized him. He looked the other two over on his way to the counter.

He ordered a drink of whiskey and downed it in one long swallow. He swore he could still hear Eleanor's voice pounding like a hammer inside his head.

Travis moved to stand on Harrison's left side and Cole moved to stand on his right side. Both brothers put their backs to the counters and stared at the strangers.

"Well?" Cole whispered. He half turned to ask, "Is he in here?"

Harrison didn't answer. Travis turned to him and said, "There are a couple of other men hanging around Belle's place. You should look them over too. They don't have any reason to be down

376

there. Belle's been in Hammond almost six months now. Everyone knows she won't be back until July. She always comes home for my birthday and stays until it turns cold again. Are you sure you remember what the man who shot you looked like?"

"What are you boys whispering about? I don't want any shooting in here, Cole. Keep that in mind." Billie was frowning with his worry.

"I was just about to tell Travis and Cole to stay out of my business, Billie," Harrison told the proprietor.

"I don't recall ever hearing anyone tell Cole Clayborne to stay out of his business before."

"I'm not taking offense," Cole said. "Harrison hasn't been feeling well lately."

Billie nodded sympathetically. He leaned into the counter. "I heard about your fainting spells. Have you had any more I should know about?"

Harrison turned to glare at Cole. The brother tried to look innocent. He failed in his endeavor.

"I didn't tell Billie," he insisted.

"He told Dooley," Travis was happy to add.

"Do you know those men sitting at the table in the corner near the window?" Harrison asked Billie.

"No, why do you ask?"

"I just wondered who they were," Harrison replied.

"Someone needs to tell them to take a bath. I can smell them over here," Cole remarked in a loud voice so he'd be sure to be overheard.

"Stay out of my business, Cole," Harrison snapped.

"I was just having a little fun."

"Do you want to go down to Belle's place or not?" Travis asked.

"Tell me who Belle is first," Harrison said.

"Why, she's the town's whore," Billie informed him. He sounded immensely proud of that fact. "Belle's a right nice woman. Isn't she, Travis?"

"Yes, she is."

Cole wasn't paying any attention to the conversation. One of the men had gotten up and walked outside. He waited to see what the others were going to do.

"Of course, she's gotten on in years," Billie continued. "She's still got a good, soft touch though. Judge Burns always stops by her place to say his hello and put his boots under her bed whenever he passes through town on a hanging spree. We all think mighty highly of her. I guess you figured that out already though, since we named our town after her."

"The town's named after a whore?" Harrison was incredulous. He shook his head and burst into laughter.

"What's so funny?" Billie asked.

"I thought you named the town after the flower," he admitted.

Billie chuckled. "Now, why would we want to do a fool thing like that? We ain't city boys, Harrison. We'd never name our place after a flower. That don't make no sense at all. I think maybe all of them fainting spells made you as loco as Ghost."

"I only fainted once," Harrison announced.

"Of course you did," Billie agreed. The con-

descending tone of voice indicated he didn't believe Harrison.

Cole was still keeping his eye on the two men
huddled together at the table. One of them was
talking in a low voice. The other kept nodding.
Then the agreeable one got up and went outside.

Cole immediately turned his gaze to the street
beyond the window. He was curious to find out
where the man was going.

"Travis, why don't you go on outside," Cole
suggested in a whisper. "Use the back door."

"Billie doesn't have a back door," Travis reminded his brother.

"Then make one."

"I told you to stay out of my business," Harrison repeated.

Cole shrugged. Travis had already left to go
into Billie's store room. Harrison tossed a coin
on the countertop. "Thanks for the drink, Billie."

He turned around and walked over to face the
man who had tried to kill him.

The stranger looked up from his drink and
frowned at Harrison. His right hand was slowly
edging toward his lap.

"I saw your face, you son-of-a-bitch."

"What are you talking about?"

Harrison told him. He used every foul, four-
letter word he could think of while he insulted
him, but the one word that finally got a reaction
was coward. Ugly-face took exception to the
word.

He started to stand up. Cole's voice stopped
him cold. "Harrison, you're talking to the scrag-
gliest looking animal I've ever seen. I can smell

his stink all the way over here. If his hand moves once more, I'm gonna have to shoot him."

"For the love of mother, don't start anything in here, Cole," Billie pleaded. He sounded like he was about to cry. "I just got my new mirror up on the wall. Go on outside, please. I'm begging you."

"Stay where you are, Cole. This is my fight, not yours. What's your name, coward?"

"I'm going to kill you. No one calls Quick a coward. And people call me Quick because I'm quick as a snake."

After giving the threat, Coward stood up and strutted outside. He was wearing two guns. Harrison was wearing only one.

Cole went to the doorway to watch. Billie hurried out from behind his counter and ran over to the window.

"Don't you think you'd best get on out there and help your friend? Everyone in town knows Harrison can't shoot his way out of a gunnysack. He's gonna get himself killed. I sure wish Dooley was here. He went fishing today. He'll be sorry he missed this."

Cole was busy looking at the tops of the buildings, trying to locate the other two men. They'd disappeared, but he knew they were hiding nearby. Men who ambushed once will do it again, or so Cole believed, and if the three of them were friends, they all thought the same gutless way. Cowards ran with cowards, didn't they?

"Now, what's Harrison doing standing in the middle of the road talking to Quick?" Billie asked.

"He's probably lawyering," Cole replied.

"His speechifying is making Quick-As-a-Snake real mad. I can see him fuming from here."

Harrison was trying to get Quick to admit his guilt before he hurt him. If he cooperated and owned up to his crime, Harrison would force himself to behave in a civilized manner. He wouldn't kill him. No, he'd let him crawl away . . . eventually. He would beat the hell out of him first, of course.

"Your bullet could have killed Mary Rose Clayborne," he roared.

Quick backed a step away from the rage he saw in Harrison's eyes. "I'm going to kill you," he repeated in a stammer. "Here and now in front of witnesses. We'll have a draw, on the square."

Harrison nodded. He was through talking. "Tell me the rules," he demanded.

"What?"

"Tell me the rules of a draw."

Quick spit in the dirt and let out a snicker. "We each take a walk backwards real slow for about ten paces."

"Can you count that high?"

Quick's eyes narrowed. "I'm gonna like killing you," he whispered before he continued with his explanation. "When one of us stops, the other one stops too. Then we shoot each other. You'll be dead before your hand reaches your gun. They don't call me Quick-As-a-Snake for nothing."

He snickered again and started backing away. Harrison also backed up. The two men faced when they were about fifteen feet apart.

Quick suddenly started shaking his head.

"Don't shoot me," he cried out.

"Why the hell not?" Harrison bellowed back.

"I ain't going to draw. I'm putting my hands up real easy. I don't want to shoot."

Harrison was infuriated. "What changed your mind?"

"I don't like the odds."

Harrison wanted to shoot him anyway. He realized he was acting like a savage. He didn't care. The bastard could have killed Mary Rose, and life without her would have killed him.

He took a long, deep breath and tried to calm his rage. "All right, put your hands up. I'm going to let Judge Burns hang you."

Quick put his hands up. Harrison started walking toward him. He happened to glance toward the walkway and saw Mary Rose peeking out at him through the window of Morrison's store. She looked extremely upset.

He wasn't altogether unhappy she'd witnessed the confrontation. He wished he'd been able to shoot the gun out of Quick's hand though. Then maybe she'd start believing he was just as capable as her brothers.

He'd take what he could get. Facing down Quick had to count for something.

God, he really needed to get the hell out of here, he suddenly realized. He was beginning to think and act like Cole.

Where was Cole? Harrison knew the answer before he turned around. The brother was standing ten feet behind him and just a little to his left. He wasn't alone. Travis and Douglas flanked his sides.

"How long have you been standing there?" Harrison bellowed the question.

"Long enough," Cole answered. "I wouldn't turn your back on Snake if I were you. He looks like he's itching to shoot you in the back."

"I told you . . ."

Harrison spotted the man leaning out a window above the empty storeroom. He was bringing his gun up when Harrison drew his gun and fired one shot.

It was enough. The gun flew out of the bastard's hand. He let out a howl of pain.

Quick seized the opportunity and went for his guns. The third man came running out from between two buildings and fired at the same instant.

Cole shot the man coming out of the alley, then turned to Quick. He was too late. Travis had already beaten him to the task. He was putting his gun back in his gunbelt before Cole had time to recock his gun. "Now, that was quick," Travis drawled out.

Douglas had already moved to stand behind his brothers with his back to them so he could protect them from any more surprises.

Harrison wanted to kill every one of the interfering brothers.

His humiliation wasn't complete, however. Cole started giving him hell for being so stupid.

"Didn't you wonder where the other two went? If we hadn't interfered, you'd be flat on your face with a bullet in your back. Start using your head, Harrison. Hotheads don't last long out here."

Harrison took a deep breath. He knew Cole

383

was right. Anger had almost gotten him killed.

"You're right. I wasn't thinking."

"Oh, you were thinking all right. You were thinking all about how Quick could have killed Mary Rose. Isn't that true?"

Harrison nodded. He was fast beginning to feel like an idiot.

"Listen up, City Boy. There's only one rule to live by out here. Someone's always going to be faster. Always. As long as you remember that, and believe it, you'll stay alive." He shoved his finger in Harrison's chest. "Got that?"

Harrison nodded. Cole let out an expletive. "We didn't kill any of them."

"I wish we had," Harrison admitted. "I guess I'll round them up and lock them up in the empty store."

"It won't do any good. They'll only get out. Let the sheriff deal with them."

"You don't have a sheriff, remember?"

Cole shrugged. "Do what you want then. You were so angry, you didn't get Quick to confess. He isn't going to now. Get ready. Here comes Mary Rose. She looks as mad as a hornet."

Harrison didn't want to turn around and look. Mary Rose reached Douglas first.

"Will you get the horses. We're going home. Now."

"Are you mad about something, Mary Rose?"

"You just shot up the town, Douglas."

"I didn't shoot anyone. They did. Harrison started it."

"I'm not in the mood for excuses. You were as much a part of it as they were."

384

"Why aren't you in the mood? Anything else happen?"

"Eleanor just called Mrs. Morrison a fat cow. That's what else. Let's go."

Cole had turned away so his sister wouldn't see his smile. Calling Mrs. Morrison a fat cow was a real mean thing to do. He couldn't help but appreciate the guts it must have taken for Eleanor to stand up to a woman who weighed four times more than she did. It was also a stupid thing to do, but Cole didn't want to dwell on that fact.

Travis wasn't smiling. He was horrified Eleanor had insulted Catherine's mother.

"I'll admit she's a hefty-sized woman, but I wouldn't call her a cow," he told Mary Rose.

"Mary Rose, come here. I need more money. I've found something I want to buy."

Eleanor shouted the order from the walkway in front of the store. Mary Rose ignored her. She walked with Douglas to get the horses.

Cole explained Harrison's plan to Travis and told him to tell Douglas when their sister wasn't within earshot.

Harrison got inside the carriage. He'd given up on the idea of rounding up the wounded men. His only hope was that they all bled to death.

The three brothers left with their sister a few minutes later. Eleanor finally realized she'd been abandoned and ran over to the buggy.

Harrison didn't help her get inside.

"Have you ever seen such rudeness in all your life?" she muttered. "How dare Mary Rose leave without me. I am her guest, I'll have you remember."

Harrison gritted his teeth and didn't say a word until they were halfway home. Then he pulled the carriage over to the edge of the road.

"You aren't a guest. You're a charity case."

She tried to slap him. He grabbed hold of her hand and then let go. "Or at least you were a charity case."

"How dare you talk to me like that."

"Get out, Eleanor."

She let out a gasp. Her hand flew to her throat. "What did you say?"

"You heard me. Get out."

"No."

"Fine. I'll throw you out."

"You cannot be serious."

He reached for her arm. She let out a stone-shattering scream.

Then she got out of the carriage. "You've lost your senses. When I tell Mary Rose . . ."

He didn't let her finish her threat. "I don't think you'll make it back, so I don't have to worry about that, do I?"

"You can't treat me this way." She burst into tears and threw her hands over her face.

"Mary Rose's brothers will cheer me. I'm making their job easier for them. They were going to give you the boot tomorrow."

Eleanor was quite remarkable. She stopped weeping in mid sob. "What do you mean?"

"They're going to make you leave."

"Mary Rose won't let them."

"Everyone voted," he said. He didn't feel at

all bad that he was upsetting her. It was time someone shook her up. She'd been acting like a spoiled little princess with a thorn in her backside long enough. The young woman needed to learn the consequences of her actions.

"Adam would vote to let me stay," she cried out.

"He would if he could," Harrison agreed. "But he's head of the household, so he always abstains. Cole, Travis, and Douglas voted against you. I would have, but I'm not a member of the family, so they wouldn't let me vote. In the Clayborne household, majority rules, Eleanor. You've been given every chance. Mary Rose was going to help you pack tonight. I've just saved her the chore."

"I won't leave."

"If you should happen to find your way back to the ranch, one of the brothers will haul you back to town and dump you there."

Harrison wasn't showing any mercy. He was a bit ashamed when he realized how much he was enjoying himself.

Eleanor became hysterical. Harrison picked up the reins and started for the ranch again.

Her screams followed him along the trail. He started whistling in an attempt to block out the noise. It suddenly dawned on him that the screaming wasn't receding. It was getting closer. He turned and saw her running toward him. Eleanor could move when she wanted to. Odd, she couldn't find the strength to come downstairs in the morning to eat with the family, but she could run up a mountain just as fast as the horses were trotting along.

She was shouting colorful obscenities at him. Harrison turned back to the road and increased the pace. According to the plan, Cole would be waiting just around the next bend. He was probably watching Eleanor now, making certain she didn't injure herself or get into trouble.

Cole would eventually become Eleanor's savior. He would make her promise to behave herself and then bring her home.

The rest of the trip was blissfully peaceful for Harrison. He forgot about Eleanor's behavior and concentrated on his own. He was having trouble accepting the fact that he had deliberately provoked a gunfight. He hadn't been acting like a civilized man. No doubt about it, the longer he stayed at the ranch, the more barbaric he became.

His thoughts turned to the confrontation ahead of him. Now that all the brothers were home, he would talk to them tonight. He dreaded the duty, and he thought perhaps his own feelings about the brothers had been yet another reason for his procrastination. They were all good, decent men. Damn, he almost wished they weren't.

Harrison refused to think about Mary Rose's reaction to the fact that he'd been acting under false pretenses from the moment they'd met.

He started down the hill, spotted the ranch in the distance, and suddenly felt as though he were coming home. Three of the four brothers were sitting on the porch. Adam was working inside the corral, riding a black horse Harrison hadn't seen before. The animal was trying to buck his rider off his back. Adam wasn't having any trouble staying on, which was a remarkable feat, given the fact that the brother was riding bareback. He looked as though he were glued to the wild animal's back. Adam's movements were fluid and graceful. It wasn't as easy as it appeared to be though. Adam had taken his shirt off, and Harrison could see the sweat from his strenuous exertion glistening on his shoulders.

Harrison waved to him as he passed him and continued on to the barn. Travis shouted to him. He pointed to a bottle he held up in one hand. Harrison nodded. He took the buggy into the barn, unhitched the horses and put them in the back pasture to cool down, then moved MacHugh outside to an empty corral so he could get some exercise, and headed for the main house. He was ready for a cool drink and was smiling in anticipation.

"Where's Mary Rose?" he called out.

"Inside," Douglas called back.

Adam had dismounted and was just opening the gait to the corral when Harrison walked past him. He stopped to speak to him.

"After supper tonight, I'd like to talk to you and your brothers."

"All right," Adam agreed. "What do you want to talk about?"

"I'll explain later," Harrison hedged. "I don't want Mary Rose to listen in."

Adam nodded. He unfolded his shirt and put it on. The two men walked together. Adam looked thoughtful. Harrison was a little surprised he didn't ask more questions.

"It's hot out, isn't it, Harrison?" Cole remarked.

"It sure is," Harrison answered before he realized whom he was talking to.

Harrison increased his pace until he was almost running.

"What are you doing here?" he demanded in a near shout.

"I live here," Cole replied.

"Where's Eleanor?" Harrison asked.

"Isn't she with you?" Adam asked from behind.

"She was supposed to be with Cole," Harrison answered. "What happened? Did you take her back to town and leave her there?"

Even as he asked the question, he knew it wasn't possible. Cole wouldn't have had enough time to take Eleanor back to Blue Belle and then make it home before Harrison.

Unless he'd taken a shortcut.

Harrison jumped on the possibility. "She's inside, isn't she?"

Douglas smiled. Cole tilted his chair back, propped his booted feet up on the rail, lowered the rim of his hat, and closed his eyes.

Harrison turned to Adam. The eldest brother looked appalled.

"She isn't inside," Adam announced. He turned his attention to Cole. "I swear I'm going to tear the hide off your backside if anything happened to her. Were you supposed to bring her home?"

"Yes," Cole admitted without opening his eyes.

Adam reached the bottom step and stopped. Harrison sat down on the top step. He decided he'd let Adam deal with the problem. He would have better luck getting answers out of Cole.

"What happened?" Adam asked.

"She's all right," Cole said.

"Don't you realize the dangers up there? Are you completely out of your mind? For the love of God, there are wild animals roaming about. What could you have been thinking?"

"She won't hurt any of the animals. Don't get all lathered up, Adam."

"That isn't funny," Adam snapped.

Harrison began to smile, but Adam gave him a hard look and he quickly forced a frown. He knew Eleanor had to be all right. Cole wouldn't have left her to fend for herself up there, and once Harrison had gotten over his initial surprise, he realized that fact. Adam would realize it, too, as soon as he got over being angry. Cole was just having a little sport with all of them. Harrison would let him have his laugh and then find out where he'd hidden Eleanor.

"The animals won't bother Eleanor," Cole assured everyone. "Relax, will you? I'm having my break. Adam, did Travis tell you he spotted those five missing steers up on the short ridge? I'm thinking about going after them in a little while. Travis can go with me."

"I'll go with you," Harrison volunteered. He wanted to keep as busy as possible so he wouldn't have to think about the meeting tonight.

"What for? You can't help," Cole told him.

"Of course I can help," Harrison argued. "Show me what you want me to do, and I'll do it."

"Where have I heard that before?" Cole said dryly.

"What have you done with Eleanor?" Adam demanded once again. He came up the stairs and sat down next to Harrison. The oldest brother must not have been overly concerned about their houseguest, however. His gaze was centered on MacHugh now. The stallion was prancing around inside the corral.

"Harrison, would you mind if I rode MacHugh?" he asked.

"I don't mind. MacHugh might. You're welcome to give him a try."

"Cole, are you about ready to answer me?" Adam asked. He kept his attention on MacHugh while he waited for his brother to answer.

"Dooley's looking out for her. I ran into him on my way past the creek. I gave him a dollar to keep his eye on her until I feel like going back."

Harrison grinned. "Exactly when will you feel like going after her?" he asked.

"In a spell," Cole promised. "It's real peaceful now, isn't it?"

Travis came outside with bottles of beer for all of them. He handed one to Douglas and then gave Harrison one.

"Isn't that Dooley coming down the hill?" Douglas asked the question. He squinted against the sunlight in an attempt to get a better look. "Yes, I do believe it is Dooley."

Adam leaned forward. "By God, it is Dooley, and he's alone. Cole, if anything happens to Eleanor, you're responsible."

"Adam, do you want a beer?" Travis asked.

The worry about Eleanor was temporarily put on hold. He accepted the bottle and took a long swallow.

"It goes down real smooth, doesn't it?"

Travis nodded. "I bartered for a dozen bottles. Sure tastes good."

"I hope Mary Rose doesn't come outside. She's bound to notice Eleanor's missing," Douglas said.

"If she asks, we won't tell her anything," Travis said. He leaned against the post and let out a yawn. "She thinks Eleanor's in her room. Let her go on thinking it."

"I don't think she'll want to talk to Eleanor for a long time," Douglas predicted.

"Why not?" Adam asked.

"She's still mad at her," Douglas said. "Eleanor called Mrs. Morrison a fat cow."

"Dear Lord. I hope Mrs. Morrison didn't hear her," Adam said. He shuddered over the mere possibility.

"I don't see how she couldn't have heard," Douglas said. "She was talking to the woman and said it to her face."

Adam shook his head. "Looks like we're going to have to go to Hammond to get our necessaries."

"Eleanor will apologize," Cole predicted. "I'll bet she's almost ready to change her ways."

"What was she doing when you took off?" Travis asked.

"Throwing rocks and screaming. The woman's got quite a colorful vocabulary."

"Afternoon, Dooley," Douglas called out. "Do you want a beer?"

"I sure could use me one," Dooley replied. He climbed down from his mount and strutted over to the stairs. Harrison had never noticed how bowlegged the man was before. Dooley walked like he was carrying a pickle barrel between his knees.

The old man sat down on the steps between Adam and Harrison. He took his hat off, wiped his brow with the back of his arm, and then said, "It surely is warm for winter, ain't it?"

"It's June, Dooley," Cole informed him.

Harrison patiently waited for one of the brothers to find out what had happened to Eleanor. No one said a word. They were still busy appreciating their beverages. Harrison assumed the drink was a rarity for them because of the scarcity.

Dooley was licking his lips in anticipation of the treat he was going to get. Harrison finally broke down and asked the question for the others.

"Dooley, weren't you supposed to be watching out for Eleanor?"

"Yes, sir, I surely was."

"Then why are you here?"

"I couldn't take it no more. She was making so much noise my head started in pounding. She didn't spot me watching out for her though. I can hide real tight when I set my mind to it. I couldn't hide from the screaming, even when I covered my ears with my hands. Then Ghost happened along. I gave him two whole dollars to sit a spell and watch over her."

"Was Ghost drinking his brew?" Cole asked.

"He ran out three days ago. He's pretty straight now," Dooley assured him.

Harrison turned to Cole. "I'm not going after her."

"I didn't ask you to."

"I'm still going to get blamed for this, aren't I?"

"Yes, sir, you surely are." Cole laughed after he answered in just the same way Dooley would have. "If Mary Rose finds out before I bring Eleanor back, it's got to be your fault."

"How do you figure that?" Harrison asked.

"It was your plan."

"Mary Rose might not find out," Travis suggested from the doorway.

"I acted in good faith," Harrison argued.

"She'll find out all right," Douglas predicted. "She'll get real suspicious in a couple of days if Eleanor doesn't come downstairs. I figure Mary Rose will stay mad at her until around Friday. Then she'll start asking questions."

"Are you going to leave Eleanor up on the mountain that long?" Harrison asked Cole.

"I don't believe Ghost could take it that long. I might have to add another dollar to keep him from balking. You willing to lend me one, Cole?"

"Sure, Dooley," Cole agreed.

"Here's your beer, Dooley," Travis said. He handed the bottle to the man. "Say, isn't that Ghost coming down the trail?"

Harrison stood up. He accepted the inevitable. He was going to have to fetch Eleanor.

Mary Rose appeared in the doorway. "Hello, Dooley," she called out.

"Howdy, Miss Mary," he called back.

She walked out onto the porch and looked around. "Has anyone seen Eleanor? I want to have a talk with her."

Everyone looked at Harrison. He didn't say a word. He sat down again and stared off into the distance.

Travis decided to lie for him. "She's up in her room. Let her stew for a while."

"What would she be stewing about?"

Travis couldn't think of anything. Douglas came to his assistance. "She must know you're angry with her, Mary Rose. She's mean, not stupid. She called Mrs. Morrison a fat cow, and she's got to know you're unhappy about that," he reasoned.

Harrison turned to look at Mary Rose. She gave him a hard frown.

"Adam, have you had your talk with Harrison yet?" she asked.

"Not yet, Mary Rose."

"Please see to it. The sooner the better."

"Talk about what?" Harrison asked her.

She didn't answer him. She turned around and went back inside. She let the screen door slam shut behind her.

Harrison turned to Adam. "What was that all about?"

"She told on you," Cole said.

"What?"

"She told Adam about the gunfight," he explained.

"Don't take offense, Harrison. She's only trying to look out for you," Douglas said.

Cole stood up. He stretched his shoulders, put the beer bottle down on the railing, and then went down the steps.

"I guess I'll go get Eleanor now. Ghost, why aren't you watching Eleanor?" he called out.

The white-haired man reached the walkway in front of the house and shook his head. "I couldn't stand it no more. It weren't worth the money. Henry heard all the racket and came looking. I gave him three dollars to sit on her for a while. I ain't never doing you no more favors again, Dooley."

Cole headed for the barn. "Harrison, have you ever used a rope before?" he called over his shoulder.

"I showed him how," Douglas shouted back. "He's been practicing."

"We'll go and rope those steers as soon as I get back with Eleanor," Cole yelled.

Harrison stood up. "Douglas, you didn't need to lie for me."

"Go and practice now," the brother suggested. "Then it won't be a lie. Come on. I'll show you how it's done."

"Harrison, you'd better eat something first," Adam suggested.

He agreed. While Douglas went to get a couple of ropes, he accompanied Adam into the kitchen. They ate at the kitchen table and talked about mundane matters all the while. Mary Rose walked into the kitchen, spotted the two men at the table, and promptly turned around and walked back out.

"Aren't you supposed to talk to me about the gunfight?" Harrison asked. "I understand Mary Rose told on me."

He was looking at the doorway and smiling.

"Yes," Adam agreed. "My sister thinks you might have deliberately provoked the man into a draw."

"I did," Harrison admitted.

He waited for Adam's lecture. The brother didn't say another word. After several minutes of silence passed, Harrison prodded him.

"And?"

"And what?"

"Aren't you going to talk to me about it?"

"I just did."

Harrison laughed.

Cole, on the other hand, certainly wasn't laughing. Eleanor wasn't cooperating with his plan. The second she spotted him coming toward her, she picked up a good-size rock and threw it at him.

Cole didn't think that was any way for her to treat her savior. She should have been appreciative, not furious.

She sure was a sight to behold. Her cheeks were all flushed and rosy, and her eyes fairly blazed with anger.

"Haven't you figured anything out yet?" he asked her. "Quit throwing things, damn it."

He dodged another pebble and nudged his horse closer. Eleanor stood in the center of the trail. She'd walked a good distance. He looked down at her shoes and thought her feet had to be getting blisters.

She didn't seem to care. She limped right past him and continued on toward the rise.

"Where are you going?"

"Back to the ranch to pack my things. I'm going to shoot Harrison because he left me stranded up here, and then I'm going to leave. I'll walk back into town."

"Mary Rose won't let you shoot Harrison. She's sweet on him."

"I don't care."

"No, I guess you don't. You don't care about anyone but yourself."

He sounded resigned. She turned around and looked up at his face to see if he was just trying to make her angry or if he really believed what he'd just said.

He looked sincere to her. She straightened her shoulders. "That isn't true. Mary Rose has four strong brothers to look out for her. I don't have anyone. I have to watch out for myself."

"You're the most self-consumed creature I've ever met."

She burst into tears. They weren't forced. She hurt everywhere, and now he was deliberately injuring her pride. It was all she had left. She couldn't cling to it any longer though.

"I've had a difficult life," she cried out.

"Who hasn't?"

"Harrison left me out here alone."

"You were never alone."

Her shoulders slumped. "I know."

She turned to the bushes. "You may leave now, Henry. Cole's here."

"Thank you, Miss Eleanor," Henry called back.

She took a deep breath. "I . . . appreciated your company."

"I didn't mind yours neither, except when you were screaming. You made my head hurt, Miss Eleanor."

"I'm sorry."

She turned back to the trail and started walking again. Cole rode by her side.

"That wasn't so difficult, was it?"

"What wasn't difficult?" She kept her attention on the ground so she wouldn't step on anything sharp. Her feet were sticky and hot.

She felt miserable and knew she looked worse. She ran her fingers through her hair in an attempt to give the curls some order and kept walking. She didn't care what Cole thought she looked like. No, she certainly didn't. She realized her top three buttons were undone and quickly latched them up.

"Being nice wasn't difficult," he said.

"Yes, it was."

He smiled because he felt the same way. "Why is it difficult?"

"You wouldn't understand."

"Try me."

"It makes me feel vulnerable."

He almost nodded agreement. The two of them were more alike than he'd realized.

"You're supposed to treat others the way you wish to be treated," he recited from memory. Lord, how many times had Adam suggested that golden rule to him?

"Now, why would I want to do that?"

He really didn't have any idea. She volunteered her own theory. "Do you think they'll then treat me nice?"

"Some will."

"What about the ones who don't?"

"You get to be mean to them."

She burst into laughter. She was amazed she

could find joy in anything, given her dire circumstances.

His words made sense, but she wasn't quite ready to admit it. She decided to try once more for sympathy.

"Everyone leaves me," she said. "Even my father ran away from me. I was abandoned."

"So?"

"I got scared."

"Who doesn't get scared every now and then?"

She gave it one last try. "I'm completely without funds."

"Too bad. Try earning some money."

"How? I'm not trained to do anything. Maybe I should just find a man and get married."

"No man would have you, even desperate ones who haven't seen a fine-looking woman like you in years."

Her eyes widened over the casually given praise. Did he really believe she was a fine-looking woman?

"Mary Rose doesn't like me. She only pities me."

"So you treat her like . . ."

"I don't want her pity," she shouted.

"Then tell her how you feel, but be nice about it. Mary Rose could be a good friend if you don't drive her away."

"It's too late. I've ruined everything. Everyone voted. I have to leave. Harrison said so. Do you really think I'm a fine-looking woman?"

"Sure. I'll bet you're real pretty when you smile."

"Travis hates me. Smiling isn't going to change that."

"You might stop calling him boy."

"I forgot his name."

"No, you didn't. You wanted to irritate him. You succeeded. Now stop it."

She nodded. He wasn't finished giving advice, however. "Say my name," he ordered.

"Cole."

"That's right. My name's Cole, not You There or Boy."

"Do I have to be nice to everyone?"

Only Eleanor would ask that question. "Yes."

She laughed again. "I was just teasing."

"I was right."

"Right about what?"

"You're very pretty when you smile."

She turned away. "Thank you. I was nice to Adam. Harrison said he didn't vote against me. Of course he couldn't."

"Why couldn't he?"

"Because he's head of the household. He had to abstain . . . didn't he?"

"I forgot."

"Do you think Adam would have voted to throw me out?"

"No."

"I didn't think so either. He's a very kind man. He can tolerate almost anything, even me."

"I'm kind."

"No, you're not."

He smiled. She was right. He wasn't kind.

"Are you going to keep on walking?"

"What other choice do I have?"

402

He leaned down, put his arm around her waist, and lifted her up onto his lap. She felt as light as a pillow. She was hot and sweaty, yet she still smelled like she'd just taken a bath.

She was all tuckered out from her strenuous walk. The mountain air had made her feel light-headed too. She was glad Cole was letting her ride with him and knew she should thank him. She tried to come up with the appropriate words. It shouldn't have been difficult, but it was. Lord, she'd really been acting like a tyrant all these past years, ordering people around . . . and never showing any sort of gratitude.

They rode along for several minutes without any conversation. Cole was comfortable with the silence. Eleanor wasn't. She wiggled around in his lap, pressing her backside against his groin every time she moved. He gritted his teeth together to keep himself from shouting at her.

Finally, he couldn't stand any more provocation. "Quit hopping around like that."

"I'm not hopping. Thank you."

There, she'd said the words. She immediately relaxed. It hadn't been difficult after all.

Unless he mocked her, of course. She tensed in anticipation.

"Why did you call Mrs. Morrison a fat cow?"

"I was helping Mary Rose."

"How?"

"Mrs. Morrison had the nerve to tell me Harrison was going to court her daughter. I informed her she was wrong. She continued to disagree with me, and one word led to another."

He changed the subject. "Didn't you learn anything useful at school?"

"I could teach."

"Why don't you?"

"Children dislike me."

He wasn't at all surprised. "Do you like children?"

"I don't know. I've never been around any."

"Then how would you know if they liked you or not?"

"No one else does."

He let out a sigh. "Can you help out around the ranch?"

"Doing what?"

"I don't know. I guess you wouldn't be any good roping steers or breaking in horses. You're too soft."

"I am?" She tried to turn around to look at him.

He tightened his hold around her waist so she couldn't move.

"What about washing the dishes, or cooking, or sewing?"

"Sewing! I can do that."

"There you are."

"But it's too late. I've been thrown out, remember?"

"If you promise to try to get along, I'll talk to everyone. I'll make them hold off for a couple of days and then take a vote again. You can't be sassy, Eleanor. If you're nice to be around, they'll forget about tossing you out."

"Why are you being so nice to me now?"

"Because you're about the prettiest and meanest and sweetest woman I've ever known."

"No one can be mean and sweet at the same time."

He shrugged.

"Did you vote against me, Cole?" she asked.

"What I did in the past is forgotten."

"Does that rule apply to me?"

"Sure it does. We'll have a fresh beginning."

She turned around to thank him for his advice. She looked into his eyes and promptly forgot what she was going to say.

He turned his attention to her mouth. He couldn't make himself stop staring at her. He was thankful the horse knew the way home because Cole was too preoccupied to guide him.

He knew what was going to happen before she did.

"Sorry," he muttered in advance of the liberty he was going to take.

Whatever had come over him? And why was he apologizing? She saw the warmth and tenderness in his eyes and was quite astonished. She hadn't ever noticed any man looking at her the way Cole was looking at her now. If she hadn't known better, she would have thought he was going to kiss her.

And then he did. His mouth settled on top of hers and took absolute possession. His lips were soft and warm against hers. He wooed her with his gentle touch. She wasn't certain if she was supposed to kiss him back or not. He was the first man to ever kiss her, and her inexperience made her shy and unsure.

All she knew was she didn't want him to stop, and when he started to pull away, she leaned into him and put her arms around his neck. Cole growled low in his throat, tightened his hold on her, and kissed her again.

He stopped long enough to tell her to open her mouth. She didn't ask him why. She let him show her. Her heart felt as if it were going to leap out of her chest so frantically was it pounding. His tongue rubbed against hers in an erotic mating game she thoroughly enjoyed.

She was a quick learner. Because of her inexperience, she didn't have any reservations or inhibitions. Her own curiosity made her bolder. She imitated his every move, wanting only to please him as much as he was pleasing her.

They were both shaken when Cole pulled away. He had enough sense to know when to stop. Eleanor didn't. At least he didn't believe she did. She wouldn't have tried to pull him back to her if she had any sense at all.

He made her turn around. Then he quickened the pace, for he was suddenly in a hurry to get home . . . and away from her.

"Did you like kissing me?"

"Now, why do women always want to talk about stuff like that?"

She shrugged. She wasn't upset by his surly tone of voice. "I don't know why. We just do. You're the first man to ever kiss me. Naturally, I was curious to find out if you liked it."

He lost his gruff edge immediately. "You've never been kissed before?"

She heard the smile in his voice. "I didn't tell you just to amuse you."

"I'm not laughing at you. You did a real nice

406

job kissing me back."

"Thank you. Why did you stop?"

"Oh, for God's sake. Do we really have to discuss the reasons now?"

She bumped his chin when she nodded. He sighed.

"Don't tempt a grizzly unless you're willing to get eaten up."

She wasn't completely ignorant. She'd heard stories about what went on in the marriage bed. Quite a lot of what she'd heard sounded possible to her. Some sounded impossible. Still, she'd learned enough to figure out what Cole had just said to her.

He hadn't wanted to stop.

Eleanor smiled all the way home.

"There's Adam and Harrison in the corral together with that ugly horse."

"Adam's going to try to ride MacHugh," Cole said. "Say hello to them, Eleanor."

Adam turned when she called out to him. He returned her greeting with a smile.

"It looks like your plan might be working. Eleanor sounded almost happy," Adam said, turning back to Harrison.

Harrison nodded, arrogantly pleased with himself. As long as Eleanor kept behaving herself, life would be pleasant for the family. Of course, Mary Rose would kill him if she ever found out what he had done. She'd think he was a heartless bastard.

Hell, what did it matter what she thought? She was going to end up despising him as soon as she found out his intent.

Roping steers sounded like a good way to keep his mind occupied, Harrison had decided. If he was too busy to think, he wouldn't have time to worry. He was suddenly anxious to get going. He wanted hard, back-breaking work.

What he got was a lesson in humility. And a hell of a lot of pain. By the time he sat down at the supper table, every muscle in his body ached. He felt as if he'd been the one to be roped and dragged out of the mud. His left hand was on fire.

Mary Rose was full of sympathy. As soon as they'd said grace, she changed places with Eleanor so she could sit closer to him. It made her task of cutting up his meat much easier.

"Did the salve help?" Adam inquired from the opposite end of the table.

"Yes, thank you."

"Why did you take your gloves off?" Douglas asked.

Travis speculated a guess before Harrison could answer. "Maybe he had an itch."

Adam turned to Cole. He noticed his smile and shook his head at him. "You were supposed to be looking out for him," he remarked.

"It wasn't my fault. Anyone with half a brain would have enough sense to let go of the rope."

Adam visibly winced over the picture he was getting in his mind. His curiosity was every bit as morose as that of a man passing by a burning building who is compelled to stop and watch.

"Were you dragged far?"

Far enough, Harrison thought to himself. "It doesn't matter," he said. "Cole's right. It wasn't his fault. I thought I knew what I was doing. I didn't. I learned a valuable lesson today."

Mary Rose was waving his fork back and forth in front of his face. Harrison lost his patience. He snatched the utensil out of her hand and told her to stop pestering him.

His irritation didn't faze her. "You haven't taken a single bite," she said.

"I'm not an invalid. I can feed myself."

"Quit worrying about him," Douglas said. "I'll bet that rope burn hurts too much to even think about eating. You're lucky it was just your left hand."

"Tell us what you learned," Adam suggested.

"To keep his gloves on," Travis answered with a grin.

"To let go of the rope," Cole volunteered next. He winked at Eleanor across the table. She blushed in response.

Adam noticed what was going on between the two of them and rolled his eyes heavenward.

"I learned I really am completely inept out here," Harrison said.

He turned to Mary Rose. "Happy now?"

She had enough sense not to admit she was. Harrison seemed to be spoiling for a fight. She wasn't going to accommodate him. If he'd been in a better mood, she would have told him she was extremely happy with him. He had finally decided to bury his arrogance and get down to the business of learning. His chances of living a long life had just improved considerably. Was she happy about that? Of course.

The talk at the table turned to a less sensitive

409

subject. Harrison was curious to find out why the Claybornes had decided to invest in cattle. Travis explained.

"We had cattle before, but with two harsh winters in a row, we had to sell them off because we needed the cash. We're in a better situation now. I guess you could say we're starting over. We got a high price for the beef."

"We had a setback when we lost our bull. Douglas couldn't cure whatever it was ailing him. But for a while we made enough of a profit to make it worth our trouble again."

"We started out with two and had close to four hundred when we sold them," Adam added. "The steers feed on free range. Travis balks because he wants to keep them fenced in. You can't fence public land though. All the ranchers come together in the spring for the annual roundup. You missed all the commotion. Travis and Cole went on the cattle drive to Salt Lake. They'd only just gotten back home when you showed up."

It was apparent to Harrison that the brothers had used patience and doing without to get what they wanted. They were obviously already wealthy men. Yet none of them seemed to realize it. All of the brothers insisted they had only just begun to build a nest egg. Travis was the most concerned about money. Cole's obsession was security. If it had been possible, he would have built a thirty-foot wall around the entire ranch to keep everyone safe.

They continued to talk about their financial situation until Mary Rose and Eleanor finally got

410

up from the table.

"Adam said you wanted to talk to us about something," Douglas said. "What is it?"

Mary Rose had just started out the doorway. When she heard her brother, she turned around and hurried back inside.

"Our sister wasn't supposed to know about the talk," Cole reminded his brother.

"I forgot," Douglas admitted. "Sorry, Harrison."

"Why wasn't I supposed to know?"

She started in worrying. Was Harrison going to tell her brothers he had decided to leave? Had the work on the ranch been too difficult for him after all? Was he giving up?

Panic nearly overwhelmed her. She forced herself to calm down. Harrison wasn't a quitter; he would never give up. If he was leaving, it was because he'd grown restless and wanted to move on. Yet if that was true, why was she being excluded from the announcement?

"What are you going to talk about?" She sat back down and waited to hear his answer.

Harrison reached over and covered her hand with his. "You'll have to be patient."

She nodded. She looked up at him and tried to read his expression, but Harrison wasn't giving anything away. He was as closed up as a newly bound book.

"Isn't it your turn to do the dishes, Mary Rose?" Douglas asked.

"Yes, of course," she answered.

Cole nudged Eleanor's leg under the table. When she looked at him, he nodded toward

411

his sister and waited.

Eleanor understood the hint and immediately stood up. "May I help you with the dishes?"

Travis did a double take. He was sure he hadn't heard correctly. Eleanor was offering her help? It wasn't possible. He started to say something, caught Cole's expression, and closed his mouth again.

Adam waited for Mary Rose to answer Eleanor. She seemed rattled, however, and so he finally answered for her.

"I'm certain she'll be grateful for your assistance. It was good of you to offer."

The table was cleared a few minutes later. Every time Mary Rose came back into the dining room, she lingered for as long as she could. She wanted to find out what they were going to discuss, but no one was giving her any hints.

She reported to Eleanor after each trip. Her houseguest was standing in front of the washbasin, washing the plates.

Mary Rose picked up a towel and started wiping the utensils Eleanor had already washed.

"Mary Rose, I have something important to say to you."

"Can't it wait, Eleanor?"

"No."

"All right then. What is it?"

"You don't have to sound impatient."

"Sorry. I was worrying about Harrison. What did you want to say to me?"

"I wanted to tell you how sorry I am about the way I've been behaving. I know I haven't made life easy for you. You're the only friend

I have in the whole world. Please forgive me."

Mary Rose smiled. "We had this very same talk not an hour ago. I haven't changed my mind since then. Of course I forgive you."

"I just needed to say it again. I want you to realize how sincere I am. I want you to like me."

"I do like you."

"Aren't I being considerate helping you with the dishes?"

"Yes, you are," Mary Rose assured her. "I'm going to be very fortunate to have you for a friend."

Eleanor nodded. "Yes, I believe you will be fortunate. I'm not being arrogant. Just honest. I hated with a passion, didn't I? Now that I'm learning the value of friendship, I shall become just as passionate in my loyalty. Don't you think that might be so?"

"Yes."

"Good. Now tell me why you're worried about Harrison. What else has he done?"

"What else has he done? What do you mean by that?"

Eleanor remembered her promise not to tell Mary Rose what Harrison had done to her, so she didn't mention being left up on the mountain.

"He made me angry," Eleanor said. "And he's always walking into trouble. Look at the bruises on him, Mary Rose. I just wondered what he'd done this time that has you fretting."

"I'm worried about what he's going to do. I think he's getting ready to leave. He's probably saying his good-byes to my brothers this very minute."

"Are you saying you'll be upset if he leaves?"

Mary Rose felt like screaming. "Yes," she whispered instead.

"You are sweet on him."

"Yes."

"I don't think he's talking to your brothers about leaving. You wouldn't have been excluded. He'd say good-bye to you too."

"Then what . . ."

"Maybe, just maybe, he's formally asking for permission to court you. Have you considered that possibility?"

"Do you think so?"

"It makes sense, doesn't it? I know Harrison cares about you. Adam told me he really went after those men who hurt you in town. He smiles at you a lot too. I noticed. Yes, I think it's very possible he is asking permission. You would be excluded from the talk. He can't ask in front of you."

Mary Rose's spirits lifted. She desperately wanted to believe Eleanor was right in her speculation. "I shouldn't get my hopes up," she whispered.

She decided to go to the doorway and try to eavesdrop on the conversation. She bumped into Adam in the hallway.

"Where are you going? Are you finished with the dishes so soon?" Adam asked.

"I was going to collect the linens," she lied. "Where are you going?"

"We're all too tired to talk tonight. Harrison decided to wait until tomorrow."

She couldn't quite hide her disappointment.

"Then I'll have to stay curious until tomorrow," she said.

"I don't believe you need to waste time worrying," Adam advised. "Finish up and go up to bed. You look exhausted."

She took his advice and went directly up to her bedroom as soon as the kitchen work was finished. She was certain she wouldn't be able to sleep because of her worries. It had been a long, tiring day, however, and she drifted off to sleep just a few seconds after her head hit the pillow.

Harrison spent the next hour pacing back and forth in the bunkhouse. He wasn't thinking about the talk he was going to have with the brothers now, however. His mind was on all the changes he was going to make in his life — because of Mary Rose. Honest to God, he was through fighting the inevitable.

He checked his pocket watch for the time, and when at last the hour was up, he went back to the house. He was the first to enter the dining room.

Travis walked inside with a full bottle of brandy. Cole followed him. Travis put the bottle on the table and took his seat. Cole collected the shot glasses from the side bar, put them on the table, and then sat down. Adam came inside next. Douglas was last. He shut the doors behind him.

"I looked in on Mary Rose. She's sound asleep. If we keep our voices down, she'll stay that way."

Douglas directed the last of his remarks to Cole. Everyone was on edge. Cole appeared to be ready for a shootout. A tightness had settled around his mouth. He reached for the bottle, poured himself a drink, and gave the brandy decanter to Adam.

Harrison was the only one to decline a drink. Adam waited until everyone was settled.

"All right, Harrison, why don't you tell us why you're really here."

"You've known I had another motive for . . ."

"Of course."

"Why didn't you say something to me if you . . ."

"I figured you would let us know what you wanted when you were ready. A man shouldn't be rushed. As long as we could keep our eye on you, we weren't worried. You seemed to be trying to work something out. Perhaps you'll tell us now what was bothering you."

Harrison was a little taken aback. "I appreciate your patience," he said. "I *was* working something out. I'm thankful you gave me the time to do so."

"Let's get one thing straight, Harrison," Cole said. "We like you just fine, but we aren't letting you take him. You got that? We'll kill you if we have to."

"Or you can stay on here and live to be an old man," Travis suggested.

"I'm not going to try to take Adam away. He isn't the reason I came here."

"Wait a minute. How did you know Cole was talking about Adam?" Travis asked.

Harrison didn't waste time giving a long-winded explanation. "You have all been protect-

416

ing Adam from the minute you found out I was an attorney. Each one of you has let me know he's the vulnerable one. You might have believed you were being subtle. You weren't."

"Were we as subtle as you were when you were trying to find out about us?"

"Yes," Harrison admitted. "I guess I was as transparent as you were."

"We all have marks on our pasts," Cole said. "Fact is, you could have come here to get the goods on any one of us. We aren't sorry about anything. We did what we had to do in order to survive. We don't expect you to understand. We are what we are."

"We make no excuses to anyone," Adam said quietly.

"And no one ever helped you, isn't that right?" Harrison asked.

"Damn right no one helped us. We didn't ask for anything, and we wouldn't have accepted it."

Harrison nodded. He understood now. He should have realized that important fact a long time ago.

"I want to tell you a story. I would appreciate it if you all would be patient and hear what I have to say."

He waited until everyone nodded agreement, then leaned back in his chair and began.

"The man I now work for was a very close friend of my father's. I might have mentioned the association to you before, I can't recall. His name is Lord William Elliott. His wife's name was Agatha. She was a good woman with a kind heart. Elliott couldn't have done better. He loved

417

her as passionately as she loved him. They had a very happy, solid marriage."

"What do they have to do with us?" Travis asked.

"Let him explain," Adam said.

"Elliott was, and still is, a brilliant man. He quickly amassed a fortune. He built several factories in England and then decided to expand into America. He came to New York City with his wife for the opening of a factory outside the city. He never would have allowed Agatha to accompany him, however, if he had known she was carrying his child. His wife's health was more important to him than any financial matter.

"The grand opening was postponed because one of the buildings didn't meet Elliott's standards. He considered it a fire hazard and ordered changes. He and his wife stayed on in America while he personally watched over the workmen. Agatha gave birth to their only child several months later. They named their daughter, Victoria, after Elliott's mother."

Harrison paused to gather his thoughts. He looked at the brothers to see if any of them had begun to guess where he was headed. He saw only mild curiosity, however.

"They had been in New York City almost a full year when disaster struck. The factory was finally ready for the grand opening. Both Elliott and his wife attended the celebration. Agatha wanted to take the baby along, but Elliott wouldn't allow it. He argued the baby wasn't yet four months old and was therefore too fragile to be taken out in the cool spring air. They left little Victoria with her nursemaid and a full staff. They were away for just two short days, but when they returned to the city, they found the authorities waiting on their doorstep. The nursemaid had disappeared with the baby. The note demanding money arrived the following afternoon. Elliott's personal secretary, George MacPherson, grabbed hold of the messenger before he could get away and dragged him inside for questioning. The boy couldn't tell them anything significant. Elliott quickly got the money together and then waited for instructions to come telling him where to take it. No other notes followed however. Elliott clung to the hope his daughter would be returned safe and sound."

"What happened to her?" Travis asked.

"She vanished."

Silence followed. Harrison realized he was holding a drink in his hand and couldn't remember reaching for it. He put it down on the table.

"Lady Agatha never recovered from the nightmare. She became quite ill, and after six months of frantic searching, Elliott was forced to take his wife back to England. He left MacPherson in New York City to coordinate the investigation. Every lead was followed, but the investigators Elliott hired and the authorities all came up with dead ends. Then, exactly six months later, the nursemaid was found."

"Was the baby with her?" Cole asked.

"No. There wasn't any evidence in the room she'd rented to give anyone a clue as to the whereabouts of Victoria. It was assumed the woman hid the baby outside the city, then returned for

419

some specific reason. Only God knows what. She was dead by the time the authorities got to her. She'd been strangled.

"Elliott and his wife didn't give up the search. Agatha couldn't regain her strength, however. She died a year or so later. The physicians said it was consumption, but Elliott understood the real reason. He told me she had stopped living the day her baby was taken. She died of a broken heart."

"Did she blame her husband because he made her leave the baby at home?" Travis asked.

"No, I don't believe she did. Elliott blamed himself, of course."

"How old were you when all of this happened?"

"I was just a boy, around ten years old," Harrison answered. "When my father died, Elliott moved me into his home. He took over for my own father, made certain I was well educated, and tried to go on with his life.

"Everyone in England knew what had happened. Elliott was a powerful voice in Parliament. He retired when he came back home, sold off his factories, and never gave up his search. I remember that each time I came back from university, he would tell me about a possible sighting."

"Sighting?"

"Someone who looked like Victoria might look today," he explained.

"Sounds like he was grasping at straws," Cole remarked.

"He was desperate," Adam said.

"Yes," Harrison agreed. "He was desperate.

He didn't give up until a couple of years ago. Then I took over his hunt for him. Finding Victoria became my obsession."

"And now?" Adam asked.

Harrison took a long breath. "I've found her."

August 23, 1866

Dear Mama Rose,
I played with Cole's gun. I was just having fun, but he still yelled at me real good. He said he was going to spank my behind too. Then I cried real good and he changed his mind. Guns are bad, Mama. Adam said so. I won't play with guns no more. Not ever. Will you tell Cole not to yell at me? I am a good girl. Adam said so.

I love you,
Your good girl Mary Rose

12

They didn't want to believe him. Cole was emphatic in his denial. Mary Rose wasn't Victoria. She couldn't be. Adam was more reasonable. He asked questions trying to find an inconsistency. Travis tore apart every explanation Harrison gave. Douglas remained unusually silent. He kept his gaze on his glass and shook his head every once in a while. He appeared to be too stunned to speak.

"Coincidence," Cole said. He pounded his fist down on the tabletop to stress his point.

"When was Victoria born?" Adam asked in a voice shaking with emotion.

Harrison had already answered the question three times. He patiently gave the date once again. "January second, 1860."

"Holy Mother of God," Adam whispered.

"Lots of people were born on January second," Travis argued.

"Be reasonable," Harrison requested.

"Explain how you came to your conclusion that our Mary Rose was the woman you were searching for."

"Travis, I've already explained."

"I don't give a damn, Harrison. Explain it again."

"Fine," he agreed. "The woman who saw Mary Rose at the boarding school reported the incident to Elliott's people. I happened to be in Chicago at the time on business. The woman lived a short train ride away, and so I went to her home to talk to her."

"How did you hear about the woman? Does Elliott have people working for him in America?" Travis asked.

"Yes, but that isn't how I found out. I received a wire from London. I had requested to be kept informed. Elliott had given up."

"But you hadn't," Travis remarked. He sounded angry about Harrison's tenacity.

"No, I hadn't given up, and neither had his staff. They notified me. I hired an attorney in St. Louis to interview Mary Rose."

"Lawyers stick together like fleas and leeches, don't they?" Cole said.

Harrison didn't respond to the insult. "What the attorney found out made me more curious."

"She didn't tell him anything," Cole argued. "She wouldn't have."

"You're right. She didn't tell him anything. It's what the attorney couldn't find out that intrigued me. The headmistress said Mary Rose's mother lived in the south. I wondered why, of course, but I didn't find it unusual enough to pursue. Sisters boast about their brothers, or complain about them. At least I thought they did, but Mary Rose wouldn't say a word about the four of you. The attorney reported she'd been on her guard and seemed afraid and somewhat agitated."

"She distrusts lawyers as much as we do," Travis told him.

"Yes, I understand," Harrison said. "Your reaction when you found out what I did for a living was another clue that one of you might be in trouble."

"We told Mary Rose not to talk about us. We didn't want folks looking into matters that didn't concern them."

"As I said before, I understand now. I didn't understand at the time."

"What didn't you understand?" Cole asked.

"That all of you have broken the law in the past. Anyway, your sister's reticence made me more curious."

"And then?" Travis asked.

Harrison held on to his patience. He knew why they were making him go over his explanation again. They were hunting for flaws. He couldn't blame them. In their place, he would have done the same thing.

"There had been hundreds of reports over the years about women who resembled Victoria's mother, or aunt, or cousin, or some other distant relative. Although the woman who had seen Mary Rose was emphatic about the resemblance, I still wouldn't have come all the way to Montana just because of a similarity in appearance. No, I came here because of the report I'd read about the interview with your sister."

Harrison reached for his glass and took a drink. He really didn't want the brandy, but his throat was dry.

"There's a portrait hanging in Elliott's library," he began.

"What? You didn't mention a portrait before," Travis said.

He guessed he hadn't. "Right after Elliott married Agatha, he commissioned a well-known artist to paint his wife's likeness. When Mary Rose came strolling down the aisle in Morrison's store, for a moment I thought Agatha had stepped out of the oil portrait and was coming to greet me. Your sister's resemblance to Agatha is astonishing. You know the rest of it. None of you made my task easy."

"I'm glad to know we did something right," Cole interjected.

"All of you gave me odd, nonsensical answers to my questions. Your resistance fed my curiosity. Only people with a secret would behave in such a manner. You told me again and again that it was dangerous for anyone to ask questions out here, yet you plied me with hundreds of them. There was also your distrust of anyone associated with the law. Believe it or not, lawyers serve a purpose, a damned good one at that. We aren't your enemy, but you behaved as though you believed we were. It was more than apparent to me that you had something to hide. My mistake was thinking you were trying to keep me from finding out the truth about the kidnapping. I didn't believe you planned the theft, but I did think you were protecting the man or woman who had taken her. Now that I've gotten to know all of you, I realize you got here on your own. You only had each other to depend on."

Harrison paused to gather his thoughts. The brothers patiently waited for him to continue.

"You decided to pull together and become a family. Then you took the baby and headed west.

Mary Rose is Lady Victoria, isn't she?"

Adam closed his eyes. He looked stricken. "Dear God, she must be."

Travis reached for the bottle. Harrison noticed his hand shook. His glass was already full, but the brother didn't seem to notice.

Cole was staring at Harrison. He looked desolate.

Harrison turned his gaze to Adam. "On your brothers' behalf, your sister's behalf, and on your behalf, give me a dollar."

The request didn't make any sense to any of them. Adam didn't move. Harrison gave his demand again, in a harder tone of voice.

The brother reached into his vest pocket, pulled out a silver coin, and tossed it to Harrison. He caught it in midair.

"What was that for?" Travis asked.

"It was a retainer. I don't give a damn if you like lawyers or not, I now represent you. Does everyone understand and agree?"

He made all of them give their verbal consent before he continued. Then he shifted positions, scanned his audience, and said, "Who's going to start explaining?"

"Do you think we stole her?" Cole asked.

"We didn't," Travis said. "Someone else did. Whoever it was must have gotten cold feet."

"We found her," Cole said.

"Where?" Harrison asked.

"In the trash," Cole answered.

"Where?" He hadn't meant to raise his voice, but surprise made him overreact.

"You heard me. We found her in the trash

427

heap in our alley. The four of us had formed our own gang. God, we were young and stupid back then."

"You were children," Harrison replied. "There is safety in numbers."

"Yes," Cole agreed wearily. He turned to Adam. "You tell him what happened."

Adam nodded. "We had formed a gang of sorts. We all lived on the street. I had made it to New York City with the help of the Underground, but I wasn't going to stay there. I'd promised my mother I'd head west. She thought I would be safer there, until things changed."

"What things?" Harrison asked.

"Mother kept up with all the news. Lincoln was talking about ending slavery. The movement in the North was growing and she knew a fight was coming. If it went in our favor, we'd be freed. It was a hope, and I clung to it.

"My brothers and I lived in the alley. We slept close together so we could keep warm. It was going on May, but the nights were still cold that year, and we didn't have many blankets."

"In 1860?"

"Yes, 1860," Adam said. "There were other gangs of displaced children roaming the streets looking for food and trouble. The alley was our home, and we were determined to defend it. We each took turns standing watch at the entrance. It was Douglas's turn that night. Travis and Cole and I were sound asleep. He whistled to us and pointed to the trash heap. Then he took off. He was curious about something and wanted to investigate.

"I heard a noise," Adam continued. "Douglas told me later he thought it was a cat inside. Travis, I remember, was worried it might be a snake."

"Inside what?" Harrison asked.

"A basket," Adam answered. "Anyway, I thought there was an animal inside too. I went over to get a better look. I saw the rats then."

"Dear God . . ."

"They were all over the thing. I had to light my torch to chase them away. One had worked his way up to the top and was chewing through the lid. If I had waited another minute, the rat would have gotten to her."

Harrison pictured what would certainly have happened to Mary Rose and blanched in reaction.

"I got to her in time, and that's all that matters. We thought she was a boy. We named her Sidney."

"She knows everything, doesn't she?" Harrison asked.

"Oh, yes, she knows how we found her. We've never kept any secrets from her. She knows all about us too."

Harrison smiled. "Now I understand why she was so upset when Cole called her Sidney."

"Yes," Cole said. "It's a reminder to her that she isn't any better than anyone else. She is though. She's pure of heart and noble and . . ."

Cole's voice belied his stony expression.

Adam cleared his throat and continued on. "We made a pact late that night to do the best we could for her. We didn't think she would make it if we took her to one of the city's orphanages. Travis was the only one who knew for certain no one was searching for him. We all became Claybornes and headed west. It took us a long, long time to get here and build a home."

"But we did it," Cole said. "Now that I think about it, I guess maybe Mary Rose's father helped us."

"How?" Harrison asked.

"Douglas took the money from the woman who threw the basket away. He was real good picking pockets. The money financed our way for a long time. Whoever took the baby must have stolen the money too."

"How old were all of you?"

Travis answered him. "I was really just nine, going on ten, but I told everyone I was close to eleven. I was afraid they wouldn't take me if I was too young. I wanted them to think I could hold my own in a fight. Douglas and I knew what it was like living in an orphanage. We weren't going back. I guess I was smart enough to realize I needed protection. Adam was big and mean-looking to me, and so I chose to hound him day and night until he finally let me stay with him. He was thirteen. Douglas and Cole were eleven years old."

"You were children," Harrison said. "Yet even so, didn't it occur to you that the baby might have been stolen?"

"Why would such a thought occur to us?" Cole asked. "We just figured her mother or father didn't want her any longer."

"You believed they threw her away? How could you possibly believe such a thing?"

Cole and Douglas looked at each other, then

turned to Harrison again.

"Why not?" Douglas asked. "We were."

Cole couldn't understand Harrison's incredulity. "How do you think the city got glutted with so many children? Do you really think they all just got lost? The authorities knew the truth. Every once in a while, they'd grab as many of them as they could, put them on trains, and send them away. None of them knew where the trains were headed."

Douglas let out a sigh. "No one wanted them," he said. "And no one wanted the three of us. Adam was different. His mother had sent him away to keep him safe. She didn't abandon him."

"I don't know if my mother would have thrown me out or not," Cole remarked. His voice was devoid of emotion now. "I heard she was a nice woman. She died giving me life. Her name was Mary, and I figured I could repay her by handing her name down to our Mary Rose. Adam had the same idea about Mama Rose. Douglas decided we should combine the names."

"What about your father, Cole? Do you know anything about him?" Harrison asked.

"He kept me around for a while. Eventually he started to favor whiskey and gin more. He tried to sell me. I heard him negotiating for two bottles and I took off."

Harrison was too stunned to speak. He couldn't imagine such bleak lives. And then he began to see the wonder in it all.

He saw the brothers in a completely different light. His admiration and his respect were evident in his expression.

431

They had done the impossible and had flourished in spite of the odds.

"You are all men of courage."

Douglas wouldn't accept Harrison's approbation. He shook his head.

"No, we're just men doing the best we can. We were all scared little boys back then who wanted to see that Mary Rose had someone to care about her. None of us really believed she'd make it. I didn't think any of us would. Still, she deserved a shot at life, didn't she?"

"It couldn't have been easy."

"Changing her drawers was a real bitch." Cole smiled when he made the comment.

"How did you know her real birth date? Mary Rose told me she had papers. What are they?"

"There were two papers tucked in the envelope with the money," Douglas explained. "Adam has them in the library. One of the papers has a lot of numbers scribbled on it. The other paper looks like a page from a book. Across the top was a baby girl's date of birth. Her weight and measurement were written down too."

"The page is from the family Bible."

"It is?"

"Yes," Harrison said. "Two pages were torn out. One was returned with the ransom note. It was proof they really had Victoria. Her full name was written on the bottom line."

"I told my brothers about the papers, but we were more curious about the money then. Adam was the only one who could read. He looked the papers over and told us what the words were. We kept the papers in the basket for years. We only saved them so that Mary Rose would have something from her past."

"Who taught you how to read?" Harrison asked Douglas.

"Adam taught all of us."

"Do you know who strangled the nursemaid?" Cole asked.

"No," Harrison said. "But Elliott never believed she acted alone. She wasn't smart enough to plan a kidnapping. She was also extremely timid. The woman had to have had an accomplice."

"Maybe he's dead now," Douglas said.

"It could have been a woman," Harrison reasoned.

"It was a man."

"How do you know?"

"I saw him."

Harrison sent his drink careening. He didn't even notice what he had done.

"You saw him?" His voice shook with emotion.

Douglas nodded. "I guess it's my turn to explain, isn't it?" he said. "A man got out of an expensive-looking carriage. There was a crest on the door. He wore a black cloak, like the kind rich men wear to the opera. He wore a hat with the rim pulled down over his forehead. I still saw his face. He stood right under the streetlamp and turned to look in my direction. He didn't see me though. He must have thought he'd heard a noise and that's why he turned. Anyway, I got a good look at him. Do you want me to describe him to you?"

"How could you possibly remember? You were

twelve years old, Douglas. Our memories become twisted and confused over the years. It was a long time ago."

"Tell him about your cut, Cole," Douglas suggested.

The brother smiled. "We were around fifteen years old, weren't we, Douglas? I was still stupid then. I went charging into someone else's business, thinking I could swipe some animal skins. We needed coats for the winter. I figured I'd get some. I was real quiet, wasn't I, Douglas?"

"Not quiet enough, Cole."

"There must have been twenty renegades in their camp. They'd been plaguing the area, stealing and killing and burning people out, for quite a spell. Everyone was afraid of them. I was too, but I wanted the skins and I figured I had to take them, no matter how afraid I was. Every damned one of them lit out after me. I got cut across my belly. It hurt like the fires of hell. I remember the pain all right. Adam had to sew me up. Mary Rose cried while he worked on me."

"She held your hand, remember?" Travis said.

Cole smiled. He remembered. "She thought it would help me to hold on to her. She was around three or four back then and as sweet and sassy as they come."

"How did you ever get away from the Indians?" Harrison asked.

"I didn't do it on my own. I was busy running and then fighting for my life, and I didn't get a look at the one who cut me. Douglas did though. He was riding toward me with his shotgun up

434

and ready. He saw the faces of the two who held me down and the third who cut me. The bastard was going to cut my guts out. Douglas started shooting just in the nick of time, and they took off running to get their guns."

Cole paused to think about the incident before continuing. Harrison was fascinated by the story, but he couldn't imagine what the incident had to do with the discussion about Mary Rose's kidnappers. He waited to find out.

"We went back. Winter set in and we had to wait. We didn't forget, and as soon the snow melted, we went after them."

"We made them admit they were the ones."

"How? Did they speak English?"

"One did a little. It didn't matter though. Douglas never, ever forgets a face."

"They boasted about cutting you, didn't they, Cole?"

"They thought their friends would get us."

"We made certain they couldn't," Travis said.

Harrison didn't ask what had happened to the Indians. He already knew.

"The tribe that threw the misfits out heard about it. They gave us wide berth from then on," Cole explained. "Now do you want to hear Douglas's description?"

Harrison nodded. "Yes."

"The man I saw in New York City had a light-colored mustache. I couldn't see the color of his eyes. He was about six feet tall and very thin. His cheeks were sunken in like a skeleton. His nose was kind of pointed, and his lips were thin. He wore shiny black shoes, not boots. I noticed the shoes because I thought about figuring a way to steal them. The man was dressed in black, formal evening clothes.

"The woman didn't want to take the basket from him. She kept shaking her head. I wasn't close enough to hear what they were saying to each other. He pulled the envelope out of his pocket and gave it to her. She snatched it up real quick and then she took the basket."

"The man got out of the carriage with the basket?"

"Yes."

"Was she already standing there on the corner, waiting for him?"

"Yes."

"What about the driver? Did you get a look at him?"

"No. Once I saw the envelope, I kept my eye on it. She put it in her coat pocket. The man got back in the carriage and took off. She waited until he was out of sight and then started looking around for a place to get rid of Mary Rose. She chose our alley. She went running inside, threw the basket, and then took off. I waited until she reached the corner again, whistled to get Adam's attention so he'd notice the basket, and then I followed her. I took the envelope from her pocket just as she was getting on the midnight train."

Harrison leaned back in his chair. His eyes had turned cold with anger.

Cole watched him closely. "Do you know who the man was?"

Harrison slowly nodded. "I think so. I'll make certain first."

"Is he still alive?" Douglas asked.

"Yes . . . if he's the one, yes, he's still alive."

"Are you going after your Indian the way we did?" Cole asked.

Harrison understood what Cole was asking. He wanted to know how far Harrison would go to gain revenge. Would he retaliate the same way the brothers had against their enemy?

His answer was immediate. "Yes."

"Have you forgotten you're an attorney?" Adam asked.

"I haven't forgotten. One way or another, justice will be served. Douglas, tell me what happened once again. Start at the beginning."

Douglas agreed. Harrison waited until he'd finished, then plied him with more questions. He was finally satisfied he knew everything they could tell him.

"Now what?" Travis asked. "When are you going to tell her?"

"I'm not going to tell her," Harrison answered. "I think . . ."

Travis wouldn't let him continue. "Why should we believe you? You've done nothing but lie to us from the beginning. You never really wanted to learn how to ranch, did you?"

"Yes, I did want to learn,'" he answered. "I had thought that I would eventually go back to the Highlands, but now I know exactly where I'm going to settle for the rest of my life. Eventually I'll have a ranch of my own. Legal work will support me over the rougher times. All of my plans have changed," he added. "When I first came here, I wasn't even certain Mary Rose was

437

Victoria. Yes, I saw the resemblance, but it wasn't enough. She also looks a little like you, Cole. Blue eyes, yellow hair. She's a hell of a lot prettier though. The more I found out, the more confused I became. She shouldn't have had any reason to be so reticent with me. All of you cleared up that mystery for me. As I mentioned before, the way you reacted when you found out I was an attorney was certainly curious. One night Mary Rose asked me why I spent the evenings talking to Adam. She seemed worried, and when she asked me if I questioned him about his past, I concluded she didn't want me to find out about something he'd done. If I'd spent the evenings with Travis or Cole or Douglas, she would have been just as worried, wouldn't she?"

"Probably," Cole answered. "We told her everything we'd done. She knows all about our sins."

"Yes," Harrison agreed. "So you've told me. It didn't take me long to figure out you all banded together to form your own family, but I couldn't accept the fact that you'd gotten to Montana Territory all by yourselves. I had no reason to trust any of you, just as you had no reason to trust me. All of us had our reasons. I made several mistakes along the way. Two surprised the hell out of me."

"What were your mistakes?" Douglas asked.

"One, I procrastinated. I could have found out what I needed to know much sooner, but I held back. I didn't take advantage of opportunities, and that, you see, isn't at all like me. I've never been one to put off anything . . ."

"You haven't been here all that long. It's only

been six or seven weeks," Cole reminded him.

"It seems much longer to me. I didn't realize I was dragging my feet until recently. I grew up pretty much on my own, and I've never really known what a real family was like. Each of you would give your life to keep the others safe. Such love and loyalty were foreign concepts to me. I loved my father and I was loyal to him and to my government. My loyalty extended to Elliott too. There's a bond between us because of what we've both been through, but it isn't at all the same."

"The same as what?" Cole asked, trying to understand.

"The bond between brothers and sisters," Harrison explained. "You constantly amazed me. You insult each other. You're loud and forceful. You argue all the time, push and shove each other, and, honest to God, how I envied you. All of these years I pictured Lady Victoria as a victim. God was certainly watching out for her though. He gave her the four of you."

Harrison paused to draw a breath. "Cole, every time you shoved me the way I'd watched you shove Travis and Douglas, and every time you threatened me or laughed at me, I felt like I was part of your family."

The brothers were moved by Harrison's honesty. Cole understood what Harrison was saying far better than the others, however. He still remembered the loneliness and desolation he'd experienced before Adam had taken him under his wing.

"What was your other big mistake?" Adam

asked. "You said you'd made several along the way, but two really took you by surprise."

Harrison nodded. He remembered what he'd said. "I fell in love with your sister."

Cole shook his head. "She's going to hate you because you deceived her."

"For a little while, I imagine she will," Harrison agreed. "It won't matter though. I want all of you to understand my intentions here and now. I will have her."

The force in his words got their full attention. No one knew what to make of his vehement statement.

"What exactly do you mean?" Cole asked.

"I'm a man of honor," Harrison began. "At least I like to believe I am."

"And?" Cole persisted.

"I'm telling you my intent."

"But what exactly are you telling us?" Travis asked.

"I've protected your sister and pretty much left her alone. I'm going to continue to protect her, but from this moment on, I assure you I have no intention of leaving her alone. I've told myself all the reasons why I don't deserve her, and none of them matter any longer. I'll never have enough money. Travis, one day I think you'll understand that truth as well. Elliott would marry her to someone far more worthy by society's standards, but not by mine. No one will ever love her the way I do. She will belong to me."

Cole's mouth dropped open. He'd never heard Harrison sound so passionate.

Douglas was just as thunderstruck. "Are you

saying you're going to seduce our sister?"

"Yes."

"You can't be serious . . ." Travis began.

"I meant every word I just said. She's going to belong to me. Forever. She'll carry my name and bear my children."

Travis shook his head. "I can't believe you've got the guts to tell us what you're planning to do."

"Do you really think we'll let you try to touch her?" Cole asked.

Harrison lost his patience. "Try? I don't ever try anything. I do exactly what I say I'm going to do."

Douglas smiled. "Don't you think Mary Rose ought to have a say about her seduction? We all know you wouldn't force her."

"No, I wouldn't ever force her to do anything she doesn't want to do. She loves me, but she hasn't figured it all out just yet. She will though. She's a very intelligent woman. She'll give me permission before I bed her, and bed her I will."

"So you say," Cole snapped. "Adam, what do you think about this?"

"She does love him," Adam replied. "Harrison's right about that."

"Harrison, you haven't already . . ." Travis was going to ask if he'd already seduced Mary Rose and then stopped himself. The look Harrison gave him made the hair stand up on the back of his neck.

Cole laughed. "Hell, Travis, he wouldn't be in such a foul mood if he'd bedded her."

"You're talking about our sister, I'll have you

remember," Travis muttered.

"What about Lord Elliott?" Adam asked. "You said he'd marry her to someone more willing. Does that mean you're planning to tell him you found his daughter or are you going to let it rest?"

"I'm going to tell him, of course," Harrison answered. "He has a right to know, Adam. His agony will finally be over. The man has suffered long enough."

No one said a word for a long minute. The brothers were all thinking about Mary Rose's father and trying to imagine what it must have been like for him to lose his daughter.

Adam finally broke the silence. "Yes, he has suffered long enough. I wouldn't have stopped looking for my daughter. I'm certain I would have been as obsessed with finding her as Elliott was. Dear God, the agony he and his wife endured. It makes my heart ache to think about it. His misery became our blessing," he added with a nod. "I wonder if he'll understand."

"I'll make him understand," Harrison assured the brother. "He won't blame you or send anyone after you. Mary Rose has a family back in England. There are aunts and uncles and cousins too numerous to count. Your sister has a title and wealth. Elliott won't come here to see her. He won't have to. She'll go to him."

"How can you be so certain?" Douglas asked. "You said a few minutes ago that you wouldn't tell her. Have you changed your mind?"

"No, I haven't changed my mind."

"Well then?" Cole asked.

"I won't tell her. You will."

No one said a word for a long while. Harrison thought the brothers were busy wrestling with their consciences.

They would eventually do the right thing. He had lived with them long enough to know without a doubt that they would be honorable.

Adam made the decision for the others. "Yes, we'll tell her."

"She won't want to leave," Cole argued.

"It doesn't have to be forever," Adam countered. "She does have an obligation, however."

"She won't see it that way," Travis said.

"You know your sister as well as I do. Do you really believe she'll let Elliott suffer any longer?"

"Damn it, she doesn't even know him," Douglas said.

"She'll have to go and meet him. She'll want to put his mind at ease. With gentle prodding, Mary Rose will do the right thing. She'll want to procrastinate perhaps, but we won't let her. You know I'm right, Douglas. I don't like this any better than you do."

Harrison was sympathetic. "You have no one to blame but yourselves," he said. "You raised her to be noble."

"When are you leaving?" Douglas asked.

"Soon," Harrison answered. "I've stayed too long as it is," he added. "Elliott is depending on me to take over the negotiations for a merger he put together."

"The sooner you leave the better as far as I'm concerned," Travis said. "You didn't have to tell us about Elliott, you know. He's an old man, isn't he? And he'd already given up. Why did you have to take over his hunt?"

"Because I felt it was my duty to take over for him. If you knew him, you would understand."

"I think you should leave before we tell Mary Rose," Adam said.

"Why?"

"It will be easier for everyone," Adam replied.

"Exactly how will it be easier?" Harrison asked.

Adam refused to explain. The set look on his face told Harrison it would be pointless to argue.

"When are you going to tell her?" he asked.

"When we're ready. My brothers and I are going to discuss the situation first. We'll decide what's to be done, and when. I don't want you to leave just yet, however. I'm certain I'll have more questions I'll want answered before Mary Rose finds out anything."

Harrison pushed his chair back and stood up. "I know you've had quite a blow. If I could have changed things, I would have. Hell, Elliott didn't ask to be thrown into purgatory. You've had her long enough. You've watched her grow up. Her father never experienced any of the joy of her childhood. Let him at least meet her now. He needs to see her, to know she's all right."

"I've already explained Mary Rose will want to do that much," Adam responded.

"Don't put it off," Harrison pressed. "I'll give you one week, two, if I can wait that long. I hope to God you decide to tell her soon. I think you're wrong to want me to leave before you talk to her, but the decision is yours to make and I will respect it. I'll wait fourteen days. If you haven't gotten all your questions answered by then, it'll be too late. Don't you dare ask me again, Cole," he added when he caught the look on the brother's face. "I've given you my word. I won't tell Mary Rose about her father now, and I won't tell her in fourteen days. I'll simply leave. I'm going back to London, and I will tell Elliott the minute I see him."

Harrison started to leave the room. "You have quite a lot to talk over. I'll leave you to it."

"Wait a minute," Cole called out. "Are you planning to seduce our sister before or after we've told her about her father?"

"I should wait, but I'm not going to."

"Son-of-a . . ." Cole whispered.

Harrison interrupted him before he could complete the blasphemy. "I've given you my intentions and my terms. I suggest you accept them."

He pulled the door closed behind him.

The younger brothers turned to Adam. Cole asked, "What are we going to do?"

"We don't have to do anything," Douglas argued. "You heard Harrison. He said Elliott wouldn't come here."

"He also said Elliott wouldn't have to," Travis interjected. "Mary Rose would go to him."

"I want to hate him," Cole whispered, his voice harsh with worry.

"How can you want to hate Elliott?" Adam asked.

"I was talking about Harrison," Cole said. "He's trying to tear this family apart."

"He isn't trying now. He's done it," Travis said.

"We have to do the right thing," Douglas whispered. Oh, how he hated having to admit it. "She's got to go and meet him."

Travis and Cole exchanged a worried look. Of the four brothers, they were the most vulnerable and the most afraid. The future was filled with unknowns, and each was thinking he would have to face it alone.

Mary Rose had been their reason for joining together and becoming a family. She was the force that held them all together. When she left, wouldn't their purpose for being a family end?

Cole had known the day would come when she married and moved away. He had stubbornly refused to think about it. England was an ocean away, however, and the possibility that he would never see his sister again filled him with anguish.

"Our sister is all grown up," he said. "It happened overnight, didn't it? I knew she'd leave one day, but I didn't . . ."

He left the sentence unfinished. "Is it time for all of us to move on?"

"It's too soon to think about plans like that," Douglas said. "Cole, you wanted to buy that piece of land near the ridge that joins our land. Weren't you thinking about building your own place there?"

"You know I was," Cole said.

"I don't see how anything changes. Travis does so much traveling around, he isn't home much.

Even if the family breaks apart, we're still in business together."

Adam let his brothers worry out loud for a long while. Finally he had had enough of their self-pity, and forced them back to the immediate problem.

"Talking about our future plans can wait until later. Mary Rose is our concern now. She's going to be upset about all of this. I don't believe she should have time to worry about it. She can get used to the idea of a father on the way to England."

"Are you saying she should leave as soon as possible?" Travis asked.

Adam nodded. "Yes."

Cole reluctantly agreed. "The sooner she leaves, the sooner she'll be back."

"If she comes back," Travis said.

Everyone worried about the possibility once again. Then Adam said, "You heard Harrison say Elliott's a very wealthy man. Mary Rose has led a sheltered life here."

"She went to school in St. Louis," Douglas interjected. "She's seen some of the world."

"The boarding school was isolated from the city. She was sheltered there as well," Adam said.

"What are you worried about?" Cole asked. "Do you think her head will be turned by all the glitter?"

"No," Adam replied. "I just don't know how she'll handle the changes. I don't want her feeling . . . vulnerable."

"She makes friends easy," Douglas said.

447

"I don't like the notion of anyone hurting her feelings. I don't want her thinking she's inadequate," Adam said.

"Who will go with her?" Travis asked.

"All of us," Cole answered.

"Be reasonable," Douglas said. "We can't leave. We have responsibilities here."

"We're her past," Adam said. "As much as it pains me to say it, none of us can go with her."

"Are you suggesting we send her off alone?" Travis asked. He was appalled by the idea.

"Harrison could take her," Travis said.

None of the other brothers liked his suggestion. Adam finally came up with another one they found more acceptable.

"Eleanor could go with her. They could look out for each other. They're getting along just fine now, aren't they? Mary Rose has a good head. She'll do the right thing. I don't have any doubts about that."

"She came back from St. Louis alone," Cole said. "She knows how to handle herself around strangers. I made sure she could use a gun too. Adam's right. She'll be all right."

"The Cohens are going back east for some sort of family celebration. I have to go to Hammond again to sell those two horses. I'll stop by and find out the particulars. Maybe it would work out, and Eleanor and Mary Rose could ride with them."

"It sure would be nice if it worked out. I trust John Cohen," Cole said.

"We have to give the money back."

448

Douglas made the announcement. Everyone turned to him. "What money?" Cole asked.

"Elliott's money," Douglas explained. "Whoever kidnapped Mary Rose must have taken the money too. We used every bit of what was inside the envelope, and so now we have to give it back. Adam, do we have enough set aside?"

"Yes," Adam said. "And I agree. The money was probably stolen from Elliott, and we should give it back. We'll be stretched tight for a while. I'm sorry now we purchased the cattle, but we already gave the money and it's too late to back out."

The brothers continued to discuss their concerns well into the night. Adam finally decided to go to bed.

"We'll tell her together," he said.

"When?" Cole asked. He stood up and stretched his muscles.

"Let's ponder the 'when' tomorrow," Adam suggested.

Travis and Cole both acted as though they'd just been given a stay of execution from the hanging tree. They had at least twenty-four more hours to pretend everything was all right.

"What are we going to do about Harrison? Why didn't you want him to stay until after we told Mary Rose?" Douglas asked Adam.

"I need to question him about Elliott," Adam explained. "I have to find out what she's walking into. I want to know all about Elliott and what kind of life he leads. I have to be able to prepare Mary Rose. Harrison is the only one who can give me the information I need."

"We're going to have to make sure he stays away from our sister," Travis insisted.

Cole shook his head. "Damn it all, a man should have to say his vows before he claims his bride."

Adam leaned back in his chair. "I believe that's exactly what Harrison just did."

February 7, 1867

Dear Mama Rose,

We have a surprise for you. My brothers and I have been tucking a little money away for this fine day. We believe we have enough now for Cole and Douglas to come and fetch you. Hear me out, Mama, before you start shaking your head. First of all, if you're worried about the cost, then don't. We have worked everything out and once you get settled here, you'll see we're just doing fine. It's still winter, of course, and my brothers won't be able to leave until after spring roundup. I have to chuckle about our herd. We started with two breeding cows and now we have ten. We'll have five more after the birthings. It won't take us any time at all to gather ours up, but neighbors help neighbors, and so we'll give a hand to the Pearlman family. They have around eighty steers now. They've been mighty generous to us. They don't charge us for the services of their bull. We've promised to buy one of our own, and when we do, we'll reciprocate the kindness.

You're worried about Livonia, aren't you? I know she's blind, Mama, and depends on you for every little thing, but we need you too. If you train someone else to take over your chores, Livonia will get along just fine. She has two sons to look after her. I know

451

they're bad-natured, but they are her sons and therefore responsible for her. Livonia will understand, Please don't argue with us. We've waited long enough and so have you. Our minds are set. Unless we hear from you, Cole and Douglas will be knocking on your door around the first of June.

Love,
John Quincy Adam Clayborne

13

$\mathcal{J}$hey wouldn't let her out of their sight. Travis, Douglas, and Cole must have organized a schedule so each would know exactly when it was his turn to follow Mary Rose around or trail Harrison. The brothers' behavior was outrageous, especially given the fact that Harrison stayed busy from morning until night and rarely even saw their sister. He took the brothers' behavior in stride and went right along with his duties.

Adam thought his brothers were acting like children. He told them they were protecting their sister from the man who had, in effect, already pledged himself to her. Harrison had vowed in front of four witnesses to love her and protect her. He had used the word "forever," and Adam translated that to mean until death did they part. In his mind, the commitment had been made.

Travis told him he was crazy. Mary Rose hadn't made any such commitment.

"Only because you haven't given her enough time alone with Harrison to allow her to," Adam replied. "There aren't any preachers around here. Are you going to go all the way to Salt Lake to get one? Mother Rose married my father in front of her family without my father even being present. A month later he spoke his vows."

"Did he have a pistol pressed against his back?" Travis asked.

"No, he didn't. He wanted to pledge himself to her. Leave Harrison and Mary Rose alone."

Adam's reasoning might have made good sense to Travis if Mary Rose hadn't been his little sister. She was, however, and that fact changed everything. He didn't care who promised what. The thought of his sister being intimate with a man just didn't sit right. He couldn't even think about it without becoming nauseated.

Mary Rose knew something was wrong, but no one would tell her what it was. There was a lot of tension in the air. Three of her brothers were acting peculiar too. While she was pleased to have their company, she couldn't imagine why they needed to be around her all the time.

They wouldn't let her spend any time at all with Harrison. She asked Cole to tell her why everyone was on edge. He muttered something about money problems. She told Cole he should have more faith in God and in himself. They had gotten along during rough times before and they would do so again.

Her disappointment over the talk Harrison wanted to have with the brothers was difficult for her to get over. Eleanor's guess that he was going to ask to court Mary Rose turned out to be wrong. Travis told her Harrison discussed business matters. He couldn't give her any reason why she'd been excluded from the meeting, though, and she guessed Harrison was the only one who could tell her why he hadn't wanted her there. He seemed to be avoiding her. He did wink at her when he passed by her every once in a while, but he hadn't spoken more than ten words to her in almost a full week. She fretted about him and finally made up her mind to find a way to get him alone. Eleanor would help her. Now that she'd softened her attitude toward the family and opened her heart, she'd become a good friend.

Mary Rose went to see Corrie three times during the week. She made the trip more often than she needed to, but she'd hoped her brothers would be too busy to escort her, and Harrison would tag along. Thus far, the plan hadn't worked. She wasn't going to give up, however.

Each time she returned from a visit, she had wonderful news to report to the family. When she arrived at Corrie's cabin on Monday, she found a rocking chair had been placed in the center of the yard. She thought it was extremely thoughtful of Corrie to be concerned about her comfort. Wednesday she found the rocking chair in front of the window next to the steps. Corrie was letting her get closer with each visit. Now when she visited, Mary Rose wouldn't have to shout every word.

Friday was the best visit of all. The rocker was on the porch, directly outside the window. The chair faced the yard. Mary Rose admitted at supper she was a little nervous going up the steps. There wasn't a shotgun visible through the open window though, and she thought perhaps Corrie was testing her to see if she had enough courage to sit with her back to her.

Harrison's quiet reserve vanished when she told everyone what had happened. His heart nearly stopped beating. He bounded to his feet and began to roar.

"Are you out of your mind? Travis, you were with her, weren't you? How could you let your sister get close to . . ."

"Calm down," Travis said. "I had my shotgun ready. It wouldn't have taken me any time at all to get to the porch."

"She could have been dead by then," Harrison bellowed. His fury didn't seem to have any bounds.

Before Travis realized what he was about to do, Harrison reached over with one hand, grabbed hold of him, and lifted him out of his seat. The chair went flying backward. Cole glanced down, saw that Travis's feet weren't touching the floor, and then looked up at Harrison again.

There was admiration in Cole's gaze for the feat of strength Harrison was showing. Travis wasn't a lightweight by any stretch of the imagination, but Harrison didn't appear to be the least strained.

"Now, Harrison, is that any way to behave at the table?" Cole drawled out.

Harrison ignored him. He kept his gaze on Travis. "Corrie could have shoved a knife into her back or slit her throat or God only knows what else. Did you think about any of those possibilities while you had your damned shotgun up and ready, Travis?"

"Let go of him, Harrison." Adam issued the order.

Harrison finally realized what he was doing and immediately let go of the brother. Travis took it all in stride. He was still too surprised by Harrison's violent reaction to work up any real anger.

Cole picked up his chair for him. He waited until Travis was about to sit back down, then tried to pull the chair out from under him. Travis was used to the old trick. He shoved Cole hard with his shoulder and got settled again.

"Since you were hot and bothered about Mary Rose's safety, I won't have to hit you. You're lucky you didn't tear my shirt," he muttered. "I'd have to hit you then."

"I would be happy to mend it for you if Harrison did tear it," Eleanor blurted out. "Wouldn't I, Mary Rose?"

She kept her gaze on Harrison when she answered Eleanor. "Yes, of course you would."

Harrison was at it again. Mary Rose didn't know what to make of him. The sweet and gentle man she liked having around so much had once again turned into a barbarian. It was happening more frequently these days, she realized. She should be used to his spells by now. She wasn't, though. At least he didn't frighten her, she considered. He just stunned the breath out of her.

She decided she didn't like his unpredictability one bit. He was becoming extremely aggressive What had caused the change?

She looked around the table for someone to blame. Her gaze settled on Cole. He winked at her.

"Harrison sure got your attention," he said. "You look astonished."

She didn't appreciate his humor. She frowned

with displeasure and pointed her finger at him.

"This is all your fault, Cole Clayborne. You've been a bad influence on Harrison since the day he got here. He used to be a perfect gentleman. Now look at him. If you've ruined him, I'll never forgive you."

"Mary Rose, don't point your finger at anyone," Adam instructed. His attempt to correct her manners was halfhearted. He was trying not to laugh at his sister because he didn't want to hurt her feelings. If she believed Cole had ruined Harrison, Adam wouldn't try to change her mind.

Cole wasn't as disciplined, or as sensitive to his sister's feelings. He burst into laughter. "He was only pretending to be a gentleman. He's just like the rest of us, Mary Rose."

"He may be like Adam, but he certainly isn't like you or Douglas or Travis."

"What's wrong with us?" Douglas wanted to know.

She ignored his question. She turned to Harrison. He was still standing at the end of the table.

"I think you should stay away from Cole from now on. He's rubbing off on you, Harrison. You've picked up some bad habits."

"Such as?" Harrison asked.

"Such as rudeness," she answered.

"Come here, Mary Rose."

She let out a sigh. The look in his eyes told her it would be pointless to argue. She put her napkin down, got up from her chair, and walked over to him.

She put her hand on his arm. "It was rude

458

of you to pull Travis out of his chair."

"Yes," he agreed. "It was rude."

She was pleased he realized it. "And you're sorry," she said, thinking to help him with his apology.

"No, I'm not sorry at all."

"Oh, for heaven's sake, Harrison. I wish you'd stop having these spells. They're very unsettling."

"He's only acting like a normal man, Mary Rose," Douglas said. "I think it's kind of refreshing."

"I'm helping him get rid of his citified ways," Cole added. "You should thank me, sister."

"About Corrie," Harrison began, ignoring all the talk about his temper.

She squeezed his arm. "I wish you would follow my advice, Harrison. It will serve you well around here."

"This ought to be good," Travis whispered loud enough for everyone to hear.

"Mind your own business, Travis," Mary Rose said.

"You can give me your advice after we talk about Corrie," Harrison insisted.

She let out a sigh. "I know what you want. You'd like me to apologize for going up those stairs, wouldn't you?"

"I would like you to use the mind God gave you. Don't take chances like that again."

She didn't argue with him. "I'll be careful."

The tension went out of his shoulders. "Thank you."

He leaned down and kissed her. It was a sweet, tender, undemanding kiss that was finished before

459

she had time to react.

"Stop kissing our sister," Douglas ordered, though his voice lacked any real bite.

Harrison responded to the command by kissing Mary Rose again. Then he put his arm around her shoulders and hauled her up against his side. He was deliberately showing his possessiveness.

He turned his attention to Travis. "If I can't trust you to protect her . . ."

"If you can't trust me? If that isn't the kettle . . ."

"Let it rest, Travis," Adam suggested. "Harrison, sit down. Mary Rose, go back to your chair."

She walked back to her seat in a trance of disbelief. Whatever had come over Harrison? He had never shown such blatant affection in front of her brothers before.

"Who made these biscuits?" Travis asked.

"I did," Eleanor replied. "Why? Don't you like them?"

"I like them just fine. They're good."

She smiled with pleasure. "I'm pleased you like them. I'll make more tomorrow if you want me to. I could even bake a cake. I'm quite handy to have around. Aren't I, Mary Rose?"

"Yes, you are," she answered.

"You're sure being accommodating," Douglas said.

"I do try to be," Eleanor replied.

"What was the advice you were going to give Harrison?" Cole asked his sister.

"What did you ask . . . ? Advice? Oh, yes, I remember now."

She was still rattled by Harrison's kiss and was trying to regain her composure. "I was going to suggest Harrison follow my advice."

"Well, what the hell is it?" Cole asked.

"Watch your language, Cole," Mary Rose told him. "First with his mind, then with his heart. He should think things through before he acts."

Cole turned to Harrison. "Where have I heard that before?"

Harrison looked like he wanted to hit his head against something hard.

"Probably from your sister," he said dryly. "Mary Rose?"

"Yes?"

"You make me crazy."

Adam started laughing. "Don't get angry, sister. Harrison didn't meant to offend you. He was just having one of his spells again."

Eleanor patted Mary Rose's hand. "He's still rude, isn't he?"

Mary Rose didn't answer her. She let the brothers have their laugh, then decided to change the subject.

"Do you want to hear about the rest of my visit with Corrie?" Mary Rose asked.

"I don't think Harrison has enough stamina to hear any more," Cole said.

"Go ahead, sister, tell the rest," Adam encouraged.

"Corrie touched me. I was telling her all the news, rocking back and forth in her chair, and then I suddenly felt her hand on my shoulder. It was as light as a butterfly's wings. She even patted me. She also pinched me, but just once."

Douglas laughed. "Why'd she do that?"

"How could Mary Rose know?" Travis asked. "The woman still isn't talking to her."

"Oh, I believe I know why she pinched me, but I don't want to bore you with the details. Eleanor, pass the biscuits, please. They look delicious."

"They taste delicious too. Travis said so," Eleanor said. She handed the plate to Mary Rose and added the suggestion that she take two.

"You won't bore us," Cole said. "Tell us why she pinched you."

"Oh, all right," she agreed. She knew her brother wouldn't stop inquiring until she explained. "I was doing a spot of complaining, and I guess she got tired of listening. I stopped complaining as soon as she pinched me."

"We should have started in pinching you years ago," Adam teased. "Had we known how effective it would be."

"You really shouldn't complain, Mary Rose," Eleanor instructed. "People don't like it."

"When did you figure that out?" she asked.

"Surely you've noticed I've stopped complaining."

"Yes, indeed I have noticed," Mary Rose assured her friend.

"I realized how tiring my behavior was when I was walking home from town. Don't you remember the blisters I got on my toes? Well, being alone and all, I had time to think about my attitude."

"I sure have enjoyed hearing you laugh, Eleanor. You're nice to be around now, and you help out so much, I'm beginning to wonder how we ever got along without you."

"Thank you, Adam."

"When were you alone?" Mary Rose asked.

She happened to look at Cole and noticed he was trying hard not to smile.

"Did I say I was alone? I wasn't," Eleanor blurted out. "Forget I mentioned it, Mary Rose."

She wasn't going to do any such thing. Something had happened on the way back from Blue Belle, and she was determined to find out what it was.

"Eleanor, will you help me clear the table and bring in the coffee?"

"Certainly," Eleanor replied. "I try to be helpful. I hope you'll remember that."

Mary Rose collected some of the dishes and went into the kitchen. Eleanor followed her a minute later with the leftovers. She put the plates down on the sideboard, then turned to collect the coffeepot.

Mary Rose wouldn't let her leave the kitchen. She hurried over to block the doorway, then whirled around, folded her arms across her middle, and said, "Start talking, Eleanor. What happened on the way home from town? Something's going on all right."

"No, honestly," Eleanor protested. "I was never alone. I'm being sincere. Please don't do anything hasty."

"Like what?"

"Don't make me leave. Please don't vote against me."

"What in heaven's name are you talking about?"

Eleanor proceeded to tell her everything.

Mary Rose became furious. It was cruel and heartless of Harrison and Cole to frighten Eleanor. She spent a good ten minutes soothing her friend. Her anger simmered all the while. Eleanor was so pleased to have her friend's sympathy and understanding, she recounted the horrible experience once again, embellishing the details as she went along. By the time she was finished, she'd gotten all worked up again.

Douglas was thankful his sister had left the dining room because he wanted to talk about Corrie without interference.

"I've had time to think about what Harrison said," he announced in a low voice so Mary Rose wouldn't hear. "Crazy Corrie could have hurt Mary Rose. You never should have let her go up on the porch, Travis."

"She wasn't in any danger. Corrie likes Mary Rose. She left the quilt in the cave for her, didn't she?"

"How do you know it was Crazy Corrie's quilt?" Douglas asked.

"Oh, for God's sake, Douglas. If you want to start something with me, just do it. Don't use stupid arguments."

"She is crazy," Cole interjected.

"How do you figure that?" Travis asked.

"Normal folks don't greet visitors with a shotgun sticking out of their window. I'm siding with Douglas. He's right . . ."

"No, I was wrong," Harrison announced.

Everyone turned to him. He let out a sigh. "I overreacted. I still wouldn't have let her go

464

up on the porch, but I shouldn't have blown up the way I did during supper."

"Then why did you?"

Harrison shrugged. "I've been a little on edge lately."

Adam leaned back in his chair. "I find it curious," he remarked to no one in particular.

"What's curious?" Cole asked.

"You boys can be quiet when you want to, yet Harrison knew you were in the bunkhouse searching through his things. He let you think he was sleeping."

"So?" Cole prodded.

"I'm finding it curious Corrie could get inside the cave, cover Mary Rose, and then leave, while Harrison was sound asleep. Yes, sir," he added with a smile. "I'm curious all right."

Cole turned to Harrison. "You saw her, didn't you?"

"Yes, I saw her."

"Why didn't you tell us?" Travis asked.

"I didn't say anything because I didn't want Mary Rose to know. She was sleeping. Corrie wasn't crazy that night. There was a look of tenderness in her eyes when she stood over Mary Rose and looked at her. I don't know if her moods change with the winds, however, or if she could in fact turn dangerous. Since I only saw her for a couple of minutes, I wouldn't be willing to put Mary Rose's life in her hands just yet. I still believe your sister needs to remain cautious."

"What did she look like?" Douglas asked.

"Like someone took a hatchet to her."

Travis shuddered. "The poor thing," he whispered.

"How come she doesn't talk?" Cole asked.

"I'm not certain she can."

"You mean her throat . . ." Travis couldn't continue. He was rattled by the picture of the woman he was getting in his mind.

Cole was the only brother who seemed to take it all in stride. "Why didn't you tell Mary Rose you saw Corrie?"

"I felt it would be intrusive. Corrie belongs to her. She should be the first to see her."

"Do you think Corrie will ever let her?"

"I doubt it, but she might," Harrison conceded.

"Mary Rose will probably faint, or scream," Travis said. "Hell, I would."

Harrison shook his head. "No, your sister will take it all in stride."

Adam nodded. "You know her well, Harrison."

"There's a storm brewing," Douglas remarked.

"Did you hear thunder?" Cole asked.

"Hell. MacHugh hates thunder."

The brothers laughed. "He hates everything," Travis said.

"He sure likes Adam," Douglas remarked. "What'd you do to make him follow you around like a puppy after you rode him today?"

"I took Harrison's advice and praised him. He likes hearing how fine he is. We're kindred spirits, Douglas."

"Will you take care of him for me when I leave?" Harrison asked Adam.

"You aren't taking him with you?" Douglas asked.

"The journey across the ocean would be too much for him."

"Let me guess," Cole interjected. "MacHugh hates water, doesn't he?"

Harrison's expression turned serious. "Promise me something, Adam. No matter what, don't sell him. If I can't get back here, you keep him."

Adam agreed. "Do you think you will come back?"

Before Harrison could answer, Travis asked him another question. "Are you still going to leave in another week?"

"No," Harrison answered. "I've decided to leave the day after tomorrow."

"Why'd you change your mind?" Cole asked.

"Mary Rose."

He didn't think he needed to say more, but Douglas wouldn't let it go. He demanded details.

"Are you trying to rush us into telling her sooner? It's our call, Harrison, not yours. Why can't you wait longer?"

"I think he should leave soon," Travis interjected. "I'm getting tired of chasing after Mary Rose. She'll be safer once he's gone."

"Let him tell us why he moved the date up," Douglas pestered.

Harrison decided to be blunt. "It's simple, gentlemen. I've reached the end of my endurance. I can't be in the same room with her and not . . ."

"You don't have to go into details," Cole hastily said. "We get the picture."

"And it's a disgusting one," Travis muttered, for it involved his sister.

"There it is again," Douglas said.

"What?" Travis asked.

"Thunder," Douglas answered. "It's coming from the kitchen."

"What the hell are you talking about?" Cole asked.

Douglas didn't have to explain. Harrison was ordered to the kitchen. Mary Rose shouted his name. Eleanor bellowed Cole's name.

The two men who had been summoned looked at each other. "I guess maybe they talked things over," Cole said.

"Maybe?" Harrison replied dryly.

Cole was reluctant to move. Harrison put his napkin down with a resigned look and stood up.

"Are you going to go in there?" Travis asked.

"Of course," Harrison answered.

"What in blazes for?"

"To catch hell," Harrison said. "Get up, Cole. You're going with me." Cole tossed his napkin at Travis and followed Harrison into the kitchen. Mary Rose started in first.

"How could you be so cruel? It was callous and mean of you to scare Eleanor the way you did. I cannot believe you dumped her out on the road in the middle of nowhere. What could you have been thinking?"

Harrison wasn't given time to defend himself. Eleanor rushed over to stand next to Mary Rose. She imitated her military stance by folding her arms across her middle.

"I got blisters on my toes. They bled for God's sake. Was Cole in on this? He was, wasn't he?"

She turned, to glare at Mary Rose's brother. "I shall never, ever forgive you."

"You two left her alone. Anything could have happened to her. There are wild animals living up there on the mountain. Did you forget about them? Eleanor could have . . . did you have your gun?" she asked her friend.

Eleanor shook her head. "No, I did not. If I'd had my gun, Mary Rose, I would have shot Harrison."

"How would you have felt if something terrible had happened to me?" Eleanor asked Cole.

He walked over to the kitchen table and leaned against it. "Nothing happened to you," he said in a perfectly calm, reasonable tone of voice.

"There never was going to be a vote," Eleanor cried out. "I've been nice for no good reason at all. I even made biscuits, damn it."

Cole shrugged. "They were good biscuits," he said. "It didn't kill you to be nice, Eleanor, so quit acting like it did."

"There was always someone watching over her," Harrison interjected. He too sounded reasonable.

"Who was looking out for her?" Mary Rose asked.

"Dooley took a turn, then Ghost spelled him, and then Henry finished up," Cole explained.

"Ghost? Dear Lord, not Ghost. Had he been drinking?"

"Yes, he had," Eleanor answered. "The man was clearly sotted."

"He was what?" Cole asked.

"Drunk," she said. "He couldn't have come to my rescue if I'd gotten into trouble."

"You can't know that," Cole argued.

469

"He thought I was an angel, for God's sake."

"He was drunk." Cole burst into laughter. Harrison had more discipline. He only cracked a smile.

Eleanor desperately wanted Cole to admit he'd have mourned her if she'd been killed. She knew she was being melodramatic; she didn't care. He had kissed her, after all. He had to feel something for her, didn't he? She thought it would be lovely if he'd admit it.

"What would you have done if I'd been killed?"

"That didn't happen. You're sure a sight when your cheeks get all flushed."

"Answer my question," Eleanor insisted.

"Fine, I'll answer. I guess I'd bury you."

"You'd bury me."

She didn't look too happy with him. He decided that wasn't the answer she'd been looking for. "I'd pick a real nice spot."

Harrison put his arms around Mary Rose. "I'd do the same for you," he promised her.

She could see the laughter in his eyes. "How thoughtful of you," she whispered.

Eleanor moved closer to Cole. "And then what would you do?"

"Do you have to raise your voice like that? You're making my head pound."

She apologized before she realized what she was doing. "I'm sorry. Please tell me what you would do after you buried me in a nice spot."

Cole pretended to have to think about it.

"Well, I'd have to dig deep when I planted you so the animals wouldn't get to you. And it's hot out this time of year," he said.

"Yes," she agreed. "It's hot."

"I guess I'd come back home and tell Mary Rose what happened. She'd feel real bad, wouldn't she, Harrison?"

"Yes, she would," Harrison agreed.

Neither Eleanor nor Mary Rose could hold on to their anger. The way Cole was going on and on in that cowboy's drawl of his made both women want to laugh.

"And then what would you do?" Eleanor asked.

"I guess I'd get a beer."

She turned around and walked out of the kitchen. She knew she was going to smile. She didn't want Cole to see it.

He caught up with her in the hallway just as she was about to push the swinging door open so she could go into the dining room.

He grabbed hold of her around the waist and forced her to turn around.

"Exactly what did you expect me to say I'd do?"

"I expected you to say you'd feel sorry about my demise. Doing any actual mourning would be too much to ask from a man like you."

"Sure I'd mourn."

"Aren't you at all sorry you lied to me?"

"No."

"Why not?"

"Because you were being a real pain in the backside, Eleanor. I like you better now. You're much sweeter when you're not yelling all the time. Besides, I got to kiss you. I wouldn't have if Harrison hadn't dumped you out on the trail. The plan was all his doing, by the way. Want

471

me to kiss you again?"

"Yes, please."

Cole's hand moved to the back of her neck. He was rough when he pulled her against him.

"There's a fire burning inside you, Ellie. You make a man want to get close to the heat. Real close. I've been thinking about kissing you again all week long."

"Cole?" Her voice was a dreamy whisper.

"Yes?"

"Will you please get on with it?"

He was laughing when his mouth claimed hers. One kiss wasn't enough. He decided he wanted more. He was having such a pleasurable time, he forgot all about leaving Mary Rose in the kitchen with the man who was determined to seduce her.

His sister was thankful for a moment's privacy from the family. She wanted to talk to Harrison and find out why he'd been avoiding her. Something was wrong, all right, and she didn't want to fret about it any longer.

When Cole left the room, Harrison went to the back door and looked into the night.

A cool breeze filtered in through the screen. "What are you looking at?" she asked.

"Paradise."

He turned and found her standing just a foot away from him. He didn't say a word to her. He simply took hold of her hand, turned around again, and went outside.

She meekly followed him. She expected him to stop on the back porch, but he continued on down the stairs and across the yard. His stride

472

was long, purposeful. He wanted to put some distance between her and her brothers so he could talk to her. He let go of her hand halfway across the yard and continued on to the corral. He turned to her then, folded his arms across his chest, and leaned back against the wooden railing.

She stood at least ten feet away from him. She wanted to run to him, to put her arms around him and hold him close. Instead, she stood where she was and waited for a sign that he wanted her to touch him.

He seemed content to stare at her. She didn't feel uncomfortable under his close scrutiny. His eyes were filled with warmth now. There was such tenderness in his gaze, she felt as though he was already stroking her. She instinctively moved closer to him, her gaze locked with his, and she didn't even try to fight her own reaction to him. He hadn't touched her, yet she still felt breathless and warm and restless with yearning.

She'd missed being held by him. She found herself wondering if he realized how much he'd changed since he'd arrived in Montana. There was a savage quality about him now, a ruggedness she hadn't noticed the day she'd met him. He had always been muscular and tall, but now he seemed Herculean to her. The sun had weathered his skin into a much deeper, bronzed color. Although it wasn't possible, his eyes seemed to be darker too, and his hair was much longer, nearly reaching his shoulders. It was still dark in color, but the moonlight made it appear to be streaked with gold.

The longer she looked at him, the more difficulty she had catching her breath.

He noticed the subtle change in her. Her eyes had turned a deep blue. She had a bemused look on her face. She was arousing the hell out of him.

He recognized the look. Her eyes always turned just that color when he kissed her. Passion had caused the reaction then. What was the reason now?

He thought he knew, but he was going to make her tell him anyway.

"What are you thinking about?" His voice was the deep, husky drawl of a Highlander.

"How beautiful you are," she whispered. "You are, you know. I thought you were handsome when I first met you, but now even looking at you makes my breath catch in the back of my throat."

She couldn't believe she'd had the courage to tell him the truth, especially given the fact that he had been avoiding her all week long.

"I was also thinking that you've been avoiding me. Have you grown tired of me?"

The question astonished him. He couldn't imagine why she would worry over such an impossibility.

"I could never grow tired of you. I think about you from the minute I wake up until the second I fall asleep. Hell, I even dream about you."

"You do?" she asked the question on a sigh.

"Yes, I do."

The caress had moved into his voice. She took another step closer. "I'll bet we think about the same things." Like kissing and holding each other and sharing our secrets and our dreams.

His laugh was derisive. "I doubt it. You don't know much about men, do you?"

"I thought I did. I have four brothers. I usually know what they're thinking."

"Is that right? Do you really want to know what I'm thinking about right now?"

She slowly nodded. Then she took another step toward him. "Yes, please. You've made me very curious."

"I'm thinking how hot you're going to be when I make love to you. I'm picturing you sprawled out on my sheets, your skin soft and golden, your hair wild and untamed, your mouth swollen and rosy because I've spent a long while ravaging it. Your eyes will be the color of blue they are right now. I'm thinking about that little sound you'll make in the back of your throat that makes me go crazy and get so hard I ache to be inside you. I'm thinking how wild and savage our lovemaking will be, and how you'll dig your nails into my shoulders when we're sealed together and I'm throbbing inside you, and how tight and wet you'll be. That's pretty much what I was thinking."

She couldn't seem to catch her breath. She was amazed she could still stand up. The erotic pictures he'd painted for her were making her knees weak.

He wasn't quite finished. He slowly unfolded his arms and said, "I won't be gentle. You won't want me to be. Understand me, Mary Rose. I'm going to have you, over and over and over again. Want me to go on?"

She couldn't manage to answer him. She felt as though he'd just set her on fire. She could feel her face burning and was suddenly in dire need of her fan or a drink of ice-cold water.

She lowered her head so he wouldn't see how red her face was becoming. He would think she was embarrassed. She wasn't at all embarrassed, though, and that surprised her more than anything else.

The man certainly had a way with words. He had been extremely blunt and completely honest with her. He deserved her honesty in return. She wasn't going to pretend she hadn't liked what he'd said to her. She thought a proper lady would probably turn around now and go running back to the house for safety. Perhaps that was the reason he wasn't holding her. He was giving her the freedom to decide if she was proper or not. His words had been lover's words and were not to be mocked but embraced, and she did exactly that.

She looked up at him, stared directly into his eyes, and whispered, "That's pretty much what I was thinking."

He looked arrogantly pleased with her. She closed the distance between them quickly. She stood between his feet, with her arms around his waist, and leaned into him.

"I'm wearing clothes in my thoughts and dreams though. What am I wearing in yours?" she asked.

"Me."

The single word flooded her mind with all sorts of erotic pictures. She became breathless thinking about the two of them in bed together without a stitch of clothing between them.

"Harrison, when you say things like . . . you make me feel . . ."

"Warm all over?"

"Yes," she whispered. "Warm all over. I'm being brazen admitting it, aren't I? I don't believe I'd act like this if any other man talked to me the way you just did."

"Hell, I hope not."

"You make me feel beautiful," she whispered with wonder in her voice.

"You are beautiful," he said. "You aren't brazen, sweetheart. You were being honest with me. You weren't telling the truth about thinking and dreaming the way I do though."

"How do you know I wasn't?" Lord, how she loved the rough timbre of his voice. It made her shiver all over with yearning.

"You don't have any experience to draw from to have such thoughts. You don't have any idea how good it's going to be between us."

She leaned back so she could look into his eyes. "Exactly how much experience have you had?"

"Enough."

He wasn't going to elaborate, and she decided not to pursue the matter. His past conquests were simply that. Past. The present belonged to her. Besides, she couldn't even think about Harrison making love to another woman without getting a sharp pain of anguish and jealousy.

"It hurts to think about you with another woman."

"I can't change the past for you. I never loved

any of the women I took to my bed, and they certainly didn't love me. We used each other because we wanted the same thing."

"What did you want?"

"Physical gratification," he answered. "I'm not proud of my behavior. Using anyone the way I did was wrong. I had to grow up before I figured it all out, however."

She nodded so he would know she understood. "Cole and Travis and Douglas haven't quite grown up yet."

"How do you know they haven't?"

"The frequency of their trips to Hammond."

Harrison smiled. "You know about the house outside of town?"

"With the women? Of course. I've known for a long time. Adam explained everything to me. Now that you've explained what it could be like in bed with you, I believe I shall start having those same thoughts and dreams you have. I won't tell Adam about them though."

"Not what it could be like in my bed, what it will be like. I mean to have you, Mary Rose."

"You do?"

"I love you, sweetheart."

She was overwhelmed with joy. Tears welled up in her eyes, and all she wanted to do was throw herself into his arms and hold him close for the rest of her life. She hadn't realized how long she'd yearned to hear those words.

He wouldn't let her hug him. He held her by her shoulders and gave her a little squeeze so she would pay attention to what he wanted to explain to her.

"I want you to listen carefully. I love you, and I'm going to keep on loving you until the day I die. I want to spend the rest of my life protecting you and cherishing you. I have a tremendous amount of faith in you. I know that once you get past your anger, you'll realize we were meant to be together. It's inevitable. No man can ever love you the way I do. I want you to try to remember that when you're hating me. Remember too that I never, ever meant to hurt you."

"I don't understand what you're trying to tell me. I could never hate you."

"Ah, love, you will hate me," he promised. "I wish to God I could prevent the heartache you're going to have to endure, but I can't. It's out of my hands now."

She wasn't frightened by his dark prediction. He loved her. Nothing else mattered to her.

"You tell me you have faith in me, but you contradict yourself by suggesting I could ever hate you. I have far more trust in you than you have in me, Harrison. Nothing you have ever done, or will ever do, could make me hate you. I love you, more than I could ever have imagined was possible. With my love comes my complete trust. I don't give it easily. When I come to your bed, it will be with a loving heart. I'm not so weak-willed to love one minute and hate the next. I don't care what heartache awaits me. If you are by my side, I shall endure anything."

He gripped her shoulders tight. "Think long and hard before you give me your pledge of love. Understand and remember every word you just said to me. Then go and talk to your brothers.

Hear what they have to say before you tell me you love me again."

She shook her head. "I don't need to talk to them. I already know what is in my heart. Nothing they can say will change the way I feel about you."

He was shaken by her trust in him. "You tempt me to damn the consequences. I need you, Mary Rose, and I know I can't continue to wait much longer. I won't ever force you. You're going to give yourself willingly to me. Don't dare tell me you love me again, for if you do, from that moment on, you will belong to me. I will not let you change your mind."

His hands moved to cup the sides of her face. His rough calluses against her skin emphasized the wonderful differences between them. She luxuriated in the power that radiated from him, the strength in his hands, the hardness in his body, the very way he towered over her. She didn't feel less because he had far more physical strength than she had. She gloried in all the amazing contrasts between them. She was his equal in all ways that mattered most to both of them. In her mind, and in her heart.

"I love you, Mary Rose."

The tenderness in his voice was testimony he had spoken from his heart.

His thumb rubbed across her lower lip. She felt the warmth of his caress down to her toes.

"You are everything I could ever want in a mate, and so much more. I was drawn to your kindness and your strength and your pure heart. Go back inside now, before I forget my promise."

His hands dropped to his sides. She understood completely what he expected her to do. He had given her a way out because he wanted her to be certain. There could be no going back once she made her commitment to him.

Oh, yes, she understood. He didn't understand though. It was already too late, for her heart had already been given.

"I love you, Harrison."

He went completely still. She repeated her pledge.

"Dear God, Mary Rose. Do you understand that I . . ."

"I love you."

He pulled her into his arms. His hands cupped her backside, and he lifted her up tight against him until her pelvis was pressed against his groin.

She wrapped her arms around his neck. She began to tremble with anticipation, for his heat and strength enveloped her now. She loved the scent and feel of him against her, and dear God, if he didn't kiss her soon, she thought she would go out of her mind.

He waited until his hunger consumed him. And then he leaned down and began to make love to her with his mouth. His tongue stroked her lips, then sank deep inside to mate with hers.

The taste of her intoxicated him. His mouth became more demanding, slanting over hers again and again until he became wild with his own pulsating need. There was only Mary Rose, the passion of his life, the love for eternity. He wrapped himself in her softness and believed he'd reached heaven.

The hot, wet, open-mouthed kisses became more urgent because her uninhibited response drove him on.

She couldn't seem to get enough of him. She wanted to touch and stroke him everywhere. His arousal was cuddled between her hips. She could feel his hardness pressed against her and began to instinctively rub against him.

The temptation to go further was beginning to override all other considerations. Harrison suddenly realized his jeopardy. And hers. If he didn't stop now, he would take her virginity in the backyard. God help him, the thought didn't repulse him.

He abruptly pulled away from her. His breathing was ragged and choppy. Every nerve in his body screamed out for fulfillment. He shuddered in reaction to the raging need coursing through him and clenched his jaw tight as he desperately tried to mentally distance himself from her.

She felt as though her anchor had just been ripped away from her. Her strength deserted her, and she collapsed against him, shaking with her own need.

She wanted him to put his arms around her again and hold her close.

"Go back inside."

The harshness in his command cut through her haze of desire. She tried to understand. "Inside? I don't want to leave you. Please kiss me again. I love you, Harrison. I want you to hold me."

"Go back inside."

He wasn't asking her to leave, he was telling her to. She took a deep breath and slowly pulled her arms away from him.

She was confused by the sudden change in him. Had she done something wrong, and if so, what?

She wasn't in any condition to try to figure anything out now. She would have to wait until later, after her heart had stopped pounding so frantically and she could catch her breath without panting, and then she would think things through.

He wasn't going to have to tell her to leave him alone again, however. As dazed as she was, she still fully understood what the word *no* meant, even when it came masked as a command.

She turned around and started walking back to the house. Irritation and frustration didn't catch her until she was halfway to her destination.

It was damned rude of him to be so abrupt in his dismissal, wasn't it? Would it have killed him to tell the woman he loved why he'd been in such a hurry to stop kissing her?

She thought he was behind her. "You're as moody as your horse," she muttered loud enough for him to hear.

He didn't respond to her barb. She turned around to repeat her insult and realized then he couldn't possibly have heard her. He was going in the opposite direction.

"Where are you going?" she called out.

"To bed."

It was late, but not that late. "Aren't you coming back to the house tonight?"

"No."

"Good night then."

He didn't return her farewell. She waited another minute, and when he reached the entrance of the bunkhouse and pushed the door open, she ran out of patience.

"Good night," she shouted. She silently added the words *damn it*.

He finally turned around and looked at her. "Mary Rose?"

His voice was forceful enough to lift her off the ground.

The fanciful, impossible notion made her smile. "Yes?"

"Don't keep me waiting."

May 4, 1867

Dear Mama Rose,
We were all heartsick after we read your letter. We have a hundred questions to ask you. Why didn't you tell us what Livonia was up to sooner? You shouldn't have had to worry alone. We're your family now, and you shouldn't ever keep anything from us.

How long has Livonia been blackmailing you into staying with her? Yes, we know and we understand how afraid the old woman is. Being blind is terrible, of course it is, and being saddled with two self-centered sons who are trying to sell everything out from under her must be just as frightening, but, Mama Rose, none of her burdens can justify what she's doing to you.

Do you really believe she'll tell her sons Adam killed their father or could she be bluffing? Has she completely forgotten he was trying to protect you and Livonia from your master's rage? Remember all the times he beat her? Livonia surely has suffered, but none of what has happened to her can make her sin against you easier for us to bear. Lincoln wanted you to have your freedom, and all the thousands of young men who gave up their lives in battle did so to ensure your freedom.

Now Mistress Livonia has bound you into slavery once again . . .

God protect us all,
Your loving son, Douglas

14

Cole and Eleanor stayed in the hallway kissing and hugging and whispering sweet nonsensical words to each other for a long while. He finally called a halt to the love play when he felt his control slipping. He was used to getting what he wanted when he wanted it, but Eleanor wasn't like any of the other women he'd kissed and bedded. There would have to be a commitment given before he slept with her, and damn it all, he wasn't about to carry things that far.

He made up his mind never to kiss her again as he followed her back into the dining room. He held her chair out for her first and then walked around to the other side of the table to take his seat. He didn't seem to notice his brothers were watching him. He was fully occupied mentally listing all the reasons he needed to stay away from the blushing virgin across from him.

"Didn't you forget something?" Douglas asked his brother.

Travis had to nudge Cole to get him to answer. "Like what?" Cole asked.

"Like your sister. She's still in the kitchen with Harrison."

Cole started to get up, then changed his mind. "Mary Rose is a big girl. She can take care of herself around Harrison. If he wants to give up his freedom, that's his problem, not mine."

"His freedom?" Douglas asked, trying hard not to laugh. He'd noticed Cole had stared at Eleanor when he'd made the comment about Harrison.

"Yes, his freedom," his brother muttered. The set of his jaw indicated he didn't want to continue with the discussion.

"I don't think Harrison looks at it the way you do," Travis interjected.

Eleanor wasn't aware of the change in Cole. She smiled at him and said, "Mary Rose is very capable. All of our teachers at school thought so. She helped me get through a perfectly horrible mathematics class. I would have failed without her."

Travis stared at Cole for another minute, then stood up and went into the kitchen to get Mary Rose. He didn't care how capable his sister was. He knew Harrison and understood exactly what his intentions were. Cole may have adopted a lackadaisical attitude, but he certainly hadn't.

He found his sister sitting at the kitchen table, staring off into space. Her face looked flushed to him.

"What's the matter with you?"

"Nothing."

"Something's wrong. You only look flustered when you're sick or angry. Which is it?"

"Neither."

"Where's Harrison?"

"He went to bed."

She wasn't about to give her brother any further details. She therefore didn't mention the fact that Harrison expected her to join him.

"Don't make me wait." Hadn't he said those

488

very words to her just minutes after he'd practically shoved her away from him?

"You're angry, aren't you?"

"I'm not angry."

"You don't have to snap your words at me. Tell me what's bothering you. Maybe I can fix it."

She knew Travis wouldn't quit pestering her until she satisfied his curiosity. She had to tell him something, even if it was only a half-truth.

"Arrogant men bother me. Can you fix that?"

Travis's grin was slow and easy. "Harrison made you mad, didn't he?"

"Please leave me alone. I need time to think."

Her brother crossed the kitchen to get the coffeepot. "Is he . . ."

He didn't quite know how to phrase the delicate question he wanted to ask.

"Is he what?"

He forced a shrug. "Pushing you to do something you don't want to do?"

"He would never push me or force me to do anything I didn't want to do."

Travis nodded. "I didn't think he would, but I still wanted to hear you tell me so. Answer one more question for me, and I promise I'll leave you alone to stew."

"I'm not stewing."

"Do you love him?"

"Oh, yes, I love him."

"You're sure?"

She smiled. "I'm sure. He's rude and bossy and arrogant and stubborn."

"A girl can't ask for more than that in a man."

"He's also kind and gentle and loving."

Tears gathered in her eyes. Travis spotted them right away. "Are you going to cry about it, Mary Rose?"

"No, of course not."

The miracle of his commitment was finally sinking in. He was going to love her until the day he died. Hadn't he said those very words to her when he'd told her what was in his heart?

She let out a long sigh. A tear rolled down her cheek just as Travis turned to look at her.

"I've loved Harrison for a long time, Travis."

Her sister's voice had taken on a dreamy quality. Travis was disgusted.

"Honest to God, you're starting to act just like a woman. Oh, I knew it was coming all right, but I still wasn't ready. I wish you'd stop it, Mary Rose."

"Exactly how does a woman act that offends you so?"

"Angry one minute, smiling the next, pouting and laughing at the same time, pretty much just the way you're aching right now. You never used to be this emotional, little sister. I don't like it."

She wasn't certain if she was supposed to apologize or not. Travis stared at her and suddenly saw her in a completely different light. She wasn't a scabby-kneed little girl any longer. She was a beautiful woman.

"You grew up on me when I had my back turned, didn't you?" he whispered.

She wasn't really paying attention to what her brother was saying to her. She had more matters to think about.

"Do you want to know when I fell in love with him? I know the exact minute when I . . ."

He hastily interrupted her. "No, I don't want to know," he muttered. "Men don't care about things like that. I'm still your brother, for God's sake. I don't want to hear any particulars about something that might have happened to you."

"Nothing has happened between us I couldn't tell you about."

"Thank God for that. I don't want to hear about it when it does. You got that, Mary Rose?"

When something happens? She leaned back in her chair and stared up at her brother. "You're being rather presumptuous," she said.

"No, I'm not. I'm just being blunt."

"Yes, you are too," she argued. "You're also just as arrogant as Harrison is."

He dismissed the remark, for he didn't believe being arrogant was all that bad, even though his sister made it sound as though it was.

He lifted the coffeepot and turned to go back into the dining room. He stopped suddenly and turned to her again.

"If he ever hurts you, I want to be the first to know about it. You'll tell me, won't you?"

"Yes, I'll tell you."

He nodded with satisfaction. "I love you, brat."

"I love you too. You like Harrison, don't you?"

"It's hard not to like him. I don't like what he came here to do. You won't either after we talk to you."

"Oh, yes, the talk," she whispered.

"He told you about . . ."

She interrupted him. "He told me you were

going to tell me something. He didn't tell me what the topic was. You can tell me now."

He shook his head. "Wait until tomorrow night. Don't frown about it. All right?"

"Travis, no matter what you tell me, I won't hate him. Do you think I will?"

He didn't believe she was capable of hating anyone. She was going to get her heart broken though. Travis was certain of that. Her entire world was going to be turned around on her, and it only seemed reasonable to Travis that she would blame Harrison. Travis certainly did.

"No, you won't hate him," he said. "Grab the cups for me, Mary Rose."

He gave the order in an attempt to take her mind off of the subject of the coming meeting. He wanted her to remain happy and carefree for as long as possible.

He decided to turn her thoughts in another direction and told her about Cole and Eleanor.

"He's beginning to realize he can't mess with her. She's the marrying kind. Cole isn't."

"Yes, he is," she said. "He just doesn't realize it yet. You are too, Travis. When the right woman comes along, you won't think twice about getting married. You're going to make a wonderful husband and father."

"And give up my freedom? Are you out of your mind?"

She laughed. It was just the reaction he wanted.

"You're sounding like Adam. Why do men think marriage ends their freedom?"

"Because it does," he replied.

He started to leave the kitchen again, but she

called him back. "Travis?"

"What now."

"It was MacHugh."

"What?"

"That's when I fell in love with Harrison."

He rolled his eyes. "I get it. You fell in love with his horse and figured Harrison was part of the package."

He left the kitchen before she could make him understand. She didn't mind. She was happy to be alone again so she could think about all the wonderful things the love of her life had said to her. He wanted to spend the rest of his life with her. She couldn't imagine anything more wonderful.

She stayed at the table for several minutes, until Travis called out to her. She took the cups into the dining room, passed them around, and then excused herself for the night.

She went up to her room and sat down on the side of the bed to think things over. She tried to forget Harrison was waiting for her. She couldn't, of course. A warm knot formed in the pit of her stomach every time she glanced out the window and saw the light glowing in the window of the bunkhouse.

He was waiting for her to come to him. He had made her aware of her own body's demands, given her a glimpse of passion, and now she couldn't pretend it hadn't happened or that she hadn't wanted him to give her more.

She wanted him because she loved him. He was still being horribly arrogant. Mary Rose stood up and began to pace back and forth while she thought about the way he'd given her his command. He hadn't bothered to ask her. No, he'd assumed. Were all men like Harrison? She shook her head, discarding the possibility. No one had ever been this possessive with her or this high-handed. He was stubborn and willful, set in his ways, and sweet and giving and wonderful. No, there wasn't anyone else in the world like Harrison Stanford MacDonald. And that was precisely why she'd fallen in love with him.

He hadn't asked her to marry him. She tried to imagine him down on one knee begging for her hand in marriage and found herself smiling over the picture. He wouldn't ask. He'd tell. He was entirely too presumptuous, of course, but she didn't mind at all.

He was also being practical about their situation. It wasn't possible to officially marry now. Blue Belle didn't even have a church, and preachers were as scarce in the area as canned peaches. Hanging Judge Burns could perform the ceremony, but he was only available three or four times a year, the rest of the time the glut of men needing hanging demanded his full attention.

Harrison had made his commitment tonight with God as his witness. And she had done the same. Now everything was going to change.

She didn't have any idea how long she paced around the bedroom, pondering over her future, but the house was dark and quiet when she finally quit worrying about all the changes in her life she was going to experience. She took her time washing every inch of her body with her rose-scented soap, then put on her white nightgown.

494

She added her pink, lace-trimmed robe Douglas had given her last Christmas, then sorted through her wardrobe in search of her impractical but lovely satin slippers.

She was still nervous and somewhat afraid of what was going to happen, yet she knew fretting about it wouldn't change anything. Loving Harrison didn't frighten her. The act of making love, however, was another matter altogether. Men liked it, she knew, because of the way her brothers ran to Hammond every other week and came home wearing cheap perfume on their clothes and silly grins on their faces. Perhaps the women liked it too. Since she'd never talked to any of them, she couldn't form an opinion. She could only hope she was guessing right. Blue Belle was experienced, but she'd always been like a fussy aunt with Mary Rose and never discussed her professional business with her.

She sat down at her dressing table, picked up her brush, and spent a long while mindlessly working on her hair, for she hoped the ordinary chore could calm her down.

She finally decided she had procrastinated long enough. She put her brush down, tightened the belt on her robe, and went downstairs.

She was trembling from head to toes by the time she reached his doorstep. She didn't know how long she stood there with her hand poised to turn the knob, but it had to have been at least five minutes before she could gather enough courage to go inside.

Harrison had left out a considerable number of details when he'd described to her how she'd looked and felt when he imagined she was in his bed. She had at least a hundred questions she wanted to ask, but she finally settled on just one he would have to answer before she let him touch her.

She took a deep breath, straightened her shoulders, and opened the door.

When she made up her mind to do something, she did it with a vengeance The door slammed against the inside wall, then bounced back and almost knocked her over. She shoved it out of her way again, though not quite as forcefully.

Twelve minutes. It had taken her exactly twelve minutes to decide whether or not to open his door. Harrison felt like laughing, but he didn't even crack a smile, because showing any amusement now would probably send her running back to the house. The love of his life looked ready to bolt. He'd heard her outside on his doorstep, muttering every now and then, and quickly realized she still hadn't quite finished working the matter through.

He hadn't gotten out of bed to go and get her. He wanted her to make the decision on her own. He had checked his pocket watch, noted the time, and then happened to glance at it again a second or two before she tried to rip the door off its hinges.

As soon as he saw what she was wearing, he knew her brothers hadn't told her about her father yet. If they had, she still would have come to him, but she would have kept her day clothes on. She would demand he answer her questions. She would look hurt, angry, and confused by his complicity. For a while, she was going to believe he'd deceived and betrayed her, and, honest to God, there wasn't a thing he could do about the hurt she would have to endure. He had tremendous faith in her, however, and he knew she would eventually understand. It was his duty to protect her, and, whether she liked it or not, when she arrived in England, she was going to need him. He fully understood what was going to happen to her, for he knew the Elliott family well. With the best intentions, they would try to tear her identity away from her and make her into one of their own. Harrison couldn't let that happen. He wanted Mary Rose to know in every way possible that he loved who she was, not what she was supposed to be.

And that was exactly why he had made his commitment to her now.

Mary Rose's heart was pounding frantically, her knees were shaking, and she was desperately trying to remember how to breathe.

Staring at Harrison didn't calm her down. He was sitting up in his bed, with his back propped against the bedpost and his long legs stretched out on top of the covers.

He wasn't dressed for sleep. He was barechested and barefoot, but he still had his pants on, though only partially. The pants weren't buttoned up. The dark, curly hair covering his chest narrowed down into the opening. The sight of him caused her heartbeat to quicken. She suddenly realized where she was looking and immediately turned her gaze away from his groin.

She noticed the open book in his hands when

he closed it. Her eyes widened in reaction. He'd been reading while he waited for her to come to him. Honest to heaven, she didn't know how she felt about that. While she'd been pacing back and forth in her bedroom, agonizing and fretting and quaking with fear, he'd been calmly reading.

Once she got over her astonishment, she thought she just might hit him.

Harrison hadn't moved from the bed. He'd seen the fear in her eyes when she'd walked inside and knew he was going to have to find a way to soothe her before he touched her.

He had meant what he'd said when he told her he wouldn't force her. If she suddenly changed her mind and went back to the house, he wouldn't stop her. It would kill him to watch her walk away from him, but he would willingly die before he interfered with her choice.

He realized he was only being noble now because, in his heart, he already knew she was going to stay. It had taken courage for her to come to him. He hadn't expected less from her.

"You were reading."

Her statement of fact sounded like an accusation. He didn't remark on it. He nodded and continued to stare at her, waiting for her to let him know she was ready to be held. The fear, he noticed, was disappearing. She appeared to be disgruntled now.

He couldn't imagine why. "Do you want to close the door?"

"No."

She didn't shout the denial, and there wasn't a trace of panic in her voice. Harrison put the book down on the table, swung his legs over the side of the bed, and started to stand up. He assumed she wanted him to close the door for her.

She stopped him with a silent command by putting her hand out to indicate she wanted him to stay right where he was.

"I have a question to ask you before you move. Why aren't you wearing your nightclothes? That wasn't the question," she hastily added.

God help her, she sounded like a twit. She forced a shrug. "I was just curious about your attire."

"I don't wear anything when I sleep."

Her knees felt weak again. She couldn't stop herself from picturing him naked. "You probably shouldn't have mentioned . . . that."

"You're going to find out soon enough. Are you going to stay with me tonight?"

She couldn't believe how reasonable and calm he sounded. "I haven't made up my mind yet." She managed to give the lie without smiling.

She had made her decision in her bedroom, but she wasn't quite ready to let him know.

She was being stubborn and didn't care, for she was still reacting to the fact that he'd been enjoying a book while she'd been dancing through the fires of purgatory.

How each one of them had spent the evening summed up all the wonderful differences between them. She had agonized. He had read.

"You're the most determined and methodical man I've ever met, and pretty much everything else I thought I would detest in a mate. I wanted a sweet, vulnerable man because I believed he would always need me. How in heaven's name did I end up with you?"

The wonder in her voice made him smile. "Because I need you, more than all those other men. You need me too, Mary Rose. It would be nice to hear you admit it."

"Yes, I do need you. I don't like arrogant men though, and I especially dislike being ordered about. I'd keep that in mind if I were you."

"Sweetheart, how long is it going to take you to make up your mind? I have to touch you."

The urgency in his voice soothed her. She watched him stand up, then promptly made him stop again.

"Stay where you are, Harrison. I still have my question to ask you. If I don't like the answer, I'm leaving."

The sparkle in her eyes told him he didn't have to worry. "It's getting damned cold in here. What do you want to ask me?"

She took a step toward him, letting the anticipation grow inside her. She was shivering now with her need to kiss him.

Oh, how she loved him. He looked like a rake to her, with his lock of hair drooped down over his forehead and his devilish smile. He was strong and commanding, arrogant and proud, solid and reliable, and she would spend the rest of her life adoring him.

She couldn't wait another minute to hold him. "When you were telling me what you were thinking and you described me in your bed . . . and we were making love?"

"Yes?"

"Was I smiling?"

He was laughing when he pulled her into his arms and hugged her. His chin dropped down to rest on top of her head, and he assured her in a tender, loving voice that in all of his erotic fantasies and dreams about her, she had been very happy, extremely happy as a matter of fact, satisfied, content, humbled, appreciative and grateful, and completely overwhelmed by his magnificence and, now that he had time to think about it, really amazing sexual prowess.

"You couldn't find enough ways to thank me," he ended.

She leaned away from him and looked up into his eyes. "I *thanked* you for making love to me?"

"It was my dream, sweetheart, not yours."

She tucked her head back under his chin, wrapped her arms around his waist, splaying her hands wide against his warm back. "Heaven help me, you're even arrogant when you dream. What am I going to do with you?"

Several suggestions came to mind, but Harrison decided now wasn't the time to share them with her. All of his ideas involved her mouth, her tongue, and her hands.

"Your hands feel like ice," he said instead.

"You left the door open. It's freezing in here. You should probably close it."

Harrison reached behind her, shoved the door closed, and pulled her arms away from him. He took hold of her hand and led her over to the side of his bed.

They stood facing each other about a foot apart and stared into each other's eyes for a long, breathless moment, letting their anticipation and their need grow between them.

She looked like an angel in the soft lamplight, with her hair spilling down her shoulders and her pale, delicate robe swaying about her feet.

The longer he stared into her blue eyes, the more convinced he became that she was indeed the most perfect of creatures.

She moved before he did. She lowered her gaze to his chin and slowly untied the knot in the belt of her robe, and then removed her wrap. Her hands were trembling quite noticeably by the time she finished the task.

She handed the garment to him. He didn't take his gaze away from her when he tossed the robe behind him.

He stopped her from unbuttoning her nightgown. "Let me," he whispered in a voice deep with arousal.

Her hands dropped down to her sides. He felt her shiver when his fingers slipped under the thin fabric along the neckline of her cotton gown and he brushed against her silky skin.

He acted as though he had all the time in the world to undress her so that she wouldn't feel at all rushed, and he had to exert a great deal of self-discipline. He wanted to pull the garment off, but he wasn't about to give in to his impatience. He wanted this night to be as perfect for her as possible.

He slowly worked his way down to her waist, deliberately pausing to caress her skin around each opening, and when he had all the buttons undone, he reached up and spread the gown wide.

The sight of her perfection took his breath away. She was so very beautiful. Her skin was smooth and creamy, her breasts were full, her nipples rosy, and her soft, womanly curves were exquisitely proportioned.

His hands shook with his need to take her into his arms, to feel her pressed up against him, but he resisted the demand for yet another minute and slowly pushed the gown down lower, until the fabric rested on the gentle flair of her hips. The palms of his hands rested against the sides of her narrow waist, and he ever so slowly caressed his way down her thighs. The feel of her skin, so cool and smooth and flawless, made him shudder with desire.

The gown pooled on the floor around her feet. He took a step back and gazed at her.

"You're even more beautiful than I could ever have imagined."

Her embarrassment vanished with his fervently given praise. The look of pleasure in his eyes made her forget all about being shy. He thought she was beautiful, and his love for her made her believe she was.

She couldn't stand still any longer. She stepped out of her slippers and then reached out to him. "Do you want me to undress you?"

"Not yet," he answered. "I want this to last. If I take my pants off now, I'll go too fast. I don't want that to happen. It has to be perfect for you."

"Is going fast wrong?"

He shook his head. "Nothing we do together will ever be wrong."

He didn't give her time to think about what he'd just said to her, but pulled her into his arms and held her close. Her hands rested against his chest, her fingers surrounded by his crisp hair. It tickled her fingers, and she knew that if she moved her arms, her breasts would feel the same sensation.

She moved before he could make her. He buried his face in the crook of her neck, inhaled her scent, and let the pleasure of feeling her soft breasts against him consume him.

Her gasp of pleasure told him she was feeling the same way.

"I knew it would be this good."

She thought it felt better than good, but she couldn't seem to find the right words to describe all the feelings rushing through her now. She noticed his breathing had become ragged and only then realized hers was every bit as uneven. Each time she rubbed against him, the feelings intensified, until every nerve in her body was tingling with heat. It felt wonderful.

He placed wet kisses along the side of her neck, teased her earlobe with his mouth and his tongue, all the while whispering hot promises about all the things he wanted to do to her.

His words were as arousing to her as his touch. She wanted to touch him everywhere. She stroked his chest, his shoulders, and his neck, loving the play of his muscles under her fingertips, and kept moving restlessly against him, trying to get closer to his incredible heat.

The uninhibited way she responded to him intoxicated him. Everything about her aroused the fever of passion inside him. He loved the feel of her hair slipping through his fingers, like threads of silk, and the little erotic sounds she made in the back of her throat when he touched her a certain way and she couldn't contain her pleasure, and, oh, how he loved having her body rubbing against him.

He held her with one arm around her waist and leaned down to kiss her. His mouth was ravenous now, for the pressure building inside him was making him wild with his need to please her. His tongue moved inside, then withdrew, only to thrust back inside again and again in the erotic mating ritual. He stroked her neck and trailed his fingers down between her breasts, and finally, when she was certain she would die if he continued his sweet torment, he cupped one breast in his hand and began to tease her even more. His thumb lightly brushed across her nipple. She instinctively arched up against him to let him know how much she liked the thrilling sensation, and when he repeated the caress, she squeezed her eyes shut and let out a moan of pleasure.

"You're driving me out of my mind," she whispered against his ear.

"There's more," he promised.

She didn't believe she had the stamina to feel more. The pressure building inside her was becoming more intense, like liquid heat it slowly spread through her middle.

His mouth slanted over hers just as his hand moved down between her thighs, and he began to make love to her with his fingers. His tongue moved inside her mouth to imitate the mock love play.

She thought she would die from the raw ecstasy his touch evoked. Her hips began to move against his hand, until the feeling became too intense for her to bear. She tried to move his hand away from her then.

Harrison was shaking with his need. The damp heat surrounding his fingers took the last of his control away. He kissed her again, a long, hot, wet kiss, and when he finally pulled back, he realized her hand was wrapped around his wrist and she was trying to get him to move away from the heat he most wanted to possess.

He lifted her into his arms, pulled the covers back, and placed her on the bed. And then he took his pants off. He was desperately trying to pretend he hadn't run out of endurance. He was overwhelmed by his need to thrust inside her and let her tight walls surround him, squeeze him, love him, but he knew he was going to have to gain her cooperation first. She was beginning to have second thoughts now. He knew what had caused the change in her. He also knew exactly what she was thinking.

The love of his life was staring at his erection.

"It's going to be all right," he promised, his voice harsh with passion. "We were made to fit each other, baby."

She shook her head and started to get up. Her breathing was choppy with her passion, but her fear was making her panic.

He didn't give her any more time to feed her

fear. He trapped her in bed by stretching out beside her and anchoring her down with his thigh. He took hold of her hands, forced them around his neck so that she would stop trying to get him to move away from her and then leaned down to kiss her.

He had to chase after her mouth. She turned her head away from him into the pillow, but his soothing words of love finally calmed her enough to look at him again.

Her eyes were still hazy with passion, and he knew it wouldn't take him long to rekindle the fire inside her.

"Will you trust me, love? Let me kiss you once more. If you still want to stop, I promise we will."

He didn't add the fact that he wasn't going to stop until he was fully imbedded inside her, unless she started to struggle against him. God help him, he would stop then, even if it killed him, and he found himself praying he wouldn't have to.

She had to think about his offer before she finally agreed. If he hadn't been in such pain, he would have thought the disgruntled expressions humorous. He was throbbing with his need now, however, and all he could think about was sinking deep inside her.

"One kiss," she whispered.

"One kiss," he promised again.

"You're going to like this, sweetheart. Honest to God you are."

She didn't look like she believed him. He wasn't at all deterred by her attitude. "Open your mouth for me, baby," he whispered in a growl just a second before he took absolute possession. She tightened her hold around his neck and pulled him closer to her, and when she began to kiss him back with just as much passion, he knew she was forgetting all about being afraid.

He wooed her for long minutes with his mouth and his hands, until she was once again moving against him restlessly, and he could feel the tension growing inside her.

His hand moved down between her thighs to help her get ready for him. He shuddered with a surge of pleasure when he felt the wetness there on his fingertips. He caressed her silky folds, then slowly pressed up inside. He knew exactly where to touch her to get her to come apart in his arms.

She couldn't fight the splendor he forced on her. She began to writhe against him, but still he continued with the sweet torment. Her nails scored his shoulders and she whimpered low in her throat.

He couldn't wait any longer. He kept his mouth firmly on top of hers while he nudged her legs apart and moved between her thighs. He lifted her hips and slowly moved inside her. He stopped when he felt the thin layer of her resistance, closed his eyes in blissful surrender, and then thrust deep.

He felt as though he'd just died and gone to heaven.

She felt as though he'd just torn her apart. Searing pain shot through her. She cried out against the invasion and tried to get away from him. He wouldn't budge. He deliberately kept her pinned down with his weight.

"Try not to move, sweetheart. Just hold on to me until the pain leaves. Soon, baby, soon. It's going to feel better. I love you, Mary Rose. Oh, God, baby, don't cry."

He sounded devastated because he'd hurt her, and that realization actually helped to ease her pain. It wasn't completely unbearable now, but she still didn't much like the dull throbbing sensation.

Passion warred with her discomfort. She couldn't seem to make sense out of anything right now. Was she actually supposed to like this?

He didn't understand the torment she was going through. He was desperately trying to give her time to accept him, but his own consuming need to move inside her was becoming unbearable. Holding back was agonizing. He could feel her tight walls surrounding him, squeezing him. It was the most excruciatingly wonderful feeling, and God help him, if he didn't move soon, it would be too late. He would pour his seed into her with a primitive shout of surrender.

He rebelled against the glorious self-gratification. She was going to experience the same fulfillment, no matter how long it took.

His brow was covered with a sheen of perspiration, his jaw was clenched tight, and his heart was slamming inside his chest. He buried his face in her neck and began to nibble on her earlobe.

"Is it starting to feel better, sweetheart?"

She could hear the worry in his voice. She instinctively wanted to comfort him, to tell him he hadn't killed her, that it would be all right.

"I'm feeling fine now," she whispered in a voice that mocked the lie she gave.

To show him she meant what she said, she put her arms around him again and began to stroke his back. He shuddered against her and let out a low groan. And so she caressed him again. She could feel the tension in him and knew it was taking a tremendous amount of self-control for him to stay still inside her. The consideration he was showing her made her pain and discomfort insignificant.

"I don't want to disappoint you."

He braced his weight on his arms and lifted up to look at her. "You could never disappoint me. I love you, sweetheart."

She was overwhelmed by the tenderness. "It's much better now. I can endure it. You don't have to wait any longer."

He surprised her with his smile. "Endure?" he asked. "We'll see about that, love."

She pulled him down to kiss her, and when he lifted his head again, he was damned thankful to see the passion was back in her gaze.

He knew that very little time had actually passed since he'd planted himself deep inside her, but the raging demand in his body made him feel as if it had been an eternity.

The intensity in his expression aroused the passion simmering inside her.

"Tell me what to do. I want to please you."

"You do please me. Bring your legs up real slow, baby, so I can . . ." His groan made speech impossible for him. The pleasure he'd received when she began to move made his control snap.

She'd expected pain, but when she drew her legs up, she felt an altogether different sensation.

The intensity of the feeling made her want more. She moved again, felt another burst of pleasure, and tightened her arms around him. It really did feel better.

"It feels good, doesn't it? And this time, tell me the truth."

He sounded as though he were in agony. "Yes," she whispered. "I still don't feel like thanking you though."

God, how he loved her.

He told her to wrap her legs around him, then shifted his position and sank deeper inside.

Neither one of them could speak again. He pulled back, then surged deep once again. He wanted to take it slow and easy, to drive her completely out of her mind with pleasure, but she was so incredibly tight and hot, and it felt so damned good to be inside her, his need to quicken the pace took control of his actions now, and it was impossible for him to think about going slow or trying to be gentle. Hell, he couldn't think at all. He could only feel.

Her whispered pleas and moans urged him on. Each time he partially withdrew from her, she lifted her hips to bring him back. Her nails scored his back as her own control vanished. She became more demanding with her caresses, her cries. The pressure inside her built until she thought she would die from the sweet agony. She didn't know what she wanted. She only knew she wanted it now.

Passion raged between them, and it wasn't long before she couldn't bear the intensity of the mating another second. She found release then, surrendered to the bliss, and cried out his name as wave after wave of splendor washed over her. She squeezed him tight inside, and when he felt the tremors of her climax, he allowed his own surrender. He poured his seed into her with a low growl of raw satisfaction.

It was the most incredible release he had ever experienced.

And all because he loved her.

He collapsed on top of her. She had taken all of his strength, and it was going to be a while before he recovered. He wanted to sleep with her in his arms, and when he awakened, he wanted to lose himself in her love once again.

It took her long minutes to recover. She was overwhelmed by what had just happened to her. She felt as though her heart, her mind, and her very soul had all merged with his in that blissful moment of surrender and she was being surrounded by the warmth of his love. Mating with Harrison had been the most wonderful and glorious experience in her life.

He made everything wonderful. From the minute she had given her heart to him, her entire world had changed. Ordinary days were magical because she shared them with him. She couldn't imagine life without him. He was loving and gentle and kind and compassionate. He was erotic and sensual and bold and arrogant.

He was just about perfect. And all because she loved him.

"Are you all right, Mary Rose?"

He lifted himself above her so he could see for himself and looked into her eyes. They were still misty from the passion she'd experienced. Her mouth was swollen. There were a couple of his whisker burns on her face as well. Seeing his marks on her gave him a great deal of satisfaction. She belonged to him, and damn but he liked seeing her like this.

"I hurt you, didn't I?"

The question sounded sincere, but the slow smile that came over his expression confused her.

"Yes, you did hurt me, but the pain didn't last long. I only cried for a second."

"The first time," he agreed.

"Why are you smiling? Don't you care you hurt me?"

"Of course I care. I love you, Mary Rose. I'm smiling because of the way you look."

His voice had taken on that gruff, sensual edge she liked so much,

"How do I look?" She sounded breathless.

"Like I've just been inside you and loved you and satisfied you. I'm feeling real possessive right now."

She was feeling incredibly warm and safe and loved.

"You've always been possessive."

"It's different now, sweetheart. I've wanted you in my bed a long time."

She reached up and stroked the side of his face. "And now that I'm here?"

The smile faded from his face. "You're mine."

She wasn't going to dispute the truth. "Yes, I'm yours."

He nodded with satisfaction. Then he leaned down and kissed her.

She rubbed her toes against his legs and sighed into his mouth when his tongue began to tease hers.

He felt the stirrings of arousal and knew he needed to stop before passion made him forget her tender condition. She needed time to recover before he took her again.

He pulled away, rolled onto his back, and then drew her up against his side.

"We have to talk, Mary Rose."

The seriousness in his tone of voice worried her. She knew better than to try to second-guess him, but her own vulnerability made her think he was about to say something she didn't want to hear. She even believed she knew exactly what it was.

Several minutes passed in silence. He stared at the ceiling while he considered various ways to discuss their future.

She spent the time fretting.

She couldn't stand the silence any longer. "I'll make it easy for you, Harrison. I'll say it for you. You're . . ."

He didn't let her finish.

He tightened his hold around her waist and said, "You can't possibly know what I'm going to say. You aren't a mind reader, sweetheart."

"No, I can't read your mind," she agreed. "I can draw certain conclusions though. From the seriousness in your tone of voice, I concluded the importance of what you want to say. Your hesitancy told me you were having trouble finding the right words. Am I right so far?"

"Yes," he answered. "What I have to say to you is serious, and yes, I want to find just the right words."

"Because you're an attorney."

"No, because I want to make certain you understand. I want to prepare you."

"Harrison, I could save you a lot of time."

She began to caress his chest with her fingers, barely aware she was distracting the hell out of him. He suddenly wanted to make love to her again.

He was going to talk to her first, however. He grabbed hold of her hand and held tight.

She promptly leaned up and kissed the base of his neck.

"Quit tempting me." The command was given in a rough, no-nonsense tone of voice.

She ignored it and deliberately kissed him again.

"I'm not tempting you. I'm consoling you. There's a difference."

"You're naked in my arms, Mary Rose. Therefore . . ."

"I'm tempting you."

"Yes."

She let out a sigh and rested the side of her face against his warm skin.

"I understand what's happening to you. You're having regrets now. I understand, Harrison, and that is why I was trying to console you. You don't have to feel guilty any longer."

He went completely still. "Exactly what am I

supposed to be regretting?"

"Our . . . indiscretion."

"Our what?"

The calmness in his voice masked his anger. He refused to believe what he had just heard. She was going to have to say it again, just to convince him.

"Our indiscretion."

She felt his long, indrawn breath. The reaction should have been a warning of the fury coming. He also tightened his arm around her waist.

She still wasn't prepared.

"How in God's name does that mind of yours work? I know you're as intelligent as everyone else. Hell, you're smarter than everyone else. Does everything shut down inside your head? How could you possibly believe tonight was an indiscretion? Answer me."

He didn't give her time to say a word, however. "We made a commitment to each other. Got that?"

Mary Rose was astonished by his anger. She wasn't at all frightened by it though. The realization made her smile. Harrison was roaring like a wounded bear, and she was feeling just as safe as always.

She didn't understand his reaction, however. He acted as though she had just grossly insulted him. And his mother. And even his dog, if he happened to have one.

She tried to keep the smile out of her voice when he finally let her speak.

"I didn't say I believed we had been indiscreet. I thought you . . ."

He interrupted her again. "Listen to me. I really don't think you quite get it yet."

"Get it? What does that mean?"

"It means you obviously didn't understand me when I said you were mine now. I didn't imply you were mine for the night. I meant forever."

"I wish you'd be logical about this. If . . ."

"You want *me* to be logical?"

She thought that perhaps it hadn't been the right thing to say to him. She was thankful she couldn't see his face now, because she knew the muscle in the side of his cheek was probably going crazy. It flexed whenever he clenched his jaw, and he always did that when he was angry. It was a dead giveaway that a storm was coming.

"It appears I can't say the right thing to appease you."

He started to tell her what he thought about her remark, then decided against it. He knew if he continued on, he would become furious all over again. Indiscretion? He still couldn't believe she'd used that word to describe what had happened tonight. It was going to take him a good week to get over it.

His silence indicated to her that he was ready to listen to reason "I'm new at this. You could be a little more patient with me. It wouldn't kill you, so quit breathing like that. I've never been intimate before. I can't help but feel vulnerable."

She was certain her explanation would gain his sympathy and his understanding. She was wrong with both expectations.

"It's ridiculous for you to feel the least bit vulnerable. It's also damned insulting to me, woman."

She was beginning to lose her patience. He was taking exception to every word she said. He really was as temperamental as his horse. She considered telling him so, then changed her mind. The comparison would probably set his temper off again.

"You didn't use to be this moody."

"I didn't used to be in love with you."

She drummed her fingers against his chest. "Cole always becomes moody when he feels guilty about something."

"I don't feel guilty about a damned thing. Do you feel guilty?"

He grabbed hold of her hand and started squeezing. He was telling her without words her answer better be the one he wanted to hear.

"No, I don't feel guilty. Happy now?"

He didn't answer her. He relaxed his hold on her hand, though, and so she assumed she'd given him the right response.

"I believe we should end this discussion. If we continue, we'll get into a full-blown argument. Then you'll have to apologize to me. Do you really want to waste all that time begging my forgiveness when we could be doing much more enjoyable things?"

He smiled in spite of his irritation. "What makes you think I'll apologize?"

"Because I can wait longer than you can. You'll give in before I will."

"In other words, you hold a grudge. Your brothers mentioned that flaw to me."

"Sometimes I do."

He started to laugh. "Mary Rose, you make me want to shake you and kiss you at the same time. Honest to God, you're going to drive me out of my mind one of these days."

She started stroking his chest again. She loved the feel of his hair curling around her fingers. She wished he'd kiss her again. Just thinking about it made her restless. She let out a little sigh and draped her thigh across him.

He let out a grunt. She realized where her thigh was then, but the heat radiating from his groin felt too good against her skin for her to move away.

If he hadn't liked it, he would have pushed her away. He didn't though. He put his hand on her knee and began to caress her.

"Harrison?"

"Yes?"

"Was tonight as nice as your dream was?"

"It was much, much better. My dreams weren't ever nice. They made me hot. Tonight, you made me burn. Understand?"

"You were satisfied?"

He could hear the amusement in her voice and knew she was up to something. He smiled in anticipation. God only knew what she was going to say.

"Yes, I was satisfied."

"Now you sound appreciative, grateful. Are you?"

Her fingertips were making circles around his nipple. It was driving him to distraction.

"Yes," he answered gruffly.

"I guess I made you happy."

"Yes. You made me very happy."

She smiled against his chest. He was mildly surprised she needed this much assurance. The way he had responded to her while they were making love should have told her how good she'd been. Maybe she really was feeling vulnerable because it had been a new experience for her.

Lord, was she beginning to make sense?

"And you can't thank me enough."

Her whispered words finally registered in his mind. She was tossing his words back at him. Harrison laughed again. "I guess you didn't much like hearing that part of my dream, did you, sweetheart?"

She was too content to answer him. A sudden thought turned her attention. "What did you mean when you said I only cried for a second the first time? Did I cry again?"

"Yes. It lasted longer."

"When?"

"When you came apart."

The memory made her blush. She really had come apart during her climax. She didn't remember crying though. Finding fulfillment had required her full attention.

"Now will you listen to what I have to say?"

"If you're going to tell me I'll hate you, then no, I won't listen."

"I want to talk about our future."

"All right."

"The next six months are going to be difficult for you."

"Do you plan to be difficult?"

"No, that isn't what I meant."

"I love you, Harrison."

"I love you too. I have to go back to England, sweetheart. I want you to join me there."

"You do?"

"Yes."

"Why do you have to go back?"

"I have to finish something I started."

"Will you want to stay there for a long time?"

"That depends on you."

She didn't understand. "Do you still long for the Highlands?"

"I long to be with you. Where I live isn't important."

"It used to be important."

He smiled. She was right about that. Returning to the Highlands had been an obsession. His plans had all changed, of course, because of Mary Rose. He could be happy anywhere in the world as long as he had her by his side.

"When do you want to leave?"

"I had thought to leave the day after tomorrow. I want you to come to me as soon as possible."

He had just overwhelmed her with all the changes he wanted to make. How could she possibly leave her brothers? England was an ocean away. Oh, God, why did it have to be so far?

Would they live in the city? How could she live like that? She wouldn't be able to breathe. The crowds would drive her wild. Would she look out her window and see pavement and buildings? How could she leave her paradise?

And how could she ever let Harrison leave her

behind? Life without him would be unbearable.

Her mind reeled with questions.

"I know you need time to think about it, sweetheart."

"Yes," she answered. "I wish . . . Harrison, would you ever consider living here?"

"If it were possible."

"Is it?"

"I don't know yet," he replied.

"What if I couldn't join you?"

"I would come back to get you."

"I don't want to think about the future now. Tomorrow we'll worry about plans and decisions. Please kiss me again. I want you to make love to me now."

She lifted up on her elbows and stared down into his eyes.

"I want to feel you inside me again," she whispered.

"We can't," he whispered. "It's too soon, sweetheart. It would hurt."

She leaned down and kissed him. She didn't care if it hurt or not. She needed him.

"Please," she whispered. Her lips brushed over his again. "One kiss, my love. Let me kiss you once and if you want me to stop then, I promise you I will."

"I love the way you throw my words back at me," he said. He wrapped his arms around her and lifted her up until she was stretched out on top of him.

"Are you planning to keep on kissing me until you've got me inside you?"

"Oh, yes."

They were the last coherent words either one of them could speak for a long, long time.

They fell asleep wrapped in a tangle of arms and legs. And love.

April 5, 1868

Dear Mama Rose,

Adam got in a fight yesterday. It was all my fault, because the Indians like my pretty hair. I am putting some of it in the envelope so you can see how pretty it is. But it's yellow, Mama, and the Indians liked it so much they tried to take it all off my head. Then one of them says to take me with my hair and that's when Adam got mad. Cole and Douglas were gone, and by the time Travis came out of the barn, Adam had punched them good and hard. Your son got a bloody nose, but the Indians he got mad at were all sleeping in our garden by the time he got done with them.

Fighting isn't good, Mama. Even Adam said so, but now he thinks the Indians will leave my hair alone.

I sure hope so.

Your daughter Mary Rose

15

Mary Rose returned to her bedroom a little before dawn. She was somewhat surprised Harrison slept through her departure. He was usually a light sleeper, but he barely moved at all when she got out of his bed, dressed, and left the bunkhouse. She guessed she must have worn him out. The possibility gave her an inordinate amount of pleasure.

She wasn't quite ready to greet the day, however. She fell asleep as soon as her head touched the pillow, and she didn't wake up again until almost ten o'clock.

She didn't see Harrison again until supper. Travis told her that Dooley had ridden out early to deliver a telegram.

Her brother was headed out the back door when he mentioned the wire. Mary Rose went chasing after him to get the particulars.

"Who was the telegram for?"

"Harrison, of course. If it had been for one of us, you would have seen it on the kitchen table."

"Who sent it?"

"I don't know."

"Travis, please slow down. Did Harrison tell you about it? Did he read it to you?"

Her brother turned around.

"No, he didn't tell me, and I didn't ask. He

didn't look very happy about the news he received though. Fact is, he looked kind of grim."

"Oh, Lord, I pray no one died."

"Now, why would you think someone died?"

"Telegrams are always for bad news, Travis. Everyone knows that. What did Harrison do after he read the message?"

Travis let out a sigh. "He put the paper in his pocket and went to the bunkhouse to pack his things. He was going to go into town to buy a trunk to ship his things back to England, but Adam gave him one of his old ones to use. I promised I'd ship it off for him."

"Harrison's leaving. I knew he was leaving," she said. "He told me."

"Don't get upset until you've talked to him."

"I'm not upset."

"Then let go of my arm. You're pinching me."

She hadn't realized she'd grabbed hold of her brother's arm. She immediately pulled her hand away. "I don't want him to leave."

Travis's expression softened. "I know you don't. Loving someone isn't pleasant all the time, is it? It's made you vulnerable."

She couldn't disagree with his assessment. She was miserable right this minute.

"No, it isn't always pleasant. When is Harrison leaving?"

"He didn't say."

"Where is he now?"

"He left with Adam an hour ago. They didn't tell me where they were going. I do know Adam wanted to have a private conversation with him though. They might have gone fishing up by

Cowan's place. The trout are thick as fleas near the bend. Don't waste your day worrying, Mary Rose. I'm sure Harrison will explain his plans tonight."

She went back to the house. She was going to have to find a way to get through the rest of the day, and, Lord, how she wished she were the patient sort. She hated waiting for anything, even bad news.

Eleanor wasn't very good company today. She dragged around the house and didn't want to do much of anything. Mary Rose decided to give the parlor a good cleaning. Keeping busy would make her day go faster, or so she believed.

She didn't stop with the parlor. She scrubbed floors, changed the sheets on all the beds, washed windows, and then went outside to work in her garden. By late afternoon, she'd worn herself out. She went into the kitchen to start supper, but the cook waved his butcher knife in front of her face and told her to get the hell out of his way. Samuel, or Pucker Face, as he was called by Douglas and Cole, was part Crow Indian and part Irish. It made an interesting combination as far as his temperament was concerned, or so Adam believed. Samuel had the expected Irish temper, but with a dignified edge to it.

Mary Rose thought he was downright adorable. She didn't dare share her opinion with Samuel though, because he didn't much care for compliments of any kind.

"Samuel, you're just as grumpy as the day you arrived," she announced.

The look in his dark brown eyes told her he

527

appreciated hearing her opinion. He waved his knife in front of her face again, added the threat that he would poison her supper, and then told her once again to skedaddle.

She burst into laughter. Samuel turned away, but not before she spotted his smile.

Since Adam hadn't written the word for the day on the chalk-board, she picked up the chalk and wrote one for him. In big bold letters she printed *blarney*.

"Look, Samuel, I've printed your name," she teased.

She continued to torment the cook for several more minutes by simply talking to him, then she set the table for supper. When the mindless task was finished, she went upstairs to get clean clothes and her soap and towels. She dragged Eleanor to the bend in the river to bathe.

She couldn't wait to see Harrison again, yet deliberately avoided looking directly at him while the were seated at the table together. She was afraid she'd start blushing over the memory of what they had done together the night before. Every time she thought about their lovemaking, she became flushed and breathless.

Her brothers would notice, and for that reason, she kept her gaze firmly on her plate. She certainly wasn't ashamed of what she had done, but she wasn't ready to discuss her affairs with her brothers.

They didn't seem to be in any particular hurry to talk about it either, and she knew that at least two of them had heard her leave the house during the night. Adam would have heard her going down the stairs, and Cole would have awakened the second she opened her bedroom door. Neither one of them had said a word to her about her behavior, however, and perhaps that was why she couldn't quite bring herself to look at either one of them during supper.

She knew they knew, and heavens, why did she feel the least bit guilty? She decided she was going to need time to figure it all out.

She didn't think Harrison was having any difficulty adjusting to their new arrangement. She knew full well he didn't believe they'd done anything to regret. In his mind, he'd made his commitment to her, and she to him, and now he was probably thinking they should start behaving like an old married couple.

They weren't married though, at least not legally, and until the union was blessed by a preacher, she was going to worry about protecting her brothers' feelings.

There wasn't much conversation going on around her. Everyone seemed preoccupied tonight, and the subdued atmosphere made Mary Rose all the more nervous.

Even Eleanor was acting peculiar. She sipped water from her glass but didn't touch her food. She didn't even move it around on her plate the way Mary Rose did to fool her brothers into thinking she was actually eating.

Douglas was the first to notice Eleanor was sick. "You aren't feeling well, are you, Eleanor?" he asked.

"I'm just a little tired tonight. I can't imagine why. I haven't done anything to wear myself out.

It's cold in here, isn't it?"

Douglas looked at Adam. "She's got a fever. You can see how flushed her cheeks are."

Mary Rose dropped her fork and turned to her friend. "You're ill?" she whispered.

Douglas got up from his chair and went around the table. He put the back of his hand against her forehead to feel for himself.

"Yes, she's got fever all right. It's high too. Come along with me, Eleanor. I'm putting you to bed." As he helped Eleanor stand up, she sagged against his side.

Mary Rose was horrified by her friend's pitiful condition and her own selfish behavior. She should have realized Eleanor was ill, and if she hadn't been so busy thinking about herself, she surely would have.

She had been completely thoughtless. "Oh, Eleanor, I'm so sorry you aren't feeling well. Why didn't you say something to me sooner?"

"I didn't want to complain."

Cole shook his head. "You don't have to sound like a martyr, Ellie. How long have you been feeling sick?"

"Since this morning," she answered. "Mary Rose made me go to the river to bathe this afternoon. The water was terribly cold, but I didn't complain then either. Adam? It was nice of me to suffer in silence, wasn't it?"

Adam saw the tears in her eyes and was immediately filled with guilt. The poor woman was obviously still concerned about being thrown out.

He reached over and patted her hand. "You should have complained," he told her. "You're part of our family now, Eleanor. We all want to know when you're ill, so we can take care of you."

"You do?" She seemed thrilled by his announcement.

Adam smiled. "Yes, we do," he insisted. "Douglas will fix you up in no time at all. Go on upstairs with him. I'll be up with some tea for you in a little while. Mary Rose, why don't you help her get settled in her bed?"

Cole waited until Douglas and Mary Rose had taken Eleanor out of the dining room before he spoke again.

"We're in for it now."

"What do you mean?" Adam asked.

"Didn't you see the look in her eyes when you told her it was all right to complain? I got the feeling she liked hearing that a little too much."

"Don't be ridiculous," Adam replied. "She's sick. You can see she is."

"Forget about the complaining stuff," Travis said. "I'm mighty interested in something else I heard Adam say to Eleanor. What did you mean when you said she was part of our family now?"

Cole nodded. "Yes, Adam, what did you mean?"

"I just wanted her to feel at home. No harm in making her comfortable, is there?"

"Exactly when is she planning to leave?" Travis asked.

Adam pretended interest in extracting a bone from his trout. "Well, now, I guess that depends on her, doesn't it?"

531

Travis and Cole shared a look. Then Travis muttered, "Hell, she isn't ever leaving, is she?"

Cole scowled. "I wish to thunder you had told me before I went and kissed the woman. I never would have dallied with her if I'd known she was going to stick around. Hell," he ended in a mutter. "Now I'm going to have to have a talk with her about my intentions."

Douglas walked back into the dining room in time to overhear the last of Cole's remarks. "Don't you mean your lack of intentions?"

His brother nodded. Douglas shook his head. "You ought to be ashamed of yourself, fooling around with Eleanor. Adam, don't take any tea up to her until I go and get some of my special powder. I want to put a teaspoonful in the cup first. I really wish you hadn't told the woman it was all right to complain. She's upstairs carrying on something fierce now. Mary Rose is getting all upset too. She's blaming herself for Eleanor's fever and keeps begging her to forgive her for being selfish. Our sister has become too damned emotional lately," he added with a meaningful glare in Harrison's direction. "I think maybe she's coming down with the same ailment. She didn't eat a bite at supper, and she didn't look at Harrison once. I noticed."

"I noticed too," Cole interjected.

"Maybe we ought to put off our talk until Mary Rose is feeling better," Travis suggested.

"No." Harrison snapped out the denial in a firm voice.

Adam nodded agreement. "We put off what we dread," he told his brother. "We cannot put

532

this off. We must tell her as soon as possible. I spent the day questioning Harrison about the Elliott family. He has given me his assurance he'll look out for her. I'm not convinced she should leave with Harrison, however. It might be better to let her stay here with us a little longer, until she's had time to adjust to the notion of having a family back in England."

Harrison wanted to argue with Adam but decided to keep silent now. He excused himself from the table and went outside to sit on the porch.

Adam followed him. He sat down in the chair next to Harrison and stretched his long legs out in front of him.

"You didn't like hearing my suggestion, did you?"

"No, I didn't like hearing it," Harrison countered. "You're putting off the inevitable. She can adjust on her way to England, Adam."

"It goes against my grain to spring something on her and then rush her off. No, she needs . . . Mary Rose, how long have you been standing there?"

"Not long," she answered. She pushed the screen door open and walked outside.

"May I join you?"

"No," Adam answered. He didn't soften his refusal with a reason.

"Let her stay," Harrison suggested. "I need to talk to her."

Adam nodded. Mary Rose leaned back against the railing, folded her hands together as though in prayer, and stared at her brother.

"Will one of you please tell me what's going

on? Why are you both in bad moods?"

"We aren't in bad moods," Adam argued.

"You're frowning." She didn't think she needed to say more.

"We were discussing serious matters, Mary Rose. They don't concern you just yet."

"The hell they don't concern her. Be reasonable, Adam," Harrison demanded.

"I'll be reasonable when the time's right. I believe I'll go and fix Eleanor's tea. Don't stay outside too late, Mary Rose."

She followed her brother to the door. "What is it you have to spring on me but don't want to rush me into?"

"You were listening to us, weren't you?"

She nodded. "Will you please explain?"

"Tomorrow," Adam promised. "I'll explain everything tomorrow."

She waited until her brother had disappeared inside and then went to Harrison. She stood between his outstretched legs, her hands at her sides, and tried to look composed. She didn't want him to see her panic. She'd been desperately trying to stay calm all day long, but from the moment Travis had told her Harrison was packing his bags, she'd been filled with anxiety.

He spoke before she did. "Are you angry with me?"

She'd been staring at his chin. Her gaze flew to his eyes. "No, I'm not angry."

"You wouldn't look at me during supper or speak to me. I thought you were upset about . . ."

She wouldn't let him finish. "You're leaving

soon. Travis told me."

"Yes."

She waited for him to give her his reason for leaving so abruptly, but he didn't say another word.

He had warned her. She reminded herself of that fact once again, and it still didn't help her.

She didn't take her gaze off him. The moonlight softened his somber expression. She wanted him to take her into his arms and comfort her. She was so damned miserable now and knew it was only a matter of minutes before she began to weep, but, God, she hurt too much inside to worry about tears now.

"You did try to prepare me, didn't you? You told me you had to leave. I just hoped it wouldn't be so soon. Are you leaving now because of the telegram you received?"

He shook his head. "No, the telegram was in regard to a financial matter. Mary Rose, come closer."

He was reaching for her even as he gave the tender command. He pulled her down on his lap and wrapped his arms around her waist.

"Are you all right?" His voice was a husky whisper.

She didn't immediately answer him. How could she be all right? He was leaving, for God's sake. Didn't he realize he was taking her heart with him?

"I know I hurt you last night."

"I'm just a little tender today," she whispered back. "Are you sorry we slept together?"

The question irritated him. He nudged her chin

up and forced her to look at him.

"Sweetheart, no, I'm not at all sorry. If I could, I'd make love to you right now. God knows, I want you."

Tears brimmed in her eyes. "I want you too," she whispered. "I wish I could be more cosmopolitan about this. I'm not sorry about what happened. I just don't like feeling vulnerable, Harrison." Or feeling I'm being abandoned, she silently added.

"Why do you think you're feeling vulnerable?"

"You're leaving, damn it."

"You're coming to England, Mary Rose. It's only going to be a short separation. Weren't you listening to me last night? I'm never going to let you go. You belong to me now."

He leaned down then and claimed her mouth for a long, hot kiss. She wrapped her arms around his neck and kissed him back with all the love and desperation she felt inside her.

When at last the kiss ended, she could barely catch her breath. She tucked her head under his chin and listened to his ragged breathing.

"I love you, Harrison."

"I know you do, baby." He rubbed her back, loving the feel of her pressed against him.

"We have tonight. Make love to me again, please?"

"I'll hurt you."

Even as he gave her his reason for not touching her, he stood up, holding her in his arms, and started walking toward the bunkhouse.

She was trying to unbutton his shirt and kiss him at the same time.

By the time they reached their destination, they were both too frantic to slow down.

Her hands shook too much to get her skirt undone. Harrison took over the chore, muttering soft curses because the tiny hooks were impossible to release with his big hands.

Their clothes ended up in a pile on the floor. They fell into bed together. He tried to brace his weight with his arms when he came down on top of her, and he let out a loud groan of pleasure when he felt her warm skin against him.

The tingling ache in the pit of her belly began to spread throughout her body. She cupped the sides of his face and pulled him down for a long, wet, open-mouth kiss.

He shifted his position and began to stroke the fire inside her. His right hand moved down low on her belly. She drew in a deep breath in anticipation of the pleasure he was going to give her, but when his fingers slid into the junction of her thighs and he began to caress her there, she felt a sharp stabbing pain.

She grabbed hold of his hand and tried to make him stop.

"It hurts more than I thought it would. We should stop, Harrison. Oh, God, I don't want to stop. I . . ."

His mouth ended her protest. He held her close and ravished her with his searing kisses and his hot words of passion.

He made her restless for more in little time at all, and her worry about pain was soon forgotten.

She was shaking with her need to mate with

him when he at last ended the kiss and began to nibble on the side of her neck. His breath was hot against her ear as he whispered erotic, arousing promises of what he wanted to do to her.

And then he moved lower still and began to kiss her breasts, then her stomach, and when he moved once again, and he was kissing the very heat of her, she let out a low gasp and tried to make him stop.

He wouldn't stop, for he found the taste of her against his mouth too wonderful to pull away just yet. His tongue caressed the folds of her smooth flesh and pushed up into the warm, welcoming opening.

She clung to him and begged him with her soft moans to give her more and more and more. Her nails dug into his shoulders, and when she felt the first tremors of her own orgasm, she cried out his name and began to weep with the sheer intensity of the shattering splendor.

He felt her come apart against him and knew he couldn't wait any longer. He would go out of his mind if he didn't move inside her. He shifted positions again so that he was once again kneeling between her thighs. He lifted her up and then sank deep inside her with one hard surge.

Pain blended with fulfillment. The pressure he'd so skillfully built inside her seemed to splinter into a thousand fragments. She surrendered to the bliss, for she was safe and protected in the arms of the man she loved.

He found his fulfillment less than a minute later. He let out a shout of raw pleasure as he poured his seed into her. He'd wanted to hold back, to let her climax a second time, to come when he did, but all his grand plans were forgotten when he was inside her and her tight walls were squeezing him. She throbbed all around him and his control was lost. Each time he pulled back, she arched up against him, urging him toward fulfillment. She drew her knees up so that he could sink even deeper inside, and, God help him, he couldn't stave off his orgasm then.

He heard himself chanting he loved her, over and over and over again, and somewhere in the back of his mind he realized she was weeping. He hoped to God he wasn't hurting her, but once he'd given her his seed, he still couldn't make himself move away from her.

He stayed embedded inside her and dropped his head down in the crook of her neck.

Reality was slow to return but when it did, he was filled with concern. He'd acted like a barbarian. Had he hurt her again?

"Are you all right?" she whispered.

He tried to make sense out of her question.

"Harrison, please breathe. You're beginning to worry me."

She squirmed under him. "Dear God, have I killed you then?"

He burst into laughter. He didn't know where the energy had come from. His pleasure made him too lethargic to move, and he could still barely form a coherent thought.

"Are you all right? I was afraid I'd hurt you." Harrison said.

She shivered over the husky sound in his voice.

Heaven help her, he could be reading the newspaper out loud and she'd become aroused, she thought to herself. It was his brogue of course. It was the most sensual sound she'd ever heard.

"I'm still alive," she whispered. "Tell me you love me again."

"I love you."

"That will help . . . if and when," she whispered.

He forced himself to move. He rolled to his side and pulled her into his arms.

"If and when what, baby?"

"If I'm pregnant and when you leave."

She thought he would try to ease her worry. He didn't though. "I hope to God you are. I want at least twenty children."

"Heaven help me," she whispered.

His hand moved to her stomach. It was a possessive action and one that sent shivers down her legs.

"You'll be a very beautiful mother."

"I'll be fat."

"I like fat."

"Don't leave."

"I have to leave. You'll come to me, sweetheart. We won't be apart long."

"What if something happens and I can't join you?"

"I said before I'll come back here and get you."

"And then?"

"I'll drag you to England if I have to," he promised. "Dooley told me Judge Burns is on his way to Blue Belle. He's escorting Belle back

540

home. It seems he's smitten with her."

"Smitten?"

"Dooley's words, not mine," he explained with a yawn. "I think maybe we should make it official before I leave. Want to get married tomorrow, sweetheart?"

"I would rather wait and be married by a preacher or a priest or a rabbi. It doesn't seem very romantic to be married by a hanging judge."

"I don't want to wait."

"Are you worried I'll change my mind while you're away?"

"It's too late for you to change your mind. You made your commitment to me when you walked through the doorway last night. Why did you go back to your room after we made love?"

"Because of my brothers." She trailed her fingers down his chest. "I don't wish to do anything further to disgrace them."

"Further disgrace them?"

He hadn't meant to raise his voice, but her words so infuriated him, he couldn't control his reaction. "Is that how you feel, damn it? Do you think you disgraced yourself by sleeping with me?"

She tried to calm him. "Please understand, Harrison. I know it isn't possible to marry now, but we aren't truly married yet, and I must consider my brothers' feelings. If they'd found us in bed together, their hearts would have been broken."

He didn't understand. Before she had time to blink, he'd gotten out of bed and was reaching for his pants.

"Get dressed."

He gave the command in a hard, don't-give-me-any-argument tone of voice. She ignored it. "Come back to bed. Let me try to explain so you . . ."

"Get dressed, Mary Rose, or I swear to God I'll carry you back to the house in a blanket. Do you want your brothers to see you . . ."

He didn't have to go on. She jumped out of the bed and started to get dressed.

He was ready before she was. He helped her put on her blouse and thoughtfully handed her her skirt.

"Will you please explain why you're in such a hurry?" she asked.

She believed her question was reasonable. He acted as though she'd just shouted an insult at him, however.

"The word disgrace doesn't sit well with me," he snapped. "We're going to have a little talk with your brothers. Hurry up, damn it."

She turned to find her shoes. She noticed the sheets on his bed then and let out a loud gasp. Even from across the room she could see the splattering of blood.

Her face turned crimson in less than a heartbeat. She forgot all about finding her shoes then and ran over to strip the sheets.

He stood with his hands on his hips and a look on his face that told her he thought she'd lost her mind.

"You made me bleed."

"You were supposed to bleed."

"You don't have to sound so callous about it. What if my brothers had come in here? They

542

would have shot you before they listened to any explanation."

"They knew what my intentions were. Leave the damned sheets alone, Mary Rose. I want to talk to Adam before he goes to bed."

She wadded the sheets up into a ball and turned around to frown at Harrison.

"We are not going to talk to Adam. I'm going home alone. If you think you're going to tell my brother what we just did, you can just forget it. I will not be embarrassed or humiliated, Harrison. Do you understand me?"

She dropped the sheets on the floor, then put on her shoes. She couldn't believe the evening was ending this way. Harrison had been such a thoughtful, gentle lover. Now he was acting like an arrogant brute. She didn't know what had come over him, but she wasn't in the mood to placate him. The mere thought of letting Adam know she'd given herself to Harrison made her stomach lurch. She wouldn't allow anyone to shame her that way, not even the horrid man she loved.

She tried to walk past him. He grabbed hold of her hand and wouldn't let go. Then he dragged her after him, all the way across the yard, up the stairs, and into the house.

They passed Cole in the entryway. The brother gave Mary Rose a double glance, then said, "What the hell happened to you?"

He was staring at her hair. She used her free hand to try to calm the curls.

"Nothing happened," she called out when Harrison pulled her along.

He didn't knock on the library door. He threw

it open and gently shoved Mary Rose inside. He stood right behind her, and when she tried to back away, she found his solid frame blocking her retreat.

Adam was startled by the interruption. He closed the book he'd been reading and started to stand up.

Harrison told him to stay seated. While Adam watched, Mary Rose was prodded to the other easy chair and told to sit down.

She shook her head. "This is outrageous, Harrison," she whispered. "If you say one word, I swear I'll do something horrible."

He draped his arm around her shoulders and kept his gaze on her brother.

"Adam, Mary Rose and I need to get married as soon as possible. Judge Burns should be in Blue Belle tomorrow. I think we should all ride into town and . . ."

"I will not be married by a hanging judge. It goes against my principles," she interjected.

"Harrison, close the door," Adam suggested. "And both of you please lower your voices. What's all this talk about needing to get married?"

"Harrison's having a spell," Mary Rose announced. She folded her arms across her chest and stared over Adam's shoulder. She couldn't quite bring herself to look into his eyes. "Don't pay any attention to anything he says. He just feels bad because he has to leave."

His arm went around her shoulder again. It felt much heavier this time. She thought he was deliberately applying pressure so she'd quit talking.

She tried to ignore him. "We seem to have gotten into an argument. We should work it out together and not involve you, Adam. Do excuse us now."

It was a very proper dismissal, but it was thoroughly ruined because Harrison wouldn't let her leave.

"Adam, I thought Mary Rose understood, but now I realize she didn't. She seems to think she might have disgraced her brothers by sleeping with me. Since she feels that way, I suggest we get married with all possible haste. I'll be damned if I'll let her feel ashamed of what happened between us. I've given myself all the reasons why I should wait until after you've explained everything to her, but what I wanted to do lost out to what I did do, and hell, none of the timing matters to me now. I love her and she loves me."

Adam nodded to let Harrison know he understood, but his gaze was centered on his little sister. She certainly didn't look like a woman in love at the moment. In truth, she looked like she wanted to kill her intended groom.

"Judge Burns will be happy to perform the ceremony tomorrow."

"Adam, I don't . . ."

"Do you feel disgraced, Mary Rose?"

She closed her mouth. She knew if she answered yes she'd be married tomorrow, and if she answered no, she'd be lying to her brother.

"She told me she wished she could be as cosmopolitan as I am," Harrison remarked. "I didn't realize what she meant until a few minutes ago. Should I go and get the judge tomorrow?"

"It would be nicer to have the wedding here on the ranch, and I do believe he would agree to come out here. Be sure to include Belle. She helped us with Mary Rose during her growing up years. She'll want to see her married. I don't believe you need to mention sleeping with your bride, however. The fact that you have to leave should be enough of a reason for the hurried ceremony."

"I want her to come with me."

"That's up to her. She'll have to decide after our talk."

"I think maybe we ought to have that talk now."

Cole made the announcement from the doorway. Travis was standing right behind him.

Mary Rose wished the floor would open up and swallow her whole. If they'd heard she'd slept with Harrison, she was sure she would die of mortification.

"One problem at a time," Adam suggested. "What's done is done. Tomorrow we'll have a wedding. Are we agreed on that?"

Cole and Travis nodded. "It's easy to get divorced out here," Cole told his sister. "You can hold on to that thought during the ceremony."

Harrison wasn't amused by the brother's dark humor. "It doesn't work that way. Once married, always married. Got that, Mary Rose?"

She pushed his arm off her shoulder and turned around. "What kind of marriage proposal was that? Am I to translate 'got that' into, 'Will you marry me?' You do have a way with words, Harrison MacDonald, and if I didn't love you so

546

much, I do believe I'd shoot you. Good night."

She did get the last word. No one stopped her when she marched out of the library. She ran up to her bedroom and didn't start crying until she'd shut the door behind her.

Loving Harrison was becoming a pain in her backside. Shamed or not, she was not going to be married by a hanging judge. No sir, no way, she thought to herself, using one of Cole's favorite nonsensical replies.

She felt better now that she had her mind set. She fell asleep with her brother's words echoing in her mind.

No sir, no way.

August 18, 1869

Dear Mama Rose,

Travis, Douglas, Cole, and I were glad your letter to Adam was stern. None of us have ever heard you sound so angry, but your oldest son needed to hear you tell him to stay put. His crazy notion to take off for parts unknown so Livonia wouldn't be able to keep on blackmailing you into staying with her was a foolhardy one, just like you said.

Cole keeps thinking there's a way out of this mire, and he clearly doesn't understand your compassion for Livonia. He wonders why you don't hate her, but Adam says you don't have it in you to hate anyone. Why won't you let any of the rest of us come and see you? Livonia's sons can't hurt us, Mama.

I sure would like to hug you.

Your daughter, Mary Rose

16

She came armed to her own wedding. Judge Burns didn't cotton to the notion of guns in his courtroom or his marriage parlor, and he therefore insisted she remove the six-shooter from her pocket. He would have frisked her if Adam would have allowed it.

The judge wasn't an altogether unlikable man. He was young by a judge's standards, or so Mary Rose believed, for he wasn't quite fifty years old yet and had been a hanging judge for nearly fifteen years.

He cut a handsome figure. He was tall, only slightly stoop-shouldered from age, and had brilliant green eyes the condemned believed were the very color of Satan's. The judge didn't have horns though. He had a full head of dark auburn hair. He was given to an Irish temper and an English practicality.

He and Harrison got along quite well from the minute the two men met. Burns had distant relatives living outside of Canterbury, and so he felt he had something other than the law in common with Harrison.

The way the intended groom treated Belle softened the judge's heart as well, for Harrison treated the woman with a deference reserved for statesmen. It wasn't an act. Belle had helped in the raising of Mary Rose, and Harrison was therefore

549

as beholden to her as the others were. He didn't care what her occupation was. She had a good heart, and that was all that mattered to him. The older woman's love for Mary Rose was very evident, and when Belle was asked to stand up as a bridesmaid and witness, she burst into tears.

Belle was dressed in blue. Judge Burns told Harrison he'd never seen her in any other color in all the years he'd known her. Why, even her lacy undergarments were blue, he whispered to Harrison while they waited for Mary Rose to join them.

Belle had gone upstairs to help the bride. Her advanced age and her occupation hadn't hardened her features. She was very pretty, with gray-tinged brown hair and warm brown eyes. And when she came back into the parlor with Mary Rose on her arm, the town's pride and joy looked more radiant than the bride.

Mary Rose looked miserable. And beautiful, Harrison thought to himself.

"Eleanor won't be joining us, I'm sorry to say," Adam explained. "She's still burning with fever, though Douglas assures me she's improved somewhat today."

"Belle, can you play at the piano?" the judge asked.

"No, honey, I can't," she answered.

"I'll play," Mary Rose suggested.

"Now, that don't make no sense, child," Belle told her with a laugh. "You've got to say your vows. John, why don't you place us where you want us and get the wedding done. It's warm in here. Boys, you line up behind your sister.

Which one of you is giving her away?"

Belle handed Mary Rose a nosegay of wild-flowers. Then she took hold of her hand and placed it on Harrison's arm.

"We're all giving her away," Adam told the judge.

"Well, now, I reckon that's all right."

"Wait. Judge Burns, did you hang anyone this week?"

"Not that I recollect, Mary Rose."

She let out a sigh. "All right then. Harrison, you still haven't proposed. He didn't, Judge. He just told me we were going to get married. He never asked." Her voice sounded downright puny to her. She hoped no one noticed. The flowers were shaking in her hand too. She gripped them tighter and tried to act composed.

"Honey, you ought to ask her nice," Belle insisted.

Harrison turned to his bride. "Will you marry me, Mary Rose?"

"No."

"She means yes," he told the judge.

"She's got to say the word."

Harrison looked at Mary Rose once again. "Do you love me?"

"Yes."

"Do you want to spend the rest of your life with me?"

"Will you try to get over your spells if I say I do?"

"Yes."

"Then, yes, I want to spend the rest of my days with you."

"Sounds like she's agreeing to me, John, honey," Belle said.

The judge cleared his throat, opened his book, and began to read.

Harrison and Mary Rose became husband and wife less than five minutes later.

He looked relieved when it was over. She looked bewildered. Harrison gently drew her into his arms and kissed her. She clutched her flowers to her chest and kissed him back.

"Now you can leave," she whispered. "I'm no longer a disgrace to my brothers."

"That isn't amusing," he whispered against her mouth. He kissed her again, harder, and then draped his arm around her shoulders and pulled her into his side.

Two of the brothers, Douglas and Travis, had tears in their eyes. Cole looked pleased, however, and that surprised Harrison.

"You're happy about this?" he asked.

"If she's pregnant, she's married. She might want to stay here, Harrison. You should think about that on your way to England."

"She'll come to me."

Cole frowned. Harrison sounded damned sure of himself.

The rest of the afternoon was spent in celebration, though Mary Rose wasn't given any time alone with her husband. She went upstairs with a piece of the cake Samuel had prepared, but Eleanor didn't have the stomach for food just yet. She cried for a minute or two because she'd missed the wedding and fell asleep almost immediately. Mary Rose left the cake on the dresser

552

and then went back downstairs to thank Belle and the judge.

Harrison was waiting for her on the steps. He pulled her into his arms and hugged her.

"I promise as soon as possible we'll have a preacher bless the union. Will that make you feel better?"

"Yes, thank you."

"I love you, sweetheart."

"I love you too."

"I realize you'll want to spend the night with your bride, Harrison, but there's a matter I'd like to ask your opinion about, seeing as you're an attorney and all. Could you spare me a few minutes in the library?"

Judge Burns made the request from the bottom of the steps. Harrison couldn't deny the request, of course; though, in all honesty, the last thing he wanted to do now was talk about legal matters. He wanted to get Mary Rose naked again.

She would have to wait, however. He winked at his bride and followed the judge into the library.

The judge was a pipe smoker. He took a long while to get a proper fire lit, then leaned back in Adam's chair and smiled at Harrison. He motioned for him to take the other chair.

"This here is the most peculiar family I ever did encounter. Now that you've married into it, I guess you must be peculiar too. Are you, Harrison?"

"I guess I am," Harrison agreed. "They're all good men, Judge, and they're certainly a family. The brothers have done well for their sister."

"Sweet Belle had a little hand in it too. She

sewed up dresses for Mary Rose. I don't remember much about her as a young'n. When I called on Belle, it was usually close to nightfall and of course the child was back at home where she belonged. I recall a mop of curls though. She's still got plenty of those, doesn't she? You love her fierce, like you should?"

"Yes, sir, I do."

"I got to hear a trial day after tomorrow in Hammond," the judge remarked. He shifted his position in his chair, folded one leg over the other, and then continued on. "It's a jury trial, and everyone in town is dead set against the defendant. He won't get a fair hearing. I got the feeling he's being railroaded by the vigilantes. Ever hear of a man named Bickley?"

"I'll never forget the bastard," Harrison said. He explained how he'd met the man and what he'd done to him.

The judge didn't seem surprised by Harrison's admission. "You wanted to kill him because he hurt your Mary Rose, but you didn't kill him. That's the difference between civil and animal. Are you an ignorant lawyer, or do you really know how the law works?"

"I know how the law works.

"I'd like to see you prove it to me. Will you come to Hammond tomorrow and talk to George Madden? He's the man they plan to condemn."

"What's the charge?"

"Stealing a horse. We don't take kindly to stealing anything out here, but when a man's horse is taken, well, then, folks tend to think the death sentence is the only possible punishment. You won't have long to work up your case, I'm sorry to say, but I've got a strong feeling that after you talk to Madden, you'll know who really took the horse. I won't say anything more to taint your mind, but the man deserves a fair hearing, and unless you come to Hammond with me, he won't get one. You can't bring your bride with you because the town's worked up over this business. The vigilantes have everyone all lathered up and ready for a lynching, and the sheriff has his hands full trying to keep order. I can't put off the trial date, so don't go asking me for any favors. The sheriff would sneak in my room and shoot me in my sleep if I decided to delay things. He's putting in twenty-four-hour days now, and his jail is bursting at the seams with men in need of my attention."

"They call you the hanging judge," Harrison remarked.

"That's nice to hear."

Harrison laughed. "You're a fair man, aren't you?"

"I like to think I am. If a man needs hanging, I'm not squeamish about seeing he gets it. It doesn't always matter what's right though, especially when a man is given a jury trial. His peers are mostly an ignorant breed."

"When do you want to leave?"

The judge smiled with satisfaction. "How about noon? It will take me that long to get up the strength to leave Belle's bed. I'll meet you outside her place tomorrow then, if that's agreeable."

"Yes, sir," Harrison said as he stood up. "Now,

if you'll excuse me, I have a bride waiting to be kissed."

The judge stopped him at the doorway. "Mind telling me why she carried a pistol to her wedding? I've been mighty curious about that."

"I'm not completely certain, but I think she was letting me know she wasn't going to be coerced into doing anything she didn't want to do. I guess you could say she was trying to even up the odds. Her brothers and I were stacked up against her. She was also hoping to be married by a preacher. She wanted the union blessed, I suppose."

"Well, hell, son, drag her on in here. I'll be happy to bless her. Will it matter that I'm not a preacher?"

"I'm afraid so, Your Honor."

He left the judge snorting with laughter. Mary Rose was upstairs with Belle. The two women were looking in on Eleanor. His bride didn't come back downstairs until nearly three o'clock. Harrison sat on the porch and drank beer with her brothers. When Mary Rose came out to the porch, Harrison told her about the trial in Hammond.

The judge left with Belle an hour later, and Mary Rose went into the kitchen to help set the table for supper.

All four of her brothers seemed genuinely happy for their sister, and try as he might, Harrison couldn't understand why. Their turnabout confused him. He knew they had a motive for wanting the marriage; he just couldn't figure out what it was.

Cole sat in the chair next to Harrison. He turned to him first.

"How come you went along with the wedding?"

"It's like Douglas said," Cole drawled out. "No use closing the barn door after the horse got out. She loves you and you love her."

"And?"

"You'll bring her back home, where she belongs."

"Do you mean here? To your ranch?"

"The area at least. She belongs in Montana. The land's a part of her. You won't take that away from her."

"Where we live is in her hands," Harrison said. "She might change her mind after she meets Elliott."

Cole and Douglas exchanged a look Harrison couldn't quite interpret.

"And?" he persisted, determined to get to the end of the maze and find out what their true motive was.

"He can't keep her, can he?" Cole asked the question in a whisper-soft voice.

Harrison straightened in his chair. "Meaning what, Cole?"

Douglas answered. "Elliott can't keep her in England or marry her off to some rich old lord and make her stay in England for the rest of her life, can he? She's already married to you. We kind of think of you as our insurance."

"You met her here," Cole reminded him. "Like it or not, you're also a part of her past. You know all about us, but Elliott doesn't. Mary Rose is going to need to rely on your strength and your honor, and we all think you'll probably bring her back home. Yes, sir, that's what we think."

"Elliott isn't your enemy. If you knew him the way I do, you'd realize he would never make Mary Rose stay anywhere she didn't want to stay."

"So you say," Douglas replied. "We still wanted some protection for our sister."

"So you let her marry me. You've used backhanded logic. Haven't you considered the possibility that I might want to keep her in Scotland?"

Cole smiled. "You know what your problem is, Harrison? You're too damned noble for your own good. If she wants to come back to Montana, you'll bring her. You couldn't live with yourself if you made her unhappy. It's a shame, really. Love does have its price. Pleasing Mary Rose is going to be difficult, but you'll try."

"Just keep your eye on her," Douglas ordered. "Don't make us come after you. I know you believe Elliott's a good man, but we don't know him, now, do we?"

Mary Rose interrupted the discussion. Harrison stood up when she walked out onto the porch.

She'd changed her clothes. She'd worn an ivory dress for the wedding ceremony, but now she had on a pale pink dress with white trim. Her hair was pinned up behind her head. She looked very prim and proper to him, and suddenly all he wanted to do was pull the pins out of her hair, take her clothes off her, and make love to her.

She had other ideas in mind. She had a white apron in her hands, and while he stood there watching her, she unfolded the thing and tied it around her waist.

"I guess Harrison's finally going to see the second floor of the house," Cole remarked.

"No, he isn't," Mary Rose blurted out. "Of course, he could if he wanted to, but I thought it would be nice if he and I stayed in the bunkhouse tonight. Do you mind, Harrison?"

"No," he answered, wondering over the quick blush that covered her cheeks. He couldn't imagine why she was embarrassed, but he decided he would have to wait until later to find out what was bothering her.

"Why are you putting an apron on?" he asked.

"I was going to help with supper."

He noticed her hands were shaking then. Her brothers must have noticed too. Douglas frowned with concern. "Are you feeling all right, Mary Rose? You aren't coming down with Eleanor's ailment, are you?"

"No, I'm fine."

Harrison decided not to wait to find out what was wrong. He took hold of his bride's hand and half dragged her to the other side of the porch.

"What's the matter with you?"

"Nothing," she whispered. "I'm just a little nervous."

"Why?"

"I just got married." She all but wailed out the fact.

Harrison tried to take her into his arms. She glanced over her shoulder to look at her brothers, then backed away from him.

The audience obviously embarrassed her. Harrison held on to his patience.

"I just got married too."

"Yes, of course you did," she agreed. "It happened awfully quick, didn't it?"

"Why don't you want to sleep in your room tonight?"

She looked horrified. In a low whisper she said, "They'll hear, Harrison. My brothers hear every little sound."

He nodded. He finally understood. "We need a proper honeymoon."

She gave him an exasperated look. "You have to go to Hammond tomorrow."

He nodded agreement. He hadn't forgotten. "Know what I think we ought to do?"

He leaned down close to her. She edged a little closer to him and tilted her head back. "What do you think we ought to do?"

"Go tell Corrie."

"Tell her what?"

"That you're a married woman," he explained. "Let's spend the night in the cave. Do you think you could find it again?"

"Yes, of course I could find it. Harrison, do you really want to sleep on a rock floor tonight?"

"I want to get you alone, Mary Rose. Got any better ideas?"

He could tell from her expression that she was warming to the idea. "I've been thinking a lot about that cave," he whispered. "I want to go back, but this time, when you start to take off your clothes, I won't stop you."

Her blush intensified, and she hastily looked

over her shoulder once again to make certain her brothers hadn't heard.

"Go and pack your things," he whispered. "I'll tell Adam where we're going."

"Samuel would be happy to fix a basket of food for us," she said. "Let Adam ask him, please. He'll hide from you."

Harrison still didn't believe they had an actual cook, but he went along with her game.

They left for the ridge an hour later. Mary Rose insisted on taking Corrie another basket of gifts, and Adam let her include a book written by a popular fellow named Mark Twain with the condition that Corrie return the book when she was finished reading it. Only then would he lend her another one of his treasures to enjoy.

His bride spent less than an hour talking to her friend, and they reached the cave a little before dark.

She'd carried along a thick quilt, and they used it for their mattress. They didn't need extra blankets that night, for the heat of their bodies pressed against each other kept them warm.

It was the most romantic night either one of them had ever experienced. It was also quite educational for Mary Rose. There weren't any inhibitions, and because they were isolated from the rest of the world, she felt free to do whatever she wanted to do. Harrison taught her how to pleasure him, and she was eager to learn. She was awkward and timid, but only in the beginning, and when she saw how he reacted to her touch, she became bolder and more sure of herself.

By morning light, husband and wife were too

exhausted to move. They slept in each other's arms until nearly eight o'clock, made love once again, and reluctantly returned to the ranch.

Harrison left for Blue Belle to meet the judge a short while later. Mary Rose kissed him goodbye and then went up to her room and slept the rest of the morning away.

She walked around in a haze of bliss for the rest of the day. Eleanor was back to complaining about every little thing, but Mary Rose was too happy to be bothered by her grouchy friend.

Cole carried Eleanor downstairs for supper. Her fever had finally broken, and although she looked pale, she had regained her appetite.

She made Cole carry her back up to her room after she'd eaten, and he stayed inside her bedroom a little longer than was necessary. He had told Douglas he was going to have a talk with her about his lack of intentions.

Eleanor didn't take kindly to the news that Cole wasn't the marrying kind. She didn't much like hearing he'd only been dallying with her because he thought she'd be leaving soon, either, and by the time he left the room, she was shouting every raucous curse she had ever heard. She threw a porcelain vase at him and clipped him on the shoulder on his way out the door.

Mary Rose decided to give Eleanor time to calm down before she went upstairs to try and console her. She helped Douglas with the dishes. She thought it was odd that her other brothers continued to sit at the table, and after she'd finished the kitchen duties, she was invited to sit back down.

Adam explained there was an important matter to talk about.

She sat in Harrison's chair and faced the eldest brother. Her hands were folded in her lap. She leaned back and smiled, relaxed now, for she believed the matter concerned family finances. The brothers only wore such grim expressions when they were worried about money problems.

Cole began the discussion. "Harrison came here with two motives in mind, Mary Rose. He wanted to learn about ranching because he wants to eventually retire from law and build up a ranch of his own, either in the Highlands or maybe even around here."

"Yes, I knew what he had in mind," she agreed. "But you say he had another motive as well?"

"He was looking for someone," Douglas explained. "That was his other motive . . . and, I guess you could say, his primary reason for coming to Montana."

She waited a full minute for her brother to continue before she realized he wasn't going to say another word. She turned to Travis.

"Who was he looking for?" she asked.

"You," Travis blurted out.

He couldn't or wouldn't expound further.

The duty of explaining fell on Adam's shoulders. He cleared his throat and then proceeded to tell her all about a baby girl named Victoria.

She never said a word throughout the story Adam told her. She shook her head several times, silently denying the possibility that she was indeed Lady Victoria someone or other from England, of all places, but she listened with an open mind and tried to make sense out of what he was telling her.

It took Adam a good twenty minutes to give her the full story, and when he was finally finished, all the brothers waited for her to show some sort of reaction.

Cole expected her to be angry. He was somewhat surprised when she continued to look only mildly curious.

Douglas was more perceptive. He concluded she wasn't convinced she was Elliott's long-lost daughter.

"Don't you believe us?" he asked.

"Do you believe I'm Victoria?" she countered.

All four brothers nodded. "There is substantial proof," Adam explained. He then outlined the facts for her once again.

"How do you feel about meeting your father?"

"I don't have a father. I have four brothers."

"Don't be stubborn, Mary Rose," Adam said. "Think this through. I know it's a surprise. Of course it is. You have an entire family back in England. You can't pretend they don't exist. Your father has been searching the world over for you."

"Don't you want to go and meet him?" Travis asked.

She lowered her head and stared into her lap. There was so much to think about, she didn't know where to start.

"I feel compassion for the man. I cannot imagine what it must have been like for him and his wife to lose their infant daughter."

"You were their infant daughter," Douglas gently reminded her.

"Yes, so you say," she whispered. She gripped her hands together and tried to remain composed. "But I don't *know* him, Douglas. I feel sorry for him, but I don't have any love in my heart for him. He isn't my family. You are. It's too late to start over."

"Aren't you curious to know what he's like?" Travis asked.

She lifted her shoulders in a shrug. "Not really," she admitted. "I don't understand Harrison's involvement in all of this. He works for Elliott, doesn't he?"

"Yes, he does," Adam said.

The truth was slow to settle in her mind, but once it did, she began to feel sick to her stomach. "And you're telling me that he came to Montana because of the interview I suffered through with the attorney in St. Louis? All of this started because a woman thought I looked like Elliott's wife?"

"Yes."

"Then . . . Oh, God, then everything Harrison told me was a lie. From the very beginning he had this other motive. He never said a word to me. Not one word. If I am Victoria, as you all seem to believe, why didn't Harrison tell *me?*"

Cole grimaced over the anguish he heard in his sister's voice. "He didn't trust any of us for a long time," he explained.

"No, he never trusted any of us," she agreed.

She seemed to wilt before their very eyes. The desolation on her face made her brothers ache for her.

"Mary Rose, listen to me," Adam ordered.

"You had been kidnapped. Harrison didn't know if we were part of the plan to take you from Elliott. We were just boys, yes, and so he discarded the notion that we had planned the kidnapping, but he had to keep silent until he found out who was the mastermind behind it. He was being cautious."

"He betrayed me, didn't he? I'm his wife now, and yet he kept this from me?"

The younger brothers looked to Adam, hoping he would be able to calm their sister.

"You and Harrison will have to work this out together," Adam advised. "I want to know how you feel about going to England to meet your father. Harrison has to leave soon, but I had thought to give you more time to get used to the notion of having a family over there before sending you off. Eleanor could go with you. Mary Rose, don't shake your head at me. Try to be reasonable about this. You owe it to the man to at least go and meet him. He's had a lifetime of suffering. Let him see you and know in his heart that you're all right."

"I think maybe we ought to give her some time to think about all of this," Travis suggested. "She looks kind of stunned."

She looked furious to Cole. He knew Harrison's behavior was the reason she was so upset. She knew and loved him. Her father, on the other hand, was still a foreign concept to her, and one that would take time to get used to before she could decide what she wanted to do about him.

"Sleep on it, Mary Rose," Cole said. "You don't have to do anything until you're ready to."

She was suddenly too tired to think about anything. Her stomach felt like it was on fire, and all she wanted to do was go up to her room, get into her bed, and pretend none of what she'd just learned was true. Like the ostrich she'd once read about, she wanted to bury her head in the sand and let the rest of the world scurry on by without her.

Tears streamed down her face. Cole handed her his handkerchief before she could ask for it. Lord only knew how many times her brothers had seen her cry before. She didn't have to hide anything from them or pretend to be someone she wasn't.

She stood up, braced her hands on the tabletop, and asked, "Am I supposed to go to London and become a member of a family full of strangers? What do you expect of me? Tell me what the right thing is that you're so sure I'll do."

"We'll talk more about this tomorrow, after you've had a good night's rest," Adam suggested.

"Harrison is your family now, Mary Rose. You married him, remember? You don't hate him, do you?" Douglas asked.

She had to think about his question a long minute before she answered. "No, I don't hate him. How could I? It appears I don't even know the man. Oh, God, Douglas, I'm married to a stranger. I don't know what's real about him and what isn't. Was everything a pretense?"

"Granted, Harrison did have an ulterior motive," Douglas argued, "but after you've had time to think about the situation, I'm sure you'll realize . . ."

She cut him off. "I'll realize he never, ever trusted me, and I sure as certain can't trust him. He deceived me. He pretended to be someone he wasn't."

She was suddenly too furious to go on. She grabbed Cole's handkerchief and began to wipe the tears away from her cheeks.

Had he been pretending to love her? Oh, God, had that been a fabrication too?

"Harrison wasn't always pretending," Cole insisted. "He did turn out to be real inept, didn't he?"

"Try not to overreact, Mary Rose," Travis suggested.

"Why are all of you defending him?" she demanded.

"We've had time to think about his reasons for proceeding slowly," Adam explained.

Travis tried to come up with a suitable parable or comparison that would put it all into perspective for his sister. It took him several minutes to think of something that made a little sense to him. He waited until there was a lull in the discussion, and then said, "Do you remember all of the stories we read to you about the knights who lived back in the middle ages? The baron sometimes killed the messengers who carried bad news. Well, Harrison's sort of like a messenger. None of what happened was his fault. He didn't steal you out of your crib and throw you in the trash. I think you should remember that."

Cole liked Travis's comparison. He latched on to it with the tenacity of a child holding on to a piece of forbidden candy.

"If you had lived back in the middle ages, do you think you would have killed the messenger?"

She glared at her brother. She thought his question was a stupid one at best.

"No, I wouldn't have killed the messenger, but I sure as hell wouldn't have slept with him either."

None of her brothers felt like correcting her unladylike language. They understood how upset she was. If cursing made her feel better, they wouldn't stop her. Their little sister looked stricken, and devastated.

"What about your father?" Adam asked her once again.

"You said we would talk about him tomorrow," she reminded her brother. "If I do decide to go to England, will all of you go with me?"

The younger brothers made Adam answer for them. He leaned back in his chair and shook his head. He suddenly felt as weary as an eighty-year-old.

"We can't go with you. We're part of your past."

"You're my family," she cried out.

"Yes, of course we are," Adam hastened to agree. "That won't ever change."

"We aren't making you go," Cole said. "We love you, Mary Rose. We could never throw you out."

"Then why do I feel as though you are? All of you believe I should go to England, don't you?"

"You've got to give yourself time to get used to the notion of having another family," Travis said.

She nodded agreement. Oh, yes, she needed

time. She straightened up, asked to be excused, and ran up to her bedroom. She spent the next hour sitting on the side of her bed, trying to make sense out of her life.

Her thoughts kept returning to Harrison. She was thankful he wasn't there now because she didn't want to have to face him just yet. She didn't know what she would say to him.

He had told her she would hate him. She thought about the warning he had given her, and then became furious all over again.

What in God's name was she going to do?

She finally stood up, put on her robe and her slippers, and went downstairs to the library.

Adam was waiting for her. Even though all of their lives had been turned upside down, some things remained predictable.

Like little sisters needing to be comforted.

It was what family was all about.

She didn't feel better the following morning. She felt worse. Because she was hurting so inside, she went to Douglas. He always took care of her aches and pains, cuts and bruises, even the ones he couldn't see.

Douglas understood her need to get away for a while. He didn't believe she was being a coward because she didn't want to see Harrison, and so he took her to the Cohens' house in Hammond. Eleanor insisted on going with her friend, and since she was fully recovered from her bout of illness, Douglas agreed to let her tag along.

Eleanor surprised Douglas. She seemed to be genuinely concerned about Mary Rose. The young woman had put her own concerns aside, a first in Douglas's estimation, and really tried to comfort his sister. She held on to her hand and kept promising her that everything was going to turn out all right.

When Harrison returned to the ranch, he demanded to know where his bride was. Adam, Cole, and Travis could honestly tell him they didn't know. Douglas gave him a little more information when he realized how upset and concerned Harrison was. He explained that Mary Rose needed time alone to sort out her feelings, insisted she was safe and being looked after, and then suggested Harrison get on with his plans and leave for England.

He couldn't promise Mary Rose would follow. Harrison had expected just such a reaction from his bride, but he was still shaken by the anguish he'd caused her. He desperately wanted her to understand, and yet knew that right then she didn't understand at all.

She would come to England though. Of that he was certain. He told Douglas to wire him as soon as Mary Rose and Eleanor were on their way. And then he said his farewells, reminded Adam to take good care of MacHugh, and began his long journey back to England.

Walking away from the woman he loved was the most difficult thing he'd ever done, and even though the separation was to be temporary, he was still in agony. He felt as though his heart were being torn out of his chest.

She would come to him. He repeated the belief until it became a chant.

And he never, ever doubted. His belief in her was every bit as strong as his love for her. She would do the right thing. She was noble and good and kindhearted.

And she loved him.

No, he never doubted.

Mary Rose was both relieved and heartbroken that Harrison had left. She knew she wasn't being reasonable, but she was too distraught to think straight.

She refused to discuss her father for a full week. Thoughts of the man kept intruding, however, and once she'd gotten past her own self-pity, she began to feel guilty because she was being cold-hearted toward him.

It took her another week to come to the conclusion that she would have to go and meet him. It was the only decent thing to do, and when she informed her brothers of her decision, she qualified it with the announcement that she had no intention of staying in England long. She planned to visit him, meet his relatives, and then return to her ranch, where she belonged.

She wouldn't talk about her plans for a future with Harrison, and her brothers wisely decided not to prod her into making any decision about her husband she might later regret.

Mary Rose insisted on saying good-bye to Corrie. She made Travis go with her and extracted a promise from him that he would take supplies to Corrie once a week until Mary Rose returned. She would introduce her brother to the woman after she'd visited with her, so that Corrie would know what Travis looked like and wouldn't try to shoot him.

Because it was the middle of the week, Corrie was expecting her. Mary Rose called out her greeting from the center of the clearing, and then slowly walked forward. The rocking chair was on the porch, and Mary Rose was pleased to notice that once she started toward the steps, the shotgun was removed from the open window.

She put the basket of gifts on the windowsill and took her seat. Corrie touched her shoulder, then dropped the book she'd been loaned into Mary Rose's lap.

Mary Rose still wasn't certain if Corrie could read or not, but she didn't want to insult the woman by asking her outright.

The basket disappeared from the window. Mary Rose waited a minute, and then said, "There's another book in the basket, Corrie. If you don't want to read it, just hand it back out the window."

Corrie patted her on her shoulder once again. Mary Rose concluded she did know how to read, and wanted to keep the book.

It took her a long while to work up enough courage to tell her friend she was leaving for England.

"Would you like to know how I ended up in Montana Territory?" she began.

She didn't expect an answer, of course, and proceeded to tell her friend all about how her brothers had found her in a basket in New York City. She didn't go into a lot of unnecessary details, and when she started to talk about her father and how she had to go to England to meet him, she began to cry.

While Corrie gently stroked her shoulders, Mary Rose confided all her fears to the woman.

"Why do I feel guilty because I don't feel anything more than compassion for the man? I don't want to go and meet him, but I know I have to, Corrie. I'm being terribly selfish, but I like my life now. I hate having it disrupted. Besides, I already have a family. I don't want a new one. I know it's wrong for me to feel this way, and deep inside, I'm so scared. What if none of them like me? What if I disappoint my father? I don't know how to be a proper English lady. They say my name is really Victoria. I'm not Victoria though, I'm Mary Rose. And how will I ever be able to go on with Harrison? What kind of marriage can we have without trust in one another? Oh, Corrie, I wish I could stay here. I don't want to leave."

Mary Rose continued to weep for several more minutes, and then reached up to wipe the tears away from her face.

Corrie grabbed hold of her hand and held on to it. The comfort the woman was giving her made her weep all the more. She thought about all the terrible pain and anguish Corrie had had to endure and how foolish and inconsequential her own problems were in comparison. Corrie had watched her husband and her son die. And yet she had endured.

"You give me strength, Corrie," she whispered.

It wasn't empty praise, for the longer she thought about the dear woman's suffering, the more her own life was put into perspective. Mary

Rose knew she would do what had to be done, and regardless of the outcome, she would also endure.

"I'm very fortunate to have you for a friend, Corrie."

Travis let out a shrill whistle. He was letting Mary Rose know that it was time for them to leave.

"Eleanor and I will go to the Cohens' house in Hammond the day after tomorrow," she told her friend. "They're going to Boston for a family reunion, and we'll travel with them. Mr. Cohen will make certain we get on the right ship to England, and if all my plans go smoothly, I'll be back home before the first winter snow falls.

"Travis is going to bring you supplies while I'm away. I've told you all about my brother, remember? He won't ever come closer than the middle of the clearing," she hurried to add when her friend squeezed her hand tight. "May I call to him now? He'll stand by the trees, so you can get a good look at him. I don't want you to be startled when he comes here, and he promised me he would always call out to you so you can watch him."

Corrie finally relaxed her grip. Mary Rose shouted to her brother. Travis appeared on the far side of the clearing and waved to his sister. The curtain obstructed his view of Corrie, but he noticed Mary Rose was holding her hand.

"Storm's coming, Mary Rose. We ought to leave now," he called out. "Good day to you, Corrie," he added before he turned around and walked away.

Mary Rose finally said her good-bye. She turned and kissed Corrie's hand, and then stood up.

"I'm going to miss you," she whispered. "God and Travis will take good care of you, Corrie. Have faith in both of them."

Mary Rose clutched the book in her arms and slowly walked away. The rush of the rising wind mingled with the call of an impatient cardinal and all but muffled the sound of a woman softly weeping inside the cabin.

January 2, 1870

Dear Mama Rose,

Today I am ten years old. Do you remember Adam wrote to tell you that they found papers in my basket and all my brothers think that because the words written on the top of the page said a baby girl was born on the second day of January, and since I was the only baby girl in the basket, they think it must be me.

I'm very lucky to have such a nice family. Travis is making me a birthday cake for supper, and all my brothers made presents for me. Adam said next year he would make sure they got something store bought for me too. Won't that be nice?

Why do you think my mama and my papa threw me away? I wonder what I did wrong.

Your daughter,
Mary Rose

17

$\mathcal{H}$arrison arrived in London on a Tuesday afternoon but was forced to wait until the following evening to talk to his employer. Lord Elliott was staying at his country estate, a two-hour ride from the city, and wasn't scheduled to return to the city until Wednesday morning.

Harrison dispatched a messenger announcing his return. He asked for a private meeting, for he had a highly personal matter to discuss with him. He deliberately implied it was a legal matter he'd gotten involved in, so that Elliott wouldn't include his personal assistant, George MacPherson.

Murphy, Elliott's butler for as long as Harrison could remember, opened the front door for him. The faithful servant's eyes sparkled with delight at the sight of Harrison.

"It's so good to have you back home with us, mi'lord," Murphy announced.

"It's good to be back," Harrison replied. "How have you and Lord Elliott been getting along?"

"We've missed all the scandals you get into with your criminal cases, mi'lord. We haven't had a good fight since the day you left. Lord Elliott continues to worry me, I'll admit. He's working too hard, and you know how stubborn and unreasonable he can be. He won't slow down, no matter how much I nag him. I fear he'll continue to run until his heart stops beating. You're bound to cheer him up, however. I must say, he's missed you sorely."

"Is he upstairs?"

"Yes, mi'lord, in the library."

"Is he alone?"

"He is, and impatient to see you again. Why don't you run on up?"

Harrison started up the stairs, then stopped. "Murphy, he's going to need some brandy."

"Is the news you bring bad, then?" the butler inquired with a frown.

Harrison smiled. "Quite the opposite. He'll still need a drink of brandy though. Is there a bottle in the library?"

"Yes, mi'lord, but I shall bring up another one to be on the safe side. The two of you can get sotted together."

Harrison laughed. In all his years living with Elliott, he'd never once seen him even remotely tipsy. He couldn't picture him roaring drunk. Elliott was too well bred to ever consider doing anything that would take away his control or his dignity. Getting drunk would have robbed him of both.

He hurried on up the stairs, rounded the corner, and went into the library. Elliott was standing in front of the fireplace. He spotted Harrison and immediately embraced him.

"So you are home at last," he said in greeting. He hugged Harrison, and pounded him on his back with a great deal of affection.

"You're a sight for these old eyes," he whispered. "Sit down now and tell me all about your adventure in America. I want to hear every detail."

Harrison waited until Elliott had taken his seat before he pulled up a chair and sat down. He noticed how tired Elliott looked and was saddened by his observation. The country air hadn't done the elderly man much good, for his complexion was tinged gray, and there were the ever-present dark half-circles under his eyes. Grief had taken its toll on him.

Elliott had never remarried, but the determined ladies in London society still fought for his attention. Not only was he an extremely wealthy man, he was also considered handsome. He had silver-tipped hair, patrician features, and held himself like the statesman he was. Elliott had been born and raised in an affluent family, and his breeding, education and manners were therefore impeccable. Far more important was the fact that Elliott had a good heart. Like his daughter, Harrison thought to himself. She had perhaps inherited her sense of decency from him, and that noble quality had been nurtured by her brothers.

Elliott was also strong-willed. A lesser man would have been destroyed by the horror of having his only child taken away from him, but Elliott fought his desolation in private and presented a brave front to the rest of the world. While he had retired from active participation in government, he continued to work behind the scenes to bring about change. He was as much a champion of the less fortunate as Harrison was and certainly just as dedicated to the belief that all men were entitled to equal representation and equal rights. He wholeheartedly supported Harrison when he took on unpopular causes, such as defending the common man.

"America seems to have agreed with you. Is it the new fashion not to wear a jacket, son?"

Harrison smiled. "None of my jackets fit. I seem to have grown between my shoulders. I'll have to call in a tailor before I go out in public again."

"You do look bigger to me," Elliott said. "But there's something else that's different about you." Elliott continued to stare at Harrison another minute or two, then shook his head. "I'm very happy to have you back where you belong." He gave the admission in a quiet voice. "Now, give me your promise, Harrison. There will be no more hunts. I'll have your word before we discuss your legal problems."

"No more hunts," Harrison agreed.

Elliott nodded with satisfaction. He leaned back in his wing chair, folded one leg over the other, and said, "Now you may begin. Tell me everything. Whatever this legal problem is, we'll work it out together."

"Actually, sir, there aren't any legal problems. I just wanted to make certain we had a private talk. I didn't want your assistant to overhear what I had to say to you."

Elliott raised an eyebrow. "You didn't want George here? Why in heaven's name not? You like MacPherson, don't you? Why, he's been with me for years now, almost as long as you have. Tell me what's bothering you."

"He's going to give you good news, mi'lord."

Murphy made the announcement from the doorway and then came inside with a full bottle of brandy. He placed the liquor on the table and turned to his employer.

"Mi'lord says you'll need a stiff drink when you hear what he has to say," Murphy explained. "Shall I pour for the two of you?"

"If Harrison believes I'll need it, go ahead, Murphy."

Harrison was happy for the interruption. He was suddenly feeling tongue-tied. He didn't think it would be a good idea to simply spring the news on Elliott. The shock might give him heart palpitations, but Harrison couldn't come up with a simple way to ease into the announcement.

Murphy left the library a moment later. Elliott took a sip of his drink and turned to Harrison once again.

"I got married."

Elliott almost dropped his glass. "You what?"

"I got married."

Lord above, why had he started out by telling him that? Harrison was almost as surprised as Elliott appeared to be.

"Good heavens," Elliott whispered. "When did you get married?"

"A couple of weeks ago," Harrison answered. "I didn't mean to start out with my announcement. I have other more important news to tell you. You see, I went to . . ."

Elliott interrupted him. "Nothing could be more important than hearing you're married, son. I can barely take it in. Am I to assume the young lady you married is from America?"

"Yes, sir, but . . ."

"What is her name?"

"Mary Rose."

"Mary Rose," Elliott repeated. "Is your bride downstairs? I must confess to being disappointed I wasn't in the church for your wedding. I would have liked to stand by your side when you spoke your vows."

"Actually, sir, we weren't married in a church."

"You weren't? Then who married you?"

"Hanging Judge Burns."

Elliott looked like he was having difficulty following the explanation.

Harrison let out a sigh. "I realize it sounds . . . peculiar."

"A 'hanging judge' married you. Now, why would I think that was peculiar, Harrison?"

Harrison smiled. "You'd like Burns. He's a rough-talking man with strong ideas about what's right and what's wrong. His love of the law is to be admired. I argued a case in his court, and he didn't let me get away with much at all. He's as sharp as they come."

"Did you win for your client?"

"Yes, sir."

Elliott nodded approval. "I didn't expect less from you. Was the marriage forced?"

"Yes, it was. I forced her into marrying me. I really tried to fight the attraction, sir. I didn't feel I had the right to pursue her, but in the end, I couldn't . . ."

"Well, of course you had the right to pursue her. She's lucky to have you, Harrison. Remember who your father was. Any woman would be proud to marry you. Are you telling me your bride's family didn't think you were worthy enough? What utter nonsense," he ended in a mutter.

"No, sir, that isn't what I was telling you. You see . . ."

"Where does your bride come from? I can't seem to take this in. I recall hearing you say over and over again that you would never marry, and now it appears I'm about to meet your bride. I thought your broken engagement to Edwina soured you against matrimony. I'm pleased to see it was a false concern. The right woman will change the way a man thinks."

"Sir, Mary Rose isn't with me. She's still in America."

"She didn't come home with you? Why not?"

"There were circumstances preventing her from accompanying me."

"What specific circumstances?"

"Her family."

"And where is her family?"

"She lives with four brothers on a ranch just outside Blue Belle, in Montana Territory."

Elliott smiled. The name of the town caught his fancy. "I've read quite a few books on the rough-and-tumble towns dotting the western section of the United States, but I must confess, I've never heard of a town named after a flower."

"Actually, sir, the town was named after a prostitute. Her name's Belle."

Elliot started to laugh. "Are you serious?"

"Yes, sir. Belle helped Mary Rose get ready for the wedding."

"She did, did she?" Elliot was trying hard not

to laugh again. "Then why was the town named Blue Belle instead of simply Belle?"

"Belle doesn't like what she does for a living."

Elliott couldn't control his amusement. He laughed until tears came into his eyes. He pulled his handkerchief from his pocket and dabbed at the corners of his eyes while he tried to regain his composure.

"What have you gotten yourself into, son. This isn't like you at all. You've certainly given me quite a lot to digest," he added. "I can't wait to meet your bride."

"You think I've lost my mind, don't you, sir?"

Elliott smiled. "I think you've changed," he admitted. "I knew there was something different about you, but I never would have guessed you'd marry a girl from the country. I also thought that if you did marry, you'd choose someone more . . . refined."

"Mary Rose is very refined," Harrison said. "She's everything I could ever want."

"I didn't mean to suggest she was lacking, son. If you'll remember, I also married a country girl. My Agatha was from your Highlands. I've always believed growing up on a farm was the primary reason she was so unspoiled. Of course, she had good parents," he added with a nod.

"Sir, I went to Montana in search of your daughter. I didn't fail this time."

"No, of course you didn't. Granted, it was another false lead, but one with a happy ending, because you met and married your Mary Rose. What a pretty name your bride has. You do love her, don't you?"

"Oh, yes, sir, I love her very much. You'll love her too."

"Yes, of course I will."

Harrison leaned forward in his chair. "As I said before, it wasn't a false lead this time. There's one more important thing you need to know."

"Yes?"

"I married your daughter."

Mary Rose and Eleanor arrived in England on the twenty-first day of July. It was hot, humid, and threatening to rain.

Harrison had used up every bit of his patience waiting for his bride to get over her anger and come to him, and he'd only just made up his mind to book passage back to the States when a telegram arrived from a gentleman named John Cohen, giving him the pertinent information about Mary Rose's departure from Boston and her expected arrival date.

Harrison spotted her golden crown the second she stepped off the steam tender from the ship. He shoved his way through the crowd, grabbed hold of his wife, and pulled her into his arms. As soon as he touched her, he felt an immediate sense of acute relief. Mary Rose was finally where she belonged.

His greeting wasn't very flowery. "What the hell took you so long?"

She couldn't answer him. Harrison didn't even give her time to frown. He leaned down and captured her mouth in a ravenous kiss.

She didn't resist him. She put her arms around his neck, lifted up on her tiptoes, and kissed him back just as passionately.

"For heaven's sake, Mary Rose. People are gawking at us. Do stop that. You're attracting a crowd."

Eleanor whispered her protest from behind Mary Rose. She poked her friend and then took a step away. If the two of them didn't stop mauling each other, she would simply pretend she wasn't with them. Honestly, what had happened to her friend's sense of propriety?

Harrison, she decided, was a lost cause. It wouldn't do her any good to try to reason with him. She'd seen the look of blatant love and hunger in his eyes when he reached for Mary Rose. No, there wouldn't be any reasoning with him.

Eleanor suddenly smiled. Harrison had certainly missed his wife. One day, Eleanor was determined to find a man who felt just as much love for her.

Harrison finally ended the kiss. He was pleased to see Mary Rose appeared to be as shaken by the kiss as he was.

"I missed you, sweetheart," he whispered.

"I missed you too," she whispered back. "You and I are going to have to have a long talk though, as soon as possible. Things are going to be different between us. We're going to have to start over. I'm going to try to get past this, but it's difficult."

He didn't want to talk just yet. "We'll discuss your worries later," he promised a scant second before his mouth covered hers again.

"Oh, for heaven's sake."

Eleanor's muttering finally caught Harrison's

attention. He couldn't make himself let go of his wife after he ended the kiss, however, and so he hugged her tight against him while he greeted her disgruntled-looking friend.

"How was your voyage, Eleanor?"

"Just fine, thank you. Mary Rose can't possibly breathe, Harrison, because of the way you've got her face pressed into your jacket. Do let go of her so we can get on our way. It's about to rain, for heaven's sake. We're both quite weary from our trip, and we want to get settled in before night falls. Are we going directly to her father's house?"

Mary Rose pushed away from Harrison. "I would rather wait until tomorrow to meet him. Does he expect to see me tonight? It's almost dark now, and I would like to have a little more time to prepare myself."

"You've had two long months to prepare, Mary Rose," Harrison said.

"I need one more night," she insisted.

"Your father doesn't expect to see you until tomorrow, so you can calm down. He knew you'd be tired from your trip. Both you and Eleanor will stay with me tonight."

"I'm quite calm. Why would you think I wasn't?"

"You were shouting," Eleanor told her.

"I was simply trying to make my opinion heard."

"I hope you have spacious quarters, Harrison," Eleanor said. "Mary Rose told me she's going to insist on a room of her own. I believe she's still upset with you."

"Honestly, Eleanor, I can speak for myself," Mary Rose said. She turned to Harrison again. "I am upset with you, and as I said before, things are going to be different now. We're going to have to start over."

Harrison gave his wife a hard look, then took hold of her arm and started walking toward the main thoroughfare where the carriages were lined up.

"You're sleeping with me, in my bed," he told her in a rough whisper. "I've waited two long months, damn it. I'm not waiting any longer."

"What about our luggage?" Eleanor pestered.

"It's being taken care of," Harrison answered. "Quit shaking your head at me, Mary Rose. I meant what I said."

She wasn't going to argue with him in public. She would wait until they were alone to tell him about the decisions she'd made. Harrison was an intelligent man. He would understand how she felt.

"It hasn't been two months," Eleanor announced. She was determined to set Harrison straight. "You two have only been apart five short weeks. Mary Rose wanted to wait until the end of September to make the trip, but Adam wouldn't let her procrastinate that long."

Harrison came to an abrupt stop. "You wanted to wait until the end of September?"

"Now look what you've done, Eleanor. You've gotten him upset. Honestly, Harrison, we'll all get soaked if we don't hurry. We'll talk about this when we reach your home."

Neither Mary Rose nor Harrison said another

word for a long, long while. The rain caught them at the corner, and by the time they were settled inside the carriage, they were all drenched.

They reached Harrison's town house thirty minutes later. It was an impressive two-story home with red brick facade.

The door was opened by a young man dressed in a black coat and trousers. His name was Edward, and he was currently on loan from Lord Elliott to act as Harrison's butler.

Eleanor was thrilled to have a servant attending her. She hurried inside the foyer first. Edward smiled in greeting, but when he turned around to say his hello to Mary Rose, his expression turned to a look of startled surprise.

"She looks like her mother's painting," he whispered to Harrison. "Mi'lord Elliott will have to believe as soon as he sees her. She's the image of Lady Agatha."

Mary Rose overheard Edward's comment. "Lord Elliott doesn't believe I'm his daughter?"

Edward looked embarrassed. "He wants to believe, mi'lady, but there have been so many disappointments in his life, he's afraid to have hope you are truly his Victoria."

Harrison took off his wet jacket and handed it to the young man. He didn't have anything to add to Edward's remarks.

"I simply must have a hot bath," Eleanor insisted. "Edward, be a dear and show me to my bedroom. I'm going to catch a chill if I don't get out of my wet dress."

"You can't catch a cold in July," Mary Rose told her friend. "It's too hot."

"Haven't you ever heard of a summer cold?" Eleanor argued. She then began to list her other aches and pains on her way up the stairs. Mary Rose was happy for the diversion. Each time she looked at Harrison, her heart felt like it was fluttering inside her chest. She wanted to shout at him because he'd hurt her so and kiss him because she'd missed him so much.

Edward hurried on up the stairs to see to Eleanor's comfort. Harrison took hold of Mary Rose's hand and led her down the opposite hallway to his bedroom.

It was gigantic in proportion. The colors were warm, earthy tones of brown and gold and rust. They were the hues of Montana in the autumn months, she thought to herself.

It was impossible for her not to notice the bed. It was quite regal-looking, with four posts, and it was big enough to sleep four people comfortably. She didn't believe she'd ever seen anything so grand.

Her stomach did a flip-flop. She couldn't block the thoughts of Harrison sleeping in the bed, and since he never wore anything when he slept, the images were very provocative.

She could feel herself blushing. She knew she was going to have to talk to Harrison now, before she lost her nerve. Looking at the bed was already making her weak-kneed and weak-willed.

"Harrison, we must have a talk. Now, please."

"He's left the chamber, mi'lady. Shall I have Caroline draw your bath for you?"

She whirled around and found Edward standing in the doorway. "Where did Harrison go?"

"Back downstairs. Did you wish me to go and get him for you?"

She shook her head. "I would like a bath, thank you. Why do you keep calling me mi'lady?"

"Because you're Lady Victoria. It's the proper form of address, mi'lady."

She didn't argue with him. Edward asked her if she also wanted cook to prepare a tray for her. He explained that Eleanor had requested a light meal to be served in her bedroom after she'd had her bath.

Mary Rose declined the food. She was too nervous to even think about eating.

For the next hour she was pampered by her lady's maid. The young woman's deference toward her embarrassed her. She felt as though she were a pretender to the throne each time Caroline called her mi'lady, and though she probably should have enjoyed her pampering, she found the maid only made her more nervous.

The hot bath helped, and taking the confining pins out of her hair made her feel much, much better. She soaked in the porcelain tub a long while, until the water turned too cold for comfort, and then wrapped herself in her robe and returned to Harrison's bedroom.

Caroline spoke very little English. She used gestures and incoherent phrases to explain she wanted to brush Mary Rose's hair for her. The dark-haired woman appeared to be just as nervous as Mary Rose was, for her hands shook and her gestures were awkward as she tried to make herself understood.

Her French accent was quite apparent, and so

Mary Rose spoke French to her when she explained she would brush her own hair. Caroline wouldn't let her mistress decline her assistance, however. She was even more determined than Mary Rose.

The maid kept up a constant chatter while she ushered Mary Rose to a straight-back chair. Mary Rose took her seat and clutched her robe tight over her collarbone while Caroline tended to her hair.

The last time anyone had ever brushed her hair for her was when she was a little girl, and she'd gotten peppermint candy chips stuck in her curls. Cole had had to work the sticky mess out of her hair. Mary Rose had learned a few new curses that day.

No one had ever had to brush her hair for her again. She felt so foolish sitting there like a princess while another woman took care of such a private chore.

The chair faced the bed. Mary Rose noticed one of her nightgowns had been spread out on the sheets. The covers had already been turned back, and there was a single, long-stemmed red rose on one of the pillows.

"Why is there a rose on the bed?" she asked Caroline.

"Your husband ordered it placed there, mi'lady. Wasn't that sweet of him?"

It was sweet, and therefore quite surprising in Mary Rose's estimation. It was such a romantic gesture. It wasn't like Harrison to be so attentive or thoughtful. He really wasn't the romantic sort. When he wanted something, he went after it with a vengeance. He was very like her brothers in that respect. Harrison didn't seem the type to add such an elegant touch, but then, she really didn't know him, now did she?

"Do you know what your husband told Edward when he ordered the rose? He said it was to remind you."

"Remind me of what?"

Caroline laughed. "That he loves you," she suggested. "What else could the flower mean, mi'lady?"

Mary Rose shrugged. She reached up and took hold of the brush. She had had quite enough pampering.

She thanked the maid for her assistance and dismissed her for the night. Caroline made a perfect little curtsy and bowed her head before she left the room. Mary Rose didn't know what to make of that.

She started toward the bed to get her nightgown but stopped when she heard the door open behind her. She turned around just as Harrison walked inside.

Her husband had also had a bath. His hair was still damp. He was barefoot and wore only a pair of dark trousers.

She wondered if he even owned a proper robe. He did like to walk around half-naked, and while that had been perfectly all right in Montana, it wasn't all right in London. There were maids running about, and Mary Rose didn't like the idea of any of those women seeing her husband's bare chest.

She thought about saying something to him

about his lack of attire, then changed her mind. She would take on that issue later. Now she had a more important matter to address.

Harrison shut the door behind him, turned the bolt to lock it, and went to his wife.

He had a determined look on his face. She started backing away. "You and I must have a talk," she began. She put her hand up to ward him off. "I mean it, Harrison. Stop right where you are."

He ignored her command. Mary Rose continued to back up until the side of the bed prevented her from going any farther.

"All right," he agreed. He reached for the belt holding her robe together and began to untie it. "Talk."

She tried to push his hands away. He wouldn't be deterred, however. He had her belt undone before she could draw a proper breath.

"I'm trying real hard not to become angry with you, Mary Rose."

Her eyes widened in disbelief. "What do you have to be angry about?"

"September," he answered in a near shout. "Were you really going to wait until the end of September to come to England?"

She refused to be put on the defensive. "You deliberately lied to me. Leave my robe alone, damn it."

"Then take it off, damn it."

"Do you expect me to sleep with you?"

"I don't expect you to sleep much at all. I'm going to keep you up all night making love to you. I want you, and I know damned good and well you want me."

Tears came into her eyes. "I don't trust you."

"Yes, you do."

She suddenly felt like throwing her hands up in despair. He was making it impossible for her to argue with him. He was deliberately refusing to be logical. She couldn't present a valid argument to a man who was in the process of taking his pants off.

"I've had a long time to think about our situation," she began. "We are married, and because I made a commitment to you, I don't feel it would be right for me to walk away. We're going to have to start all over, Harrison."

"And how to do you propose we do that?"

"You could court me, and in time I'm hopeful I'll eventually learn to trust you again. I don't feel I know you at all, Harrison. The man I loved broke my heart."

Lord, but she was given to dramatics. He heard most of what she said to him. He paid attention too, until she got to the part about courting her. The hell with that, he thought to himself. They had gone way beyond courting days.

He was hard and aching with his need by the time he kicked his trousers aside and reached for her.

"Am I supposed to forget what it felt like to move inside you? I've had you, remember? I've felt you come in my arms, Mary Rose. I've heard you scream my name, felt you squeeze me tight, and if you really believe I can put those memories aside and start all over again, you've got to be out of your ever-loving mind."

She could barely stand up straight by the time he finished reminding her what loving him had been like. The roughness in his voice made her shiver with desire to feel his touch once again.

"What do you suggest we do?"

"Come here and I'll show you."

She shook her head. She knew exactly what would happen if she moved into his arms. She wanted to reach some sort of understanding before she gave in to her own needs.

She kept her gaze directed on his face. "Tell me first."

He grabbed hold of her shoulders. "No, you tell me something first. Do you still love me?"

She lowered her gaze to his chest. She didn't want to start lying to him, even though she knew full well the truth would mean she would lose the argument.

"You broke my heart," she told him once again.

"I warned you, remember?"

"You should have told me about my father."

"No, the duty belonged to your brothers. It would have been wrong for me to tell you."

"Then why weren't you with them when they told me? It would have made it easier for me."

"I was in Hammond defending a man in court when your brothers finally got around to telling you, and when I came back to the ranch, you'd disappeared. Damn it, Mary Rose, you shouldn't have run away from me. I'm your husband."

Considering the fact that she'd thought about killing him, she believed running away was a minor infraction in the rules governing marriage.

"I was extremely angry with you."

He shrugged. It wasn't the reaction she'd hoped to gain. "Where did you go?" he asked.

"Douglas took me to the Cohens' house. I stayed with the family for two weeks. Are you sorry you hurt me?"

She was hoping for an apology. She didn't know if it would help her get over her heartache, but she believed it might.

"I did what was necessary under the circumstances. In time you'll realize that."

"Do you love me?"

"Yes, I love you."

He pulled her up tight against him. "Can we please hold each other now?"

He put his arms around her and leaned down. He kissed her brow, the bridge of her nose, whispering all the while how much he'd missed her.

He pulled back, removed her robe, and then lifted her into his arms and fell onto the bed.

He was careful not to crush her with his weight, and once his body completely covered hers, he braced himself on his arms so he could look down into her eyes.

There were tears streaming down her cheeks. "Do you want me to leave you, Mary Rose?"

She shook her head, and he began to breathe again. And then she leaned up and kissed him.

His mouth settled firmly on top of hers, but her tongue moved inside to explore the interior of his mouth first. The bold action aroused him as much as the feel of her silky body against him. She stroked his back and his shoulders, and made him shake with his own need in the space of a heartbeat.

He wanted to slow their lovemaking, to pleasure her completely before he gave in to his own fulfillment, but her touch soon drove him beyond reason. She was so wonderfully responsive and giving, and, dear God, how he loved her.

He ended the kiss and lowered his head over her breasts. He began to stroke and tease her nipples with his tongue. She let out a ragged sigh of pleasure, urging him now, and when he took one nipple into his mouth and began to suckle, her sighs turned to moans. She arched up against him, moved her toes restlessly against his legs, and tried to get even closer to him.

His touch became rougher, less controlled. His hand caressed a path down her belly and lower still, until he found what he most wanted to possess. He felt the damp heat between her thighs and completely lost his discipline then. His fingers moved up inside her.

Mary Rose raked her nails across his shoulders, demanding now that he stop his torment and mate with her completely.

He didn't move quickly enough to suit her. She reached down and took hold of his arousal, and with her fingers closed around him, he let out a low growl of pleasure.

There could be no more waiting. He grabbed hold of her hands and roughly put them around his back as he moved to position himself. And then he entered her with one smooth thrust.

His jaw was clenched tight, for the rush of ecstasy was almost too much for him to bear.

"God, you feel good," he whispered. "Don't move like that, not yet. Let me, ah, sweetheart, you're making me want to . . ."

He couldn't go on. She had robbed him of the ability to talk at all. He was beyond thinking now, could only feel the incredible bliss of her hips moving against him. She drew her legs up to take him more completely inside her and wrapped her arms around his neck. She craved fulfillment now, for each time he thrust deep inside her, she felt a burst of splendor rush through her. His slow penetrating movements made her demand more and more until she was mindless of everything but the feel of him delving inside her. She pulled on his hair and scored the back of his neck with her nails. Her whimpers became more insistent and drove him over the edge. His thrusts became harder, deeper, and when he felt the first spasms of her orgasm, when she arched up against him and squeezed him tight inside her, he allowed his own release. He shouted her name as wave after wave of excruciating pleasure washed over him.

She felt the splendor explode inside her. There was only a second or two of fear before she gave in to the feeling and allowed it to consume her. She clung to her husband, knowing in her heart that he would keep her safe.

It took her long minutes to return to reality. Harrison held her close and stroked her. He whispered loving, nonsensical words against her ear that she thought were perfectly logical, for he was letting her know without any doubt how much he had missed her.

She fell asleep with her husband nibbling on her earlobe but was awakened an hour later by his caresses. They made love once again during the dark hours of the night, and then yet again as the sun was beginning its ritualistic climb into the sky.

Each time she gave herself willingly to him, and when she began to come apart in his arms, she was filled with a sense of wonder because she felt so completely safe with him.

She loved Harrison with all her heart. She would be an understanding wife and learn to forgive him for deceiving her. In time she would be able to trust him again.

She fell asleep praying that was true.

Dear Mama:

Today I found out all about how babies get made. Adam told me exactly what happens between a man and a lady. He said I shouldn't scrunch up my face and look so disgusted, but it's hard not to feel sick inside, Mama. It makes me want to puke when I think about a man trying to climb up on top of me.

Travis and Douglas think making babies is disgusting too. They didn't say so, but they couldn't look at me when they tried to explain how it happens. They both got red faces too. I don't think they will ever want to climb up on any ladies. I don't know what Cole thinks about it though. He got mad at me for asking him to explain and then he sent me to Adam.

Your son told me that mating between a man and a woman was beautiful. I think he was just teasing me. What do you think about making babies, Mama? You had Adam, so I know you had to have his papa on top of you once. Was it sickening?

Cole's putting the finishing touches on the ceiling of the library of our fine home. He's so particular about his cut work on the mouldings. He works almost every night, and I know he wishes he could work on the house during the days too, but he can't because

Douglas needs his help breaking in the horses.

I had to give another swatch of my hair to the Indians again. They're very nice to me now and don't try to steal me away from Adam. They're still scared of him. Adam gives them food and tries to be polite, but I don't think he trusts them. He still hasn't forgotten what almost happened when those renegades tried to take me.

The Indians think I bring them good fortune. Isn't that silly, Mama?

Why don't you hate Livonia? Sometimes I think you should. I know she's afraid and she depends on you, but I was thinking, maybe if you're mean to her, she'll let you go.

I miss you sorely,
Mary Rose

18

$\mathcal{M}$ary Rose was nervous about meeting her father. She didn't understand her own reaction. She had nothing to fear from the man. He was a stranger to her, and she would be polite and kind and compassionate to him. Lord Elliott had suffered a terrible loss, she reminded herself once again, and, just as her brothers had suggested, it was her duty to try to comfort him.

Harrison had awakened her with the news that Elliott wanted them to move into his country home with him for an undetermined length of time.

She'd started in worrying then. She thought perhaps some of her fear was due to the fact that she knew absolutely nothing of consequence about him. Harrison had told her he was rich and he was intelligent. Neither defined in her mind what the man was really like, however. Wealth meant little to her, and while hearing that her father was intelligent pleased her, it was still all too vague for her liking. She didn't know anything about his values or his attitudes.

She plied Harrison with questions on their way to Elliott's estate.

"You explained that those who could afford to left the city during the summer months, but you didn't explain why," she began.

"It's too hot in the city. Everything sort of

shuts down until September."

She folded her hands in her lap. "I don't understand why we couldn't wait for Eleanor. Didn't you want her to accompany us today?"

"Sweetheart, she wouldn't get out of bed, remember? She'll follow us tomorrow, with Edward and the rest of the staff."

"How long does Lord Elliott expect us to stay with him?"

"For as long as you wish to stay."

He stretched out his long legs in front of him and tried to act relaxed. He knew his wife was nervous. She was wringing her hands together now, but he doubted she realized what she was doing.

She'd had difficulty deciding on a dress to wear too, and such behavior wasn't like her at all. She wasn't one to worry about her appearance, but she'd been concerned this morning, and he thought he understood why.

She didn't want to disappoint her father. "He's going to love you, sweetheart."

She lifted her shoulders in a shrug. "Will I like him?" she asked.

Harrison seemed surprised by her question. He suddenly leaned forward and took hold of her hands. "Yes, you'll like him. You're going to have to . . ."

She waited for him to continue, and when he didn't, she prodded him. "I'll have to what?"

He let out a sigh. "I was going to tell you to trust me, but that's a sore point with you, isn't it?"

She looked down at her hands. "I don't wish

to talk about trust now. You broke my heart, Harrison."

"So you've said," he replied dryly.

She looked up at him so he could see her disgruntled expression. He shook his head at her.

"You really do hold a grudge, don't you? If you'd use that logical head of yours, you'd realize . . ."

"I'd realize you could have told me but you chose not to, that's what I'd realize," she whispered. She pulled her hands away from his. "I shouldn't have worn this blue dress. It makes me look pale."

"You look fine."

"I don't want to look fine."

"England is beautiful, isn't it?" he remarked, hoping to change the subject.

"Yes, it is," she agreed. "The countryside is lovely. It isn't home though."

"Give yourself time to adjust to the changes, Mary Rose."

"I miss my brothers."

"Did you miss me after I left?"

She wouldn't answer him. He leaned back again and turned to look out the window. It had been drizzling when they left the city, but the sun was out now, and it was turning into a glorious day.

"We'll be early," he said. "Your father doesn't expect us until around four this afternoon. We'll reach his estate before noon."

"Is it true everyone sleeps in and stays up half the night?"

Harrison nodded. "It's true. Are you tired

today? I kept you up most of last night."

She immediately started to blush. "No, I'm not tired."

He grinned. "I am. Your body's forgiven me."

"You aren't making any sense, Harrison."

She looked flustered. He thought it was a telling reaction. "You can't help the way you respond to me, can you? Do you remember how you . . ."

"I was there," she blurted out. "You don't have to remind me of what happened between us. Please tell me how Lord Elliott reacted when he heard about me. I'm most curious."

"You're deliberately changing the subject. I'd rather talk about the way you felt in my arms last night."

"For the love of God, will you answer my question and stop this talk about lovemaking?"

"He didn't believe me."

"Who?"

Harrison laughed. She was rattled all right, and that realization made him feel an immense amount of pleasure.

"Your father," he explained.

She let out a sigh. Then she picked up her fan, unfolded it, and began to wave it in front of her face.

"I spent several hours convincing him," Harrison told her. "He's afraid to believe, Mary Rose. Want to sit on my lap?"

"No, I don't want to sit on your lap."

"I want to kiss you."

"You can't. I'll get all mussed."

Harrison had his way. Before she could even think about pushing him away, he lifted her across the seat and settled her on his lap. For comfort's sake, she put one arm around his shoulders, even as she glared at him for ignoring her decision to be left alone.

"I don't like your hair pinned up like that."

"Do you know why I'm glad you didn't cut your hair?"

"Why?"

She began to stroke the back of his neck, letting his silky hair thread through her fingers.

"You look more like a mountain man now and not so much like a refined Englishman."

He was kissing the side of her neck. She felt the shivers all the way down to her toes. She let out a soft sigh and tilted her head back to give him better access.

She thought she knew why he was becoming so amorous. He'd guessed she was worried and was trying to take her mind off her father.

It was certainly working. His warm breath against her ear aroused her, and all she wanted to think about was getting a proper kiss from him.

She didn't like being manipulated, however, and she thought she'd tell him just that after he'd finished kissing her.

"How come you always smell so good, sweetheart?"

"I take baths," she answered.

He laughed as he cupped her chin in his hand and turned her toward him.

And then he gave her a proper kiss. His mouth was warm and hard as it settled possessively on top of hers. His tongue moved inside to tease and taste, and it wasn't long at all before Mary Rose stopped worrying about everything but kissing him back.

He couldn't keep up the tender love play long. One kiss made him want it all. In no time at all, he was hard and aching to be inside her.

He pulled back from her and let his forehead drop down on top of hers. "Honest to God, Mary Rose, it isn't possible for me to kiss you without wanting to tear your clothes off and make love to you. Stop it now, sweetheart. Don't provoke me."

Mary Rose was kissing his neck and feeling incredibly powerful because of his reaction to her touch. His breathing was ragged, and he visibly shuddered.

She let out another little sigh of pleasure. She leaned up and kissed his chin. He told her to behave herself. She ignored the suggestion and stroked his lower lip with her tongue.

He growled low in his throat and tightened his hold around her waist. He was through trying to behave like a gentleman. He gave her a hot, wet, open-mouth kiss and then another and another. Mary Rose soon forgot where they were. She kept trying to get closer to her husband, to feel just a little more of his heat against her, and her restless movements in his lap made his own control vanish.

Making love to his wife seemed like a sound idea to him, and he didn't care at all that they were inside a moving vehicle. He wanted her, and she wanted him. Nothing else mattered.

She finally came to her senses when she felt

his hand on her thigh. How he'd managed to get under her skirts was beyond her.

"What in heaven's name are we doing?" she whispered in a voice that trembled with her need. "We're in a carriage, Harrison. What could you be thinking?"

"We're married. It's all right. We can make love wherever we want to."

It sounded logical to him. Mary Rose pulled his hands away from her and moved back to the opposite seat. Her hand shook when she reached up to secure the pins in her hair, and it was only then that she realized her curls were hanging down around her shoulders.

Harrison was responsible for her disheveled appearance. She gave him a good frown as she threaded her fingers through the mass and tried to make the curls behave.

"You look beautiful."

The way he looked at her told her he believed she was beautiful. She quit trying to improve on her appearance then.

"Lust has made you blind," she told him.

"We're here. The gate we just passed is the entrance to your father's estate. He has over a hundred acres."

She took a deep breath. "Was he happy to hear you married me?"

"He was," Harrison replied. "But he was also disappointed he missed the ceremony. He wants to have another one."

Her eyes widened. "I don't believe that's necessary."

"He does," Harrison told her. "You can discuss

it with him, after you've gotten to know him. Sweetheart, quit gripping your hands together. It's going to be all right. Just lean on me if you get scared."

"I'm perfectly capable of standing on my own two feet. My father doesn't frighten me."

It was all bluster on her part. Harrison wasn't going to argue with his wife though. If she wanted him to believe she wasn't scared, he'd pretend to believe her.

"Will the relatives be there too? Oh, Lord, Harrison, his house is huge. How many bedrooms are there?"

"Twelve, I think. I'm not certain. The relatives are scheduled to arrive late today."

"What time is it now?"

"Not quite eleven," he answered after he checked his pocket watch.

The carriage rounded a corner and then began the climb up to a circle drive in front of a large white home Mary Rose thought looked very like a palace. There were flowers everywhere and carefully manicured lawns with shrubs shaped into perfect lines.

There were tall stone lions on either side of the steps leading up to the front door. The stairs were red brick. She thought they must have cost a fortune to ship into England and then realized they were probably made somewhere around the city. Everything had to be shipped by rail and then by wagon into Blue Belle, but her father's home was only a short ride from a major city. It was completely different here. She would have to remember that, she thought to herself.

Harrison helped her out of the carriage. They walked side by side up the steps. The front door was black, with an oblong gold knocker in the very center. Two large white planter boxes were on either side of the entrance, and were filled with spring flowers in every color of the rainbow. Thick vines of lime green ivy trailed down the sides.

Mary Rose moved closer to Harrison as he reached up and knocked on the door. It was opened less than five seconds later by a thick-shouldered man named Russell. He bowed low and then hastily moved back to allow them entrance.

His reaction to the sight of her was similar to the reaction of the butler she'd met in Harrison's town house. Russell looked just as startled as Edward had been.

"Yes, Russell, my wife does resemble Lady Agatha," Harrison said before the servant could gather his wits and make the comment.

The elderly man's eyes crinkled up in a smile. "She gave me quite a start, mi'lord," he admitted in a whisper.

Mary Rose barely paid attention to the conversation. She stood in the center of the foyer and stared about her in wonder. The entrance was every bit as impressive as the outside of the house. The floor was covered with squares of black and white marble, and its area alone was as large as Mary Rose's entire house back home. There was a grand circular staircase in front of her. Hanging low from a ceiling at least three floors high was a magnificent crystal chandelier.

There were over fifty candles in the sparkling fixture, and Mary Rose couldn't imagine how anyone could reach that high to light them.

"Where's Lord Elliott?" Harrison asked. "Has he come downstairs yet today, or is he working in the library?"

"I'm not certain where he is at the moment, mi'lord. He wasn't expecting you until late this afternoon. Would you like to go upstairs and wait in the library while I search for him?"

Harrison shook his head. "It's too fine a day to stay inside. We'll go on out back and wait in the garden."

He pulled Mary Rose along after him. They went through another gigantic room she thought was probably called a salon or a parlor. There were two large sitting areas with settees facing each other, a gigantic marble-faced fireplace, and several round-backed chairs and small wooden tables with glass tops.

The fabric on all of the furniture was a rich ivory brocade. Mary Rose stopped to admire the room. She didn't believe she'd ever seen anything so extravagant.

Harrison watched her. "What are you thinking? You look puzzled about something," he remarked.

"It isn't practical," she whispered so she wouldn't be overheard by the staff. "A day's worth of dust coming in through the windows would ruin the cloth. Who would put white on their chairs?"

"Do you like it?"

"Oh, yes, but I wouldn't dare sit on such fine chairs. I might put a smudge on one of them."

Harrison suddenly wanted to take her into his arms and kiss her. She was so wonderfully unspoiled.

"Shall we go on outside?" He took hold of her hand again and pulled her along to a pair of French doors. There was a wide stone courtyard beyond, surrounded by a three-foot-high brick wall. The courtyard overlooked a garden to rival all the pictures she'd seen of gardens owned by kings.

Harrison pushed the doors open and followed her outside. "Your father likes flowers," he remarked. "He told me once that when he has a particular puzzle to solve, he goes outside and pulls weeds. He's figured out how to win many a legal case while he was down on his knees. Your father surrounds himself with riches, but it's the simple things in life he most enjoys."

Mary Rose nodded, but didn't comment on Harrison's explanation. He directed her to a cluster of chairs with yellow cushions and suggested she sit down and relax while he went to help Russell locate her father.

"Shouldn't we take our luggage upstairs and unpack our clothes? My dresses are going to be wrinkled if I don't hang them up right away."

"Staff will take care of our luggage."

She sat down and folded her hands in her lap. "Yes, of course," she agreed.

She'd forgotten about all the servants Lord Elliott employed. Harrison had rattled off at least a dozen names of men and women who worked for her father. She couldn't imagine having so many people attending to her needs. She was used to doing for herself, and she wasn't at all certain she would be able to adapt to the change very well.

Harrison leaned down and kissed her brow before going back inside. She was too nervous to sit still long. She didn't have the faintest idea what she would say to her father when she finally came face to face with him, and it had become extremely important to her that she find just the right words. She didn't want to disappoint him. He had searched for her most of her life, and a simple "Nice to meet you" didn't seem appropriate.

Mary Rose decided to walk along the stone path that led throughout the garden, hoping the leisurely stroll would help her calm her racing heartbeat and organize her thoughts.

She turned the first corner and was suddenly surrounded by the fragrance of summer. There were flowers all around her. The mingling of the scents reminded her of her valley back home, and though it didn't make much sense to her, she could feel herself begin to relax a little. She took a deep breath, clasped her hands behind her back, and continued on. She stopped several times to lean down and examine more closely a flower she didn't recognize. One she found most curious. The flower had red and pink petals that reminded her of a rose, yet when she bent down to inhale the scent, she was surprised by the heavy aroma of lilacs.

Being alone in the beautiful garden soothed her. She was pleased to know Lord Elliott liked the outdoors, and she thought that the two of them had something in common after all to talk about. She could tell him about her garden back home, and he could name all the flowers in his backyard paradise for her.

She straightened up and continued on along the path, and when she turned the next corner, she spotted an elderly man, bent down on one knee, carefully examining a flower. The man wasn't dressed like a gardener, for he wore dark Sunday pants and a sparkling white shirt. He'd rolled the sleeves up to his elbows. Mary Rose couldn't see his face because he wore a straw hat with a wide brim pulled down low on his forehead.

She thought he might be her father, but she couldn't be certain, of course, and she didn't know quite how to proceed. She almost turned around to hurry back to the courtyard, then changed her mind and continued forward.

Elliott heard the rustle of skirts behind him and assumed one of the maids had come outside to see if she could be of assistance. He reached over to his side, pulled the basket he'd already filled with flowers, and lifted it up for the maid to take.

"My daughter might like to have more than one vase of fresh flowers in her room," he explained.

He still hadn't looked up at her. Mary Rose took hold of the handle of the basket in her left hand, looped it over her arm, and continued to stand there, feeling completely tongue-tied and foolish.

Elliott didn't seem to notice she hadn't immediately taken the flowers inside. She patiently waited for him to look up at her. She thought she would probably begin the conversation by introducing herself, and, Lord, how she prayed her voice wouldn't betray her nervousness.

"I wonder if my Victoria likes flowers," he remarked.

She took a deep breath. "I like them very much, Father."

Elliott went completely still for what seemed an eternity to her, and then he slowly turned to look up.

His breath got trapped in the back of his throat and his heart felt as though it were going to explode into a thousand fragments. The first sight of his Victoria proved to be too much for him. Sunlight surrounded her golden head, giving her a mystical appearance, and for a brief moment, he thought his beloved Agatha had come down from heaven to be with him again.

She was her mother's daughter. Victoria had finally come home. Elliott couldn't catch his breath or his balance. He felt himself reeling to the side and would have fallen to the ground had she not reached down to offer him her hand.

He grasped hold of it as if it were a lifeline and held tight. And still he continued to stare up at her with a look of wonder in his gaze.

She smiled at him, a soft, beckoning smile so very like her mother's, and then she began to blur in his vision, and he realized he was weeping silent tears.

Mary Rose helped him stand up. She wanted to put her arm around his waist to steady him, but he wouldn't let go of her hand long enough to allow her to assist him.

His straw hat had fallen to the ground. She stared up at her father and thought to herself that he was indeed a handsome man, given his advanced age. In the sunlight his hair sparkled silver. He had high cheekbones and a nice, straight nose. The way he stood, so noble and proud, like a statesman or an orator, reminded her of her brother Adam, and she thought that if their skin color were more similar in tone, people would mistake them for relatives. Her brother had the blood of his chieftain ancestors coursing through his veins, and that was why he stood so proud. Did Lord Elliott come from such fine ancestors too? She would have to remember to ask him one day. Now it didn't seem appropriate.

Father and daughter continued to stare at one another for several more seconds. Elliott was valiantly trying to compose himself. He extracted a linen handkerchief from his pocket and wiped the tears away from his face.

And then he gave a brisk nod, squeezed her hand tight, and nodded once again.

The two of them turned and walked hand in hand back to the house. His voice was rough with emotion when he finally spoke to her.

"I'm very pleased to have you back home with me."

She nodded so he would know she understood and then tried to think of something to say to him in return.

She wanted to be completely honest with him,

but kind too, and so she simply spoke from her heart.

"Father?"

"Yes, Victoria?"

"I'm pleased to know you didn't throw me away."

Lord Elliott's younger sister, Lillian, was the first of the family members to arrive for the reunion with Lady Victoria.

Of all the relatives, Lillian had been the most difficult to convince that her brother's daughter had truly been found. She had suffered all the disappointments along with Lord Elliott, had seen the anguish each pretender had caused, and worried that this too would end in yet another cruel deception.

The proof had been indisputable, of course, and yet Lillian still withheld judgment. She would decide for herself if Mary Rose Clayborne were Victoria or just a schemer out for financial gain.

"William, whatever are you doing sitting out here in the heat?" she asked as she rushed outside. "You're going to become ill if you aren't more careful."

Harrison, Lord Elliott, and Mary Rose all stood up when Lillian walked toward them. Her aunt kept her gaze fully directed on Mary Rose.

"She does look like Agatha all right," she allowed. "The resemblance is quite remarkable."

Elliott formally presented his daughter to his sister. Mary Rose smiled. She didn't know if she were supposed to bow or curtsy or shake her hand, and so she simply stood there and waited

619

for Lillian to give her some clue as to what was proper conduct.

Lillian didn't look like her brother. She barely reached his shoulders. She was a thin woman with a hawkish nose and dark brown hair. She had the same high cheekbones though. Lillian would have been a more attractive woman if she didn't wear such drab colors. She was dressed in a dark gray dress that made her complexion look terribly pale. If she pinched her cheeks real hard, she might achieve a bit of color.

She also needed to quit scowling. She was all but openly glaring at Mary Rose.

"What is your name, child?" she demanded. She clasped her hands together as though in prayer while she waited for her answer.

"My name is Mary Rose Clayborne."

"She doesn't call herself Lady Victoria," Lillian remarked to her brother. "I wonder why not."

Mary Rose answered her. "I've always been called Mary Rose for as long as I can remember, madam. The name Victoria has no meaning to me."

Lillian was taken aback by the young woman's directness. Her frown intensified. "You look like my brother's late wife, but I'm still not fully convinced you're his daughter. Do you wish to try to convince me, child?"

Mary Rose decided to be completely honest, no matter how rude it made her appear.

"No, madam, I don't wish to try to convince you. I do, however, fervently wish you wouldn't call me a child. I'm not, you know."

"Lord, she's impertinent, William."

Mary Rose didn't know what to say about that. Her father came to her rescue. "She was being truthful, not impertinent."

Lillian nodded. "What are your plans?" she asked.

"Oh, for heaven's sake, Lillian. My daughter only just arrived. We needn't talk about plans now. Sit down and quit pestering her."

"I simply wanted to get to the root of this as soon as possible."

"The root of what, madam?" Mary Rose asked.

Lillian took a step toward her. "Finding out if you're really Victoria. Let me have my say, William, and then I'll keep quiet no matter what you do. Are you Lady Victoria?" she pressed again.

"They say that I am," Mary Rose answered. "For my father's sake, I would like it to be true. I would like to give him some peace, and I understand he's been looking for me for a long, long time."

"And for your sake?"

Mary Rose didn't understand what she was asking. She looked up at Harrison, then returned her attention to Lillian. "I would like to spend a few weeks with my father, and then I will return home."

"It's far too soon to know what your plans are," her father interjected. He patted her hand. "You might wish to stay on here with me."

She didn't want to deceive him with false hopes. "I have four brothers back home. I must go back, Father."

"We'll discuss this later," he decided. "You need time to get to know all of us first. Lillian's the most difficult member of your family, my dear. You can see you've left her speechless. I must confess I didn't believe anyone could rattle my sister, but you certainly have."

Mary Rose was thoroughly confused. "I didn't mean to rattle you, madam."

"Harrison, doesn't she understand her father's worth?" Lillian asked.

"No, she doesn't understand," he replied. "Her values are different from those of the young women in England."

"Shall we go into the drawing room?" Lord Elliott suggested. "My sister looks in need of a refreshment."

"You and Harrison go on ahead. I want to have a word in private with my niece."

"I won't have you bullying her, Lillian."

"She won't bully me, Father."

Harrison didn't want to leave his wife with Lillian either. He knew how abrasive Elliott's sister could be. He didn't want Mary Rose upset, and if there'd been time, he would have taken her aside and explained that Lillian was all bark and little bite. She had a good heart. She just made certain no one knew about it.

"My daughter and I have been apart too long. Sorry, Lillian, but I must insist we all go inside together."

"We'll be along in just a minute, Father," Mary Rose said. "I also wish to have a private word with my aunt."

She didn't wait to gain the men's permission.

She sat down again and suggested Lillian also take a seat.

Both women waited until they were alone. "Shall I start or would you like to, Aunt Lillian?"

"I shall start first," her aunt insisted. "Age has its benefits," she added with a smile. "I would like to trust your intentions, my dear, but I find it difficult. Yes, I've heard all the proof your husband has collected, and while it should seem to be positive that you are indeed our Victoria, I still have my doubts. I can certainly understand why you would wish to be my brother's heir."

"You can? Will you tell me why you believe I would wish to be Victoria?"

"Why, the position, the wealth, the . . ."

She was still so surprised by the question, she could barely gather her wits.

"I could give you just as many reasons why I wouldn't wish to be your niece. Being someone else certainly complicates my life, madam. I have a family in Montana. Is it selfish of me to be homesick?"

"Do you come from a wealthy family?"

"Yes, I believe I do. I have everything I could ever want."

"Are the members of this family as wealthy as your father?"

"I'm not certain," Mary Rose answered. "It's a different way of life, and a different kind of wealth," she tried to explain. "Why don't you want me to be Victoria?"

Lillian stared at Mary Rose for a long moment and then whispered, "You have your grandmother's eyes."

"My grandmother?"

Lillian nodded. A smile softened her expression. "I never heard Agatha say an unkind word about anyone, least of all her own mother. Your grandmother was a mean old bat, but she did have pretty blue eyes. Agatha is probably rolling over in her grave because I'm talking ill about her mother, but I'm speaking only the truth. She really was difficult to be around."

Mary Rose burst into laughter. Lillian looked extremely prim, but her remarks weren't at all proper.

"I don't want to see my brother hurt again."

"I will try not to hurt him," Mary Rose promised. "I want only to get to know him and then return to my home. I would correspond with him, of course, and hopefully one day he would wish to come and see me. I would like him to meet my brothers."

Lillian didn't know what to make of her. "Don't you realize what your father could give you?"

"Yes, I know exactly what he could give me. A father's love. I will protect his heart. And I will try to love him just the way a daughter should love her father. I haven't had any practice, but I'll learn."

"My dear, you're now a married woman, and therefore you are under your husband's control. Harrison's home is in England. Surely you realize you must stay here with him."

She didn't realize any such thing. She wasn't about to share her views with Lillian though.

"Are you married, Aunt Lillian?"

"I was. My dear Kenneth passed on five years

ago. We weren't blessed with children."

"I'm sorry for your loss," Mary Rose said.

"I keep busy. I have my charity projects and of course the family requires a great deal of my time and attention. Robert has seven children. They're always getting in trouble. Barbara's a sweet woman, but she can't control her brood. They have six girls and one boy," she added with a nod. "You will meet all of them in another hour or two."

"Who are Robert and Barbara?"

"They're your uncle and aunt. William, your father, is the first-born, then I came along, then Daniel, and finally Robert. Barbara's his wife. Do you have a more suitable dress to put on before we dine, my dear?"

Mary Rose looked down at her skirts. She didn't see any smudges or wrinkles that were overly noticeable. "Is something wrong with this dress?"

"It's hopelessly old-fashioned."

"I paid a bloody fortune for the material," she argued.

Lillian let out a loud gasp. Her hand went to the base of her throat. "You mustn't talk like that, Victoria. One simply doesn't use the word 'bloody' unless one is common. We'll have to start work on improving your manners immediately. We have so much to do before you're presented to society. You mustn't forget who your father is."

She wasn't certain what her aunt was telling her, but the intense look on her face indicated it was important.

"No, I won't forget who my father is," she

625

agreed. "Why haven't you remarried, Aunt Lillian? You're such a pretty woman. If you lived in Montana, you would have been pursued by at least ten men before your dearly departed was even in the ground."

"Good heavens, child. Don't be impertinent."

"I'm not being impertinent," Mary Rose countered. "Just honest."

Lillian reached up to make certain her bun was intact, then stood up. "You'll have to remember to keep your opinions to yourself, Victoria. You're bound to shock people if you say what's on your mind."

It suddenly occurred to Mary Rose that Lillian was accepting her as her brother's child.

"You couldn't have changed your mind so quickly, madam," she remarked.

"The proof's difficult to argue with, but I shall reserve judgment. I'm giving you the benefit of my doubts, my dear."

"Why?"

"It's rude to ask so many questions, Victoria. Come along inside. Your father and your husband have waited long enough for your company."

"I have a favor to ask of you first."

Lillian turned back to her niece. "Yes?"

"Please call me Mary Rose."

"But you aren't Mary Rose any longer, now, are you? You're Victoria. You're going to have to get used to hearing your name."

She latched on to Mary Rose's arm and pulled her along. "I understand your friend will be joining you tomorrow. What is her name?"

"Her name is Eleanor," Mary Rose explained.

"I believe you'll like her, Aunt Lillian. Her manners are better than mine."

"We shall see about that," Lillian replied.

Mary Rose followed her aunt inside the salon. Neither Harrison nor her father noticed her. They were in the midst of a heated debate.

"They want you to have this money, sir. I believe you should take it," Harrison said.

He stood in front of the hearth with his back to his bride. Mary Rose walked over to her husband and stood next to his side.

"I will not take it," Lord Elliott announced for the third time. "Send it back to them, Harrison."

Harrison shook his head. Mary Rose brushed her arm against his. He immediately took hold of her hand.

"Are you talking about the money my brothers sent?" she asked.

"Yes," Harrison answered. "Your father doesn't want it back."

Lord Elliott was sitting in a wing chair adjacent to the hearth. Mary Rose turned to him.

"It would please my brothers if you would take the money back, Father."

The look on Elliott's face indicated he was going to be stubborn about it. He started to say something to her, then changed his mind and turned to his sister for assistance.

Lillian immediately hurried forward. "You shouldn't involve yourself in this discussion, Victoria. Let the men sort it all out. Shall we go upstairs and look through your clothes? I'm sure we'll be able to find something a little more suitable for you to wear tonight."

Mary Rose heard Harrison sigh. He squeezed her hand and looked down at her. "Go ahead, sweetheart. We'll talk about this later."

She'd been properly dismissed. If she'd been back home, she would have argued something fierce about being excluded from "men's talk," but she wasn't home now. She was in England. The rules weren't at all the same here, and she was suddenly feeling unsure of herself. She had promised her brothers she would try to get along with all of her relatives, and so she meekly followed her aunt out of the room. She paused at the entrance to give Harrison a good frown just to let him know what she thought about being excluded, but his reaction wasn't at all sympathetic. He actually winked at her, and that only pricked her temper all the more. She let out a sigh then and went on up the stairs. She would have to wait until later to let Harrison know how she felt.

She spent the next hour arguing with her aunt Lillian about her wardrobe. The woman seemed obsessed with clothes. Mary Rose found her behavior puzzling. She thought it was ridiculous that Lillian couldn't find anything suitable for her to wear. Why, she showed her eight perfectly lovely day dresses. Lillian looked them over, then shook her head. In a haughty tone of voice, she emphatically rejected every single one of them.

Mary Rose tried not to let her feelings get involved. Things were different here, she reminded herself. Still, she had personally chosen the fabric and the style of two of the dresses her aunt had found so distasteful. She couldn't help but feel a little embarrassed.

She ended up keeping her blue dress on. Lillian went back downstairs to send a messenger to a dressmaker.

She paused in the doorway. "Tomorrow, after you've had your examination by the physicians my brother has scheduled, you and I will go over fabrics and begin to build your wardrobe."

"I don't need to see a doctor," Mary Rose protested. "I feel fine, really."

"Don't be difficult, Victoria. It's for your own good. I shall make certain you're seated next to me at the table tonight so that I can assist you with your table manners. You may rest now for an hour, and then come downstairs. Robert and his family should be here by then."

"Aunt Lillian? You mentioned another brother, Daniel. Will he be visiting?"

"Daniel and his wife are in the south of France. They'll be back home in another week or two. You'll meet him then. His wife's name is Johanna. They have three children, all fine boys. Have your nap now, Victoria. I'll send Ann Marie in to assist you."

Mary Rose didn't ask why she needed a maid to help her rest. Lillian would only tell her she was being impertinent again. She didn't argue about taking a nap either, though she couldn't imagine why anyone would want to sleep during the day. She wasn't at all tired, but, Lord, she was weary. There were so many names to remember, and so many rules she must try to obey.

How in heaven's name was she going to meet

everyone's expectations? Mary Rose had never run away from a challenge, and she wasn't about to start now. She decided she would do whatever was required to please her relatives.

Ann Marie came into the room to help her remove her dress, then turned back the covers on the bed. Mary Rose was really expected to rest, she supposed, when the young servant pulled the drapes closed.

The room was quite spacious and was done in rich gold tones. She found it quite soothing. She stretched out on the bed wearing only her chemise and stacked her hands behind her head. She stared up at the ceiling while she tried to sort out her feelings.

She thought about her father and what a kind man he was. She liked the way he smiled. She liked his voice too. It was soft, yet commanding. When she wrote to her brothers she would tell them Lord Elliott was a very nice man.

Harrison came inside just a few minutes later.

"Your father's being stubborn," he told his wife. "He seems to think the money your brothers sent should go right back to them. He called it payment for letting you live with them. He doesn't understand, of course."

Mary Rose rolled onto her side so she could look at her husband. "He didn't like it when I mentioned my brothers. I could tell by the way he looked at me. He seemed . . . disappointed."

"Give him time to get used to the idea of you having another family," Harrison suggested.

"Did you know I must have an examination tomorrow by two physicians?"

Harrison took off his jacket, tossed it on a nearby chair, and then sat down on the side of the bed. He bent over to take his shoes and socks off. "Your father mentioned it to me," he remarked.

"Why must I be examined? I feel fine."

"The doctors will give your father the assurance he seems to need. It can't do any harm, can it? I'll put a stop to it if you really don't want to be looked over."

She thought about it for a minute and then decided to appease her father. Her husband was right, she supposed. There couldn't be any harm in being examined.

"It's a waste of good money," she said in a halfhearted attempt to protest. "But I'll go along with his plans. You haven't asked me what I think of my father. Aren't you curious?"

He half turned to smile at her. "I already know what you think. You're curious about him, of course. I've noticed the way you stare at him when he isn't looking at you. You already like him, and I think you'd like to love him."

She nodded. Harrison was as observant as ever. "I'm his daughter. I should love him, shouldn't I?"

"Yes."

"Can I trust him?"

He was surprised by the question. "Yes," he answered. "You can trust him. You can trust me too, you know."

She didn't want to talk about that. She tried to change the subject then, but Harrison wouldn't let her.

"I realize I shouldn't have demanded you trust me. It was probably a little arrogant of me."

"Probably?"

"You haven't figured it all out yet, have you?"

"Figured what out?"

"That love and trust go hand in hand. You couldn't love me if you didn't trust me. And you do love me, don't you?"

She didn't answer him. The issue of trust was still tender for her to talk about. Harrison had hurt her by deliberately deceiving her. She understood why he'd kept silent about his reason for coming to her ranch . . . in the beginning. Yes, she understood his motives, but after they'd given their pledge of love to one another, he'd continued to keep silent. He'd explained that the duty of telling her about her father belonged to her brothers. She understood that fact as well.

Yet he had deceived her, and, though she was afraid to voice her fear, she didn't know if he would ever deceive her again.

Trust between them would have to be rebuilt, stone by stone, and Harrison was going to have to be patient with her until she got over her fears.

"I'm not ready to discuss this with you," she announced. "You're going to have to give me time to sort it all out, like it or not. Yes, I do love you," she added when he gave her such a ferocious frown. "And while you're waiting, you might think about learning how to trust me," she added.

"You're making me angry, Mary Rose."

"But you love me, don't you?"

"Yes, I love you."

He didn't sound happy about the fact. She wasn't upset by his attitude. Harrison liked to have everything in neat little compartments, and having to wait for anything went against his grain. He'd been logical with her, and he fully expected her to behave and think in the same manner.

"I hope I can remember everyone's names tonight."

She was deliberately changing the subject. Harrison went back to the task of removing his pants. "I'll help you remember. We need to talk about George MacPherson, sweetheart. He's your father's personal assistant. He won't be here tonight; he still isn't back from his holiday yet. I don't want you to tell him how Douglas saw a man and a woman together on the street corner with the basket. Act as if you don't know anything about that night."

"Is he the one who took me?"

"I think so, but I still haven't proven it. I've been poring over the old ledgers. MacPherson couldn't have saved up thousands of dollars to give to his accomplice, so he had to have taken the money out of one of Elliott's accounts. I haven't found the discrepancy yet. I will though."

"Wasn't MacPherson investigated at the time of the kidnapping?"

"Yes, he was. I don't believe the authorities looked at the books as thoroughly as they should have though."

"Could I help you?"

He started to deny her request, then changed his mind. She was his wife now, and although he was used to working alone, he found he wanted her to be involved. Working together would be a novel experience.

"Yes, you can help."

"You do realize that if we simply asked Douglas to come to England, he could point MacPherson out as the culprit."

"Memories change over the years and so do appearances," Harrison replied. "The defense would shred Douglas's recollections. It wouldn't be reliable without supporting evidence."

"Have you told my father about MacPherson?"

"Not yet," Harrison answered. "I don't think he'll be able to work with the man if he knows I plan to tell him everything, of course, just as soon as I find proof. Do you want me to tell him now?"

"Would you if I wanted you to?"

"Yes."

She was pleased that Harrison would do what she wanted. She considered the problem and then decided he was right to wait.

"It would be difficult for him not to show his hand, and then MacPherson could very well become suspicious. Why, he could disappear on us, and we can't have that, can we? No, I think we should wait to tell him. He'll understand."

"The way you understood why I waited to tell you the reason I'd journeyed to Montana?"

"This is different," she argued. "I don't know my father well, but I can't imagine he would have a poker face."

Harrison raised an eyebrow. "A poker face?"

"He'd let his feelings show. A good poker player

never lets others know what he's thinking. I'll bet you win lots of games of chance, don't you? You rarely let anyone know what you're thinking. Does everyone rest during the afternoons?"

The switch in subjects didn't faze him. He was getting used to how his wife's mind worked.

"Most women do."

"What about men?"

Harrison stripped out of the rest of his clothes before answering her. "Some men rest, but I'm not going to. I want you too much. You about finished talking, sweetheart?"

She rolled onto her back just as he came down on top of her. She put her arms around his neck and stared up into his eyes. Her fingers caressed the back of his neck. "Do you like my clothes?"

"Hell, no. I hate your clothes. I like you naked."

He wasn't giving her the assurance she needed. She decided not to worry any longer about anything as foolish as her wardrobe. She had something far more important to do now. She was going to make love to her husband, and she was determined to drive him completely out of his mind first.

"How long are we allowed to stay in our room and rest?"

He nibbled on the side of her neck while he answered her. "A couple of hours. Why?"

"That should be long enough. Please get off me."

His head snapped up. "You don't want me to . . ."

"Oh, yes," she answered breathlessly. "I want you to, but I want to first."

"I don't have a prayer of ever figuring out what you just said, do I?"

"Do you want me to explain or would you rather I showed you?"

He immediately rolled onto his back. "Show me."

She was blushing like a virgin but behaving like a temptress. Harrison stacked his hands behind his head and waited to see what she would do.

Mary Rose sat up and then leaned forward on her knees. The look in her husband's eyes helped her get past her shyness. She slowly untied the satin ribbon holding her undergarment together over her breasts, and then pushed the straps down.

She took her time disrobing, and she was pleased to notice Harrison's breathing had become uneven.

Once she'd completely removed the chemise, she leaned forward and let her breasts rub against his chest. Her hair spilled down across his shoulders.

"Are you ticklish?" she whispered the question as she trailed her fingertips down his hard, flat middle.

He inhaled sharply. "No."

She moved down his body then, and he fully expected her to find out for herself if he was telling the truth by kissing his stomach.

She kissed his arousal instead. He almost came off the bed. He clenched his jaw tight and closed his eyes. She caressed him with her fingertips and with her mouth, and, dear God, he couldn't stand the torment long. When she took him fully into her mouth and began to suckle him, he let out a loud raw shout and forced her to move away from him.

He wasn't gentle with her. He was close to gaining his release, and he was determined to give her pleasure first. He lifted her up, roughly parted her thighs, and forced her to straddle him.

"Take me inside you," he ordered in a voice that sounded as though he were in acute pain.

She shook her head. "Not yet," she whispered. She leaned forward and put the flat of her hand on his shoulder. And then she began to torment him with sweet kisses. The tip of her tongue rubbed across his lips. Harrison cupped the back of her neck and leaned up, forcing her to deepen the kiss. Her tongue moved inside then to stroke the roof of his mouth.

Harrison couldn't stand being passive any longer. His hands moved to fondle her breasts. She moved restlessly against him, letting him know how much she liked the way he touched her.

He stroked her stomach, and then his hand moved down between her thighs, and he began to ready her with his fingers. When he felt her wet heat, his hands moved to her hips. He lifted her up until the tip of his erection penetrated her and slowly forced her to take him deep inside her.

She wasn't certain what she was supposed to do now, but the urge to move made her begin to rotate her hips.

He let out a low groan and clasped her hips tight. It was all the encouragement she needed.

She focused all of her concentration on pleasuring him and gaining her own satisfaction. Her movements were instinctive now, though certainly awkward, but Harrison didn't seem to mind.

She stayed in control until he reached down and began to caress her into gaining her own orgasm, and when he couldn't hold out any longer and he thrust up hard inside her and spilled his seed, the silky walls surrounding him began to spasm and tighten. She cried out his name in a near shout as she found her own fulfillment.

Moments later she collapsed on top of him. The side of her face rested against his chest. His heartbeat thundered in her ears and seemed to be as erratic and loud as her own.

It took him a long while to come back to reality. He held her in his arms and couldn't seem to stop stroking her while he slowly regained his strength and his wits.

When he was finally able to speak again, he said, "What was that all about?"

She suddenly felt embarrassed by what she'd done to him. "You didn't like it?" she whispered.

He heard the worry in her voice and started to laugh. Not like it? Just thinking about her sweet wet mouth coming down on top of him made him want to make love to her again. Hell, he was already beginning to feel the first stirrings of arousal.

He twisted her hair in his hand, forced her to lift up her head and look at him, and then grinned at her. "Yeah, I liked it. Couldn't you tell?"

She smiled with pleasure. "I thought you did.

I like the way you taste."

He let out a low groan. Then he pulled her down for a long kiss. One wasn't enough, and so he kissed her again and again, and it wasn't long at all before they were both restless for more.

They made love a second time, though the pace was much slower. Harrison wouldn't let her have much control. He was determined to torment her in just the same way she'd tormented him. They were both thoroughly undone and satisfied.

When at last it was time to get dressed, Mary Rose was yawning. Harrison looked just as tired, she was happy to notice.

Ann Marie insisted on putting her hair up in a cluster of curls behind her head. Mary Rose gave in once the servant explained she was following Lady Lillian's instructions.

Harrison told her she looked beautiful. After three hours of being gawked at and questioned by a horde of well-meaning relatives, she wasn't so certain how she looked. Everyone seemed to have an opinion about the way she walked and talked. The evening was a strain on her, for she wasn't used to being the center of attention, but she held on to her smile and tried to be understanding about their curiosity.

Her Aunt Barbara was a force to be reckoned with. The woman was tall and very well endowed. She accepted Mary Rose as her niece the moment she saw her. She took her into her arms, smashed her face into her bosoms, and began to pound her on her back as though she were a crying infant in need of calming.

"You poor, poor child," she repeated over and

over. "It's all right now. You're home with your family. Everything's going to be fine. We're all here to love you and take care of you."

Aunt Barbara wouldn't let go of her. Uncle Robert finally came to her rescue. "You're smothering her, Barbara," he announced a scant second before he pulled Mary Rose into his arms and hugged the breath right out of her.

She looked at Harrison while she was being embraced and saw his amusement. He stood across the drawing room with her father, watching her being pulled in three directions at once.

She smiled at him and then turned her attention back to her extremely affectionate aunt and uncle. Their acceptance of her was humbling, though several of their comments were most bewildering. Her Aunt Barbara seemed to think Mary Rose had suffered some deplorable injustice over the past years. She wasn't a victim, for heaven's sake, but by the end of the evening, she realized all of her relatives thought she was.

She tried not to become angry with them. They didn't understand what a rich and full life she had with her brothers, she reasoned, and that was why they all thought she'd been deprived.

She was introduced to her cousins and found them all perfectly delightful. The oldest was just fourteen and getting ready for her introduction to society. Her five younger sisters were like stair steps in age and appearance. The youngest was a boy, named Robert after his father. He was seven years old and didn't want to be bothered meeting his cousin. The moment he'd run into the drawing room, he'd spotted Harrison and hadn't left his side since. The child obviously adored Mary Rose's husband.

The children weren't allowed to dine with the adults and were sent upstairs when supper was announced.

Mary Rose thought it was odd to exclude the children, but she didn't make her opinion known, for her Aunt Lillian had already cautioned her to guard what she said.

She was seated between her Aunt Barbara and her Aunt Lillian. Harrison was at the opposite end of the table.

Dining, she soon realized, was a solemn affair. No one spoke above a whisper, and waiters hovered about while they served the food from beautiful silver platters.

Mary Rose made her first error before she'd even begun to eat. She asked her aunt if they were going to say grace. Her father heard the question and suggested she lead them in a prayer of thanksgiving.

She did just that, but didn't finish her prayer. No one would have heard her anyway, given the fact that her aunt Lillian was screeching like an attacking Indian.

"Dear God, William, they raised her Catholic. What are we to do?"

"You poor child," Barbara interjected. "You poor, poor child."

"I'm not Catholic yet," Mary Rose said. "I haven't made up my mind which religion I shall embrace."

"You haven't made up your mind? Victoria, the Elliott family have been faithful members of

641

the Church of England for years and years. You're an Elliott, my dear," Lillian explained.

"Can't I be an Elliott and a Catholic at the same time? Or Jewish or . . ."

Lillian's loud gasp of disapproval made Mary Rose stop. She guessed she'd rattled her aunt with her opinions, she concluded, when the dear woman knocked over her water glass.

"I didn't wish to upset you," Mary Rose said. "My brothers and I decided to study all the different religions before we made up our minds."

"We have our work cut out for us, Lillian," Barbara announced.

Lillian nodded agreement. "It's difficult to know where to begin. There's so much to change."

She turned to her niece. "If your mother or your grandmother could hear you talk about other religions, why, they'd both die of fright."

"They're already dead," Elliott snapped. "I find it admirable Victoria would wish to learn about other religions. Indeed I do. I'm certain, of course, that she'll decide to join the Church of England."

Mary Rose didn't argue with him. She wasn't certain she'd do any such thing, but she didn't want to get into a lengthy discussion at the table.

Harrison was irritated by Elliott's decision. "The choice will be hers to make, won't it, sir?"

Elliott shrugged. He decided to change the subject to a less upsetting one. Lillian's face was bright red. She'd had enough surprises for one evening.

"Victoria, did you know you were named after your grandmother?"

Her eyes widened. She leaned toward Aunt Lillian and whispered, "I was named after the old bat?"

Lord Elliott heard his daughter. He tried hard not to smile. Lillian let out a loud groan and her hand went back up to her throat again. Mary Rose realized she'd spoken out of turn, and she tried to think of something to say to redeem herself.

Her father seemed to take it all in stride. His voice was droll when he said, "No, Victoria, not the old bat, the other grandmother."

And then he smiled at her and suggested they eat.

The rest of the meal was subdued. Mary Rose had been hungry when she sat down, but now her stomach was too upset for her to even think about eating. She moved the food around on her plate and pretended to enjoy herself.

She didn't care for the formality. Suppers were supposed to be loud and chaotic. It was the only time all her brothers were together, and each would catch the others up on what he'd accomplished during the day. They would argue and tease each other, and there was always something they could all laugh about.

She felt as if she were at a funeral now. She wanted to go upstairs to bed. She didn't dare ask to be excused, however, and dutifully followed her aunt Lillian's instructions all through the long, seemingly endless meal.

Her father made a lovely toast in honor of her return and her marriage to Harrison. Barbara came up with the idea that a reception held in late September would be a wonderful way to celebrate the union. Lillian embraced the notion.

They began to make their plans in hushed voices. Mary Rose was soon lulled half asleep.

She wasn't allowed to go to bed for another hour, and by then she was so exhausted, she could barely make it up the stairs.

Ann Marie was waiting for her. And so was the rose. The long-stemmed red flower had once again been placed on her pillow. The sight of the rose made her smile.

She was sound asleep by the time Harrison joined her. He leaned down to kiss her good night and was inordinately pleased to see she was holding on to the flower while she slept. He removed the rose, got into bed, and let her hold on to him instead.

Tonight had been difficult for her. He had seen how confused she looked, and at times he was certain she was overwhelmed by all the attention she was receiving.

She hadn't eaten any of her supper. He noticed, of course, and thought that the constant criticism she received was the reason for her loss of appetite. It had certainly destroyed his.

Mary Rose had handled herself well. She'd reacted to the chaos much better than he had. He'd been shaking with anger over her relatives' thoughtless remarks, but she'd been quite gracious to all of them.

Harrison fell asleep worrying about his wife. Yes, this evening had been difficult.

And it was only going to get worse.

October 3, 1872

Dear Mama Rose,

Will you please quit hounding me to take a bride? You know I'm not in a position to even think about marrying. I could be carted off to jail or hung off a tree branch, and I don't want to make a woman a widow or force her to live the way I've had to live.

Besides, I like it just fine the way things are now. I keep to myself and don't have to answer to anyone. The last thing I need is a woman pestering me.

Your letter explaining about a woman's monthly arrived in the nick of time. Mary Rose suffered terrible back pains and hid up in her room for two whole days. She still won't talk about becoming a woman, but I know your letter telling her what to expect helped her. She doesn't like being a female, Mama, but we both know one of these days she'll change her mind. She's going to have to learn to quit punching all the boys who come calling.

She still doesn't realize how pretty she is. None of us think she'll ever turn vain. With four older brothers constantly harping at her, it isn't possible for her to develop airs. She certainly turns the men's heads in town. Wait until you see her, Mama. She's a piece of work, all right. She's sassy and smart, and those blue eyes of hers are going to break quite a few hearts.

Lord, how I hate to see her grow up.

Love,
Adam

19

$\mathcal{M}$ary Rose spent the next day being poked and prodded and pinned. Dr. Thomas Wells and Dr. Harold Kendleton arrived at eleven o'clock in the morning and spent two full hours with her. The physical examination didn't take any time at all, and the rest of the time was spent interviewing her about her past.

She was happy to answer their questions, for she enjoyed talking about her family and her life back in Montana. She was proud of her brothers and wanted everyone to know how wonderful they were.

As soon as the doctors left her chamber, the dressmaker and three assistants hurried inside to begin work on her new wardrobe.

The doctors sought out Lord Elliott to give him their expert opinions. Mary Rose's father included his sisters and their husbands in the conference and thought to include Harrison a short time later.

Dr. Wells was a stout man with thick, gray whiskers. He rubbed them constantly while he spouted his opinion. Harrison found the man a bit too pompous. His know-it-all opinions were all wrong too.

The meeting took place inside the library on the second floor. Harrison came in just as Wells was explaining how important he believed it was to help Victoria make a smooth transition into her new life. Harrison shut the door behind him and then leaned against it with his arms folded across his chest.

"She mustn't be allowed to dwell on her past," he dictated. "Both Kendleton and I noticed how loyal she is to the men she stayed with. Why, she's actually accepted them as her brothers," he added with a nod. "We found it impossible to make her admit they weren't, in fact, related."

Dr. Kendleton nodded agreement. He squinted at his audience over his thick glasses. "I don't believe it's a good idea to let her talk about what happened to her. You must help her let it go. In time she'll forget, once she's settled in to her new life here. Your daughter is most intelligent, Lord Elliott. She shouldn't have any difficult finding her place here, and once she gets over this strange loyalty she feels toward those men, her adjustment will be complete."

Harrison listened to the experts and vehemently disagreed with every suggestion they made. Elliott, he noticed, was hanging on their every word. He was looking for guidance, but in Harrison's estimation, he was listening to the wrong people.

He couldn't keep silent any longer. "Sir, why don't you talk to your daughter about your concerns? If you think she'll have difficulty adjusting to her life here, then ask her what you can do to help her."

"I've just been advised not to dredge up her past, Harrison. We all want to help her move forward, son. Didn't you hear her last night? She believes she'll stay here only a short while and then return to America. She does feel a tremendous loyalty to those four men." He addressed the last of his remarks to Dr. Wells. "You were right about that."

"You cannot undo what happened to her," Dr. Kendleton announced. "But with work and patience, your daughter will have a full, rewarding future."

Harrison was hard-pressed not to let his anger show. "Why do all of you believe she's been through some godawful ordeal? She wasn't a prisoner all those growing up years. She had a good life. She was given everything she needed, and she was certainly loved. You're making a grave mistake not letting her talk about her brothers, sir. They are her family. Of course she's loyal to them."

"We must listen to the experts," Lord Elliott insisted. "They know better than you or I how to help Victoria."

Harrison didn't know what more he could say to the man. He was astonished by his behavior. It wasn't like Elliott to ever be unsure of himself. He was usually a very disciplined, methodical man, and certainly reasonable. If he'd only think about it, he would see the rightness in accepting Mary Rose for what she was.

If the two of them had been alone, he would have asked him to tell him what he was afraid of.

Elliott must have guessed what Harrison was thinking, for he suddenly said, "I will not lose her, son. I will do whatever it takes to make her happy."

"We all want what's best for her," Lillian interjected.

Harrison let out a loud sigh. "What I want is for all of you to realize what a lovely young lady my wife is. She doesn't need to change. You can't erase her past, and if you listened to her talk about her growing up years, you would realize what a mistake it would be to try to make her pretend none of it happened."

"We don't want to change her," Barbara said. "We only want to broaden her education and her experiences."

Dr. Kendleton took the floor again to offer a few more suggestions for "handling" Victoria.

Harrison couldn't listen to any more of their drivel. Without a word, he left the library. He had an almost overwhelming urge to pack up his wife and take her back to Montana. The thought of anyone trying to improve upon perfection appalled him.

He decided to wait a few days before he had a talk with Lord Elliott. He would give the man time to get used to having his daughter around, then take him aside and remind him of something he'd obviously forgotten. A father's love should be unconditional. Mary Rose didn't need to change. She needed to be loved and accepted for who she was. Harrison fervently hoped Elliott would come to his senses soon and start being reasonable again.

He looked in on his wife, just to assure himself that she was all right. Mary Rose was standing on a footstool in the center of the bedroom with her arms out at her sides, while two women took her measurements. She was staring up at the ceiling and looking bored with all the fuss going on around her.

He whistled to get her attention. Lillian came hurrying past him just as he let out the shrill noise.

"My dear man, one doesn't whistle to get noticed. Where are your manners?"

"Harrison has wonderful manners," Mary Rose called out. "May I please get off this stool now? I wish to speak to my husband."

"No, dear, stay where you are," Lillian ordered. "You can talk to Harrison later. We have work to do."

"Sweetheart, I have to go back to London to pack up some papers. I'll be back by nightfall."

She wanted to go with him, but her request was refused by her Aunt Lillian.

"I wish to kiss Harrison goodbye," she announced.

"No, dear," Lillian replied.

Harrison ignored the aunt. He crossed the room, cupped his wife's chin in his hand, and kissed her. He lingered over the task, but Mary Rose didn't seem to mind. Much to her aunt's consternation, she put her arms around him and kissed him back.

He left a few minutes later. He spent most of the afternoon in the storage area adjacent to his London office. There was a pile of paperwork on top of his desk, and he knew he had at least a month's work waiting for him. While he sorted

651

through boxes of old ledgers and correspondence, his assistant went over his list of questions about more pressing business matters.

Harrison didn't return to Elliott's country home until well after sundown. The house was packed to the rafters with relatives and close friends.

His wife looked relieved to see him. She was seated between her father and her friend Eleanor on one of the long sofas, but hastily stood up when he entered the drawing room.

Showing open affection in front of guests wasn't considered acceptable behavior, but neither Harrison, who knew better, nor Mary Rose, who didn't know, worried about convention. They wound their way around family and friends to get to each other. He was reaching for her when she threw herself into his arms and hugged him tight.

"I missed you," she whispered.

He leaned down and kissed her on her forehead. "How was your afternoon, sweetheart?"

"Hectic," she answered. "Lillian's frowning at us. I wonder what I've done wrong now."

"We aren't supposed to let anyone see how much we like touching each other," he explained.

"It is a hard and fast rule?"

He shrugged. He finally let go of her, but then draped his arm around her shoulder and hauled her up next to him.

Lord Elliott was looking at him in astonishment. Harrison surmised he was going to once again hear how much he had changed.

The two of them made their way over to her father. Lillian frowned with displeasure.

"It isn't like you to make a spectacle of yourself, Harrison. Let go of your wife."

"Leave him alone, Lillian. He isn't a little boy you can order about any longer. Come and join us, son. Eleanor was just telling us how much she enjoys being in England."

Mary Rose and Harrison sat down on the settee across from her father and her friend. Lillian was seated in a round-backed chair adjacent to the sofas.

"I do love it here," Eleanor announced enthusiastically. "I have my very own lady's maid and everyone has been quite gracious to me."

"She loves being pampered," Mary Rose whispered to her husband.

"Victoria, a lady doesn't whisper secrets while in the company of others," Aunt Lillian dictated.

"Yes, Aunt Lillian."

She wasn't through correcting her niece, however. "Quit slumping in your seat, dear. Straighten your spine with pride. You're an Elliott, I'll have you remember."

"She's a MacDonald," Harrison interjected, just to set the record straight.

"But also an Elliott," Lillian insisted.

Mary Rose tried to sit the way her aunt was and found it painfully uncomfortable. Lillian reminded her of a general. Her back was ramrod straight. She looked as if she were about to snap. Lillian had her hands folded in her lap. Mary Rose imitated the action and was rewarded by a nod and a smile from her relative.

"It's difficult to know what a lady is here," Eleanor interjected. "The rules of behavior are different than in America. Lady Barbara was telling me that a true lady never squints. Did you know about that rule, Mary Rose?"

"No, I didn't."

"Her name is Victoria. Please address her by her proper name," Lillian instructed. "The rules shouldn't be different," she continued. "Just remember, a lady is a lady no matter where she resides. Jane Carlyle defined a lady as one who has not set foot in her own kitchen in over seven years. I believe she's right."

Mary Rose felt like throwing her hands up in despair. She'd never heard of such rubbish. She noticed Eleanor looked devastated by Aunt Lillian's opinions. She'd obviously taken the definition to heart. Her friend flipped open her fan and waved it in Mary Rose's direction.

"I used to be a lady, and I would still be, if Mary Rose . . . I mean Victoria hadn't forced me to go into her kitchen back home. I even had to cook, Lady Lillian. Must I now wait seven years before I'm deemed a lady again?"

Lillian appeared stunned by Eleanor's confession. "You cooked?"

Mary Rose looked at her father. He seemed bewildered by the turn in the conversation.

She decided to change the subject. "I would like to see Harrison's home," she blurted out. "He has boasted that his Highlands are as beautiful as my valley back home, and I would like to see for myself if he . . ."

The expression on her father's face stopped her from going on. He looked angry. Now what had she said wrong?

"I've upset you, Father?"

"No, of course not," he replied. "I was thinking about something else, my dear," he added. "The Highlands are beautiful. Harrison was right about that."

"I would like to see his home before I go back to Montana. Will there be enough time?"

She posed the last of her question to her husband. He nodded. "We'll make time."

"What is this nonsense about leaving? You've only just gotten here," Lillian stammered out. "Victoria, this is your home."

"Quit pecking at her, Lillian. My daughter needs time to . . . settle in."

Elliott gave his sister a hard look. She immediately closed her mouth.

Mary Rose could feel the tension in the atmosphere, but she didn't have any idea what had caused the change. Her father and her aunt both appeared to be upset about something.

Mary Rose felt the need to apologize. She would have to find out what she'd done first, she supposed. She knew she was somehow responsible for the sudden silence and their quick frowns.

She almost let out a loud sigh of frustration but caught herself in time. She didn't wish to be criticized by her aunt again, and so she remained silent.

Harrison suddenly reached over and took hold of her hand. She realized she'd been gripping her fingers together then. His touch comforted her.

She held on to her husband and edged a little closer to his side. The conversation turned to the latest styles in women's fashions. Mary Rose wanted to talk about her father's work instead. Harrison had told her that Lord Elliott used to be a member of Parliament, but had retired from that duty when his wife had died. He was still active behind the scenes and had brought about several important changes in government. Mary Rose was curious to know what the changes were.

She was afraid to ask, fearing she would once again be sanctioned for talking out of turn. And so she listened as her aunt lamented over the news that trains, or rather the cascade of cloth creating a train behind a woman's gown, were on their way out. Lillian didn't much care for the short fitted jackets currently in style either, for the covering shamefully emphasized a woman's hips. That was all good and fine for a young, narrow-hipped lady, but not at all suitable for the older, more dignified woman.

Barbara and her husband, Robert, came over to join the discussion. Supper wouldn't be served for at least another hour, which meant sixty more minutes of hearing about clothes. Weren't the men bored? Mary Rose looked at Harrison to find out. His expression didn't tell her anything, though, and then she realized he was staring beyond her Aunt Lillian's shoulder. She guessed he was thinking about something else and only pretended to be listening to the talk going on around him.

She decided to follow his example, then realized what a mistake she'd made, because her thoughts immediately turned to her family back home. She pictured what her brothers would be doing right about now and was suddenly melancholy for her valley.

"Do you, Victoria?" Eleanor asked.

She was jarred back to the present by her friend's shrill voice. "Do I what?"

"Play tennis," Eleanor explained. "Weren't you listening?"

No, she hadn't been listening. "No, I don't play tennis."

"We shall have to teach you how, my dear," Uncle Robert insisted. "It's quite the rage now."

"She plays the piano," Harrison informed the group. His voice sounded with pride.

She squeezed his hand tight. "No, I don't," she blurted out.

He raised an eyebrow and leaned down close to her. "You don't?"

"No, I don't play the piano in England," she explained. She squeezed his hand again, silently begging him to go along with her.

Harrison couldn't figure out what had come over her. He could tell she was upset, but he didn't have any idea why. She should be proud of her accomplishments, not hide them. He decided he would have to wait until later to find out what was wrong. For now he would go along. "All right," he agreed. "You don't play the piano in England."

She relaxed her grip on him. She knew she would have to explain her motives when they were alone, and she wasn't at all certain she could make sense out of her feelings so that he would understand.

She remembered how she and Adam would sit

side by side on the piano bench and play their duets together. They would laugh when one of them missed a note, and sometimes she would quicken the pace and try to finish the piece before Adam did. It was a joyful time, and she sought only to protect the memory. If any of her relatives in England mocked her technique or her ability, Mary Rose felt they would be mocking her brother too. She wasn't about to let that happen. Thus far, her aunt Lillian had found fault with just about everything about her. Mary Rose had tried to be gracious and put up with the criticism, because she wanted to make her father and her aunt happy. If they didn't hear her play the piano, then they couldn't find fault with her skill, could they?

In less than one week, her own behavior had changed radically. When she first arrived, she wanted to tell her father all about her brothers. Now she didn't want any of the relatives to know anything about her family. She sought only to protect them from the cruel little comments she was constantly suffering.

She knew she wasn't making much sense. Her brothers would never know what was said about them. That didn't matter though. It would devastate her to hear any negative remarks about the men she so loved.

She suddenly wanted to run upstairs and write a long letter to her brothers. She knew she couldn't leave the room now, however. She was going to have to wait until dinner was over.

Mary Rose hadn't quite adjusted to the change in her daily schedule. She was used to waking up at the crack of dawn each day and was always in bed by nine or ten o'clock each night.

No one in England seemed to want to eat his supper before bedtime though. It was half past nine when the servant finally chimed the bell. Mary Rose almost fell asleep at the table. Needless to say, her Aunt Lillian had quite a lot to say about her behavior. She nudged her with her elbow so many times Mary Rose was certain her side was getting bruised.

The gentlemen lingered in the dining room to drink their coffee while the ladies withdrew to the drawing room to have their after-supper tea. Mary Rose was so sleepy she wasn't paying attention to what she was doing. When Aunt Lillian stood up, she stood up too, and then picked up her plate to take into the kitchen. She was just reaching for her Aunt Barbara's utensils when she realized what she was doing.

Lillian looked horrified. Mary Rose felt like a ninny. She quickly put her plate down, straightened up, and slowly walked around the table.

Her face felt as though it were on fire. Eleanor was sympathetic. She looped her arm through Mary Rose's and whispered, "Don't be embarrassed. You're doing just fine, really you are. Smile, Mary Rose . . . I mean Victoria. Everyone's watching. Isn't your aunt Lillian wonderful?" She pulled Mary Rose along while she sang the praises of her relative. "She only wants the best for you, Victoria. Surely you realize that."

"Exactly why do you think she's so wonderful?" Mary Rose asked.

Eleanor was bubbling over with excitement.

"Your dear aunt has decided that I must also have a new wardrobe. She told me I couldn't accompany you about town dressed in rags. I'm to be measured tomorrow."

Mary Rose looked back at her husband on her way out of the room. He smiled at her and pretended all was right with the world, but as soon as the servant closed the dining room doors, his expression turned to a dark scowl.

Lord Elliott cut him off before he could get started. "Quit glaring at me, Harrison. I know you don't like the way my sisters are pestering Victoria. They're only trying to help. Surely you can see how well meaning they are. You don't want your wife embarrassed when she's introduced to society, do you?"

He didn't give Harrison time to answer his question but plodded on ahead. "I have asked you for your cooperation, and now I will plead for it."

Harrison's uncle-in-law Robert interrupted the discussion when he came back into the dining room. He'd gone upstairs for the third time to get his son to settle down for the night. The boy was being difficult, he explained as he took his seat.

"What have I missed?" he asked.

"Lord Elliott was asking me to cooperate," Harrison answered.

"Yes," Elliott agreed. He lowered his gaze to the tablecloth and in an unconscious action began to smooth out an imaginary wrinkle as he gathered his thoughts.

"I'm going to be stubborn about this," Elliott

660

announced. "My daughter's happiness is at issue, and in this instance, I believe the end will more than justify the means. You've done a marvelous thing, son. You found my Victoria and brought her home to me. Now let me become her father. Allow me to know what's best for her. I want to help guide her into her new life. Don't fight the family. We all need your support now. Victoria looks to you for approval and if you also encouraged her to let go of her past, I believe she'll adapt in no time at all. She resists the truth of who she is. When you two are together, do you call her Mary Rose?"

"Yes, I do."

"Her name is Victoria," Robert reminded him. "She should get accustomed to hearing it."

"She isn't a child," Harrison argued. "She knows who she is."

"Didn't you hear what she said tonight?" Robert asked. "She expects to go back to America."

Elliott nodded. "My daughter hasn't even settled in here and already she talks of returning to the States. I will not lose her again. Please help me."

Harrison was shaken by Elliott's emotional plea. He was hard-pressed to deny his request. He saw the wisdom in supporting his wife's father, and if he focused on the fact that Elliott sincerely wanted what was best for his daughter, it all made good sense. He still found it difficult to agree, because it seemed to him that all the relatives were determined to change Mary Rose.

"I'll do whatever I can to make my wife happy," he promised. "But I would once again urge you to let her talk about her brothers. She needs the connection with them, sir. Surely you can understand how she feels."

Elliott didn't understand. "Why do you doubt the advice of experts? It isn't like you to be unreasonable. Kendleton and Wells aren't novices in their field of expertise. They have both strongly recommended that we help Victoria move forward. I won't listen to any more objections, and I would appreciate it if you would also try to encourage my daughter to think about her life here."

Harrison felt as though he were caught in a vise. His instincts told him the path Elliott was taking was wrong, but how could he argue with the experts? Were they right in their evaluations after all?

He finally acknowledged the truth. He liked Mary Rose just the way she was. He didn't want her to change, and that fact put him in direct conflict with her father. Hell, it was complicated, and Harrison couldn't even begin to imagine the confusion Mary Rose must be feeling.

She was caught between two worlds, and as her husband, wasn't it his responsibility to help her make the transition?

The talk at the table turned to other matters, and the men didn't join the ladies for a long while. Mary Rose couldn't stop yawning, much to her aunt's consternation. She was finally allowed to go upstairs a little before midnight.

She wasn't about to go to bed without first talking things over with her brothers and her Mama Rose, and so, after the maid helped her change, she sat down at the elegantly appointed desk and wrote two long letters. She included a long note for her brother to read to Corrie too.

There was another long-stemmed rose on her pillow. She was pleased by her husband's gesture, even though she still didn't understand the motive behind it. She didn't ask him why he was suddenly becoming romantic because she knew he would only insist that he'd always been thoughtful and tenderhearted.

Her husband had a reason for every little thing he did. In time she would figure out what he was up to, and she admitted she liked the mystery in this game of his. What had the maid told her Harrison had said when he ordered the flower? Oh, yes, she remembered. He wanted to remind her of something important. Mary Rose let out a loud, thoroughly unladylike yawn and got into bed. She fell asleep seconds later holding two precious gifts. The locket her Mama Rose had given her was in one hand and Harrison's flower was in the other.

Her husband came to bed an hour later. He put the locket and the flower on the bedside table and then pulled his wife into his arms and fell asleep holding her. He tried to wake her up during the dark hours of the night, but his gentle little wife was dead to the world and couldn't be awakened. He finally gave up and went back to sleep. She kissed him awake at dawn and gave him exactly what he needed and craved, and much, much more. He was so sated, he fell asleep again.

Mary Rose quietly got out of bed so she

wouldn't disturb Harrison. She washed and dressed and then went downstairs in search of breakfast.

The staff wasn't used to early risers, and when Lady Victoria strolled into the kitchens, she caused quite a stir. Edward quickly ushered her into the dining room, pulled out a chair for her, and begged her to be seated.

She turned down the offer of deviled kidneys with eggs and crumpets and asked for two pieces of toast and a cup of tea. Breakfast was quickly finished, and then Mary Rose asked the butler if she could go into her father's library.

He thought it was a fine idea. "You haven't seen the portrait of your mother yet, have you, Lady Victoria? Your father had it delivered from his London residence yesterday afternoon. It's a comfort for him to have it close. Shall I show you the way?"

She followed the butler up the stairs and down the second corridor. The house was quiet, for everyone was still fast asleep.

"What time does my father usually get up?" she asked in a soft whisper so she wouldn't disturb anyone.

"Almost as early as I do, mi'lady. Here we are," he added when they reached the library. He pushed the door open for her and then bowed. "Will you be wanting anything further?"

She shook her head, thanked him for his assistance, and went inside. The library was shrouded in darkness. The scent of old books and new leather surrounded her as she made her way over to the double windows. She pulled the heavy drapes back and turned to the mantel.

The portrait of her mother was lovely. She stared up at it a long while and tried to imagine what she'd been like.

"My goodness, Victoria. What are you doing up so early?"

Her father stood in the doorway. He looked startled by the sight of her. She smiled at him. His hair, she noticed, was standing on end. He had obviously just gotten out of bed. He wasn't dressed for company yet, but wore a long black robe and brown leather slippers.

"I'm used to getting up early, Father. Do you mind that I'm in your sanctuary?"

"No, no, of course not." He hurried over to his desk and sat down behind it. Then he began to stack and restack a pile of papers.

He was nervous being alone with her. Mary Rose didn't know what to make of his reaction. She wanted to put him at ease though, but wasn't certain how.

Her attention returned to the portrait. "What was she like?"

Elliott stopped shuffling his papers and leaned back in his chair. His expression softened. "She was a remarkable woman. Would you like to know how we met?"

"Yes, please."

She sat down in a chair and folded her hands together in her lap. For the next hour she listened to her father talk about his Agatha. Mary Rose was curious about the woman, of course, and interested to learn all she could about her, but when her father finished talking, she still didn't feel a link with Agatha. She looked up at the portrait once again.

"I'm sorry I didn't know her. You've made her out to be a saint, Father. Surely she had some flaws. Tell me what they were."

Lord Elliott proceeded to tell her all about her mother's unreasonable stubborn streak.

Mary Rose interrupted to ask him questions every now and then, and after another hour passed in pleasant conversation, she believed her father had gotten over his nervousness and was feeling a little more comfortable with her. The mother she had never known drew the two of them together.

From that morning on, it became a ritual for her to go into the library and read until her father joined her. They would have their breakfast from silver trays the servants carried up, and they would spend most of the mornings together. Mary Rose never talked about her past, because she had been told several times by her aunts how much it distressed her father to hear her talk about her brothers, and so she encouraged him to tell her all about his family. She thought of their time together as a history lesson, but still found it very pleasant.

She slowly began to relax her guard, and after several weeks passed getting to know him, she realized how much she liked him. One morning, when it was time for her to leave him and go to her Aunt Lillian to find out what the day's schedule was, she surprised her father by kissing him on his brow before she left the room.

Elliott was overwhelmed by his daughter's

spontaneous show of affection. He awkwardly patted her shoulder and told her in a gruff voice not to keep her aunt waiting.

He informed his sisters that evening that his Victoria was settling in quite nicely.

Quite the opposite was the case. Mary Rose was becoming an accomplished actress, and no one, not even Harrison, realized how miserable she was. She was so homesick for her brothers, she cried herself to sleep almost every night, clutching her locket in her hand.

Harrison wasn't there to comfort her. He had been given a mound of work to complete for Lord Elliott and was, therefore, forced to spend the weekdays and weeknights in the city. She saw him only during the weekends, but then the country house was always bursting at the seams with relatives and friends, and they were rarely allowed to be alone.

Harrison had become obsessed with finding the evidence to condemn George MacPherson. Whenever there was an extra hour available, he went up to their bedroom and poured over old ledgers he'd brought from London looking for the hidden discrepancy. Douglas had stolen the money from the nursemaid, and she had to have gotten it from MacPherson. Where in thunder had he gotten it, Harrison would mutter to himself. It was driving him crazy that he couldn't find it.

Mary Rose still hadn't met her father's assistant. MacPherson, she'd been told, had left on holiday just as she was reaching England. He had wired for an extension and still hadn't returned to work.

She told Harrison she supposed she would never

meet the man because she fully expected to be back in Montana before the first hard snow, and it didn't look like MacPherson planned on returning to England any time soon. Harrison didn't agree or disagree with her assumption.

As time went on, she became more and more withdrawn. She'd written to her brothers at least a dozen times and still hadn't heard a word from them. She didn't want to bother Harrison with her worry that something had happened and her brothers were trying to shield her from bad news, and so she fretted about it in silence.

She hadn't heard from her mama either, and she knew Cole had sent her Mary Rose's address. Had something happened to her? Dear God, what would she do if her mama needed her and she couldn't go to her?

Worrying about her family put her on edge, of course. Her relationship with her Aunt Lillian became increasingly brittle. Eleanor had become the aunt's darling, and Lady Lillian was constantly comparing the two young ladies. Eleanor cooperated; Mary Rose didn't. Eleanor appreciated what the family could do for her. She adored her new clothes and realized the importance of looking smart at all times. Mary Rose would do well to learn from her friend's example. No one ever saw Eleanor with a smudge on her dress or a hair out of place. She never, ever ran anywhere. Why, when all the official functions began, Eleanor would be ready, but would Lord Elliott's own daughter? Could any of them bear it if she embarrassed them?

Mary Rose couldn't understand her aunt's obsession with such superficial matters. The behavior of the upper crust puzzled her. Women, it seemed, spent most of their days changing their clothes. Mary Rose was expected to wear a riding habit in the morning, then change to a day dress, then a tea gown, and finally put on an elegant dinner gown. It seemed to her that she was always running up the stairs to put on something different.

Women weren't supposed to engage men in conversation about political matters either. It wasn't considered ladylike to show one's intelligence. Did she wish to embarrass Harrison by behaving like an equal? No, no, of course she didn't, her aunt decreed. Mary Rose must learn to talk about home and family. She must present a smile to the world, and if she wanted to argue or criticize, well then, that was what her staff was for. It was perfectly all right to find fault with the servants.

Mary Rose didn't tell her aunt what she thought about her opinions. She knew she frustrated her relatives. She wanted to please her aunts and her father, and so each morning she vowed to try a little harder to live up to everyone's expectations. Her Aunt Barbara suggested she think of herself as a blank canvas and let them create a masterpiece.

August and most of September were spent preparing her for her place in society. Mary Rose learned all about the hierarchy amongst the titled gentlemen and ladies, who was interested in what, those she should avoid and those she should be especially nice to, and on and on and on, until

her mind became cluttered with all the unimportant details she mustn't dare forget.

She spent her afternoons being tutored while
she sat with her cousins in the conservatory of
her father's home learning how to do needlework
and other crafts.

Lord Elliott continued to pile work on Harrison.
He was sent from one end of England to another
on business matters, and on those rare occasions
when he returned to his wife, she inevitably
broached the subject of going home. Harrison put
her off by telling her to wait a little longer before
she made her decision.

He also gave her constant praise, so much so
that she began to wonder why he liked what was
being done to her.

Her last spurt of rebellion came just the day
before she was to attend her very first ball. She
found her Aunt Lillian in her bedroom going
through her clothes.

"What are you doing, Aunt Lillian?"

"Ann Marie told me you're still wearing these
crinolines, Victoria. They're out of fashion now.
Don't you remember, dear? The tighter skirts
are in. Shouldn't you think about throwing them
out?"

Mary Rose was appalled by the idea. Throwing
away perfectly good underskirts had to be sinful.
She vehemently argued with her aunt.

A tug-of-war resulted. The underskirt her
aunt was trying to take and Mary Rose was
trying to keep ended up being torn in half.
In the midst of the struggle, buckshot clattered
to the floor.

"What in the name of God is that?" her aunt wanted to know.

"It's buckshot, Aunt Lillian. My friend Blue Belle suggested I sew some into the hems of my underskirts to weigh them down. The wind can sometimes become strong enough to blow a lady's skirts up over her head in the West."

Lillian was so appalled by her explanation, she had to sit down. She ordered Ann Marie to fetch her smelling salts and then patted the seat next to her and suggested to Mary Rose that they have another nice long talk.

Mary Rose knew what was coming. Her aunt wanted to assure her for the hundredth time that she and the family only had her best interests at heart. She would also tell her never to mention putting buckshot in her skirt hems again.

The family moved into their London quarters late that afternoon, and the following evening she was duly presented to her father's friends and associates at a formal ball in honor of her marriage.

She wore a beautiful ivory evening gown with matching gloves. Her hair was swept up into a cluster of curls and secured with sapphire clips. The dress was dangerously low cut, in keeping with the current fashion, and her maid had to assure her several times she really wasn't going to spill out of the bodice.

"You look like Lady Victoria," she whispered once she'd finished fussing with her mistress's curls.

Harrison almost missed his own party. He had just returned to London two hours before. He looked exhausted to her. Her husband stood with her father in the entryway and watched her walk down the stairs. Elliott was fairly overwhelmed by his daughter. He grabbed hold of Harrison's arm to steady himself and whispered, "I see my Agatha when I gaze upon Victoria."

Mary Rose could see how happy her father was. She reached the bottom of the steps and executed a perfect curtsy. Her aunts and uncle stood in the background watching. Tears filled her Aunt Lillian's eyes as she watched her niece.

"Well done, Victoria," she praised. "Well done."

Harrison was the only one not pleased with what he was seeing. He wanted his wife to go back upstairs and put on something less revealing.

"She'll catch a cold," he argued.

"Nonsense," Aunt Lillian scoffed. "She'll wear her new jacket and be just fine."

Eleanor kept them waiting another fifteen minutes. She finally came down the stairs dressed in a pale green evening gown. She stared at Aunt Lillian for approval, and when the woman gave her a brisk nod and a quick smile, Eleanor beamed with pleasure.

Harrison was helping Mary Rose put on her fur jacket when Aunt Lillian spotted her gold chain.

"Where are your sapphires?" she asked.

"Upstairs," Mary Rose answered. "I wanted to wear my locket and Ann Marie told me I couldn't wear both."

"It won't do, dear. Why, the chain looks tarnished. Take it off this instant. Edward, run upstairs and fetch the sapphires."

"She wants to wear her locket," Harrison announced. "It has special meaning to her, and to me."

Her father also decided to champion her cause, and two men against one woman should have weighed the outcome in their favor. It didn't though. As usual, Aunt Lillian was a force to be reckoned with. A battle would have ensued if Mary Rose hadn't graciously given in.

She asked the butler to take her locket upstairs and put it on her desk. She also added the request that he be careful with it.

Aunt Lillian stopped frowning once the sapphire necklace was clipped around Mary Rose's neck.

"Do you ever get to win?" Harrison asked her on the way out the door.

"No, but that isn't important," she answered. "My aunt has my best interests at heart."

Harrison wasn't at all certain about her Aunt Lillian's motives, but because Mary Rose didn't seem upset by the woman's constant bullying, he decided not to make an issue out of the necklace now.

Mary Rose was filled with excitement. She felt like a princess in a fairy tale. She was determined to make her father proud of her and said several hasty prayers that she wouldn't do anything to embarrass any of her relatives.

The ball was held at Montrouse Mansion. Mary Rose stood between her husband and her father as she was introduced to well-wishers. She met the Duke and Duchess of Tremont and found them both delightful. The duke was quite old, befuddled too, because he kept calling her Lady

Agatha and whispering what a miracle it all was.

No one corrected the man. She looked up at Harrison to see what he thought about the man's misconception. He winked at her.

She didn't believe she made very many mistakes. Her father and her aunts seemed pleased with her performance. It was a strain, though, to suffer everyone's curiosity. A baron with sideburns nearly reaching his mouth begged for a dance, and while she was being twirled about the floor, he asked her if she had ever seen any of those savage Indians he'd read about. He didn't give her time to form an answer, but added the comment that he supposed she hadn't, given the fact that she was raised by a God-fearing family in St. Louis.

Mary Rose didn't set the baron straight. When the dance was finished, she went in search of her husband. She spotted him standing in front of the French doors that led out onto the balcony. He was in deep conversation with another man she hadn't met yet. Whatever the topic was, it obviously irritated Harrison, for his jaw was clenched and there was a frosty look in his eyes.

Aunt Lillian intercepted her. "Your Uncle Daniel and Aunt Johanna have just arrived. Come and meet them, dear."

"Yes, of course," she agreed. "Aunt Lillian? Did you tell the baron I was just dancing with that I used to live in St. Louis?"

Her aunt didn't immediately answer her. She clasped hold of Mary Rose's arm and led her around the dancing couples. Mary Rose was too curious to let the subject go. She made the assumption her aunt was responsible and prodded her into telling her why she'd lied.

"It wasn't a lie, my dear, just a little fabrication. It's easier for everyone to accept you. St. Louis isn't as primitive, and there aren't many uncouth people living there. I have it on good authority they're quite cultured. I won't have anyone mocking you, Victoria. After tonight, no one would dare, of course. You're the most refined young lady here. I'm so proud of you. We all are. Your mother's surely smiling down on you with pride. There's Daniel now. He doesn't look at all like your father, does he?"

Mary Rose gave up trying to make sense out of her aunt's convoluted motives. She wasn't ashamed of where she'd grown up, but Aunt Lillian seemed to think she should be. The older woman didn't understand what a wonderful life she'd had, of course. How could she? Mary Rose was never allowed to talk about it.

Her father's brother seemed to be genuinely happy to meet her. His wife stood by his side, and after she'd gotten over her surprise and made the comment, as everyone else had, that Mary Rose looked so very like her mother, she embraced her niece and welcomed her into the family.

Mary Rose liked Daniel, but she decided to wait before she formed an opinion about Lady Johanna. If her aunt joined the others and began pecking at her, she wasn't going to like her much at all.

As was her habit, when she felt herself becoming nervous, she reached up to touch her locket. The link with her family comforted her. She felt a moment of panic when she touched the jeweled necklace, then took a deep breath, told herself she was being foolish, and tried once again to pay attention to what her Uncle Daniel was telling her about his family's exhausting holiday.

Mary Rose's glance kept returning to Harrison. She was finally able to excuse herself and go to her husband. She wanted to tell him to stop frowning, but the other gentleman was standing next to him, and she wasn't about to criticize him in front of a stranger.

Harrison's friend, Nicholas, joined her. He introduced himself, bowed low, and then smiled at her. He was an extremely handsome man, with dark hair and eyes. He was almost as tall as Harrison was, wire thin, and oozed charm.

"Congratulations, Lady Victoria. I wish you and Harrison the best."

"Thank you, sir," she answered.

"Shall we go and save your husband from the biggest gossip in London?"

She put her hand on his arm and walked by his side. "What is his name?"

"The bore," Nicholas answered.

Mary Rose laughed. The sound of her amusement turned several heads. She quickly schooled her expression. "He isn't boring Harrison."

"No, he isn't," Nicholas agreed. "Your husband is trying to hold on to his temper."

Mary Rose was introduced to Sidney Madison a moment later. She had already decided she didn't like him because he was a rumor spreader, and his manners only confirmed her opinion.

Adam would have called him a fop, and Sidney Madison wouldn't have lasted five minutes in Blue Belle. He was an effeminate man with overly long fingernails she thought distasteful. His manners were very affected too.

She put her hand on Harrison's arm and stood by his side while Madison finished telling a story about his recent experience in New York City. Nicholas stood on her other side with his hands clasped behind his back. The sparkle, she noticed, was gone from his eyes. Nicholas seemed to be as miserable as Harrison obviously was. Her husband gripped the glass he was holding in his right hand, and she noticed his other hand was fisted at his side.

It had been a perfect evening thus far, and Mary Rose didn't want to have it ruined for her husband or her father. Harrison was the guest of honor, after all; he shouldn't have to suffer the bore's presence another minute.

She decided to separate the two. "Might I have a word in private?" she asked her husband.

"I've taken up too much of your husband's time, haven't I?" Madison asked. He turned to Harrison once again. "Congratulations to you. It was very clever of you to marry Victoria in America before she found out. Very clever indeed. I commend you."

Harrison knew he was being baited by the son-of-a-bitch. He silently counted to ten and vowed not to say another word.

Nicholas leaned forward. "Before his wife found out what, Madison?"

"Why, what she's worth, of course." He smiled

after giving the insult.

Mary Rose heard Nicholas's indrawn breath a scant second before Harrison succumbed to one of his spells. He kept his gaze directed on the crowd in front of him, but she could see the hard glint that came into his eyes. Harrison suddenly reminded her of Cole. Her brother always got that peculiar gleam in his eyes just before he was doing to . . .

Dear God. "Don't," she whispered to her husband.

It was already too late. If she hadn't been watching him closely, she would have missed his attack on the Englishman. With lightning speed, the back of Harrison's fist slammed into Madison's face. The man flew backward into the doors, put both of his hands up to his nose, and let out a low cry of alarm.

Harrison didn't even blink. He did smile, though, and acted as if nothing out of the ordinary had just happened. He didn't even bother to look at Madison to find out what damage he'd caused.

Nicholas's mouth dropped open. Just as Madison was recovering his balance, Harrison's friend whispered, "What did you just do?"

"This."

And then he struck Madison once more. The Englishman again went staggering backward. Mary Rose was horrified. Harrison turned and smiled at her.

"Shall we dance, sweetheart?"

And so they did. Nicholas's laughter followed them onto the dance floor.

678

"You're having one of your spells, aren't you, Harrison."

He took her into his arms and began to move to the music. "It's about time, isn't it? How are you holding up? I've missed talking to you. Are you all right?"

"I'm fine," she answered. "Did my father see what you did?"

"If the expression on his face is any indication, I would have to conclude he did. He just dropped his glass."

"Oh, Lord," she whispered. "If you've gone and ruined it for my father and his sisters, there will be hell to pay."

Harrison pulled her close. "Ruin what?"

"Their evening of course."

"The night belongs to you, sweetheart, not your relatives. Did I embarrass you?"

She had to think about it a long minute before she admitted the truth. "No, you didn't embarrass me. Quit gloating, Harrison, and try to look contrite. My father's on his way over to us."

Elliott blocked their retreat. "What in heaven's name have you done, son?"

Mary Rose grabbed hold of her husband's hand. "Don't ask him. He'll want to show you. He's having a spell, Father. I believe I should take him outside for some fresh air."

She wanted to get him alone so she could order him to behave himself. He wasn't living in the West now. He was in London, for the love of God.

Mary Rose wasn't given the opportunity to be alone with her husband until they returned that night to her father's London house.

Ann Marie helped her get ready for bed, and she was just getting under the covers when Harrison came in.

She bolted upright. "Did you break that man's nose?"

"Probably."

"You aren't sorry?"

"No, I'm not. He insulted me. How was I supposed to react?"

"You were supposed to think before you reacted," she instructed him.

He shrugged, dismissing the incident. "I have to go to Germany the day after tomorrow."

"Why?"

"On business for your father. I'm trying to get everything tied up for him. I know it's been difficult for you. I wish I could stay here to help . . ."

"May I go with you?"

"No, your father isn't about to let you out of his sight, sweetheart. He's already planned your schedule for the next four months. He wants to show you off. I'm trying to let him enjoy himself and not have to worry about his business concerns. We have some pressing cases to settle. Try to understand."

"Is that why we moved into his city house and not yours?"

"Your father doesn't want you to be lonely while I'm away."

He couldn't give her the exact length of time he would be away. She tried not to feel abandoned. As his wife, she realized her duty was to support

680

and encourage him.

"I will be understanding," she promised.

Harrison sat down on the side of the bed and pulled her into his arms. "I wish . . ."

"What do you wish?"

She leaned into him. "That we had more time together. When am I going to see your Highlands?"

"Soon," he promised. "Try to be patient with your father, all right? He still hasn't recovered from the surprise of having you back. He needs time to get to know you."

Mary Rose didn't argue with Harrison. She tried to push her own wants aside. Her father had suffered long years, and it was her duty to give him as much peace and joy as she could. Adam had told her she had a responsibility to comfort him. Surely she could stand a little more homesickness, couldn't she?

It wasn't going to be possible for her to go home until next spring. The snow would soon cover the passes, making it impossible to cross. She reminded herself she was a strong woman. She could stand a few more months of loneliness for her father's sake.

And Harrison's. "You once told me that you liked living in Montana, that you could be happy and content there. Were you . . . exaggerating with me?"

She was really asking him if he'd lied to her or told her the truth. He tried not to get angry. He didn't have anyone to blame but himself for his wife's uncertainty.

"Listen carefully to me. What happened is behind us. I know it was wrong of me to demand you trust me, but I'm going to once again promise you I will never, ever lie to you again. Do you believe me?"

"I believe you."

He relaxed his grip on her and began to slowly stroke her back. "Give yourself more time with your relatives and try not to think about making another change now. You've only just come home."

He was trying to be reasonable and logical. How could she make him understand? Home was with her brothers. She felt isolated amongst her English relatives and was constantly battling her own guilt because she wasn't living up to everyone's expectations. They all wanted the best for her, and every time a wave of homesickness struck her, she tried to remember that fact.

Harrison was exhausted, but he still found enough strength to make love to his wife. She fell asleep with his body pressed up against hers.

She was loved and cherished. And scared.

April 28, 1873

Dear Mama,

I have to spend the rest of the afternoon in my bedroom as punishment because I punched Peter Jenkins in the stomach. Do you remember I told you he's always trying to pester me. Well, he dared to kiss me today. I was so disgusted, I spit and wiped my mouth. I know I wasn't being ladylike, but spitting is better than throwing up, isn't it?

I heard my brothers talking about sending me to boarding school. Will you please write to all of them right away and tell them to let me stay home? I don't need to be refined. Honestly I don't. I'm turning out to be a lovely young lady. You told me so, remember?

I love you,
Mary Rose

P.S. I'm getting bosoms. They're a bother, Mama, and I don't think I like being a girl much today.

20

George MacPherson reminded Mary Rose of a ferret. He was a tall, lean man with a long, pointy nose and skinny eyes. She felt a little guilty thinking he looked so much like the homely animal, because MacPherson was extremely kind and solicitous to her. He seemed to be genuinely thrilled to make her acquaintance, and she could have sworn there were tears in his eyes when he spotted her standing in the entrance of the drawing room.

Douglas would have called MacPherson dapper, but he would have made the comment in a mocking tone of voice.

Her father's personal assistant was dressed to the nines in a brown suit, with a gold pocket watch chain looped just so, and brown shoes that were so shiny from spit and polish, she thought that if she looked down, she would have seen her face reflected in the leather. He carried a folder full of papers in one hand and had a black umbrella hooked over his other arm.

Elliott introduced her, then suggested she sit with him and MacPherson while they looked over the monthly vouchers.

"Your father is a very generous man, Lady Victoria. These vouchers release funds from his accounts to support charitable organizations in England. We make the disbursements once a month."

Mary Rose nodded to let the man know she understood, then decided to engage him in conversation about the past.

"Mister MacPherson, you said it was nice to make my acquaintance, but we have met before, haven't we? I was just a baby at the time."

"Please call me George," he insisted. He sat down on the sofa facing her, straightened his jacket until there weren't any visible wrinkles, and then said, "Yes, we certainly did meet before. You were a beautiful infant."

"I was bald."

MacPherson smiled. "Yes, you were bald."

"Father, will it upset you to talk about what happened the night I was taken? I'm very curious about it."

"What did you want to know?" Elliott asked. He was already beginning to frown.

She turned back to MacPherson. "I was told the nursemaid took me from the nursery."

MacPherson nodded. "Your parents had gone to the opening of the new factory. They weren't expected to return until the following day. We still don't know how Lydia pulled it off. The house was filled with staff. We believe she took you down the back stairs and out the back door."

"Lydia was the name of the nursemaid?"

"Yes," her father answered. "George was eventually put in charge of the investigation. Your mother had taken ill, and I wanted to get her back to England and her own personal physician. She trusted him, you see."

"The authorities gave up the search after six months of intense looking, but your father had already hired his own team of investigators. I simply coordinated their duties."

"How long did the investigators work for you, Father?"

"Until four or five years ago. I finally put it all in God's hands and tried to accept the fact that you were lost to me. Harrison wouldn't let me give up though. He began to take over. He followed every lead that came our way."

He reached over and clasped her hand in his. "It's a miracle he found you."

"I understand from your father that you were found in an alley by some street thugs, Lady Victoria," MacPherson said.

She was grossly offended by his choice of words. "*They weren't thugs.* They were four good-hearted boys who had been tossed out on their own and were doing the best they could to survive. They weren't thugs," she added again in a much harder voice.

"Yes," her father agreed. He patted her hand and then let go of her. "We don't need to talk about those men now, do we? We have you back home. That's all that matters."

Mary Rose didn't want to let the subject go. She turned back to MacPherson and asked, "Did the nursemaid plan it?"

George looked at his employer before he answered. He could tell Lord Elliott was becoming distressed. He obviously wanted to put the ordeal behind him.

"Sir, do you mind if I answer her?" he asked.

"No, I don't mind. She's curious. It's only natural."

"At first, we thought there must have been one or two others involved, but as time went on, we became convinced she acted alone. I wish I could tell you more, Lady Victoria, but after all these years, we still don't have any more information. I believe it's going to remain a mystery. If Lydia had lived, perhaps she could have been persuaded to tell us."

"The woman's references were impeccable," her father interjected. The frown on his face intensified while he thought about the treachery.

"We now know she'd gotten rid of you, mi'lady. She must have had cold feet at the last minute. She didn't have any money to support herself without a job. The authorities found her in a tenement building. She'd been strangled. It's believed she came home and interrupted a robbery."

Elliott abruptly stood up. "That's enough talk about the past. George, I'll sign these vouchers tomorrow."

Mary Rose could see how distressed her father had become.

"Will you have time to go riding today, Father?" she asked, thinking to turn his attention.

He believed it was a splendid idea. Mary Rose excused herself and went up to her bedroom to change into her riding habit. She found Harrison hunched over the desk, pouring over old papers again.

"I met MacPherson," she told him after she'd shut the door behind her. "Are you certain he's the one behind the kidnapping? He seems to be too refined and timid to ever do anything so bold."

687

He rubbed his neck to ease the stiffness, rolled his shoulders, and then stood up. "Hell, I don't know anymore. Douglas told me the man he saw was dressed in evening attire, and MacPherson was supposed to have gone to the theater with friends."

"Everyone dresses for the evening."

"Not staff."

She sighed. "You're looking for the discrepancy in one of the charitable donations, aren't you? Have you had any luck yet?"

"There are almost a dozen organizations I've never heard of," he answered. "I'll check them out to make certain they exist."

"And if they are all credible?"

"I'll start looking somewhere else."

"Why is it so important for you to find out?"

"Are you serious?"

"You seem to be obsessed with this, Harrison. It happened years ago, and if the authorities weren't able to make a connection between Mac-Pherson and the nursemaid, why do you think you can?"

"None of them talked to Douglas," he answered. "Your brother's description of the man he saw sounds like MacPherson, doesn't it?"

"He could have been describing a thousand men. Have you looked at yourself in the mirror lately? You're exhausted. You can't keep up this pace much longer. Every spare minute you have you spend poring over old documents. Why is it so important to you?"

He didn't know how to make her understand. "I have to finish it," he snapped.

She tried not to be offended by his irritation. Exhaustion was the reason for his behavior.

"Do you have to leave tomorrow?" she asked.

"Yes."

"Where are you going now?" she asked when he reached for his jacket.

"To the office, sweetheart. Quit worrying about me."

"I wanted to talk to you about our future. Will you have time tonight?"

"I'll make time," he promised. "Now, quit worrying about me."

He had become as abrupt and agitated as her father had been when she'd asked questions about that night so many years ago.

He kissed her good-bye and then left the room. His own personal demons followed him. He felt he had a debt to pay, and if he had become obsessed, it was only because he owed it to his savior to finish what the jackals had started. Harrison couldn't rest until he knew for certain that MacPherson wasn't the mastermind behind the crime. He had to at least try to solve the mystery because of the kindness Elliott had shown his father.

The debt consumed him.

The following afternoon Mary Rose happened to be crossing the entryway when the mail was being delivered. She was so eager to find out if any of the letters were from her brothers, she all but snatched them out of the butler's hands.

She spotted Adam's handwriting right away, of course, and let out a cry of joy. Then she ran back upstairs to read his letter in privacy. She knew she was going to weep and didn't want anyone to see her.

Adam wondered why she hadn't written. He told her he realized she must be busy, but it wasn't like her to be unthoughtful, and she surely must know her brothers worried about her. Couldn't she spare a few minutes to pen them a note?

She was horrified by the anguish her brothers must be going through. She was disheartened too. Why hadn't her brothers received her letters?

Had they been intercepted before they left the house? No, of course they hadn't been. Her relatives wouldn't deliberately be cruel, and it would be a grave insult for her to ask.

She wrote back right away, sealed her envelope, and then tucked it into the pocket of her coat. Ann Marie came into the bedroom then.

"Where are you going, mi'lady? Have you forgotten your lessons?"

Mary Rose smiled. "Missing one afternoon learning how to run a household won't upset my aunt, will it? Will you send Eleanor to me?"

"She's helping to organize your aunt's invitations. Do you wish me to interrupt her?"

"No," Mary Rose replied. She was already going to suffer Aunt's Lillian's ire for missing her lessons. Taking her pride and joy away would only send her into a lather. Eleanor was making herself indispensable to her relative. Mary Rose was glad the two women were so fond of each other, for while her aunt was busy giving Eleanor orders, she left Mary Rose alone.

"I feel like a nice, brisk walk. Would you like to come with me?"

The maid eagerly nodded and went to fetch her coat. Mary Rose had an ulterior motive for asking her to accompany her. She wanted to send a wire to her brothers letting them know she was all right, and she needed Ann Marie to help her find the telegraph office.

She also had another favor to ask. "You have Wednesday afternoons off, don't you?"

"Yes, mi'lady," Ann Marie answered. "And every other Saturday morning as well."

"Would you be willing to post my letters for me when you're away from the house? I would really appreciate your help, Ann Marie."

The maid looked surprised by the request, but didn't argue with her mistress. She agreed to do as she was asked and promised not to mention the favor to any of the family.

"Please don't mention I'm sending a wire either," she asked.

"Is there some reason you don't trust the staff, mi'lady?"

"No, of course not. I just don't want my letters . . . lost. My father becomes upset when I talk about my family back in Montana. Seeing my letters on the hall table would only distress him."

"And upset your aunts as well," Ann Marie added with a nod.

Mary Rose felt much better after she'd formulated her plans. Adam's letter made her smile all the rest of the day.

Her days and nights fell into a pattern throughout the winter months. She was always sure she

691

lingered in the foyer until the mail was delivered so she would be certain her letters weren't accidentally misdirected, and twice a week she gave her letters to Ann Marie to post for her.

Her sleeping habits drastically changed. It wasn't possible for her to dance half the night away and continue to get up from her bed at the crack of dawn.

There were other noticeable changes about her as well. She became extremely quiet and nervous, jumped at the drop of a hat, and never, ever made a comment without first weighing every word.

Her relatives couldn't have been happier with her. They obviously didn't notice the strain she was under. They believed she was making the transition to her new life as Lady Victoria completely.

She was the rave of London society. Her circle of acquaintances extended, and some days she received three invitations to parties being held on the same night. She was constantly coming or going or changing her clothes. Some days there wasn't even time to think. She liked those days most of all because when she was occupied rushing about, she didn't have time to worry about what was happening to her.

There were many lavish, wonderful things for her to enjoy, and she certainly appreciated the luxurious life she suddenly had. She began to soften in her attitude toward her Aunt Lillian as well. When the dour woman wasn't in one of her bossy, you-mustn't-ever-say-that-again moods, she was actually likable. She had a bizarre sense of humor too. She shared stories with her niece about the mischief she'd gotten into as a child, and some of the incidents she recounted made Mary Rose laugh.

She didn't share any of her childhood memories with her aunt, however, for that would have been breaking the unspoken rule never to talk about her past life.

Her aunt loved her. All her relatives did, especially her father. She tried to remember that important fact when the hollowness inside her welled up, and she didn't think she could stand it another minute.

Yes, they all loved her. And yet none of them knew her at all.

Harrison wasn't making life easy for her. He was rarely home to comfort her or assure her that she was doing the right thing and that everything really would be all right. Lord, how she needed to talk things over with him. Her father had him popping from city to city like a flea from dog to dog. When he wasn't home to hold her in his arms during the nights, she held her locket in her hands. The link with her mama and her brothers comforted her as much as a security blanket comforts a baby.

It would have been easy for her to blame Harrison for her misery. It had been all his fault that her life had been turned upside down, hadn't it? He'd come to Montana and found her, damn it.

But she'd also found him. She couldn't imagine life without Harrison, and, oh, how she missed the man she'd fallen in love with. Her husband was under quite a strain too. She could see it in his eyes and in the way he looked at her. A good wife would have been more understanding, she told herself over and over again. Harrison had asked her to be patient, to give herself time to get to know her relatives, and he always gave her the same reason why. He needed to finish it. He wouldn't explain further. There never seemed to be enough time.

She received a letter from her mama on Monday, and Travis's note arrived the following day. Her brothers, he told her, were getting ready for the spring roundup because the snow had melted early this year and the passes were almost completely bare. He added the postscript that Corrie was doing all right, at least he thought she was. The basket of supplies he left in the clearing was always empty and waiting for him when he returned. The woman still wouldn't let him get close to the cabin though, and he felt like an idiot having to read Mary Rose's letters to Corrie in a shout.

While her brothers were getting ready for the annual roundup, her relatives were preparing to move to her father's country house for the rest of spring and all of the summer months. Aunt Lillian and her prodigy, Eleanor, had also been invited to join them. Mary Rose didn't have any idea if and when Harrison would be able to join her.

She became more and more frightened of what was happening to her. She kept remembering what Harrison had said to her when they spent the night in the cave near Corrie's home. They'd been talking about honor and integrity at the time, and she recalled his exact words. If you begin to give away parts of yourself, eventually you'll give it all. And once you've lost yourself, haven't you lost everything?

The words haunted her.

It wasn't possible for her to keep up her pretence forever. Two incidents sent her world careening.

The first happened quite by accident. She was pacing back and forth in the entryway, waiting for the mail to be delivered, when Eleanor came hurrying down the stairs.

"I have wonderful news, Victoria," she cried out. "Lady Lillian wants me to become her assistant. She likes me, really likes me, and thinks my organizational skills are just what she needs. She leads such a busy life. She's needed someone to help her for a long time. Do you know what else she told me? She's going to help me find a husband. She will too. Your Aunt Lillian can do anything she sets her mind to. She told me I was like a daughter to her. Yes, she did. Isn't it all wonderful?"

Mary Rose wasn't surprised by the news. She wanted to be happy for her friend. Eleanor had had a difficult past. She'd never known her own mother, and Aunt Lillian hadn't had any children. They were two lonely people who could help each other.

"It is joyful news, indeed," she told her friend. "Does this mean you'll never want to go back to . . . America?" She'd almost asked her if she had made up her mind not to go back to Montana, but quickly changed her mind.

"There isn't anything in America for me, Victoria."

"What about Cole? Didn't you care about him?"

Eleanor took hold of Mary Rose's hand and smiled at her. "I'll never forget him. How could I? He gave me my very first kiss. He won't ever marry me though, and I'm grateful I found out he wasn't the marrying kind before I gave my heart to him. Besides, we really don't have anything in common. I'm much better suited to life here, Victoria. So are you," she added with a nod.

Mary Rose ignored her last comment. "I'll miss you."

Eleanor frowned. "Miss me? You aren't going anywhere, and we're always going to remain fast friends. Do you know I'm accepted by your friends because of who you are? You're Lady Victoria, for heaven's sake. Why, just look at yourself in the mirror. You have become your father's daughter all right. No one could ever know you didn't grow up here. I'm so proud of you. Your aunt's proud of you too. She loves you with all her heart. Honestly, she does. I must run now. There's so much to do today in preparation for our move."

Mary Rose watched her friend hurry back up the stairs. Edward walked into the entryway then. She was thankful the younger butler was in attendance today and not her father's other "man" as he was called. Russell, the senior staff member, had been in Elliott's employ much longer, and she knew it wouldn't be as easy to get information out of him.

"Edward, may I have a word with you? In confidence," she added so he would know she wouldn't tell anyone about the conversation. "I need to know something. Has my Aunt Lillian been intercepting my letters from home?"

Edward's complexion visibly paled. "No, Lady Victoria, she hasn't."

She was going to have to accept what he said as fact, she supposed. She nodded, then turned to go up the stairs. She stopped suddenly when Edward blurted out, "They only have your best interests at heart, mi'lady, especially Lord Elliott."

She slowly turned around. "My father's been taking my letters, hasn't he?"

He didn't answer her but turned his gaze to the floor. She thought his silence damning. "I thought it was my aunt," she whispered. Her voice sounded bewildered. "I don't know why, but I never considered my father would do . . . How long has it been going on?"

"From the beginning," he answered in a low voice.

"And the letters I wrote to my brothers and left on the hall table to be posted? Did he intercept those too?"

Edward looked into the drawing room to make certain they weren't being overheard, then answered her. "Yes, but you had already figured everything out, hadn't you? I'm not being disloyal by confirming your suspicions, am I?"

"No, you aren't being disloyal."

"Your father was only following the physician's advice, mi'lady. He was very happy to notice you'd stopped writing to those men. I heard him tell his brother-in-law that the advice had been sound. You were letting your past go."

"The physicians advised him?"

"I believe so, Lady Victoria."

The staff apparently knew more about the workings of the family than she did. She would have to remember to ask Edward her questions in future. She would get the truth from him.

She was too disheartened to continue the conversation. She thanked him once again and then went up to her bedroom.

Her father believed she'd left her past behind her — and her brothers, she thought to herself. Mary Rose hadn't forgotten, of course, and she hadn't quit writing. She'd known someone was intercepting her mail after she'd read Adam's letter asking her why she hadn't written. Thank God for Ann Marie. The sweet lady's maid was quietly making sure her letters were posted.

She was so furious she could barely form a coherent thought. She knew she was going to have to get past her anger before she even tried to talk to her father to find out why he would do such a cruel thing to her. After an hour of pacing and thinking about the situation, she decided not to talk to him at all. He would only tell her he was doing what was best for her, and God help her, if she heard those words just one more time, she thought she would start screaming and never be able to stop.

Her anger wouldn't go away. She begged off

going to the theater with the family that evening, giving the excuse she was tired.

A hot bath didn't soothe her nerves. She put on her nightgown and her robe and reached for her locket. She kept the treasure in an ornately carved Oriental box on top of her dresser. She wanted to wear the locket to bed. Perhaps a good night's sleep would put everything back into perspective, and she would once again have enough stamina to be understanding.

The box was empty. Mary Rose didn't panic, at least not right away. She carefully retraced her steps around the room. She remembered she'd taken the necklace off that morning just after she'd gotten out of bed. Yes, she was certain she'd done just that. And she always put it in the little box for safekeeping during the day.

The locket had vanished. An hour later, she was tearing the bedroom apart for the second time. Harrison came home and found her on her knees looking under their bed. He collapsed into the nearest chair, stretched his legs out, and thought that if he didn't get some sleep soon, he would pass out.

His mind was still reeling from the information he'd found damning MacPherson. He felt tremendous anger as well, and now that he was close to tying up all the loose ends and finally going to the authorities, the tension inside him was building to an explosive level. He was as edgy as a caged bear. Lack of sleep was surely the cause, he knew, for he doubted he'd had more than three hours' rest each night for the past week.

MacPherson was never far from Harrison's thoughts. Rage would wash over him every time he thought about how the bastard calmly worked by Elliott's side all these past years. Elliott had trusted him completely, and all that while, Mac-Pherson had witnessed his anguish and his desolation. The son-of-a-bitch knew . . .

Harrison forced himself to block his thoughts. He was too agitated to go to bed right away and decided to tell his wife what he'd found out.

She hadn't noticed him yet. "I found it, sweetheart," he called out.

She bumped her head when she bolted upright on her knees. "Where is it? I've looked everywhere. Oh, thank God. I thought I'd lost it."

Harrison heard the panic in her voice and only then looked at her face. Tears were streaming down her cheeks.

"I don't think we're talking about the same thing. I was trying to tell you I found the discrepancy I was looking for. What have you lost?"

"My locket," she cried out. "It's disappeared."

"We'll find it. I'll help you look. Just let me get my second wind." He let out a loud yawn after giving her his promise.

"What if it was thrown away?"

He closed his eyes, and began to rub his brow. "I'm sure it wasn't. Come and kiss me."

She couldn't believe his cavalier attitude. "You know how important my mama's locket is to me. I think they took it. I'll never forgive them if they did. Never."

His wife was shouting. Harrison straightened in his chair, braced his elbows on his knees, and frowned at her. He was determined not to let his weariness make him impatient.

"After a good night's sleep . . ."

"We have to find my locket before we go to bed."

He decided to try to put it all in perspective for her. The locket was important to her, yes, but they would eventually find it.

"Will you calm down? No one took your locket. You've simply misplaced it. That's all there is to it."

"How would you know if they took it or not? You're never here long enough to know anything that goes on."

"I've been busy," he shouted out. "I was trying to tell you . . ." He stopped before he went into an explanation about MacPherson. Now wasn't the time. She was too distraught to hear a word he said.

He let out an expletive then. "You could be a little more understanding," he said.

She staggered to her feet. She was so furious, her hands were in fists at her sides. The dam inside her burst, for it was suddenly all too much for her to endure. All those months of trying to be someone she wasn't was finally taking its toll.

"Understanding? You expect me to be understanding about their sneakery? My father takes my letters before I can mail them, and I'm supposed to be understanding? How long do you want me to be patient, Harrison? Forever? When you aren't working day and night finishing whatever in God's name you're determined to finish,

701

you're running around looking for evidence to convict MacPherson. You've been scratching the wrong itch for months now. Oh, shame on me. I've used another expression my relatives find distasteful."

"What are you talking about? What's distasteful?"

She didn't answer him. He wouldn't understand. No one did. She turned her back on her husband and stared out into the night.

"They all love you," he assured her in a calmer tone of voice.

She whirled around again. "No, they don't. They love the woman they're all creating. Do you know what Aunt Barbara told me? I'm supposed to think of myself as a blank canvas and let them create their masterpiece. They don't love me. How could they? They don't even know me. They love the idea of having Victoria back, and now everyone's trying to pretend I've lived here all my life. What about you, Harrison? Do you love me or their masterpiece?"

The implication behind her question sent him to his feet. If she wanted to argue, then by God he would accommodate her.

"I love you," he roared.

The argument didn't end there; it escalated. She was distraught and terrified by what was happening to her, and he was simply too exhausted to reason anything out. The combination was explosive.

What the hell had she meant about a canvas, for God's sake? She started shouting again when he demanded she explain. They said some unkind

702

things to each other, though nothing that couldn't be forgiven, and when Mary Rose realized she was going to start weeping again, she pointed to the door and ordered him to leave.

He did just that. Then she got into bed and cried herself to sleep. She was awakened by her husband's fervent apology.

"I'm sorry, baby. I'm sorry," he told her over and over again.

She believed she could forgive him anything. She loved him and would do anything to protect him and their marriage.

They made love, each desperately needing comfort from the other, and when he was just drifting off to sleep, he heard her whisper, "I love you."

"I love you too, Victoria."

Dear God, he'd called her Victoria.

She went home two days later.

August 14, 1874

Dear Mama Rose,

I have to spend the rest of the afternoon in my bedroom as punishment because I didn't act like a lady today. I punched Tommy Bonnersmith in the nose and made him bleed. He had it coming, Mama. Cole had taken me into Blue Belle, and I'd just walked outside the general store when Tommy grabbed hold of me and planted his mushy lips on top of mine.

I didn't tell Cole what Tommy had done to me. He came outside and spotted Tommy sitting on the ground holding his nose and crying like a baby. My brother would have shot Tommy if he knew what happened and I don't want him shooting anyone else. He's getting a bad reputation.

I'm not at all contrite about my behavior. Adam and Cole are always telling me I shouldn't ever let any man take liberties with me. Tommy was doing just that, wasn't he?

Are you disappointed in me?

Your loving daughter
Mary Rose

21

$\mathcal{H}$arrison returned to Lord Elliott's house just as the ship Mary Rose was on sailed for America. He didn't know she'd left, of course. No one did.

He walked into the conservatory, where Elliott sat with his assistant going over transactions.

"Where's my wife?"

Elliott looked up at Harrison and smiled. "She went shopping with her lady's maid," he answered.

"Will you excuse us, MacPherson?" Harrison asked. He clasped his hands behind his back and forced himself to look composed. He wanted to grab MacPherson by the neck and send him hurling into hell for what he'd done, and it took every ounce of his willpower not to give in to the impulse.

"Why don't you go and order some tea for us while I talk to my son-in-law?"

MacPherson bowed to his employer and left the room. Harrison pulled the doors closed behind him.

"I doubt anyone will hear us talking, Harrison. Everyone's gone out for the day, and the staff is busy packing. Something's wrong, isn't it? You've got that look in your eyes."

"We have company, sir. The authorities are waiting in the hall to arrest MacPherson. God willing, they'll get him to confess everything. There's enough evidence though to convict him of embezzlement, and one way or another, the son of a bitch is going to be locked away. He's the one who planned the kidnapping."

Elliott dropped the papers he'd been holding in his hand. His mind raced to keep up with the information Harrison had given him.

He couldn't seem to take it all in. "George . . . George took my Victoria from me? No, no, he couldn't have. He was fully investigated, and no one found a thread of evidence to connect him to my daughter's disappearance. Now you're suggesting . . ."

"Douglas saw him get out of the carriage and hand the basket to a woman."

"Douglas? Who is he?"

Harrison was taken aback by the question. Dear God, Elliott didn't even know the names of her brothers.

"One of the men who raised her," he answered. "Douglas is one of her brothers in every damned way that counts. You'd better come to terms with that reality before it's too late."

Elliott was so stunned by what Harrison had told him about MacPherson, he couldn't think about anything else. He didn't even notice how angry his son-in-law was becoming.

"There was embezzlement?"

"You've been making donations to an orphanage that doesn't exist. The place did exist at the time Victoria was taken, of course, but it closed a couple of years later. I doubt any of your money ever got past MacPherson's pockets."

"But embezzlement and kidnapping are two different . . ."

"MacPherson was behind it, sir. There isn't any doubt."

Elliott doubled over in pain. He was so sickened by the truth, he thought he was going to throw up. He desperately tried to compose himself.

"Give me a minute, son, just a minute," he whispered.

Harrison sat down beside him and put his hand on Elliott's shoulder. He didn't say a word, but patiently waited for the man to sort it all out in his mind.

It only took Elliott a short while to calm down enough to want to know everything.

"Start at the beginning and don't stop until you've told me everything."

"We know MacPherson took a large sum of money from one of your accounts the day before your daughter was kidnapped. He took Victoria late the following night, and delivered her to the nursemaid. I suppose the money he'd stolen was for the woman to use to support herself and the baby while he milked as much ransom out of you as he could. The papers he'd taken from the Bible were probably going to be sent back to you as proof he had your daughter."

"But what happened? We never received a ransom demand . . . just that first note . . ."

"It all went sour on MacPherson," Harrison said. "That's what happened, sir. Douglas told me the woman didn't want to take the basket. He saw her shake her head at MacPherson, but her mind was changed when he produced the envelope full of money and waved it front of her eyes."

"And then?"

"The nursemaid got cold feet, and after Mac-Pherson left, she found the nearest alley and threw Victoria into a pile of garbage. Then she ran away."

"Can you prove all of this, Harrison?"

"I can prove he embezzled, sir. It's enough to put him away for the rest of his life. Douglas insists he'd recognize MacPherson today. I'm not so sure myself, but I think your assistant will be convinced by the authorities to talk."

"If the nursemaid hadn't had second thoughts, would I have gotten my daughter back? No . . . no, of, course I wouldn't have. He would have killed her, wouldn't he?"

"Probably," Harrison agreed.

Elliott began to shake with fury. "All these past years that monster has been sitting by my side, calmly acting as though . . ."

He couldn't go on. Harrison nodded with understanding. "Sir, it was damned clever of him. He must have been in a real panic when the nursemaid and the baby disappeared. He didn't bolt though. He stayed right where he was. How better to control the investigation than to be in the center of it? As long as he continued to work for you, he could see whatever came across your desk before you did."

Elliott suddenly bounded to his feet and rushed toward the door. "I'm going in there and I'm going to . . ."

Harrison stopped him by grabbing hold of his

arm. "No, you aren't going anywhere. They've already taken him away. I know what you want to do, and it's all right to think it, but you can't kill him."

He gently led Elliott back to the settee and helped him sit down. He didn't leave his side for a long, long while, until he was convinced Elliott was under control and wouldn't do anything he would regret.

Harrison had wanted to talk to him about his own plans for the future, but he realized now wasn't the time to burden the man with anything more. He would have to wait until later to tender his resignation.

He went up to the bedroom so he could spend some time alone to think about exactly what he wanted to say to his wife. The words had to be right, and if he needed to get down on his knees and beg her forgiveness for all the pain he had inadvertently caused her, then he would do just that.

Elliott didn't know the names of her brothers. The realization still staggered him. In the name of love and fatherhood, he had deliberately tried to erase her past and mold her into the daughter he wanted. What must Mary Rose be feeling now, and how had she endured all of their insufferable righteousness?

Her note was waiting for him on top of the desk. A feeling of dread came over him the minute he saw it, and he was almost afraid to touch it.

He read her farewell three times before he reacted. And then anguish such as he had never known before welled up inside him until it consumed him. He bowed his head and gave in to the pain, welcomed it because he had no one to blame but himself, and now it was too late.

He had lost her.

Harrison didn't have any idea how long he stood there holding the note, but the room was cast in shadows when he finally moved. Edward was pounding on the door and shouting the request to please come downstairs. Lord Elliott needed him.

He almost didn't answer the summons, and then he realized he had quite a lot to say to his father-in-law. He no longer gave a damn if the man understood. Harrison still needed to talk to him about his daughter.

Elliott was standing in front of the fireplace. He was looking down at the note in his hands.

"Did my wife say good-bye to you too?"

Elliott slowly nodded. "She had everything," he whispered. "Why wasn't she happy? Did you know she was planning to leave? Harrison, I don't understand. She says . . . here, let me read it. The last line . . . yes, here it is. I love you, Father, and I think if you got to know me, you might love me too."

Elliott lifted his head again. "I do love her."

"Yes, you love her, but from the moment you took her into your arms and welcomed her, you've been trying to change her. You don't have any idea what you've lost, do you? I suggest you sit down while I introduce you to your daughter. I think I'll start with Corrie," he added. "Crazy Corrie. You haven't heard of her before, have you, sir? No, of course you haven't. You wouldn't have listened. You will now though. I'm determined to make you understand."

Elliott walked over to the sofa and sat down. He couldn't make himself let go of his daughter's farewell note, and so he continued to hold on to it.

Harrison talked about the friendship between the two women. Elliott blanched when he heard the description of what the recluse looked like. Tears came into his eyes a short while later when Harrison recounted how Corrie reached through the open window to stroke his daughter's shoulder.

"Her compassion for those in pain humbles me," Harrison added. "I think maybe that's why she put up with us for so long. God, I kept telling her to be more understanding, to give you time to accept her. You weren't ever going to accept who she was though, were you? You can't make it go away, sir. It all happened. Those men are her family. Your daughter plays the piano and speaks fluent French. You should be damned proud of her."

It was too late in the day for Harrison to put his own plans into action, and so he stayed with Elliott well into the night and told him most of what he knew about her background.

They were given privacy. Lillian had tried to intrude, but her brother's harsh command to get out sent her running.

"A father's love should be unconditional," Elliott whispered. "But I . . ."

He couldn't go on. He began to weep and buried

his face in his hands. Harrison handed him his handkerchief.

"Every morning she would sit with me and listen to me talk about the family. She never talked about her friends."

"You wouldn't let her."

Elliott bowed his head. "No, I wouldn't let her. Dear God, what have I done? What have I done?"

Harrison was drained both physically and emotionally. He couldn't give Elliott the compassion he probably needed now.

"I quit."

"You what?"

"I quit, sir. I've finished up all the work you gave me. It was deliberate, wasn't it? You wanted time alone with your daughter and so you had me running back and forth across the country. I don't blame you. I was so damned busy trying to repay the debt I owe you, I let it happen. That's why I've been so obsessed about MacPherson," he added with a nod. "But it's finished," he whispered. "If you'll excuse me now, I'm going upstairs and pack."

"Where are you going?"

Harrison didn't answer him until he reached the doors. "I'm going home."

Adam Clayborne was going to be tried for murder. Harrison found out about the atrocity when he reached the livery stable. He'd planned to purchase a wagon and two horses so he could cart his possessions to Blue Belle, but once the old man who ran the place started telling him what was going on, Harrison's plans drastically changed.

"Yes, sir, we're going to have us a hanging. Two fancy-dressed southern boys brung their lawyer with them. I heard tell they expect Hanging Judge Burns to hand Adam over to them so they can haul him back down where he came from to stand trial, but folks around here don't believe the judge will cotton to the notion. He'll want to try the man hisself or get hung for disappointing everyone. That's why my place is half deserted today. Come tomorrow, everything will be shut down tight. Folks will make a day of it in Blue Belle; treat it like a holiday. Some will picnic while they watch him swing, others will cheer. The women will mostly cry I reckon. Anyway, dancing won't start in until sundown. It's going to be a big shindig and you ought not to miss it."

Harrison had heard all he needed to know. He quickly purchased a horse, tossed twenty dollars at the old man and asked him to hire someone to cart his things for him.

He had just saddled the black horse when the old man said, "I can see from your hurry you don't want to miss it. You got time," he assured him. "I ain't leaving for another couple of hours. I'll bring your things down for you. Might as well earn me twenty dollars as not."

"Adam Clayborne's innocent." After making the statement, Harrison swung up into the saddle.

"Don't make no matter. He's a blackie and them two accusing him are white. Clayborne's going to hang all right."

The old man turned around and only then realized he'd been talking to thin air. Harrison had already taken off.

He rode toward Blue Belle at a neckbreaking pace, for he was terrified of what might have already happened. He had to stop the momentum before it got completely out of hand. He'd never seen a lynching mob before, but he'd read enough vivid descriptions about them to send chills of dread shooting down his spine. He didn't have any idea what he could do to save Adam, but with God's help, he would find something. Legal or otherwise.

Harrison wouldn't allow himself to think about Mary Rose and what she must be going through. He forced himself to center his thoughts on Adam. He had known there was something lurking in his background, but Adam hadn't told him what it was.

Murder? He couldn't imagine the soft-spoken man killing anyone without just cause.

Although Harrison wasn't much of a praying man, he pleaded to God for His assistance. He was so damned scared.

Don't let it be too late. Don't let it be too late.

The hearing took place in the empty storefront across the road from Morrison's store. The room was packed to capacity. Mary Rose sat at the table on one side of her brother. Travis was seated on his opposite side. Douglas and Cole were both outside. They hadn't been allowed in because the judge was concerned about tempers getting out of hand.

Adam's accusers sat at a table across from the Claybornes. There were three of them in all. One lawyer and two vile, disgusting reptiles who called themselves Livonia's kin. Mary Rose couldn't stand to look at either of them.

Judge Burns was pounding his gavel and ordering everyone to shut the hell up or he'd make all the spectators leave. Mary Rose was in such a daze of disbelief, she could barely understand a word the judge said.

Everyone outside of Blue Belle had all turned against her brother. All of them. As quickly as one could snap his fingers, they'd turned from smiling acquaintances into a group of angry vigilantes. Adam had helped most of the men inside the courtroom. His kindness and his generosity meant nothing to any of them now. He was black, and the man he supposedly killed was white. No one needed to hear anything more. Adam was guilty, regardless of circumstances. If the mob could have taken him outside and crucified him, Mary Rose believed they would.

She didn't know how to stop it. Adam was so stoic and dignified about it all. Even though he knew what was going to happen to him, the expression on his face showed only mild curiosity. Was he raging inside? She reached over and brushed her hand over his. How could she help him? How could anyone?

The judge slammed his gavel down once again. He was ready to render his decision about taking Adam back down south.

"I've looked your papers over and they appear to be legal."

The attorney Livonia's sons had brought with them hastily stood up. His name was Floyd Manning, and when he'd introduced himself to the judge, he'd added the fact that his family had lived in South Carolina for over a hundred years. He seemed to think that that somehow made him more qualified.

"Of course they're legal," Manning said. "Shall we take Clayborne with us now? You have no recourse but to follow the law."

A howl of alarm went up. The coyotes wanted to be fed. "Don't let him take him, Judge," someone shouted from the back of the courtroom. "It ain't fair. I got my family waiting outside. I promised them . . ."

"Shut the hell up," the judge ordered the complainer. "What I was saying before you tried to fast-talk me into rushing, Floyd Manning, is that I got a little problem with this here legal paper. The law is the law, but telling me I don't have any recourse, well, now, that's mighty bold talk coming from an outsider. Let me set you straight. I'm the law here. What I say goes, and now I'm saying Adam Clayborne isn't going to be handed over to you. You want to see him hang, then you'll have to wait around to find out if he's rendered guilty or not."

"But, Judge, in South Carolina . . ." Manning began.

"We ain't in South Carolina," came the shout from the back. "Go on ahead and try him now, Judge. It's getting on to noon."

The judge looked as if he wanted to shoot someone. Since he was the only one with a gun inside

716

this courtroom, he figured he might do just that if folks didn't settle down pretty soon.

He glared at the crowd before turning back to the citified lawyer with hundred-year-old relatives. "We're in a territory, not a state, and like I told you before, what I say goes."

Mary Rose bowed her head. She was desperately trying not to cry. Her anger made her shiver so much her arms had goosebumps everywhere. Would this nightmare ever end? Her brothers had hoped that Judge Burns would hand Adam over to the southerners. They planned to grab him outside of town and hide him up in the mountains until future plans could be made.

The crowd was in a frenzy waiting for the judge to tell them he would go ahead and try Adam then and there. Burns wasn't about to lose control of his court. He reached down into his lap and pulled out his six-shooter. He was going to put a couple of bullets in the ceiling to get everyone's attention.

The tactic turned out to be unnecessary. Just as he was cocking his weapon, a hush came over the crowd. Burns looked up and spotted Harrison roughly shoving his way through the angry men.

Mary Rose noticed the silence and gripped her hands together even tighter. What more had happened? Were they bringing in Douglas and Cole? She was afraid to look.

Harrison walked right past her. He didn't spare her or her brothers a glance as he made his way to the table Judge Burns sat behind.

"I have business with this court."

Her head jerked up. She blinked. He didn't

disappear. Harrison? Harrison was in Blue Belle? She couldn't seem to catch her breath, couldn't make herself understand.

"State your business," the judge commanded.

"My name is Harrison Stanford MacDonald . . ."

Burns didn't let him continue. "Why are you telling me your name? I know who you are."

"For the record, Your Honor."

"What record? We don't keep records here, leastways we don't very often. We're more casual in the Territory. State your business," he repeated.

"I represent Adam Clayborne."

A sparkle came into the judge's eyes. He leaned back in his chair and rubbed his jaw. "You do, do you?"

"Yes, Your Honor, I do."

"Then you might as well get on over there and represent him. I'm about to try him for murder."

"Is a man entitled to a fair trial in the Territory?" he asked.

The judge knew Harrison well enough to understand he wasn't trying to bait him or insult him.

"Yes, of course he's entitled."

"Then I request sufficient time to confer with my client."

"How much time?"

"One month."

A roar of discontent went up. The judge calmly shot his gun into the air. "Can't wait a whole month, Harrison."

"Your Honor, I must have sufficient time

718

to build my case."

"Where we gonna keep him until you figure out what you want to say?"

"He should be released into my custody," Harrison said.

"He'll run, Judge. The darkie will run. Just you wait and see."

Judge Burns leaned to the side so he could see past Harrison. "Is that you, Bickley, disrupting my courtroom? I swear to God I'm gonna put a bullet in your butt if you don't shut your trap. You got two weeks to prepare, Harrison. You willing to put up money in the event Adam runs?"

"Everything I own."

"A hundred dollars will do me now. You can pay up the rest in two weeks, unless of course he doesn't run."

"Yes, Your Honor."

The judge slammed the gavel down once again. "Adam's got to stay under house arrest until trial. Anyone doesn't like it can watch he doesn't leave from the edge of the Clayborne property line. All of you hear what I'm saying? Bickley, if you don't have anything better to do with your time than sit around and watch, you do it from the trees. You got that? I'm declaring here and now if any of you set foot on Clayborne land, it's legal for them to shoot you. We're going to have us a trial in two weeks. Court's adjourned."

The judge slapped the gavel down against the tabletop one last time. "You've got your work cut out for you, Harrison," he remarked in a low voice. "I have a folder full of evidence against

Adam. You can have a gander at it until I leave to go fishing. I'll be at Belle's place until Sunday next. Bring your hundred dollars over there."

Floyd Manning walked over to Harrison. "Nigger lover," he hissed.

The judge heard him. "You got no more business here, Manning. Go on back home. I do my own prosecuting here. It'll be trial by jury, and I'll be the one picking the twelve."

Manning's bushy eyebrows came together in yet another scowl. "That boy don't deserve a fair trial. They all ought to be dragged out of here and strung up."

The attorney's face had turned a blotchy red. He was furious the hearing hadn't gone his way.

Judge Burns looked at Harrison. "Who exactly does he think we ought to string up? The town or just the Claybornes?"

Manning was happy to answer him. "The Claybornes, of course, especially that white girl living under the same roof with the nigger. She's trash."

"You got something to say about that, Harrison?" the judge asked.

He counted to ten before he answered the judge. Stalling didn't help him change his mind. "How much for the charge of assault, Your Honor?"

Burns's eyes sparkled with merriment. "Five dollars, given the special circumstances."

Harrison reached into his pocket, pulled out five dollars, and dropped the money on the table.

What happened next so surprised the southern attorney, he didn't have time to protect himself. Harrison punched him hard in the face.

He coldcocked him. Manning collapsed on the floor in a dead faint. The judge leaned over the table to get a better look at the man, then turned back to Harrison.

He was trying hard not to smile. "Well now, that's premeditation. Cost you a dollar more."

Harrison handed him the money and went to his wife and her brothers.

He kept his attention on the crowd. The men were slow to leave, and Harrison had plenty of time to study their faces. He didn't recognize any of them.

Travis started to get up. Harrison ordered him to stay in his chair.

"Mary Rose, get up and come over to me. Look damned happy to see me."

She didn't hesitate. She quickly got up and walked around the table. He pulled her into his arms, leaned down and kissed her brow, and then hugged her tight.

"Welcome back, Harrison," Adam whispered.

"When the hell did all this happen?" he asked.

"They woke me up yesterday," Adam answered. "And here I am. You got here in the nick of time. In another hour, it would have been too late. They would have waited until tomorrow to hang me, but once a sentence is handed down, no one can do anything."

The last of the strangers filed out of the storefront. Douglas and Cole came charging inside.

"Shut the door," Harrison called out.

"Let's get the hell out of here," Cole muttered. He tossed Travis his gun as he came storming down the aisle. "Adam, you okay?"

"Yes," his brother answered.

Harrison finally relaxed his grip on Mary Rose. She didn't move away from him, however, but continued to lean into him. She was shaking almost violently now. She'd had one hell of a day, and he knew it wasn't going to get much better.

He had so much to say to her, but now certainly wasn't the time or the place. Getting Adam back to the ranch alive was going to require everyone's full concentration.

"I say we run now," Cole said.

"We'll all get bullets in our backs if we try," Travis argued.

"He's right," Douglas agreed. "Now isn't the time to leave," Douglas said.

"I'm not going anywhere but home," Adam announced. He pushed his chair back and finally stood up. "Harrison, I don't know if I should thank you or hit you. You've just given me two full weeks to think about that rope going around my neck."

"You don't have much faith in your attorney," Harrison remarked dryly.

"I've got plenty of faith in you. It's the rest of the world I have trouble with. You're an honorable man, Harrison, but that seems to be a rare quality these days. I told Mary Rose you'd come back. She didn't believe me. I guess she does now, doesn't she?"

Harrison was stunned. Had she thought he'd stay on in England and go right about his business? Didn't she realize she'd taken his heart with her?

"Harrison, are you going home with us or over to Belle's to look at the evidence?" Travis asked.

"Home," he answered. "I want to talk to Adam before I do anything else."

It was a solemn procession that filed out of the storefront. The locals were there to greet Adam and offer him words of encouragement. It was good to see the people of Blue Belle hadn't turned against him.

Harrison was given the duty of watching their backs on the way home. He stayed well behind the family, and when they started down the last hill, he stopped and waited until they were safely out of gunshot range. He made a quick detour then, found what he was looking for, and continued on.

Mary Rose sat with her brothers at the dining room table. They were all whispering and worrying out loud about the two-week reprieve.

She was thinking about Harrison. Seeing him again had filled her with such incredible longing. Why had he come back? She couldn't be the woman her relatives in England wanted her to be. Didn't he understand that? Oh, God, what was she going to do? She'd been so miserable from the moment she'd left him . . . until today. She'd felt as though she were dying inside, and when he'd calmly walked into the courtroom and made reason in the midst of madness, she'd started living again.

She heard Harrison come inside the house and go upstairs. Doors squeaked open and closed. He was looking for her room, she thought to herself, and did that mean he expected to stay with her?

He finally joined the family. "Adam, I want to talk to you alone in the library."

He didn't even look at her.

"My brothers and my sister know everything," Adam replied.

"Alone," Harrison suggested once again.

They weren't disturbed by anyone and stayed closeted together for over two hours. Harrison had insisted Adam tell him everything he remembered about his daily routine while he lived on the plantation and everything he knew about the family who had owned him.

"Mistress Livonia was married to Walter Adderley. They had two sons. You saw both of them in court today. Reginald's the baby. He's a couple of years younger than I am. Lionel is the older one. He's the spitting image of his father. Walter was a drunk. He'd start in around noon every day, and by evening, he'd have to be carried up to bed. He got real mean when he drank, which meant he was mean most of the time. He would pick fights with his wife. Something must have happened between them, because when he was drunk, he couldn't abide the sight of her."

"Would he strike her?"

"Oh, yes, he'd use his fists. She wasn't any match for him. He was over six feet, and she was just a little tiny bit of a thing. He'd hit my mama too. She was Livonia's companion, and so she got her share of abuse as well.

"On a late Friday afternoon, just around suppertime, I was passing by the house on my way in from planting, and I heard Mistress Livonia screaming. Adderley was beating both of them. I put myself between Livonia and my owner because when I walked into the room, he was pounding on her. I remember thinking that if I could just get him to turn his rage against me, Mama and Livonia would be all right. Mama's nose was bloody and one eye was already swelling closed. Livonia was in worse shape. She was trying to stand up and had almost made it when he struck her again. She collapsed on the floor. She kept begging him to stop. He started kicking her then. She was pleading for mercy, and praying, Harrison. She begged me to help her . . . and so I did."

Adam paused to take a shaky breath before continuing. "I put my arms around his waist and pulled him back while Mama ran over to help Livonia to her feet.

"Adderley went crazy. He told Livonia he was going to kill her, shrugged me off of him, and went after her again. That's when I hit him. He stumbled back about ten feet and then started to charge me. He lost his footing and crashed into the edge of the mantel. I think he was dead before he landed on the floor."

"Where did you hit him?"

"In the chin."

"Not from behind? You said he had turned away from you . . ."

"Yes, but I was quicker than he was. I put myself in front of Mistress Livonia again to try to protect her and struck him when he tried to kick her."

"And then what happened?"

"Mistress Livonia gave me money and told me to run. She and Mama were going to tell the authorities I'd been sold. When the authorities

725

arrived, Livonia told them it had been an accident. Neither woman mentioned me at all. I hadn't done any damage to Adderley's face with my punch. I was just thirteen and didn't know how to fight. Everyone in the state knew what a drunk Adderley was. No one doubted Livonia. She told them how her husband had stumbled and crashed into the mantel. It was ruled an accidental death."

"Did anyone else see what happened?"

"No."

"Why would her sons come after you now? What evidence do they have?"

"The letters I wrote to my mama. She saved all of them. Adderley's sons must have found them. I mentioned the past in several of the letters and told Mama I was afraid for her."

Harrison let out weary sigh. "You aren't guilty of a crime, Adam."

"I was a slave, and I dared to raise my hand against my owner. I touched him. His sons believe I should be killed just for that."

"Do you think Adderley's sons went to their mother and forced her to tell them exactly what took place?"

"Oh, yes. Lionel's turning out to be just like his father. Mama's letters are filled with her worries about Mistress Livonia. None of it matters, does it? If two white men accuse me of murder, we both know I'll be convicted."

"Not without a fight," Harrison promised. "I have to ask you something else. Do you want to stay here and fight this, or do you want to run?"

"Would you let me run if I wanted to? You

put up everything you own to ensure I would stay around."

"I didn't put up my most valuable asset," he answered. "I'll still have Mary Rose, if she'll let me stay."

"What do you advise?"

"In my heart, you've become my brother, Adam, from the day I married your sister. I don't want to see anything happen to you. As your attorney, I would advise you to stay and fight."

"So the brother in you wants me to run, and the attorney wants me to face it."

"Something like that," Harrison agreed. He happened to notice the framed words Adam had copied down and hung on his wall. It made sense to him now, the reason Adam so loved the passage.

"Make me a promise, Adam."

"What is it?"

"When this is over and we've won, you'll take the passage down and put it away."

Adam stood up and stretched the muscles in his shoulders. "I've lived my entire life hiding and waiting. I don't want to live like that any longer. I always knew the day would come, and now that it's finally here, I'm going to stay around and face it. 'For whom the bell tolls,' " he added in a whisper. " 'It tolls for thee.' "

"Hell, that's grim."

"I'm feeling grim. I'm entitled tonight. Are we about finished talking?"

Harrison smiled. "We've only just begun. We're going to talk about what you're going to say when you're on the stand, and what I don't believe would be a good idea to say. Sit down, Adam.

It's going to be a long night."

Harrison started taking notes. Cole carried in a tray with cheese and biscuits and beer. Since he wasn't asked to leave, he stayed inside the library and leaned against the edge of the desk while he listened to Harrison question his brother.

Travis and Douglas joined them an hour later, but Mary Rose stayed behind. She thought Adam would speak more freely if he didn't have to worry about her.

She couldn't eat anything, her stomach was too upset, and after sitting at the table all alone thinking about Adam, she finally got up and went to her room.

Her thoughts kept turning to Harrison. What in heaven's name was she going to do? He'd called her Victoria. Who did he love? Didn't he know he'd broken her heart when he'd called her that name? Why couldn't he love her just the way she was?

There was a flower on her pillow. It wasn't a rose, but a brilliant red fireweed.

She finally understood what he had been trying to remind her of from that first night in England when he'd had a long-stemmed rose placed on her pillow. He knew what it would be like for her in England, how difficult the transition would be for her to make, and so, while everyone else was diligently trying to change everything about her, Harrison had been quietly reminding her that he loved her just the way she was. He accepted her, flaws and all.

She was his Rose.

She was overwhelmed by her husband. How

could she have ever doubted him? And how could he ever forgive her for not having enough faith in him?

She sat down on the side of the bed, and while she gently pressed the flower to her heart, she bowed her head and cried.

"The flower was supposed to make you happy, not sad."

Harrison was standing in the doorway. Her heart felt as if it had just done a somersault. He looked so worried and tired . . . and vulnerable.

"You love me."

"Yes."

"Thank you," she whispered.

"For loving you?"

She shook her head. "For putting up with my uncertainty. I love you so much, and I've been so afraid inside. Wait," she added when he started toward her. "I have to beg your forgiveness first."

A slow smile caught her by surprise. She shouldn't be smiling now. She needed to be serious so he would believe her when she promised to never doubt him again.

"You have the patience of Job," she began. "All this time you've been waiting for me to understand, haven't you?"

"No, you always understood. I was just reminding you."

"You called me Victoria."

"I did?" He looked astonished by what she'd just said.

"You broke my heart."

Harrison closed the door and went to her. He

stopped just a foot away.

"I love you, Mary Rose MacDonald. I don't care what name you go by. If you want to change it every other week, that's okay with me. You'll always be my Rose."

She didn't want to hold the flower any longer. She wanted to hold her husband. She put the fireweed on the side table and stood up. "I love you too," she repeated. "I'm so sorry I doubted you. Can you ever forgive me?"

"I should have been there for you. I knew what you were going through, and I should have quit working for your father a long time ago. I shouldn't have wanted to finish everything first. Can you ever forgive me?"

"You quit?" she whispered.

"You didn't do anything crazy when you came back here, did you, sweetheart?"

"Crazy? Like what?"

"Like getting one of those divorces I read was easy to procure here."

"I'm not answering until you kiss me. Oh, Harrison, in the midst of all the confusion today, you remembered I used to think fireweed was a rose. Please kiss me."

"I'll only marry you again if you did get a divorce. Forever, Mary Rose. I meant it."

And then he finally pulled her into his arms and kissed her with all the love and tenderness he possessed. The ache he'd been suffering during their separation vanished, and now he felt complete again.

She placed fervent kisses on his face. "Why did you wait so long to come to me?"

"Sweetheart, if you had looked behind you while you were on ship, I could have waved to you," he exaggerated. "I got here as soon as I could. Let me kiss you again."

They were both shaking with their need for each other when they pulled apart. Mary Rose rested the side of her face against his chest. She loved the way his heart hammered in her ear, loved everything about him. Even when he was driving her crazy with his stubbornness and his arrogance, she loved him.

She wondered if he knew how perfect he was.

"It isn't easy to get a divorce here. You've read too many dime novels, Harrison. And no, I didn't divorce you. It's forever, remember?"

His chin dropped to the top of her head. Lord, he was content. He felt whole again, complete, and all because of her magical love.

"Are we going back to England? I will go anywhere in the world with you. As long as we're together, I shall be content."

He was overwhelmed. She would give up paradise for him and do so willingly because she loved him.

"No, we aren't going back. We're going to live here. I'll buy some land close by and build a house."

She started crying again. She assured him they were tears of joy, of course. And then she pushed herself away from him and insisted she couldn't speak another coherent word until she'd taken her clothes off.

He was happy to accommodate her. He thought he set a record of some kind for stripping out of his clothes and getting her out of hers without tearing anything. One of them pulled the covers back, and then they fell into bed together.

He covered her completely and kissed her softly until he felt her mouth open under his. The tip of his tongue rubbed against hers and then gradually slipped inside. He was determined to go slow and not give in to his hunger now, but she was making it impossible for him. Her hands caressed him everywhere, and when she began to stroke his arousal, he forgot all his good intentions.

He twisted her long curls around his hands and shifted his position. His tongue thrust deep inside her mouth. With one motion, he penetrated her. The pleasure of feeling her walls squeezing him inside made him close his eyes in ecstasy.

She drew her knees up to bring him deeper inside her and let out a little whimper as the wave of pleasure washed over her. The intensity took her control away from her. She was mindless now to everything but finding fulfillment.

He had more stamina than she did. She reached utopia first, and when he felt the tremors of her release, he quickened his pace and gave in to his own.

And it was as perfect as he had remembered.

He didn't have the strength to move away from her for a long, long while. He hoped to God he wasn't crushing her, and just as soon as his mind could get his body to cooperate, he'd find out.

She didn't cry this time. She laughed. The sound proved contagious, and he found himself smiling in reaction.

He finally lifted himself up so he could look into her beautiful eyes.

"Felt good, didn't it?"

She slowly nodded. "Better than good."

"I behaved like an animal in heat."

She laughed again. "So did I. The memory of what happened is already fading. Do you think you could remind me again?"

"You're killing me, Mary Rose."

She almost did too. Harrison fell asleep an hour later believing he had died a happy man.

January 2, 1876

Dear Mama,

Today is my sixteenth birthday and I am finally allowed to wear my beautiful locket for the very first time. I've been waiting for such a long time. Thank you, Mama, for giving me the treasure. I will value it forever. I'm so lucky to have you. Adam says that God has been watching out for all of us from the day they found me in the alley. He's right, Mama. He gave me four brothers to love and protect me, and He gave me you.

I've saved half the money I need to make the trip to Carolina. If all goes well, I'll be able to come and stay with you next year. It's my dream, Mama. Please let me. I so need to hug you.

Your daughter
Mary Rose

22

$\mathcal{M}$ary Rose awakened Harrison around one in the morning when she tried to ease out of the bed.

"Where are you going?" he asked in a sleepy whisper.

"Downstairs. I'm starving. I didn't mean to wake you. Go back to sleep."

Harrison decided he was hungry too. He put on his pants, stubbed his toe in the process, and hopped around the room muttering expletives.

"Hush," she whispered in a laugh. "I don't want to disturb my brothers."

It was already too late. Harrison had made so much racket complaining about his foot, he got everyone up.

Cole was the first to join them at the kitchen table. Mary Rose was cutting slices of cheese while sitting on Harrison's lap.

She scooted onto her own chair as soon as her brother walked in.

"I couldn't sleep," he explained. He straddled the chair across from Harrison and gave him a hard look. "You going to be able to fix this?"

"If you want a guarantee, I can't give it to you, Cole."

"Then you've got to help me convince Adam to run."

"I can't do that. The decision has to be his,

and his alone. Back him up on this, Cole. He'd do the same for you."

The brother shook his head. "He wouldn't stand by and watch me die. I'm telling you here and now. If he's condemned, I'm getting him out."

Mary Rose was quickly losing her appetite. Fear tightened her stomach into a knot. "I think we need to have faith in Harrison, Cole. Trust him to do everything he can to save Adam."

Harrison reached over and clasped her hand in his. "I'm not a miracle worker, but thank you for having faith."

"The hell with faith," Cole muttered.

Douglas joined them in time to hear his brother's remark. He'd put on pants and a long-sleeved flannel shirt. He had it buttoned up all wrong. Mary Rose smiled when she noticed.

"Have you figured out a plan yet?" he asked Harrison.

"I'm going to send a telegram tomorrow to the attorney I used in St. Louis. He's with a large firm. He might know the name of an attorney in South Carolina. I'll find one, even if I have to go there myself."

"For what purpose?"

"To get a sworn statement from Livonia and Rose. Time is critical now. It will work out though. I'll make it work."

"What good will their statements do?" Douglas asked.

"They'll confirm what Adam told me. Right now it's two men against one. I'm evening the odds. I hope to God Livonia cooperates. She may

736

be too frightened."

The brothers nodded. "Adam will balk at this. He knows what will happen to the woman when the sons get back home. I don't think he'll let you go after her for a sworn statement."

Harrison didn't argue with the men. He would do what he had to do to make certain Adam was given a fair trial.

"Let's talk about something else. Mary Rose is becoming upset."

"No, I'm not."

"You aren't eating."

She shrugged. "What would you like to talk about?"

Travis came in and answered for Harrison. "What happened after she left London? Did all hell break loose? Did that aunt call her ungrateful? Mary Rose thought she might."

Mary Rose stared at her plate. "I hurt my father, didn't I?"

Harrison didn't soften the truth. "Yes."

"I wish he could understand," she whispered.

"Sweetheart, he had plenty of time to try. He never gave you a chance. I think I might have made a sound argument. He seemed to understand when I was finished. I'm still not sure. I didn't want to wait around to find out."

"Why didn't they like her?" Cole asked.

"They wanted Victoria back. None of them could accept the fact that Mary Rose hadn't been a victim all those years. In their minds, they believed she'd been deprived because she hadn't been surrounded by riches. None of them took the time to get to know her. They were too busy trying to create someone else. It was crazy, all of it. They had this image of how she would have turned out, and they were all trying to mold her into what they wanted her to be."

"Their masterpiece," Mary Rose said.

"Why didn't you punch your aunt when she told you to think of yourself as a blank canvas?" Harrison asked.

Doing such an outrageous thing was absurd to her. She burst into laughter just thinking about it.

"My Aunt Barbara gave me that suggestion. I could never have hurt her. She had my best interests at heart."

"Are you going to take her back to England and try again, Harrison?" Douglas asked.

"No."

The brothers smiled. They didn't need to know specific plans tonight.

They stayed at the table another half hour or so talking. The discussion eventually circled back to Adam, but Mary Rose had finished eating by then.

"What can we do to help?"

"Quite a lot," Harrison answered. "I'll give you all the particulars as we go along. When we're inside the courtroom, I don't want Mary Rose sitting by Adam. Cole, you sit on Adam's right side and I'll sit on his left side. Travis and Douglas will put Mary Rose between them in the first row behind the table. If there's a recess called, when you sit down again, sit in the same places."

"Why can't I sit next to Adam?" she asked.

"I want you to separate yourself from him as

much as possible," he answered.

His bluntness took all of them by surprise. None of the brothers looked angry though. They looked curious to find out his reason.

"If you put your hand on his or hug him or pat him, all everyone is going to see is a white woman touching a black man. People know all about your family, and they somewhat accept Adam now. Don't push them, Mary Rose. I don't want anyone to forget he's your brother. We aren't just fighting a murder charge now. Hell, that would be easy. We're fighting prejudice too. I don't want to hear any argument about this," he added when she looked like she wanted to disagree with him. "You'll all show your support for Adam as a family, but not as individuals."

"Why did you choose Cole to sit next to Adam instead of Travis or me?" Douglas asked.

"For intimidation purposes. He makes people nervous."

Cole smiled. "I do, don't I?"

"Yes, you do. The jury will hear all the evidence, and Cole's going to stare at every one of those twelve faces and act like he's memorizing each reaction."

"Couldn't that backfire?" Douglas asked.

"In a more sophisticated courtroom, it probably would backfire, but not out here. Mary Rose once told me people are more concerned about surviving than worrying about what other people do. I want the jury to think about surviving Cole's wrath if they let their prejudice guide their decision."

"You fight dirty," Cole said. "I like that."

"I might remind all of you that what I'm now saying is privileged information. Got that?"

Mary Rose yawned. Harrison immediately took her back up to their bedroom.

"I have a surprise for you. Sit down on the bed and close your eyes."

She did as he ordered. She peeked once and saw him pulling clothes out of his satchel.

"Are they closed?" he asked.

She squeezed them tight. She felt him brush her hair away from her face, and then she felt something cold around her neck.

She knew what it was before she opened her eyes.

"Mama's locket," she cried out. "Where did you . . ."

She couldn't go on. She'd started crying again.

"It was wedged between the mattress and the headboard."

She threw herself into his arms and thanked him over and over again. It didn't take him any time at all to want her again. They fell on top of the covers and made wild, passionate love.

He knew the blissful interlude would have to last them a long time.

The storm was coming.

Mary Rose saw little of Harrison during the next week. He spent most of his days over at Belle's house, pouring over the letters they'd all sent to Mama Rose that the Adderley boys had taken. At night he sat in the library and read the letters their mother had written them. He took page after page of notes, and when he wasn't working, he sat on the porch to think and plan.

She didn't have to ask him what progress he was making. His grim expression told her everything she needed to know. She felt completely useless and powerless. She asked him every single morning if there was some little thing she could do to help him. His answer was always the same. If he thought of something, he'd let her know.

The closer to trial the more preoccupied he became. She didn't feel at all slighted, even when he would go up to bed without telling her good night. He was thinking about the case, and that was all she wanted from him.

They came together as a family on Sunday for supper. She made a promise that no matter what, the meal would be pleasant, and so, every time someone mentioned anything having to do with the trial, she quickly changed the subject.

Everyone caught on to her game. They went along with it too, and in no time at all, Travis was even able to smile about something she'd told him.

"Cole, you never asked me about Eleanor. Aren't you curious what happened to her?"

He shrugged. "Is she happy?"

"Yes," Mary Rose answered. "She went to work for my Aunt Lillian."

"The general? Eleanor's got more guts than I thought. Good for her."

Harrison smiled. "You call your aunt a general?"

"She acts like one," Mary Rose admitted. "Corrie left me a note yesterday. Would you like me to read it to you?"

"No." All four brothers shouted the word together. Then they burst into laughter.

She wasn't put off by their rudeness. "I'll be happy to read it to you, Harrison."

"Sweetheart, I've already heard it three times. Corrie wants you to bring her another book."

"And?"

"She's happy you're home. You're sure pretty when you blush."

"I'm not blushing. I don't mind my brothers laughing at me. They can't help being uncivilized at the table. Ignore them."

"I think I missed being uncivilized most of all while we were in England."

"Oh, Lord. Have I married someone just like my brothers?"

"I hope so. It would be the highest compliment you could give me."

"I told you he liked us," Cole drawled out, embarrassed by his own reaction to Harrison's praise.

"Someone's coming up to the house," Douglas announced. "He's dressed in a suit and driving a buggy."

Harrison stood up. "It's Alfred Mitchell," he guessed. "He's the attorney we hired to do some work for us. You wait here," he told the brothers when they all started to get up. "I want to talk to him alone first. You can meet him later."

He left the room before Adam could ask him to explain the work this Mitchell fellow was doing for them. He posed the question to Cole.

"Harrison wanted to get some information about Livonia's sons. He sent a wire to an attorney in St. Louis, asking for a recommendation, and Mitchell was suggested. The man must have ridden day and night to get here so soon. I can't imagine how he did it."

"Should we listen at the door?" Travis asked.

"We'll do no such thing," Adam dictated. "We'll give Harrison privacy."

They all heard the screen door open once again. A few seconds later, Harrison came back into the dining room.

He looked stunned.

The reason was standing right behind him.

Mary Rose staggered to her feet. "Father?"

Her brothers all stood up. Their attention was focused on Lord Elliott.

Harrison was watching his wife. Her complexion had turned a stark white, and he thought she was going to faint.

He hurried to her side and took hold of her arm.

Elliott stood there in the entrance staring at the family. He still didn't know what he was going to say to them. He'd worried about it all the way here. How could he let her brothers know he accepted them as part of his family and hoped they would accept him?

Harrison saw the worry in his eyes and decided to help the reunion along. He leaned down close to his wife's ear, and whispered, "Your father's very nervous."

He knew he wouldn't have to say another word. Mary Rose's heart immediately went out to her father. She hurried to his side, leaned up on her tiptoes, and kissed him on his cheek.

"I'm very happy to see you again."

He came out of his stupor with a start. He took hold of her hands. "Can you ever forgive me, daughter? I'm so sorry for all the pain I caused you."

Tears gathered in her eyes. Her father had spoken in such a passionate voice that she knew the words had come from his heart.

"Oh, Father, I love you. Of course I forgive you. I love Harrison, and I have to forgive him all the time. He forgives me too. It's what family is all about. I'm so sorry I hurt you by leaving."

"No, no, you made me come to my senses. You did the right thing."

Her brothers heard every word of his apology. None of them showed any outward reaction. Harrison thought their expressions could have been set in stone.

"Father, I'm called Mary Rose here."

"All right then."

"All right . . . It's all right?" She threw herself into his arms and hugged him.

"When you come to England to visit me, I may slip now and then and call you Victoria. Will you mind?"

"No, no, I won't mind at all."

Elliott patted her shoulder, a soft smile on his face. His worry eased away. He had done the right thing.

Mary Rose finally remembered her manners. She pulled away from her father and smiled up at him.

"Father, I would like you to meet my brothers," she announced, her voice filled with pride.

Elliott closely studied all of them. Harrison moved to stand with the brothers. Elliott realized why he'd done so. He was helping him remember what the pecking order was in Mary Rose's heart. Her husband came first, then her brothers, and finally her father. He didn't mind being last on her list because he now knew she had enough love for all of them.

The time had finally arrived for him to acknowledge her brothers as family. He didn't feel rushed. He stared at the strapping young men and suddenly felt as though he were in the presence of giants. He was both humbled and in awe of them.

They were God's answer to his prayers. All those years of anguish and terror, in the dark hours of the night when desolation threatened to devour his very soul, he had prayed for a miracle.

And all along God had already given him four.

He had been truly blessed. He had a wonderful daughter, a noble son-in-law, and now . . .

"It appears I have four sons."

November 28, 1877

Dear Mama Rose,

It was voted on and I got stuck writing this letter to beg you to let up. Mama, we think it's wrong for you to keep pestering us to get married. We know you think Adam should marry first because he's the oldest, but he's not going to do it, and that's the way it is. Adam likes it just fine the way things are, and so do we, so please let go of your ideas about grandchildren.

We all expect Mary Rose to get married one day. Now that she's away at school, we can all relax our guards a little. The men around here are constantly fighting for her attention. None of them mind that smart mouth of hers either. We miss her though, more than we thought we would. You don't have to worry about her at all. I taught her how to take care of herself if any of the men in St. Louis try to bother her. She packed her six-shooter and two boxes of bullets. That should be enough.

I hope you aren't angry with me because I had to be so blunt with you. We all love you and wish you could come here and live with us.

Cole

23

God definitely had a sense of humor. Elliott came to his conclusion after observing the behavior of the brothers for an hour or so. Mary Rose's guardian angels were rough and rowdy, argumentative and wary at the same time, and loud. Lord, they were loud. They had the peculiar habit of all talking at the same time, and yet they were all able to hear what everyone else was saying. Elliott felt as if he were sitting in the center of a rally.

He was having the time of his life.

After he'd spoken to the men, they'd come forward to shake his hand. They were hesitant to accept him as part of their family, of course, but Elliott wasn't discouraged. In time they would realize that, like him, they had little choice in the matter. God had pulled them all together, and together they would stay.

He met Adam first. "You're the one who likes to argue, aren't you?" he remarked as he shook his hand.

Adam immediately turned to Harrison. "Did you tell him that?"

"I said you liked to debate," he explained.

Elliott nodded. "Same thing," he announced. "I like to argue too, son. You'll find I always win."

A gleam came into Adam's eyes. "Is that so?"

"You were wrong about the Greeks' motives, you know. I'll have to set you straight."

"I welcome the challenge," Adam responded.

Elliott met Travis next. "You're going to be an attorney," he announced.

"I am?"

"Yes, you are. Harrison says you've a natural ability to sort through quagmire."

Travis grinned. "You just used yesterday's word of the day, sir. I've always wanted to shoot lawyers, not become one."

Douglas shook his hand next. "What did Harrison tell you about me?" he asked.

"That you work magic with your horses. You could make a fortune in England working with thoroughbreds. Animals trust you and that tells me you have compassion. I wondered where my daughter came by hers. Now I know."

Cole waited for his turn. He had already made up his mind he wasn't going to roll over as easily as his brothers had. Elliott had hurt Mary Rose. He should have to pay before they started being hospitable to him.

"Where's the mean one?" Elliott asked.

"Right here, sir," Cole answered before he could stop himself. Then he smiled. "Harrison told you I was mean?"

"It was given with a great deal of admiration," he assured the brother. "I've heard a great amount about you. Some of the remarks were made by a young lady named Eleanor. She seemed to believe you would try to shoot me and told me to be careful around you. As to Eleanor," he continued. "I was wondering . . ."

Cole raised an eyebrow. "What's that, sir?"

"Would all of you mind taking her back?"

The brothers shouted the word *no* at the same time. Elliott laughed. So did Cole, "Sir, you're stuck with her," he said then.

"She's happy there," Mary Rose insisted. "Father, you must be hungry. We've already had our supper, but we'll sit with you while you have yours. Take a chair now. You must be weary from your journey."

She didn't wait to hear his agreement but hurried on into the kitchen. She couldn't quit smiling. She was going to have to get down on her knees and give God a proper thank you for helping her father.

Harrison caught her around the waist and pulled her up against him in the hallway. He leaned down and kissed her ear.

"It's good to see you happy again," he whispered. "Turn around and make me happy. I need to kiss you."

She put her heart into the task. She wrapped her arms around her husband's neck and drew him down for a long, passionate kiss. One wasn't enough, and it wasn't long before they both realized that if they didn't stop now, they wouldn't stop at all.

She was breathless and flustered when she pulled away from him. She was just the way he liked her to be.

"You made him understand, didn't you? Thank you, Harrison."

"No, you made him understand when you left. You gave it all up, and once he realized what you considered valuable, he began to understand. I'm happy he's here too, sweetheart. I've been looking for an edge."

"For Adam?"

Harrison nodded. "Elliott won't let me miss anything. He's the edge I need."

"Let him have his supper before you tell him about Adam. I don't think he'll feel like eating . . . after."

Harrison knew the brothers wouldn't mention it to Elliott. He went back to the table and sat down next to Cole. Adam was seated adjacent to Mary Rose's father. They were talking about the sleeping arrangements.

Cole grinned at him. Harrison should have known something was up. He had a feeling he wasn't going to like it either, because Cole only smiled when he had sorry news to give.

"It's already been decided, Harrison. He's taking Mary Rose's bedroom. You two can sleep in the bunkhouse. You'll have more privacy out there."

"When you were out of the room," Travis told him. "We voted."

Harrison wasn't about to sleep in a bunk bed with his wife. He started to argue, but was waylaid when Mary Rose came back into the dining room. She didn't look happy.

"Cole, Samuel's waving his butcher knife at me again. He won't let me feed Father. Do something, for heaven's sake."

"I'll do something," Harrison roared. He started to stand up. Cole shoved him back down.

"Now, Harrison, he'll only cut you if you go

in there. He's not quite ready to like you yet. I'll go."

Elliott looked stunned. "Someone's in the kitchen with a knife . . . threatening my daughter?"

"Yes, sir," Cole answered on his way to the door. He paused to draw his gun, cock it, and then shoved the door open.

"Samuel, you're sure a trial to my patience," he bellowed.

"Good Lord." Elliott couldn't think of anything more to say.

Harrison relaxed. He turned to Elliott and smiled. The man looked completely befuddled. "They pay him a wage too. Makes you want to pound your head against something hard, doesn't it, sir?"

Elliott nodded. Harrison burst into laughter. Honest to God, there was never a dull minute at the ranch. Adam shook his head and looked sheepish. He guessed maybe to outsiders it did seem crazy to put up with Samuel.

"Samuel's our cook," he explained.

Mary Rose stood tapping her foot against the floor while she waited. Cole finally called to her. She let out a little sigh and went back into the kitchen.

Her father was given a proper supper a few minutes later. The men drank coffee while they waited for him to finish. Mary Rose took his empty plate back into the kitchen.

"I'll be a while. I have to make up with Samuel. He's going to make me beg. I just know it."

"You going to tell him?" Cole asked Harrison

with a nod towards Elliott.

"Yes. Sir, we're all a bit irritable these days. You see, next Friday . . ."

Adam interrupted him. "I'm going to be tried for murder."

Elliott blinked, but it was the only outward reaction he showed to the news.

"Did you do it?"

"Yes, sir."

"That's the last damned time you're going to admit it, Adam," Harrison snapped.

"Don't curse, son."

"Yes, sir."

"Were there extenuating circumstances?"

Adam nodded and then proceeded to give him a full explanation. Elliott listened intently without once interrupting.

"Harrison, are you prepared to defend him?"

"Not quite yet, sir, but I'm getting there. I still have quite a lot of work to do."

Elliott gave him a piercing look. "Do you have a specific plan of action?"

"Yes."

"Will I like the approach you're going to take?" he questioned.

Harrison stared right into his eyes when he answered him. "No, sir, you won't like it at all."

Elliott nodded. "I need paper, pen, and ink. We're going to start all over again, Adam. Harrison, I would like to see your notes."

"Tell us your gut feeling," Cole requested. "Do you think . . ."

Elliott slammed his hand down on the table. "I won't have it. That's what I think."

752

He leaned back in his chair and waited while Harrison went to get the writing supplies and his notes.

No one said a word. They all knew Elliott was thinking about the case, and they didn't want to interrupt him. Mary Rose came back into the room and joined them at the table again.

The silence continued. The air became charged with anticipation. The brothers and their sister sat on the edge of their chairs while they waited to hear Elliott's opinions. They all felt something was about to happen but couldn't explain why. They just *knew*.

When Elliott finally spoke, he addressed Adam. His voice was whisper soft and somewhat chilling.

"He's the best there is, you know. I almost pity your accusers. He won't show any mercy, not in a courtroom, and not after the grievous insult done to his family. Oh, yes, I almost pity them."

Goose bumps covered Mary Rose's arms. "Didn't you train him, Father?" she asked.

"I taught him the law. He has his own unique way of arguing it. He's brilliant, yes, but he's also ruthless. He becomes a predator when he walks into court. I've seen him, watched him, and I'll tell you now, there have been a few instances when I've actually feared him. I would never go up against him. You see, I've only just figured out what he's going to do, and when he's finished, your accusers may not be able to get out of this town alive."

Harrison came back into the dining room a few minutes later with his notes and the writing supplies for Elliott. He noticed the silence immediately. They were all staring up at him, and he knew something significant had happened. He waited for someone to tell him.

No one said a word. And then he noticed something else. He saw it in Adam's eyes.

Hope.

Mary Rose saw very little of Harrison during the next week. He and Douglas went into town together on Monday and didn't return until twilight. Douglas had the five rental horses from the town's stable with him. Neither her husband nor her brother explained why they'd taken the horses.

On Tuesday Travis accompanied Harrison into Blue Belle. They both looked grim when they returned home. Harrison made love to her that night. He was far more demanding than usual. He did things to her she hadn't thought were possible, and she climaxed three times before he gave in to his own fulfillment.

On Wednesday Harrison spent all day going over his notes. The next morning Dooley rode out to the ranch to pass along the news that Judge Burns got tired of fishing and was back at Belle's house again. Elliott was anxious to read the evidence against Adam, but Harrison didn't take him into town until almost eleven o'clock. He was fully occupied taking care of his sick wife.

She'd been throwing up since ten. She tried to get him to leave, insisting she was fine, really, but then she'd start in gagging again, and Harrison got all worked up.

She started feeling better an hour later. She knew she looked like hell. She was draped over the bed, flat on her stomach with her hair hanging down over the side. Harrison squatted down beside her while he mopped her brow with a cold damp cloth.

"This is all my fault, sweetheart. I hurt you last night, and now . . ."

"You didn't hurt me . . . well, you did, but it was a nice kind of hurt. I liked it. I've been feeling nauseated for several days. It isn't your fault. It's the trial. I can't help fretting about it."

Douglas came in the bunkhouse to check on his sister.

"Where the hell have you been?" Harrison demanded. "She's been sick for over an hour now. Do something, for God's sake."

Douglas was a bit taken aback by the fury in Harrison's voice. "She scared you, didn't she? She doesn't get sick very often. I'll take care of her. She's got some color back in her face. I think she's already recovering. Dooley's getting ready to leave. Didn't you want to talk to him?"

"Your sister is going to have to promise me that when I get back this afternoon, I'll find her in bed. Give me your word, Mary Rose, or I'm not going anywhere."

She let out a dramatic sigh. "All right. I'll be in bed."

He lifted her hair away from her face so he could kiss her. Then he let it drop back down again.

Douglas waited until he'd left before broaching

a rather delicate subject.

"Do you know what this is all about?" he asked.

"I'm sick. That's what it's about."

He sat down on the side of her bed. "What kind of sick? Did you eat something that made you ill?"

"No. I'm just worked up about the trial, Douglas."

"Could you be pregnant?"

The question astonished her. She had to think about it a long while.

"Have you missed your monthly?"

She turned beet red in less than a minute. "You're embarrassing me. You're my brother, for heaven's sake. You shouldn't ask such personal questions."

"Have you?"

"Yes."

"How many?"

"Two . . . no, three."

Mary Rose lifted her head off the pillow. "Do you think . . ."

She couldn't go on. The wonder of it all was just settling in. A baby. She might really be having a baby. She was suddenly overwhelmed with joy.

"I think I'm going to become an uncle," Douglas said. He patted her on her shoulder and smiled down at her.

"We can't tell Harrison. Don't tell anyone until I'm certain, Douglas. My husband has enough to think about. He'll be happy about my news, but he might become distracted. We can't have that."

Douglas agreed. Harrison left an hour later to

take her father over to Belle's house so he could look over the evidence against Adam. Then he went back into town again. He spent the day there and didn't return to the ranch until suppertime.

He went directly to the bunkhouse to make certain Mary Rose was where he'd left her. He took one look at her and knew she'd gotten out of bed.

She wasn't about to admit it.

"Did you rest all day, sweetheart?"

"Yes, I did."

He smiled. "You stayed in bed?"

She smiled back. "You should be happy with me," she answered, which wasn't a proper answer at all. "You didn't think you'd find me in bed, did you? I could tell you were surprised. How did your day go?"

He decided to force her to lie outright. She hadn't yet. She'd evaded his questions. She looked damned proud of herself too.

"Did you rest in bed all day?"

She didn't miss a beat. "Now, why would you ask me that again? Don't you believe me, Harrison? You'll have to trust me, I suppose."

He shook his head. His sweet wife had completely disregarded his instructions. He didn't know what he was going to do about that. He let out a loud sigh. There really wasn't a damned thing he could do about it. She was stubborn and willful, and unless he tied her down to the bed, she'd do what she thought best.

"Just promise me that when you feel ill, you'll rest. All right?"

She sat up in bed. "Why don't you believe me?"

He didn't answer her. "I'm going up to the house. You might want to put something on your face before you join me, sweetheart."

He knew she'd ask him why, of course, and he couldn't wait to tell her. He started counting to ten as he opened the door and started out.

"Wait," she called out. "What's wrong with my face?"

"It's sunburned."

She wasn't the least bit contrite, but she was thoughtful. He'd give her that much. She waited until he'd pulled the door closed before she started laughing.

Was it any wonder why he loved her?

Everyone had just finished supper when Alfred Mitchell came riding down the slope.

"Stranger's here. Take a look, sir. Is he one of your relatives?"

Elliott squinted out the window. "Can't tell from this distance, but I don't believe I know the man."

"Then it's Alfred Mitchell. Harrison, do you want us to wait inside while you talk to him?"

"Yes."

"Offer him some refreshment," Mary Rose called out.

She wasn't sure if Harrison heard her or not. He'd already gone outside. Harrison didn't wait for the attorney on the porch. He went down the steps and kept walking. The two men met halfway across the meadow.

Mitchell let out a loud groan when he dismounted. The two men shook hands and introduced themselves.

"You look worn out," Harrison remarked.

Mitchell nodded. He looked up at Harrison, for Mitchell was quite a bit shorter. He appeared to be several years younger as well.

"I am worn out," he admitted in a slow southern drawl. "I've gotten what you asked for, but I also bring you some terrible news. Can we walk while we talk? I'd like to work the cramps out of my backside before I ride back to my campsite."

"You're welcome to stay the night here, Alfred."

"I'm afraid I won't be able to keep quiet about what's happening if I do stay. I've made camp close to town. I think I'll stay there tonight, if you don't mind my being unsociable."

"You'll have to testify tomorrow," Harrison reminded him.

"Yes, I know. I'm eager to do so, sir. Very eager to tell what happened."

Harrison and Alfred started walking toward the mountains. Mary Rose watched from behind the screen door.

Harrison was strolling along with his hands clasped behind his back for several minutes, then he suddenly turned to Mitchell.

"You can't hear anything from here," Douglas whispered behind her back.

She jumped. "Harrison doesn't like what Mitchell is telling him. Look how rigid both men are. I don't think it's good news, Douglas. It's bad."

759

"The only bad thing would be that Mitchell didn't get the signed papers, Mary Rose, and you can see Harrison's holding something in his hand. My guess is that Mitchell couldn't get Livonia to sign one."

Harrison and Alfred continued to talk for over twenty minutes. Mary Rose thought the conference was over when they turned and started walking back. She went outside and stood on the porch to wait.

Alfred shook Harrison's hand and climbed back up in his saddle. Mary Rose almost called out to the man to invite him to stay for the night. Harrison turned toward her, and when she saw the look on his face, she couldn't have spoken a word to anyone. Her husband looked devastated.

He walked closer, then stopped and stood there staring at her.

He wanted her to come to him. Mary Rose didn't hesitate. She ran to him.

He didn't say a word to her, but took hold of her hand and turned around again.

They walked clear across the meadow before he stopped.

"I'm going to lie tomorrow."

Her eyes widened. "You're going to lie in court?"

He didn't answer her. "I won't lie to you unless you give me permission to."

She didn't know what to say. They started walking again, their heads bowed, as each thought about tomorrow.

It only took Mary Rose a few minutes to understand. "You would never lie in court. No,

760

you'd never do that. It's unethical . . . and so, you're going to lie to my brothers. You'd like to lie to me too, but you . . ."

"I promised you I would never lie to you again. I won't ever break my word."

"Unless I give you permission."

"Yes."

"All right."

She turned and smiled at him. "I trust you. Do what you must. Now isn't the time to worry about me."

He was humbled by her. He closed his eyes and slowly nodded. "Thank you."

"For trusting you?"

"And loving me . . . and being who you are."

"Kiss me, and I'll know you mean it."

He did just that.

They walked back to the house in silence. "I'm going for a ride. Do you want to go with me?"

"You need to think about things. I think maybe you need to be alone now."

He kissed her again and then went to the barn. Mary Rose leaned against the porch railing and watched.

Harrison came out just a minute later. MacHugh was by his side. The stallion wasn't wearing a saddle or a halter, but he stayed right by Harrison's side as they crossed the meadow.

Harrison suddenly turned to the animal, grabbed hold of his mane, and swung up on his back. MacHugh went into a full gallop up the first slope.

"He rides like an Indian," Travis remarked.

"Where's he going?"

"To think."

"Your father would like you to play the piano. Are you feeling up to it?"

"I'm fine," she said although it wasn't true.

Playing would help her forget about her worries, she decided, and so she went inside and sat down on the piano bench.

Her father was standing close, eagerly waiting. "What are you going to play, daughter?"

Her brothers had seen her expression when she walked into the parlor. They knew exactly what she would play.

"The Fifth," they all told him at the same time.

And so she did, over and over and over again.

It was sunny and bright Friday morning. Mary Rose was disappointed to see blue skies. She wanted a good storm with thunder and lightning, because she thought bad weather might keep some of the curious in their own towns where they belonged.

She rode with her father in the covered buggy. Neither one of them felt like talking. She spent her time praying and worrying about Adam and Harrison. Her brother's nightmare was finally taking place, and she was powerless to stop it.

It was all up to Harrison. God help him. He'd looked so grim when he joined her in bed. He'd held on to her all through the night.

She tried to talk to him before they got dressed, but he cut her off before she'd even gotten started. She wanted to tell him she loved him and she trusted him, and that no matter what happened today, she would go right on loving him and believing in him. Harrison wouldn't listen. He was abrupt and distant. She became really scared then, but as he was leaving, he turned and gave her the most wonderful and surely the meanest order she'd ever heard.

He told her he'd put a gag in her mouth if she said or did anything to make him feel good. And if she told him she loved him, he just might lock her in a closet and leave her there all day.

"In other words, you don't want to be distracted."

He nodded.

They left for Blue Belle an hour later. Harrison led the family, and Travis rode shotgun.

Harrison stopped the procession just outside of town.

"Mary Rose? Do you feel all right? I don't want you throwing up in court."

"I won't throw up," she promised him.

"Adam, I read somewhere that slaves weren't allowed to look directly at their owners until they were ordered to do so. Was that true?"

"Yes. It was considered insolent . . . uppity. Why'd you ask me that question?"

"Because I forgot to ask you last night," he snapped. "When you sit down at the table in court, I want you to stare at Livonia's sons. Keep your expression bland, but let them know you're staring at them. Look at one brother all the while he's testifying. Look him right in the eyes, Adam. When the other one gets up there, do the same thing. When I give you the nod, let them see disdain on your face."

"They'll hate it," Adam warned him.

Harrison nodded. "I hope so. Does everyone else remember what I told you?"

He waited until they nodded and then gave them one last piece of information.

"Don't believe anything you hear from *anyone* while you're in court."

"Not even you?" Mary Rose asked.

He repeated his earlier statement. He wasn't going to tell them he planned to lie, because he had no such intent. He didn't want them finding out bad news until after the jury had been sequestered by Judge Burns.

"No matter what I say or do, don't look surprised or angry. You hear me, Cole?"

"I hear you."

"Let's get it done."

Harrison led the way down the last slope and across the flat into town. It was slow going down the main road because a large crowd had already gathered. None of the gawkers would be allowed inside the storefront until Judge Burns opened the doors for them.

It was a mixed group of people waiting. Some yelled encouraging cheers, while others tried to drown them out by shouting filthy obscenities. Mary Rose tried to pretend she couldn't hear, but it was a difficult task at best.

The crowd separated so that they could go forward. Mary Rose held on to her father's arm and let him guide her inside.

Judge Burns was already seated behind the table at the end of the room. He faced the door. He motioned the family to come forward. Chairs of every sort from households around Blue Belle had been carried in and placed in neat rows facing the judge. A wide aisle led down the middle.

About fifteen feet away from the judge's table on the right side of the storefront were two rows of chairs, six in each, for the jury.

"You can take your seats now. Hello, William," he called out to Mary Rose's father. "I didn't see you standing behind all those tall boys of yours. It's a hell of a sorry day, isn't it?"

"Yes, Your Honor. It certainly is."

"Harrison, that suggestion you gave me yesterday and tried to make me think it was all my own idea? Well, I've decided to go along with it because it makes good sense to me. I don't want a bunch of strangers in here. They'll only disrupt me, and then, by God, I'll have to start in shooting. Can't abide chaos in my court. Cole, get on up and hand me your guns. I'll look after them for you. The rest of you boys do the same. Mary Rose? You carrying a pistol?"

"No, Your Honor."

"All right then."

The judge waited until all the Clayborne guns had been placed on his table.

"Harrison, Morrison's agreed to help me figure out which ones live in Blue Belle or in a ten-mile circle around the town. No one else is getting inside, especially that no-account vigilante group from Hammond. I'll head on outside in a minute. First, I got to ask you what objections you have to any of the jury members. Do you mind women along with the men if I decided to pick one or two? I might be ornery enough to do it."

Harrison smiled. "I don't have any objections to letting women sit on the jury, Your Honor. Whatever you decide will be fine with me."

"Well, now, that's mighty accommodating. Anything you don't cotton to?"

"No, Your Honor. I've compiled my own list of people who live in and around Blue Belle. I've taken the liberty of putting a check mark next to the ones who came from down South."

The judge grinned. "Any ringers in this here list of yours?"

"Excuse me, Your Honor?"

"Never you mind. I spoke out of turn. I know how you operate, now that I've watched you pontificating in my courtroom in Hammond. You wouldn't stoop to buying anyone off. I'll be happy to use your list. It will make my job sorting everyone out much easier. I'm making John Morrison foreman. You got any objections to that?"

Harrison pretended to ponder the matter. He didn't want Judge Burns to know what a piece of luck it was. Adam had come to Morrison's aid when the roof of his store caved in. He hoped to God Morrison remembered.

"No, Your Honor. I have no objections. Morrison's an honest man."

"If everyone's ready, I'll let folks trickle in."

"Your Honor, will you have someone stand in front of the door to keep everyone else out?"

"I will," the judge answered.

"I'm expecting an important telegram. If it arrives . . ."

"I'll see you get it. That's cutting it a little short, isn't it, Harrison?"

"The telegram will help, but it isn't needed to present my case."

Burns stood up. "I'm bringing in those southern boys last. Since they're witnesses against Adam, I'll sit them over on the other side of the defendant. I put the two chairs at an angle so the jury and the crowd can get a good look at them."

Harrison waited until the judge was on his way down the main aisle before joining Adam at the table. He sat down, leaned close to the brother, and whispered something into his ear.

Mary Rose couldn't hear what her husband said, but she was able to see her brother's reaction. Adam looked astonished. Then he smiled. It was the first time in weeks he'd shown any joy. She couldn't imagine what Harrison had said to him.

Her husband leaned back in his chair. He wouldn't look at her when he asked her once again if she was feeling all right.

"Yes," she whispered.

Harrison had ordered all of them to keep quiet during the trial, and so, when the first man walked in and went directly to the chairs reserved for the jury, everyone hushed.

There weren't any women sitting on the jury. Mary Rose recognized most of the men, but she couldn't remember some of their names. None of the twelve was smiling. They all had solemn expressions, which she thought were appropriate, given the seriousness of the case they were going to hear.

Lionel and Reginald Adderley were the last two men allowed inside. They stomped their way to the front and took their seats.

Both of the men had blond hair. Reginald was older than his brother by several years. He had gray streaks in his closely cropped beard. His eyes were hazel but with more yellow than green in them. He reminded her of a lizard.

His brother was just as ugly. His eyes were brown. His skin was pasty like his brother's, suggesting to her that neither brother had ever worked outside a day in his life.

Dooley was given the duty of guarding the door. Billie was told to spell him.

Harrison continued to stay seated until Burns got to the end of the aisle. Harrison immediately stood up. So did Adam.

So no one else moved. The judge seemed pleased by the deference Harrison and Adam were showing him.

"With Your Honor's permission?"

Burns guessed what he was asking. He eagerly nodded. "Wait until I get on in the storeroom," he whispered. "This is gonna be a first, and I want to enjoy every minute."

Adam started to sit down. Harrison wouldn't let him. "Stand," he whispered.

Harrison waited until the judge had disappeared into the storeroom, and then called out in a loud, booming voice, "Hear Ye, Hear Ye. All rise. Court is now in session. Judge John Burns is presiding."

The crowd immediately got out of their chairs. The judge peeked around the corner to make certain everyone was standing, then strutted into the courtroom, looking as pleased and proud as a peacock. He obviously loved formality and rarely got it.

He took his time going to his table and taking his seat.

"All right. Sit yourselves back down."

"I'm only going to say this once, so all of you hear me good. I won't tolerate shouting or cheering or making any other noises while my court is in session. This here is sacred ground right this minute cause of me squatting on it. First, I'm going to tell the jury the evidence against Adam Clayborne. Then I'll call two witnesses."

The judge paused to take a drink of water.

"John Quincy Adam Clayborne has been charged with murdering Walter Adderley. Adderley was the man who owned Adam during the slaving years. Adderley's sons brung me letters the Clayborne family had written to Adam's mother, Rose. Now Rose still lives down south on that same plantation with Adderley's wife, Livonia. She takes care of her 'cause the woman's plumb blind. In six or seven of the letters, there's mention of Adderley's death. Ain't nothing damning though. Adam don't admit to killing Adderley, but he does admit to being in the house when Adderley died, and Adam also admits in writing that he ran. I'll question Adam all about that when he takes the stand. He is taking the stand, isn't he, Harrison?"

"Yes, Your Honor, he is."

"Fine. Now I got one last thing to say to you, jury. I want to see justice done here today. If any of you have already made up your minds that Adam's guilty, raise your butts off them chairs and get on out of here. A man's innocent until proven guilty, and I ain't allowing no man to railroad him.

"Harrison, it's your turn now. You got something you want to say to the jury?"

"Yes, Your Honor," Harrison answered.

He stood up and walked across the room so he could face the twelve men.

"My client has been accused of a crime he didn't commit. If you listen to all the testimony, you will give Adam his freedom. Open up your hearts and your minds, rid yourselves of any feelings you might have regarding the color of his skin, and see that he gets a fair hearing. Abraham Lincoln believed in equality, and so did hundreds of thousands of valiant young men who willingly gave their lives so that slavery would be abolished. Don't mock the memories of those courageous men. Remember how they died and why. Adam's life is in your hands, gentlemen, and I will prove to you, without a doubt, that he is innocent."

Harrison turned and slowly walked back to the table. Mary Rose thought he was finished. She had to force herself not smile. She was so proud of her husband. His speech had impressed her, yes, but it was the extra touch he'd added that made it more forceful. There was a very, very subtle western drawl blended in with his deep resonant Highland brogue. She didn't think anyone else noticed the change in his speech though, and she thought she knew why he'd done it. He wanted the jury to think of him as one of their own.

"I'm going to tell you a little bit about John Quincy Adam. I'll start by telling you why his

770

mother gave him the name. Some of you might recall your history and already know John Quincy Adams was the sixth president of the United States. That isn't why Adam's mother so admired the man though. She'd heard a story about President Adams and found out later it was true. After Adams retired from being such a fine president, he went back on home, thinking he'd lead a nice, peaceful life, and he did just that until he heard about a shameful incident going on in our very own country. In 1835 or about, some Spanish pirates kidnapped fifty-two Africans and headed for Cuba. Two Cubans purchased all of them and headed for the sugar plantations to sell them. Well, now, the Africans didn't much like the notion of being slaves, so they revolted. They killed one of the crew too. When the ship reached Long Island, the Cubans had them tossed in jail and charged them with revolt and murder.

"Now, why do you think the incident bothered President Adams so much? Slavery was legal back then, wasn't it?"

Several of the jurors nodded.

Harrison's western drawl become a little more pronounced as he continued. "I sure was confused, I'll tell you, so I went and looked it up and found out why it was wrong. Slave trade with other countries had already been outlawed by 1835. A lot of other countries put the same law into effect too. So here's the law. A black man born in America in 1835 would be a slave, but it was illegal to bring slaves into our country from outside.

"Well, now, President Adams couldn't help but get riled up about it. He believed everyone should obey the laws they had all gone to so much trouble to write down. He didn't keep quiet about his opinion either. No, sir, he didn't. His friends told him to stay away from the issue because it wasn't popular to argue in defense of a black man. Of course that only got Adams more riled up. Know what he said?"

Several jurors shook their heads. "He said, 'May I walk humbly and uprightly, on this and all other occasions, flinching from no duty, obtruding no officious interposition of opinions, and prepared to meet with firmness whatever obloquy may follow the free expression of my thoughts.' Now, what he meant was that the law was the law, and he guessed he was going to have to kick a few backsides if he had to in order to protect his country's honor. The law is the law. If one or two men disregard it, and no one does anything about it, well then, pretty soon there's more and more folks willing to bend the rules to suit them. Before you know it, all the rights the forefathers gave us in the Constitution are plumb ignored . . . even yours."

Harrison paused to stare at each one of the jurors before continuing. "Adams was seventy-four years old, but age and ill-health didn't stop him from marching into the Supreme Court and having his say. He defended those black men, and when he was finished, the Africans were sent back home where they belonged. The law is the law. Adams remembered that. I want all of you to remember it too. Adam's mother sure did admire the gumption of President Adams, and that's why she gave her son his name.

"My client was born into slavery. The law said that's what he was from the minute he took his first breath. He lived and worked on Adderley's plantation. Now Walter Adderley didn't think much of his slaves. He didn't think much of his wife, Livonia, either. I can prove what I'm saying. I have signed documents from southern white men who remember seeing Livonia all beaten up. Her husband liked drink, and when he got drunk, he got mean. He was a big man, over six feet tall. His wife was a little bit of a thing, around five feet on tiptoes. She certainly couldn't defend herself against her beloved . . ." Harrison sneered the word as though it were a blasphemy, "hus-band. Walter Adderley beat her pretty regularly according to all the accounts I gathered. He liked to hit her about her head. She's blind now, and the doctors all say the blows her beloved" — he sneered the word once again — "husband gave her caused the condition. Do any of you think it's all right to beat your mama or your wife?"

Harrison knew he wasn't supposed to ask ques-tions, and before he could be reprimanded by the judge, he hurried on. "No, sir, it makes you plumb sick to think about it, doesn't it?"

Every single one of the jurors nodded. Harrison held them in the palm of his hand. He wasn't about to let them get away.

"It made Adam Clayborne sick too. Livonia wasn't the only woman who got regular beatings. Adam's own mama took her share. She tried to protect her mistress, you see, and one time she got her nose broken for her interference.

"When Adam was around thirteen years old,

he heard terrible shouting going on inside the house. Livonia was calling out for help. Adam went on in to see what was wrong. He didn't like what he found. His mistress was down on the floor. Her beloved husband was kicking her. You'll hear Adam tell you all about it, of course. He knew Adderley was drunk 'cause he reeked of whiskey, and so he put his arms around his waist and pulled him back. Adam wasn't big for his age, so Adderley was able to shrug him off. He started in on Livonia again, and again Adam pulled him back. Adderley lost his footing then. He tumbled across the floor and went headfirst into the mantel. Adam didn't kill him. No, he did not. Drink and meanness destroyed Walter Adderley. Why did Adam run? Because his mistress begged him to run, that's why. She knew what would happen if her sons found out. Adam was a slave, remember, and slaves were never allowed to touch their masters. He'd be killed by those sons for doing a kindness and trying to keep their own mama alive."

Harrison turned around and started back to the table. He suddenly stopped. His voice turned hard, angry. "If a man ever was in need of killing, Walter Adderley surely was. Any man who beats a woman ought to die. Adam didn't kill him though. The evidence I've collected and will show you will prove his innocence. I'll tell you one thing though. If I were wearing his shoes, and someone, even my father, was beating on my mama, I don't believe I would have been honorable. I think I'd have to kill him if he raised a hand against my mama. Yes, sir, I would."

John Morrison and two others gave quick nods.

Every one of the jurors remembered his own mother. In most instances, mamas were sacred to their sons. None of them liked Walter Adderley much now.

It was just the beginning. Harrison wanted them to hate the man, and then he would slowly turn that hatred toward the two sons.

It was still a black man up against two white men. The odds weren't in Adam's favor yet. Harrison was going to turn the focus. People who didn't know any better tended to hate anyone different from them, and Harrison was assuming that while the jurors might be sympathetic to Adam, they'd hang him all the same.

Unless there was someone else they could hate more.

His next task was to get all of them to like Adam. His voice took on a story-reading tone when he said, "I'm only going to take another minute of your time. I think you ought to know a little about Adam Clayborne. Fact is, I think you have to be real curious about all of them. The Claybornes don't like talking about themselves. They're private, just like all of you, but I think you should hear how they all got together and formed their own family.

"After Walter Adderley died, Adam went to New York City. He slept in an alley with three other boys. Douglas and Travis and Cole were younger than Adam was, so they looked up to him to take care of them. It was quite a responsibility for a thirteen-year-old boy to take on, wasn't it? Well, he'd saved every one of them from near death, and he figured he'd go on doing just that until he got caught and taken back down South. He was scared all right, but not because Walter Adderley had died. That was his own accident, not Adam's doing. Adam was scared because he'd touched him when he'd put his arms around his waist. He knew they'd kill him for that insolence. Yes, sir, trying to save a mama would have been called insolent."

Harrison paused to shake his head. "Well, now, one night they found a basket someone had thrown into the trash. Rats were climbing all over the thing, but Adam was able to get the basket away from the vermin. Little Mary Rose was inside. Like Travis and Douglas and Cole, she'd been thrown away. Lots of kids roamed the streets back then because their daddies didn't want them around any longer. Some were gathered up, tossed on trains, and sent west. Others died of starvation. Well, now, little Mary Rose was just four months old. The boys didn't want to take her to an orphanage because they knew what went on inside those places, and they all believed she wouldn't last long. They wanted her to have a chance at life. And that's when they decided to all take the name Clayborne and head west, where people have such fine morals and values. It took them a long while, but they made it to Blue Belle. Adam was the only one who could read, his mama had taught him how, and so he taught his brothers. They wanted to be educated for their sister. They wanted her to have a good life, you see. They had help too. Sweet Belle made little dresses for her and showed her how to be a little girl.

Then families started settling into the area, and pretty soon Mary Rose had friends to play with. And family. She had family, just like everyone should be entitled to. The boys scrimped and saved and did without so she could have piano lessons. When she was old enough, they sent her to a boarding school in St. Louis. None of them had an easy time of it. No, sir, they didn't. But they had neighbors helping, and whenever one of their friends was in trouble, every one of the Claybornes came running to help.

"Mary Rose knows all about how she was found. She gets mad when one of her brothers calls her Sidney. It was the first name they gave her until they found out she was a girl. She was bald, you see, and so, because the boys were so young themselves, they figured she had to be a boy."

The jurors were smiling now. Harrison decided he'd said enough. "So now you know how they became a family. Mary Rose wasn't the thread that held them all together though, like the brothers believe. No, Adam kept them united. He's honorable and honest and good-hearted. If he'd killed someone, he'd be the first to admit it. Remember that, gentlemen. You're judging an honest man. Listen to what he has to say. Thank you."

There was a thunderous round of applause as Harrison took his seat. Even Judge Burns clapped for him.

He nodded to Harrison, took another gulp of water, and then called John Quincy Adam Clayborne to the stand.

Adam moved to the chair at the end of the judge's table. He sat as straight as a general.

"Did you kill Walter Adderley, Adam?" the judge asked.

"No, sir, I did not."

"Tell me what you recollect of that day."

Adam did just that. He spoke in a low voice. The room was as quiet as an empty cathedral, and the people in the back rows barely had to strain to hear his every word.

Adam left out the fact that he'd struck Adderley in the chin. The blow hadn't done any damage. The big man he was trying to get to leave Livonia alone didn't even flinch when he'd hit him. Besides, Harrison had told him to keep that information to himself.

"I got one last question to ask you before you go back to your chair, Adam. How come your mama didn't come here to live with all of you after the war was over and all the slaves were freed?"

"Mistress Livonia was almost blind back then and very dependent on my mother for every little thing. If you knew my mama, you'd understand she couldn't have turned her back on the helpless woman. She stayed on to take care of her."

"Livonia Adderley has two sons sitting right over there. Didn't they help their mother?"

"No, sir, they didn't."

"All right. You can get on back now."

The judge waited until Adam was sitting down at his table before he called his next witness. "Lionel Adderley, it's your turn to talk. Sit your-

778

self down in the chair. I'll ask you questions as we go along, and when I'm done, Harrison will have his turn questioning you. What's all that commotion going on at the door, Dooley," he shouted.

"It's Miss Blue Belle, Judge. She's saying you told her she could come on in."

"Let her in then," the judge bellowed. "She can squeeze herself in next to Travis on the aisle there."

Everyone paused to watch Blue Belle stroll down the aisle. She smiled at the judge and sat down where he directed her.

"Thank you, Judge," she called out.

"You're welcome, Blue Belle. You sure look pretty today in your blue dress."

"Judge, honey, you know I always wear blue. I'm glad it pleases you."

He nodded, then turned to Lionel. He and Harrison both noticed the disgust on the southerner's face. Lionel was staring at Blue Belle while he sneered.

The judge's back arched in reaction, and his lips puckered.

"Tell me what you know, Lionel. Be quick about it."

"My brother and I found the nigger's letters to his mother. When we read them, we knew Adam had killed our father."

"Hold on now. I just read those same letters, and I didn't come away with that notion."

"The nigger admits running, doesn't he? He grabbed hold of my poor daddy too, didn't he? He knew the punishment for touching a white man, but he did it anyway. He should die for his murder and his insolence, and I'm here to see that he does. I'll admit he didn't write down that he killed my father. My brother and I went to our mother to find out exactly what happened. You've got the paper we wrote the facts down on as she told us the truth, and then we put a pen in her hand and she signed it. She says the nigger killed my father. That's all the proof you need."

"It's damning evidence all right," the judge agreed. "Were there any witnesses to your mother's confession?"

"Yes, my brother Reginald was there . . . and the nigger's mother. She didn't count though. A southerner knows better than to trust anything a nigger says."

Harrison could feel the hate oozing out of the man. He looked at the jury to see how they were reacting. They seemed uncomfortable, for several squirmed in their chairs, but they didn't hate Lionel Adderley. Yet.

It was time for him to go to work.

"It's your turn, Harrison."

He leaned close to Adam. "Don't believe a word I say. If I *nod,* you'll know I'm lying. Tell your brothers and sister, but don't let anyone else hear you."

Harrison made a lot of noise scraping his chair back to distract anyone from overhearing Adam speak to the family.

He walked to the judge's table first. "Well, now, maybe that's damning evidence, and then again, maybe it isn't. We're going to have to see about that, aren't we?"

"We surely are."

Harrison turned to Lionel. He stared at him a long half minute. He wanted the jurors to see the look of repulsion on his face.

His voice was mild and mellow when he began his interrogation. "I like to think I'm like my father, God rest his soul. He was a good man. Are you like your father, Lionel?"

"I suppose I am. I'm his proud son."

"Well, then, you admire him."

"Yes. Everyone admired my daddy."

"What happened after he died? Did things change around the plantation?"

"The war came. That's what happened."

"I'll bet you think your daddy could have stopped it from happening. You think so too, don't you, being such a proud-of-your-daddy son and all."

"We'll never know, will we?" Lionel sneered. "He might have stopped it. He would have made a difference in our lives though. We lost everything and Daddy never would have let that happen."

"How old were you when your daddy died?"

"Seventeen."

"And your younger brother? How old was he?"

"Twelve."

"Seventeen's old enough to fight. Did you sign up for duty, Lionel?"

"No, but only because I have a physical ailment that prevented me from serving in the Confederate Army."

"What might that ailment be, Lionel?"

781

"Do I have to tell, Judge?"

"Yes, you do."

"My feet," he snapped. "They're flat. I broke the arches. I can't walk long distances."

"Flat feet kept you out of the Confederate Army?"

"Yes."

Harrison didn't believe him. He knew no one else in the courtroom did either.

"Did your father ever strike you?"

"No, never."

He was lying again. Harrison walked over to the table, picked up a Bible, and held it out for Lionel to see.

The judge hadn't bothered with the formality of swearing everyone in. Harrison decided to correct that error now.

"When this court was called into session and Honorable John Burns walked inside, it was more than showing him the respect he's due. It was the signal to everyone here that what was said from that moment on would be truthful. I don't have any patience with perjury. You're wasting the jury's valuable time as well as the judge's. I now ask you once again, did your father ever strike you?"

Lionel shrugged. "A slap every now and then. Nothing like . . ."

Harrison leapt on the opening. "Nothing like what he did to your mother?"

"She provoked him," Lionel shouted. "A man's wife should be obedient. Mother knew that. She liked to pick fights with him. She knew he had a temper."

"Were some of the fights about you boys?"

"Maybe. I can't say."

"You can't? Well, now, I've got a signed statement from one of your neighbors who happened inside your house one day and saw you and Reginald hiding behind your mama's skirts while your father beat on her. She let him pound away so she could protect you."

"I was very young."

"You were sixteen. Almost a man. You were already bigger than your mama."

"You make it sound worse than it was."

Lionel turned to the judge. "My daddy's behavior isn't on trial here. That nigger boy is. Do your job and remind your attorney."

"Don't you go telling me my job," Burns growled.

"That's telling him, honey," Blue Belle called out.

The judge smiled. "Harrison?" he said then. "I guess you know where you're headed."

Lionel was on edge. Harrison decided to let him relax a minute before he went in for the kill. He nodded to the judge before turning to the witness again.

"I agree with you, Lionel. Your daddy's behavior isn't on trial. Are you an honest man?"

"Every southern gentleman is an honest man."

"Was Livonia's confession forced? Did you coerce her into signing the paper?"

"I most certainly did not. She wanted to tell. She'd held it inside for a long time. She was afraid."

"Afraid of what?"

"The nigger taking care of her. My mother knew that if she told, the nigger mama would kill her."

"Disregard that last stupid remark, jury. He's speaking what he can't know for certain," the judge ordered.

"If Rose was as mean as you paint her to be, why didn't she kill your mother a whole hell of a lot sooner and leave?"

"She didn't have the guts, that's why. She had opportunity. She was too stupid to know it."

"You weren't around your mama much after your father died, were you?"

"It was difficult to watch her losing her sight. My brother and I stayed in the main house. She and her nigger moved into a cottage on the edge of the property."

"Did you take over for your father?"

"I tried."

Harrison nodded. He walked over to the jury and looked at them. "Here's the way I see it. Lionel says his mother's confession wasn't co-erced, and he expects all of you to believe him. He's white, after all. We should believe him over Adam, shouldn't we? Well, now, I think maybe I ought to find out if Lionel is telling us the truth. If he lies about one thing, he's gonna lie about another, isn't he? That's the way I see it. Yes, sir, I do. Lionel, what do you think of our little town?"

"I like it just fine."

"You like the people here?"

"Yes, I do. They're very pleasant."

"Did you spend a lot of time this past week in town?"

"My brother and I had to stay. We wanted to go riding up in the mountains, but there weren't any horses available to rent, and we'd come here by stagecoach."

"Did you spend some time in Morrison's nice general store?"

"Yes."

"Did you spend some time in the saloon?"

"Yes."

"So you met quite a few nice people, didn't you?"

"Yes."

"Did you meet anyone you didn't like?"

Lionel pretended to have to think about it. "No, I liked everyone just fine."

"Even our own Blue Belle? Did you like her too?"

Lionel must have figured where he was being led. He gave the judge a quick glance, then closed his mouth.

"Answer his question, Lionel," the judge ordered.

"Yes, I liked her just as much as I liked everyone else."

Harrison's voice changed then. He let his disdain and his anger sound in his tone.

"You got a strange notion about what's nice and what isn't. Fact is, you're lying, aren't you, Lionel? You hate every one of us."

"That isn't true."

"And Belle?" he prodded once again.

"I like Belle fine."

"He's lying, Judge," Blue Belle shouted. "He called me a filthy, nickel-dollar whore. He said it in front of Billie too."

"She is a whore." Lionel defended.

Harrison smiled. He turned around. "Thank you, Blue Belle," he drawled out. "It was right nice of you to help out."

"Now, we got us another problem, Judge. It seems what we consider nice and what the southern boys consider nice are two different things. Lionel, you think maybe nice means disgusting to you boys?"

Lionel didn't answer him. Harrison continued to press. "What about the other women in town? What about Mary Rose?"

"She's trash. She's living with a nigger, isn't she?"

Harrison didn't lose his control. He wanted to punch the son-of-bitch for insulting his wife, of course. He was going to destroy him instead.

"Harrison, what's this about? Why are you questioning him about the town folk?" the judge asked.

"Goes to character, Judge," Harrison answered. "If a man says he's telling the truth, I have to find out if I can believe him."

The judge agreed. "What about Catherine Morrison? What nice thing did you have to say about her to Dooley and Henry and Ghost?"

"I don't recall."

"Well, now, I do. I had Henry write it down, too, and sign it. We'll get him on up here if we need to and let him say what happened."

Harrison walked back to the table and took the top paper. He handed it to the judge. "Lionel called our Catherine a man-sniffing whore, and that he was sure she'd had most of the men in Blue Belle. He suggested to Henry that she go into business with Belle. He had a few things to say about her mama too. I'm not going to repeat them. They're too foul. You can read them to the jury if you want."

The judge did just that. Harrison deliberately avoided looking at John Morrison. He went back to the table and collected four other signed papers, and when the judge had finished reading what Henry had written down, Harrison handed him the other evidence.

He went back to Lionel. "The fact is simple for all of us to understand. You hold all of us in contempt, don't you, Lionel. We aren't citified and probably not very sophisticated by your southern boy standards, and so we're lower than snakes to you, aren't we? You've spent the last week mocking all of us and laughing at us. Half the town heard you."

Lionel straightened up in his chair and glared at Harrison. His hatred was more than evident now. "So what if I think you are? I've suffered intolerable conditions this past week so that I could see justice served. Yes, my brother and I think you're all dirty, uncivilized swill. What we think doesn't change a thing. My mother signed the confession, saying the nigger's guilty. That's all that matters."

"But you just perjured yourself, now didn't you, Lionel?"

"I merely tried to be tactful."

"Why now? You've been anything but tactful all week. Did you coerce your mother into signing that paper?" Harrison shouted his last question.

"No, I did not, and you can't prove otherwise," Lionel shouted back.

"Your Honor, when this is finished, I want this man locked up for perjury. I'm not finished with him, but I would like to call him back to the stand after you hear from another witness."

The judge was glaring at Lionel. "All right. Get out of the chair, Lionel, but don't leave the court."

Harrison called Alfred Mitchell to the stand. He took the time to swear him in by having the man place his hand on the Bible.

The judge took over. "Do you swear to tell the truth?"

"I do."

"I don't believe the Bible's necessary. Once court's in session, everybody's got to tell the truth."

"Tell who you are and why you're here, Alfred," Harrison began.

"My name is Alfred Mitchell. I'm an attorney in the law offices of Mitchell, Mitchell and Mitchell. My two brothers are the other two Mitchells," he explained.

"I received a wire from you, Harrison, asking for certain information. You wanted quite a few things done, and you also wanted me to get here before the two weeks were up, so I enlisted the assistance of my brothers, and we all went to work. I got everything you wanted . . . and more,

I'm sorry to say. I gave you the signed and witnessed documents yesterday."

Mitchell turned to the jury. He was young, but he'd already learned how to charm people.

"I happen to like Blue Belle. I've only seen a little bit of your town, but it reminds me of a town near the one where I grew up. I'm a farm boy at heart. I like having dirt under my nails because it's proof to me I put in a hard day's work."

Harrison didn't smile, but he felt like it. The jury responded to Mitchell's candidness. Morrison even grinned.

"Tell me about Livonia Adderley," Harrison ordered.

The smile left Mitchell's face. "She wasn't in her cottage. A neighbor told me she was in a nearby hospital, and so I went there to interview her. The doctor stayed with me the entire time, and Livonia told me what happened. I wrote it down the way she told me to, then read it to her, and Livonia signed it."

Harrison paused in his questioning to go back to his table. He took the signed paper and gave it to the judge.

Burns read it to the jury. "John Quincy Adam was not responsible for my husband's death. Walter Adderley stumbled and hit his head on the edge of the mantel. The blow caused his immediate death."

"Please read all of it, Judge," Harrison asked.

Burns looked at Cole and then Adam before he agreed. "Are you sure about this?"

"I'm sure."

"All right then. She says, 'I do not hold my sons responsible for their behavior and I will not press charges against them. Rose has also made this same promise to me, and my faithful friend will keep her word. I love my sons. They frighten me only when they allow their anger to get the better of them. They didn't mean to hurt me, but I had refused to sign their paper, and they then felt they had to force me to. They didn't want the truth, and I couldn't take any more of the beating because I'm a weak woman, just as Walter Adderley always believed, and so I signed the paper. God forgive me my lie.'"

A hush fell over the crowd. Judge Burns looked sick. Harrison thought everyone did. He didn't let up though. There was still more to tell, and he wanted all of it out.

"Besides the doctor, was there anyone else in the hospital room with you?"

"Yes," Mitchell answered. "Mama Rose was there. Livonia calls her that and she gave me permission to call her Mama Rose too."

"Where was she, in Livonia's room or was she waiting outside of the hospital?"

"Sitting in a chair next to the bed. She was holding Livonia's hand and comforting her."

Harrison took a breath. He hated what he was going to ask now. "And how did Mama Rose look?"

Mitchell shook his head. "She was almost in as bad condition as Livonia was. Her face was swollen. She had two black eyes and bruises on her arms and legs. She should have been in a hospital bed herself, but she refused to leave

Livonia's side. Each time Livonia would wake up, she would call out to Rose. As soon as she heard her answering voice, she would smile and go back to sleep again."

"Did Mama Rose also sign a document saying Adam was innocent?"

"Yes."

Harrison handed the paper to the judge. "Will Livonia recover?"

"The doctors don't believe she will. She was severely beaten. Her poor body may not be able to regain any strength."

"And Mama Rose?"

"The doctors take care of her while she sits in the chair. It was against hospital rules to let her sleep there, but after one or two days, the nurses saw her kindness and they carried in a cot for her to sleep on. It's going to take her a while to recover, but she's getting the best of care."

Harrison turned to Adam. Mary Rose's eldest brother looked frantic. His hands were flat on the table, and he was about to jump to his feet.

Harrison waited until Adam was looking at him, and then he slowly nodded. The brother immediately calmed down again. Adam remembered Harrison was going to nod when he lied.

Cole's hand had gone to his empty gunbelt, and he was thinking hard about snatching his gun from Burns's table and putting a bullet through Lionel's heart. He too saw Harrison's nod and quickly pulled himself together again.

When he nodded, it meant he was lying. Cole had to repeat what Adam had said three times before his breathing settled down.

"Tell the jury who was responsible for beating Livonia."

"Lionel Adderley."

There were several loud mutters in the room. Harrison ignored the noise and turned to Lionel. "Like father, like son."

He turned back to Mitchell. "How do you know it was Lionel?"

"Mama Rose and Livonia both told me Lionel had beaten them. The doctor saw Livonia's son the next afternoon. He came into the hospital room while the doctor was there. I have his signed statement. He said that when Lionel leaned down to kiss his mother, he saw the cuts and bruises on his fists. He asked Lionel directly if he'd done this to his mother, and Lionel told him to mind his own business. He never came back after that day. I believe he hired an attorney and set out for Montana Territory with his brother a couple of days later."

"Thank you, Alfred. You may step down now." He turned to the jury and added, "Folks, Mitchell is living proof there are some honest men living down south."

"Lionel Adderley, get back on the stand."

Lionel's face was beet red when he took his chair. He looked sullen and angry.

"You lied to me, to Judge Burns, and to this jury, Lionel Adderley. You lied more than once too. I asked you specifically if you coerced your mother into signing the document. Both times you told me you didn't."

"I didn't coerce her. I merely helped her see

the rightness in telling the truth."

"By breaking damned near every bone in her body?" Harrison roared. "That's helping her?" Harrison shook his head in disgust. "I have no more questions."

Lionel stupidly glared at the jury on his way back to his chair. Harrison called Reginald to the stand next. He didn't soft-pedal his way through his questions with the younger brother. He was demanding, forceful, and somewhat threatening. He got down close to Reginald's face when he was finished prying out of him what he needed, and told the man what he thought of him.

He then dismissed Reginald.

It was now time for his summation. He positioned himself right in front of the jury, just far enough away so that none of the six in the first row would have to stretch up to look at him.

"The proof is unquestionable. Adam Clayborne has been cleared of the murder charges by two witnesses. Lionel and Reginald Adderley have come into our community and pointed their fingers at Adam as a criminal. They're outsiders, and so they believe they know better than simple, ignorant country folk like us. Adam isn't an outsider. He's one of us. He's a neighbor and a friend. He's been there when someone's needed help, and he's been loyal. He's a good man. You all know that. He didn't like hearing sweet Catherine Morrison being called a man-sniffing whore any better than the rest of you. He didn't like what they called Catherine's mother either. They were foul, crude words used by city boys. And all of them untrue. Do we turn the other cheek and pretend we don't mind outsiders telling us our business? There are criminals sitting in the courtroom today. Have a good look at them, gentlemen. Lionel and Reginald Adderley. Picture what they did to their own mama, and then think about your own. We'll all pray Livonia makes it, but I doubt she will. She won't press charges while she's alive, but the doctor plans to bring in the authorities and charge both boys with murder if she dies. Do the right thing. Let justice, our justice, decide the day. Thank you."

Judge Burns wasn't quite certain what to do with the jury now. He didn't want anyone inside the courtroom to leave because he'd have to go through the sorting-out process all over again. He settled on sending the jury into the storeroom instead.

"Pick up your chairs and go on in there," he ordered. "We'll all wait here for as long as it takes you. I'll give you an hour before I let anyone out of here."

Harrison didn't look at the jury as they made their way into the storeroom. No one said a word in the room, not even the spectators. Harrison hoped they were all silently seething over the facts he'd presented.

Hate. It was all about hating. He was sickened by the reality. Evidence wasn't as strong to a man who wanted to hate. He would latch on to any little piece of possible truth and condemn his enemy. Reason was forgotten, along with compassion and understanding. Hate, like a gnawing tumor, devoured it.

He was disgusted by the theatrics he'd used, but he'd used them all the same. He knew they needed to hate someone, and so he fueled their fire until the simmering coals roared into life. And then he'd turned the flames away from Adam. He gave the jurors someone else to hate more.

He sat down at the table and turned to his wife. He needed to look at her, to assure himself she was there. He needed her comfort, and, dear God, inside he was so scared and uncertain, he could barely speak to her.

She had tears in her eyes. "Are you feeling all right?" he whispered.

"May I tell you now, Harrison?"

He felt the warmth of her comfort around his heart. "Yes, tell me."

"I love you."

"I love you too. Sir, give Mary Rose your handkerchief."

He turned around again. Adam was looking at him. "When you nodded, it meant you were . . ."

"Yes, that's what it meant."

John Morrison came back into the room and called to the judge. Burns immediately got up and hurried over to the door. He listened for just a minute, gave Harrison a nod, and hurried on into the storeroom with the twelve men.

Harrison and Adam both stood up. "All rise. Court is now in session," Harrison said.

The judge led the jury back inside. The men left their chairs in the storeroom but lined up in their same positions.

"Have you reached a verdict, John Morrison?"

"We have, Your Honor."

"On the charge of murder, how do you find John Quincy Adam Clayborne?"

Morrison looked directly at Adam when he answered. "We find him not guilty."

The crowd went wild. People jumped to their feet. They cheered and they clapped over the decision.

The judge pounded on his table. "All right, that's enough. We're all mighty happy justice was served today. Lionel and Reginald Adderley, you get the hell out of town. You don't call our namesake a dirty nickel whore and think you're gonna live long. I might just put a couple of bullets through your foul mouths myself. Harrison come up here. All right now. Court's adjourned," he added with one last swing of his gavel.

Harrison hurried over to the judge. Burns was standing now, stretching his arms.

"Tell me about the wire you were expecting. What were you hoping for?"

"I wasn't hoping, Judge, but Mitchell's brother was going to wire me when Livonia died. I'm sorry for her. She'd had one hell of a life. Maybe she'll find peace in the next one."

"If a woman ever deserves to get into heaven, Livonia surely does," Harrison said.

"She's lingering, is she?"

"Just barely. It's inevitable. She's bleeding inside."

"You wanted the boys to know they had murder charges hanging over their heads, didn't you?"

"Yes, Your Honor. I did."

"They were the first ones out the door. Let me shake your hand, son. You did a fine job."

Harrison did just that. Mary Rose caught him from behind. She wrapped her arms around his waist and hugged him tight.

She inadvertently gave Burns a notion of his own. "Sugar Belle, come on over here and give me one of your happy-to-see-me kisses."

Harrison had to peel his wife's hands away before he could turn around.

Tears of joy were streaming down her face. "I'm so proud of you, Harrison."

He kissed her on the mouth, long and hard. "You can tell me all about it in bed tonight, sweetheart. We have to get Adam home first. Bickley's still outside, remember?"

"Let Cole shoot him," she suggested.

Harrison laughed.

Belle stopped to kiss him on her way out the door. "I've got to hurry on home and get ready for the judge," she explained. "I'll come on out to your ranch tomorrow to celebrate with you."

"We'd love to have you, Belle. Bring the judge with you," Mary Rose called out.

She couldn't make herself let go of her husband. Family and friends surrounded her brothers. Adam looked as if he was in a daze. Harrison doubted he'd even remember what was now being said to him by John Morrison.

They went outside together. The road was almost deserted. Once the outsiders had heard the disappointing news that there wouldn't be a hanging anytime soon, they'd gone on back home.

Bickley and five others in his vigilante group stood in the center of the road. Harrison noticed they were all armed. He shoved Mary Rose behind him.

"Sir, go on and get in the buggy. Cole will make certain you get there. Take Mary Rose with you."

She started to go to her father, but she kept her attention on Bickley. He wasn't looking at Adam now. Harrison seemed to be the target of his anger.

Bickley went for his gun. Mary Rose didn't hesitate. She threw herself in front of her husband to shield him.

Harrison shouted, "No."

Everyone drew his gun at the same time. The judge was quicker than all of them, for he already had his pistol out and cocked. He'd had a pretty good notion of what Bickley planned to do, and so he'd waited by the side for his opportunity.

The bullet went right through the center of Bickley's forehead. He flew backward and landed in the dust.

"Any of you other boys want some of this here gun?" the judge roared.

Bickley's friends shook their heads and put their hands up. "Then get the hell out of my town," the judge ordered. "And haul that trash on the ground with you. Git now."

Harrison was shaking. He grabbed his wife and squeezed her. "You damned near got yourself killed. What in God's name were you doing?"

"Making sure you didn't get killed."

"If you ever . . . dear God, Mary Rose, I

can't go on without . . . how could you . . ."

Cole started laughing. "Give her hell at home, Harrison. You know why Bickley tried to kill you, don't you?"

"I'm guessing he hates lawyers like everyone else does. Harrison, are you sure I have to become one?" Travis asked.

Harrison wasn't amused. He let Cole pull his horse after him and squeezed into the buggy with his wife and her father.

Travis and Douglas and Cole rode in a half circle with Adam in the center all the way home. They didn't trust Bickley's friends, of course, and they weren't about to let one of them kill Adam or Harrison now.

Harrison's jaw was clenched tight. Mary Rose knew he was still trying to recover from Bickley's attempt. She decided she would take his attention away from the matter by talking about the trial.

"Father, wasn't Harrison wonderful?"

"Yes, he was wonderful. I'm glad he didn't have to get brutal. It worked out just the way he planned it."

"He wasn't brutal?"

"Oh, heaven's no. I thought he was very agreeable."

"Harrison? How did you get Mitchell to lie?"

"I didn't."

"Then . . ."

"He told the truth . . . as he knew it to be," he deliberately added to mislead her.

"Was it a plan of some sort?"

"Yes."

She leaned against him. "Quit talking in such

clipped tones. I know you're mad at me. It's a wife's duty to protect her husband. Do try to get past it."

He lifted her up onto his lap and shoved the side of her face down onto his shoulder.

"I'm proud of you, son," Elliot told him.

"It was easy, sir. Adam was innocent."

"But that wasn't what this trial was all about, was it?"

"No, sir. It was about hate."

Elliott nodded. They all fell silent as the buggy climbed the road. Elliott was thinking that he couldn't wait to get Harrison alone and find out what the plan had been. He knew how Harrison's mind worked, and he also knew, without any doubt, that he would never, ever lie in court. He wouldn't get anyone else to do it for him either. So how had he pulled it off?

Part of the answer was smiling up at her husband. Harrison hadn't lied in court, but he had lied to Mary Rose and her brothers. Elliott understood why he'd done it, of course. They wouldn't have been as calm and controlled if they'd known beforehand what Livonia's sons had done to their Mama Rose.

Elliott wondered if Harrison would ever tell them the truth. He'd ask him just that question tonight, he decided.

"I'll have to get back to England soon," he announced.

"You can't leave yet. I have so much to show you. I want to introduce you to Corrie, and I want to show you my mountains. I'll show you where the ghosts are buried if you stay."

Elliott was pleased she didn't want him to leave. His eyes became misty, and he slowly nodded. His voice was shaky when he said, "All right, daughter. I'll stay another couple of weeks. You and Harrison can come to England to visit me next summer. I'll add on another week if you promise me now."

"But you have to come back here next summer. I can't leave then," she said.

"Sweetheart, we can take a month and go back. I want to show you Scotland," Harrison insisted.

"I won't promise until I talk to Harrison, Father. Can you wait until tomorrow?"

He agreed. "I don't want to wait to hear about the ghost graveyard. Tell me all about it now. Who did you bury there?"

"Monsters from under my bed," Mary Rose answered. "When I was five or six, I wouldn't sleep in my own bed. I'd always wait and sneak in with one of my brothers. I always did sleep with them when I was younger, and they were trying to break me of the habit.

"Douglas hung a curtain up to separate me from the living area. We were still living in a cabin then. Anyway, I was sure I heard monsters under my bed. All my brothers but Cole tried to convince me I was imagining things.

"Cole took a different approach. He got down on his knees, looked under the bed, and then let out a whistle. 'Well, I'll be. There's a monster under here all right. Mary Rose, close your eyes real tight while I haul him out. He's too ugly for you to see.' "

Harrison and Elliott were both smiling. "Cole

801

had already taken his gun out. He shouted to Douglas to open the door. He went running outside so I couldn't see him. Then I heard a shot."

"He killed him for you."

"Of course," she answered. "He promised me he'd let it stay there all night so other monsters would know what the Claybornes think about them, and in the morning, we'd bury it. I was very young, and of course I believed him. I made him shoot a monster about once a week. I figured I was safe then. Cole would put an empty box out on the stoop. He told me not to look inside or it would scare the curls out of my hair."

She laughed thinking about it. "I was very vain about my hair. I didn't dare take the chance. We walked across the meadow and up the first hill and gave the monster a burial. We didn't pray over him because I didn't want the thing to get into heaven."

Harrison pictured the little girl holding on to a gunfighter's hand. "You were surrounded by love," he whispered.

"Yes, she was," Elliott agreed. "Tonight you must tell me another story. I found out quite a lot about you from the letters. Your mother didn't hold a grudge. I wonder where you came by that trait?"

"I think from Cole," she answered.

"And Douglas and Travis," Harrison supplied.

"I wasn't a perfect child, Father. I complained, and I always told Mama Rose if my brothers did anything I didn't like."

"Will I have to shoot monsters for our children?"

"Of course. It's a father's duty. If we have a boy, I'll name him Harrison Stanford MacDonald."

"The Fourth," he added.

"The Fourth," she agreed.

"And if it's a girl?"

"I think I'll name her after the two women who loved me so much. Agatha Rose. It's pretty, isn't it?"

Elliott was too emotional to speak. He nodded to let her know how fine he thought the name was. And fitting.

All three of them thought about the traditions that would endure and continue.

They reached the ranch a few minutes later. His brothers wouldn't let him take Mary Rose into the bunkhouse. They wanted him to answer some questions for them first.

They weren't going to give in. Harrison sat down on the porch, pulled his wife onto his lap, and waited for the questions to begin.

Travis was first. "How did you get Alfred Mitchell to lie on the stand?"

"I'm going to give you one week to figure it out on your own. Then I'll tell you."

Douglas asked a question next. "I understand why you had me bring all the rental horses home. You wanted Lionel and Reginald to be stuck in town."

"Yes."

"You knew they'd hate it. How did you know that?" Cole asked.

"Adam told me about their way of life down south before the war came. The brothers were used to luxury. I wanted them to be miserable and start complaining."

"What else did you do?" Douglas asked.

"I talked to Billie and Henry and Dooley. Adam, you've got some loyal friends here."

Adam smiled. "Yes, I know."

"Billie fed them every meal. He made sure it was awful. Henry substituted Ghost's homemade brew for Billie to use whenever he served them, and Dooley kept track of what they were saying about folks. Then he'd tell me."

"And you'd go tell the folks what they said and get them to sign a paper?"

"No, Dooley would have already gotten them riled up. I would merely give them my sympathy and hint at possibly being willing to bring suit against them."

"Slander?" Cole asked.

"Something like that," Harrison answered.

Elliott stood up. "I'm going to get out of these city clothes. I don't believe I'll be able to figure out what you did, Harrison. You're going to have to explain about Alfred Mitchell's testimony in a week, I suppose. I know you well, son, and you wouldn't do anything underhanded."

"One week, sir. Please wait that long. Adam, how does it feel to be free? You've had the worry hanging over your head for a hell of a long time."

"It feels good," he whispered. "I don't believe I've taken it all in yet. I believe I'll go on inside and take that poem off the wall now. Tell me something, Harrison. Why were the words so special to you? You memorized them, remember?"

"I remember. I read the passage to my father

almost every night. He liked it. It gave him comfort."

Adam nodded. Harrison suddenly felt drained. Mary Rose looked exhausted. He told everyone good-bye and took his wife back to their "home." He needed her to give him strength again, in body and in spirit, so that he could go out and slay the monsters again.

He stood inside the door of the bunkhouse and watched her take off her clothes. She was just about to remove her chemise when he asked her to sit down on the side of the bed.

He knelt down in front of her and took her hands in his.

"Your Mama Rose is fine. Alfred Mitchell didn't lie on the stand."

"I know. You never would have asked him to lie. Is she really all right?"

"Yes, she is. I lied to your brothers because I didn't want them to hear the truth without at least questioning it while they were sitting so close to the men who'd hurt their mother. I knew what would happen."

"What will happen to Livonia when her sons return home?"

"Sweetheart, Livonia's dying. One of Mitchell's brothers is going to wire us when that happens. Alfred hired a man to guard her day and night. He'll watch after your mother too, but I don't think Lionel and Reginald will be in any hurry to get back. They have to be worried about facing charges."

"Why didn't you explain to my brothers on the porch?"

"What do you think Cole would have done if he'd known the truth?"

"He would go after them."

Harrison nodded. "I'm giving Livonia's sons a week to disappear. Otherwise I might have to defend Cole on two murder charges."

She pulled her hand away from his and gently stroked the side of his face.

"Cole would do something foolish. At least I think he would. You were balancing my brothers' reaction against Adam's defense. You did the right thing."

"Thank you for trusting me."

"You needn't thank me. I believe in you. Don't you understand yet? You're part of my family now. We'll argue and bicker and kiss and apologize; we'll lecture one another and offer comfort at the same time; we'll do all the other wonderful things families do. Love is all the strength we'll ever need.

"It's what family is all about."

Dear Children,

Livonia is at peace now. She was given a proper burial last week. I stayed outside the church during the service, and then followed her to the cemetery. I stayed awhile with her after every one else had left, and I said my farewells to her. I shall miss her.

I've found a companion to travel with me, and at long last I'm coming home. There's a town in Kansas, filled with black people who left the South and settled there. I'll rest there a few days and see old friends before I continue the journey.

God keep you until I get there.

Your Mama,
Rose

Adam, dearest, I'm bringing your bride with me.

Of all flowers, Methinks a rose is best.
It is the very emblem of a maid;
For when the west wind courts her gently,
How modestly she blows, and paints the sun
With her chaste blushes! When the north
  comes near her,
Rude and Impatient, then, like chastity,
She locks her beauties in her bud again,
And leaves him to base briers.
She is wondrous fair.
. . . Methinks a rose is best.

— from *The Two Noble Kinsmen*,
by William Shakespeare
and John Fletcher